"What a handsome face he had: but if he
were naked you would forget he had a face,
he is so beautiful in every way."
– Plato

Main cover illustration from Kevin Kramer's private collection; secondary illustration courtesy of Bel Ami Video (see acknowledgements). Bel Ami videos are also available from STARbooks Press.

Worldwide Praise for the Erotica of John Patrick and STARbooks!

"John Patrick is a modern master of the genre!
...This writing is what being brave is all about.
It brings up the kinds of things that are usually kept so private that you think you're the only one who experiences them."
— *Gay Times, London*

"'Barely Legal' is a great potpourri...
and the coverboy is gorgeous!"
— *Ian Young, Torso magazine*

"A huge collection of highly erotic, short and steamy one-handed tales. Perfect bedtime reading, though you probably won't get much sleep! Prepare to be shocked!
Highly recommended!"
— *Vulcan magazine*

"Tantalizing tales of porn stars, hustlers, and other lost boys...John Patrick set the pace with 'Angel!'"
— *The Weekly News, Miami*

"...Some readers may find some of the scenes too explicit; others will enjoy the sudden, graphic sensations each page brings. Each of these romans á clef is written with sustained intensity. 'Angel' offers a strange, often poetic vision of sexual obsession. I recommend it to you."
— *Nouveau Midwest*

"Self-absorbed, sexually-addicted bombshell Stacy flounced onto the scene in 'Angel' and here he is again, engaged in further, distinctly 'non-literary' adventures...lots of action!"
— *Prinz Eisenherz Book Review, Germany*

"'Angel' is mouthwatering and enticing..."
— *Rouge Magazine, London*

"'Superstars' is a fast read...if you'd like a nice round of fireworks before the Fourth, read this aloud at your next church picnic..."
— *Welcomat, Philadelphia*

"Yes, it's another of those bumper collections of steamy tales from STARbooks. The rate at which John Patrick turns out these compilations you'd be forgiven for thinking it's not exactly quality prose. Wrong. These stories are well-crafted, but not over-written, and have a profound effect in the pants department."
– *Vulcan magazine, London*

"For those who share Mr. Patrick's appreciation for cute young men, 'Legends' is a delightfully readable book...I am a fan of John Patrick's...His writing is clear and straight-forward and should be better known in the gay community."
- *Ian Young, Torso Magazine*

"...'Billy & David' is frank, intelligent, disarming. Few books approach the government's failure to respond to crisis in such a realistic, powerful manner."
- *RG Magazine, Montreal, Canada*

"...Touching and gallant in its concern for the sexually addicted, 'Angel' becomes a wonderfully seductive investigation of the mysterious disparity between lust and passion, obsession and desire."
-*Lambda Book Report*

"Each page of John Patrick's 'Angel' was like a sponge and I was slowly sucked into the works. 'The Kid' had the same effect on me and now 'What Went Wrong?' has blown me away!"
-*P. K. New York*

"John Patrick has one of the best jobs a gay male writer could have. In his fiction, he tells tales of rampant sexuality. His non-fiction involves first person explorations of adult male video stars. Talk about choice assignments!"
-*Southern Exposure*

"The title for 'Boys of Spring' is taken from a poem by Dylan Thomas, so you can count on high caliber imagery throughout."
- *Walter Vatter, Editor, A Different Light Review*

*Book of the Month Selections in Europe and the U.K.
And Featured By A Different Light,
Lambda Rising and GR, Australia
And Available at Fine Booksellers Everywhere*

More than just a pretty face...

Beautiful BOYS

A New Collection of Erotic Tales
Edited By
JOHN PATRICK

STARbooks Press
Sarasota, Florida

Books by John Patrick

Non-Fiction

A Charmed Life: Vince Cobretti
Lowe Down: Tim Lowe
The Best of the Superstars 1990
The Best of the Superstars 1991
The Best of the Superstars 1992
The Best of the Superstars 1993
The Best of the Superstars 1994
The Best of the Superstars 1995
The Best of the Superstars 1996
The Best of the Superstars 1997
What Went Wrong?
When Boys Are Bad
& Sex Goes Wrong
Legends: The World's Sexiest Men, Vols. 1 & 2
Legends (Third Edition)
Tarnished Angels (Ed.)

Fiction

Billy & David: A Deadly Minuet
The Bigger They Are...
The Younger They Are...
The Harder They Are...
Angel: The Complete Trilogy
Angel II: Stacy's Story
Angel: The Complete Quintet
A Natural Beauty (Editor)
The Kid (with Joe Leslie)
HUGE (Editor)
Strip: He Danced Alone
The Boys of Spring
Big Boys/Little Lies (Editor)
Boy Toy
Seduced (Editor)
Insatiable/Unforgettable (Editor)
Heartthrobs
Runaways/Kid Stuff (Editor)
Dangerous Boys/Rent Boys (Editor)
Barely Legal (Editor)
Country Boys/City Boys (Editor)
My Three Boys (Editor)
Mad About the Boys (Editor)
Lover Boys (Editor)
In the BOY ZONE (Editor)
Boys of the Night (Editor)
Secret Passions (Editor)
Beautiful Boys (Editor)

Entire Contents Copyrighted © 1997 by John Patrick, Sarasota, FL. All rights reserved.

Every effort has been made to credit copyrighted material. The author and the publisher regret any omissions and will correct them in future editions. Note: While the words "boy," "girl," "young man," "youngster," "gal," "kid," "student," "guy," "son," "youth," "fella," and other such terms are occasionally used in text, this work is generally about persons who are at least 18 years of age, unless otherwise noted.

First Edition Published in the U.S. in April 1997
Library of Congress Card Catalogue No. 96-070310
ISBN No. 1-877978-88-4

Contents

Introduction:
THE POWER OF BEAUTY
John Patrick
LOOKING FOR LOVE
John Patrick
THE STRANGERS WE'D MEET
John Patrick
THE PIMP'S BOY
John Patrick
HARD ALL OVER
Frank Brooks
THE COMPANY OF
BEAUTIFUL BOYS
P. K. Warren & John Patrick
COUPLINGS
James Wilton
THE TWINS
Grant Adams
SON OF DAKOTA
Peter Eros
CODY'S COCK
John Patrick
THE BOYS IN THE FENS
Leo Cardini
SEDUCE ME, PLEASE!
Thom Nickels
FIRST LESSON
Kent Dawson
NOTORIOUS
Thomas Holm
DOOGIE:
CLASSICALLY
BEAUTIFUL
Jarred Goodall
THE RED-HAIRED
PROFESSOR
Greg Bowden
PORTRAIT OF A
FRESHMAN
David Patrick Beavers
TOOLS
Peter Gilbert
MISSING YOU
John Patrick
STRIP BOY
Dan Veen

THE GENIUS OF ALL
BEAUTIFUL BOYS
Orland Outland
THE SMELL OF SEX
Bruce Lee
HIS FAVORITE PHOTO
Kevin Bantan
MAGIC
Rick Jackson
MIKEY LIKED IT
William Cozad
THE SECRET OF THE RUE ST.
GERMAIN
Charles Willard Scoggins
THE LAWNMOWER BOY
Jesse Montegudo
ABSOLUTE BEAUTY
John Palgrave
PRACTICE
MAKES PERFECT
John Patrick

Plus Bonus Books
Leo Cardini's
THE BLESSING
Being extremely well-hung ran in
this family, and the possibilities
were staggering!
AND
John Patrick's
Expose
FANTASY LOVERS:
THE GOOD, THE BAD, AND
THE BEAUTIFUL
Including:
GORGEOUSNESS-TO-GO
STARRING KEVIN KRAMER
Confessions of a Sex Pig
With Excluisve Photographs
BODIES FOR SALE

And
Poems by
ANTLER
DENNIS COOPER
B. N. PRICE

Editor's Note

Most of the stories appearing in this book take place prior to the years of The Plague; the editor and each of the authors represented herein advocate the practice of safe sex at all times.

And, because these stories trespass the boundaries of fiction and non-fiction, to respect the privacy of those involved, we've changed all of the names and other identifying details.

Seeing a boy in a bookstore
I go in to get a closer look.
One glimpse is all I can stand.
The love of beautiful boys
Is as beautiful as beautiful boys.
Just looking for two seconds
Too much for me.
I feel faint, breathless,
Dazed as I rush back out
Plunging into the crowd.
Yet the air smells of spring.
I see flowers blooming.
I realize I am still
A creature of the woods.
A wild animal untamed.
Yet I think a beautiful boy
Might coax me
With gentle talking
And a soft song
To come closer,
To eat from his hand.

– Antler

*How beautiful your feet in boots,
your thighs in faded jeans,
your biceps in that flannel shirt,
your forearms' sweaty sheen.*

*I watch you from my living room
as you unload your truck:
You reach and bend, and through my window,
I am passion-struck.*

*Your body is a dinner bell
that makes me salivate.
I'm starving for a taste of you.
May I fellate?*

— B. N. Price

INTRODUCTION: THE POWER OF BEAUTY

John Patrick

While it is said that youth is wasted on the young, beauty certainly isn't. In this collection we have assembled stories that celebrate the undeniable power of beauty.

"Because women are raised to deny beauty so as to ward off others' envy," Nancy Friday suggests in *The Power of Beauty*, "we never really learn its full power, its effect on people, how we might better use it." Her thesis is that (gasp!) beauty is a double-edged sword that causes envy even as it gives women a leg up in the bedroom and the workplace. This thesis applies equally to gays, of course. It would seem, though, that gays are better able to use the power of beauty than women.

That ability is beautifully evoked in *Like People in History*, wherein Felice Picano writes, "...Every time I looked at him, I kept finding new aspects of his beauty. The creaminess of the skin on the high insides of his arms. The massive, almost tumorous, solidity of his biceps. The extraordinary soaring architecture of his shoulder blades seen from behind. The seemingly Chinese delicacy and porcelain hardness of his clavicle. The tornado swirls of dark-colored hair around his navel, and their vectors south into a hurricane of pubic bush, then north and thinner, reduced to a virtual pencil line pointing toward each perfect areola surrounding a nipple atop his breastbone. The auricular curlicues of modestly fuzzed cartilage that composed his ears. The slight dimple at the end of his nose that could only be noticed close up, and which made it seem so much more defined from farther away. The astonishing definition of his upper lip, almost a line, and its cherrylike coloring, as though someone had applied lipstick in embryo and it had never rubbed off. The near-agate mosaic of his eyes, corneas mostly a silver-gray, but speckled lighter, a star-burst pattern at the center in paler gray, ice green, turquoise, sienna, amethyst, even lemon yellow. From the tiny perfect knob under his knee that connected the two long muscles running beneath his thigh down into the one that ran below his calf, to the nearly feathered tiny V's of hair that made up his sideburns, I'd never before encountered such an idealization of form, or, more impressively, such a lavish extravagance of detail! As though once he'd been shaped, his Creator had been so surprised, so pleased with the result, He'd come back again and again, dotingly, to touch up His work."

Speaking of God's work, many homosexual men believe the erect penis to be the most beautiful part of a man's anatomy, at least so says Alex Jeffers in *Safe As Houses*. "Myself, I'm of two minds – I look at hands, I look at faces, at the overall shape and form of the body, and the phallus by itself I find not so much beautiful as endearing, clumsy and intent as a small child."

At one point in the book, the narrator, Allen, cannot ignore young Jeremy's phallus, beautiful or not, but, alas, his heart isn't in it: "'Oh,' then 'Yes,' (he) raised his hips a little and pushed my head down. He was still half-asleep, groggy, faltering, as, between us, we shifted our positions, he sat up, I half-knelt, half-crouched between his legs.

"In my mouth, Jeremy's cock knew what it wanted. 'Suck on it,' Jeremy muttered, 'do it good, give that big prick a wild ride,' but his heart wasn't in it because he giggled, but his heart was in it because he held my head firmly between his hands, pushed his thumbs into my ears. 'Cocksucker,' he said. He said, 'Allen.' And then, puzzled, he said, 'You didn't put a condom on me?'

"By now I was suckling blindly, drawing up the length of his penis which by now tasted mainly of my own saliva, palping it with my tongue, pressing down, while with one hand I extended the grasp of my lips, with the other poked and pulled at Jeremy's nipples, as erect and attentive as the flesh in my mouth. He brushed that hand away. 'Don't.' His voice was uneasy, thin. 'Don't, Allen.' He moaned, as though I'd done something especially clever. 'I'll come, Allen, I don't want to come in your mouth.' I pushed him down and concentrated.

"A new flavor filled my mouth now, barely perceptible at first, a slimy, fluid saltiness. What I wanted was for his semen to flood my mouth, and what I wanted was to swallow it, but this was only a preliminary leakage. I closed my eyes. His hands grasped my ears, pulled me off, and he said, 'Allen!' If I could see my own face I would have seen a slack, open mouth, flushed cheeks, inflamed lips dribbling spit, I would have seen nostrils wide for breath and dopey, bloodshot eyes. Instead I saw Jeremy's face, excited and distraught at once, and I said - as if I might have said, the check's in the mail - 'It's what I want, Jeremy, this time.'

"At last he came, and it was bitterer than I remembered, and I gagged, but I swallowed. 'You're out of your mind,' he said, more sad than angry, as I sat up between his legs. "You don't know what you're doing." He moved his head on the pillow, glancing away although from his position there wasn't much to look at but me, said sadly, 'I won't do it for you.' Then, angry, focusing, 'You don't even have a hard-on...'"

In his novel *The Beauty of Men*, Andrew Holleran addresses the power of beauty, as it relates to his protagonist Lark:

"Ten years ago he'd be going home with an organ. Ten years ago, men used to follow me in their cars when he drove away from the bar; now that his hair has gone entirely gray, I am allowed to disappear unchased. I don't feel there's any point in even going inside. After all the bars he would have walked into, Lark thinks, every time with a little thrill, I am sitting in a Buick Skylark in a parking lot in Gainesville, Florida, wondering what is the point.

"He watches two men leave the bar together, get into separate cars, and drive off - to another bar? The University Club? Or home to an apartment to have sex? Is it possible that they have actually met each other in the bar and are now going home to do it? Of course it's possible: They're young. The blond had that gorgeous haircut that looks like the helmet the guards at Buckingham Palace wear - the Roman helmet, with the plume. All done in human hair. He watches two other men get out of their cars and walk to the bar, passing under the light in the colonnade at the entrance, one of them hitching his belt up, the other patting his dark cloud of hair, the last nervous gesture before - Making an Entrance. For them the bar *is* exciting. The rewards are Sex and Pleasure. No wonder Youth has fun - it has so much time to reproduce. Or not reproduce, as the case may be. With this thought he backs out. A man in a white tank top standing under the colonnade follows him with his eyes – a kindred spirit, Lark thinks, a man who also finds the bar beside the point, or the parking lot easier to cruise – but he does nothing about that either.

"...On this sunny afternoon, the bus stops again and a solitary youth descends with his blue plaid shirt unbuttoned in the heat, a bookbag slung over his shoulder, and a torso that reminds Lark of the Elgin Marbles: the problem of Beauty. He watches the young man take off his blue plaid shirt and walk down the dirt road, the youth obviously aware that everyone in the cars stopped behind the bus can see him – as if they've stopped, thinks Lark, not to ensure his safe passage but to pay homage to his beauty; and he thinks of all the years he has expended in pursuit of this quality distributed so randomly among the populace, as likely to be found at two-thirty in the afternoon on a dirt road in Florida as in some bar in New York. You can't keep track of it, he thinks."

"...*Quel burden*: Beauty. A curse, said Juvenal. And not just Beauty – that aspect of a person has nothing to do with sexual gifts; I've been to bed with beauties...and wondered, How do I bring this to an end? 'Beauty,' my friend the bartender said when I complained, 'seldom comes without a price tag.'"

This sentiment was echoed in *The Bitterweed Path*, wherein Thomas Hal Phillips spins a sad tale about how great a price its hero must pay for being beautiful. The novel, written in the '50s and recently reprinted, is about two boys in the Deep South who grow up loving each other. The one boy, Darrell, is the more attractive of the two; he is in fact, beautiful, at least according to Miriam, sister of the other boy, Roger. Miriam once caught the boys kissing and when Roger goes away to school, Miriam sees her chance to get to Darrell:

Eagerly and quickly Roger embraced his father and then his mother and then Miriam. For a moment he stalled before Darrell and the sureness in his face was gone. "Hug him too'" Miriam said, and the smoke from the train blew down over them and the cinders, like small shot, touched their faces. "Maybe Darrell doesn't want him to," Mother said.

"Do you?" Miriam said.

"Will you hand my bag up to me?" Roger said.

Darrell nodded. Roger went ahead of him and climbed up to the vestibule. When he reached down for the suitcase his face seemed full of the train smoke and his hand caught Darrell's hand and held it. Finally he took the suitcase and said: "Good bye, Darr."

"Goodbye."

The train pulled away and they could see Roger through the window but he did not once look around to them... They were halfway home before Miriam began to talk to Darrell. He could feel her beside him and finally she began to whisper, "Roger will come home Christmas. That won't be so long." He did not say anything and she said, "Hold my hand." He held her hand. It was warm and small. "Will you think more of me now that Roger is gone?"

"Yes," he said. He looked at her and he was glad that she was beside him, but he was not sure he had spoken the truth.

"I don't think Father cares much that Roger has gone away, because you're here."

"Why do you say that?"

"The first day you ever came to our house and I told on you and Roger – do you remember?"

"Yes." His thumb began to feel her hand.

"Father told Mother that night that you were the finest looking boy he had ever seen. And Mother said she hoped he never said that before Roger. I think Father got angry at her because he thought Roger wouldn't care if he said it. He came and picked me up and asked me what I thought."

"What did you say?"

"I said you were beautiful."

He held her hand tight. She seemed very sad to him and he was sorry for her because she did not have Roger now...

When he got home that night he went into his grandmother's room where she sat beside the sewing machine with her back to the long oval-shaped mirror and with the lamplight falling over her shoulders. He walked across the room and stood near her before she finally lifted her eyes and closed the book on her fingers. He gazed into the mirror and let his forefinger rake across his chin. "Grandmother, do you think I'm beautiful?"

"Beautiful?" She got up and took the shawl from her shoulders and spread it out on the foot of her bed. And while she bent over with her back to him she said, "Now what a pretty thing to ask." Then suddenly she faced him. "But I'll tell you the truth. Yes. You're too much so. You're too beautiful Darrell Barclay, and any time the Lord gives a body too much of anything he has to pay and pay and pay..." Darrell began to laugh, quietly at first and then very loudly. He threw himself across his grandmother's bed and said, "Beautiful... haaaaaaaa... beautiful... haaaaaa... beautiful ..."

In *Young Man from the Provinces*, Alan Helms says he had learned how to be "a Universal Type of Desire, or (to be on the safe side) an Almost Universal Type of Desire, or (to be as clear as possible) I'd learned how to cooperate in being considered an Almost Universal Type of Desire. That caused such confusion that even now it's hard for me to make sense of it. It meant that my looks & charms, such as they were, could be turned to so many advantages. In a culture where everything considered valuable is commodified, being desired can bring you so many benefits. If you're considered attractive in America, your attractiveness, like money, becomes fetishized, & if you're not a total fool, you become aware of the fact, which means you develop an acute & omnipresent self-consciousness about being desired.

"At least I did, so much so that even when alone I used to check myself out in the mirror to make sure the gift of the look was still intact. I had learned well the lessons of my culture – to use my attractions as a means of exchange & to subvert the pleasures of sex through the mentality of profit & loss. But perhaps I'm not a good example of how beauty can be made to turn in on itself since I was such a self-conscious young man to begin with. Coming out into the gay world of New York in the late '50s & finding myself in demand simply exacerbated a psychological problem I'd developed in childhood. And yet, the beautiful Americans I've known have all spoken of the same self-consciousness, along with the fear that they're not really up to snuff, not as fully beautiful as they're made to feel. Get a beautiful American to relax enough to become confidential & you always discover a rift of diffidence – the eyes are too close or the calves too thin, the butt's too big or too small, the hair too curly or too straight or the wrong color, the lips too thin or too full.

"'Better to be born a hunchback than to be born beautiful,' says Voltaire, but my friend Ira used to say 'Let Voltaire try hunchback for a week & get back to us.' *Pace* Ira, I suspect Voltaire understood the self-consciousness that comes with the gift of the look, & also the envy it inspires. That was perhaps the most unsettling part of being considered desirable, all the envy lurking in the admiration & the way it could turn to anger & rejection before my eyes. I saw it in so many men's faces – not just I want to be with you, get to know you, maybe even sleep with you, but I'd like to be you, or be like you, know what it feels like to be the living embodiment of others' desires."

Most guys who are beautiful don't believe they are, which is probably just as well. Consider: "The boy sitting across from me is, by anyone's definition, beautiful," says William J. Mann, gay author and columnist. "He's barely 18, with dark hair, dark eyes, long lashes, pouting lips. Anyone's definition, that is, but his own."

"'I'm ugly,' he says.

"I am dumbfounded. This is what he's stressing about. Call it a case of typical teenage insecurity, but it's more than that.

"'You're not,' I protest. 'You're very attractive.'

"I struggle with boundaries: how far do I go in detailing his physical beauty before I cross the line between advice and lust? But that particular dilemma is swiftly replaced by another.

"'Here,' he says, standing up and walking over to my bulletin board, where I have tacked up a photo, torn from a gay newspaper, of Mr. Gay Hotlanta 1994. 'Here,' he says, taking it from the wall and handing it to me. '*This* is attractive,' he tells me. 'I'll never have a body like that.'

"I take it and look at it, remembering the compulsion that prompted me to tear it out and tack it up. A thought stikes me hard: am I part of this boy's oppression? Have I contributed to his feelings of inadequacy? And what should I tell him now? That of course he could have a body like that? That all he needs to do is work at it? Or do I take the opposite tack, and tell him that such bodies are not – or at least, should not – be the only barometers of beauty?

"But I suggest neither. All I say is: 'Who does?'

"'Lots of guys,' he tells me, and he's right. 'I've got to start working out,' he says, 'or I'll never be attractive.'"

During a trip to Berlin, Stan Persky (writing in *Boyopolis*) had a "Death in Venice"-type of encounter: "The boys are beautiful and capable of consent, you desire them, you're otherwise not a monster, they're there (in a bar), conditions are proposed which you're prepared to meet (the famous cash nexus), why be so bourgeois as to accede to the qualms of those who refuse to recognize the ways-of-the-world? And anyway, you're older now, longer in the tooth, and your knee hurts. It's a tempting view, but just as I'm about to be tempted, the other side of the dialectic, the human city, invariably hoves into sight.

"There were all sorts of kids hanging around. Small ones, and teenage boys too. One boy in particular attracted me. He was in his mid to late teens, blue-eyed, with pale sandy hair and a quick smile. He was with a couple of his friends, and at first all I noticed was the boys' friendliness among themselves, the way they leaned against each other, casually draping an arm over the other's shoulders. Then the blue-eyed boy and I exchanged glances and there was a brief, wordless encounter, the sort of meeting I might have forgotten if nothing else had happened. Our eyes met again, he offered a smile. It was nothing, really. But as he passed behind me on the veranda, he touched me. He ran a feathery hand across my shoulders, just as he did with the other boys he was with. And as quickly as he'd appeared, he was gone."

Eventually, Persky goes to a popular bar: "A dark-haired boy with a faint, downy moustache wandered in and ordered a beer in heavily accented English. I had been vaguely expecting to see a blond boy I'd noticed in Tabasco's once or twice before. When whoever it is (invariably unexpected) begins the conversation – he's Portuguese, his name is Jose, he's travelling in Europe, wants to know if I'm looking for a good time – all that matters is to recognize: this is what I requested from the world. Many miss it altogether, deny they've asked for anything, mistakenly decide that this is not exactly what they asked for..."

On another night, Persky returns to the bar where he meets another beauty, Manuel: "When midnight rolled around, Manuel walked me outside, which I took to be a local courtesy. I was thinking, in a self-congratulatory way, little more than 'This is all very pleasant for starters.' Found a bar, negotiated my way into another language, got dazzled. Not bad for a night's work. That's when I realized that Manuel was making an offer. 'How much?' I asked him. 'It's up to you,' I took his reply to mean. 'A hundred marks?' Had someone told me that that was roughly the going rate? Manuel said that he usually got somewhat more, but that if I would pay for the room, it would do. Almost without thinking about it, I followed him up the stairs of a by-the-hour hotel. 'Berlin's a sex world,' Manuel said. 'Morning, noon, night...'"

For us of ordinary looks, being around someone beautiful might well be intimidating. In *Brutal*, Aiden Shaw discusses this when he spots a beauty on the dance floor at a club in London: "It was full and dark. All of the people seemed to merge into one as though they were simply a crowd. I walked through them towards the flashing lights which were absorbed by the muddy movements of the people. As I got through, a twirling head caught the light then dodged out of sight. When finding my space I watched as a young boy spun with his hands beside his face, so pretty and completely mad looking. He tossed and posed, kicked and shone amid a sea of darkness. He saw me as soon as I stood still and seemed to play up even more as though there was no one else around him although I thought he must be doing it for them, or rather against them. Whatever, it looked beautiful. He was beautiful, but a real beautiful, which did not intimidate but drew me in. This may have been because it wasn't sexual or that it was before I was bothered by such things. Maybe it was as simple as I was attracted to him and went with it. I wanted fun but couldn't compete with this star so caught him as he came off. This wasn't difficult because he happened to come off right beside me as though there was no other space in the whole club. 'Excuse me,' he said and kind of fell into me.

I got hold of him by his arm half helping him but pulling him towards me so that he had to look at me to see what was going on. 'You're a beauty,' I said close in his ear.

"He stopped as though timing his response to the second, then kissed me on my lips. Off he shot towards the bar and then suddenly was with me again with two drinks in his hand.

"Marcus came home with me that night. We didn't have sex but I don't think it was for the more complex reasons that developed later in my life. Marcus swears that I said he was too beautiful to have sex with. Although that's exactly the kind of explanation he would give. All I know now is that I wanted him around and it turned out that so did lots of other people. Marcus was very popular and seemed to know everybody in London. I lured him home with the possibility of having sex. This was one of the ways in which I attracted people. Some say this is manipulating but if the goal is friendship how wrong is it?"

Some find a fragile beauty more desirable, perfect for contemplation. Researcher and columnist Thom Nickels points out that F. Holland Day, an American photographer born in 1864 to a wealthy manufacturer, snapped many a willing beauty – most of them boys along the Mediterranean coast. "Day started out as a publisher of experimental authors," Nickels says, "and with his partner, Herbert Copeland, formed Copeland and Day, publishers of Oscar Wilde's 'Salome.' Besides befriending Wilde, Day knew William Butler Yeats, Aubrey Beardsley and philosopher George Santayan. He was an ardent advocate of aestheticism, or art for art's sake. A Yankee dandy in every sense of the word, Day liked to dress in eccentric costume, and loved mystical religions, Balzac, Egyptology and Keats memorabilia. His entry into the world of photography was influenced by the so-called father of gay photography, Baron Von Gloeden (1856-1931), an upper-class Prussian who photographed sensuous Mediterranean youth in classical settings. (Von Gloeden befriended and photographed the 13-year-old Kahlil Gibran.) Whereas Von Gloeden's photographs were heavy-handed in their evocation of ancient Greece, Day's approach was more austere."

As Allen Ellenzweig notes in his book *The Homoerotic Photograph*: "Day limited the evocative objects to but a few, so these do not compete with the central artistic conception: the young male figure in isolated study." Ellenzweig added that Day "looked for boys who were on their way to manhood and who had the appropriate measure of fragile beauty perfect for contemplation." Before his death in 1933, Day traveled to Maine where he began photographing adolescent boys. That he had relations with his models can be assumed. In Day's biography, *Slave to Beauty*, author Estelle Jussim noted: "Day never documented his homosexual activities in terms of sex ...

but after his death, letters to Day from Oscar Wilde and Aubrey Beardsley were discovered that confirm what we can easily suspect."

In *Queer Geography*, Frank Browning talks about what united Greek men with adolescent boys: "They saw in that erotic bond an exquisite grace exemplified in the unblemished bodies of eighteen-year-old boys, but more, they saw in the classical relations of the *erastes* and the *erameno* a code of ethical proportion that could justify and give guidance to their homosexual longings.

"And, of course, they found the flesh. In the paintings of Caravaggio, lustrous and ripe with desire. On the ceiling of the Sistine Chapel, where Michelangelo draped pubescent boys across every spare hillock. In the poems of Michelangelo written to his own beloved Cavalieri. And on the streets of fishing villages or in the fields of peasant farms where impoverished families were all too eager to offer their sons' services to the rich Northerners.

"Boys and young men born into poverty and confronted with opportunity easily dismissed the moral pronouncements of distant archbishops (themselves widely known for their taste in comely lads). For those who exist on the boundary between survival and sacrifice, the body is always the last defense and sex its most versatile tool. If Northerners like Norman Douglas or J. A. Symonds saw in these 'Praxitelean youth' the physical vestiges of Ganymede and Apollo, the young men saw something decidedly more tangible: the promise of food and shelter. At a time when vast numbers of their brothers and cousins were shipping off to Ellis Island to find a future in sweatshops and factories, these boys found a method of survival more or less at home, which, on occasion, even offered warmth and affection."

And speaking of survival, in one of his historic essays, Charles Shively challenged the premium the gay community placed – and still places – on physical beauty. Shively praised random promiscuity, arguing that to choose a sexual partner based on his physical attributes is to commit an act of discrimination. Shively wrote, "No one should be denied love because they are old, ugly, fat, crippled, bruised, of the wrong race, color, creed, sex or country of national origin." For a man to demonstrate equal respect toward all men, Shively reasoned, he should have sex with any man who wants it. To do otherwise, Shively said, was to be a bigot. This broad net encompassed young men as well, with *Fag Rag* further solidifying its radical position through an article titled "Molestation of the Young Is the Start of Politics."

Someone that we'd hope would be open to having "sex with anyone who wants it" is the porn star Johan Paulik.

Mike Esser of Pride Video in London says that just having Paulik's photo on the sleeve of a video guarantees sales of at least 8,000 copies. Mike says that "apart from being stunningly beautiful and having the most fabulous personality, Johan's a dream to work with. He kisses beautifully – I could watch him kiss for hours, he gets a hard-on in a second, he doesn't need much direction and he instinctively knows how to look amazing on screen. It's hard, if not impossible, to shoot him badly, which is why he's so hard to edit - every shot of him is beautiful. I've worked with some of the world's most beautiful specimens - but never with anyone as perfect as Johan Paulik."

"'Beauty is youth, youth beauty': so a friend of mine used to say in a jocular variation on Keats," Bruce Bawer said in *The Advocate* in his criticism of Holleran's book. Bawer says, "Though only in his 40s, he considers himself old and finds that young men's beauty, though as enticing as ever, is now also a torturous reminder of his own lost and irrecoverable splendor.

"I've talked and corresponded with hundreds of gay men in towns and cities around the country, and my distinct impression is that in the lives of most of them, such ambitions and fears have figured either very marginally or not at all. I think it is safe to say, in fact, that the great majority of gay men who are today in their 40s or older don't look to the downtown club scene, in New York or anywhere else, for affirmation of their identity and worth; most, I suspect, would say that over the years they haven't declined but have, rather, grown in confidence and self-respect. And perhaps even in the joys of the heart and the flesh...

"Few of us, to be sure, are crazy about aging. And there e re many gay men who feel ancient and invisible at 50. This is a genuine issue with which gay America has not yet begun to grapple. But Holleran is mistaken when he suggests that the pain and loneliness of older gay men is an inevitable by-product of their homosexuality. The issue here is not really about age but about youth – it is about the ways in which some young gay people are encouraged to think about their identities, both as individuals and as gay men. Young urban gay men who never come to value themselves as complex, precious individuals and who, desperately craving affirmation, learn to yoke their entire sense of who they are to the number of heads they can turn at this week's downtown hot spot, will find their sense of self suddenly unsteady when youth and beauty fade.

"...Granted, youth is glorious. Beauty is wonderful. And when you're young and beautiful and privileged, being a fixture at trendy gay hangouts can be a harmless enough diversion, provided you don't take it too seriously and don't stay too long at the fair. The important thing is to recognize that such things do not amount to the ultimate meaning of gay life – or of any life."

David Leddick, in his novel *My Worst Date*, sums it up best: "...And I realized something about Glenn. And people like him. Beautiful people: Sexy people. People everyone loves. Maybe I'm one of those people myself except that I don't think or act the way they do. They're sort of like things in nature. The Grand Canyon. Sunset over the ocean. A beautiful cliff where the water breaks. They just stay still and let everybody rush and crash around them. You can love them but you can't make them act. They are just there. They don't see life like I do at all. As going somewhere, becoming something. They just exist.

"I guess if you've been beautiful all your life there doesn't seem to be any reason to make plans to try to interest someone in you, create something. You are the subject of so many people's fantasies you don't have to have any of your own. You *are* the dream. You don't have to have any."

When first I met you
in all your sudden beauty
your eyes sparkled like
diamonds
on a jeweler's black velvet.
Elongated corners
of delicate ellipses
hinting at noble lineage
sprung from antiquity
...Quickly you go into thick velvet night
the waiting world
barring from me your
most exquisite beauty.

– *Christopher Maynard*

. . .

"I tested various combinations of boy and girl, trying to find a pair who worked really well together. The boy turned out to be less of a problem than I feared. Lila de Nobili, who was in London designing a production for Peter Hall at Stratford, told me to look out for a young actor called Leonard Whiting. I did so, and sure enough, he seemed ideal. He was beautiful in that Renaissance page-boy way that was revived during the 1960s; he could probably act; and, as was obvious when I met him, he was very ambitious . . . his looks were perfect for the role; he was the most exquisitely beautiful male adolescent I've ever met."
– Franco Zeffireili, on casting his "Romeo"

. . .

"The phone: 'How will I recognize you?' 'I'm beautiful.'"
– *from Ned Rorem, The Paris Diary of Ned Rorem (1966)*

LOOKING FOR LOVE

John Patrick

I don't know why but I always seem to end up in the produce section at the supermarket. All those lovely thick, long bananas and zucchini – I can't resist squeezing them. I ignore the stares.

My shopping done, I wait in line, pay the cashier what she says I owe.

"Paper-or-plastic?" the bagger offers.

I look up, directly into the most beautiful dark eyes I've seen in years. "Oh, paper, please."

The boy, so smartly dressed in his tight white and red uniform, nods and puts my bananas and oats and other provisions in two sacks, drops them in my cart, then moves on to the next items rolling off the belt. His name tag says "Tony."

"Have a nice day," he says, which, I presume, he says to everyone who passes his way. I stop at the entrance to take one last good look at Tony. I tend to favor boys with exotic semi-Mediterranean looks and Tony is perfect: thick, curly, almost black hair, warm olive-tinted skin and, of course, those magnificent eyes. Tony turns around, as if he knows I am here, making a fool of myself over him. He smiles, turns, and starts making his way to the back of the store.

Of course, it would have to be raining, I mutter to myself as I leave the supermarket. "Have a nice day!" Shit!

It doesn't help to improve my mood that I had to park at the far end of the lot. The rain is becoming heavier; there are puddles on the pavement. Gritting my teeth, I step out, pushing the cart in front of me, groaning when the wheels jam. I grab my two stuffed bags (paper, not plastic) and run to my car. By the time I'm in the safe cocoon of the leather-upholstered Mercedes, I am quite beside myself. Like I always do when things overwhelm me, I take several deep breaths, attempt to rest. Tony or no Tony, this is most definitely not going to be my day. I take a pill and turn on the stereo, one of the "Quiet Moments" tapes.

After about ten minutes, the rain has let up and I'm feeling better. I back the car out of the line and head toward the exit. I stop at the mall entrance and start to turn left when I see him. The bagger, Tony, is standing up at the corner, and he has his thumb out. I make a quick lane change and speed to the corner.

Tony gets in the car, wipes the rain from his face and says, "Thanks." Now he really looks at me for the first time. "Oh, bananas."

"Yes, bananas." It's a perfect opener but I ignore it.

Even all wet Tony's gorgeous. Oh how I'd love to – but that would be lust, not love. It's love I really need.

My friend Charles, who teaches college level history so he should know, says, "Everything is a bargain if you consider it from a certain perspective." He says there are only two important things to know in life: First of all, if the shoe fits, don't wear it; it's probably a trap. Second, it's a lie about needing to wear clean underpants when you're in a car wreck or any other time for that matter. It's really better not to wear any at all.

"What you need is to get out more," he adds. "Or order someone in." Charles thinks rent boys are just the ticket. "No fuss, no muss." No love, either, I counter.

When the time is ripe, Charles says, everything will happen at once, like that time in 1984 when all the planets lined up in a row. I can hardly wait. I've been looking for love for about two years now. Last week I got close. I met this guy in the library of all places. I followed him to the john and we lingered at the urinals, comparing notes. But it was doomed. I think he knew I was looking for love.

Charles says, "If you're looking for love you have to be cool about it."

I fight it, but I remain cool in the scant few minutes it takes to get to Tony's place. I listen patiently to the story of his short life, how he's just moved to town with his mother and how they found this "neat manufactured home at Shady Acres." When we arrive, I see it is a rather nice little place, but it is, to me, still a mobile home in a trailer park and I always heard horrifying stories about what happened to people who lived in those things during our terrible summer storms, and how they were real fire-traps.

After wishing me yet another nice day, Tony bounds from

the car and makes a dash to the steps of the trailer. As I pull away, he turns and waves. He doesn't know it but, for me, the sun is shining all of a sudden. My heart is thumping chaotically, because when you're looking for love even the faintest glimmer of it makes you go wild.

A week later. I'm in the store again, getting more bananas.
I wait so Tony can bag my bananas, even though the line is longer. He says, "You must love these things."
"Sure do."
"Have a nice day," he says.

Another week passes. Tony's moved up to cashier, apparently. He rings up each thing in a way I admire. His nice hands cradle the items as if they were gems of some kind, especially the bananas. "Can't get enough, eh?" Then he sticks the receipt in my palm. This, I think, will be the closest I'll ever get to him.
I beat him to the punch: "Have a nice day," I say, pushing my cart ahead of me.
"See you later," he says, winking.
I stop in my tracks, check my watch. Yes, it is exactly the same time it was two weeks ago when it was raining and I gave him a lift. *See me later?* And he winked at me. I ponder this as I make my way to the car.
Today it's clear and the sun is setting on the horizon, the sky a lovely pink. I sit in the car and wait. Before long I see him leave the store. He looks right, then left, then straight ahead. He sees my car. He ambles over, not too fast, not too slow.
I lower the window. "Going my way?" I ask.
"What way is that?"
I shake my head. "Why don't you get in?"
He nods, comes around to the passenger side, makes himself comfortable.
"It's gonna be a beautiful night," he says.
"Yes, isn't it?" What's beautiful is Tony. He is *so* beautiful tonight that I have to grip the steering wheel.
He looks over at me. "Something wrong?"
I smile. "No, no. Absolutely nothing."
I start the engine, head for the exit. I turn left this time, not

right. Tony says nothing. I'm home free.

"Dinner?" I ask as we pass a few fast-food places.

"Yeah, sure. That'd be nice."

The Via Sorrento appears as if by magic on the right. I pull into the parking lot.

Tony orders the lasagna special. I do the same. My voice is losing a little of its normal husky thread of amusement and becoming instead cool and just a little withdrawn. I have no clue as where this is heading. I do not want to get my hopes up. I order some red wine. Tony seems pleased. After a glass or two, I begin to loosen up again, but still I can't read this one. He doesn't make it easy. He talks about going to night school to get his GED. I allow as that's a smart move. He tells me about his studies.

I am non-plussed. He has not even alluded to anything queer.

Finally, once back in the car, he asks, out of the blue, "Where do you go?"

"Where do I go?"

He chuckles. "Yeah, you know, to satisfy your, eh, urges."

"I have plenty of urges, but seldom any satisfaction."

He nods. "Me too. I had a steady girl back in Gainesville. I miss her."

"I'll bet." I am confused, but don't know why I should be. I am heading toward my house, not his trailer park.

"I mean, I *really* miss her."

"Desperately?"

"Yeah, that's the word. Des-per-ate-ly." He breaks the word into parts, rolls it over on his tongue as if he's just discovered it, which maybe he has.

"I get pretty desperate myself."

"Oh?"

"You know how it is. You're not stupid." I am in an attack-mode now, frustrated with this charade. The wine has done its job loosening my tongue.

He laughs, wickedly, rubs his hard belly. "That was a good dinner, man. I really enjoyed it."

"The fun's not over yet."

"No?"

"No." I am mad, crazy with desire for this kid.
"You mean, we're going to have dessert at your place?"
"I am. I don't know about you."
He laughs again, a belly laugh. He's a barrel of laughs this kid.

He walks through the house as if he's been here before, as if he belongs here, which he maybe does, in a way. There is a tight, sensual grace in his movements. Here I was looking for love and I get this.
He fiddles with the CD's, picks out one of my "Quiet Moments" albums. "This help?"
"Help what?" I sit on the edge of the couch, my eyes wide at the sight of his buns as he leans over the player.
"Calm you down, man. You're a nervous nelly."
I do not think I act nelly, but I don't argue. "It can help maybe. But other things work a lot better."
He turns, grins. "Other things?"
"You know," I say, my eyes dropping to the crotch of his jeans. I detect a bulge that wasn't there before. Slowly he steps toward me until the bulge is right in my face. There is no doubt now, and no turning back either.
He ignores my determination to pretend that he isn't here, standing before me.
"Time for dessert?" he asks, slowly unsnapping the buttons on his 501's.
I refuse to answer, but my mouth gapes open. As he is undoing his pants, his hands, impossibly slender and well-formed, touch my face. His fingers are hard and warm as just for a second they touch my cheeks.
Because of my memories of so many other episodes with trade such as this, I start shaking my head. This is not what I want. I have had enough of lust, of satisfying some supposedly straight kid's need. But this is no ordinary straight kid.
He wears no underwear and as the pants drop away, his semi-flaccid cock pops in my face. It is long, thick, heavily-veined and brutal looking. A generous sleeve of skin covers his big knob and droops a good inch beyond the tip. His ballsac is packed with egg-sized globes and spiked with coarse black hairs. It is a generous slab of uncut meat, perfect in every

detail. Tony holds his prized manhood with both hands, intentionally stroking himself to full erection.

An intense burning begins in my gut. I reach out to touch it, but snatch back my hand, curling my fingers closed, but not quite able to stifle my small betraying gasp of awe at the sheer magnificence of his cock.

Now he reaches down and flicks my tits through my Polo shirt with his thumbnails. His roughness makes my own dick surge with blood. He waves his cock in my face, lets go of my tits and brings his hands to the back of my head. He pushes my head forward. I open my mouth as wide as it will go. The head of his cock enters my mouth. I cannot help myself; I grip his strong thighs and burrow deeper into his crotch. Moaning, he takes his hands off my head. I let up on him. The rigid shaft plops out of my mouth and rises up to curve against his belly. I begin stroking the cock up to the sticky tip.

I start licking the shaft, then go for the head again, sucking and tonguing on it, nibbling on the foreskin. I look up into his dark eyes. He smiles; he loves watching me adore his penis. I wrap my hand around the part I can't stuff in my mouth. I tighten my grip so that the foreskin slides back and forth over the head as it leaves my mouth. He shudders as I drive him crazy by running my tongue underneath the folds of skin, teasing the tender skin of the head beneath. Then I peel the foreskin back all the way and shove his cock deep in my throat. It is now out to its full eight inches. I love this cock, I decide. If I was looking for love, well, I have found it. I love this big dark cock.

I pull off and he straightens up, holding his cock by the base and looking down at it. He whips my face with it. Then I wrap my mouth around it again and start a slow suck, working the whole thing. Playing with his ass, taking his cock all the way down my throat each time, running my tongue around the shaft now and then. Teasing him, I remove the cock again and begin licking his balls, using my tongue to work one of them into my mouth.

"Oh, fuck, yes! Eat my balls," he cries.

I take one ball into my mouth, tongue and suck on it, let it slide out and go for the other one.

"Oh, fuck, yes!"

He's getting close. I let up on him. His cock lies across my face as I look up to see the lightly furred expanse of his chest and tight stomach above me as he tears off his shirt. I go back to sucking slowly again, taking it all the way down my throat, sliding off to the head, giving it a tonguing, then going back down again.

Now he starts a slow face-fuck that matches my mouth stroking. His hands move to my shoulders, then up to my head, and he starts fucking faster. He's very close when he pulls his prick out of my throat, rubbing it along my tongue. It throbs.

"Oh, man, I'm gonna come!" he screams, filling my mouth with jism. I am gulping like mad, but keep sucking. I drain the cock, not letting go until he has gone limp. I rise up, wiping cum off my lips with the back of my hand, letting his dick flop down. Finally I am able to work my own cock. I nuzzle my face into his groin, kissing and licking the soft shaft as I begin my orgasm.

He returns his hands to my head, runs his fingers through my hair. "Yeah," he says, "do it," as if he is granting me permission to jack-off.

By the time I am finished coming, cupping my load in my hand, he is hard again. I pull away, catching my breath.

With my cum-covered hand, I stroke his sopping erection. "God, what are we going to do with this?"

He smiles, takes my head in his hands and guides me forward. "Gee, I guess you're just gonna have to keep doin' it till you get it right."

Here I was looking for love and I end up with this.

. . .

Three weeks later. He's here again. It's been the same routine: dinner, wine, back here, a blowjob in the living room. An orgasm for me after his first, and then a more leisurely suck of his meat and another orgasm for him.

It's been fun, I'll admit, but I want more. I think he knows what I want: I want to get fucked by this cock I have grown to love. But he said, "Nah, I don't think so."

Tonight he wanted a shower, he'd been helping his mother

fix up the trailer. God knows, that old trailer needed it. Anyway, I met him at the entrance to the park. "No sense gettin' Mom curious."

"No, certainly not."

All this sneaking around was at first repugnant but I'm getting into now. After all, Tony is cheating on his girlfriend, even though she's three hundred miles away.

He comes out of the shower and goes to the living room looking for me.

"I'm in here," I shout. I've undressed, lubed myself and am relaxing on my stomach on the bed. As I hear him approach, I turn out the light.

"What's going on?" he asks. He's still drying his cock and balls with the big blue towel. After all, there's so much to dry off.

"Change of scene will do us good."

"I don't know – "

I scramble over to the edge of the bed, pull the towel out of his hand. All his cleaning has made his cock semi-hard. I wrap my arms around him, pulling it into my face.

"Oh," he moans as I take it between my lips.

I do my best with it for several minutes, until he says, "Nobody's ever sucked me like you do."

He's close, so I let up on in. "Okay, so give me what I want."

"My cum?"

"Yes, up my ass."

"I don't know."

"C'mon, it's tighter 'n any pussy."

"I know, but – "

Soon he's squirming under my oral assault, making me ache for him to skewer me on the throbbing spear of his prick. I have a good feeling in my gut that Tony can meet all of my needs without breaking stride.

"I want it," I moan.

All pretense is gone now. It is just me, a male in heat, sprawled naked on the bed, hard-on dripping, my asshole aching for him.

He grins, then mounts me like a fucking dog. I feel his knob batter my assring, then he finds the mark and rams into me brutally. I know he's afraid he'll lose his hard-on if he stops to think about it.

"Aaarghhh!" I cry, all my consciousness focused on the churning, burning pain in my guts.

He begins pummelling me, gradually opening me till I am taking him easily from tip to balls. As the pain subsides, an incredible rush of warmth rushes through me. I start to sweat. I can also feel the sweat dripping off of Tony, splashing onto my back and ass.

I start bucking back against him and he reaches down to grip my ass, holding me steady. My head goes down against the mattress, changing the angle of thrust so he gets me in the prostate on every stroke. He loves to fuck, this Tony, and it shows. I've never been fucked like this in my life! I shoot my first no-hands load and Tony feels my asshole clenching and starts pounding me even harder than before. Soon he is shuddering as he pumps my asshole full of his delicious cum. I collapse and Tony sprawls out on top of me, panting raggedly. We rest there for considerable time. I would love to kiss him now, but I know that would be asking for too much at this point.

I feel him moving inside me again. His cock is hardening. I groan. "What are we going to do with that thing?"

He lifts himself up and grips my asscheeks. "Guess we're gonna have to keep doin' it till we get it right."

"Oh, I love it," I sigh. Content now that I was looking for love in all the wrong places.

THE STRANGERS WE'D MEET

John Patrick

My relationship with Henry started off rather simply, at least as simple as anything could be with two gay males involved – one so young, the other, well, not so young. I'm sure that strangers we'd meet used to wonder just how things all fit together – but some of them sure found out in a hurry.

I was giving Henry (he hated being called Hank) a massage on a weekly basis and then he took me under his wing, so to speak, after his wife died. He told me he liked to go to concerts and plays and fancy restaurants, and once we got there he'd go on and on about how great his old lady'd been to leave him so well-fixed. So money was never a problem with Henry.

Sometimes what *was* a problem was deciding just what strangers we wanted to meet.

One night we went to one of our favorite haunts, Chez Paul, and we were delighted to find Paul had hired three new waiters, none of which I would ever have kicked out of bed.

Our black-tied waiter for the evening, Carl, was the cutest of the bunch, and he almost never quit *being* cute. Henry wasn't even trying to shock or scandalize that night, it was just that two drinks were his limit and he'd already had three, and the new waiter was so very receptive.

I ordered from the right-hand side of the menu like I always did when Henry was paying, and all in all, it was a very elegant dinner, beautifully served. Finally dessert time rolled around and Henry got Bananas Foster, then excused himself to go to the bathroom. Carl bowed before me. "And what would *you* like for dessert this evening?"

"Well, I certainly don't want anything that has to be set on fire at the table."

"No, I think you're already on fire."

"That noticeable, eh?"

He nodded. "I get off at midnight."

I handed him Henry's card. "Henry has a lovely, *very big* apartment."

"I'll be there."

Just then, Henry returned and the waiter withdrew.

Henry sipped some water, then looked over his shoulder to be sure Carl was gone before he asked me if I'd made any progress. I said only one word, "Midnight," before suddenly the waiter reappeared at Henry's elbow. He was as polite and formal as could be. Henry almost snapped at him but not quite. "What do you want now?"

"Pardon the interruption, sir, but I regret we are out of bananas."

"Out of bananas? At Chez Paul's?"

"They've gone bad, that's all."

"Soft?"

"Very."

Now Henry was giggling. "That'll never do."

The boy grinned. "I know."

"Well, what *do* you have?"

"That's hard?" Carl asked, grinning mischievously.

That broke Henry up and he decided to just have another drink.

By the time we left the restaurant, I was exhausted from listening because Henry was not a phony. He was really an authority on any subject – and he loved to talk.

The sky had cleared. It was a beautiful night, Henry said.

I said, "Yes, this part of the country is always pretty right after a rain."

And that got him started on rain. He knew the average rainfall of every county in Florida and every state in the Union. He talked about land mass, air currents, the hurricanes that were sure to come. Just about the time he started in on the importance of rainfall to the level of Lake Okeechobee and the Everglades, he was parking his Cadillac in the underground garage at the condo he owned on the beach.

I suggested he take a nap, maybe even let me give him one of my massages, but Henry would have none of that. He was too excited about the pending arrival of Carl. When he got in that state, all he could do was clean up things in the kitchen. As for me, I didn't want to get my hopes up. Carl was just too good to be true. He was the youngest boy we'd ever managed to finagle into coming up to the condo.

Henry had grown pretty possessive of me by this time, but

he had more sense than to act like that even a little bit when one of these "special" evenings was in the offing. Our sex had never progressed beyond what one might expect of a nude masseur and his customer. Henry still liked to suck me while I rubbed his back, and then let me jerk him off once he rolled over. But when we had company, Henry was able to watch me perform as I would if I were back in my own bedroom, and he loved every minute of it. He said it was like having a porn flick come to life in his bedroom. Having Henry sitting there was unnerving to many of our guests but eventually I won them over. Some of them even let Henry blow them while I was otherwise engaged.

But it was I who was growing possessive after Carl got there and was given a drink by Henry.

I had taken a shower and hadn't realized the kid had arrived as I wandered into the living room towel-drying my hair.

"Well," Henry laughed, "Jake isn't wasting any time tonight."

Carl didn't say anything, he just stared at my cock and balls.

I mumbled something about being sorry, how I didn't know Carl was here, blah blah blah, but nobody was listening. I wrapped the towel around my waist and fixed a drink for myself.

Henry resumed his questioning of how Carl ended up at Chez Paul, in a vain attempt to get the boy to admit that Paul had one of the most active "casting couches" in town. As I listened to the two of them talk, I could tell right off Carl was classic – very mature for his age, discreet, and knew his way around.

I took up residence next to Carl on the couch. He was still wearing his black trousers and his white dress shirt was unbuttoned to the navel, revealing nice, reasonably hairy pecs. He was, I decided, even cuter than he'd been at the restaurant, if that was possible. Trouble was, he either was terribly interested in Henry or was incredibly polite. He kept Henry talking and talking and I was getting restless. I surely didn't need any more to drink. All I wanted was to get between Carl's thighs and see what was hidden inside those black trousers.

"You two been together long?" Carl asked finally, looking directly at me for a change.

"Oh, I don't live here. I'm Henry's masseur – "

"And what a masseur he is, too," Henry said. He was tending to slur his words by this time and I knew he'd probably pass out if we ever made it to the bedroom.

"Oh, really? I haven't ever had a massage," Carl said, his eyes dancing now.

This was perfect, couldn't have been better. There I was sitting next to this adorable youth with nothing but a towel wrapped around me and he was practically begging me to do what I do best.

"Well, tonight's the night then," Henry offered, "if you're game."

"It's not me, it's Jake," Carl said. "I mean, maybe he doesn't feel like... *working?*"

I laughed at that. "Silly boy, I *always* feel like it." I bounded off the couch and headed for the bedroom. "It'll only take me a moment to set up the table." I could have done it on the bed but this boy deserved the best.

"Yes," Henry said, finishing his drink. "Jake loves his work."

"You've been staring at Carl's ass like you were trying to memorize it," Henry chuckled. He was sitting on the bed in his bathrobe, watching my every move. He had poured himself another drink. It wouldn't be long now.

"Yes, it's beautiful. You should see it up close."

Henry stood up – at least he tried to. "Later," he said, falling back on the bed.

Yes, Carl's ass was luscious, a perfect bubble butt, the pouty lips soft and pink. I had just started rubbing Carl's smooth skin when he writhing his ass in my face. Now I kissed the quivering bud of flesh, ran the tip of my tongue all around the rim. When I began poking at the opening, Carl was whimpering and his asscheeks were flexing against my forehead. I reached under him and began fingering his swelling dick. I had not seen his dick at this point. I had gone to the bathroom while he made himself comfortable on the table. I've found it's easier that way, especially for virgins. But while Carl was new to massage, he was no virgin to mansex. His cock was responding wholeheartedly and I squeezed it. He didn't resist when I lubed my fingers and invaded him, still stroking his cock with my other hand.

The last time I had done this, Henry had come over and taken over at the crotch, sucking the trick to orgasm before I even got my cock in his ass. But tonight when I looked over at him I saw Henry had passed out – finally. I had Carl all to myself.

I was soon pressing the head of my stiff cock against the lubed hole. I slipped easily inside Carl. Together we let out small moans of shared ecstasy, and Carl gratefully rotated his ass against my cock. "Oh, yeah," he groaned when I reached around and grabbed his cock again, jerking it back and forth until it throbbed. Carl cried out as inch by inch of my unusally thick meat slid up his ass, all the way to the balls. But Carl pushed back, hungry for even more. I worked my dick back and forth, twisting and plunging into the upturned ass. I let Carl jerk himself. My fucking was relentless. Nearly out of control, my cock slipped almost out, then back inside Carl.

Carl cried out while he furiously beat his meat. I groaned as I felt the first gush of my cum. Carl moaned loudly, clenching his ass muscles to squeeze out all I had to give. He bucked and thrashed against me. His cum blasted onto the towel I had laid out on the table. Then, exhausted, he lay flat against the table. I lay on top of him, then slowly removed my cock from his ass, lovingly rubbing each cheek. I stood up and rested my head on top of Carl's still quivering ass and kissed the skin.

"Poor Henry missed the show," I said softly.

"Then I guess we'll have to do it again," Carl suggested.

"Tomorrow night?"

"If I can get the rest of my massage."

"Oh, I'm sorry."

He rolled over. "I'm not," he said, grinning. He began stroking his cum-covered cock. It was a cock that was every bit as luscious as his ass, so I decided to massage it a little. I mean, the kid deserved it.

THE PIMP'S BOY

John Patrick

"Once you've had black, you won't go back."
– Old Queer Saying

Sometimes when Linc is pounding into him, like now, Donny makes himself think about the way it had started between them, when he had thought Linc was so nice, coming to his rescue.

Donny was walking out of Max's with some deli instead of a real dinner because he didn't have much money and his mother was working late at the drug store up the street when some young thugs started following him, teasing him as they had always teased him. Donny keeping his head down, trying to walk faster, crying to himself. He was always nice to people. Why did they have to pick on him?

"What you got there, cutie-pie, some cock slaw? You didn't have to buy it, I'd given ya some." Ha. Ha. Ha. They were soon snatching at his clothes, making sucking noises, grabbing at his package of deli food.

And suddenly there was this big kid, chasing them away. Big, bad black Linc. Nobody messed with Linc. Linc was soon walking Donny home, through the streets where burnt-out junkies waited in the doorways, watched from their squads by cops nibbling on donuts and drinking their coffee. The cops only interfered if the druggies trespassed on the school yard, or if the mayor was in the neighborhood. Linc saw Donny all the way home, to the apartment house on Maple Street in a nicer part of town. They stood out front, talking. Donny looked up at Linc. He was no longer afraid, but he was embarrassed at his tears, at his looks. Donny wanted to just thank him and go upstairs to his mother's apartment. But Linc seemed to want more. And he was so caring, or seemed so then, brushing away Donny's tears with a gentle smudge of his thumb. "Don't cry, little one," Linc said.

"I want to thank you," Donny said. He gulped. "Somehow."

Donny began opening up to him, in more ways than one. Telling him that he hated himself, his unruly mop of blond hair, his cowlick, everything, on the way up to the apartment. And Linc saying, "But you're cute. Beautiful, in fact. You are one beautiful boy."

"Do you think so?"

"Prettier than any white girl I ever screwed, I'll tell you that."

"Honest?"

"Honest."

Life was difficult for Donny and his mother after his father had disappeared, scraping to pay rent, eat, wear decent clothes.

Linc made it sound so easy. He knew all kinds of guys who would pay for a beauty like Donny. This surprised Donny. But Linc had to have some payment upfront, some sign of good faith.

But Donny didn't have anything. Linc put his hand on his ass right there – the first time anybody had touched him in that way, grabbing it, pulling the cheeks apart – and said that that was worth more than a hundred. Then Donny was pulling away, scared. But Linc said he didn't want him to be hurt and he could protect him.

Every afternoon they met there, to get Donny ready for what Linc called, "the big time," but if anyone was bigger than Linc, Donny couldn't imagine it. Up to that time, Donny had never seen a black boy's cock hard. He'd seen some in the showers at school, dark coils of snake in a curly tangle. He looked away, embarrassed. Donny had seen a couple of his friend's cocks, but they were as puny as his. Linc was hung, or as he put it, "built for fuckin'." Donny discovered that was true enough. The only thing that stopped Linc was the threat that Donny's mother might come through the door. He'd come, rest a minute, and go right back at it again.

Linc had taught Donny how to suck his cock, but he preferred fucking – and Donny did too. Lying on his stomach as Linc "made love" to his body was as close to heaven as Donny had ever gotten. He even managed a couple of orgasms himself during these episodes.

But eventually Linc had to be making some money off his investment in Donny's education. He met Donny's mother and charmed her. He convinced her Donny should stay with him awhile. She was dubious but Donny said it would be a little summer vacation for him. Besides, he wouldn't take no for an answer, he simply packed a duffel bag and left. Once he had Donny in his apartment, Linc began making phone calls. Everyone was interested in meeting Donny.

Linc wasn't happy. He had never lost a boy before. He went looking for him, saw Lewis sitting in a coffee shop.

"I've been lookin' for you," Linc said, choking rage in his chest.

"You wanted to see me?" Lewis said as he put his cup down and fiddled for a moment with a short cigar, which Linc lit for him as it got to his mouth. "Well, you've been busy, have you?" he asked through the smoke.

"Not very," Linc said.

Linc waited. Lewis smoked some more. Linc took a drink of the coffee Lewis had ordered for him.

"Whatever it is, I'll fix it," Lewis said. "But I don't have Donny any more."

"Where'd he go?"

"I had a friend come in. He took a liking to the kid. They became...how shall I say it, inseparable? Yeah, inseparable."

"So where is he now?"

"With my friend."

"But where?"

"That's not important."

"No?"

"No. What's important is that you get what you think you're due."

"You don't understand. I got used to that."

"Yes, I could see how that would happen. But you treated him like shit, Linc, if you don't mind my saying so."

Linc clenched his fists. "What did he tell you?"

"How you had to have it, even after he'd done maybe two or three tricks. You always had to have it."

"He made me horny."

"He made me horny, too. Just to think of him now makes me horny. But you have to learn moderation in all things – "

"Have you checked your messages?" Lewis asked into the phone.

"No," Larry answered, knuckling his eyes. It had been a long night.

"I've called five or six times."

"What's the matter?"

"Real trouble. Linc's looking for Donny. Don't take him home. Not till you're done with him."

Donny lay on a blanket looking at the clear blue sky. Suddenly, Larry's head was in Donny's lap.

"I wish," Larry said.

"Oh, stop it," Donny said, rolling away from him. "How many days like this do we get, and you just won't give it a rest."

Larry didn't want to risk running into Linc, but it was too nice a day just to stay inside. Now he was nervous, and horny at the same time. He, like Lewis, like Linc, wanted Donny all the time. "You're right. That's all you can do with troubles," Larry said. "Just let them go. What's gonna be is gonna be."

But that was about as comforting as it was original. They were sitting on a blanket littered now with the remains of the lunch Larry had made before they left the apartment.

Donny was reasonably happy. He finally had friends who kept doing nice things for him – but only if he put out. Still, after Linc, these guys were easy.

A light breeze blew high in the trees over them.

Larry stared down at Donny. Most of the other people Donny's age struck him as hopelessly immature in the way he valued the most – in bed. Donny knew tricks Larry had never experienced. He had never been with a boy who *wanted* to get fucked.

Donny, drowsy, closed his eyes. He felt Larry caress his freshly-cut blond hair. Larry was so nice, so gentle, that he pushed Linc out of his mind. He dozed for a few minutes, but a car backfiring in the street awakened him.

"You want to leave?" Larry stood and stretched his back. "I don't think you've been getting very good sleep these past few nights, staying up watching those old movies. Couldn't hurt to catch up a little – in bed."

"I guess." Donny shrugged, gathering up the blanket.

Larry noticed Donny had gotten hard during his nap. He touched it lightly.

"I think you're great," Larry sighed. "You should know that."

"Okay."

"And now you're embarrassed." Donny leaned back against a tree. His eyes were bright green under his shining blond hair. He was happy, but knew this wasn't going to last. Larry would introduce him to someone else and it would start all over again.

"I wish I could take you right here," Larry said, stuffing the trash into a grocery bag.

Donny's eyes always seemed to shine with the threat of tears, but he held them back, scrunching his nose up and forcing a smile. Larry walked up to him, put his arms around him and hugged him hard. "My boy," Larry gushed.

Donny felt something turn over inside of him. He looked out through the trees, trying to decide what it was.

...Now Donny looks over his shoulder at Linc, eyes closed, rocking back and forth, taking his time, loving it...

Larry objected to taking the long way home, to allow Donny to drop in on his mother at the drug store, but he finally agreed. He couldn't tell Donny the reason he was afraid.

Larry waited outside the drug store. He had never laid eyes on Linc but knew he would know him when he saw him. He lit a cigarette and waited. Before long, Donny appeared, clutching some movie magazines his mother had saved him with the covers torn off. Donny's mother was delighted to see Donny looking so nice. But she worried that perhaps Linc was getting Donny involved in drugs. Donny told her no, that wasn't it at all. And left it at that. He said he was enjoying his vacation.

They sauntered along in the fading light and Larry slipped off his windbreaker. He was thin, almost frail, and not much taller than Donny. He knew he would be no match for Linc if they met him. But maybe Linc's just seeing Donny would keep things calm. That was all he could hope for.

They crossed Main Street and turned on West Avenue, only

a block from Donny's apartment. Larry was nervous. He had reason to be, because they were being followed. Linc had seen Donny leaving the drug store. He had been staking the place out for days and it finally paid off. He held back, waiting until the pair got to a secluded place. Now he was sure they were going to Donny's apartment, but they didn't, they kept on walking up the avenue.

Linc liked what being kept had done for Donny. He liked the new haircut, the new clothes. Donny was doing exactly what he told him to do. Trouble was, Linc wasn't getting any. None of the other boys Linc met had affected him the way Donny had. Linc could take 'em or leave 'em; he *had* to have Donny. And now he was just wasting time.

Finally Larry and Donny stopped to look at TVs in a store window. They were laughing. Linc came up behind them. Larry turned and knew immediately who it was. Linc, at six foot three, towered over him. His biceps bulged in his tank top. His jeans fit tightly and bulged incredibly at the crotch. Larry would have been terribly attracted to him under another circumstance, but now he feared for his very life.

Donny began trembling when he saw Linc. He clung to Larry. "Don't hurt him," Donny said to Linc. "He didn't do nothin' to you."

"No, only stole my meal ticket."

"I'll pay you whatever you think is due – " Larry offered, reaching for his wallet.

"You couldn't afford it," Linc huffed, grabbing Donny by the sleeve of his new Polo jacket.

Donny did not resist. He started walking, Linc behind him, shoving him. Larry stood still on the sidewalk, sweating profusely. He had avoided a fight, but he had lost Donny.

...Linc is speeding up now, and Donny gets into it a little, leaning back into it, maybe hurry him along. He reaches back between his legs and runs his fingers along the bottom of Linc's scrotum and Linc makes that sound that means it won't be too long now...

Donny was still trembling when they got to Linc's little apartment. As soon as the door was closed, Donny collapsed on the sofa in tears. Linc had still said nothing. He stood over Donny, began undressing.

Donny looked up, wiped away his tears. Linc's cock looked bigger than he had remembered it. He had been treated so well, but the men's cocks could not compare to Linc's. Linc took Donny's head in his hands, smudged the remaining tears into his cheeks. Donny looked up at the man's body, dark as ebony. He felt the hair on the chest and legs, so different from his own smooth skin and that of the johns. He leaned forward and pushed back the foreskin. He took the head between his lips. The cock began to sink into his mouth. He closed his eyes, letting Linc's prick fill him. As he sucked gently on it, the shaft began to swell. He worked his eager mouth along the length of the now fully erect prick, choked on it, then returned to it, overcome now by the pleasure.

Donny brought his hands to Linc's asscheeks, pushing him against his face. He grasped the man tightly. As Donny sucked his dick, Linc began to thrust slowly in and out, fucking steadily. Linc placed his hands on Donny's head to steady the boy.

...Linc pulls out. He doesn't want to come yet. No, he wants to make this last a bit longer. He wants Donny to beg him for it. He hasn't had this big dick for three weeks. He knows he missed it; he wants him to say it.

Linc rolls the boy over. "What's wrong?"

"You don't like it any more?"

"What?"

"You get better from those men?"

"No, no."

"I didn't think so."

Now for the first time, Linc wants Donny from the front. Donny takes his own erection in his hand only to pull it against his belly so that he can more easily watch Linc's enormous member slide into his ass.

Linc kneels between Donny's thighs and pulls Donny's nearly hairless legs up over his shoulders. Donny moans when he feels the tip of the cock against his asshole. As Linc shoves into him, Donny cries out in pain, but as inch after inch is slowly fed into him again, he begins moaning with pleasure. Finally he feels Linc's thick bush against his ass.

The monster cock retreats and enters in long motions, the heavy balls slapping noisily against Donny's butt as Linc fucks the boy. Donny's fingers dig into Linc's skin, holding his thighs. Linc thrusts harder, forcing his cock deep into the asshole, pulling almost all of the way out before sinking in again.

Donny reaches for his own cock now. He can't help himself. As he comes, Linc batters the ass until Donny is finished.

Donny is disoriented. He has missed this more than he realized. "Oh, yeah," he moans when he feels Linc is close.

"Oh, oh, motherfucker. Motherfucker!" Linc says the litany every time he comes. Collapsing onto Donny's chest, he wraps around him, kisses him full on the mouth. Donny groans. Linc has never kissed him before. Linc's thick cock is still large inside him, and it is stirring.

Donny starts to cry again. But now they are tears of happiness.

THE BLACK GOLIATH: HARD ALL OVER

Frank Brooks

Back in the days when Arnold Schwarzennegar, Sergio Oliva, and Franco Columbu were battling yearly for the Mr. Olympia title, Jason, Danny, and I, three teenagers, were training daily in the well-equipped garage gym we'd set up together, having accumulated, over our years together in high school and junior high, the weights and benches and gymnastics apparatus needed for serious bodybuilding.

We were a dedicated threesome, all of us having built classically proportioned, defined, and hard-all-over physiques over the years, but despite all our years of dedication and hard work we all realized, in the back of our minds, that our small-boned frames would never pack on those big slabs of muscle that would make us look like real bodybuilders. All three of us, at five-seven and 130 pounds, resembled well-trained gymnasts.

We kept dreaming, however, imagining ourselves up there on the posing platform at the Mr. Olympia contest, flexing and writhing before thousands of cheering fans, our oiled bodies clad only in the tiniest bikini posing briefs. All three of us were naturally hairless, with only the tiniest tufts under our arms and on our groins, tufts that we could and did whisk off in seconds with a razor. And we all resembled each other to an uncanny degree, all three of us being towheaded and blue-eyed with pageboy haircuts, our thick bangs hanging to our eyebrows in front. People called us the three musketeers, because we were always together. We'd been inseparable since grade school.

The walls of our garage gym, the areas of wall, anyway, that weren't mirror, were plastered with color centerfolds and cutouts from bodybuilding magazines. Arnold, Sergio, and Franco, of course, were our main heroes, with Sergio, not Arnold, being the king, as far as we were concerned. They say that opposites attract, and maybe that's why we were so wild about Sergio, the beautiful black Cuban giant with the biggest slabs of dense muscle ever to be packed on a human frame. To us three young blond boys, his dark brown beef looked good enough to eat, and the three of us spent hours gazing up at his pictures, our mouths salivating, our young bodies throbbing.

And our three stiff peckers oozed pre-cum into our bikini trunks, when we were wearing them, or onto the mat if we'd stripped off our trunks to let our peckers throb free in the air. And it never failed that we'd end up pounding our throbbing prongs in unison, gazing up at Sergio, wishing we could somehow see him without those trunks on. We just knew he had a mammoth black fuck-snake packed inside his posing briefs, a beautiful black cock that matched his beautiful black body, a cock that spewed gallons of thick white fuck-cream when he came. We imagined Sergio filling a bathtub with his hot jism and the three of us swimming in it. We'd certainly shot more cum from our seven-inch boycocks while lusting over Sergio than over any other of the massive bodybuilding heroes we worshipped.

One day, though, Sergio had to step aside. Another black giant appeared in the magazines and immediately found a place on our gym wall up there beside him. Although a newcomer on the contest scene, Goliath Black (dubbed immediately The Black Goliath by his fans and the bodybuilding press) had surely spent years, maybe decades, heaving tons of barbell plates or even railroad cars to develop slabs of dense beef that rivaled even those of Sergio. Apparently Goliath had decided to stay quietly behind the scenes, training for years until he'd acquired a full-blown Mr. Olympia physique before going public with his body.

Goliath was taller than Sergio, his skin darker, his muscles more deeply cut. And, if it were possible, he looked even more serious and intense than Sergio, and he had a bulge in his posing briefs that dwarfed not only Sergio's bulge, but that of any other bodybuilder we'd ever seen. We guessed that his stud meat had to be at least ten inches long, maybe eleven, and proportionately thick, and we were convinced that it was uncut. All three of us being cut ourselves, we had a fascination for uncut man-dick.

Soon we were jacking off with our three pairs of blue,

worshipful eyes turned up and focused on Goliath, with Sergio and Arnold and Franco still up there, but only within our peripheral vision. Our hearts pounded as we imagined Goliath's sweat-streaming body naked, our pink tongues lapping at his slabs of black muscle, our tongue tips probing the tasty, salty crevices of his cuts. As our legs nearly gave out under us and we grunted in boyish ecstasy and shot cum onto the gym mat and against the wall mirrors before us, our glazed eyes remained trained up at the most beautiful, muscular black man any of us had ever seen. Soon Goliath was all we talked about or dreamed about, and that's why, when a bodybuilding magazine let slip that Goliath was now living in our very own city and had been training for months at Quinn's Pro Gym downtown, we nearly went into shock.

Here we'd been living in the same town as Goliath for months and we hadn't even known it! As soon as we found out, we squeezed into our tightest white muscle shirts and our tightest faded blue-jeans and our white leather Nikes, well-scuffed and worn without socks, and we headed down to Quinn's Pro Gym, hoping to catch sight of our hero in person.

Unfortunately, Quinn, the red-headed, freckled-skinned, massively muscled owner of his own professional iron-pumping factory wouldn't allow anybody inside the gym except members, and to be even considered for membership you had to already look like a Mr. America competitor. Quinn and his gym had a national reputation and drew serious bodybuilders from all over the world. The closest we could get to these men, who came and went via the private back door and the private gym parking lot in back, was to watch them through the large plate glass windows out front, through which you could hear the muffled crashing of barbell plates and the grunts and screams of bodybuilders bombing and blitzing to the limit.

We arrived at Quinn's Gym at ten o'clock on Saturday morning and spent the whole day on the sidewalk out front, ogling bodybuilders in action through the windows. We spotted several famous faces and a few big stars, but none of them was Goliath. The magazines claimed that he trained twice a day, six days a week, and by four we were beginning to wonder if Saturday was maybe his day off. At 4:15, though, Goliath's massive, nearly naked black frame strode into view. We couldn't believe it!

Talk about excitement! The three of us had to hold onto each other to keep from fainting. Our three wildly throbbing dicks squirmed in our jeans and nearly creamed. Goliath looked twice as big and black in person as he did in his pictures. His biceps and calves were bigger than our heads. His posing briefs hardly covered his ass cleft or contained his massive cock. To warm up, he did about fifty rapid presses with dumbells, each of which weighed as much as a barbell we would use for deadlifts. As he began his heavy-duty bombing and blitzing, the sweat flowed in rivers over his swelling, bulging, writhing black muscles, and we three admiring boys moaned out loud, fighting the urge to pull out our dicks and squirt cum against the plate glass.

About an hour into his workout, Goliath noticed us watching him, our freckled noses nearly pressed to the window, and he started glancing at us between sets, his face serious and unreadable. Jason claimed that he saw Goliath smile, but neither Danny nor I had noticed. To me, Goliath appeared so deadly serious about his workout that he seemed almost angry, and I guessed that the smile Jason thought he saw was a grimace of concentration or pain.

Then, all at once, Quinn was talking with Goliath and the two men both looked toward us. A minute later Quinn stepped out the front door.

"Can I help you dudes?"

"We're just watching," we mumbled.

"Yeah? Well, you been out here just watching all day. Maybe you oughta think about moving on. My window ain't a TV set."

"We thought maybe we could get Goliath's autograph," Jason said, surprising both Danny and me, as we'd never even considered trying to get that.

"My guys are here to train, not give autographs," Quinn said. Then he shook his head as if we were hopeless and went back inside. We watched him talk with Goliath and suddenly the black giant was striding like a panther toward the front door.

He stepped out into the sunshine, dripping sweat all over sidewalk. He wasn't exactly smiling, but he wasn't glaring either. "I hear you guys are fans of mine."

"Yes sir," we managed to croak, all three of us shaking.

"You must be brothers, and I can see you all pump iron."

We laughed, assuring him that we weren't brothers. Jason mentioned that we worked out daily in our garage gym.

Goliath's eyes moved up and down our bodies, appraising them, lingering here and there. He would have had to be blind not to notice our hard cocks throbbing in our jeans.

"Nice physiques," he said. "Small, but nice. Well, hand over your writing pad and I'll sign it."

We all turned red, and Jason finally admitted that we had nothing to write on or with.

Goliath appeared amused. "Maybe you want me to sign the sidewalk with sweat then."

"No sir," we all mumbled.

Then Goliath said something that shocked us speechless. "Meet me out back at the parking lot entrance in 45 minutes. I'll have an autograph for each of you, and then maybe we can go over to that garage gym of yours so I can take a look at it."

Forty-five minutes later we boys packed into the front seat of a sports car hardly large enough to contain Goliath, let alone Goliath plus us. We had to sit on top of each other and just about wrap around each other. Goliath had thrown on shorts and a sports shirt and was still dripping sweat from his workout. He evidently hadn't showered. We got to our garage none too soon, just as the three of us were about to suffocate.

"Cozy," Goliath said, looking around our gym. He smiled at his picture prominently displayed on the wall between posters of Sergio and Franco. "Real nice place you boys got here."

We stared bug-eyed as he stripped off his shirt and shorts and kicked off his shoes, revealing his magnificent body clad only in posing briefs. He struck a frontal biceps pose, watching himself in the wall mirrors. Then he turned around and looked at us. "Well, what're you dudes waiting for? Strip down and we'll do some pumping."

We stumbled out of our shoes and peeled off our shirts, but then we hesitated. None of us was wearing anything under our jeans and if we took them off we wouldn't be able to hide our rampant cocks.

"Well, get on with it," Goliath said. "You can't work out in pants tight as those, you'll bust the seams."

When we still hesitated, each of us waiting for one of the others to go first, Goliath smiled and shook his head. He went over to Jason, undid Jason's jeans, and yanked them down. Jason's hardon snapped up, whopping Goliath on the chin.

"Whoa!" Goliath said. "What's this?" He gave Jason's cock a twang. "Fucking billyclub. Working out must get you worked up."

He yanked down Danny's jeans next, then mine, and all three of us stood there shaking, our young cocks pointing ceilingward and throbbing with our rapid heartbeats.

"Well!" Goliath exclaimed. "What have we here? Looks like all three of you boys get turned on working out. To tell the truth, so do I."

Easing his fingers under the waistband of his tiny silk posing briefs, he bent over and pushed them down, sliding them off over his huge black feet. As he straightened up, his massive cock came into view, standing straight out and curved slightly upward, with half of its gleaming, purplish-black knob bulging from its foreskin. The huge fucker looked as long and thick as my forearm, and the black sac that hung from its base bulged with balls as big as peaches.

Goliath rubbed both hands between his legs and spread ball-sweat up onto the massive, deeply cut slabs of his abdominals. Then his hands slid to his hips, resting there, and he began to flex his cock up and down as we watched, goggled-eyed.

"What're you waiting for?" he asked. "Warm up them stiff motherfuckers. You gotta exercise 'em if you want 'em to be strong. Come on, flex 'em. One, two, three, four!"

With our hands on our hips in imitation of Goliath, we began to wiggle our seven-inch cocks up and down, flexing them as Goliath counted out the repetitions and flexed his own cock to the same beat. Our pissholes opened up and started to drip pre-cum. We exercised our cocks until we couldn't perform another repetition.

"I believe in working every muscle in the body," Goliath said, showing us his white teeth in a grin. He picked up a ten-pound barbell plate, laid it on its side on top of his cock, and, using his thumb and forefinger to keep it from falling off, he began to flex his cock and lift the plate up and down. It seemed impossible.

"If you don't want to balance a plate on your cock," he went on, "you can tie a cord around it, then tie the other end to a plate and do your lifts that way. Or – " He dropped the plate on the mat and pressed his hand down on top of his cock. "You can apply hand resistance." He flexed his cock against his down-pushing hand.

"Why don't you boys help me out." He took our hands and drew them to his cock. "Hold it down if you can."

His powerful cock felt like a hot rattlesnake struggling to spring up under our hands. It was so strong that I imagined chinning myself on it. As the massive black fucker bucked against our palms, tickling them, we began to stroke it, to feel it all over, to slide its foreskin up and down. Its pisshole gaped so large that I could have inserted a half inch of my little finger up it. Pre-cum oozed out, hot and slippery, and our fingers slicked it over the apple-sized knob and black, veiny shaft.

"Nice," Goliath said. "Real nice. Soft hands. Keep it up, don't be shy now."

We were all hypnotized, watching and rubbing Goliath's fucker, our tongues flicking between our lips, and suddenly we were dropping to our knees, rubbing against Goliath's bulging thighs, our tongues and lips, our fingers and freckled noses sliding all over his cock and balls, moans and mutters of appreciation escaping our mouths.

Goliath stroked our blond heads. "You white boys like that big black cock, huh. You like all this black muscle." He flexed his abs, making them dance. "Come on, give this black muscle a tongue bath. Go on, lick me all over." He took a step back, sat down on the mat and lay back, stretching out fully, his arms above his head. "Go on, lick."

He was the hottest, most beautiful man any of us had ever seen, and there he lay, naked and stretched out for us to play with. Every part of him had been shaved below the neck, including his groin and armpits, so his skin was as smooth as silk and looked almost translucent stretched tight over his muscles. We fell on him like three ravenous lion cubs, devouring him, lapping up his sweat, sucking at his black flesh. We licked his toes, chewed his nipples, sucked his armpits, all of us delirious with lust for him.

Goliath caught us in his arms and crushed us down on top of him. As we squirmed against him and humped, he kissed us, feeding us his tongue, which we sucked greedily. His lips caught each of our tongues in turn and sucked, and we drooled into his mouth. I was so excited that I was going to squirt at any moment, but Goliath rolled us aside before I could and got up to sit on a bench.

"Okay babies," he said, spreading his legs wide, his huge fucker throbbing upright between his thighs, "let's see who can swallow the most big meat?"

Jason went first. Kneeling between Goliath's legs, gripping the huge black cock in two hands, he pulled the foreskin down tight and licked the knob. Then he stuffed his mouth with cock flesh. He was able to take the head and about three inches of shaft before choking. It looked at if he were trying to swallow a black baseball bat. His blond head hardly moved as he sucked, his spit trickling down Goliath's shaft and balls. Growling, smacking his lips as he munched cock, he jerked his own cock rapidly, his eyes glazed with pleasure and excitement. From the expression on his face, I expected to see him squirt jism in about two more seconds, but Goliath seemed to sense Jason's imminent orgasm and pushed him away before it began.

"Next," Goliath said.

I grabbed Goliath's cock before Danny could. My mouth gaping, I engulfed Goliath's spit-wet knob and slid my lips down his shaft until I was choking. I'd never had anything so huge in my mouth. I could feel Goliath's heart beat in his cock and could sense the strength of the gigantic fuck-tool as it pulsed. I imagined that if he flexed his cock, it would tear my head off.

I growled, sucking with ravenous hunger, my spit trickling down his cock shaft. I was able to bob my head only slightly and to wiggle my tongue, but my jaws felt about to dislocate and my lips to tear from being stretched like rubberbands around the thick cylinder of man-meat. My entire head felt like it was filled with cock. I was beating off in a frenzy.

Again, before I could shoot off, Goliath pushed me away and

Danny took over. He had trouble swallowing as much cock as Jason and I had, and he choked several times before his throat adjusted. Once he got going, though, he couldn't get enough cock, and when Goliath tried to push him away, he resisted, growling as if he would bite Goliath's cock right off.

"Easy boy," Goliath said, gently lifting Danny's head off his cock. "You babies are all natural cocksuckers. Now it's my turn to show you what I can do."

We lined up to get our cocks sucked, and Jason went first, sticking his cock in Goliath's huge mouth. From the way Jason's eyes rolled back and he groaned, I could tell that Goliath knew what he was doing. After a few minutes of hot sucking, Goliath pushed Jason aside and went down on me. I moaned as he took my seven inches to the balls and sucked with long, hot, deep strokes, nearly sucking the cum out of me with each smack of his lips. Just as I was getting into the rhythm of Goliath's pleasuring me, and hoping it would never stop, he pushed me aside and devoured Danny's dripping young fucker. Danny grunted, his tight little ass dimpling as his loins humped.

After sucking Danny for a few minutes, Goliath resumed sucking Jason, then me, then Danny again. He kept moving from one cock to another, repeatedly sucking us to the verge of orgasm, but stopping just before we could pop. It drove us nuts. He had the hottest mouth I'd ever sunk my cock into, his fat tongue and lips thrilling me in ways that sent pleasure coursing through my asshole, nipples, and toes. I came to the verge of creaming in Goliath's mouth a half-dozen times before he decided he'd had enough cock for a while and wanted something else.

"OK boys, turn around now and show me them cute little white butts," Goliath said. "That's it, turn around. Oh yeah, now that's what I call grade-A young ass."

He parted our buttcheeks with his thumbs as we wiggled our asses in his face, muttering about "pink holes" and "boy-pussy" as he sniffed our puckers and licked up and down our sweaty cracks. The tip of his tongue probed our tight, twitching assholes and wiggled its way up into them. Three inches of hot tongue worked its way up my shitter and I thought I'd die with pleasure. After rimming us silly, he asked us where we kept the fuck-grease.

We looked at each other, all three of us thinking the same thing: that he'd kill us with that enormous cock if he tried to fuck us. We were used to each other's seven-inch cocks up our butts, not an eleven-inch monster as thick as a Coke can.

"Quick now," Goliath said, stroking his cock, "get the grease. This big old black rattlesnake can't wait much longer. It needs to fuck some tight young ass before old Goliath loses his mind." Giving Danny and me a look of "what else can I do," Jason fetched the Vaseline we used for jack offs and fucking and handed the container to Goliath, who smiled and smeared a handful of the greasy lube from the tip of his black cock to his balls. Goliath told Danny, who was nearest him, to turn around and he shoved a greased middle finger up Danny's asshole. Danny gasped as the thick black finger pumped in and out several times. Goliath's finger was almost as large as our cocks and soon Danny was gyrating his ass and moaning as if Jason or I were fucking him.

"Hot baby," Goliath said. "And tight. Nothing I like better than a boy who's hot for a dick up his tight young ass." He slipped his finger out of Danny, grasped Danny's hips from behind, and sat the boy down on his rigid, standing cock.

Danny looked as terrified as he was excited and was panting a mile a minute. Goliath's naked cockhead throbbed between his asscheeks. Jason and I watched wide-eyed as Danny began to absorb the enormous black cock into his body. As the head disappeared inside him, he gasped, his mouth wide open, and his dick flexed wildly. Several more inches of Goliath's cock sank into him before he could take no more. At least three-quarters of the monster cock was buried inside him.

"Baby, that's beautiful!" Goliath said, looking at his gleaming stud-pole nearly buried to the hilt up the kid's ass. "Now ride me, baby! Easy now."

Danny, taking deep breaths like a woman giving birth, eased himself up and down. As his asshole adjusted to the stretch, his movements quickened. Goliath groaned, several inches of his vein-bulging black fuckmeat reappearing, then disappearing again up Danny's white ass.

Goliath slicked the middle fingers of both his hands with Vaseline and held them up, grinning as he gave Jason and me the finger. "Show me your asses, boys."

It was like receiving an electric jolt as he slipped his thick finger up my asshole, and I could tell that Jason felt the same way. We both moaned, wiggling our butts and jerking on our cocks as Goliath pumped his fingers in and out of us.

"It's – so – fucking – big!" Danny gasped, impaling himself deeper on Goliath's prong, his right hand pounding his own cock as he rode the man. "Oh fuck!" Incredibly, nearly all of Goliath's cock was up his ass now.

Goliath rolled his eyes with pleasure, rubbing his black ass against the sweat-slick seat of the bench, grinding his cock in Danny's sizzling asshole. "What an ass!" he grunted. "Fuck me, boy, ride me!"

"Oh, I'm gonna come!" Danny moaned.

"Not yet, baby!" Goliath popped Danny off his cock just as Danny ejected a few watery drops. He stopped Danny's jerking hand. "Not yet, baby, save it for me." Then he grabbed Jason from behind and pulled Jason's ass onto his cock. "Sit on it, boy."

Jason, moaning, wiggled his butt and screwed himself down on Goliath's cock, pounding away at his prick as Goliath's fuck-snake disappeared nearly totally inside him. I expected to see Goliath's cockhead pop out of Jason's mouth.

"Man!" Jason panted, gyrating his ass and fucking himself silly on the gigantic black crowbar. "Oh shit!"

"Ride it!" Goliath grunted. "Fuck my cock!" The black man humped, thrusting his shining black fuck-sword up into Jason's down-fucking white ass. As he screwed Jason, he pulled Danny nearer, stuck a middle finger up Danny's asshole, and took Danny's cock into his mouth.

"Oh yeahhh!" Danny grabbed Goliath's head, plunging his cock between Goliath's smacking lips and deep into his mouth. His blue eyes turned back with delirious pleasure and his toes curled against the mat. In seconds Danny was jerking like a puppet on a string, squirting boy-jizz in Goliath's mouth. "I'm coming! Coming!"

Danny clung to Goliath's head, his body spasming, his cum squirting down Goliath's throat. Goliath gagged a few times, trying to gulp the hot sperm, until his throat adjusted to the forceful spurts. All though Danny's orgasm, Goliath's thick finger rammed in and out of Danny's asshole, driving Danny nuts.

When Goliath released Danny, Danny collapsed onto the mat as if he were melting, and there he sprawled, cooing, his cock still hard.

Goliath pushed Jason off his cock and pulled me onto it. His huge hands easily encircled my waist and hips and I felt his cockhead burning between my asscheeks. Gently but firmly he pulled downward as he thrust upward and his cock slipped into me. I gasped with surpise and pain as his cockhead stuffed me. It felt like a fist going up my ass, then like a baseball bat as the rest of his cock followed. I thought I'd split down the middle.

"Yeahhh!" Goliath sighed. "Now ride me!" His hands still encircling my waist, he started me moving, sliding my asshole up and down the entire length of his cock as if I were a fuck-toy. "Tight hot ass! Oh baby, ride me!"

If I hadn't been as excited as I was, I'd have screamed. As Goliath's cock stuffed me again and again, I jerked on my cock in a panic and soon the splitting pain in my loins gave way to pleasure. Muttering out of my head, I started rotating my ass and fucking myself faster on the powerfully flexing man-cock. Soon I was literally bouncing.

"That's it!" Goliath grunted. "You got it now, baby!" He let go of my loins as I took over riding him and he shoved the finger that had been up Danny's asshole up Jason's and he started sucking Jason's cock.

Jason's fat balls flapped against Goliath's black chin. His fingers dug into Goliath's scalp. He humped as Goliath finger-fucked him and sucked him. In half a minute it was all over.

"Take it!" Jason panted, his cum exploding into Goliath's mouth. "Drink it!" He squirmed as if he were being whipped, shooting his youthful spunk down Goliath's throat.

Goliath cooed his appreciation, his lips smacking, his adam's apple bobbing. As he drank Jason's load, he began to thrust up into me in earnest. His black toes curled against the mat, toenails digging in as he rammed me faster and faster. Then he groaned loudly and his cock shuddered.

For a moment my feet left the floor and I was literally lifted and waved in the air, my body impaled on Goliath's powerful, spasming cock. The huge fuck-organ shuddered again and suddenly an explosion of liquid heat flooded my loins. My toes touched the mat again and Goliath's second explosion of pleasure-juice splashed in my guts and his cock again lifted me. The spurting, powerfully flexing cock inside me sent me into ecstasy. I yelped as jism shot from my cock and splashed against the wall mirror six feet away.

"Beautiful!" Goliath groaned, watching my jism fly. "Shoot that hot juice!" He crushed me in a bear hug, fucking the rest of his load up my ass as my own cum splashed across the mat and I whimpered in ecstasy.

When the fireworks were finally over, Goliath slid off the bench and crouched on the mat, lapping up the puddles of my spunk. We all watched him as he crawled along, the muscles of his sweat-drenched black body bulging, the jism dripping from his lifting tongue. When he reached the mirror, he licked his way up it until he'd cleaned off every drop of my spunk.

"Can't get enough cum," he said, wiping his mouth and grinning at us. "It builds muscle like nothing else."

So that's how it happened that back in the days when Arnold and Sergio and Franco were battling for the Mr. Olympia title, that Jason, Danny, and I got to know Goliath Black, who everybody said was headed for Mr. Olympia himself. He never made it, though, and that was possibly our fault. After meeting us he cut his twice-daily workouts at Quinn's to one morning session per day so he could work out with us in the garage afternoons, where he exercised his powerful black fuck-muscle to the exclusion of his other body parts – and left feeling more drained than possibly was good for a world-class bodybuilder in training.

Goliath never complained, though, and neither did we. Mr. Olympia or not, he remained our number one hero, surpassing Arnold and Franco and even the great beautiful black Sergio.

THE COMPANY OF BEAUTIFUL BOYS
P. K. Warren & John Patrick

"For a moment, he'd worried. Maybe it came from being imprisoned. In jail, heterosexuals mutated, he'd heard. Due to the company of beautiful boys? Who, in steamy bathrooms, bizarrely became gorgeous girls? Something like that. Toby didn't want to pursue the line of thought. He found it disturbing."
— Lewis Gannett, Magazine Beach

Dear J.,

Since my last letter the riot is over, but the fun continues. Buses have been leaving and arriving here around the clock. They are transferring the gang leaders/trouble makers, and, hopefully, transfer in a better stock. So, generally, we're being overwhelmed with new faces. It's the adminstration's own fault. It used to be it would take you a few years to make it to this joint but now fairly recent numbers are showing up – nothing but young punks fresh off the streets and bent on making trouble.

But the big news is that your little girl here has got herself a - can you believe - a new Daddy!

But this isn't one of the transfers. I've known D. since I got here. We weren't exactly buddy-buddy, if you know what I mean, but always polite to one another. Too, it isn't as though he hasn't k-n-o-w-n about me either. He's not a runway model, nor Mr. America, but rather the kind of guy you can just glance at and tell just as quick that "Oh, honey, he's Daddy material!" D. is five-eleven, 6', 185 lbs., with brown hair that he wears in a brush cut, and a goatee - neatly trimmed. He's sorta like a trucker, biker, redneck all rolled into one.

In the past we've always kidded one another, always teasing and joking. He'd drop in where I work and start in. Whenever I attempted to call his bluff, make a move, he'd say "see ya later" and run for the hills. Then one day, after D. had fled, one of the guys in the shop (who everyone knows is a big girl at heart) came up to me and whispered, "Girlfriend, what on earth are you doing? Don't you know that boy wants you, and you're too busy to give him an ounce of your time?" He snapped his fingers at me. "Sweetheart, open your eyes."

Well, I cut him short on the "girlfriend" business, though pretending dumb with him is a losing battle because he's got his eyes open and on everything. Before his husband showed up and he trotted off to keep house, he said, "You could use the darkroom. Let me know when you're ready and I'll keep watch for you."

By the following Monday I knew some insider trading was done over the weekend. Before I could shake D. from the area he asked, "Hey, beautiful, when're you gonna give me a personal tour of the darkroom?" As he left, before I could even answer, he passed behind me and, accidently on purpose, brushed my ass with his arm.

The next day when he showed up I took a smoke break and asked him to join me in the Rest Room area.

"You know, D.," I said, fighting to control my nerves, "I'm scared shitless over what's coming. I know they're going to riot and if it gets ugly I'm gonna need protection, because I'm a lover - not a fighter. Can I count on you?"

"Shit, beautiful, who's gonna protect *me*?" he asked with a stern face, then started laughing.

"Well, I'll do what I can to keep you safe, but I'm an old softy."

"How soft is that?" he asked.

"Like the texture of an abused pussy, only worse."

"Pussy. God, I haven't had one of those in years."

"I know," I said, my gaze drifting to his crotch.

He smiled. "Yeah, a little head right now wouldn't hurt any." He groped his crotch. "How 'bout that darkroom tour?"

"C'mon, stop fucking around – I'm serious."

"So am I." He was vigorously massaging it now.

I got up for a drink of water at the fountain and returned. "Are you serious," I said, "or it this just another passing fancy of yours?"

He glanced up and his face was a blank. Clearly my question had caught him off guard. He got up and made to leave, then stopped at the door and stood a moment glancing up and down the length of the workshop. "You really fucked up this time, beautiful."

Then he walked off to the urinals, unzipping to take a piss. Or so I thought.

I waited a couple of minutes, then realized I was stretching my break too far. Passing the rest room, I noticed D.; instead of pissing, he had turned so I could see that he was stroking his stiff cock. It was a risky on his part because anyone can look right into the rest room.

Even before he said "C'mon," I was giddy as a school girl on her first date. D. stepped up to the largest stall of two, opened the door, nodded for me to follow. I nearly ran.

There is barely enough room for two people in the stall. When it's in use, the person's knees are practically against the door when sitting on the bowl. So it wasn't the easiest stunt to do, but it had to be done to ward off the curious: I dropped trou and sat on the bowl so my booted feet could be seen. With D. standing to the far back of the stall I had to twist my torso to a painful degree in order to reach him. I hadn't had a stiff dick, in my mouth in so long that I gobbled up D.'s like it was a last meal. I gagged once, but after that it was like the old saying; once you learn to ride a bike you never forget!

D.'s not hung like a stallion, but, D.'s got the right size cock - the type you can suck and fuck with for hours on end and never get tired of. In short order D.'s T-shirt was hooked up behind his head, pants and boxers down around his feet with his hands holding and caressing my head as it bobbed over his full length. You remember how good I was at deep-throat? Well, I haven't lost my touch; I was going down on him with a quest of feeling that plum-like cock head poking around the walls of my stomach, while my fingers were busy with a set of balls the size of hen's eggs.

Eventually, D. held my head still and fucked the depths of my throat. As he did so, I reached up to attack his nipples with my fingers, which really set him off. I thought for sure he'd make mashed potatoes out of my nose the way his pelvis kept bouncing off it. When his breathing turned to short labored rasps I knew it was time for some focus on my own throbbing cock. In just three strokes I had to bend my cock down into the bowl to let it fire and be overwhelmed by it all. Just as I did, D. pushed down my throat and held fast as the first volley shot down my gullet, then drew up to my mouth to fire the second, then rammed it and the third down my throat.

The after-shakes took hold of me and it was a bitch pulling myself half-assed together once D.'s softened cock left my mouth. As I stood up to draw up my drawers, D.'s big hand took hold of an asscheek and I could have dropped a second load right then.

"Next time," I promised, then walked back to my station.

The next time I saw him, conditions weren't favorable for an encore. But we did have a smoke together. "You learn to relax your asshole in prison," D. told me. "You just have to." After his arrest as a teen, he was dumped in a cell where he was repeatedly raped and urinated on by inmates over a two-day period. He was finally able to escape his tormentors by posting bail and was released. But eventually he was tried and convicted and, in prison, he was trained as a sex slave by four prisoners who had joint ownership of him. Being a punk for these men prevented him from being molested by other prisoners. He eventually began to see his being pissed on as a form of baptism. Now, as these things work out, I was his punk. I was not about to admit how much I had dreamed of having his cock up my ass. It was more fun to have him think he had to convince me.

I guess with all the tension in the air over the forced close-down after the riot, it made for doing some crazy things. Anyhow, last Tuesday, it was finally back to the rest room and the same stall. More or less, D. didn't ask for it – he took it and staked his claim. I thought it was going to be just a repeat show, but, no sooner were my buns bared, to sit on the bowl, D.'s hands were all over them. "You promised," he reminded me.

He straddled the bowl and pushed up behind me and I was all prepared for some incredible pain, but it never happened. I'll put it this way: his cock and my boy-pussy were made for each other!

We really didn't have time on our side, but he took it anyway. He eased himself in and drew off and waited for me to get comfortable before starting again. D. did just about everything he could to help me relax without touching my cock. This sounds selfish on his part, but I've had enough trade to know that's how it has to be sometimes. He got completely in me and it was as if we'd left this world and entered one of our own. He pushed my shirt up my back and hugged me from behind, massaging his sweat into my skin like an exotic oil, all the while he sawed his cock in and out of my stretched, yielding ass. The problem was, we were not only cramped for space, we were restricted from really losing ourselves in one another. It got to the point where his legs were beginning to cramp and I was getting wrecked quicker than would have liked to. If anything, I wanted him to sit on the bowl with me sitting on his lap.

Finally D. came, pulled out and we left it at that, although before we left the stall he grabbed hold of my ass and whispered, "This is mine!"

Busy pulling myself together, I didn't bother responding. After all, what could I say?

Love, P.K.

. . .

I missed my visit to P.K. because I had a deadline to meet (a piece about these cactus flowers that bloom one night a year, conduct their whole sex lives, and vanish by dawn) and the one after that because the prison was locked down. There'd been a stabbing, and a hostage-taking, and rumblings of a hunger strike. I wrote to P.K., concerned about his health and safety. He wrote the above letter in response.

I needn't have worried about him; I could see that now. We had never been lovers exactly; more like fuck-buddies who exchanged stories the next morning. We shared a common interest in keeping company with beautiful boys, but he always had more chances than me because he worked at the Club, a bar that is closed now. The government said they were selling drugs and laundering the profits. I knew this to be true, and P.K. got caught in the web. We both fell into despair when there were no more strings to pull to keep him out of prison.

We grew very close during that ordeal and somehow I harbored the notion that P.K. would end up being my last lover. I would, I pledged, be faithful to him (in my fashion) until his release. Reading that he now had a Daddy in the joint annoyed me for a few days, but, on the other hand, it freed me. He had, at long last, released me.

Dear P.K.,

. . . I've been spending a lot of time at the Playroom. All the old gang from the Club goes there now, but there are many new faces. You know me, the beauties are what attracts me and they have several new strippers that have caught my eye. I'd been going there for a couple of weeks before one of them made his move.
"I've seen you here before?" the cute young stripper said. Good sign, his having to speak first. Me, I kept silent, but moved closer, getting my thigh up close against his thigh. He cleared his throat, shifted about on the bar stool.
I said nothing, creating more tension. His fingers began to play with my lighter. My fingers moved over his hand, taking it from him. He looked up at me.
"You are very beautiful," I said, and fell silent again.
He had light eyes, a rim of darkness around the pupil. He was younger than I thought, more vulnerable. He passed his tongue across his lips. Looking up at me, looking away, his eyes drawn back to mine, he finally said, "Thanks."
He glanced at the man next to me, then across the bar, assessing the possibilities. He flicked his ash with the edge of his thumb, put his cigarette between his lips, straightened his shoulders.
I took a drink from his glass of beer without saying a word, so now he laughed. "Thirsty?"
"Oh, I'm sorry. I'm just nervous."
"Nervous?"
"Yes. I'll buy you a fresh one."
I signalled the bartender.
Imperceptibly, he leaned toward me, closing the tension, locking it between us.
He put his right hand on my shoulder. Now there was no

turning back. I glanced down at his lap. The bulge in his G-string was bigger than it was while he was dancing. He wanted to impress me. And god, did he impress me. His hand grew heavy on my shoulder.

A few years ago, on a good night, when I was new to it, this was enough, sometimes.

My hand moved to his slim waist, came to rest on the G-string. I began to fondle him. My hand moved slowly, willing him to stop me if he wanted. I stroked along his bulge, around it, pretending this wasn't serious. That it was up to him. My touch was delicate, and he could ignore it if he wanted to. I stroked, sizing him up, tracing his shape. Then I cusped him with my whole hand as though ready to take him. He drew in his breath with anticipation. He was sweating, and pushed against me, desperate. The bulge became even larger, so eager to be gripped.

I kept my eyes on my fresh mug of beer while he lifted himself on his bar stool to press himself again, then again into my hand.

We went to the rest room. The stall was vacant. I pulled down the G-strip, curled my fingers around him, stroking. "Don't come, make it last, don't come," I begged.

But the minute the lovely cut cock slid into my mouth, he started to come. His eyes glazed with the effort to pretend nothing was happening, but his body started to shake. He jerked back from me, his cum spewing into my face.

On a scale from one to ten, I would say it was an eight plus orgasm. I stood up and he held me, cupped my ass. "Next time," I said.

I waited for him at the bar, shoved a fifty under his mug of beer. "Thanks," he said as he slid onto his stool.

I asked him when he was dancing here again. We made a date for the following Tuesday.

Tonight he looked even younger. His skin was lightly tanned and very smooth. His face had a kind of puckish look with its tiny nose and pointed chin. His cheekbones were the only feature that indicated he was nearly a man. They were square and prominent and they did not quite fit his face yet. He seemed much too young for what I really wanted him to do.

"Hey, Barry." A lanky dark-haired boy came up and punched the kid in the arm. "This your new girlfriend?" His tone was mocking. I had seen him here before. He was a jerk, and I loathed him.

"Fuck off." But Barry said this with a smile, pushing into me, cupping my ass. He was so hungry tonight. Almost as hungry as I was. I bought beers, and we listened to the music. He had already danced so he was free to "circulate."

My hand went back to the bulge. "You are so cute," I said. "And your cock is very beautiful."

"Thanks," he said, smiling.

We finished our beers and he said he needed to take a piss. I followed, knowing a piss was the least of it.

The stall was occupied so we waited. Barry peed, I combed my hair. The wait was short.

I took a condom from my pocket and handed it to him. He cupped my firm buttocks in his big strong hands, and I braced myself against the wall. "It's ready for you," I said. "Just slide it in." He fumbled with the condom for a moment and then he was smooth and hard and in me to the hilt. He held me motionless and then all of a sudden, he was slamming for all he was worth, ripping my ass hard, scraping me against the wall, burying his glorious cock in me, filling me. His long dirty blond hair slapped his shoulders with each long stroke.

He was an incredible fuck but all too quickly I was coming and he was coming with me, glowing, shuddering, spasming, shattering. Together. He had another eight plus orgasm.

He eased his length out of me, pulled the condom off, and tossed it in the toilet. As I pulled my pants back up, he squeezed a cheek of my ass. He squeezed so hard it was as if he was leaving his brand on it.

It sounds like we have both found guys who have taken possession. Funny, eh?

Love, J.

COUPLINGS

James Wilton

My home in Florida has seen a parade of beauties who live here for a few months and then move on. They flop in one of my guest rooms, loll around the pool, and have open use of my kitchen and bar. We occasionally take shopping trips to keep them attractively dressed, on my plastic, of course. And, miraculously, fifty-dollar bills appear in dresser drawers if they are good. My only expectation is that they are always receptive to my urges. Knowing what a good deal they have, they are usually more than attentive to my friends, as well. It's nice.

One week, a particularly handsome and horny friend named Dan came down from Connecticut to escape the February cold. He's in his early forties, blond, big-boned, and thick-necked; a real football player type. At the time of his visit I had Jack, Greg, and Larry keeping me company but I hadn't told Dan about them or my general situation when I picked him up at the airport.

On his first morning, Dan got up early, still being on hypertime, I guess. We sat clad in poolwear, eating breakfast and enjoying coffee by the pool when the first of the boys showed up. Dan's eyes bugged out at this cute youngster plopping down on my patio. Before long, numbers two and three joined the circle. Dan was obviously enjoying the scenery but was too polite to ask me "what's the fuckin' story?" The three boys were groggy, in their morning fog, and were only partially aware of the attention Dan was giving them. They were dressed only in their Speedos and, without doubt, Dan was enjoying the delicious view of three young men exposing almost all of their attributes.

When my guest went inside to use the bathroom, Greg asked who that was sitting by "their" pool. When I told them it was a friend from the North they asked if he was fair game. Upon hearing that he was, Greg began whispering with the other boys and I suspected that Dan was in for an interesting morning.

Upon his return poolside, his excitement was about to be

significantly increased. Each of the boys pretended to be dosing. Jack lay on his stomach and began to very slowly grind out an erotic humping of the inflatable raft. Greg lay on his back with his legs spread and ran his right hand over his chest and stomach, absentmindedly. The gently brushing of his nipples and the idea of what he was doing to our guest caused his bathing suit to fill and eventually tent up. Larry was probably the sexiest of the three. He lay face up on the patio with his hands behind his head and his legs spread wide with Dan facing right up that arousing vee. He didn't move or touch himself in any way yet his dick rose up in his pouch and worked the head out of the elastic until it was fully visible to any lookers. Meanwhile, Larry acted oblivious to the rest of us.

Dan couldn't miss the sexual heat displayed before him. He began to squirm and adjust himself shyly. Soon he realized the ridiculousness of his modesty and arranged his growing erection so it could rise with a minimum of discomfort, decorum be damned. He ogled one and then the next of the boys. Without saying anything he looked over to me for an explanation but I wasn't going to let him off the hook that easily. I played dumb to the whole show but did let on that I was enjoying it, too. My own growing woody would have made any attempt at indifference an obvious lie.

Finally I broke the silent tension by asking Dan how he liked the boys who were staying at my place. With a crack in his voice he said the thought they were real cute. At this, Greg slipped his hand down lower than before and rubbed it back and forth along the length of his erection. Jack peeked out of his closed eyes at Greg to see what the stirring was all about. Larry, though, did not break his demeanor and really seemed to be asleep, though having an erotic dream.

Exchanging a wink, the two boys got up and approached Dan. One stood on each side and pressed their aroused baskets against his sizable biceps while they ran their hands down his chest, causing his nipples to rise in excitement. Dan sat enjoying the stimulation while he watched the glory of the hot vista at his feet. He reached his hands up between the legs of the two boys and grabbed their asses, pressing them harder into his shoulders. In reply, they leaned down and began nibbling at his neck and ears. This was turning into a midmorning orgy. Dan became so turned on to the work on his neck that he began to ignore the view before him and rocked his head from side to side as the boys turned up his sexual heat. As if on signal, the two of them reached down beyond his waist and massaged the tubular basket that held his dick. At first they worked the member through the fabric but soon their hands were inside the cloth and were manipulating his cock and balls. This drew serious moans from Dan as he arched his back and pushed his erection up into the hands playing with it.

Without any of the three of them noticing it, Larry had figured that the sleeping ruse was up and he was missing some action. He crawled the short distance from his spot on the concrete to between Dan's legs where he began licking the thighs from knee to crotch. This had the obvious effect of furthering this man's excitement. As the other two began to uncover Dan's equipment, Larry was there to lick the newly exposed genitalia. First, he performed the needed task of laving the precum off the head of Dan's dick. Next he licked the length of his shaft, to the delighted response of my guest. Finally, as the entire package was exposed, he treated the balls to an oral massage, leaving the pulsating erection to Greg and Jack's attention.

At this point, Dan stood up and called an end to the proceedings. He announced that he was too close to cumming and wanted to wait until later to spill his seed. At our age, the excitement can be phenomenal but there is a limit to the number of episodes in a day. He pulled up his trunks, dashed across the patio, and dove into the pool, followed by the three boys. They weren't about to give up on this hot man even though he had managed to cool down his equipment. They cornered him in the deep end and pecked at all parts of his body like feeding guppies. This foolishness got him laughing and the tension of the morning was broken. The five of us turned the episode into and splash and dunk fest.

After lunch, Dan got me aside and worked out the lay of the land. He wanted my permission, freely given, to dally with any or all of the boys. So, when we returned to poolside, I had the three line up and gave Dan his choice for a companion during his siesta. He took over and had them pull down their bathing suits and work up an erection.

First there was Jack, a tall, slim, brown haired boy with smooth skin. He was the cutest of the three; a real boyish look to him. His cock was long and thin, to match his build. His balls hung real low in a nice, silky sack.

Greg was the shortest of the three. He had that Latin, seductive look about him. He was also the darkest and the only one with much hair on this body. He had the classic triangular body with broad shoulders and narrow hips. His dick was quite big and curved noticeably upwards.

Last was Larry. He was medium in height and also smooth. His dark blond hair was cut very short and his heavy beard always looked like he needed to shave. He had a broad jaw and a dimple in his chin. His body was like a hockey player's. He had broad shoulders, big arms, a barrel chest, big buns and powerful thighs. His dick was not as long as Jack's but was the thickest of the three.

Dan enjoyed handling the three of them. Their bodies were all hard and well defined so the testing was as good as the selection. All three of them had nice hard ons and my friend pulled each of them down and released them to snap back up to the hard stomach above. The boys were thoroughly enjoying the event. They were exhibitionists to begin with and they were also getting turned on by watching this hunk enjoy himself so much.

The final choice was Larry. Jack, Greg, and I lay back on our lounges as Dan proceeded with his matinee. Later on, he told me all about it: He wanted to get fucked and took Larry because his thighs promised a power fuck and his thick dick would fill him up without punching in too deep. His instincts had been right because Larry truly was a fuck machine.

After the preliminaries, Dan had the boy grease up his hole and then he sat on the dick. This gave him the chance to ease down on it and open himself gradually before the real assault began. Once Dan was comfortable with the equipment, they rolled into a doggy fuck. Dan said that Larry rammed him so forcefully that they actually moved across the bed. Finally, they changed to a classic missionary position where Dan could enjoy the hunk's body above him. He felt his way over the huge chest and caused extra hard jabs with each tweak on those erect nipples. He said he especially liked looking up into that sexy face as it was contorted with the agony of sexual arousal. As he sensed the stud above him approaching climax, Dan reached down to his own hard erection and brought himself to ejaculation just as he felt the dick up his ass filling its condom with jism. After that came the real siesta and the two of them finally reappeared late in the afternoon.

Cocktails and dinner were times for Jack and Greg to openly flirt with Dan and try to be the next to win his affections. Neither of them was very subtle and Dan didn't mind a bit. He was eating up the attention. By bedtime, which was unreasonably early since the three of them were so horny, Dan couldn't decide on a bedmate so he took both of them. That left me with studly Larry.

After his experience with my northern friend, I didn't want him too self-impressed so I took the mega-top role. I had been turned on several times during the day but had not yet gotten my nuts off and I was ready for some heavy action. Once we were in my bedroom I had Larry remove his Speedos and kneel at my feet with his hands behind his ass - my boys know this as the submissive pose. As soon as my order was given I saw Larry's cock jump and begin its hardening. He knew what was ahead and it obviously excited him. Without using his hands, I had the big boy mouth my dick through the shorts and get me even more turned on. Next, I had him lower my shorts using only his mouth. As my jockeys were pulled down my thighs Larry was hit in the face by my very aroused dick. This got him even more into the action and he went for the spot he knew would turn me on: my balls. After a long tongue-massage, he worked his way up the length of my erection and eventually gave me the blowjob I had expected.

Being near to an explosion, I had him stop pretty quickly. While I got a condom, I had Larry kneel in the supersubmissive pose; face and shoulders on the floor, ass in the air, and hands spreading the cheeks for easy viewing or access to the rectum. I got quite a bit of pleasure out of seeing this little toughy presenting himself so meekly to me but, my cock wouldn't let me savor the view for long and I soon mounted him. In spite of his top demeanor, Larry did enjoy bottoming, too. As I inched my way into his tight anus, he moaned and gasped in pleasure. When I finally hit bottom he bounced back against me as if to force that extra millimeter into his hole. As I fell into a steady rhythm of fucking I reached around and felt his hard fire plug jutting out from his belly. I could barely grasp its circumference but its size was truly a turn-on. While I humped his ass, I jacked that hot piece of manmeat. The nearer I got, the nearer I sensed he was. Finally, I arched back and rammed myself as deep and as hard as I could while I blew out my seed and I felt his erection stiffen even more and blast his cum over my fist and the floor. Without wanting to dismount, I collapsed over his broad back and let my dick slowly shrink in its warm crevice. Eventually it was ejected by Larry's strong ass muscles. Both of us were sorry the coupling was over and we rolled onto our sides in a long back-to-front embrace.

The next morning, Dan told me that his experience had been totally top, too. Both boys had such enticing asses that he couldn't decide between them so he became a pig and used both boys in turn. At first he had both of them kneeling on the edge of his bed, presenting their asses to him. He played with both at once and the two of them competed for the more satisfied reaction. At this point he decided to sample each. He had Greg lubricate Jack's slim ass as he sheafed his own cock. Then, as he mounted the taller boy, he had Greg climb under him and suck his cock to keep him aroused. This was no burden for our dark friend who was an inveterate oralist. Before things climaxed, Dan chose to reverse their roles and had Jack sucking that dark, big dick as Greg got his ass plowed. This time things did not end prematurely and my friend shot his load inside Greg's ass, sending the dark boy over the top as he sprayed Jack's face with his love juice.

Once they recovered from the intensity of their eruptions, Dan realized that Jack was still erect and ready to blow. Wanting to watch a rut, he had Greg roll onto his back and throw his legs up for Jack to enter him. Dan took hold of Jack's throbbing cock and guided it into Greg's recently used entrance. Things were loosened and lubed for that long, slim tool and it gently slid its full length to the bottom of Greg's love pit. With direction from his finger tips against Jack's thighs, Dan was able to choreograph an ever intensifying mating. Quickly he had a powerful rhythm going as Jack's long, thin dick drove deeply into Greg. At the bottom of each thrust, Jack's lowhangers bounced off Greg's tailbone. As the end approached, Dan reached between Jack's thighs and felt the root of the boy's dick as it pulsed out the staccato of an ejaculation. After such an intense session, all three of them slumped into a heap and slept the night away.

With this stable of willing sexualists at his disposal, Dan had the vacation of his dreams. He has since come down every winter for a break from the New England winter and to sample the latest delights Florida has to offer.

THE TWINS

Grant Adams

With his binoculars pressed to his eager eyes, Steven stood at his upstairs bedroom window watching the Thompson twins frolic in their swimming pool next door. Ever since the Thompsons moved into the house a month ago, Steven was spending more and more time admiring the boys' incredible beauty. He couldn't tell one from the other, both identical and each as perfect as the other. And he couldn't stop thinking about them. Nor would he miss an opportunity to look at them unobserved from his bedroom, particularly when they were wearing their tight little bathing trunks which failed to fully conceal their luscious apple asses and their surprisingly mature cocks which were temptingly outlined through their wet trunks.

Their hair was pale yellow, streaked by the sun. Their eyes were a ridiculously vivid blue, and their skin was flawless and slightly bronzed. They were grace itself as they tossed and tumbled in the pool, laughing and grabbing at each other, delighting in each other's company as if no one else existed, just the two teens in their own perfect world. Their names were Kevin and Keith, but Steven didn't know which was which, nor did it matter to him.

Steven had never before been attracted to males so young. He had always preferred men older than himself; in fact, he had been in a successful relationship with an older man for over seven years now. What was this new, embarrassing impulse he was experiencing? he asked himself. The seven-year itch? But he couldn't ignore whatever it was. Each morning before dressing to go to the local middle school where he taught math and coached the track team, he found himself hoping to glimpse the twins in their pool before they themselves dressed for the expensive private school they attended.

He hadn't met the father who was away on business much of the time, but he and his lover Frank had met the mother Liz who was attractive, witty, and warm, always dressed in casual elegance. She worked at a museum in town, and the Thompson house was filled with avant-garde paintings and stunning objets d'art from all over the world. But nothing in the house compared to her beautiful boys.

Steven had spent very little time around the boys. The few times he had been in their home they had been busy elsewhere, either upstairs in their room or at the pool. He had been introduced to them, and they had acknowledged him with courteous smiles, laughing and whispering between themselves as adolescents do. And he hadn't wanted to show them too much attention in front of their mother, fearful he might reveal his overpowering desire for them.

As he stood at the window watching the twins emerge from the pool, familiar hands encircled Steven, first around his waist and then down to his stiffening cock. Frank had come from the bathroom and had once again caught Steven at what seemed to be his favorite pastime.

"I should be jealous," Frank whispered in his ear before taking its lobe into his mouth and gnawing on it gently.

"You have no reason to be," Steven said, dropping the binoculars onto the bed and turning to face Frank who was naked and still damp from his shower and whose own cock was standing erect. "I look at those boys as I would a beautiful sunset, or a mountain range, or a rose garden. I simply admire their beauty."

"When did a rose ever give you a hard-on?" Frank laughed teasingly.

"I don't want to corrupt those boys," Steven lied, not wanting to jeopardize his stable if too predictable set-up with Frank whom he loved. "It's you I want to corrupt. Now."

"We don't have time," Frank said, pleased that Steven seemed to be so turned on so much of the time lately, much like their first few years together. He wondered if the twins had anything to do with this renewed fervor, not realizing they had everything to do with it.

Before Frank could protest further, Steven dropped to his knees and gulped his lover's family-size cock into his mouth. These spontaneous sexual outbursts were happening more and more frequently, at unexpected times in unexpected places. Their walk-in closet had been the scene of their coupling a few days ago, and last night it had been the kitchen floor while dinner was over-cooking on the stove. Frank didn't complain though. He loved sex, and he loved sex with Steven after all their years together. Nobody could suck cock like Steven: he managed to always thrill Frank with his ability to take all of Frank's nine inches deep into his throat and massage each hard inch with incomparable skill. Today was no exception.

Steven finally stood and pushed his lover down across their unmade bed, immediately returning his attention to the spit-slick cock. Frank wanted to get at Steven's tempting prick, but Steven pushed his hand away. Frank knew what this meant. And he was right.

Steven eased his knees under Frank's firm butt and raised Frank's legs into the air to facilitate his entrance into his lover's puckered asshole. He was unbelievably able to push his cock into Frank without missing a beat munching Frank's delicious meat. Frank went crazy, as he always did, by being sucked and fucked at the same time. His chest heaving with passion, he wrapped his hairy legs around Steven's back, encouraging him to increase his pace by bucking his hips. Frank's handsome head twisted from side to side, and he felt that he was being turned inside out by Steven's eight-inch rod which rammed deeper and deeper into him, seemingly growing even larger as it touched those hot, secret recesses in his convulsing rectum.

As he was driving his steaming cock into Frank's asshole and while his mouth was filled to the brim with Frank's delectable club of man flesh, Steven closed his eyes and imagined that it wasn't Frank beneath him but one of the twins. This is what he wanted to do to each of them, to feast on their flesh until he had had his fill, to somehow recapture his own youth by capturing and partaking of their perfection with his hands, his mouth, his cock, even his ass. Yet he knew this couldn't be, that his fantasy was just that, an insubstantial dream that couldn't and shouldn't come true.

Frank began the familiar whine which signaled his approaching orgasm, and Steven was more than ready to swallow his lover's consistently copious cream. Frank reached down and grabbed Steven by the hair, pulling it hard as he yelled out, "I'm coming! I'm coming! I'm coming!" And he shot deep into Steven's mouth and throat the luscious hot cum which Steven relished. Then Steven wondered what the twins' cum would taste like, probably quite sweet, he imagined, with the innocence of their youth. He immediately chided himself for such an unfaithful thought, but he also realized that the thought had pushed him to the edge, and he burst into his lover's depths, filling Frank's chute with the fruit of his fantasy. Without withdrawing his cock completely from his lover's twitching channel, Steven swallowed the last of Frank's profuse emission and leaned forward to kiss Frank on and in the mouth, their tongues embracing to acknowledge their mutual love.

. . .

Days passed, and Steven's sexual appetite and spontaneity were slowly replaced by an unusual and troubling lethargy. Frank questioned the change and accepted Steven's explanation that he wasn't feeling all that well, that he was working too hard and not sleeping enough. Their sexual encounters diminished in both frequency and intensity. And in truth Steven wasn't feeling himself. His desire for the twins had become an obsession which kept him awake at night. He found himself daydreaming about them, often not listening to what was being said to him, ignoring or forgetting the simplest responsibilities, and dreading his time away from the house when he knew they would be home and probably in their pool.

Worrying about his lover, Frank insisted that he see a doctor, but Steven said he'd be fine, that he just needed some rest. Frank suggested a vacation together, a long weekend away from home, a change of scenery, a different environment. But Steven rejected such a plan, saying he couldn't take the time from school. In truth, he didn't want to be away from the twins for that long a time even though he hated their hold on him and knew that they could ruin his life.

Not having slept at all the night before, Steven left school early one afternoon and came home to rest and to grade the papers that had been ignored for the past several weeks, much to his students' dismay. As he was working at his desk in the makeshift office he and Frank shared in what was once a guest bedroom, the doorbell rang. Not wanting to see anyone about anything, Steven went to the door reluctantly. Standing at the door was Liz, looking as if she had just stepped out of a magazine, as always.

She was all smiles. "I thought I heard you drive up a while ago. You're home so early. Are you ill?" she asked.

"No," he replied, "just tired. Too much work, I guess. Won't you come in?"

"Thank you, but I can't. I'm helping to host a reception at the museum this evening, and I have a thousand things to do." She paused for a moment, obviously with more on her mind. "I came to ask you a favor, but now I hesitate since you're overworked as it is."

Steven asked, "What is it?"

"My boys aren't doing at all well in math. They're usually straight-A students in all their courses, but for some reason they're having trouble with their math this term. Since you teach math and live right next door, I was wondering if you'd be willing to tutor them. Of course, I'd pay you, whatever you want."

Steven's head reeled. Here was the opportunity he'd waited for. But was it? Wouldn't his problems be simply aggravated by such close proximity to the twins? Why put himself through such torture? And yet . . . .

"Yes," he finally said. "I'd be glad to help, and I don't want you to pay me anything. I'll do it as a neighbor, as a friend."

"Aren't you the sweetest one?" Liz gushed.

"When do you want me to start?"

"Whenever you can," she said, beginning to move from the door. She then turned back to Steven. "Keith and Kevin have an important exam tomorrow, but this is such short notice. You surely have other plans tonight."

"No, tonight's fine." And it was arranged for Steven to go to the twins' house after supper while Liz was at the reception, while her husband was out of town, and while Frank was working late.

. . .

Steven was nervous as he hurried next door after having showered and shaved and slipped on a polo shirt, shorts, and sandals. He wasn't looking his best, he thought, not having slept well in over a week. He was being ridiculous, he told himself, thinking the twins wouldn't care how he looked.

He rang the doorbell and took several deep breaths. His heart was beating faster than usual, and he was beginning to sweat. He chided himself for such childish foolishness as he waited on the porch. After a moment or two he rang the bell again. Still no answer. He leaned his ear against the door and thought he heard the twins' laughter coming from the patio. He went to the side gate which was unlocked and walked to the pool where he found the twins stretched out on lounge chairs, wearing their wet swim trunks and giggling about something.

The twins looked up, and one of them said, "Hi, Steven. May we call you Steven?"

Steven almost blushed. "Of course, you may."

"Mother said you'd come over to help us with our math," the other one said. They both stood and moved to Steven. "I'm Kevin, and this is Keith."

"I know your names," Steven said, shaking their extended hands, "but I can't tell which is which." He had never been this close to them before, and he had hoped that close proximity would somehow dispel his fantasy, that he would see that they weren't the paragons he had envisioned and cherished. But they looked even better than Steven had imagined, more beautiful than they had any right to be. A perfectly matched pair.

"People who don't know us well always have trouble telling us apart," one said. They then looked at each other and laughed. "There is a difference between us though, but it's in a private place that nobody sees." And again they laughed.

Steven said smiling, "I guess I'll have to remain at a disadvantage then."

The twins excused themselves to change clothes, and Steven glanced up at his bedroom window and wondered if the twins had ever seen him standing there watching their every move. Surely not. They were too busy with their own playful antics.

"Do you want to swim?" one of twins asked coming from the house in a T-shirt and shorts.

80

"No, thank you," Steven said, becoming aware of his thickening cock. "I think we'd better get to the math."

"Would you like something to drink? We have beer. We have real cold beer."

Against his better judgment, Steven accepted a beer, thinking it might calm him down, and then followed the boys upstairs to their bedroom where they were to work. The room was quite large with two twin beds at one end and bookcases, a stereo and TV, desks, and two computers at the other. It was typically decorated with sporting equipment and posters of prominent rock stars. The twins obviously had everything they could possibly want.

The boys positioned themselves on either side of Steven at one of the desks, their bare arms and legs touching him slightly, sending chills through him. Steven knew this wasn't going to be easy for him, and he regretted having agreed to help the boys. He could even feel their sweet breath as they began to work on a particularly complex problem. He then noticed that the boys were spending more time looking at him than at the book before them. And was pressure being applied to his legs by their legs? Of course not, Steven told himself. His vivid imagination was kicking into high gear, nothing more.

He tried to concentrate on what he was doing, but he was having difficulty expressing himself clearly. The twins seemed to be moving even closer to him, and he fought to keep his self-control, knowing he would have to leave as soon as possible and cursing himself for having come in the first place. He was too old, too smart, for this kind of nonsense. He also realized after going through several problems with the twins that they were much more proficient at math than he had been led to believe.

He pushed his chair back from the desk and stood. "What's all this about needing help with your math? You both seem to be doing fine." The boys smiled at each other and their rosy cheeks turned ever rosier. "I'd better be going."

"Do you have to?" one asked.

And the other added with a knowing smile, "Do you want to?"

The twins stared at him, and Steven saw something in their beautiful blue eyes that belied their young age. He could have sworn it was a look of sexual hunger. He had seen it at the bars often enough. But he had to be wrong, he told himself. His imagination was playing cruel tricks again.

"Dad's out of town, and Mother won't be home for hours, till after midnight at least," one said. Then almost pleading, "Don't go, Steven. Please."

"But shouldn't you guys be getting to bed soon?" Steven asked.

"Only if you'll go to bed with us," he heard one whisper.

Steven couldn't believe his ears. He was stunned, as if he had been kicked in the chest. The twins continued staring at him, neither speaking, and Steven felt as if he had been transported to another world that bore no semblance to reality or to time.

The twins began to move slowly toward him, carefully gauging his reaction. Steven tried to step back, away from them, his mind racing into overload. He was speechless, not knowing what to say, not knowing what to do. Something inside him told him to leave, to run from the room. But something else, something more powerful, more demanding, kept him rooted to the spot. The twins threw their arms around him, toppling him to one of their beds. They tore at his clothes like desperate scavengers until he was down to his jockey shorts, his cock engorged and straining against his white cotton briefs.

One of the boys attacked his upper body, biting and licking his stiff nipples and pulling at the chest hair with insistent teeth, while the other worked on his legs, rubbing them with his young, hot hands and kissing and drooling on his inner thighs, careful to avoid the swollen cock, still encased in cotton.

Steven's body twitched and squirmed. He threw back his head in rapture, knowing he should make them stop but unable to say the words or to make the moves. The one at his chest raised his body to feed at Steven's neck and then his ears. Steven took the boy's gorgeous head in his hands, holding him inches from his face, to look into those unbelievable eyes, and then to taste his unbelievably soft lips. The other twin joined them, and the boys darted their ravenous tongues into Steven's mouth, crooning and chirping like baby birds at their mother's beak.

Trying but failing to control what was happening, Steven surrendered to his assailants, his hands ripping the T-shirts from their firm young chests. They in turn maneuvered their way out of their shorts, neither wearing underwear and both hard as rocks.

When Steven finally managed to break from their searing kisses that tasted of almonds and honey, he raised himself up slightly on his elbows. "Do you know what you're doing?" he asked, breathless and panting.

The boys sat back on their haunches, their faces flushed as they tried to catch their breaths. One spoke for them both. "You want to have sex with us, don't you? We've seen you watching us from your upstairs window. Why do you think we went swimming every morning before school?"

"And we want to do sex things with you too," the other piped in. "We even asked Mother to get you to help us with math." He smiled and giggled. "We're really good at math, the best in our class."

"We think you're really sexy, Steven, and we thought it would be fun to find out what it was like with a man. So far we've only done stuff with each other. That's fun, but we talked about it and decided we wanted you to be our first real man." He suddenly turned shy. "Is that okay?"

"Yes. Oh, yes," Steven moaned, still unable to grasp the reality of his dream but more than willing never to wake up, to give the boys whatever they wanted.

He reached for their gorgeous young cocks and massaged them gently in his hot hands. He then bent down to sample their taste, knowing they would be as succulent as they looked. Both cocks were perfect, and both were identical except one had a tiny crescent moon just to the side of the pisshole.

"Now you can tell the difference between us," the twin with the crescent moon said with a giggle. "I'm Kevin."

"And I'm Keith."

Giving vent to his pent-up lust, Steven took Kevin into his mouth, gulping the entire length of the boy's penis into him. He rolled his tongue around every delicious inch, savoring the sweet, salty flavor of adolescent cock, something he had never tasted before. Kevin ran his hands through Steven's thick hair and finally said, "Now Keith."

Impressed by the boy's willingness to share, Steven moved from Kevin to Keith whose pulsing cock told him he was more than ready. Steven repeated his oral undulations on Keith who began to push frantically against Steven's face, making little grunting noises as he face-fucked the older man.

"Not yet," Kevin warned, pulling his brother away from Steven's mouth. He then explained his actions to Steven. "Keith comes real fast. The slightest thing sets him off. I can control myself better."

"But not much," Keith said, defending himself. Steven smiled at their precocious innocence and took both of them into his arms, delighting in their marvelous young bodies, all angles and bones and incomparable sweetness.

"Can we play with your thing?" Kevin asked hesitantly.

"Of course, you can," Steven said, slipping out of his briefs and opening his long, muscular legs to facilitate their endeavors.

Both boys moved close to his throbbing cock, one on either side, and he could see that both were impressed. Kevin touched the base and then wrapped his hand around it, barely able to encircle it. Keith leaned forward and tongued the top of the slick, leaking glans, his little tongue probing into the slit and tasting the almost colorless juice that was oozing there.

Looking up at his twin, Keith said, "Gosh, Kevin, this is wonderful. It tastes better than your cum." Steven wondered what they'd think when he delivered the real cum instead of this thin, watery prelude. "And look at this big vein, Kevin." Both boys inspected the pulsing vein that ran the length of Steven's cock as if they were making an extraordinary discovery. Kevin leaned in and ran his tongue up and down the vein, sending thrills through Steven who was still unable to believe that the two boys were seducing him with such casual ease.

"Let me lick it," Keith insisted, pushing Kevin away and tonguing the vein with even greater determination than his brother.

"And look at the size of these balls," Kevin exclaimed. "They're really cool." He took one into his hand and weighed it before squeezing it slightly. He then looked up to Steven who almost felt as if he were undergoing a sexual dissection. "Can

I taste them?" Kevin asked.

Steven quickly agreed. "You can do anything you want to do."

The two boys looked at each other, delighted with the permission they had been given. Kevin licked and sucked the balls, first one and then the other, unable to get them both in his mouth at the same time. Keith began to take more and more of Steven's cock into his mouth, teasing the base with his hands as he happily slurped at the rigid meat.

"Turn your bodies around so I can get to your cocks," Steven instructed. The boys quickly complied without taking their eager mouths from their newfound treasures.

Steven was beside himself with an embarrassment of riches. Here at his mouth were the two most beautiful cocks he had ever seen on the two most beautiful boys he had ever known. He licked one and then the other, dividing his attention between the two of them. He then sucked Kevin into his mouth, amazed by the girth of so young a prick. And after a few moments he turned his attention to Keith, tonguing his beauty with great gratification as the boys were administering to his genitals with a competence beyond their years. They must have been practicing on one another for some time, he surmised. And he envied the many times they must have enjoyed each other's wonderful bodies in the past.

Going from one cock to the other, Steven felt the two boys close to the brink of expulsion. Their legs began to quiver and their hips began to buck furiously. He pulled them closer to him so that he could get most of their two cocks into his mouth at one time, an experience he had never had before and one that delighted him.

Both the twins squealed suddenly and let fly their tasty loads of fresh, young boy cum into Steven's overstuffed mouth. Their delicious discharge triggered Steven's own orgasm, and as he began to shoot his hot spunk into Keith, Kevin relinquished Steven's churning balls and eased Keith slightly to one side so that he too could drink his first man cum. The two boys shared the wealth, drinking every gushing geyser that Steven shot into their greedy mouths with a fanatic enthusiasm.

Before Steven was able to catch his breath, Kevin pulled his prick from Steven's mouth and twisted his body to sit on

Steven's lower torso. The boy rubbed his butt crack against Steven's still-swollen and sticky cock and then reached behind himself to grab the enormous prick as he tried to force its formidable head into his tiny, puckered asshole.

"No," Steven protested. "I'm too big for you. I'll hurt you."

But the boy was determined. "I want you to fuck me," he demanded. "I want to feel you inside me." And he pushed himself down with such force that Steven's cockhead popped into the tight chute with less difficulty than Steven could have imagined. "I want to suck your cock, Keith, while Steven fucks me," Kevin told his twin. And in a flash Keith jumped to his brother and stuck his ready rod into Kevin's open mouth.

Steven was astonished as Kevin was able to take more and more of his eight inches into his ass, and he was equally astonished that he was able to keep his dick so hard in the boy after such an explosive orgasm just moments before. As Kevin squirmed down farther and farther on his cock, Steven delighted in the hot, excruciating tightness that gripped his burning tool. And before long, he knew he was going to erupt again as he watched the two boys so entirely caught up in their frantic passion for each other and for the act of sex itself.

"Here I come!" Keith shouted, emptying himself into his twin's mouth, and Steven, not knowing where his endurance was coming from, shot his load into Kevin who had miraculously managed to accommodate most of Steven's massive member.

It was then that Steven pulled Kevin to him so that he could again take the boy's sweet juice which was already beginning to spurt from his quivering young prick. This was indeed the nectar of the gods, Steven thought to himself as he drained the tasty cock of its final drops.

. . .

After a quick shower, almost reluctant to wash away the pungent smell of the evening's shocking but fulfilling encounter, Steven tenderly kissed the boys goodnight but not before they made him promise that they would again enjoy each other's physical delights.

As he was leaving, Kevin asked, "What about your friend? Would he like to fool around with us too?"

"Yeah," Keith joined in enthusiastically. "A four-way would be fun."

Steven shook his head, again surprised by the boys' open acceptance of their sexual explorations and discoveries, embracing it as readily and as eagerly as the air they breathed.

"I'll ask him," Steven said, not knowing if or how he was going to relate this experience to Frank to whom he had vowed fidelity, a vow he had been able to keep until this evening. But he also knew how much Frank would enjoy a romp with these two earth angels. Not much more than children, they certainly wouldn't threaten what Frank and Steven shared, Steven told himself; in fact, they might enhance the seven-year relationship.

As he walked into his house, he heard Frank puttering in the kitchen, humming to himself, happy to be home after a long day at the office.

"What have you been up to?" Frank asked when he saw Steven smiling as if he had swallowed the proverbial canary.

"Remember that vacation you talked about?" Steven said, taking Frank into his arms. "How about a vacation next door? It'll be a lot cheaper. And, believe me, you'll never want to come back."

SON OF DAKOTA

Peter Eros

"Hi! What kind of dog is that?" the roller-bladed kid asked as he stopped abruptly. He looked about eighteen, with sandy blond hair flopping over a high forehead. The cheek bones were high and prominent, the eyes gray-blue, the nose aquiline with prominent flaring nostrils, over a wide, full-lipped inviting mouth. The chin was firm with an appealing cleft, framed by cute dimples. He truly was a beauty, Chad thought to himself, as he contemplated the kid through his mirrored sun-glasses.

"He's a bit of a mixture actually," Chad glanced down at the dog, so he could take in the kid's crotch on the way up again, without being too obvious about it. The bulge on the inside left leg was prominent and inviting. It looked wonderfully hard with a well-defined head under the faded and threadbare jeans. The bottom button was teasingly undone. Chad removed his glasses and caught and held the kid's eyes, detecting a distinctly recognizable hungry look. "He's part spaniel and part Basset," he said, trying to keep his voice steady and reassuring.

"My Gran's got two Bassets. That's her house three doors back, where the caravan is in the front yard. I live with her. They'll go crazy barking when they see your dog," and his hand strayed to his crotch, his eyes taking in the quiet sidewalkless street behind and on either side of Chad, checking that no one was observing them. The pink tip of his tongue poked out and licked his lips. "Would you like to see the Bassets? Gran's not home right now. She won't be back till tonight."

Chad was a bit worried that this was so close to home, but his dick was expanding down his leg. "Sure, why not?" The kid turned and led the way. "My name's Tye. What's yours?"

Chad told him and the kid chattered on, "I've often seen you walking the dog, but you don't normally come down this street - or I haven't seen you down here, anyway."

Chad agreed that he'd not often walked down Laurel Canyon that far, but that he did try to walk a different route each day to keep it interesting.

They were at the gate of the small stuccoed thirties house which was shaded by two huge eucalyptus trees. The Bassets indeed began to bay loudly, but soon settled down to nose-to-tail inspection once they'd established that the intruders were friendly.

"You can leave your dog with them. I reckon they'll get on OK." Chad felt his swollen dick spontaneously self-lubricating. The wetness ran down his thigh. This kid was obviously not undiscovered territory. They walked round the side path to the back of the house and the kid unlocked the door. "C'mon in," Tye bent down and unsnapped the roller-blades, then turned into Chad's arms. "Hi," he whispered as he turned his face up to Chad and caressed then clutched his buns. Chad held the appealing face in his hands and kissed the pouting lips. The kid emitted a relieved sigh and responded voraciously.

They fumbled with each others clothes, feeling mounting excitement. Tye led Chad through the house to his room where one whole wall over the bed was devoted to pinups and posters of desirable guys, mostly movie and pop stars with a sprinkling of hunky jocks.

They had already stripped off their tops. Now they ripped open each others fly buttons and Chad pushed the kid back on to the bed and knelt between his legs, admiring the erection which was the most substantial thing about him. Pink and quivering it stood out against the pale parenthesis of his body. Chad breathed in the yeasty smell of the kid's groin and sucked in the tumescent and rampant cock, at the same time pulling the Levi's down from the slim but shapely thighs. Then he slid his tongue along the underside of the bobbing prick and gobbled the bulging sack. The boy's eyes were wide with excitement. He purred. "Oh yeah, chew my nuts," he moaned. His hands clutched Chad's head, encouraging the pumping action. "Oh yeah, oh Chad, yeah man! Oh man!"

Chad slid his own jeans down to his knees then levered off his shoes without interrupting his swallowing. He slid round onto the bed, kicking off his Levis as he did so and straddled the galvanized boy, his hugely stimulated cock brushing Tye's face. Impassioned lips and salivating mouth engulfed it amid gratified gurgles. All restraint went out the window as they gobbled each other with gusto. The boy would have shouted his ecstasy had not his own throat been plugged with more meat than he'd ever tried to manage before. He shot his bountiful load deep in the gullet of his benefactor in rapid spasmodic jets as he gurgled and slavered and tried to deep throat the delicious salami, though his mind was focused on his own convulsing midriff.

Milked dry, Tye was still erect and stimulated as Chad pulled away from him then licked up his arching torso, sucked and nibbled each nipple a little, nuzzled and nipped the thrown- back neck, wolfed an ear, reaming it with his agile tongue, then slid down and fastened his mouth to the gasping lips and tongue wrestled the glowing boy till they both had to come up for air.

Tye emitted a long satisfied sigh, then fondled Chad's resplendent weapon. "You haven't come yet." He looked up into the big sable eyes that seemed to drink him. "Do you want to fuck me?" he asked, stroking Chad's muscled thigh with his long shapely fingers. Chad nodded and grinned appealingly. His rod hadn't been this pumped-up in years. He was wet with heat. "You're a lot bigger than anyone I've been with," Tye responded, "but I did try it with a Chiquita banana once," and he chuckled. "Just be slow and careful, please."

Chad kissed him tenderly on the eyelids and nibbled his nose. "Kid, you are a sex-maniac, and so am I, thank God. Have you got some KY or something? I wasn't prepared for this. I'm HIV-negative, but if you want me to use a condom, I always carry a couple."

"No I don't like condoms if I don't need to use 'em - I want to really feel you inside me." He pulled a tube of KY from under his pillow and handed it to Chad. "I've seen you riding your Harley or driving by lots of times when I've been going or coming from school and I've seen you walking the dog and wanted to talk but couldn't think of what to say before. You've got a great body," and he caressed the pumped pecs with their taught and erect nipples, speculatively fingered the gold rings that pierced them, then his fingers strayed to the hard ridges of the firm abdominals. Chad admitted that he had noticed Tye also; had in fact admired the chiseled pneumatic buttocks bulging through unfashionably tight denim; but like Tye hadn't known, on the spur of the moment, what to do about it.

Chad anointed his cock then rolled the unresisting lad on his side and greased his puckered butt hole with first one, then two, then three fingers. The kid sighed and gasped and thrust back a little, enjoying the penetration. His whole being seemed suffused by a rosy glow. "How do you prefer it? Do you want to try it on your side? Or would you rather put your legs over your head? I'm easy. I don't want to hurt you," and Chad gave him a tender kiss.

Tye grinned dreamily. "Gee, I just knew you'd be great. But I was scared you mightn't be gay. I like it on my side, but you being so big it might be easier with my feet up - first time, anyway. I know you'll be careful. I really trust you," and he grinned contentedly as he lay back and raised his feet, with a pillow under his butt, and rested his ankles on the broad shoulders. Chad liberally greased the hole once more then pushed his swollen glans very slowly into the tight orifice. The boy groaned as it squeezed through the tenacious isthmus of the sphincter and his legs slid down to grip behind the muscular back, urging the desired connection. Their mouths engaged and they tasted sperm and breathed vibrant life into one another.

Tye felt the slow grind of the swollen prick sliding in and out and his feet gripped behind Chad's waist, urging him to deeper penetration. Chad quickened his pace, fucking Tye hard and fast in staccato thrusts angled and timed to bring the kid the most immediate and muscular orgasm his aching sphincter could muster. Tye's hands grasped his own cock and captured the motion, his body vibrating as Chad's passion overflowed deep inside him. Semen jerked from Tye's cock in great spurts, spattering on his chest and his chin then dribbled back from the flat smooth pecs to pool on his solar plexus from which Chad sucked it up hungrily.

Chad withdrew with an audible plop and they fell back together on the bed, stretching and yawning, feeling languid and warm, basking in the afterglow. Tye's hand snaked across and fingered the line of hairs on Chad's stomach, then the long fingers encircled the enormous schlong, remembering every detail of the feel of it at the very core of his being. "Wow," he husked in awe. "You're built like a horse." The hand cupped

the still swollen sack beneath. "Your balls are all stallion."
    Chad smiled and pulled the roving hand up and pressed it against his belly.
    "Your not bad yourself, cutie pie. How old are you anyway?" Chad asked with a hint of a frown. "I hope I'm not robbing a cradle?"
    "I turned eighteen a coupla' months ago." The kid grinned shyly and blinked appealingly. "I enroll at college in the fall. I've been out a while now, but not at school. I know a couple of kids who are out and obvious and they have a rough time. I haven't had a lot of experience with other guys. I usually get off at the movies or a park; sometimes at the Mall. I prefer older guys; they know what they're doing. How about you? You obviously don't have no dull nine-to-five job."

    So Chad launched into his well-rehearsed and oft repeated history; how he'd been raised by his widower father, doing men's work on his father's farm so that he had a pretty hard muscled bod; how he'd been thrown out at fourteen by his homophobic Dad, when he was caught being fucked by a hunky farmhand, twenty years ago; how he'd hitched, with sympathetic truckies, happy to sexually initiate him further, from the corn-belt of Ohio, first to San Fran, then to LA. How he'd fallen in with other runaways or shoved-outs who'd told him where to crash and how to market his butt on Selma Street in Hollywood; how he'd been picked up by a jovial, plump little Mexican who turned out to own one of the major gardening businesses, tending the grounds of the wealthy in Beverly Hills and who after a romp with him assured him that, "For big success in this town you carry everything you need between your legs."
    Pedro gave him a gardening job and urged him not to wear a shirt, but to give himself a Vaseline sheen and to wear very short cut-offs with no underwear.
    By the end of his second week a randy employer had tweaked the tip of his heavy dick poking out the bottom of his shorts and raced him to his bedroom and then his payroll as a pampered love toy. But Chad had wanted more. With his employer's largesse he joined a leading gym and trained really hard. He liked the gym. He thrived on the high energy of

bodies in motion. He built his body into a work of art, and let other wealthy patrons, contribute their share to his growing bank account and portfolio. He pumped their brains too and learnt all he could about business. When he felt he knew enough he left his patron, who in any case was looking to new bods to excite his interest, and started doing porno films with a producer who'd been after him for months. He'd held out for the highest fee any porno stud had ever been paid and a legal contract. He starred as Johnny Dakota, a name he'd chosen because his grandmother was an Oglala Sioux from that part of the country. But most people just called him Dakota. Round the studio too he learnt all he could and the following year started his own modeling agency, specializing in porno movie talent and short-term escort duty. "Now I own my own studio and publishing house. Our videos and books are distributed all over the world through a company in Amsterdam, in Holland. But you haven't told me about you. Why do you live with your Gran?"

The slim body tensed and the kid sighed. "My folks are dead. My old man was a Marine, but when he left the service he became some sort of mercenary in Central America somewhere and from that he got involved in the drug trade. He was killed in prison a coupla' years ago. That's when Mom went haywire. She got hooked on more and more drugs and one day, five months ago, when she was high on speed she threw herself off a cliff down where they make 'Baywatch' now." A dry sob racked his frame and tears began to flow. "I loved her, Chad, and I think I was a good kid, but I guess that wasn't enough," and he was convulsed with deep wrenching keening sobs.

Chad drew him into his arms and cradled and crooned. He kissed the wet eyelids and brushed the wavy tresses from the stressed forehead. He crushed the clinging boy to him and rocked him like a baby. He licked at the tears and smothered the hungry lips of the boy with his own. He whispered sweet nothings and nibbled his ear lobe, coaxing a rueful smile. Tye snuggled into him like a contented and well-fed puppy.

"Would you like to do movies?" Chad rose on one elbow and gazed at the kid's amazed face. Chad caressed the perfectly formed pecs and traced the hard nipples, which seemed to salute him as warmly and seductively as the boys glowing eyes. "You don't have to decide right now. You'd be a big hit," and he caressed the boy's face and kissed him again, his long black tresses brushing the delicate body. He slid down licking and nibbling, as the sap-like odor of ejaculate led him back to the resurrected and wet organ waving its signal of preparedness. His mouth fastened on it and sucked it deep as the panting boy arched and thrust, his eyes dilating.

Then Tye gazed in wide-eyed wonder as Chad straddled his aching tumescence and lowered his butt, guiding the waving weapon to stab his gaping hollow. The kid slid in easily and as Tye arched and thrust Chad opened his asshole further to suck the kid as deep as he could, feeding the hunger that permeated his core. Chad's fingers gripped the mahogany headboard as his butt pounded them both to the hip-wrenching orbit of rampant mutual pleasure. Tye shoved up into him with a frenzied final set of thrusts. Sweat rained from Chad's forehead. His shoulders ached from holding himself up. He could feel a new numbness growing in his testicles. Sweat puddled in the depression of Tye's abdomen and chest. Chad spent himself with a guttural cry as at last the release and the reverberation in their bodies climaxed and rocked them. Tye came with a sharp agonized sigh as Chad's warm rivulet ran over his fingers. Chad fell forward onto him and they clung to each other, still trembling and convulsing as the final ecstatic sensations ebbed.

They lay a long time cuddling and fondling each other, the boy murmuring his gratitude and confessing that he hadn't been with anyone for months. He admired the small tattoo of a dragon on Chad's right buttock and asked him what it signified. "I was born in the Chinese Year of the Dragon, so I had the tattoo put on when I was in Thailand. That's where I met my houseboy Tran. He's originally from Burma, but he escaped into Thailand and I got him a work visa as my personal servant. You'll like Tran. He's a cute kid too."

Tye glanced up at Chad and confided that he'd like to try a movie but didn't know how to without arousing his Gran's suspicions. "I wouldn't want to hurt her. I'm the reason she's working. My grandad was a Marine too, a thirty-year man, so Gran has a good pension, but not enough to put me through college."

"Not to worry," Chad said, smoothing the hair back from the damp forehead and kissing him again. He held the cleft chin and gazed into the troubled eyes, more blue now than gray. "I put all my guys through college, or whatever other vocational training they want to do. I've set up a non-profit, the Zia Educational Scholarship Fund. The Zia is an Indian sun symbol. Any guy who wants it has his movie wages paid to him through the fund so he doesn't pay taxes and I can claim it as a tax write-off, a donation to a registered non-profit. If you agree we could save your Gran a lot of hard work. All she'll need to know is that you've received a scholarship from the Fund. You know, I might just return to the screen myself. I think I'll be too jealous to let anyone else enjoy the pleasure I've just had with you Tye, at least for a while. What do you say?"

The kid was sniffling again as he mumbled "Yes, oh yes. Thank you!"

Tye clutched Chad's still impressive weapon, unable to stop admiring. They both glistened as though they had been oiled down, basking together in the sunlight spilling from a high window.

Chad caressed the back of the boy's neck and pulled him down into an embrace. He engulfed the boy's mouth with his own and thrust his tongue between the unresisting lips. They savored the taste and smell of each other. Then Tye pushed himself up on an elbow and gazed at his handsome new lover. He looked bashful and a hint of a blush tinged his cheek. "Could I try what you just did, Chad? I haven't ever done that."

Chad couldn't help chuckling at the blush, after what they'd already done together. "What? Ride my dick, you mean?" The kid nodded, with a rueful grin. "Sure, if you're really up to it. My poor old dick hasn't had this much of a workout for quite a while. But let me prepare you a little first." And he pulled Tye round to squat over his face. The practiced tongue rimmed the finely-haired ass, flickering in circles round the swollen bunghole, before entering deeply; juicy lips sucking voraciously, as the kid bucked and sighed.

Chad disengaged, eased Tye up and pushed gently, sliding him down along his torso to the object of the kid's desire. Tye rocked his butt into position, grasped the rampant penis and eased it into his orifice. A sharp gasp was followed by a murmur of relief as Chad entered his body. Chad pushed up as Tye bobbed up and down with the rhythm of the thrusting groin. Chad raised his midriff and shoved a pillow under himself, his penis jammed into the kid deeply.

With each upward thrust the kid's head fell back further as gasping throaty gurgles and whimpers accented the staccato rhythms of his premier ride. Then from somewhere deep inside him he groaned, "Oh, man! Oh, puleeze, fill me up! Oh, yeah, man!" He settled into a slow rhythm, unraveling his craving. Chad circled Tye's engorged nipples with a wet fingertip then squeezed and kneaded them, as the boy slammed down onto him, responding to his mounting pangs of pleasure.

Tye could feel the sensations building up through his torso and traveling into his arms. He could feel Chad pulsating deep inside him and could hear only the sound of sliding, slapping fornication and his own harsh gasps. At last the feeling focused in his prostate and a flash of intense pleasure shuddered through his body. He was incredibly, overwhelmingly aroused. He felt Chad shoot his load, pulsing in volcanic jets deep within him, still hard, stimulated by the tight contractions of Tye's sphincter.

Chad cupped the boys pecs in his hands and squeezed, as his climax began to duplicate itself in the boy. Guttural sounds started in Tye's gut, pushing through his lungs and throat. Each shriek of ecstasy accompanied by a contraction of his sphincter around the joyous probe. He cried out loud as his body shook uncontrollably, bucking on Chad's distended penis, and Chad let out a gasp as the reverberations shook him. The orgasm hit with spasmodic aftershocks that lasted a couple of minutes.

Tye collapsed forward onto Chad, still impaled; delirious with the after-effect, his whole body alive with ecstatic sensation. They both gasped for air, exhausted but tingling with joy. The kid lay back contentedly and let Chad explore him with his mouth till the agile tongue once more traced his lips then forced entry. They breathed each other, giving each other the kiss of life.

Chad glanced at his watch. "Shit! I didn't realize it was so late. I need to phone Tran to come and collect me with the car.

Would you like to come up to the house for a while?"

"Sure," the kid grinned. "The phone's in the kitchen. Would you like some juice?"

Chad nodded and as he called from the wall-phone by the fridge Tye poured him a glass then stood naked on one leg, his foot propping open the fridge door, drinking orange juice from a quart container, his perfect little passed-out dick swinging between sinewy legs. He screeched and giggled when a splash of cold juice hit his bare chest.

And that's how Son of Dakota was born.

CODY'S COCK

John Patrick

Maybe I'm growing older less gracefully than I thought, growing older rather badly in fact. So often these days, my memory plays tricks on me, and I begin to recall objects of beauty that when I go back and look at the pictures I took of them, they aren't really as beautiful as I had imagined.

But one object that cannot trick my memory is Cody's cock. It's been a couple of years now, and not a single day goes by when I don't think of Cody and his cock with ever-agonizing longing. I scream in my sleep, I cry inside while I amble down familiar streets and cities, praying for the day Cody no longer intrudes and I can put the whole episode away for good. But now every cock I see reminds me of what I lost when I lost Cody.

Yes, I remember it all. Of course, his body, his utter blondness, his voice, the way he said, "Fuck me." And the good things, the bad things, the silly, irrelevant things. But most of all, the cock. I remember so well how my fingers, my tongue, my very soul languished over, across and along it and I could hear his moans, his sighs, the pleasure I gave him. Cody's cock. How glad I was that I paid him an extra hundred occasionally as "spending money," just to let me photograph it. Ah, yes, tousle-haired, soft-spoken Cody, who let his cock do his talking for him.

I often recall the time we spent together, the number of times we had sex, the places we did it: on the floor, over my desk, in beds, in T-rooms, in and out of the hot tub.

I still cherish his prowess, all the ways he had to make the pleasure last, his long legs held up over my shoulders as I dug my cock ever deeper into him, while I played with his beautiful cock. He would cry "Oh, god!" as he came, and nobody ever came as intensely as he did.

I knew Cody was a rebel, often governed by his fierce temper, always getting involved in stupid, useless rows with the men who adored him, but I was willing to put up with him to gain access to that cock. His parents had always given in to him, and he expected his men to do the same. I indulged him, but only if he was good.

I would have laughed if someone had told me that I would become painfully enamoured with a mere schoolboy, especially one who, at first glance, had so little to offer. Cody was just eighteen, and cute in a way, but it was his cock that was really beautiful. Of course, I didn't know that when I first laid eyes on him on that day long ago. I remember what I was doing right then: marveling at the hunks on the beach in front of the Marlin Beach Hotel in Fort Lauderdale.

After watching these guys romping around in Speedos, I was desperate in my need for quick release. It was warm for February and Cody was sweating profusely as he approached me. I looked down at his body, at the bulge in his Speedos, then up again. His eyes met mine. As we walked along the beach, I smelled his sweat, a pungent aroma.

Of all the beauties at the beach, he was the only boy who showed any interest in me. He came up to me, engaged me in conversation, offered to buy me a Coke. I said, "Let's go."

I knew what the game was but enjoyed playing his way for once. Little did I realize I would have to play it *his way* always, or not get his cock.

The power of his cock first manifested itself after we had Cokes and burgers and slowly made our way back to my hotel room overlooking the Ocean. There had been no discussion of price to that point. I thought once we reached the room, he would make it plain exactly what my relief was going to cost me, but, no, nothing was said.

Cody did say he wanted to take a shower and I turned up the air conditioning to high and closed the drapes. I laid on the bed and dozed off. I opened my eyes to see Cody's cock. What a sight! He was kneeling on the bed, his crotch in my face. He was drying his hair, and his cock bounced in my face. Even semi-hard it was a good eight inches. I reached up, closed my fingers gently around the shaft, and pulled him toward me. I rolled onto my back and he straddled my broad chest, the hair on his legs tickling along my sides as he settled himself against me. The head of his big cock brushed against my lips, and I licked at the hooded knob. He gasped and his prick twitched violently for a few moments before settling heavily against my mouth once again. I gently took the silky foreskin between my teeth, tugging it forward and away from the swollen, shiny glans hidden inside. I slipped my tongue between the sheath of skin, probing and digging in the tight, hot space. He groaned, and I felt the muscles of his legs tighten against my sides as he thrust forward, forcing himself into my mouth. When I dug my tongue into his gaping piss slit, searching for the pre-cum, he squeezed his cock from base to tip, letting some free. I licked it, then raised my head slightly, urging him to probe my mouth deeply.

He leaned forward, bracing himself against the headboard and tilting his pelvis so he could more easily slide his erection into my throat. I played with his ball, and other hand wandered up along his sun-browned torso, pulling teasingly at the thin line of hair which bisected his slender body. I rubbed the ball of my thumb against the thick brown points of his tits and felt him shudder against me. His hips soon kicked into action, pumping his long shaft in and out of my mouth.

I would have been content to suck him till his cum gushed down my hungry throat, but Cody had other ideas. He scrambled back between my legs, roughly pushed them apart, and bent his shaggy head to my crack. I clenched my fists as he nipped at my asshole, tugging the short hairs around my sweaty, puckered flesh till I ached with pleasure and my prick snapped up tight against my gut. Soon his breath was warm on my balls. He rubbed his spit around my asshole, then pushed a finger into me. I pulled his head down. He sucked me for a bit, until I was nearly ready to shoot.

"Fuck me," I begged.

Soon he was guiding his long, thick prick into my asshole, then pushing forward with all of his weight, jamming deep into me with one thrust.

I wrapped my legs around his narrow waist, opening myself up to his incredible thrusting. I was overwhelmed by him, by the way his pelvis ground hard against my ass, his balls slapping against my tailbone, his hands clamped hard on the headboard behind me.

I could have kept this up all day as well, but he again had other ideas. Just before he came, he pulled out and joined his cock with mine, bringing us both off in a flash.

He collapsed next to me and my hand went to his sloppy cock. It was semi-hard. "God, what a cock," I purred.
"Did I hurt you?" he asked.
"A bit, at first," I replied.
He stood up, his tall beauty towering through the now frigid hotel room. He shuddered and grabbed his T-shirt. Tugging it on, it reached to just below his navel. His sex exposed, his backside bare. He turned away from me, moving toward the bathroom. His cock now hidden from me, my eyes lingered over the expanse of the moon-shaped twin hemispheres of his ass.
That was the next surprise. That night, after dinner, we returned to the hotel room and he asked me to fuck him. But his sphincter muscles rebelled against the intrusion. It took awhile to get him relaxed. I also wondered how I could get in, after having come earlier. I was more than twice Cody's age, of course, and was good for only one a day – normally. But this was not a normal circumstance. My cock is medium in length but quite thick when totally engorged, and to enable the final thrust to break through Cody's resistance, I began to hold the stem of my cock hard between my clenched fingers to force more blood toward the tip and make the cock rigid at the moment of entry. Once I was in him, I was fine. This managed to sustain my erection through his orgasm, then pulled out to jerk off, my cum joining his in the puddle on his chest.
Upon my departure, I asked him how much I owed him. That was when the photography started. He posed willingly, came for me as I gave him a farewell blowjob, and made three hundred dollars for two days' work.

A month later, I went back to Fort Lauderdale and found him at the beach again. I asked Cody to travel with me. He accepted. "Besides," he said, "season's almost over." He would have to move on anyhow, I took it.
In every city on my book tour we acted like animals in heat, rutting, moaning, sighing, screaming, oiling our bodies with fragrant lotions.
Then, in New Orleans, we went to the Bourbon Pub. We went upstairs and he began dancing with a black boy. They were joined by two more black boys. I went downstairs to

freshen my drink and when I went back upstairs, Cody – and the blacks – were gone. I waited around, figuring he was just having some fun in the john, but he had vanished. I stayed on in New Orleans looking for him, but finally I had to leave.

One of my favorite fantasies was that of a blond boy being ravaged by black men. Now I began to think of Cody, somewhere on a bed, servicing two black men with massive cocks, one in his mouth, one in his ass, screwing like a maniac with his instrument of torture, while the third waited his turn. The idea of it got me off, but it also saddened me. I prayed he was okay. I missed him terribly, but, most of all, I missed his cock. The object of my desire. COCK: A four-letter word of sheer beauty. Cody's cock.

THE BOYS IN THE FENS

Leo Cardini

The problem I have with sucking cock is it always leaves me wanting more, kinda like an addiction. Oh, I know there's lots of guys who, once they get a steamy hot load of the stuff down their throats, can turn their attention to other matters and move on with their lives. Well, not me.

Like here I am in bed with Coach Douglas first thing in the morning. You see, last night me and Norm met up with him at Sporters and the three of us made a night of dropping into every gay bar in Boston. Even Playland, down in the Combat Zone, though it's really too sleazy even for my tastes. Of course, by the time we'd closed the bars and had a late night snack at Ken's we'd missed the last trolley back to Jamaica Plain - which is where me and Norm have lived all nineteen years of our lives - so we slept over at the Coach's apartment at 114 The Fenway. Pretty fancy address, huh? It's right next door to the Boston Museum of Art.

Well, yeah, of course the three of us had sex together!

Anyhow, as usual, Norm's the first to wake up. Since he always has a morning hard-on that won't go away until he shoots his load, he starts jacking himself off, which wakes me up. So I suck him off, and then he leaves for his daily workout at the Back Bay Health Club. Bodies like his - and mine, to be honest - don't come from nowhere. And we've been spending so much time hanging out with the Coach we keep extra gym bags at his place since he's just a ten-minutes walk from the Club.

Well, I fall back to sleep again with the thought of Norm's fat, Polish dick in my mouth, and then when the Coach's alarm goes off, I wake up again and we suck each other off.

And what am I doing now? Sucking on his soft dick, of course. Fuck, I don't even care whether or not he gets another hard-on, considering what a great piece of meat he's got. So here I am flat on my belly chomping away between his spreadapart legs as he lies back on his pillow with his hands behind his head, and all I can think of is how wonderful it would be if I could spend the rest of my life just like this, sucking on big fat dicks like his and Norm's, draining the cum out of them as fast as they can manufacture the damn stuff.

But all good things must come to an end, and soon I hear, "Sorry Tony," as he takes my head between my hands and gently pulls me off his dick with, "but I gotta get ready for summer school."

So while he showers and shaves, I get up and make breakfast for us, thinking if even just a couple of months back you predicted I'd end up so chummy with Coach Douglas, I'd call you crazy.

Actually, his first name's Steve, but me and Norm still call him Coach Douglas even though we graduated from J.P. High fifteen or sixteen months ago. Yeah, class of '76. What happened is we bumped into him one Sunday afternoon at the beginning of the summer right outside of Chaps, this gay bar behind the Boston Public Library. Turns out he and Mike Franzi - that's this other guy who was in our class before his family moved to Malden - had been kinda like fuck buddies for several months.

Well, you know how it is. One thing led to another and before you knew it, the four of us end up at the Coach's apartment getting stoned out of our gourds and fucking and sucking to our hearts' content. Since then we've all been hanging out a lot together, so it's been one helluva summer.

"So," says Coach Douglas, sitting down to breakfast, "What are you and Norm up to tonight?"

"Well, I can't speak for Norm..."

"Oh?"

The way he says it. As if we're...but we're not, of course. We weren't even that close until he came out. Sure we've known each other all our lives, but he was just another one of the neighborhood kids, that's all. At least until four months ago, when I got him stoned for the first time in his life and the next thing you know he let me suck him off. Now that would've been no big deal, except the next weekend he made it a point to turn up at my place with some grass he got himself, and once we got stoned, he fucked me. Well, since then, the adventures we've had together could fill the kind of book that'd be banned in Boston, so we'd never get to read it anyhow.

Well, I don't know what we'll be up to tonight. And right now, I'm so cockhungry I can't think beyond how long it's gonna take me to clean up, shower and shave and hustle my ass over to the Fens.

Now in case you don't know what the Fens are, they're this long stretch of tall reeds across the river from Steve's apartment, just behind the Victory Gardens. Yeah, a stone's throw from Fenway Park, where the Red Sox play. (If they only knew!) And barely a five-minute walk from the Ramrod and the 1270, which makes it a very popular cruising spot once the bars get out. And not only that, but everyone has sex right there in the bushes!

It's networked with what seems like hundreds of narrow paths of packed-down dirt leading into all sorts of interesting dead ends, some barely large enough for two, others big enough for the orgy of your dreams, though on a warm Saturday night sometimes you can barely squeeze in.

Call me a romantic - or a pig - but I think the Fens is the greatest place on earth, especially during the daytime. I mean, you're absolutely surrounded by pure nature, like you were back in the garden of Eden (that is, if you ignore the used condoms and soggy tissues that sometimes litter the place).

Anyhow, Steve leaves to teach his summer school classes, I clean up, and barely a half-hour later, here I am, strolling along the paved walkway that separates the Fens from the Victory Gardens, my hard nipples stabbing the half a white tank top I'm wearing. I ripped the bottom half off a long time ago so I can show off my abs. I figure I got the body and I worked hard enough at it, so why not? Some of the guys at the Club even call me Angelo, which I kinda like because it's short for Michaelangelo and he's this old artist who carved a statue called David that looks just like me, except that my dick's bigger.

So here I am, sauntering along pretending I'm admiring the scenery, my hands dug deep into my 501's so I can touch myself, when who should I see leaning against the tall old oak tree by the most conspicuous entrance into the Fens, but Norm!

He's wearing snug-fitting, faded blue Levi's that emphasize his powerful calves and thighs and strain against that wonderful piece of equipment in his crotch, and a tight, white tee shirt stretched across the muscular terrain of his torso, looking like it'll rip into a thousand shreds if he so much as coughs.

Every time I see him I get that same fluttery feeling in my chest, and that same tingly sensation in my crotch. I mean, he's so well-built. And so good-looking in a fresh-off-the-farm kind of way, even though he lives in J.P. and works at his father's gas station. He's got the smoothest, whitest skin you'll ever see, a broad forehead, full, sensual lips, brown puppy-god eyes, and a thick mane of wavy, dark brown hair that he parts in the middle.

He spots me, he buries his hands in his pockets as he lowers his head and kicks an imaginary pebble in front of him, and then he looks up at me again with a sheepish grin.

"Hi Norm," I say, walking right up to him. "Whatcha up to?"

"Oh, hi Tony. I was just over at the Club, you know...and uh...uh..."

"Norm, maybe I'm not the smartest guy in the world, but I think I can figure out why you're here. You're always listening to me and Mike and Steve talk about the Fens and you decided to check it out for yourself. Right?"

"Well, yeah, that's part of it. The other part is..."

I've never seen him look so embarrassed.

"Norm, I don't think you could say anything that'd shock me."

"I think I need practice sucking cock."

I wanna laugh, he's so serious about it, but I cover with a cough and then repeat, "Practice?"

"Yeah. I mean, I've seen the way you suck cock. And Mike and Steve."

"You've more than seen us suck cock."

"Yeah," he says with a broad smile, "and that's why I know you guys do it better than me. Especially you."

I'm flattered.

"I guess it takes practice," he continues, "which is probably why you're so good at it, considering you've been sucking dick ever since you were..."

"Okay, okay. I guess you're right."

"Besides," he says, smiling again, "I've gotta make up for lost time."

Like he hasn't been making up for it all summer long!

There is one thing, though. Maybe I'm only nineteen, and maybe I'm not very bright, but one of the things I've learned is that each and every one of us has a preference for either cock in his mouth or dick up his ass. Not that most of us don't get into both, but there's always that preference. I mean, think about it. When you're in bed alone jacking off and you pull up the image of some heartthrob of a guy, bet you think either of taking his dick in your mouth or letting him plow you up the ass. Am I right?

Well, give me cock down my throat. But Norm... well, you should just see the blissed-out look that comes over his face, and you should just hear the way he moans when something makes its way up his ass, be it tongue, fingers (I've seen him manage all five), dildo or dick, which, considering his firm, creamy white asscheeks, and that pink, puckered butthole of his, is a real blessing to the rest of us. One look at it and if I wasn't such a horny bastard all the time, I'd be inspired to write a poem about it.

"So you been inside yet?" I ask, nodding towards the Fens.

"No. I thought I'd...you know...kinda warm up to it."

I know what he means because the first time I went into the Fens - it was at night - I was scared out of my britches. Well, I did end up out of my britches, after all, but not because I was scared!

"C'mon," I say leading way in as I peel off my tank top and stuff it into my back pocket. Norm follows, doing the same, and as many times as I've seen him bare-chested, I can't help glancing back to admire his broad, armor-like pecs, and the narrow line of hair that descends the tight terrain of his abs into the heavenly regions below.

Well, there's not much action inside yet, though we do come across this guy in a Boston University tee-shirt leaning against his bike, and this kid I recognize from the bars down on his knees blowing him. The one giving the blowjob sees us out of the corners of his eyes and beckons us to join them without the slightest deviation from the deepthroat, suckstroke rhythm he's established. But the guy on the bike holds up his hand in gentle protest, so we continue along, heading for my favorite section of the Fens, passing several men on the way worth keeping in mind once we settle down to business.

We finally make our way to the northernmost extreme of the Fens, near the Boylston Street Bridge where the reeds grow tall and dense. The paths are narrower, the reeds arch over you, and you feel as far away from Boston as if you were in the Amazon.

I lead Norm into the enclosure I like to think of as my own. It's circular and cozy as a hut, underfoot it's got a nice mat of fallen brown reeds, and it fits five comfortably. Believe me, I know.

"So now what do we do, Tony?"

"We wait for someone to come along. And if we're interested and if they're interested...well, you..."

I'm trying to figure out how you describe all the nuances of cruising in the bushes - the looks you exchange, the ways you posture yourself - which, is a whole lot different from cruising the bars, when Norm interrupts with, "Could I suck on your dick in the meantime?"

Well, it's as good a way as any to draw attention to why we're here, so I smile at him, unbutton my Levi's and pull out my cock and balls.

Norm gets right down onto his haunches and holds my dick in the palm of his hand, examining it as he kneads his own denim-enclosed crotch.

"Jesus," he says, "every time I see it...I mean, it's so big..."

It begins to lengthen.

"...so brown and fat and..."

My dickhead makes its way off the edge of his palm.

"...and all those veins..."

My piss slit peeks up at him, and then the whole thing begins to levitate off his hand.

"...Oh!"

And with that he goes down on me, sucking up and down the first several inches of my cockshaft as it completes its growth in his mouth reaching its full nine inches in record time.

Moaning in response, I place my hands on his head, working my fingers through his beautiful, soft brown hair.

Then I hear the crunch of fallen reeds being trampled on that's a sign someone's approaching. And who should come around the bend in the path but Jesse, an old flame of mine!

If this wasn't Boston, but instead some West Coast beach town, one look at Jesse and you'd peg him for a surfer. Long blond hair, bright white teeth, an open, accepting smile, deep blue eyes bright with excitement, and a lean, tight-muscled body - that's Jesse. I don't know how he does it but his body always seems aglow with a deep, golden tan. Even his body hair - a mere sprinkling of it on his chest, contrasting with the dense overgrowth of his pubic bush and the fine fur that grows on his ass and legs - seems transformed into thin threads of spun gold.

His look might be surfer, but his dress is definitely gay: snug-fitting 501 cutoffs as short as can be, a tight white tank top, sweat socks and scuffed construction boots

We used to date a couple of years back when he was a senior at Northeastern. I really fell for him. But he's the kind of guy who, when you're with him, he can think of no one else, but when you're not, it's like you don't exist. I mean, he'd never think to call you up to chat or arrange for a date, but if he ran into you someplace, you might spend the next several days together, kicking around from bedroom to brunch to bar. Anyhow, after he graduated he went off to Katmandu (I had to look it up on a map to discover where the fuck it is) and when he came back six months later, well, we were into different things, like he'd hang out in the Cambridge bars, and I'm just not fond of the whole Harvard-M.I.T. crowd, since I always feel like they think I'm not smart enough for them.

"Hiya, Tony," he says grabbing my hand and shaking it, like it's no big deal there's some guy down on his knees sucking me off. "What you been up to?"

Norm, of course, stops to look up at us, my hard-on sticking up side by side his face as if it too was busy checking out this intruding visitor.

"Jesse," I say, "this is my good friend Norm."

Norm gets up, leaving my self-centered dick to sulk alone in abandonment, downcurving into softness, and the two of them exchange hiya's and shake hands.

"Norm just came out a couple of months ago and we're here because he wants to perfect his cocksucking."

Norm blushes in embarrassment, but Jesse says, "Hey, that's cool. Wanna practice on me?"

He says this with such an eager smile lighting up his face that Norm immediately replies "Sure!"

"Good. But first," Jesse says, bending over to retrieve a joint and a matchbook from inside his left sock, holding it up for our inspection. "This stuff will fucking blow your mind! And it's a real physical high, so it's great for sucking cock!"

He lights up and the three of us pass the joint around, filling up the time talking about not much of anything. Soon I realize I'm very, very stoned - I can't help playing with my balls and thinking what it'd be like to shave them. I mean, really, can you just imagine? And Jesse's right, it is a real physical high. Which is why, I guess, Norm takes to running his hand across his chest, back and forth, back and forth, and then with both hands begins tugging on his nipples.

When Jesse see this, he says, "Stoned, huh?"

Norm's response is a cautious, "Say, you guys wouldn't mind if I like take off all my clothes, would you?"

"Hell, no," Jesse says for the both of us.

So Norm turns his back to us, strips, and gets down on his knees to make a neat pile of his clothes, wedging them in-between the reeds. When he stands up again and turns around, I can see from Jesse's reaction he's as taken by Norm's manly beauty as I am, even though I've seen Norm like this many a time. From his broad shoulders, to his rippled abs and all the way down to his bulging calves, he's just too much of a good thing. And then there's that huge pale dick of his hanging down heavily between his legs below the thick bush of dark brown pubic hair that spills over onto the base of his cockshaft in such contrast to his light skin.

"God, you're beautiful," Jesse mutters to himself.

Norm gets down on his haunches in front of Jesse, his big, broad hands dangling between his legs, and looks up at the two of us. Now, me and Norm have had enough threesomes for me to know this is my cue, so I step behind Jesse and pull his tank top up over his chest. He cooperatively raises his arms and I slip it off him in no time, draping it over the fork of a nearby reed.

Below, Norm's already unbuttoned Jesse's cutoffs, pulling them down to his ankles. Jesse's majestic, half-hard dick comes flopping out, quivering like a diviner's rod that's just detected a mother lode of water. The surprising thing is he has no tanline - even his dick's tan! - which probably means he goes up to Crane's Beach a lot. I can just see him lying there stoned and naked under the summer sun.

"Wow!" Norm says, reaching into Jesse's crotch to fondle those two big balls that hang low in his loose ballsac.

Jesse's dick gives several twitches and I see that Norm's absolutely entranced by the spectacle of his fat, buoyant dick capped with a purplish, shiny cockhead.

"Why don't you join him, Tony?" Jesse urges me. "After all, there's no one more qualified to teach Norm the fine points of sucking cock than you," he coaxes, undoing the final, top button of my 501's and giving them a tug. They fall to my ankles and I kick off my sneakers so's I can pull them off. Then instead of putting my sneakers back on, I peel my socks off, too. As naked as Norm, with a showoff cock all a-throb, I get down on my knees next to him.

"Hiya Tony," Norm whispers to me before slipping his tongue between my lips.

I close my eyes and reach into Norm's crotch to play with his hard-on. Next thing I know, there's something pressing against the side of my mouth. Pulling away from Norm, I see it's Jesse's dick, drooling with pre-cum and impatiently twitching as it makes its way center-stage between our faces.

Norm looks into my eyes. He smiles at me and then runs his tongue along the underside of Jesse's cockhead. It responds with a massive jerk upwards, which encourages Norm to tongue-tease it again and again and again. Soon Norm's got it bouncing up and down like an acrobat on a trampoline, each downward plunge less than the one before as it reaches its full nearly nine inches.

When Norm stops, Jesse's dick curves gracefully upwards in front of our eyes and Norm and I stare at it in rapt contemplation.

"So go ahead, Norm." I finally say to him. "Take it in your mouth. Start off with just his cockhead."

Which Norm does. And I can tell from his cheek he's giving it a real thorough tonguing. Jesse's lets out with a moan and his hand falls lightly on Norm's head.

"Now go down on it," I prompt.

Norm shuts his eyes and slides his lips down along Jesse's cockshaft.

"Ooh!" from above, as Jesse's beautiful dick disappears into Norm's mouth.

But then "mmph!" and I know Norm's gagging.

Dismounting Jesse, he says to me. "How come that never happens to you?"

"You gotta relax your gagging muscles, Norm."

"Yeah, Norm," Jesse says, lowering himself to his haunches so the three of us are in a huddle. He takes Norm's balls in one hand and plays with them. "But you'll get the hang of it. Try again, because until you coughed you were doing real good. Real good."

And with that, he gives Norm's balls an encouraging tug and rises to his feet again, once more gracing us with a mouthwatering view of his throbbing, pre-cummy dick.

So Norm wraps his lips around Jesse's cock and I say, "Just take as much in as you can before it reaches your throat and then stop."

Norm slides down Jesse's cockhead again and then stops mid-shaft, turning his eyes towards me. You should see him there with his mouth full of dick.

"Now just relax, like when you're about to get fucked, except now we're talking about your throat, though I guess the principle's the same."

Norm closes his eyes again and after a meditative pause his lips slide down the remaining length of dickshaft until his nose is buried in Jesse's pubic hair.

"Ohh!" Jesse enthuses.

Norm opens his eyes and looks at me again. I give him an approving nod. He slowly dismounts Jesse, except for his cockhead, and then begins sucking up and down his shaft with even-paced, deepthroat suckstrokes, and I know he's learned how to relax his gagging muscles.

Well, I figure he can solo for a bit, so I kneel down low, managing to crane my neck in-between the two of them to admire Norm's jacking off and the way it causes his big balls to flop around. I pull his hand off his dick and go down on him, thanking my lucky stars I'm as limber as I am. Oh, that familiar feel of his over-sized Polish sausage in my mouth! And you can bet your ass I don't have a problem with gagging. No sir. If anything, giving Norm the advice I just did makes me even more aware of the sensation of dick in my throat - and just how much I crave it.

Soon I'm working my way up and down Norm's cock as I fondle his balls, lost in the world of his crotch. From above, I can hear the sounds of slurping suckstrokes and moans of pleasure and I'm in heaven.

That is, until, "Hey Tony, get up here."

So I do. While Norm continues to suck him off, Jesse runs one hand over my ass, the other across my chest and plunges his tongue into my mouth.

"Mmmm," he purrs when he pulls his tongue out again, "I didn't realize how much I've missed you, baby."

Before I can think what to say back, I'm suddenly distracted because now Norm's sucking on my dick taking the whole of it with surprising ease.

Jesse's tongue makes it's way into my mouth again. Then I realize Norm's struggling to get both our dicks in his mouth at the same time!

I'll tell you something about sucking on two dicks at once. It's a real hot idea, right? Well, the fact of the matter is you can only get so much double helping of dick inside your mouth at the same time - three inches maybe, four inches tops. And then there are occasions, like say you've got an up-curver and a down-curver, when you just can't do much at all except hope one of them pulls out to move on to something different.

But it's fun to try. And who can't resist, given the opportunity?

Well, Norm does manage both our cocks inside his mouth, but of course only the first few inches. And since we both have dicks that stick upright and don't have much give to them, he soon dismounts us, pulling our cocks close together and furiously tonguing doubletime back and forth just below our piss slits.

Well, the sharp stabs of pleasure this generates mix with Jesse's tongue's probing around inside my mouth while his left hand tugs on my right nipple and his free arm supports me as I arc slightly backwards from the force of his kiss. I close my eyes and all these sensations wash over me, pulling me out of time and place, adrift in passion.

But then I hear the crunch of approaching footsteps and I'm back again in the Fens.

The guy who interrupts our threesome is this short, muscular Latin type; smooth, light-brown skin with not much body hair but a thick, wavy black mane combed back, pronounced eyebrows and long, delicate eyelashes that emphasize his bewitching black eyes.

In no time we've got his black, low-scooped tanktop up over his head, and his white Levi's down to his ankles, discovering a lush pubic forest, from which sprouts an uncut dick. So what if it's only about six inches when it's hard, because at its barely visible base, it's nearly fat as beercan. Well, you know these all take, no give types. All they want to do is stand there while you worship their body and bring them to orgasm. But that's okay, since he has such suckable brown nipples and lickable armpits and this tight little bubble butt that's really a challenge for me to pry apart to get my tongue inside his hole. And all the while, there's Norm on his knees sucking him off after fooling around with his foreskin until the guy clamps his hands down on either side of Norm's head and takes control of his own orgasm, groaning with pleasure as he shoots his seed down Norm's throat with stab-like hipthrusts.

Well, once he's drained his dick, he pulls his clothes back on, casts us a sly smile and goes on his way.

So Norm goes back to blowing Jesse and I go back to blowing Norm, and in seconds along comes this kid who's as tall and skinny as can be, and, to be honest, kinda plain, with a prominent Adam's apple. But he has huge hands and feet, foretelling a big dick. We easily get his pants down to his ankles - all a-smile, he offers no resistance - and it turns out it's bigger than big, a huge, rugged horsedick hanging heavily between his legs, looking as it had drained his body of every extra ounce of flesh possible, behind which rests a loosehanging ballsac weighted down with two nuts the size of billiard balls.

Well, you know what big dicks are like. Sure they're a challenge to stuff down your throat, and you can only manage so much of them inside your mouth, but the real problem is they never really get rockhard. To his credit, Norm does a damn good job, given the size of the kid's dick, working on him with hand and mouth combined until he slips his huge member out from between Norm's seriously stretched lips and takes over, stroking himself until he shoots what looked like quarts of cum all over the place.

Once he's done and his dick hangs soft in his hand, he shakes off the final drool of cum stretching towards the ground and, pushes it back into his pants and goes on his way with, "Gee, thanks, guys!"

We're not a dozen suckstrokes back into me blowing Norm blowing Jesse, when along comes along this guy with short black hair, a trim mustache, and darting black eyes who's packed his gym-perfect, disco-trim body into tight black Levi's, shirtless except for a black leather vest. I peg him for a New Yorker, because, well, you know these New York types. They go right after what they want. As soon as he sees us, he pulls out his already half-hard dick and quickly strokes it into a good nine inches of perfectly-formed, cut cock looking raw-red from overuse. He steps right over to us with no hesitation, plunging his dick into Norm's mouth the moment Norm dismounts Jesse, taking control and pushing Norm's face up and down his dick. You can tell by the way Norm's stroking his own cock how much he's liking this. Then the guy shoves Norm off his dick and shoots his load all over Norm's face. He barely pauses to recover from his orgasm before he gives Norm a quick wink without smiling as he stuffs himself back into the pants and leaves.

Well, by now Norm's got this wide-eyed, sex-crazed look on his face. He's on his knees running one hand across his chest and stroking his dick with the other. He looks up at us, breathing heavily, with beads of sweat on his forehead, and all that cum running down his face.

"One of you guys' gotta fuck me!" he says desperately.

Remember what I said earlier? About how some guys need to have dick in their mouth, and others dick up their ass? So even though Norm cruised into the Fens with the object of sucking cock, and suck cock he has, he's gotta finish off the morning with a good fuck.

Of course he's gonna get his way, but I can't help thinking, what about me? I haven't had a fraction of the cocksucking I'd looked forward to. But I guess that's the kind of sacrifice you make for friends like Norm.

Anyhow, Jesse positions himself behind Norm, who bends over, mooning him with, I swear, the world's most perfect, creamy-white butt. Jesse, descends onto his haunches, pulls Norm's asscheeks wide apart, and rims Norm until he's got him moaning out of control. Then he stands up, leaving Norm with a nice, wet hole, hawks a gob of spit into his palm, and slathers it all over his dick. When he sticks it up Norm's ass, it slides in easily and he gets a nice, steady rhythm going in no time.

During all of this, Norm manages to drag me by my dick in front of his face and deepthroats me. Is it my imagination or has his cocksucking really improved? Never before has my dick felt so good in his mouth.

And then, when Jesse begins to work on my nipples - half tugging, half holding on for balance as he slams his dick in and out of Norm's butthole - well, it doesn't seem to matter anymore that I didn't get to suck as much cock as I'd set out to do this morning.

Soon, I'm on the verge of coming, that thick, oozy feeling building up inside my balls.

"Ah!" I keep going in a breathy whisper as the feeling takes over my will until nothing else matters but shooting my load.

Jesse begins intoning "ohh!" as his mouth falls open and he stares at me with the same, tortured look I'd seen on Norm's face when he said he needed to get fucked.

And the next thing you know, the cum blasts out of my balls and I scream a strangulated "AAAH!" you can probably hear all the way down to Copley Square.

Norm's "mmphing" like there's no tomorrow, but he's got me by the hips and refuses to dismount me.

And at that very same time, Jesse lets out with "Oh! Oh! OHHH!" and begins thrashing his head back with force as he moves his hands down to Norm's hip to ride him like a broncho buster.

When we've shot our loads, I push Norm off my dick and plunge to my knees to suck him off, while Jesse embraces him from behind with his cock still up Norm's ass.

Norm's dick is rockhard and ready and it doesn't take much deepthroating before I feel his hot seed spurting down my throat as Norm struggles against Jesse's restraining embrace to allow his orgasm to work itself through his body.

By the time the three of us disentangle, spent and exhausted, we're a sweaty mess.

Jesse breaks away with a "Whew!" Pulling on his clothes again, he says to me, "You know, Tony, it's great seeing you again. I didn't realize how much I'd missed you. Give me a call sometime."

I know I won't, but of course I say, "Sure."

"Actually, I live over on Hemenway Street now, barely across the street from here. If you guys would like to drop by we could have some beer, more grass and then maybe we'll be ready to..."

"No thanks," says Norm. "I think I've had enough sex for one day."

"You, Tony? Like old times?"

"Nah."

"Well, if you ever change your mind... See ya guys."

And with that, he disappears down the path.

"Funny, how no matter what, we always end up together like this, huh Tony?"

"You're the one who turned down Jesse's offer."

"Why? Would you've said 'yes'?"

"I'm not saying that. I'm just saying..."

I hesitate because I don't know what I'm trying to say. It's not like we're lovers or anything. I mean, lovers wouldn't fool around like this in the Fens.

Would they?

Well, just when I think I'm getting like really confused about all of this, Norm pulls me into his embrace, taking possession of me with a great big kiss.

I guess I'll sort out my feelings some other time, 'cause right now, whatever Norm wants, well, that's what he's gonna get!

SEDUCE ME, PLEASE

Thom Nickels

In the spring of 1971, I christened my new room in Cambridge by entertaining a blond AWOL soldier I met in Harvard Yard. I was returning from my job in a local hospital reeking of ether when I saw him: sexy, lanky, with an eye hungry for contact as he stood in front of a statue of a stuffy academic.

"I'm trying to find a chick I know. She lives in one of these dorms, but I can't remember which one. She said she would help me," he said.

"Help you?"

We were both about 18, a bit pimply, and rather despondent. I was feeling low because it was a Friday afternoon and I had no plans for the weekend; he was feeling glum because he couldn't contact the student who was supposed to help him get to Canada.

"She said I could stay with her tonight, and now I have nowhere to go. I'm AWOL from the Army," he added, his thumb wedged inside his belt buckle.

The prospect of helping an AWOL soldier appealed to the conscientious objector in me. It also helped that he was a lordly specimen of American youth in tight green trousers. "I might be able to help you out. I mean, I can't promise an overnight stay but we can at least talk about it, you can get your bearings at my place," I said.

"Sounds good," he said.

At my place I fixed him some sandwiches and opened a six-pack.

We talked for some time before I began plotting the inevitable seduction. Not that he had to be seduced. Any AWOL soldier who hung around Harvard Square in those days was definitely not naive or orthodox in behavior or morals. Not that my having sex with him would in any way be immoral. To the contrary: I knew it would invigorate him, give him vision and bounce, improve his mental attitude besides bringing him good luck.

After a beer or two I finally found the nerve to touch him when he stood in front of me looking at a map of New England.

"No, man," he said, pushing my hand away. "Let's listen to some music. Do you have a radio?"

Of course I had a radio, but what was this? I'd met this type of cockteaser before. They egg you on just to cut you off at the crucial moment. Other brands of cockteasers like saying "no" until it's time to say yes (that way they think you'll appreciate them more). Getting the solider – his name was Jim – to drink more beer was probably the answer, as well as talking a lot of sex talk – liberated sex talk along the lines of my lectures to the local neighborhood urchins about the sex life of the most interesting poet in America, Allen Ginsberg.

"Well," I said after a couple hours of listening to Jimi Hendrix, Cream, the Rolling Stones, as well as snippets of a Nixon speech when the News was on. "It's time to go to bed. It's really late."

He'd already exhausted me with tales of the Army, his girlfriend Ru Ru Somebody who climbed rope and weaved dresses in Vermont, his trying to get to Canada by hook or crook. At random points in the conversation he'd slouch down on the sofa, assume a come-seduce-me-pose and then straighten up when it looked like I was going to make a pass. I was upset because when he slouched he always had a hardon of considerable length showing in his pants.

"Enough is enough," I thought, attack-stroking its plump juiciness at the stroke of midnight, a time when most of the people in my rooming house were already in bed or getting in their jamies.

"No," he said, pushing my hand away again with an antiseptic vengeance.

In today's lingo, no means no but in those halcyon days of glib marijuana smoke and blurred Bob Dylan lyrics, it often meant "Maybe later," or "I'll see," or "Get me stoned more and I'll reconsider." With men, of course, the timing had to be right.

The cockteasing went on for the length of our conversation, so that by the time we went to bed, I was quite bleary-eyed. But not too tired to try again, mind you, since I believe it's always smart to send out erotic reminders in case there's been a mind change.

"It's best that you sleep with me," I said. "The sofa is not comfortable. You're not afraid to sleep with me, I hope..."

"Afraid?"

"Well, it does seem a little odd that you're not afraid to go AWOL and risk years in the slammer but that you are afraid to have sex with another man. Isn't that twisted logic?"

He looked at me funny so I dropped the subject and suggested that he take the double bed while I hit the sofa. I knew that if he took the bed it'd be easy to sneak in beside him, whereas if he took the sofa it'd be impossible to get a hand in edgewise.

I watched as he stripped down to his underpants, his nice blond boy's body not too hairy and with just the right hint of muscularity. I also tried not to notice that his ivory colored skin emitted a sweet scent.

He climbed into bed and pulled the top sheet over himself but then very quickly cast it aside. Did this gesture, I wondered, signal the end of his cockteasing? Had I worked a conversion in Allen Ginsberg's name? Of course, under no circumstances would I have thrown him out if he refused to have sex with me. This also was in Ginsberg's Bible: be kind to uptight men who cannot give of themselves, let then sleep the sleep of Pollyanna though you may try to hump them one more time in the morning.

In no time he was curled up like a fetus and facing the window. I felt he placed himself in this position because it was his way of saying I could sleep with him; he just didn't want to be trapped on the side of the bed facing the wall. He said nothing when I slid in beside him (it was my bed, after all), curling up close to him but not too close. When I placed a hand on the rim of his jockey shorts, he jerked forward a little.

"No. Please, remove your hand."

"You are one tough cookie," I said. "Think of all the lonely men in the world clamoring to get a massage. I'm not asking you for anything. All you have to do is lay there. It'll please you, believe me."

By now I was feeling pretty disgusted. Why did he have to be such a diehard straight arrow?

Morning, however, was bright with stiff projectiles. For what seemed like hours – as perspiration covered our faces and wet the bed sheets – we explored each other's bodies. What brought on the change? I'm not sure, I only know that one orgasm was not enough and that he became a fountain of giving.

Later, after he showered in the bathroom at the end of the hall, he returned to my room with a towel draped around his waist, a cigarette dangling from his lips. Through the open window I smelled spring flowers and freshly mowed grass. Life was promising after all.

"Let me treat you to breakfast at the Pewter Pot. They have good omelettes there," I said, still tasting his Ivory-ness and wanting more.

As he stared into space though columns of cigarette smoke, I caught psychic glimpses of his Company drill sergeants, Vietnam, napalm, dying or dead soldiers with their insides exposed. I thought of Jim realizing too late that the war was a farce and how there was only one thing to do: head north on the freedom trail, the new underground railroad tended by anti-war activists like myself. Had he been a different sort of fellow, of course, a strong determination on my part might have kept him in Boston, our domestic menage becoming as cozy as anything in *House and Garden*. But he was straight, a Vietnam war criminal of sorts, and on the run. Hardly the ingredients of a happy marriage.

"How long have you been AWOL?"

"Two months. They're after me now. I know I'm on the FBI's list. Couple of times I was followed. I was at the MBTA stop in the Square when I saw a man spying on me. He reached up for something and I saw handcuffs dangling from his belt." He took another drag on his cigarette and blew out a long column of smoke. For some reason I envisioned napalm rising to the ceiling and killing 100 children in one fell swoop.

Everybody in those days was paranoid, claiming they were being followed by the FBI or CIA. You'd hear it from anti-war activists, ex-Black Panthers, Socialist Worker Party members, Gay Liberation activists. People who merely sympathized with the revolution complained that their phones were being tapped, as if the FBI had nothing better to do than wire all the phones of the people in Boston who were reading Jerry Rubin and getting stoned at outdoor rock concerts. There were more stories than I can count of men in dark sunglasses peeking around corners or following people as they marked time before the Big Bust.

"Do you know the way to Canada from here?" I asked him.

"Just hitchhike north. I don't know what it'll be like at the border," he said, scratching his crotch.

"You know anybody else in town?" A part of me was afraid I was his only Boston contact. I was afraid he'd expect me to take care of him or provide him with shelter until going to Canada was feasible. But there was no way I could leave him alone in my place. Despite all the chattering we'd done, he still hadn't revealed enough about himself for me to trust him. Outside of sex, there was nothing that interested me about him, a rather unpleasant realization. Still, because I had sex with him I felt obligated to help him in some way. How could a registered conscientious objector like myself allow a beautiful blond pacifist to fall into the hands of the FBI?

"Well, let's go to breakfast," I said, glad to have a companion by my side.

As we walked up Kirkland Street, I hoped we'd pass a fellow roomer so they'd see me with my new friend. As it happened, a fellow roomer was coming towards us. He was coming back from his Armenian Orthodox Sunday liturgy, dressed in a suit and tie, so out of place in 1970.

The Orthodox roomer was careful – closet case that he was – not to look at my friend. He was carrying the *New York Times* like it was a parcel of valuable boyflesh.

In the Pewter Pot, students, activists and hippie-types sat huddled over coffee and muffins plotting the course of the revolution. Women in long hair and granny glasses moved their lips as serious young men in huge mustaches or beards contributed to the babble. In Boston, Pewter Pot waitresses dressed in Dolly Madison costumes, but not in eccentric Cambridge, where the waitresses all looked like Radcliff girls with their hair up like Emily Dickinson.

My friend ordered a salad with fresh broccoli in it. I tried not to look at him eat, averting my eyes when he forked the tiny raw heads and dipped them into a kind of blue cheese dressing. I was devouring English muffins, sliding them across my plate in order to scoop up remaining egg yolk. His crunching on the broccoli heads made me nervous.

"Is there something wrong?" he asked.

"No, I was just wondering if you would be safe going to Canada...I mean, with all those FBI men chasing you and all. It's a major undertaking, leaving the country of your birth..."

He forked a tomato, then a wedge of lettuce. For a moment he put the salad aside and took a bite out of a blueberry muffin. He handled his teabag with his hands, pressing it with his fingers over the tea. The waitress came by and set down his entree, a bacon and cheese omelette. I contemplated his fingers: beautiful long fingers, slender like ebony and in some sense resembling his prick. I would miss him, yes, but at the same time I wanted him gone. Every act of sex brought with it humiliating sessions of begging as he pushed my hand away and said "no," until he decided he had tortured me enough. Then he'd unzipper and take out his dick. I was worn out.

After the meal, I called someone I knew at the hospital, a radical straight black activist who was interested in all aspects of the revolution. His view of homosexuality was positive, only he believed that everyone should be gay only when they reached old age. "This would match the way human hormones work. Women with mustaches, men losing their beards and muscle tone and turning soft like women," he said. "When this happens, then people should be homosexual."

His ideal world left out the youthful and vibrant middle years, when sexuality peaked, but I never raked him over the coals on this. He was being honest; at least he insisted there was a place for Queerness, even if it was at the end of a person's life. Of course, his insistence that a person could just switch-hit once they hit old age probably tapped into his own inherent bisexuality.

He told us to meet him in one of Cambridge's bar/cafes. There, he'd give the guy the address of people willing to feed him and pay his way until he got another address, and so on until he arrived in Canada. Once across the border, he was on his own, although there were anti-war organizations set up to help people like him hide. Jim was quite thankful for this arrangement, though back in my room he resisted my advances once again, making me think that perhaps he was only a morning sex person. His sex rationing irked me, and the prospect of being stuck with him in my tiny L-shaped room until our appointment with the black activist was unsettling too. What to do with him? Keep buying him beer? Listen to more inane talk about Ru Ru and her Vermont weaving?

After much coaxing and fretting on my part, we once again became a pile of twisted limbs and sprouting projectiles: so much so that I imagined our cocks pointing north towards the white polar caps of Canadian freedom.

During a break in our lovemaking, I went downstairs to get him more beer when I ran into Debbie, whom I'd met several weeks prior to meeting Jim. Debbie was 19 or 20, a young woman of impossible good cheer with beautiful teeth, impeccable skin and white blond hair. She was, I knew, a heterosexual boy's dream.

"Good afternoon," I said.

Our budding friendship had a lot to do with her being from Wisconsin. It was her first time away from home and her first year in college. It should come as no surprise that she reminded me of the little Oz girl forgetting to tap her shoes together.

Previously, we'd spent some time in my room drinking coffee and telling stories. I told her about the morgue autopsies I was seeing, as well as the great architect, Walter Gropius, I brought into the OR. "His huge feet stuck over the end of the mattress. They were long, thin feet, the feet of an artist," I told her. "He talked about a great shock – 'You will experience a great shock!' he said. I thought he was talking about himself but he was talking about me. Imagine that! Gropius just smiled, and that was that. The surgeon said it was the medication," I told Debbie.

In the communal kitchen she asked me if I would put her brother up for a night when he came out to visit her in a few days. The question caught me off-guard. First of all, Jim was still in my room lounging around in his BVDs going over maps of Canada. I was blowing him in hour intervals, stroking him through his underpants and then sticking his cock through the slit in his shorts. We had time for one more beer before we had to split to meet Howard, get the address, and then walk Jim to the subway.

That would be it. During this time, Jim seemed to lose all inhibition. I no longer had to struggle to have sex with him but he offered himself willingly so that these last hours together were the nicest we spent.

A part of me was beginning to mourn Jim's going away and I was fearing a season of sexual starvation when along came Debbie with this tempting offer.

"Todd's never been to the big city before," she said. "He's only lived on the family farm. He's nineteen, a year younger than me. I think he'd feel more comfortable with you. It'll just be for one night. The next day he's taking a bus to Maine to go fishing with a friend."

I agreed, and set off upstairs, wondering at this extraordinary change in luck.

When I got to my room, Jim was dressed and ready to go. We drank the beer quickly and then headed to the Square where we met Howard on the subway island. He handed Jim the piece of paper with the name and address of some people in Maine. With the address was an envelope with thirty dollars inside, money from Cambridge activists. Jim took the money and the paper, thanked us both, and then headed into the subway without so much as a last good-bye or affectionate nod. I don't know why I expect people to give a little extra in situations like this, but I do.

When he was gone, I was feeling quite empty and not at all eager to go back to my lonely room.

Fortunately Debbie's brother appeared a few days later. She knocked on my door and introduced the strapping farm guy who stood about six-one with short dark hair, brown eyes and home-on-the range muscles. Todd's boyish shyness and square all-American features seemed out-of-place in Cambridge. He might as well have been from the moon.

Debbie said they were going out to dinner and would return later. I said okay – and yes, it was fine if Todd left his overnight bag in my room until they returned. When they left, I could still see the handsome boy who had teeth as white as his sister's. He was a marvel; a sinewy gift from Middle

America. What to do until they returned became a nerve wracking decision. I sat on the sofa, looking at Todd's bag, debating whether to open it. My intention wasn't to steal but to look for personal affects of this most interesting young men: underarm deodorant, underpants, shoes, socks, any article that might have touched the body of this virginal country boy.

I opened the bag. Bleached white underwear stacked like cans of white tuna were piled next to T-shirts, socks, folded shorts and jeans. There was man's man Old Spice, a shaving razor, a toothbrush. Everything was clean and folded and smelled of duffle bag and laundry detergent. Then I uncovered an old sock, size 13 or so, rolled up in a ball and stuffed in a corner of the bag. I unraveled it and held it at arm's length, imagining tractor boy's monster foot, wide beyond measure, delicious, forceful.

"Well, I see you two survived dinner," I said, opening the door two hours later after hearing a knock. I was happy that it was still early in the evening. "Where did you guys eat?" I asked. "Guys" was an attempt to put brother and sister on equal footing, to mask my happiness at having Todd, and only Todd, in my bedroom for the night. Todd radiated the look of green pastures, golden thighs, pails of milk after a few pulls on a cow's udder. "The Pewter Pot? Oh yeah, I always go there. I've eaten so many of their corn muffins I feel like a corn muffin myself. How do you like Cambridge so far, Todd?"

"He does." Debbie glanced at her brother and smiled. Todd looked around the room, his eyes focusing on my small bookcase. Earlier, I hid all of my gay books. Whatever happened, had to be a surprise. Todd could not know. He must not have a chance to fortify himself.

"Sit down if you want. Can I serve you something?"

"Oh, I can't be staying," Debbie said. "I have to study. If we're here too early, just say so. I can bring Todd back later."

Todd was already seated on the sofa. I could see that he had squarish knee caps, almost always a sign of muscular legs. His hands were folded politely over his crotch. "Todd can just come to my room tomorrow morning when you go to work," Debbie said. "Have fun you guys."

"You really have a nice sister. She seems to be one in a million," I said when Debbie had left. I reminded myself to watch the Pollyanna stuff. Brother and sister knockdown fights were traditional, and I wondered who screamed the loudest. And how close was close? Was there ever a question of incest between the two? "I just remembered I have a few cold beers in the kitchen. Would you like one?"

Todd said yes. A good sign. If he'd get a little drunk, he'd loosen up and relax. I came back with four beers. We talked about his engineering major at the University of Wisconsin. Todd told me that he planned on leaving his parents' farm after graduation but that he wanted to make his home in some little town in the Midwest.

When we finished the first beer, I watched for signs that he was relaxed. I wanted him to sit back, spread his legs. But his body language was tight, constricted. I was afraid that he saw through my over-enthusiasm. "Have you been here before?"

"Nope."

"Have you noticed anything different about the people here? Anything about them shock you a little bit? I mean, here it's pretty much do your own thing – whatever turns you on, that philosophy."

"I've sort of noticed."

His answers were flat, methodical, and he volunteered little. 'Whatever turns you on' was a subtle reference to bisexuality, but he didn't seem to get the connection.

"Do you go to anti-war demonstrations or rock concerts in Wisconsin?"

"Nope."

"Do you think you're going to investigate what life's like here?"

"Oh, I don't think there's time for that. I'm going fishing tomorrow."

"Tell me about the farm you grew up on," I said, cocking my head sideways and stealing a quick glimpse of his crotch. Of course, I'd read Dr. Kinsey's report and knew the startling stastitics concerning farmboys, of how they had done different things with livestock, sheep, pigs, etc. Why should Todd be any different? Looks were often deceiving. I had even heard a story about one horny teenager who attached his cock to a milking machine and got it ripped off because the jerking motions were too violent.

Todd talked about his parents, about his chores – driving the tractor, bailing hay, feeding – the livestock, helping Dad. He had almost finished his second beer. Just a hint of relaxed body language was evident now. He was slouching against the sofa back, running his thick fingers along the sides of the beer bottle in a masturbatory fashion. The position of the bottle was, ironically enough, provocative enough to make me slide closer to him. After talking about the farm, there didn't seem to be anything else he wanted to say, so I went to the bookshelf and pulled out same poetry by Ginsberg and Walt Whitman. I asked him if he'd like me to read aloud. He said yes, so I got down on the floor in front of the sofa.

"If I'm boring you, just let me know. These poems are very sexual, so I hope you don't embarrass easily. Ginsberg is what hip people here are reading. It's probably important that you get a taste of it. It's like the old saying: 'When in Rome do as the Romans do.' I laughed, hoping to see a smile on his face. He did smile – tolerantly, but looked at me as if he were coming to a conclusion about something.

My first selections were tame, but the heat soon intensified. Mentioned was cocksucking, vaginal lays in Denver backlots, New York orgasms, LSD orgasms, heterosexual loveboys, sodomy in Newark and Camden, jacking off on Amtrak trains, Whitman's poem "We Two Boys." I was really piling it on. Positioned on the floor in front of him, within arm's reach of his crotch, I was waiting for him to stretch out his legs but he held them snug against the sofa as if he were in a Baptist church. His crotch showed no tenting. He might as well have been listening to readings from the works of Bertrand Russell.

Suddenly I wished Jim were back. Jim had been difficult but at least the ice broke at the eleventh hour. This boy reminded me of stone, the heart and soul of American Gothic – or an FBI agent.

"I'll stop now," I said, "since I don't want to bore you. Anyway, that's what's being read here nowadays. At least you got a little sample of it." I took another swig of beer to bolster my courage. "Listen, I have an idea. I give a great back massage. It's a wonderful relaxer. It makes tension disappear." Square-jawed, broad shouldered Todd was just my type, and I was ready to please.

When there was no response, I thought of slow oxen in the fields: shy and retiring, they needed heavy coaxing. Was it only city boys who readily jumped at offers of sex? "Well, would you like a back massage?" I held my breath. I had a quick vision of him punching me out, upsetting the sofa and walking out John Wayne-style. I imagined him going to Debbie and pounding his fist on her wall, shouting "You sent me to a faggot's den!" Instead, he merely shook his head and gave a simple 'no,' as if he'd rehearsed the line earlier in his mind. Firm resolve fluttered in his eyes like the sails of a great flagship – this truly was a future FBI agent, and something had to be done.

I wished then that I had the power to transform myself unto a long haired Radcliff girl, blouse open, buttery bosom flopping. I imagined the intensity of Todd's passion as he then joined me on the floor.

"Ah, Thomasina, let me inside baby. Ah, you're sweet. Hmmmmm..." Or something like that.

"Well, how about a foot massage?" I ventured. "If your feet are tired my kind of massage can work wonders."

I knew he was still thinking of me as his sister's boyfriend when he said he just wanted to go to sleep. I watched as he stripped down to his boxer shorts and lay on the sofa. I observed how he stretched out on his stomach and let his feet dangle over the edge of the sofa. Very reluctantly I turned off the lights and stretched out on my own bed for a while, but when I couldn't sleep I got up and went over to where he was.

I got down on the floor next to him and watched him sleep. Tomorrow he would tell his sister everything.

"Are you awake? Listen, who will it hurt? Who will know? We are alone and the only thing you will feel is pleasure. Allow yourself the experience!" I stared at the print on his boxer shorts. Had I only maneuvered my hand and taken the plunge as I had with Jim, but I was tired of taking risks and tired of begging, and very tired of hearing the word 'no,' even if 'yes' came later.

In an abrupt about-face, he turned on his back, pulling the top sheet over his middle section as he placed his hands over his crotch. What struck me most about this protective maneuver was the placement of his feet. They were on the sofa's edge aimed in my direction, as if he wanted me to touch them.

I moved closer, positioning my head a few inches from the big clodhoppers. Rubbing my hands together to generate warmth, I grabbed his right foot and began stroking the fine underside down to the heel before massaging the toes. He did not resist but lay still as I rubbed in firm up and down strokes. Within a few minutes, he even moved his feet near my mouth, making it easy for me to lick both of them at the same time.

Throughout the session, he did not remove his hands from his crotch but held them in a fixed position. My work on his feet aroused him. I could see he had a huge hard-on though he kept it hidden under his hands and wouldn't let me go near it. My massage lulled him to sleep.

I kept my head near his feet until the wee hours of the morning, licking and stroking them all during the night. Todd never resisted, even when he was on his stomach and when I did his feet from behind.

By the time dawn came, I did not care that I had never seen Todd's cock. A night with his feet had done the trick; for some reason they had excited me as much as the cocks of the neighborhood urchins had a few months earlier. More than that, I knew I was onto a new thing. I was entering a new sexual cycle – the post-penis phase which had very possibly been predicted by Walter Gropius as he lay dying.

If a foot massage can quell the nerves of a straight farm boy from Wisconsin, what might it do for other straight men?

There are benefits to having a foot fetish. It means an increase of prospects: overweight men who I'd ordinarily reject because of weight might – if they're attractive and have nice feet – become objects of desire. Less attractive men and boys, including bald men without muscles, can also become erotic possibilities. On the other hand, conventionally beautiful men who have ugly feet might not make the grade. Having a foot fetish also broadens the scope in terms of seducing so-called minors: what can the law say about sucking a teen boy's toes if no other part of his body was handled?

Todd left me with these words: "That foot massage was neat. I never thought all that could come from handling feet. Thanks."

When Todd left, Debbie began giving me more energetic

hellos than before. Obviously Todd had told her good things about his stay. Just what I didn't know until Debbie came to my door, took off her shoes and asked me if I wouldn't mind massaging her toes. "Because they hurt, and my brother tells me you are a professional reflexologist," she said. Which was far from the truth, but Todd had to tell her something. But massaging a woman's feet did not interest me. In fact, when she took off her shoes and when I saw her dainty, porcelain-like toes and marshmallow heels, I felt squeamish. It was like having my nose forced into a jar of cold cream. Women's feet were just not erotic, Debbie's feet especially. They had no veins. They might as well have been amputated feet floating in a jar of formaldehyde.

Still, I couldn't turn her away. I obliged, resting her feet on a footstool and rubbing them with aloe lotion. She closed her eyes and said how relaxed it made her feel. I felt no tingling sensation in my groin, and I was not tempted to put my mouth over her miniature toes.

When I finished the massage, her feet had turned a scarlet red, which for some reason reminded me of the good old red, white and blue – and of Jim hiding out in Canada.

FIRST LESSON

Kent Dawson

He was standing by himself, not quite in one corner of the bar, but certainly not in a spot that would have attracted the kind of attention his looks deserved. Fine-featured, blond, curly hair lightened by copious helpings of sunshine, golden skin stretched tight over the high cheekbones, the slightness of the torso, and right down to the beginnings of the flat stomach that dived below the waistband of his skimpy denim shorts, his was the kind of classic beauty that could have had you thinking of great masterpieces of sculpture by Michelangelo, but right at that moment my mind was far away from anything classically sculptured or otherwise. It was easy to imagine him shooting the waves, but my eyes had travelled lower, taking my imagination off in a completely different direction.

From where I was leaning on the bar, I was getting a slightly side-on view of the gash in those skimpy shorts that slashed across a patch of equally golden skin towards a sweet little bullseye. And as my eye travelled across that gorgeous golden bun towards the crack of his ass, it was all I could do to stop drooling. I gulped down another mouthful of beer to wash down that excess saliva.

"Nice, huh?" I wasn't the only one giving him an eyeful. On either side of me Hal and Jake had shifted slightly to get a better view of the scenery. Hal's eyes were still fixed at torso level, but Jake's stare was on exactly the same spot that had captured my attention. I knew he'd be drooling just as heavily as I was.

The kid had obviously felt our eyes on him because he looked up and glanced across at us for a microsecond before he turned his attention back to his glass. The three of us held the gaze in unison for a long second, maybe more, until he looked up again. This time, before the eyes dropped away, there was a slight, nervous smile. That was all Jake needed. A couple of strides across the bar and he was beside the kid before he looked up again.

"Name's Jake." He offered that strong paw that spent most

days controlling a jackhammer and the kid took it, with just the slightest hesitation - which was more than you could say for Hal and me. We moved in even before the kid got to open his mouth. "Randy ... Randy Harris." The words came out quickly, with a slight tremble to them. Considering the reputation the place had, the fact that he was there meant he had to know something of the score, even if the soft blue eyes, now they'd lost some of the hesitancy, were lit with a sweet kind of innocence that was enough to drive a man crazy. "This is Hal and Peter." The kid took each of our hands in turn. Now that Jake had the introductions over, he wasn't about to waste any time. "Ain't seen you around here before, Randy."

"We just moved here, a couple of weeks back. My old man's got a promotion with his bank, and so here we are."

"Looks like you haven't been spending too much time around banks," Hal said appraisingly. "Been catching some waves by the looks of it." Randy blushed prettily.

"I've been trying, but I'm not good at it. Weren't no waves where we came from - nothing but sand and dust." That had to be one of the best cues I've ever been handed.

"You ought to drop by and talk to Hal some time. He's got the board shop down at the end of the beach." The kid blushed again and looked straight at Hal.

"I know. I've seen you there." He smiled and the eyes lit up even more. "Gee, could I really? I bet you could teach me lots of things."

The grin that Hal gave him confirmed that he would probably be able to teach Randy lots of things, but all three of us intended that, if we could manage it, the kid's lessons were going to start long before he ever got near a surfboard. Before long we'd grabbed some beer and headed back to my place. Jake's never been one to waste time on idle chatter, and my place was the obvious choice since it's the most functional for the kind of scene we had in mind; it might not win any prizes in the home decorating stakes, but the bed is solid, and big.

For a while we sat around drinking, making idle conversation, and just settling the kid down. Randy was rapt in the idea of going out with Hal for same extra lessons, but after a couple of drinks, he seemed to forget about the waves, and I noticed his eyes kept flicking from Hal and me, and always ending up back on Jake. Not that I blamed him. I've never minded looking at Jake either. He'd stripped off his shirt and was sitting in a chair by himself while Hal and I kept company of either side of Randy whom I'd installed in the middle of the sofa.

Jake is literally a mat of hair and muscle – thick pecs, a heavy covering of black hair on his chest tapering down to his waist where skintight jeans stretched over the hips, and strained at the bulge that looked like it had been carefully arranged for maximum effect.

Randy could hardly keep his eyes off it. Both Hal and I could have told him there was nothing at all arranged about Jake's crotch. It wouldn't have mattered how that guy dressed, it was one part of Jake that was always going to be impressive.

Not that either Hal or I felt we had anything to be ashamed of in the body stakes. Hal was stockier than Jake, covered in a fine mat of golden hair that almost vanished into his deep tan. The time he spent in the waves kept him well toned. As for me, well, I might be leaner, smoother, but I spend enough time at the gym to make sure I can match it with Hal and Jake when the three of us went out together.

For a while we sat around drinking and talking, and then Hal produced the joint he always keeps for this kind of occasion. Never rely on the lure of a board alone, that's always been Hal's motto. It's another reason we've always worked so well as a team - Jake provides the body, Hal was the bait, while I've got the bedroom.

After the second drag, there was no way I could hold out any longer, especially with that cute little asshole virtually dangling before my eyes, not more than an arm's length away. I moved closer, and started my hand on an exploration of the golden skin. Randy looked up at me and smiled, slightly nervous, and I let the hand go further, across the ass cheek that poked up through the tear in the shorts, then under the denim so I could start to finger along the crack, and across the tightness of that sweet little hole. At this stage I didn't need a beer or a smoke - nothing but the feel of that tightly closed crack, quivering like a mound of Jello as I began my initial explorations.

Jake and Hal had moved just as quickly. Hal's fingers were

at work on the flesh around Randy's nipples, pinching the mounds into tight little erections before he bought his mouth down and nipped lightly on the flesh.

Randy moaned softly, shifting his body and spreading his legs to get more comfortable. With a single movement, Jake cupped one hand under the boy's backside and lifted him easily, while the other hand stripped off the shorts leaving the finely chiselled young body, gold all over, spread out before us like a meal at a table. With the shorts gone, the flat belly had dropped to show six inches or more of cock shaft rising from its nest of golden hairs, coming up from a tight little ball bag - definitely the kind of scene Michelangelo would have had in mind when he worked on David. But right at that moment, none of us needed culture. Jake brought his head forward and took that sweet little ball bag and shaft into his mouth in one practiced swallow, pressing his lips hard against the hairs at its base. Randy moaned more loudly. I lifted his leg so my mouth could gain access to that sweetness that was showing so much promise under my fingers. Practice, they say, makes perfect, and I sure as hell have had plenty of practice at this sort of thing. It wasn't too long before that tight little sphincter had begun to relax, letting my tongue begin its probing exploration as I savored the first delicious flavors of the kid's ass juice.

By this stage, Jake's rod was screaming for release from the tight restriction of his jeans, so I ran my fingers down his zip. It sprang out, just over ten inches of hard anger, rising from the tight mattress of black hair. I heard Randy's gasp as his small hand flew towards the stiffened rod, the fingers closing around the shaft as they strained to meet the thumb and failed miserably.

Randy's other hand came down to caress the apple-sized cock head that had reared out of the foreskin, the pisshole already glistening with Jake's precum.

We'd gone past the stage where the sofa was of any further use. This was now a job for the bedroom.

As if he was reading my mind, Jake scooped up the naked boy, holding him easily in one arm as he headed for my bedroom, the free hand shedding his jeans as he went. Hal and I followed, leaving behind a trail of discarded garments.

Jake threw Randy down onto the bed, and the three of us

stood around him, our cocks stiff, reaching out hungrily towards this delicious morsel that lay on the mattress before us. Slowly Randy's gaze moved from first one cock to the other. The words came out in a quiet whisper. "Jesus, you guys are big."

He was only stating the obvious, but it's always nice to hear it again. When you've got close to a yard of cock between the three of you, it's hard for these young guys not to be impressed. I might not have been as thick as Jake, but I made up for it with the extra length, coming in at just over the eleven inch mark, and while Hal only just made the ten inches, he more than compensated for it with a thickness that filled a pair of swim trunks the way that most men could only dream about.

There have been lots of times when I've been turned on by both Hal and Jake, but right now I wasn't interested in anything other than the sweet little ass my mouth was aching to get back to.

While my tongue began its first serious probing, reaching deep into that ass muscle to make it wet and ready for what was to follow, Jake moved so he could swallow me whole, taking the full length of my long shaft so the cockhead pressed a deep against the sides of his throat in one practiced motion that I'd got to know a long time ago, but which gives its own fresh thrill every time. As I came up for air, I saw that Randy's mouth was working hard, stretching to take as much of Hal as he could, his hand out fondling Jake's shaft, while Hal's mouth moved in quick darting bits from the kid's tiny cockhead to the tight little ballbag, each nip causing the slender body to tighten as one spasm of pleasure followed the other.

Some precum was now dripping steadily from Jake's pisshole, so I moved away, knowing that the time had come to put that hole I had so enjoyed filling with wetness to another use. Jake moved into position, placing the dripping knob at the entrance to the little hole that now glistened. He moved it back and forward a couple of times, finding the center of that tight target, then like an arrow released from a crossbow, he brought himself forward. Randy's head snapped back off Hal's cock, and his scream rang across the room.

Jake's large hand had reached around to the front of that

hard, slender belly and he pressed the boy back, holding him tight against the throbbing rod until the ass could adjust to the sudden invasion. Then Jake began the first of the fucking with long slow strokes, taking the shaft back so the knob almost left the now gaping asshole, then sliding it back to its full length. I'd positioned myself beneath them so my exploring tongue could follow along the shaft each time it made its exit, drinking the excess juices that now covered Jake's thick piston.

Randy had gone back to work on Hal's cock, while Hal turned his attention to my throbbing rod, covering the entire length with quick small nippings before he returned to swallow each of my balls in turn.

Jake's breathing became heavier, faster, matching the movements of his cock as he quickened the pace and began slamming the glistening shaft into the waiting hole time and time again. I moved back to watch as the gigantic ballbag exploded with its load, following the first signs as the spurtings began their long journey as Jake pushed his cockhead deep for one last thrust, pulling the slender body against him more tightly so the first load could find its home deep in the young gut. Jake pulled out and rolled on his back. I was on him in an instant, wrapping my mouth around that large knob, now covered with a mixture of cum and ass juice, with Jake's last drops of fresh cum still oozing into the mixture. My mouth worked up and down that shaft, savoring every drop that had been left behind after Randy's first fucking.

By now, Randy's ass was getting an extra stretching as Hal moved into him, plunging short sharp stabs of thick throbbing rod, almost the same size as the boy's forearm, while Randy lay there letting the pleasure sweep over him. "Oh, man, fuck me hard!"

Hal increased the speed, and from past experience I knew I didn't have a lot of time to finish working on Jake's cock before I'd need to be doing the same thing to Hal.

Hal pulled out, his shaft covered with a mixing of his own cum with Jake's, with Randy's ass juice adding to the sweetness of the cocktail. After I'd taken as much as I could from that still rock-hard shaft, I turned my attention to the now gaping asshole, the source of that delicious mixture and began to drink more deeply, sucking away at the juices that now oozed back to my eager mouth. Randy had his lips around my cock and was trying to follow Jake's example, forcing the length deep down into his throat. Once again the kid was proving to be a fast learner. While he might not have had Jake's experience, for a beginner he wasn't half bad, and I was willing to give him plenty of opportunity to practice.

I could have stayed there a whole lot longer, but I knew Jake was keen to release a second load into that hole that still throbbed with promise, and besides, that extra cum could only add to its sweetness. I moved my mouth away and Jake's slipped in as though it had always belonged there.

Jake rolled on his back, taking Randy over with him. I moved myself into position, lying full length along Randy's smooth hairless body, bringing my cockhead up between Jake's gigantic ballsac, and then following along his shaft as I plunged with him into the warmth of that hole that had now stretched to take the two of us in a steady fucking.

Hal had moved his cock to Randy's mouth, and the kid was stretching his jaws to match his ass, taking that thick muscle down into his throat, occasionally gagging and coming up for air, but every time going back for more.

I could have gone on like that forever, but my cock had other ideas. My balls tightened out of control, and I felt my load welling up, demanding to be free. Jake's shaft, thrusting in unison with mine, became even harder, and I knew he too was about to spill his second load into that sweet warmth that was giving us both so much pleasure.

He exploded just below my cockhead, hot bursts that seared along the tip of my knob as my own jism spurted in one long hot stream into the very heart of Randy's gut. Hal had dropped his load into the boy's mouth, and Randy was now trying to swallow cock and juice at the same time, with stray cum dribbling down his chin.

Against my belly I could feel a throbbing wetness, and I knew it was Randy's cum, sticking our stomachs together as we lay there, our energies spent.

It was Randy who finally broke the silence. "Geez, I thought you guys could teach me something, but I didn't guess it'd be so much."

"Don't worry, kid," Hal replied. "That was just the first

lesson. There's a lot more to come."

That second lesson came a few hours later, after we'd snatched a broken sleep. Hal, Jake and Randy each dozed with a cockhead in his mouth, while I spent that time in a delicious half sleep with my lips against that well-stretched asshole, my tongue lapping at the cum oozing out from it. Together we made a comfortable mass of entwined bodies, but then, that's one of the advantages of having such a large bed.

NOTORIOUS

Thomas Holm

Baron Henri de V., notorious voluptuary, sat with his boy of the moment in his box at the Opera. He was attending the premiere of a production of "Tosca," the latest work by Puccini, to the financing of which the Baron had substantially contributed. He raised a pair of opera glasses from time to time to his heavy-lidded eyes, when he wished to focus on some detail that was directly or indirectly the fruit of his largesse. But for this occasional movement he remained quite still, rapt as he was in the music.

His companion, Laurent, remained almost as still, but only with great effort. He was not rapt, he was far from enthralled by the music and by the incomprehensible shenanigans on the stage: He was bored, and resentful at being bored and resentful of the shackles of financial dependency which bound him to the Baron and which had resulted in his spending so many evenings in this overheated opera box while unattractive people in odd garb warbled in a foreign language on the stage below.

Laurent was in an unusally bad mood this evening. His otherwise beautiful face was sulky and pouting. He could sense his own bad mood and sense how it affected him, how it made him somehow effeminate. He noticed this more and more these days, heard it in the voice he raised to complain, caught sight of it in the mirror's reflection of his tetchy frown, his pursed lips. He noticed this change and he noticed the Baron's displeasure at it, and there was nothing he could do. Though the Baron's tastes ran to pretty, they didn't extend to girlish, and Laurent's sulks and tantrums were dangerously close to the limits of what was tolerable. Laurent knew that the Baron was tiring of him, was irritated with him; Laurent had been forced to accompany him to the opera three times already this week. There was something indolently sadistic about the Baron's insistence, for he well knew how little Laurent cared for the opera. It was as if the Baron were tenderizing the boy before administering *the coup de grace*.

Most of the activities for which the Baron was notorious - the gargantuan suppers in the city's finest restaurants, the extended drinking sessions with cronies, the vast sums gambled in the casino or at the Longchamp racecourse - were pleasures only, pleasures he permitted himself, because he could so easily afford them, part of the cycle of conspicuous consumption that had more to do with class, heredity, geography, and the manners of the age. It was a kind of behavior which, though entirely selfish, was in fact anti-individualistic, conformist. What set the Baron apart from other famed gluttons or spendthrifts of the Parisian *belle epoque*, the point at which his own personality held sway, was in two fierce and fiercely individual passions: for grand opera and for gorgeous boys.

When possible, being a man who liked to experiment with sensations, he would endeavor to combine, or as he liked to say *synthesize*, these two passions; and few things gave him greater pleasure than to have the favored boy of the moment installed in his box during a performance of, say, "Tristan," immaculately clad to the eyes of the auditorium below, naked from the waist down, lolling cock ready to receive the Baron's attentions. Many times he had sat entranced through some favorite aria or duet while a beautiful youth knelt between his legs, mouth plugged onto his ecstatic erection.

The Baron was an honoured friend of the opera house, having devoted so much of his great fortune to maintaining its artistic excellence, and the gratitude of its directors was frequently expressed in the form of the handsome opera-house stewards, who were instructed to enter the Baron's box with complimentary bottles of champagne or trays of cakes and remain long enough to provide any other oral gratification he demanded.

He had brought Laurent here in the early days of their liaison. Though they had met at a supper at the Comtesse M's house in Neuilly, and the Baron had bedded him first in one of the Comtesse's many bedrooms (and later that night skewered him repeatedly in his own house on the Ile Saint-Louis), still his passion for the boy was not really fully underway until the evening when the boy gave him a masterful blowjob in his box during Brunnhilde's immolation in "Gotterdammerung."

Now, several months later, Laurent would have been glad of

some sexual commerce. It would have mitigated his boredom with the opera and reassured him of his continued attraction. He was even moved, as the first act progressed, to rub his crotch in frank indication of his readiness. But the Baron sat quite still, seemingly oblivious to his companion, absorbed in what was happening on the stage, moving only to raise the opera glasses to his face.

At the first act curtain, the Baron laid down the glasses, drew deeply on his Romeo y Julieta cigar, and tugged on a tasseled bell-pull. At once a steward entered, a handsome dark-skinned boy, faintly Iberian in appearance, who had serviced the Baron on many a previous occasion. This time, however, the Baron showed no interest in him save as a functionary. He took out a pen, scrawled a few words on his programme, folded it, inscribed the name of the producer, and handed it to the steward. Then he turned to Laurent with an air of surprise, as if astonished to find such a person sharing his box. "What do you think?"

"Very fine," said Laurent, caught watching the well-formed ass of the steward as he retreated. "Oh, very fine indeed."

The Baron burst out laughing. "Ah, yes," the Baron said, glancing behind him. The steward had vanished. "Well, seriously, I think it is a terrible production. It should have had another four weeks of rehearsal." He drew out a bottle of cologne, poured a measured drop onto his handkerchief, and dabbed his forehead.

Laurent, feeling small, said, "Was that the message you sent just now?"

The Baron glanced at him with his torpid, reptilian eyes. "A word to my friend, the producer. Relating to certain possible changes of cast he may make in the near future." He sat back, content, and brought together his white-gloved fingertips in an attitude of prayer; an obscenely large sapphire ring glinted on the little finger of his left hand. He was evidently not inclined to pursue this conversation with his lover.

Laurent began to panic. "Perhaps we could leave early. We could have so much more fun at home."

The Baron turned to him, eyebrows ironically raised.

Laurent continued hastily: "If, as you say, of course, you don't care for the production..."

"The production may improve," said the Baron blithely. "Besides which, I largely paid for the production, and I intend to have my money's worth this evening."

There followed a long silence during which Laurent felt awkward and unnecessary, and the Baron leaned over the edge of his box and glanced at the inhabitants of the other boxes who seemed as if arranged in tiers of celebrity and privilege. To many he gave a little wave of his gloved hand; at others he nodded; at others merely smiled. The Baron knew everybody and was related in some way to half the crowd. The excesses of his private life had not proved sufficient to alienate him from Parisian society, and besides, almost all were somehow in his debt.

There was a discreet rap at the door. The steward entered and announced, "Monsieur Charles Desporges." A youth, no more than eighteen, entered the box and greeted the Baron. He made a great play of humility and confusion in the presence of the great man, clearly not intended to conceal the real amused confidence of one who had traded for some time on his sexual attractiveness. The Baron had noticed him as a chorus member towards the end of the first act of "Tosca." There had been something wonderfully perverse in this lubricous youth's impersonation of a young Roman acolyte engaged in holy office. He had stood out from his colleagues by his sheer inability to look as if he might ever have a religious vocation, it had been as unconvincing as his feint of deference and honor on being presented to the Baron. He was one of the myriad small details of the production that the Baron would have wished to change.

He stood now beside the Baron's seat, his legs a little too wide apart. Clearly he had changed hurriedly from his stage costume, and had contrived to give the impression of having imperfectly dressed, as if the clothes he had thrown on in such haste might just as easily fall away from him. He ignored Laurent, to whom his attention had in any case not been drawn.

The Baron drew on his cigar and gazed at the boy, up and down. Charles looked back with his dissimulating insolence. "So, you mean to make a career in the theatre?"

"I have no fixed plans, Monsieur le Baron."

"But you have ambition? You want to go far?"

"As far as I am allowed, Monsieur le Baron. I am not yet sure where my talents lie."

The Baron laughed at this, delighted, his eyes gazing at the boy's abundant crotch.

The boy dropped a hand to his crotch and asked: "What are your estimates for my future?"

"I may be interested," said the Baron. "Indeed, I may be interested in making some use of your talents myself."

The boy rubbed his crotch gently. "In what capacity would that be?"

"I may have an opening that you are well qualified to fill," said the Baron, choosing his words, his *double-entendre* with care, anxious to see if the boy would respond further.

Charles' mind was as filthily disposed as the Baron had hoped. "I'm sure you have, Monsieur le Baron," he said, "and I'm sure I would endeavor to give satisfaction in that area."

The Baron picked up the ivory-handled cane that lay at his side, inserted it between the boy's knees, lifted it upwards; Charles parted his legs. The Baron brought the tip of his cane to the boy's crotch; Charles was now obviously excited. "I'm not convinced," said the Baron, "that your talents lie strictly in your voice."

Charles made no attempt to withdraw the bulge of his trousers from the exploring tip of the Baron's cane. "Perhaps not in my voice," he said, "but surely in my throat."

"You will kindly stay here for the remainder of the performance – "

"Unfortunately, Monsieur le Baron, I am required in both the following acts."

The Baron snapped his fingers for Laurent's programme. Laurent, furious but powerless, did as bidden, the Baron scrawled a few words, then rang for the steward with instructions to take the message to his friend the producer. In fact, his earlier message had already made quite clear that he intended to keep Charles for the rest of the evening; this was no more than a demonstration of his power for Charles' benefit and also for the mortification of Laurent. "Your problem is solved," he said, "you may remain here." He lifted his cane, inserted it under Charles' collar, and drew him round, behind the seats, to a corner of the box where a curtain hid him from the audience's view. "The second act is about to begin. It would perhaps be a distraction to the worthy people who have actually paid for their seats, if your presence here were to be known." He drew the point of his cane down over the front of Charles' shirt, paused at the buckle of his belt. "I, on the other hand, am only too happy to be distracted."

"Henri!" hissed Laurent, outraged, from his seat.

The Baron turned his heavy lidded gaze onto his lover. "My dear Laurent, you will of course be free to participate if you so choose at a later moment. If you do not wish to do so, I suggest you concentrate on the performance. This is the best part, as the Chief of Police is preparing to exact a terrible price from the unwilling Tosca." He turned his attention back to the young singer, who appeared to be willing to pay the terrible price exacted of him. The tip of the cane nudged his belt. "I do not think this costume will be necessary for the rest of your performance."

The boy, grinning, unfastened his belt, unbuttoned his fly, and dropped his trousers. The Baron traced the tip of his cane over his underwear. "Take off your shoes, then your trousers," he said.

Charles obeyed, then presented himself to the Baron's devouring gaze. The Baron drew his cane up the inner side of the boy's leg, his thigh, probed the evident erection within his breeches.

Charles looked down at the cane that was exploring his crotch. He chuckled. "I'm sure Monsieur le Baron is aware how much I will enjoy this evening's performance."

The Baron inhaled deeply. "You will not require that garment as part of your uniform."

Charles slipped his hands inside his breeches and pushed them down, in one swift movement, to his ankles. His cock sprang up. The Baron's cane traced its length. "This seems quite adequate for my purposes," he said. He swallowed hard. It was a magnificent cock. "More than adequate, my boy. Do you think you can maintain this standard?"

"I will endeavor to offer satisfaction," said Charles, stepping forward so that his cock was within range of the Baron's face. "But you yourself are the only one who can guarantee that."

"I have teased you quite long enough with the tip of my cane," said the Baron, blinking at the gorgeous apparition before his eyes. "Come closer."

Charles stepped forward, and the head of his cock brushed against the Baron's lips. It was suddenly impossible to keep up the lewd banter of the last few moments; the Baron, breathing deeply, ran his tongue once over his dry lips, then pressed his face into the boy's crotch, drinking in its full gamey scent. He groaned as his mouth found Charles' cock, insolently hard, throbbing and smooth.

Over the Baron's head Charles caught Laurent's eye and gave him an outrageous wink. Laurent glared back poisonously.

The Baron pulled his face away and examined the singer, who looked calmly down at him with that impudent pretense of innocence: a wily street-boy, a thing of the gutter, but with a few God-given talents of which his voice was not perhaps the least significant, and the intelligence to play them for all they were worth. A youth of strangely corrupt beauty, with flawless skin, scrubbed, groomed, and with enough sleepy impudence in his eyes, enough hastily-flattened unruliness in his hair, to suggest a wanton boy-whore dragged warm from bed and into church. The upper part of his body chastely clad In white shirt and dull burgundy waistcoat, the lower half gapingly nude. His hands respectfully clasped behind his back, his engorged prick, pre-cum glistening on its slit, rudely pointed into the Baron's face. The Baron took the boy's cock in his gloved hand and began to stroke it, pulling back the foreskin, marvelling at its elasticity. His habitual languid sophistication had vanished; a harsh rasp of lust underlay his every breath. He felt at that moment that he had never seen any sight so beautiful as this boy's cock, a judgment with which the boy might easily have concurred in so far as he had never seen any sight so beautiful as his own cock clasped in that white-gloved hand with the huge sapphire glinting on its little finger.

He suffered the Baron to inspect him fully, then thrust his cock up to the older man's mouth. The Baron gorged on it, took its full tensile length in his mouth, then drew back to tease and nibble the head. Charles worked his hips to meet the Baron's eager mouth, and the two gloved hands closed on the cheeks of his ass: it was as if he wanted to possess the boy through every sense available - through the touch of that firm young flesh, through the sight of that pulsing cock, through the scent of that tangy crotch, through the taste of that moist cockhead, even through the sound of his own mouth sucking away greedily. Meanwhile, Charles raised an ironic eyebrow and stared over at Laurent, who, furious and offended as he was, could not help but be aroused by what was happening a few feet away, and was working away with one hand inside his trousers.

It was perhaps fortunate that the Baron already knew the opera so well, otherwise he would certainly have lost the convoluted thread of the action unfolding on the stage. As it was, the action in his own box was of consuming interest.

The Baron had Charles turn around and present his ass for the Baron's approval. With a moan of longing the Baron held the boy's cheeks apart, ground his face between them, drove his tongue into the crack. The boy gave what may even have been a spontaneous sigh of pleasure, which was, for the Baron, invitation enough: he tore furiously at the fly of his trousers and at the undergarments therein, freed his own aching prick, and pressed Charles down over the brocade chair. He shot out an impatient hand behind him: "Laurent!"

The glowering Laurent fished a small bottle of perfumed lotion from the Baron's vast fur coat where it hung, and placed it in the Baron's hand. Laurent stepped away, but abruptly turned and stood near, discreetly observing the sight. The Baron drew the top of the bottle, smeared a generous quantity of the fragrant lubricating fluid over his cock and in the boy's crevice, then, incapable of holding back any longer, dropped the unstoppered bottle to the floor, where the ointment seeped into the carpet. He sighed as his cock slid into the ass without stopping.

"Hmmmm," Charles moaned.

The fucking was fast and furious. The obscenities he muttered into the boy's ear as he felt the cream rise within him, the clenched groan of his violent climax as he thrust his prick one last time up the boy's sweet ass and held it there, were drowned out by the vengeful shrieks of the heroine on the stage, as she drove the dagger into the brutal chief of the Roman police. The sex so excited Laurent that he took out his prick and stroked it to orgasm even before the Baron had completed the act. By the time the Baron recovered and was helping Charles dress, Laurent was back in his seat watching the opera.

After the opera they went for supper at one of the Baron's favorite restaurants on the Boulevard des Capucines, together with the producer, the conductor, the soprano, and her Bulgarian-born husband. Laurent sat at the Baron's side, while Charles, a mere chorus member, was placed at the end of the table and virtually ignored.

But when supper ended at two in the morning, Charles was to the Baron's mansion on the Ile Saint-Louis, and Laurent was dispatched to his small *garconniere* where he had not slept for some weeks.

There was no question of Charles' returning to the theatre the following night: his brief musical career was over almost before it had begun. After breakfast the next day, taken in bed, the Baron, having worked the boy to yet another fresh erection, after a total of three during the previous night, took a spoonful of honey and proceeded to drip it onto Charles' cock. When it was completely coated, the Baron applied himself to sucking it clean, then pressed his own aching prick into the boy's eager mouth. The Baron found the boy's talents were worthy of great rewards, and, being a generous man when it came to his pleasures, the Baron presented him with some token - jewelry, a costly trinket. But Charles refused, and continued to refuse as the weeks wore on: he did not seem to want a reward, nor did he seem interested in the Baron's fortune. And when the Baron offered him a large apartment on the fashionable Quai Voltaire, still he refused. He spent his nights in the Baron's bed, but on evenings when the Baron was away, he returned to the mysterious place he called "home."

In this he was different and wiser than all his predecessors, whose sexual compliance had always been conditional on the Baron's largesse. No, Charles gave every appearance of enjoying the sex as much as the Baron himself, enjoying it for its own sake, and this was his masterstroke. The Baron was beside himself with joy at his find, at the boy's easy carnality, at his readiness for sex. Charles did not have to be begged, bullied, bribed or blackmailed into sex, like the venal creatures who had gone before. And Charles would do anything that was asked of him, he had no limits and no prejudices. And the Baron's obsession with the boy was fuelled by suspicion, by jealousy: for if Charles enjoyed sex so much with him, surely he must be enjoying it elsewhere, at the place where he went so mysteriously when not with him? The idea tormented him and, curiously, excited him.

The Baron was keen to show Charles off to friends of his who shared his tastes. There were select dinners in the house at Ile Saint Louis, and he would have Charles sit on his right, naked from the waist down, and the Baron would delightedly register the surprise, the gulping lust on the face of each guest as he first caught sight of the boy's great curving cock. "And now dessert," the Baron would announce, smearing Charles' crotch with creme de chantilly. The Baron would permit each of his favored guests to approach and kneel before the boy, then suck his cock clean. "A taste, only a taste," the Baron insisted, wanting to tantalize his guests with this treasure, no more, and it was always the Baron who drew out Charles' own cream, later in their private chambers. And all this Charles accepted, willingly, loyally, good-humoredly, honored to give satisfaction to so many great members of society.

Charles stayed with the Baron for two years, and when they finally parted it was on the best of terms, and with the Baron's gratitude intact. Charles had been prevailed on at last to accept some of his patron's munificence, and he was a quite wealthy young man when he struck out on his own. Furthermore, the Baron helped launch him into society where he scored notable success, he was quick to learn, eager as ever to please, and amusing: furthermore, in his two years as the Baron's constant companion he had absorbed enough of the manners and arcane knowledge required to enter the most exclusive circles.

The Baron had many other partners in the years that followed, but none replaced Charles Desporges in his affections. And when the Baron died, quite unexpectedly, in a riding accident, he named Charles as his sole beneficiary. Charles was on a holiday in Switzerland when he heard the news: it caused him to weep with sincere grief, though he had not seen the

Baron for five years. He cut short his holiday and returned to Paris for the funeral.

And when after a long absence he visited the opera house that he had first entered as a chorus boy, he came as a patron and benefactor, taking the Baron's box. It was on that night, towards the end of the first act of "Tosca," that he noticed a comely lad in the chorus...

DOOGIE: CLASSICALLY BEAUTIFUL

Jarred Goodall

You know how you keep running into a boy time after time, a kid you actually don't know from Adam, and you wonder why you bother to notice him, until one day you realize you've developed a thing for him? Then you remember you've always seen him in a certain place at certain times, so you start arranging your life to be there when he is.

I should describe the kid I'm talking about, as I saw him then. Late teens. Chestnut-colored hair, slightly wavy. Hazel eyes. Summer-tanned skin of amazing purity. Classically beautiful features. Proud and, I suspected, a bit of a loner. Not given to smiling. A kid with disappointments in his life. And goals. I kept meeting him on a certain path I took through the neighborhood park on my way back from work.

A kid that striking must defend himself. Some people attempt to get intimate with him - and most of the time he won't want that, especially if it suggests "queer stuff." Other people (males) resent his good looks and want to fight him - and so he learns to be tough.

Inevitably one day he noticed me. As we were passing he spat - not in my direction but into the bushes on the other side of the path. His message was clear: "Quit staring at me. You're crowding me too close." He walked on, quickly.

I looked to where the spittle had gone, and there it was, hanging coherently on one big leaf, a kind of tilted, colorless ameba thing with pseudopodia slowly flowing downwards under gravity, its main mass decorated with multiple bubbles encapsulating some of the kid's spent breath.

Without giving it more thought, I went to the bush and gathered all I could of it onto the palm of my hand and brought it to my nose. Mostly the scent was of green - green leaf, green sap of nature - but also, not totally masked, was a hint of his human, boy/mouth scent itself.

I was so absorbed in all of this, and the feel of my cock

stiffening inside my trousers, that it was a moment before I realized the kid had stopped only fifteen feet away and was staring at me over his shoulder. He shot me a cold, if not contemptuous, look and stalked off down the path.

That encounter did wonders for my masturbatory pleasure a little later. Vivid in my mind was the sight of the boy, his alluring scowl, traces of his personal scent in what he had flung into the bushes and I'd retrieved. We had at long last made contact with each other, in a way. My solitary sex life was definitely looking up.

I made it a point to be on that path the next afternoon at the same time. And there he was, school bag on his back, walking briskly as though he had no time for the sunny weather, the sweet scent of spring, the song of the birds about us building their nests. He saw me, gave me the same look of withering contempt - and once again spat in the bushes.

Why are teenage boys always spitting? Is it aggression? Is it a way of marking territory, like dogs, but with a different substance? Whatever, I again found his spittle, robbed the leaves of it. This time I was very much aware that he had stopped and was watching me in his proudly scornful way.

My trouble has always been that I'm usually too shy, too frightened, to take up a sexual challenge. There's that old story about the boy who claimed the secret of his numerous conquests was that he just went up to whomever turned him on and said, "Let's fuck." Didn't he get his face slapped a lot? "Yeah," he explained, "but I get in a lot of fucking, too." I determined now to be less of a nerd.

"That's my spit you're goobering yourself with, isn't it?" he said.

I smiled. "Why, you want it back?"

He wasn't amused. "I seen you hanging around here, looking at me funny. I always figured there was something pervy about you."

I shrugged. "Everybody's got his own tastes."

"Not everybody is interested in my spit."

I'd now come to just outside that invisible boundary of his defensible space. The boy's face, seen close up, was even more sexy than I'd anticipated. "Not everybody is you," I said.

"Meaning?"

"What do you think? - you're a nice looking kid."

He accepted this as his due. "What's that got to do with my spit?"

"Looks like it's all a guy's going to get."

The kid had to think that over for a minute. Then his eyes narrowed. "It turns you on?"

I shrugged - meaning, what do you think?

"I've always wanted to spit on a creep," he said.

Oh, those tensions and frustrations in a teenage boy, those resentments - hatreds, even - of adults and the adult world! They were working for me, now. All I had to do was stroke them the right way.

"Go ahead," I said. If I couldn't get a kiss from the kid's lips, I might at least get a sample - direct - of what was behind them. I wasn't proud.

"All right, mister, you asked for it. I hope you're going to enjoy this, 'cause I'm sure going to!"

Breathless, testosterone of the most perverse sort humming in my ears, I watched him suck the saliva forward in his mouth until he had it charged just behind his pursed lips. And then he spat!

Well, let me tell you, there are jerk-offs and jerk-offs, and my jerk-off a few minutes later raised me to within sight of nirvana. Tearing off my tie, flinging away my business suit, I lubed up my cock with my own inferior saliva, grasped it firmly in my right hand, and in my reeling mind brought back into focus the kid's face, the explosion of his spittle, its scent and the scent of his breath.

The sensual charge that encounter had built up in my balls could not be relieved by one ejaculation, nor a second, nor a third. Even then there remained a plangent longing for another meeting with The Spitting Boy, as I'd come to call him, to inhale again his fresh schoolday scents.

Our paths didn't cross for a week, although every afternoon I haunted that park around the time the high schools let out. Then one morning, on the crowded bus I was taking to work, I spied a pair of lanky adolescent legs stretched out over the one unoccupied seat. The legs withdrew as I maneuvered myself into position to sit down - and then I saw that the legs were attached to The Spitting Boy.

"We better not do a repeat here," I said to him pleasantly.

He shot me a look of pure adolescent scorn and, resting an elbow on the window sill, turned his attention outside, tapping his front teeth impatiently with a fingernail.

"Seems we both got something out of the other day," I continued.

"How you figure that?"

"I got my thrill - and you got rid of some of your..."

"Chrissake," he growled, interrupting me, "there's people here."

"...anger. Don't worry, I'm not about to embarrass you socially. Or me."

We rode on in silence for a while, the kid staring out the window, me trying to work out my next gambit. Then I had it. "You know what one very wise and experienced man once said?"

A faint shake of his head.

I leaned towards him so I was almost whispering into his ear. "Every teenage boy needs a blow-job right now."

"That's bullshit!" he exploded. "Besides, this is my stop." He got up and darted out the door of the bus almost before it opened.

Well, I'd planted a seed in his mind, or maybe a germ in his neuro-genital gestalt. How it would germinate I didn't dare guess.

The next time I saw The Spitting Kid he was clearly in trouble. I was cruising through a sleazy part of town in my sporty Triumph when I spotted him outside our one and only adult bookstore being hassled by an aggressive bunch of wrong-side-of-the-trackers. There was a scuffle. He tried to move away. They came after him, yelling the kind of insults minorities and the underprivileged reserve for the advantaged. He started to run - in my direction. When he came opposite me, I yelled, "Jump in!" And he did, vaulting over the tiny door and crashing down on the other bucket seat. Blood was streaming out of his nose.

"There's Kleenex in the glove compartment," I told him.

He extracted one and cleaned up as best he could.
"Thanks."
"It's all a fellow can do," I said.
Now he recognized me. "Oh, shit!" he said. "You been following me again?"
I shook my head. "Just chance. And lucky for you, it looks like. What were you doing outside our one and only porn emporium?"
"None of your business. Where we going?"
"You want to show up at home looking like that?"
He scowled at his bloody knuckles. "I suppose not."
"Besides, I have better erotica at my house than you'd have found in that store."
"Sure, guy-guy stuff."
"Not only."
Once home, I led him to the shower and started to do some touch-up work on his blood-smeared shirt and Levi's. A little later he emerged in my bathrobe, hair tousled, belt tightly drawn up around his middle.
"Look," I said, "we got off to a bad start out there in the park. I'm not going to rape you or anything. Sit down." I told him my name and put out my hand.
"Doogie Douglas," he said, lowering himself down onto my couch.
Doogie, huh? Well, that was better than The Spitting Boy. I clicked the video remote controller and suddenly on the TV screen naked male and female bodies were writhing in simulated porno ecstasy. Doogie's jaw dropped, eyes bugged, color mounted in his face.
"Aw shit," he said, "look at that!"
I decided to leave him alone with my home entertainment for a while and went out into the kitchen to make us some snacks. I was pretty sure what he would be doing pretty soon - and I was right, if a little late. He hastily whipped my bathrobe shut as I came in with Cokes and scones and then gave a grin that was both embarrassed and a smirk. "You show that sort of stuff in your house, you oughta provide Kleenexes or something."
"An accident?" I asked.
"Naw, it was no accident - it sure wasn't no accident - but I

pretty well soaked your dressing gown."

"That's okay!" I said enthusiastically.

He leveled me with his sober gray eyes. "Is there nothing you don't like that comes out of a kid's body?"

"Just about."

"Flob, jizz. How about pee?" His former contempt was beginning to be cut with a bit of humanity, and a trace of amusement.

"Are you serious? Is that a proposition?"

He thought for a moment, chewing his mouth. "How much is it worth?"

"A buck?"

"Five bucks."

"Two. You have to get rid of it somewhere."

More thinking, more mouth-chewing. Then, "Fuck, why not? You want to lie down in the tub or something?"

Good Lord, how, I wondered, could a man be so lucky? I led him upstairs to my bathroom, stripped in a hurry and folded my rather long frame down into the bathtub while the boy pretended to avoid looking at me.

"Okay," I said, "I'm ready."

But Doogie was having some last minute doubts. "Jeez, Mister, I don't know as I ought to do this."

"Why?" I yelped. "You can't stop now!"

"It's just that... guys don't piss on guys..."

"They do, yes, they do!"

"You sure you really want me to?"

"Completely sure. A hundred and one percent sure!"

He set that worried mouth of his and moved in to the tub, bending slightly so that his knees were resting on the rim, and pulled the bathrobe slightly open.

And now for the first time I saw his cock - long, circumcised, not completely softened after its recent spill - and smelled it, too. The tip, the crown, the glans, was a lovely lilac, still a bit smeared. The loose skin drooped a ways behind and beneath it. Doogie leveled the instrument with his right hand and pointed it at my chest and... let go.

Oh, that lovely piss! If his spit had been nice, it was only a come-on to this, a low foothill to the Real Thing. The pee sprayed out of his urethra and splattered over me, first on my chest, then my stomach, then my groin. I scooped some of it up and poured it over my face. What a strong, raunchy odor it had, what a salty, bitter taste! I wrapped my fingers around my wet cock where pre-cum (mine) mixed with piss (his) and began to jerk. "Oh, God!" I moaned, "Doogie, Doogie, Doogie!"

And came, wildly, the sperm actually burning as all those little zygotes clawed their way up my urethra, desperate for release.

As the last globs of cum made it up onto my prick-head, the last spurts of Doogie's piss washed them away. A great sense of fulfillment and contentment washed through my body. I slumped. "That was incredible," I mumbled. "And you actually flush that stuff down the toilet! You ought to bottle and sell it!"

"Come on, Mister, don't be gross!"

"I'd buy it."

"I suppose you would. I gotta get home." - closing the bathrobe and drawing tight the belt. "And you are going to give me the two bucks?"

We made an arrangement, came to an agreement. Afternoons, after school, if he felt like it, he would stop by at my house and we would have a repeat of him jerking off to a porno video (I was never allowed to do it for him) and then relieving himself upon me in my tub. I came to rely upon it, only he came only intermittently. At work I would be troubled by a persistent hard-on which also accompanied me on the bus ride home. By the time I reached the front door my cock would have been leaking pre-cum so long that my undershorts would be as slimy inside as a masturbating hand. I would wait, pacing back and forth in my living room. Four o'clock would come and go. Four-o-five. Four-ten. And then, if I was lucky, I would see him sauntering up to my porch, books clutched under one forearm, wrist bent under.

And so it went for the next couple of weeks. Every afternoon I'd be waiting, heart in my mouth, with a monstrous erection pouring slime into my Jockey shorts. About every third day he would appear. I would hand over the payment, which soon increased to five bucks, he would settle down in front of my TV, beat off to a favorite video, and then we would go upstairs and he would deliver.

Some poor souls are addicted to heroine, others to cocaine, or tobacco or alcohol. And I? In the course of only a couple of weeks, I'd become just as addicted to Doogie's pee.

One afternoon, with his mission accomplished, he paused as he was about to go out the front door and asked, "You got a hundred bucks?"

Fear stabbed me in the gut. This was blackmail. Doogie was going to threaten me with exposure.

He saw my distress and scowled. "Fuck, man, this is no shake-down. What kind of a guy do you think I am?"

"I don't know," I said. "You come at me with a demand for a hundred dollars..."

"I didn't demand it. I asked if you had it."

"There's a difference?"

"I think a whole lot."

"So, for what?"

"Oh, fuck, forget it."

"That's going to be pretty hard to do."

His mouth twisted as he thought. "Okay, I'll lay it out. You been paying me five bucks for me to piss on you, right?"

"I have."

"On our basketball team there's twenty guys. Twenty times five is a hundred."

"So?"

"We have practice tonight. And afterwards we gotta shower, right? Coach trusts us and goes home to his family. He doesn't really like night sessions."

"And?"

"You're invited. I talked to the guys."

My heart did flip-flops in my breast. "About... piss?" I gasped, incredulous.

"Yeah. They're cool."

This was totally unexpected - and totally exciting! Would twenty teenage boys peeing on me be twenty times as good as the one Doogie doing it alone?

"Any trolls?" I asked.

"Come on, mister, get real. Nerds don't make it on our team."

I know nothing about basketball, less about football, and as for baseball, I think it's the dullest pastime invented by mankind, after dangle-fishing for pleasure on the banks of a muddy river. Yet that night, viewing it as ballet, a kind of semi-strip-show, the practice session was a nice appetizer: twenty boys running and dodging about on the court, sometimes falling, their shorts and numbered undershirts clinging to the slick sweat which coated their bodies and made arms and calf-muscles glisten in the overhead lights. And then there was their heady odor, as a tangle of kids rushed by close to the railing where I sat. My cock was stiff long before the practice was over and the coach, admonishing his charges to "pick up and lock up" after them, bade me good night - I passed off as a visiting uncle of one of the boys.

Doogie extracted from me the agreed-upon hundred dollars and the whole team ushered me politely into the shower room.

"Um, get comfortable," Doogie said. I stripped, folded my clothes carefully and left them on one of the wooden benches. I assumed they would be doing the same but depositing their sport attire in the lockers which lined the other side of the shower room, and I was looking forward to seeing their strong, sinewy bodies and their adolescent cocks. But it seemed they intended to discharge their obligation to me before cleaning up. And so there I stood, the team members still in their sweaty shorts and tops stinking up the shower room, me the only one naked, with my expectant pole pointing skywards. They urged me over against the tiled wall, under a convenient shower-head, and lined up casually, laughing at themselves and at me.

The first kid was a big, handsome blond. "Doogie says you got to know each other collecting his flob. That right?"

What was I supposed to say? It was true enough, but that wasn't the reason I'd come to the basketball practice tonight. Sure, a handsome boy's sweat, tears and saliva are all turn-ons, but...

"Well, yes, but..."

"Right, here's for warm-ups."

I must say he showed no emotion - anger, disgust or pity. If you're indifferent to spit yourself, I suppose you can work up a few feelings about a commercially transacted spit-and piss-down. He was simply keeping up his end of the bargain and made little drama of what he did. He came to a stop before me, his face about a foot from mine. His lips pressed briefly together and then burst open. I felt his breath, hot and damp, scented with all the mouth aromas of a teenage boy, but it was transient, brushing my face and then gone in a fraction of a second. The saliva driven by it splattered on me in heavy, slimy, bubbly clots. Before I could blink some of it out of my eyes, his place was taken by a shorter, younger looking kid with a spray of freckles across a small snubbed nose. He spat once, hard, a very big mouthful, said, "Good riddance. I was about choking on the stuff!", then spat again, grinned and gave me a mock salute before his replacement elbowed him out of the way.

Player followed player, sweaty, smelly boy followed smelly, sweaty boy. I became a spittle sponge, torn clots of spit and air trapped in bubbles, viscid, mucoid, personal, intimate, clots clinging to my eyelashes and having to be blinked away, then watching the boys' proud, still-sweaty faces. I found myself becoming surprisingly, enormously aroused, stretched emotionally to the breaking point.

After the first two, the individual players of that basketball team tended to merge into a maze of spittle-blurred vision. Twenty mouthfuls is an awful lot of spit. Within minutes I was completely soaked: not just my face, but my chest and my arms and even my hair. By the time the whole team had passed, and spat, I was as sopping as if I'd fallen in a river.

And there was the smell, faint at first but growing with time. Some of the spittle had an acrid and musty odor, for not every boy on the team was overly careful about keeping his mouth clean. Some had a sweet, sometimes spermy scent, like hay, or spring flowers, touching and innocent.

So what about my cock? All this time I hadn't touched it, saving my cum for the promised piss-down. I'd gritted my teeth and held out until the last kid had splattered onto my face his last mouthful of saliva. I found I could hold out no longer. I lubricated my hands with what was flowing freely down my chest, wrapped my fingers around my dripping cock and balls, and in just two ecstatic slides orgasm grabbed me, shook me like a shark in feeding frenzy and extracted my sperm in long squirts which shot across the room and decorated the tiled floor in multiple milky globs. And as I came I howled.

"Fuck, man, shut that off!" said one of the kids. "You want to bring in the night watchman?"

I hardly heard him. I slumped down on my butt and closed my eyes. The boys on the team left me alone, now. They stripped, showered, taking their own sweet time and talking about basketball and cars and girls and an up-coming pop concert. Steam billowed from multiple shower-heads.

I just lay there in post-orgasmic wipe-out, leaning against the shower wall, sprawled out over the spit-slippery tile floor, inwardly moaning. I'd fucked up. I'd really fucked up. A hundred dollars wasted. The kids were just giving me a little foretaste tease of the Main Thing and I'd blown it like a thirteen-year-old that couldn't keep his hands off his cock once it got hard.

Then, suddenly, I looked up and saw a tall dark-haired boy standing over me, naked, rosy and sweet-smelling - Number 7, as I remembered, the team captain or something.

"You don't really want to go home all goobered up, do you?" he asked.

"No," I said, "I guess not." They were going to call it a day, or a night, taking my money which they knew I'd never dare demand back. I expected someone to turn on the shower above me. But nothing happened and then I became aware of an unnatural stillness in the shower room. I looked up again. Number 7, backed by a ring of other naked boys, had moved in close. He had his down-hung cock in hand and was pointing it at me, aiming it right at my eyes.

And then, to my amazement, and, of course, my delight, he let go. A hard, hot, wet gush of piss sprayed out of its tip and splattered into my face. I gasped, choked, gurgled, for some of it had penetrated my lips and was filling my mouth. How did the kid know? How did the boys know that at my advance age of thirty-five I would recover so fast, which I soon found myself doing? Kids, when it comes to sex, aren't as dumb as some people (especially psychiatrists) think they are.

The hot pee came and came, foaming in my hair, playing on my ears, spilling into my mouth. I raised my face to meet the ragged yellow jet, to allow Number 7 to train it on first one closed eye, then the other, then my nose, then my lips.

Yes!

This was it! This was the ultimate. I found myself in total, wicked, perverted bliss, thrilling to another unexpected turn of the screw that wouldn't result in a screw. The boys' spit-down had been sweet, subtly scented, gentle and lubricious. There was nothing gentle about the hard jet of Number 7's hot, stinking pee!

I grabbed my cock, now in termination stiff. The kids laughed.

"Remember the guy back in the dunes that day?" one of them said.

"Another piss-freak."

"Only he didn't like it."

"Or so he said. That cock he'd been pullin' on didn't seem to go down any."

Number 7's jet sputtered out to a trickle. He shook the last drops off into my hair and backed away. Now the whole semi-circle behind him closed in, surrounding me - one quarter of the team, all handling their cocks, pointing them down at me, aiming....

First one penis started up, then another, then two more. After a second or two, all were spurting out yellow boy-piss, hitting me on all sides, up and down. When I took a breath, the stink was awesome - sometimes rancid, sometimes surprisingly sweet, or scented with coffee, over-all sharp and pungent. Again, I raised my face into it, parted my lips, let one strong stream splatter on my teeth.

When that circle was pissed out, another formed in its place, and then another. Soon all traces of the boys' saliva were gone; my face, my body, my cock were awash only in bright, bitter-tasting urine.

I jerked furiously off! There was no lubrication now. Urine is a poor lubricant. And yet my hand moved and moved and I jerked and gasped and gargled and bubbled and felt myself getting close, careening towards a climax just as intense as the first.

But someone was talking to me. Yes, it was Doogie, my old friend Doogie. "Let go of it, mister," he ordered. "We'll take care of that."

Good heavens, what were they going to do? Was one of them actually going to grab it - me covered with the urine of all his team mates? I couldn't imagine such a thing happening, but tonight had been full of surprises.

I obeyed and opened my hand. My cock snapped back tight against my belly.

Doogie stood in the center of the fourth and last circle of pissers. Now they let go, all of them. They turned their jets not on my face, not on my chest, but, to my amazement, upon the front of my cock! It felt like a fire hose - no five fire hoses - trained on my glans and foreskin. By-spray tickled my balls. It was the most devastating penile friction I'd ever endured!

When the cum came it was like a hot wire being pulled through my piss tube. White bullets of sperm shot out into the yellow deluge. I started to howl again, but the boys were prepared for that: three of the jets raised to my mouth and my nose, jets I didn't seem to be able to avoid, for however I turned my head, one or another seemed to be trained right on target. I gurgled, snuffled, shuddered, hammered that shower room floor with my fists and heels. And then I simply re-collapsed and let the weakening jets wash away the last pulses of sperm.

Well, if there's one thing teenage boys are good about it's taking care of a drunken buddy who has messed himself up and needs a shower. After that second cataclysmic orgasm, I was too dizzy even to open my eyes. I felt myself being lifted - which was pretty brave because it meant someone had to get his hands in all that pee - and stood under a warm shower, gentle and pure and sweet.

Afterwards I was dried off with a bath towel, then helped into my clothes. One of the boys actually knelt at my feet and put on my shoes and tied the laces.

Dressed at last, the team cleared out, leaving only me and, I soon realized, Doogie.

"Come on, get up," he said. "I'm taking you home. My car's just outside."

I remember little of the drive back to my house, except that the radio was blaring away with the kind of music teenagers like and the car smelled old.

"Thanks," I told him when we reached home. "You know, you really are a good kid."

"Don't let anyone hear you say that," he grinned. "I got my reputation to think about."

Sex for all of us comes in waves. The biggest wave of all time had broken over me that night in the high school shower room and for a good week afterwards I lay calmly in its swash.

Then one evening as I was preparing to make supper for myself the doorbell rang. Standing on the porch was Number 7, long and lanky and looking extremely attractive in his team jacket and 501s.

"Um, is it okay if I come in?" he asked.

"Oh sure, sorry. I was just surprised to see you," I said.

"Not pissed off, I hope." He walked into the living room with the typical lope of a lanky adolescent athlete. I sat down on the couch. He remained on his feet. "That was a real party we had, wasn't it?" he said, giving me a big grin.

"You could say that."

"What I want to ask you is... You know what it's like when you're in high school - you're broke and you got a hard-on all the time."

"It was a while ago," I said, "but I remember."

He pulled up a foot stool in front of me and hunkered down on it and locked his fingers and cracked his knuckles, staring into my eyes. "After that... session... we got, some of us, talking, and we figured maybe you'd give a guy some worthwhile pocket money for a solo gig. We figured in your own home, where you didn't have to worry about time or being seen, well, it should be worth more than five bucks."

"Whoa, wait a minute, slow down! You guys have been talking about - doing more?"

He nodded.

"So you're not the only member of our high school basketball team...?"

"Hell no, long as you're not too stingy with the bread. We come to an arrangement, I'll put the word out and I'll guarantee you there'll be some kid here on your porch just about every afternoon. And, well, you'd be able to do some real stuff, too."

I raised my eyebrows. "What do you mean by that?"

Number 7 looked a little sheepish. "Suppose I let you play with it for a while, and then you gave me a real good B-J - suppose I did that, we did that, do you think it would be worth a tenner? I don't mean that's all I'd do. Like afterwards, I haven't taken a piss for hours. I guess I can pee as good as any kid in town, including Doogie, who you'll see one of these days again anyhow. Come on, mister, what do you say?"

THE RED-HAIRED PROFESSOR & ME

Greg Bowden

The summer I turned eighteen I talked my dad, who was an economics professor at the local college, into getting me a pass for the Men's Swim Season at the college gym. In those days the men (you had to be over eighteen) got to have the pool to themselves every afternoon Monday through Friday while the weekends were given over to families and little kids. I was a fairly serious swimmer in those days and my dad agreed that my kind of swimming would be much easier without the splashing and playing that went on all weekend.

All of that was true, of course, but the real reason I wanted to swim with the men was that I had heard that some of them swam in the nude. I knew, even then, that my fascination with naked men wasn't usual and my looking at the guys in the shower after gym class was much more serious than the casual checking out the other guys did. They were making quick comparisons and joking about it while I was memorizing.

My first day of the Men's Swim Season was more than I'd ever hoped for. For one thing there were all different kinds of men there, from my age to my dad's age and older and all but one or two of them were swimming without anything on. The other thing was I'd never been in the pool naked before and didn't know how wonderful it felt. I got a little embarrassed at first because the feel of being naked in the water made me go hard as soon as I got in. I was afraid someone might notice but I don't think anyone did and it pretty much went down after ten fast laps.

When I finished my program I sat up on the edge for a while, pretending to rest but really I just watched the naked men for as long as I thought I could get away with it. Then I hit the showers. The shower room was just that: a big room with about twenty showers sticking out of the walls. I took one next to a good-looking muscular guy, probably a graduate student. He was just soaping himself up and I guess he liked it because every time he put more lather on his cock it seemed to get a little bigger. He caught me looking at him and turned his back, facing into the corner. Some other men came in and I tried not to stare at any of them but it wasn't easy, especially since there were a couple of them who still had their foreskins, something I'd only heard about and I thought was fascinating.

I was just about to turn my shower off when the guy next to me, the one who'd caught me looking at him, let out a little bark and flexed his buns five or six times, making dimples in them. Something told me to wait and after a minute or two he turned around to rinse and I saw that his cock was kind of puffed up. It was only then that I realized he'd turned his back because he'd been jacking off. Right there, standing next to me! I had to shut the water off quick and get out of there but I didn't make it. My dick was stiff and sticking straight out in front of me before I could even get out of the shower room and grab a towel to hide it.

It took a few weeks but I finally got used to swimming and showering with a bunch of naked guys although I always got stiff when I first got in the pool and I still had to be careful about staring in the showers. Don't get me wrong, I did a lot of looking – but I did a lot of swimming, too.

One Monday, in mid-July, I stayed in the pool late and most everyone had gone by the time I went for my shower. Since there wasn't anybody else in there I just rinsed and went in to get dressed. I was sitting on the bench in front of my locker trying to remember the combination when two guys came out of the restroom, talking about some physics experiment one of them wanted to do. They stopped at the aisle where my locker was and finished their conversation. The older man, who I thought was probably one of the new teachers at the college, hadn't dressed yet but the other guy, who had to be one of his students, was all dressed in jeans and a white tee shirt. I remember thinking how very naked the man looked, standing there talking with someone who was fully dressed.

I tried not to stare at the naked man but it was difficult. He had reddish hair which was long and thick on his chest and then narrowed into a bright coppery line that ran down his belly and connected to another, thicker patch in his crotch. Every few seconds he would unconsciously run his fingers through his pubic hair and tug at it which made his cock flop around over his balls. And his cock... it was long and thick and, best of all, it still had its skin. Like I said, I tried not to stare but I know I did.

After a little bit the red-haired man patted the student on the arm, said his ideas were good and told him to come to his office the next afternoon so they could finalize the project. The student left and the red-haired professor walked straight down the aisle to where I was sitting.

"Having trouble with that locker?" he asked. He hit the door with his fist, right under the lock. "Now try it. Usually that's all these things need."

I reached out and ran the combination without thinking about it and the door popped open. He worked the combination on the door just above and to the left of mine but it wouldn't open so he banged on it and then tried again. This time it opened and he began rummaging through the stuff inside, looking for something. When he found what he wanted he turned and began writing on something taped inside the door. While he was busy I got to get a good look at his equipment which, with the way he was standing, was hanging about a foot in front of my face.

Pretty soon I realized the man had stopped writing. When I looked up he was looking right at me and had a big smile on his face. I got really embarrassed at being caught and I guess I must have blushed.

"Hey, don't worry about it," he said, smiling. "It's just another piece of anatomy. Go ahead, check it out all you like." He tugged at his wiry pubic hair the way he had when he'd been talking to the other guy and then he laughed. "It's the foreskin, isn't it? You don't see many of them around here although I don't know why. You missing yours?" He reached down and took away the towel I'd thrown over my lap. I hadn't realized it before but I had gotten a real stiffer looking at his equipment and I felt my face go all red and hot with embarrassment.

He put his hand on my shoulder. "Don't sweat it, kid. It happens to everyone sometimes and it's nothing to be ashamed of – especially when it's as beautiful as yours. But I see you are missing your skin. Too bad. Tell me, you ever really looked at one with the skin still on, seen how it works?"

I shook my head dumbly, still staring at his cock.

"Well, no time like the present to satisfy your curiosity. See? The skin is double and forms a little pocket for the head. If you pull it clear back, well, then it looks just like yours." He demonstrated, pulling the skin back until the dark colored head was out in the open. Then he let go and the skin slowly crept along the shaft until it swallowed up the head again. He stood for a long moment, letting me look at it. Then he said, "If you want to try it, go ahead. Really. I don't mind."

It was like I had no control over my hands. They just reached out, shaking a little, and very gently took hold of the man's cock. It was the first time in my life I'd ever had another man's cock in my hands and I couldn't get over how warm and alive it felt. I let it rest in my palm and then, with my other hand, I took hold of it, just behind the head, and moved the skin. It slid back easily, like maybe it wasn't connected to anything inside. When it was completely back I let it go but it just stayed there and didn't try to cover the head again. I was suddenly afraid that I'd somehow broken it.

I looked up and the man laughed. "It won't move by itself when you've got it in your hand. You have to slide it back with your fingers."

I didn't want to let go of it so I used my hand to slide the skin forward again, until it had slipped back over the head, hiding it. Then I slipped it back, to see how it worked. I guess he saw what I was doing because he pointed at my crotch.

"See there," he said, running his finger along the line between the dark and light parts of my cock. "That's where your foreskin was, before the doctor cut it off. See? I don't have a line or scar like you do." He moved my hand along his cock. "My skin is smooth all along the shaft."

"Does... I mean... When you get..." I was almost tongue-tied.

"You asking if the head comes out of the skin when I'm erect? Stays out?"

I nodded.

He laughed. "Well, you just keep sliding the skin back and forth that way and you're bound to find out. A man can't take too much of that before it makes him hard."

I dropped his cock like it had suddenly become red hot but he took my hand and gently put it back around his cock. "It's okay. Go ahead and find out. As I said before, it's something that happens to all of us. Nothing to be concerned about."

His cock began to grow in my hand as I worked the skin back and forth along the shaft and it didn't take long before it stretched out and got a lot thicker and felt like there was an iron bar growing inside it. I found that even when it was really hard I could still pull the skin back over the head but only just barely; left alone the skin slipped back and covered just the bottom part. I loved the feel of it, the way the skin slipped back and forth along his thick cock and I began pulling it as far back as I could and then back up, to cover the head.

I leaned closer, to see how it looked from in front. I don't know what came over me or what made me do it but suddenly I stuck out my tongue and licked the head as I pulled the skin away. Then, I don't know why, I just kissed the head and took it into my mouth.

The taste, the feel of that man's cock in my mouth made me weak it was so good. The man liked it too because he groaned and pushed it in a little further. I moved my tongue all around the head, tasting it and feeling the smoothness of it and then he pulled it out a little ways and then pushed it back in, letting me wedge my tongue between the head and the skin. He groaned again and his sweet, salty taste got stronger and stronger and I knew he was going to shoot off.

"Better let go," the man said. "It's time..."

I didn't care. I wanted him to come in my mouth, to see what he would taste like. I almost missed it, though, because the minute I felt his cock begin to swell and pulse mine shot off too, so hard I almost blacked out. That wonderful feeling just went on and on but so did the man, shooting hot, bittersweet cum into my mouth faster than I could swallow it so some of it ran down my chin.

When he finally stopped shooting he held still for a time, until I felt his cock shrink up on my tongue and he began to go soft. When he pulled it out of my mouth I didn't want to let it go. "Well," he said when it was hanging down over his balls again, "that was quite something. I hope..."

A door banged open and someone yelled, "Hey, anybody in here? The gym is closed." One of the campus security guards came down the aisle, looking important. The red-haired professor wrapped my towel around his waist and went to meet him.

The security guard stopped and nodded. "Oh, it's you, Professor Elich. You know it's after five o'clock? Gym closes at five."

The man -- Professor Elich -- looked up at the big clock over the doorway to the shower room and laughed. "So it is, John. So it is. Somehow time has a way of getting away from me these days. Listen," he said, putting a hand on the guard's shoulder, "my friend and I haven't even had our showers yet. Do you suppose you could let us have a few minutes -- just enough to rinse the sweat off? I promise we won't be long."

"Well, seeing it's you, Professor, I guess it's okay. I'll just slip the outside lock now and then do the dead bolts when I come back around in an hour. You'll be able to get out but not back in so be sure you take all your stuff with you." He shook hands with the Professor and left with hardly a glance at me.

The professor reached out and smeared the sticky stuff around on my chest. "You want a shower? I know I need one. You made several direct hits on my balls and it's a wonder ol' John there didn't smell it on me."

Walking to the shower room he put an arm around my shoulders and said, "You okay with this? I don't want you to have any bad feelings about what happened back there." He squeezed my shoulder. "After all, it's just one of those things that happens between guys sometimes."

I thought about it for a minute. "No sir, Professor Elich, I thought it was great. I mean, as long as you didn't mind... you know, what I..."

He laughed and turned on one of the showers. "Well, that did kind of take me by surprise but no, I didn't mind at all. That sort of thing -- well, it just comes naturally to some guys. Oh, and call me Bob. I think we're well enough acquainted to drop the professor nonsense." He picked up a bar of soap and put me under the hot shower so it beat on the back of my neck. "I will expect you to call me Professor, though, if you ever take one of my courses." He took the soap and began rubbing it over my chest. "By the way, just for the record, what are you called?"

"Rog. Uh, I mean, Roger. Roger Campton." I was having trouble thinking because he was rubbing the soap in my pubic hair and my cock was getting hard again.

"Professor Campton's boy? I thought you looked familiar somehow."

He ran a soapy finger along the top side of my cock and then took the whole thing in his fist and stroked it a couple of times. My knees seemed to go weak and I thought if he didn't stop I was going to come right there in his hand. I reached out and found his cock with my hand. It was as hard as mine and I bent towards it.

"Oh, no," he said, "you've already had that pleasure. Now it's my turn." He turned me into the steaming water for a moment to wash off the soap. Then he got down on his knees and slowly pulled me to him, until my cock was all the way in his mouth and I could feel his breath in my pubic hair. It was wonderful! Better than anything I'd ever felt before, better than the time I pushed it into the can of Crisco, better even than with the hot mud.

Then he started playing with my balls, gently at first and then pinching the sack a little and pulling on the hairs. And then he pulled me even closer, his thumb pressing up between my balls and one finger right over my asshole. I felt it there, touching me, holding me close to him. After a while he began to rub his finger around my hole and suddenly that was all I could feel, that finger touching my asshole, pushing on it a little, and then I shot off in his mouth, the biggest pop I'd ever had in my life. I guess he popped too, because when he stood up his cock was mostly hard with a little of his stuff still dripping out of it.

"Amazing," he said. "You are quite the horny lad, aren't you? And it seems to have rubbed off on me a bit." He laughed in that really nice way he has and messed up my hair even more than it was. "Well, I suppose we'd better get with it and get out of here before John comes back and catches us with sweat still on us."

He ran the soap over himself, rinsed, made sure I was clean and then shut the shower off. We took fresh towels from the pile by the door and went back to our lockers, drying off on the way. When we were dressed he tossed the towels into the big laundry basket and put a hand on my shoulder.

"I assume we're keeping this between ourselves," he said. I nodded, wondering who I would tell even if I wanted to. Then I really surprised myself by asking if maybe we could do it again. I mean, the man was a professor, just like my dad, and I didn't know if it was okay to ask like that but he just smiled at me and said sure, we could do that. Any time I wanted. Then he patted me on the butt, just the way Uncle Jerry sometimes does, and led me out of the locker room.

As soon as I got home I had to go up to my bedroom and jack off, I was so horny from thinking about what had happened. I did it again when I went to bed too, thinking about how good everything had felt, especially when the professor had touched my asshole. When I jacked off in the morning that was all I could think about, the feel of the professor's finger rubbing around my ass.

I went to the pool on Tuesday and Wednesday, of course, but I didn't see Professor Elich. I looked for him all afternoon but he never did show up. I guess I swam about a thousand laps, trying to keep my mind off him, but I couldn't and I was stiff almost all the time thinking about what he'd let me do.

On Thursday I got to the pool before it even opened, sure he still wouldn't be there but he was. He was standing by the door, almost as if he was waiting for someone. "Hi, Rog," he said as I pushed my bike into the rack.

I was so, I don't know, relieved I guess, that I didn't know what to say so I just said 'hi' back.

He came over and put his hand on my shoulder, which felt really good for some reason. "Sure is a hot one, don't you think?" he said, looking at the sky.

I didn't think it was but I nodded anyway. I mean, it was pretty warm but it wasn't all that hot.

He looked at his watch and said, "It's a while yet before they open. You want to come over to my place for a cold drink or something?"

"Okay." I was surprised when he pulled a bike out of the rack. It was a nice one with about twenty-five gears and it was painted a beautiful shade of red. He only lived a couple of blocks from the campus and it didn't take long to get there and when we did he told me to put my bike up on the porch, behind some kind of thick vines he had growing there. So it wouldn't get stolen I guess.

"Coke or iced tea?" the professor asked, looking in the ice box. We ended up with the tea but it wasn't like the stuff mom makes at home. It was kind of orangy with maybe some cinnamon or something in it and I really liked it.

After a couple of minutes he grinned at me and said, "Well, now. I guess we'd better get back pretty soon. Unless you'd rather take your shower here with me?"

I had to gulp my tea because my throat had gone all dry and I could hardly speak. Finally I managed to say something and the professor grinned again, refilled our glasses and led me upstairs to where his bedroom and the bathroom were. In the bedroom he had this enormous bed, bigger than any I'd ever seen and I wondered what it'd be like, sleeping in a bed like that. I got all embarrassed when he started to undress because my cock was up and stiff, from thinking about what might happen, but the professor just laughed and said don't worry. "Give yourself ten or eleven years, 'till you're my age. Then maybe you'll get it under control. Well," he pushed down his pants and showed me he was hard too, "sometimes, anyway."

He took me into the bathroom and turned on the shower which was easily big enough for both of us and even had two sprayers. As soon as we were in it he began washing me all over with a wonderful smelling soap. He let me touch him, too, while he scrubbed me but when I started to kneel down he stopped me. "Let's save that for after, when we can do it properly," he said, handing me the soap.

When we were rinsed and dried he led me out to his bedroom and pulled the covers back on the enormous bed. We laid down on the cool sheets and he reached out and took my cock in his hand. It felt so good I was afraid I was going to come right then and I guess he knew because he said, "You're very close, aren't you. Maybe we'd better just go ahead and get you off right now so you can enjoy the rest of it without worrying about coming too soon."

With that he leaned over and took my cock in his mouth,

sucking down on it all the way to the end so his nose was rubbing in my hairs. At the same time he gently touched my asshole, rubbing his finger around as if he was going to push it into me. When I thought about that I couldn't help myself and I shot my wad, harder than I think I've ever done it before. Then the professor began to swallow with my cock still in his throat and that made it even better.

When my cock finally stopped shooting he eased off and looked at me with a grin. "I think you liked that," he said, stretching out next to me. "So did I. I love it when a guy really gets into it. You want to rest for a while?"

I shook my head. I didn't want to rest; I wanted to do to him what he'd just done to me. I didn't know if I could take his cock all the way down my throat the way he did mine but I wanted to try. I crawled down the bed and kneeled in between his legs. His cock looked bigger than I remembered, the dark head pushing out from his skin with just a tiny bit of white stuff coming out the pee slit. I slid the skin back, letting the whole head come out into the air and the little bubble of white stuff got bigger. I licked it off and found it was sweet, not salty like I expected.

I kissed the head and slowly took it into my mouth. It felt so good, warm and firm but still a little bit flexible. I sucked in more of it and I knew I wasn't going to get the whole thing in my mouth but I thought I could, someday, if he'd let me practice on it enough. I held his balls in my hand while I took in as much of this cock as I could and then I slipped my hand back, under him so I could touch him between his buns. That made him groan and spread his legs further apart.

"You learn fast," he said when I started pushing my finger into his hole. He groaned again and said, "That's only one of the reasons for a shower first but it's a good one." With that he lifted my head off his cock and pulled me up so I was lying on top of him, our cocks lying next to each other and touching.

He put his arms around me and looked me in the eyes. "You like it when I touch you down there, on your ass? You don't think it's dirty or anything?"

I shook my head. "No, it just feels good in a funny kind of way. I... Well, I sort of tried putting my finger up there once when I was jacking off..." I got all embarrassed again because that was the first time I ever said I jacked off to anyone.

The professor acted like everybody jacked off – which I guess maybe they do – and fooled around with themselves, trying out different stuff. He said, "What'd you use, spit? It probably didn't go in very easily if you did." He was right, it didn't and it almost hurt more than it felt good. "What you need," he said, "a good, slick lube. And for some things you want a lot of saliva too, just to get started."

"Is it true... I mean, could a guy really take another..." I didn't know how to say it but the professor seemed to know everything I was thinking and he said it for me.

"Can a man take another man's dick up there? Sure he can. And for some guys it's about as pleasurable as anything can get. It takes a little practice but once you get the hang of it -- well, it can be a lot of fun." He rolled me off him, onto my belly, and began to play with my buns.

I didn't know what he was going to do but the way he was feeling and licking my buns felt so good I didn't care. Then he pulled my buns apart and kissed me right on my hole. It was like, I don't know, later I thought it was like he had pushed an electric wire in there but at the time I don't think I even knew what it was like, just that it wasn't like anything anyone ever did to me.

He didn't stop, either. He kissed and licked me and even forced some of his spit into me. Then his tongue started pushing against me, like a little hammer stabbing in and pulling back to do it again and again and I felt myself go limp and begin to open, letting his tongue in me a little ways. And all the time there was this... this feeling running through me, something that was turning my insides to jelly.

I didn't want him ever to stop but he did, pulling himself up and laying across my back, kissing the back of my neck. "Well," he whispered in my ear, "what'd you think of that? You like it?"

I knew what I wanted him to do now but I didn't know how to ask. Finally I just said, "Do the rest. Go inside me."

He rolled off me and turned me on my side so he could look at me. "You sure about that, Rog? Sometimes that hurts pretty bad, at least the first few times and I wouldn't want to hurt you."

I nodded, and said please. I didn't care. I wanted to feel him – his cock – up inside me.

"Okay," he said. "We'll try. But if you want to stop, want me to pull out, you just say so. We might have to try it a couple of times before it's comfortable for you so don't be disappointed if it doesn't work the first time. Okay?"

I nodded again and turned on my belly and spread my legs. The professor went back to kissing and licking my hole for a while and then I felt something slick and cool in my ass. After that he pushed a finger against the hole and it slipped right in. He moved his finger around a little and then put another one in. "Okay, Rog. But I think you'd better control it."

He turned on his back and motioned for me to get on top of him, squatting right over his cock. "Now you just take your time and let yourself get used to it as it goes in. And if it hurts you just pull off. As I said, it might take a couple of tries before you can get it in."

When I felt the head of his cock touch my ass and saw the way his face broke into a grin I knew it was going to be okay. I slipped down on it, just enough to let the head inside me and it did hurt a little, kind of like burning but I didn't care. There was too much else going on that felt wonderful.

I let myself move further down on it but I had to do it very slowly. The professor thought I was doing it so slow because it hurt but I wasn't. I was slow because it felt so good. The burning had gone away and something else, something I'd never felt before, took over instead and I knew if the feeling got any stronger it was going to make me come. And then it did, just as I felt his hairs against my ass and I knew he was all the way in. That bubble inside me just got too big and it burst, making me yell and shoot my stuff all over the professor.

"My, my," the professor said, wiping off his face. "It seems this sort of thing agrees with you, doesn't it, Rog. You okay? You want to get off?" He sort of flexed his cock inside me which started the bubble growing all over again. I shook my head and began to slide myself up and down on him. He threw back his head and began to make funny noises in his throat and I knew he was liking it as much as I was.

He took hold of my nipples and rubbed them between his fingers which felt really good and then he wrapped one hand around my cock and began jacking me off, slowly, just the way I was sliding up and down on his cock. After a while I reached out and took his nipples in my fingers, just the way he was doing to me and when I did he groaned and said to be careful because he was very, very close.

I was closer though, and when I leaned forward to play with his chest his cock hit something up inside me and I felt the bubble begin to burst only this time it was really slow and seemed to take a long time before I finally started to shoot off. As soon as I started that the professor made a real funny sound in his throat and began shooting off inside me and that made me come even harder.

After it was over, when I felt the professor begin to go soft inside me, I let him slip out of me and lay down beside him. He got a little towel from the bedside table and wiped us off and then rolled me up on my side so I could rest my head on his chest and I guess maybe I dozed off for a while it felt so good with his arms around me, holding me that way.

I was stiff again when I woke up but I didn't care. Besides, I could see that he was, too, so I started playing around, sucking on one of his nipples and rubbing my cock against his leg. "Careful, Rog," he said. "Keep that up and you'll get me started again." I sucked his nipple harder and he pulled me up so I was lying on top of him, my cock pressed against his balls. "Okay, you're asking for it." He spread his legs and I slipped between them; then he pulled his legs up and handed me the tube of slippery jelly that he'd put in me. "Well, go on. Turnabout is fair play, especially in bed."

It felt so good spreading the slick jelly on my cock that I had to be careful so I didn't build up the bubble too much. When I put my finger in the professor's hole he squirmed around on the bed and said, "Oh, yes, I'm ready for it, Rog. Go ahead. Put your dick in."

I pushed his legs back so I could see and I thought how impossible it looked, that my cock could ever get through that tiny little pucker. But it could. I just pushed against it and it opened right up and seemed almost to pull my cock in. When the head was in and maybe a couple of inches too, the professor groaned so I stopped, thinking it might be hurting him. I guess it wasn't, though, because he grabbed me by the buns and pulled me all the way into him and held me there for a second. Then he said, "Do it, Rog. Let me have it, hard and fast."

I started pulling my cock almost out of him and then shoving it back in as fast as I could. He reached back and took my balls in his hand, squeezing them and tugging on them until I had to make him stop so I wouldn't come so fast. Then he began playing with his cock, putting spit on it and rubbing it against my belly. Pretty soon he groaned, "I think it's all over, Rog. I can't last much..." I felt his stuff shoot against my belly and I guess that made my bubble burst because then I started shooting off inside him.

While I was still shooting he pulled me down to his face and started kissing me. Right on the mouth. When he pushed his tongue in my mouth it was like a new bubble was bursting and I was starting to come all over again.

When we finally stopped shooting and coming he let my cock stay in him as long as I wanted. He said he wanted to feel it go soft in him but then he kept kissing me so it wouldn't. After a while it all felt so good that I started moving in and out of him again, only this time real slow and kind of lazy. He let me play with his cock and showed me how when I hit that one certain place up inside him it made his stuff leak out. I couldn't do that too much though because he said it would make him come and I didn't want to do that. It was too good just sliding in and out of him and kissing him and playing with his cock.

After while, though, I could only move a little bit because, no matter what, I was very close to coming. Finally I couldn't stand it and I told him I just had to do it, I had to let the bubble burst and shoot off in him. He clamped his muscles down on my cock and said go ahead because he was at the same place.

We didn't make much noise this time but I could feel how good it felt to the professor just by the way he looked at me and by the way he kissed me. I tried to let him feel how good it was for me, too, and later he said I did a good job of it.

After, we took another shower and then it was time for me to get on home for dinner. The professor asked again if this was just between the two of us and I said it was. He smiled and said we could do it again if I wanted to. Any time.

I wanted to all the time.

I still got in some swimming practice though. The professor made me. We'd meet at the pool, take a quick shower and then I'd do my laps. Afterward we'd go back to his house and fool around for the rest of the afternoon.

It was a great summer.

PORTRAIT OF A FRESHMAN

David Patrick Beavers

Jeff looked around the space of the shop. A space he was supposed to somehow fill with paint and paper, tile and enamel molding. Space. He wasn't a designer. He wasn't an architect. He was just a former switch technician working on large PBXs and small key systems.

To any and all clients, it didn't matter that he'd a degree in communications, with telephony as his specialty. It didn't matter to screaming clients bitching about their bad speaker phones, their lost voicemail messages, whatever, that he had certification in a vast variety of complex telecommunications and data systems. He was just "the phone man" to them all. The guy they could curse at after they'd chewed up some poor customer service person. He was just a former phone man who'd taken a chance to pursue a hobby and hopefully make some sort of career out of it. Painting was the hobby. Portraits, abstracts, realism, surrealism, whatever. He'd studied art in college. Had a few minor shows and exhibits. Sold some work here and there. But it was never enough to survive, so he'd earned his degree in communications and fell, by happenstance, into a job with a telephone company. That's how life worked. Still, he found a creative outlet within his condo. Walls he owned that he found to be canvases waiting for a brush.

His unit became a bit of a showplace. More often than not, people liked his work. He did a few gigs for friends, painting scenes on walls in their apartments and houses. Word of mouth travelled fast and now, here he was, with virgin dry-wall he was being paid to paint. Paid well, too. That's what was scaring him most. When people pay, they want to like what they pay for. The owner of the shop had no idea what he wanted painted on the walls, so he suggested that Jeff run with the flow and follow his instincts. Walls, counters, tiles, whatever he needed to use. The shop was to be a curiosity shop. A place where local talents could peddle their wares on consignment. Jeff wasn't sure just what those wares would be, though.

He finally stopped thinking and started on one wall, painting it a base color of indigo. He didn't use a pan or a roller, though. Rather, he used a wide brush and dribble-painted the thinned-down oil wash over the space, creating a strippled effect, like a tight latticing of navy vines. The wall would've normally taken a half hour to paint in standard fashion. It took Jeff almost three hours to complete.

Even though he was tired and a dull headache was forming due to paint thinner fumes, he decided to do the counter as well. He had a brilliant grass green he wanted to use on it. His favorite color. And within an hour and a half, the entire counter was as vibrant as a pasture at the height of spring. Satisfied with his base colors, he realized the rest of the walls would be in primary and secondary hues as well. Perhaps it would seem trendy, but his painting technique made the flat surfaces seem softly textured. Still, he was unsure about what to paint atop the base colors. Images popped in and out of his mind quicker than second-hand thoughts and none quite fit the bill as far as he was concerned. He didn't want anything cheeky or cute, or anything that would be considered trendoid chic. Then he thought about hitting the street with his camera in hand in search of some sort of inspiration.

He locked up his supplies in a tool bin provided him by the shop's owner. It was the type of tool bin one normally sees bolted down behind the cab of a pick-up, anchored to the side walls of the bed. He washed the residual paint off his hands with thinner, then scrubbed them again with an abrasive soap.

Cleaned up and packed up, he left the shop, climbed into his car and drove back to his home. His cave, he called it. His friends had taken to calling him cave-dweller as he rarely ventured out with them to parade around the bars and clubs of the city. He was too old for such nonsense, he thought. He wasn't twenty-one, or even thirty-one anymore. He was thirty-something. He'd done his time on dance floors, at the tubs, in bars in almost every state. He'd resolved himself to the fact that Mr. Right was always only going to be Mr. Right-for-the-Moment. Since his personal life was going nowhere at an alarming rate of speed, he made the brash decision to change his occupation. That was the only thing that was seeming to go correctly. At least for now.

He was lucky in that his unit had a balcony. Not some

microscopic speck of space jutting out from the building like a giant pouting lip, but a real balcony, where he'd forested himself in with leafy plants and where he'd placed a small patio table and chairs. He liked to sit outside. He could see the hills just beyond the city's edge. He could see most of the pool area below. He could see one side of the wing of the complex that housed him. Not much ever happened beyond those windows, though. His voyeuristic tendencies kept him ever on the alert for motion and movement, especially at night. But, in the years that he lived there, almost all his neighbors kept their shades and curtains drawn at night. Occasionally, he glimpsed a backlit silhouetted shadow hidden away, but none of them ever intrigued him enough to keep watching.

He went into the bathroom, stripped down and climbed into the shower, relishing the hot blast of the water kneading the muscles in his shoulders and back. This was one of his places to think. One of the places where his mind fell blank and time was often forgotten, at least until the hot water turned cold and reality charged back into his life with a bracing, awakening call. Yet he didn't linger in the shower this time.

As soon as he stepped into the tub, he knew he really wanted to immerse himself in water. He wanted to do laps in the pool. He killed the shower, patted himself dry then dug in the adjacent closet for his swim suit, a pair of old black trunks as short as running shorts that were getting so shot from chlorine and sun that the fabric was nearing the point of giving up the ghost in the most critical of seams.

Still, the trunks suited him. They made his average legs look longer and enhanced his tanned skin. Besides, he spent all his time in the water, only surfacing to dry land when he was ready to head inside. Lingering on a chaise longue in the sun like some sea lion on a rock jetty wasn't his idea of fun.

Directly across from his front door was the stairwell. He opted to bound down the three flights of steps, then exit through a side door that led directly to the back of the building, near the pool. It was a quick walk that dumped him square at the shallow end of the pool, where he dropped his towel, stowed his keys in his shoes, then removed his shirt and jumped into the water. Down like a rock he went, submerging himself. As he broke through the surface, he realized that the pool's heater was obviously not working up to snuff, for eighty-degree water felt like it was much, much colder. Nonetheless, it stimulated him and he fell into his pattern of lazy laps, gliding through crystal clear wetness like an experienced, old dolphin. And he thought. Thought with sharp focus on the bare walls of the shop. And images came to mind. Images that flew through his head like a high speed slide show. Images, he realized, that were similar to every other work he'd scene or done. He sighed a bubbly exhalation as he felt his arms and chest expanding with blood fed muscles as he swam. He let his mind go blank again, focusing on nothing more than the pale blue walls of the pool, on the reflecting light and shadow of gently rippling waves all around him. He finally stopped to rest, letting a deep, cleansing breath wash through his lungs. The sun was moving on and shade was overtaking the water.

"Hi!"

The voice startled Jeff. Usually, the moment the sun's rays wane, any and all into heliotropic therapy scampered away to higher ground. Jeff turned around slowly, expecting to see one of his many neighbors, whom he knew nothing about save for the occasional chat in the hallway or at the mailboxes. There before him was a hereto-unseen young man with sandy blond hair, brilliant blue eyes and the coppery-est tan he'd ever seen on a pale haired form.

"Hi," Jeff said without a smile.

"I just moved in last week. Up on the fourth floor."

"Ah! Welcome to the maze."

The young man grinned. "The maze?"

"All the hallways and fire doors," said Jeff, referring to the large scale, confusing corridors of Navajo white walls and doors that somewhat segmented the complex.

"Oh... It can be confusing." The young man stared at him. "My name's Shawn."

"Jeff." Jeff extended a damp hand. Shawn crouched down to shake it. "What brings you here?"

"School," said Shawn. "The condo I'm in actually belongs to my uncle. He just rents it out, though. When the couple in there moved out, he offered it to me."

"Couple?" Jeff thought. "The McAllisters?"

Shawn nodded. "I think that was their name. He was a

doctor, or something?"

"They were a nice couple," said Jeff. He gripped the side of the pool and hauled himself out, quickly grabbing his towel to soak up the wetness and to cover his midsection.

"You swim a lot," said Shawn.

"It's therapeutic. Clears my mind."

"Maybe I'll come down and do laps with you sometime."

"Company's always welcome," Jeff said as he slipped his shirt on and stepped into his shoes. "I'm in 306," he said.

"427," said Shawn. "You got a balcony?"

"Yeah... Don't you?"

"No."

"Oh..." Jeff looked around at the building. He'd never quite noticed that not all the units had balconies. He'd just made the assumption that since he saw many balconies, they all had one. "That's weird."

"My uncle said that there are two on each floor that don't have them," Shawn said matter-of-factly. "Each unit that's a 27 or a 29 all the way up. There's a stairwell. Fire exit type of thing."

"Well, that's kind of idiotic," Jeff said. "I mean there are plenty of dead, unused spaces to utilize."

"Kinda sucks, but hey, beggars can't be choosers."

"Ah, balconies have their drawbacks. Gotta keep'em swept. Birds land and shit on 'em..."

"Can I see yours?"

Jeff was unsure whether this was an honest request or perhaps an introduction to a come-on. Or, he thought, it could be some kid sizing up his possessions. He always had a certain healthy dose of paranoia when it came to people's motives. Still, he thought it's a populated building. He could always point a finger.

"Okay..." Jeff acquiesced. He led the way up the stairs to his unit. He opened the door and let Shawn inside. The young man moved almost directly into the middle of the living room, surveying Jeff's vividly painted walls.

"Whoa..."

"Kinda weird, huh?" Jeff said as he moved to open the balcony doors.

"I like it," said Shawn with a grin.

One wall was a mural of a series of faces, each of which where only three quarters seen, the remaining quarter being hidden behind the face of the first. The first in line was a somewhat large portrait, about two feet by three feet, of a young man who looked a lot like Jeff. Behind him ran an arching succession of faces of men and women, all of them young, that ran from the lower left corner of the wall up to the high right corner, as if the portraits were slipping away into oblivion. Another wall was an abstract montage of mens' forms. So many that they bled together obfuscating the beauty of each separate piece. Another wall was simply a wash of colors that blended, somehow, smoothly together. When the eyes focused on it, one could make out an entire landscape of a flowering meadow. Yet another wall was simply "a-la-Mondrian." Panels of colors, all framed in a networking of black lines. Jeff could tell that Shawn was indeed impressed with his work.

"I got tired of hanging pictures and seeing white walls get yellowed within a year. At least the colors here will take a long while to seem faded."

"You're an artist?" Shawn was surprised.

"Only as a hobby, until recently, that is."

"What'd you do before?"

"Phone man," said Jeff.

"The phone company?"

"Many phone companies," Jeff said with a sigh. "I was a service technician."

"God..." said Shawn. "Didn't think they made that kind of money." He realized what he'd said. "I mean, these condos aren't cheap."

"Yeah, but I worked a ton of overtime to support the government and me," said Jeff. "And I'm single. Had no real debt to speak of, except for student loans."

"I know all about those," Shawn said as he followed Jeff out onto the balcony. "This is cool!"

"Actually, even with sweeping and bird shit, I like it best out here. Warm nights, cool days, even when it's lightly raining, I enjoy sitting out here."

"See? It's a plus to have a balcony." Shawn peered over the railing. "You can see the pool."

"Yeah, but there's rarely anyone in it when I think to look."

"Lousy for boy watching?"

Jeff felt his face turn red. The kid was a bit ballsy, he thought, making an assumption about Jeff's sexual inclinations, even though he was correct. Jeff sat down and pulled a cigarette from the pack on the table. "You into boy watching?" he asked.

"Sometimes," Shawn said. "But boys aren't my speed."

"No?"

"I like men."

"Some boys are men," said Jeff. "And some men are mere boys."

"Oh let's not get pseudo-philosophical about this," said Shawn. "Guys my age are out for a party, an orgy, a good time in general, which is okay, if you're into it."

"I know I was when I was your age."

"Did you have affairs with only guys in your age bracket?"

Jeff laughed to himself. "No, it was a different time. And I was an equal opportunity slut."

"Very different back then, wasn't it?"

"Yeah, but some of your generation is bringing our old ways back, I hear, even though perhaps they shouldn't be."

"I know," he said. "I'm not into all that."

"Then what are you into?"

Shawn shot him a dubious smile. "As I said, men."

Jeff just let it go. The kid was pretty. The kid seemed focused. Still, he wasn't ready to jump into anything quick and dissatisfying. "Well, there are plenty of men in this city."

"True." Shawn leaned against the balustrade. "But not all of them are my type, if you know what I mean."

Jeff felt a shiver run up his spine. While it would be convenient to blame it on a chill from the cooling air, he knew full well it was because of Shawn. The young man was most decidedly focusing on him at the moment. Jeff snubbed out his cigarette and rose, hoping that the tails of his shirt were concealing the swelling organ in the pouch of his trunks. It was awkward to try to walk in a dignified manner with an erection popping up. Still he managed to lead the way inside.

"Well, my young friend, I need to get dressed," he said as an excuse.

Shawn followed him inside, settling in a chair. He stared at the wall of faces. "Who're they?"

"Friends. Enemies. Acquaintances." Jeff thought that this was silly. He should boot the boy out. Rush him along. Get back to the tasks at hand.

"I can understand painting your friends, but your enemies?"

"Why not?" Jeff asked. "They're as much a part of your growth and who you are as your friends are."

"I don't think most people would see it that way," Shawn said. He leaned back in the chair, studying the faces, while his legs spread wide with lazy ease.

Jeff could make out the slight swell of the young man's basket molded comfortably to fading denim. He didn't need this. Not a young trick for the night. Especially not one who lived in his building. He tugged his shirt tails lower, trying to cover his rapidly rising erection.

"Excuse me..." he said as he slipped into his bedroom.

Shawn regarded Jeff's quick exit curiously. He liked the guy. Short, but shaggy dark hair, with a slight peppering of gray throughout. A very slight peppering, it was. Just enough to soften the dark. Big brown eyes arched by heavy, expressive brows. Jeff had that wide kind of face. Wide with a very strong jaw whose five o'clock shadow was not quite a blue beard of youth, but almost white, from what he could tell. The light reflected faintly on the hint of whiskers. Yet his moustache, a neatly trimmed cookie duster of masculine virility, was as dark as his hair. And he had that ruddy tan. Coopertone brown-red that could go as dark as a native of Bombay. Swarthy is what his friend, Mike, called the look. Swarthy. Shawn loved swarthy men. Loved the smell of their bodies after a full day's work. Loved the feel of skin and hair that covered their forms. He especially loved a hairy stomach and ass. He'd duly noted that Jeff's legs were blanketed by pale brown strands that had been faintly bleaching a deep golden brown from too much chlorine and a fair amount of sun. He wanted to get up and to peer in on his new neighbor. He wanted to see Jeff stripping away shirt and trunks. He wanted to see, but he was just a bit too timid to be so forward.

"Well," said Jeff as he returned from his room, barefoot, but clad in jeans and the same damp shirt. "You want something to drink?"

"Water, if you have it."

"Bottled water, you mean," Jeff said. "I do have it. You want it cold or room temperature."

"I hear cold water helps burn fat faster."

"When you're my age, a little fat's going to be keeping you company, too," Jeff said as he meandered into the kitchen.

"I didn't mean you!" Shawn said. He got up and padded after Jeff. "I meant me."

Jeff pulled a litre from the refrigerator and poured two tall glasses. He handed one to Shawn. "Like you're really fat."

"I was," Shawn admitted. "Up until my junior year of high school. I dropped thirty-plus pounds."

Jeff quickly scrutinized the young man's frame. He was about five-eight. Broad shoulders, he thought. Somewhat of a V-taper at the waist. The lad's legs weren't long, nor were they particularly meaty. More like a runner's build. Or a swimmer's. He stared at Shawn's face. A wonderful crown of blond locks that shifted hues from light to dark. Then there were the bright blue eyes. The boy only had a whisper of lashes and brows, but they were just a deep enough shade of pale, pale brown to be enhancing. Narrow face. Narrow nose, sort of patrician, with very clean, lines. It was the kind of nose people pay plastic surgeons to get. The young man had a thin, almost Aryan upper lip, while the lower lip was plump with brownish-pink freshness. One thing, though, he was sure that Shawn would be the type whose wonderful tan would fade to milk white come winter time.

"Thirty-plus pounds?" Jeff repeated.

"Yeah. I was kind of stocky all over, but had this gut, ya know?" Shawn said with an embarrassed grin. "I still have a problem with the sidecars."

"Sidecars?"

"Love handles?"

"Primary storage facilities - PSF - that's what I prefer to call'em."

"I don't like'em on me."

"I'm sure no one notices," Jeff said. "So, what're you doing in your uncle's apartment?"

"School."

"Ah!" Jeff said. "That's what you meant by understanding

student loans."

Shawn nodded. "They suck. But, they're necessary."

"What're you? Sophomore?"

"Freshman," Shawn said. "Second semester. I killed some of my general ed requirements at a junior college up north, then transferred down here."

"Smart move."

"I thought so. I was going to do a full year at the J.C., but I got bored. Small town an' all."

"There's some nice people in small towns."

"Yeah," Shawn conceded, "but everyone knows your business."

"So, you have a job?"

"Kinda. Work in the Administration Office as a general lackey," Shawn said with a slight snarl. "They're okay, I guess, but I need something else to pad the cheque book, ya know?"

Jeff stuck upon his image for one of the shop's walls. Like the faces on his wall that started distinct, then faded into oblivion. He would do a portrait of movement. Some sort of movement. He looked at Shawn and wondered. It would seem like a hokey excuse, but nothing ventured, nothing gained.

"I've got a wall to paint," Jeff said. "Well, actually a bunch of walls."

"Is that a job offer?" Shawn said with a skeptical smile.

"Actually, you'd be the model."

"Right..." Shawn said.

"No, really!" said Jeff. "I just got the idea for one of the murals. A movement shot."

"Of me."

"Sure! Maybe walking, or throwing something... No... Tumbling!"

Shawn was surprised by Jeff's exuberance. "You're not kidding, are you?"

"No! What I do is shoot you on eight millimeter. It's cheaper. Then I blow up the frames of the movement and sketch those onto the wall."

"And I'd be naked, I suppose?"

"You don't have to be," said Jeff. "After all, it is a store. You should be in shorts, though. Maybe a tank top. Maybe a full shirt with the tails hangin' out."

Shawn thought for a moment. "But what if I wanted to do it naked?"

"I don't know," Jeff said thoughtfully. "I think it would be a cleaner image, but then again, we're talking about a type of retail business that isn't a sex shop, if you know what I mean."

"What kind of retail?"

"Different craftsmen, artists, designers, whatever, hawking their wares, so to speak."

"So why would they mind a naked form?"

"Well, I guess if the owner doesn't like it, I can paint clothes on you."

"God, just like the old Christians hammering marble fig leaves onto the crotches of all those ancient statues."

"Fair enough."

Shawn thought again for a moment. "How much?"

"I can give you two-fifty."

"Up front?"

"The day we shoot."

"What about tomorrow?"

"Tomorrow? That's soon."

"Too soon?"

"Well, I haven't even prepped the other walls yet with a base," Jeff said.

"Think you can make me look better than this?" said Shawn, indicating his entire form.

"You look fine, Shawn."

"I've got no real definition," he said. "Not like you."

"I didn't even start to get any definition until I was twenty-nine. That's when I started doing the gym."

"Still, you got a few years head start."

"A few?" Jeff laughed. "More than that."

"How old are you?"

"Thirty-nine. I'll be forty in September."

"Virgo or Libra?"

"Libra."

"I'm an Aquarian, myself."

"Should I know what that means?"

"Didn't you see the original version of 'Hair'?"

"Hardy-har-har." Jeff set his glass down on the counter. "I'm not quite that old."

"Well," Shawn said as he set his glass down as well. "Maybe you should see me first."

Jeff's antennae shot up, along with his dick. "You want to strip down?"

"Either now or later," said Shawn. "And later you'll have to pay."

Jeff grinned awkwardly. "Later might be... safer."

"Safer?"

"You don't need to show me your body, Shawn. I'm sure it will work just fine for the shoot."

Shawn was a little disappointed. He wasn't usually so forward, but when opportunity invited itself in, he decided to go for it. Or at least he attempted to. Maybe Jeff wasn't interested in him. He felt himself flush with the shade of embarrassment.

"Sorry..." he muttered.

"About what?" Jeff asked.

"I just thought that... You might wanna see what kind of model you're getting."

"I don't want you to think... Um..." Jeff wasn't sure how to say it.

"You're not trying to get me in bed," Shawn said. "I know the offer's genuine."

"Yeah..." Jeff was both relieved and disappointed.

"Still..." Shawn unbuttoned his shirt. "I think you're handsome."

"Handsome's a pretty exaggerated word." Jeff felt his own face turning a brilliant crimson as he watched Shawn carefully peel off his shirt. He went and draped it over one of the dinette chairs, then stepped out of his shoes and with slightly cockeyed grace, out of his pants. He stood there in a pair of white Jockey's and all his flesh. The coppery tan seemed to bleed right into the young man's shorts. Jeff noted the sleek curve of Shawn's erect cock snaking up the side of the briefs, riding up on his right hip.

"Well?" Shawn asked simply.

"Well..." Jeff's cock was pushing hard at the zipper. He was so painfully erect that to walk would have snapped his dick in two. "You've got a beautiful body."

Beautiful it was. The young man's form was lithe, with very

minimal definition in his arms and chest. Skin so even colored and soft that it almost shimmered like satin under the light. Delicate brown aureoles peaked into tightly pinched nipples. Shawn's body was form still being defined, somewhere between adolescence and manhood. Light brown wisps of short, silky hair led from his navel to the nest of youthful need in the pouch of his underwear. That same light brown hair delicately covered slim thighs and well formed calves. Even his ankles were both delicate and masculine, like an agile sprinter's. Jeff felt himself to be a thick, cumbersome bear by comparison. He stepped closer to Shawn, studying the youthful face and body. He gingerly combed his fingers through the boy's hair, righting it's somewhat chaotic sweep.

    Shawn slowly drew his head back, his face up, letting Jeff's fingers come to trace gently the contours of his expression. One of desire. One of wanting. One of need. Jeff let his fingertips dust a scant shadow of flesh. The young man closed his eyes as his tongue licked Jeff's fingers and palm.

    Young, slender hands caressed Jeff's arm, then wrist, guiding the man's fingers to lips that were soft and eager. Jeff shuddered as Shawn drew two fingers into his mouth, sucking them gently, slipping his tongue between them. Jeff let his free hand roam the kid soft skin of Shawn's shoulder, then chest, letting his thumb rub lazily over the young man's nipple. And further down this free hand slid, over ribs, down the stomach to the slight indentation of a navel as he slipped his other hand, his fingers, wet and warm, from his young model's mouth. Firmness grasped Shawn's chin, holding it fast, as Jeff's thick lips and soft moustache pressed against the lad's lips. Tongues spoke to one another in a silent, snaking dance, and Shawn felt the gentle strength of his man beneath the sheath of Jockey cotton, forcing it down and drawing him out. His cock pulsed instinctively in Jeff's hand.

    The young man tasted like warm peppermint and lust and Jeff swallowed hard the blasts of panting breath rising from Shawn's lungs as he manipulated the long, slender shaft of his groin. He could sense the mounting euphoric high within his young friend. He pulled away quickly, leaving Shawn to gasp breaths of clear air as he dropped to his knees and swallowed whole the youthful cock, slamming his face again and again into the tangle of downy threads.

Shawn felt as if his cock had been thrust into a vacuum of velvet drenched in heated oil. Jeff's tongue swabbed all around the underside of his shaft, tickling it as he sucked and warm spit dribbled all over his balls and down his thighs and he felt himself blacking out to silent, red and white pulsations of hallucinogenic lights that danced like fireballs, and he felt his abdomen contract sharply as his scrotum hiked up into his groin as his knees trembled to failing beneath him and he shot hot white spunk deep down the throat of this man. This artist. This guy's guy.

Jeff felt the first blast of jism strike his throat like a thick ball of sticky warmth, then another two shots of liquidy cum washed down the wonderful thickness and he sucked hard, drawing yet another shot of watery load out of the young man. This final taste being delivered right on his tongue.

Shawn winced slightly as Jeff's strong lips nursed on the head of his tender prick. He was softening in the man's moist mouth. He liked the feeling of hot spit and slick cum bathing his cock. He looked down at the handsome man, letting his fingers rake through the thick, dark hair. Jeff let his head fall back slowly, Shawn's spent cock slipping easily from between his lips. The man raised himself and wrapped his arms around the youth, pressing Shawn into him, wanting to make them merge into one.

"Take off your clothes," Shawn said softly. "I want to smell you. Feel you."

Jeff pulled back slightly, his fingers fumbling with buttons, wanting to seem calm. The shirt was open. Shawn helped him guide it off. Then Shawn unfastened Jeff's jeans, deftly skimming down the zipper. He slid his hands beneath the waist band, skiing around hips to that point where lower back and buttocks meet. Jeff almost caved in as Shawn pressed the heel of his palms into his ass cheeks, kneading the muscles deep beneath the skin. Then with swift force, Shawn forced down Jeff's jeans, he himself going down onto his knees in the process. He bruskly nuzzled his face into Jeff's groin, savoring the faint mix of chlorine and sweat between his thighs, beneath his balls. Hairy balls. A scrotal sack that hung low with walnut sized testicles that slipped comfortably into his mouth. He loved sucking nuts. Loved the feel of fleshy fullness lolling on his tongue as his nose pressed into the base of a cock. And Jeff's cock was thick and full with loose foreskin that still covered most of the head of the erect shaft.

Jeff gently pursued Shawn to relinquish his mouthful. He wanted to pick up the young man and take him into the bedroom, where it was cooler and more pleasant, but Shawn gripped his prick firmly, pushing up his foreskin even further over the head. Shawn stabbed the slight pucker of prepuce with the tip of his tongue, then licked all around wiping away all of Jeff's precum ooze.

Jeff involuntarily twitched a pleased response, which encouraged Shawn to continue his exploration. He pulled the foreskin back, exposing the fat, flushed cock head, then fastened his lips around it, sucking on it like a Tootsie Pop. Spit dripped down his chin as he feasted on the salty knob.

"Let's go into the other room..." Jeff said softly.

Shawn either didn't hear him or refused to. Jeff watched Shawn swallow him whole as one hand slipped around to knead an ass cheek while the other snaked between his thighs. Jeff left out a pant of surprise as he felt Shawn's finger bore up into his hole and strike his prostate dead on the money. He felt his knees buckle and he reflexively gripped Shawn's head, reining fistfuls of golden mane. Shawn's free hand flew back behind him, landing atop on of Jeff's. Palm to hand, he silently encouraged Jeff to take control, to fuck his face and to fuck it hard. Jeff was reluctant at first, then Shawn's finger probed his prostate again, massaging it vigorously. An electric charge coursed like lightning up Jeff's spine as he felt his balls retracting inside him as cum churned and boiled. He grabbed Shawn's head harshly and his hips started pumping, slamming his cock deep into the boy's mouth. He could hear Shawn panting choked gasps as he sucked feverishly on the thick stick of man meat. He rocked on his knees as Jeff's balls slapped his chin again and again. His finger jammed deeper into his man, exciting him more, egging him on. Jeff pounded violently against his boy's face as sweat ran freely from his pits and head, running down his chest and stomach, drenching the blond bangs the poured sweat freely, too. Jeff's legs locked as he bucked hard, shooting a heavy, thick load deep in Shawn.

He thrust again. And again. Releasing all that he had. And Shawn fed eagerly on the creamy jism, sucking hard on the knob of man cock, licking the piss slit clean with the tip of his tongue.

As he released his lip lock on Jeff's cock, Jeff loosened up and slipped down onto his knees to kiss this young friend he'd made. He relished the taste of his residual cum coating Shawn's tongue. He loved the taste of the young man who'd tasted him. He wanted more. He wanted this young man to slip his slender cock into his ass, to fuck him hard, to fuck him slowly as they lay in a tangle on the floor, on the bed, on the balcony.

Shawn pulled back a bit, then scooted back and turned away. He stretched out onto the kitchen floor and spread his legs wide, hiking his luscious small butt into the air.

"You like ass?" he asked.

Jeff pressed his face into the crack, sniffing the slightly heady scent of unwashed flesh. His tongue pressed flat against the puckered hole and he wiped the boy clean, licking the day away until only the sweetness of deep recesses remained. He pried the pink ass cheeks apart with his hands, pulling the youth's crack taut so that the ridges of his sphincter protruded a bit and the faintest glimpse of tender interior could be seen. His mouth watered. As he stretched out his tongue to probe the tasty hole, saliva ran down its tip, lubricating the orifice, aiding his tongue's entry inside.

Shawn shivered with anticipation as the slick, rough tongue drilled its thickness into him. He shifted his hips slightly, press back, pushing his ass into Jeff's face. And Jeff responded well. Tongue inserted, he pressed his lips around the hole and sucked hard, drawing the puckered muscle just into his mouth. Shawn gasped. Groaned a throaty groan of pleasure. Jeff relaxed his lips, his tongue, letting the now slick hole go free. He gingerly probed inside the boy's ass with the tip of his finger, feeling the tightness, the warm silkiness inside him. He wanted to feel this cock up there, as he wanted to feel Shawn's cock up inside him. He smiled to himself and pulled himself back, massaging Shawn's ass and thighs. Shawn twisted around a bit, a bent arm and hand supporting his grinning face.

"You do like ass," he said.

"I do," said Jeff.

"But you stopped?"

Jeff smiled and swatted his friend's ass gently. "This is the kitchen. The floor needs mopping."

"I got another deck you can swab."

"And I've one for you."

"Well?"

Jeff stood up, pulling up his pants. He extended his hand to Shawn, drew him to his feet, then held him fast. "If we do everything now, there won't be much to do after I shoot you."

"You really want to use me for a model?"

"Yeah. I think I'll shoot you tumbling. It'll make a very interesting portrait of movement on the wall."

"Shoot me once clothed, then once again naked?"

"No clothes," said Jeff. "This portrait should be in the nude."

"Okay..."

"I'll be at the shop tomorrow until about five."

"I can be there around four-thirty," said Shawn as he grabbed his shirt.

"I've got some old gym mats. There's a long wall that's still basically white. Just the gypsum. It'll service as a clean background."

"This'll be interesting."

"I should hope so."

Shawn put on his shirt, then stepped into his pants. "We could go for a swim after."

"I'd like the company."

"So would I."

The two stood staring at each other for a moment, then Shawn hugged Jeff hard and gave him a quick kiss. "I'm glad my uncle suggested I move in here."

"Me, too."

TOOLS

Peter Gilbert

"What are they for?" asked Luke.
"Don't ask me. Our job is to make the bloody things, not ask questions," said his older companion. "Anyway, we're here. Look sharp." The truck drew up in front of the classical portico. The pillars gleamed white. The last time Luke had seen them they were a dirty yellow color. For years the manor house had been derelict, standing in a wilderness of thorn bushes and surrounded by forbidding coils of barbed wire. But there was a way in. Luke felt himself blushing at the memory as he climbed out of the cab. He rang the door bell and waited. Nothing happened.

"Push it harder," said Bert from the cab. "If you'd only get yourself a girl friend, she'd tell you how to do it!" He cackled with laughter.

Luke rang again. Bert's coarse jokes got on his nerves sometimes but the job at Lakeside Furniture was a job and he hadn't had a proper job since he left school. He was eighteen now and at last the car he had always dreamed about was a possibility.

"He must be in," said Bert. "I called him to make sure. I don't want to take the bloody things back. Ring again."

Luke did so. He looked down at his feet. Same feet; same steps, only this time they were scrubbed. The last time he had seen them they were covered with dead leaves. He was fifteen then. He'd gotten through the wire and fought his way through the undergrowth because someone had told him that there were bats nesting in the ruins. In those days he had been interested in animals.

The man caught him climbing up a rusty drainpipe. He said he was a watchman. It was his duty to report Luke to the police. He wouldn't go to prison but he would be prosecuted for trespassing and his parents would have to be told. There was an alternative....

Luke shuddered at the memory of standing in that roofless

ruin with his pants round his ankles and looking down at the man's balding, grey head as he slavered on Luke's cock. It had been horrible at first but he had closed his eyes. That made it much better. He had even promised to return the next day. The man had squeezed his buns affectionately.

"You're a good boy," he said and added, as an afterthought, "You've got a nice fuckable little ass too."

If he hadn't said that, Luke would probably have gone to meet him again. The man had given him a pound. A pound was worth having. Even in those days, Luke was dreaming about owning a car.

The door opened. Luke jumped.

"Er... Lakeside Furniture. We've brought your cubicles," he stammered. Bert clambered out of the cab and took over.

"Hey! That's great!" said the man.

Luke had heard that he was an American. A millionaire according to some.

"Where do you want them?" Bert asked.

"In the great hall. I'll show you." They followed him through the door, down a passage and into the very room in which it had happened. What Luke remembered as a leaf and rubbish strewn concrete floor was now parquet so highly polished that it reflected the huge roof rafters in its surface. There wasn't much furniture; just a few expensive-looking leather sofas along one side. Luke guessed it was used for dancing.

"If it's alright with you, we'll assemble them here, sir," said Bert. "I'll leave my lad here to do that and come back for him later."

"Leave him here as long as you like," said the man. He didn't seem to be in the least distant as Luke imagined a millionaire would be.

He actually helped them unload the three heavy panels and carry them into the hall. "Now just you be careful not to scratch the floor," said Bert.

"Doesn't make any difference," said the man. "Scratches can be polished out."

"Yeah, well, he's a new lad, sir. You make sure he's careful. I'll be back in about an hour for him." Bert touched the oily cap he always wore and left.

"What's your name?" asked the man. Luke told him. The man's name was Darrell Simpson. Darrell J. Simpson to be exact. He was just telling Luke about his company in the United States when the doorbell rang again.

"Richard Loxley," said Mr. Simpson. "Excuse me."

Luke continued to work, joining the panels together. Carefully, he raised the three sided structures and stood inside one to put in the final screws. It was the most extraordinary order the firm had ever received. Thirty booths rather like telephone kiosks, each with a two inch hole in the centre panel three feet from the bottom. The hole had to be absolutely smooth. The man who placed the order was insistent upon that. They need not be painted, the man had said, but each had to have a number on the front.

He crouched down to tighten the screws at the bottom. He heard footsteps. He peered out of the hole in the front. Mr. Simpson was standing in the centre of the room with the man who had placed the order.

"Typically American!" said the younger man. "Think big. Thirty of them - and those holes are far too big."

For a moment Luke panicked. He couldn't afford to lose this job. Bert had said two inches. He hadn't actually looked at the specification himself. Bert wasn't the sort of man to take the blame. It would all be his fault.

"They swell, you know," said the man.

"Yes, but not to that extent. We British are pretty good but we aren't supermen."

"Did you bring the pictures?" Mr. Simpson asked.

"Yes. They're in my briefcase." Luke stood up in the structure and in doing so dropped his screwdriver. "Let's go into the study," said the younger man who seemed suddenly disconcerted at the sound.

Luke finished. He put his tools away and wondered what to do. Should he wait there or outside? Should he tell Mr. Simpson that he had finished? He wandered out into the corridor and stood in front of a mirror. He combed his hair. Bert was always teasing him about his hair. "Hardly worth doing if you haven't got a girl. A good-looking lad like you without a girl! I don't know what the younger generation is coming to." Was he good-looking? Well... perhaps. The teenage spots had gone from his face certainly but he had his doubts.

He heard voices through a closed door on his right. Should he knock and say that he had finished? Perhaps Mr. Simpson ought to check them before he left. Maybe he'd like to make sure there were no scratches in his floor too. Luke put his head against the door.

"We'll have to give him something to stand on. A stool or something." That was Mr. Loxley's voice.

"Yeah. Okay. No problem. Hey! This one is nice. Can't you get any more like that?"

"It isn't easy," said Mr. Loxley. "I'll try but I warn you now, it's going to cost a hell of a lot of money. I'm having to offer two hundred pounds a head and quite a few have said it's not enough."

"Make it two fifty. Make it three hundred. Hell, Richard, make it five hundred if you have to. This is going to be some party. Spend what you like. Just make it good."

"I've only got a fortnight!"

"A what?"

"Two weeks. Fifteen days to be exact."

"Do the best you can. Saturday week."

"What time do you want me here?"

"Get here when you like. I guess we'll need quite a time for preparation and rehearsal. We start at 7 pm. The guy is fixing the cubicles now."

"Yes, I heard him. I'd better get going."

Luke heard the sound of a chair scraping on the floor. Not wanting to be caught listening, he stepped aside rapidly and stood against a massive cupboard. Mr. Loxley came out, closed the door behind him and walked rapidly down the corridor. Luke tapped on the door. "Yeah?" He opened the door and went in. Mr. Simpson was sitting at a huge desk. "I've finished, sir," said Luke. "Do you want to look at them?"

"No. I'm sure they'll be fine."

"And I haven't scratched the floor."

"I'm sure you haven't. Thanks a lot." Luke was about to leave when he spoke again. "Tell me," he said, "Do you do private jobs?"

"How do you mean?"

"Like hanging pictures, a bit of painting, a bit of repairing. Handyman stuff."

"Well I could..."

"If you're too busy, just say so," said Mr. Simpson. "I'd pay well."

"Well, yes. If I can do it."

"I'm sure you can do a hell of a lot. I guess you don't have a business card, eh?"

Luke shook his head. Mr. Simpson took a piece of stiff card from a pile. "Write your name and address on the back of one of these," he said. "I guess we shan't be using all of them."

It seemed a shame to write his name, address and telephone number on the back of a card with gilt edges but he did so and, as he went to hand it over, he dropped it. It fluttered to the floor. He excused himself and picked it up. It had turned over as it fell. On the front, in bold type, he just had time to read: "A TANTALUS PARTY, at the home of Darrell J. Simpson. The Manor House, Cokington. Saturday, 15th July. 7 pm."

Mr. Simpson seemed to want to talk and even offered him a chair but Luke felt uncomfortable to be in those surroundings in overalls. He made his excuses and waited for Bert in the portico.

"What's a tantalus party, Bert?" he asked when he was in the more familiar atmosphere of sawdust and machinery.

"Beats me," said Bert. "Why?"

"Those cubicles are for a tantalus party."

"Sure you got the word right?"

"Quite sure. I read it on an invitation card."

"Well, I know what a tantalus is. We used to make a lot of them in the old days before the firm fell on hard times. It's a gadget to hold drink decanters but it's locked so you can't get at the drink. Sort of teasing. You can see it but you can't get at the drink."

"Perhaps he's going to put drink in it so that people can look at the bottle," said Luke.

"More likely to be diamonds or something like that on velvet cushions," said Bert. "It's a bloody awful design for either. And fancy not having them painted or varnished."

Luke was perfectly certain that he was going to get that job. The firm had charged so much for making them that it was small wonder that Mr. Simpson had decided to use casual labour.

The expected message came the next day. Extraordinarily, Mr. Simpson didn't want any jobs done but said that if Luke felt like using his swimming pool, he was to feel free to do so. Luke thanked him but declined the offer. Then Mr. Loxley rang. Would Luke like to go over to the Manor House one evening for a drink? His mother was probably right. Eighteen-year-old trainee woodworkers didn't drink with millionaires. Luke didn't go.

Saturday, the fifteenth of July was a very hot day. Luke spent it as he spent most Saturdays; playing his records, reading through his collection of automobile magazines and watching television. At about half fast five in the afternoon, he decided to stroll up in the direction of the Manor House, just to see the guests arrive. Their cars, he thought, would be worth seeing. He wondered if the fence was still broken. Fortunately, it was. He clambered through the gap. The area he remembered as being a wilderness was flower beds now. He skirted round them and found himself at the back of the house. He had never seen so many limousines at any one time. It was like being at a show. He was admiring a superb and brand new Mercedes when a hand touched him on the shoulder. He nearly had a heart attack!

"What are you doing here? You should be getting ready." It was Mr. Loxley.

"I... er... I...."

"I would have thought the instructions were plain enough," said the man. "Come with me."

Meekly, Luke followed him into the house, and along a corridor. Mr. Loxley opened a door. "In here," he said. "You're too late to take a shower. Just get undressed as quickly as possible."

Luke couldn't believe his eyes. The room was furnished like a football changing room with a concrete floor and wooden benches. At one end there were shower cubicles. It was full of young men and boys and all were as naked as they day they were born. The steam - laden atmosphere smelt like a perfume shop.

If there was one thing which Luke hated, it was undressing

in front of other people. It had gotten so embarrassing in school that he pleaded with his parents to let him leave at the earliest possible opportunity. He'd never told them why; never mentioned the shouts of "Here comes the elephant!" and "You got a license for that thing?" Worse still, it had a habit of rising at such times. The situation had gotten so serious that just the smell of steam and sweating bodies was enough to make it spring to attention.

"You're late," said a blond-haired young man.

"Yes I sort of got caught up," said Luke. "What's the idea?"

"Search me. Richard will tell us." He uncrossed his legs. Luke caught sight of the biggest cock he had ever seen. It was at least an inch longer than his own and considerably thicker. The young man seemed unconcerned about either his own nudity or its size.

Luke began to undress. Fortunately, nobody seemed to take any notice.

"Is that right that the money has gone up?" somebody asked.

"Four hundred I heard. More if you stay overnight," said another.

"Hmm. I'll see who I get before I decide. It might be an idea. I can get out of this forever then."

"What for?"

"I've had enough. Since I was fifteen I've been a schoolboy in short pants, a gladiator, a Roman slave and God knows what else. I'm fed up with it."

Luke took off the last of his clothes, folded them and sat down, managing to trap his rising cock between his legs as he did so. The door opened and Mr. Loxley came in.

"All here?" he said. "Good."

"Where are the costumes, Richard?" somebody called.

"No costumes. It's a question of come as you are. Don't worry though. Nobody will see your modest blushes. Follow me."

He led them back down the corridor and towards the great hall. Things began to click together in Luke's mind. Cabinets with holes in the front...'Nobody will see your modest blushes'... He caught sight of himself in the same mirror he had used on his first visit. He was blushing slightly. It seemed odd to see pale flesh reflected instead jeans and a shirt, even odder to see it, still half hard, swaying in front of him as he walked. Amazingly, and he couldn't help noticing the fact, one or two of the others were in the same state. He suddenly felt better.

There was one great advantage, he thought. Whatever a tantalus party might be, he wouldn't be recognised by Mr. Simpson. There would be no need to tell lies about why he was there.

"You're to stand in them," said Mr. Loxley, pointing to the cubicles. "Let them hang out of the holes. That's all anyone will see of you. You're not to speak or say anything. In you go. Let's see what it looks like."

Luke followed the others and nipped into the first empty cubicle he could find.

"Right. Let's see them."

He put his penis through the hole.

"Mmmm." said Mr. Loxley. "Get up as close as you can. That's good. Stay like that. No talking, mind."

A door opened. There was a babble of voices and some laughter.

"Hey! That's a sight for tired eyes!" said someone.

"Trust Richard to come up with a good idea." That was Mr. Simpson.

Luke wished he hadn't come and cursed his curiosity. If only he hadn't been so curious! He'd known what he was letting himself in for on the previous occasion in that very room. The sudden friendliness of the 'watchman' and the way he had patted Luke's butt as he led the boy into the ruins had been pretty clear indications of what he had in mind. He wanted to run away.

It was too late now. Surrounded by marine quality four ply secured by screws to substantial battens and with his penis projecting through a hole (chamfered and smoothed and of two inches overall diameter) he was a prisoner in a cell of his own making. Besides, there were men out there on the other side. He couldn't tell how many. Quite a few certainly. But he couldn't see them and they couldn't see him - not all of him anyway. It was just as well Mr. Simpson hadn't ordered clear, plastic cubicles!

Somebody's fingers touched him. He winced. "Substantial,"

said a voice, "but not my taste. He's twenty five at least."

Different fingers wrapped round it. He felt the cold metal of a ring. "Now this, George, is what I call a cock," said a quavering, upper - class, English voice.

"Delighted to see that you've still got your faculties even at your age," said another man.

"Very much so," replied the first man, "but this one is not for me I think. He is a rather ugly boy."

"X-rRay vision too!" said the first. "When did you acquire that gift? On your sixtieth birthday perhaps?"

"There is no need to be bitchy, dear. It doesn't become you. When you've seen as many cocks as I have you get to know what sort of boy goes with a particular cock. This one is short and fat. He has the most ghastly protruding teeth and bad breath. I can guarantee it."

Luke felt himself going red again. This time with anger rather than embarrassment. He would have liked to tell the silly old fool that he was just an inch off six feet, that he weighed a hundred and thirty eight pounds and his teeth were admired by the dentist on every regular inspection. The bony fingers released him and the voices faded as the two of them walked away.

Another hand grabbed him, squeezed him, and was removed. Then another, and another. Bony fingered hands which felt as if a particularly large bird had come to settle on it, younger hands, some soft, others hard and calloused. At any minute, Luke thought, one would come to rest, possibly to masturbate; possibly one of the evil old sods would slobber over it again. The panel which he had sanded down so carefully would be splattered with his semen. Queers were weirdos but four hundred pounds was a hell of a lot of money and at least his contribution would be anonymous.

"Aha! I recognise this one," Another set of fingers wrapped round it. "Young John! Hallo John, it's me, Simon."

Luke said nothing.

"Oh come on, John. You can talk to me!"

Luke stayed silent.

"Please yourself," said the voice. Luke felt his foreskin being pushed back. "Recognise him anywhere," said the man. "Remember the slave party at Anthony's place about two years ago?"

"Of course," said another man.

"That's where I had John. Lovely lad. Nice long hairy legs and very accommodating."

"So are you going to have him again?"

"I think not. I'll stick to that number seventeen. It's always been my lucky number. He'll be gorgeous." The hand ceased manipulating Luke's cock.

Other, cooler fingers wrapped round it; much more gently than the others. Luke felt his foreskin being pulled back. He could hear whoever it was breathing. Not a word was spoken.

"Everybody ready?" Mr. Loxley's voice rang out through the hall. "Good. Number one, you can come out."

There was some applause.

"Number two!"

More applause.

"Number three!"

"I told you I was always right," said a familiar voice.

"Number four!"

Luke was horrified. Did they expect him to get out and stand in front of them in that condition? Surely not! And he had no idea of the number of his booth. It was somewhere in the middle of the line.

"Number five! Number six! Number seven!" and so it continued, sometimes to applause; sometimes to astonished gasps. One boy, number eleven, was greeted with "Oh shit!" What would they say to him? Their voices and their footsteps came nearer and nearer. It was like being on death row, waiting for them to come and get him. His cock subsided as fear gripped him.

Number twelve! Number thirteen! Number fourteen! Number fifteen..... Number fifteen.... Number fifteen!"

"Perhaps he's asleep," said somebody.

"He might be. His cock isn't," said another man. Somebody tapped on the wood. "You can come out now," It was Mr. Simpson's voice!

What to do? Say 'Fuck off!' or plead a headache? Make a run for it? Tell them that it was all a mistake? An expensive mistake. Four hundred pounds was more than he earned in a month at Lakeside. He took a deep breath, stepped backwards and emerged.

Someone gave a long, admiring whistle. Mr. Loxley, in his white tuxedo was standing in the middle of a throng of men, most of whom were clapping. Luke put his hands down to hide his embarrassment. He felt slightly faint. A friendly arm went round his waist.

"I'll be damned!" said Mr. Simpson. "So you managed it after all!"

"With some difficulty," said Mr. Loxley. He stared hard at Luke.

"I'm amazed," said Mr. Simpson. "What would I do without you?"

There was no mistaking the meaning of Mr. Loxley's stare. 'Say nothing' it said.

Mr. Simpson drew Luke closer. The material of his tuxedo felt smooth and cold against Luke's naked flesh.

Behind them the count proceeded. Luke shuddered again.

"You're cold," said Mr. Simpson. "Better get you upstairs."

"If it's alright with you...." said Luke.

"What?"

"Er...I'd rather..." Then the figure 'Four hundred' flashed through his mind. "I'd like a drink first," he said.

"Plenty upstairs. Come on."

A few minutes later, Luke was sitting in a comfortable armchair in a very luxuriously appointed bedroom with a beer in his hand. He felt slightly better.

"I just can't believe it!" said Mr. Simpson. "I tried every known way to get to know you and then you appear. Not only that but I got the lucky number."

Luke took a swig from the can. Some of the beer splashed down on to his front and he shivered again. "Perhaps we were meant for each other," he said. It was a phrase his mother often used and it was only when he said it that he realised how stupid and sloppy it sounded.

"Do you think so, Luke?"

"Could be. I never knew you were gay though."

"It's not a thing to be publicized and you can be sure I'll always protect your reputation. Another beer?"

"Yes please," said Luke. Anything to delay the awful moment.

"In the cabinet by the window," said Mr. Simpson. Luke got up, took a can from the cabinet. Mr. Simpson left the armchair in which he had been sitting and sat on the bed. He patted the quilt. "Come and sit here," he said. "It's more comfortable."

Feeling strangely mesmerised Luke did so, pulled the ring on the can and put it to his lips. So, what of it? he thought as a hand began to glide up and down his thigh and Mr. Simpson began to whisper in his ear. The beer was free and he was going to get four hundred pounds. Why worry?

"Why didn't you come and see me?" asked Mr. Simpson.

"I was busy," said Luke lamely.

"No matter. You're here now. That's the main thing. Good old Richard. That guy is a miracle worker!"

"Actually, Mr. Simpson...." Luke began.

"Call me Darrell."

Luke remembered Mr. Loxley's stare and decided to say nothing.

"I just remembered," he said, "My mother is expecting me home tonight. Maybe I ought to go."

"Like hell. What's her number?" Luke told him. Darrell picked up the phone next to the bed and dialed the number. He explained to an obviously dumbstruck Mrs. Landon that Luke was helping with odd jobs at the Manor House and, with her kind permission, he had offered him a bed for the night.

"There!" he said, putting the phone down. "She seems a nice lady."

"She is," said Luke. "Odd jobs indeed! Odd is the right word!"

Darrell laughed. Then he began to undress. At first Luke averted his eyes but then, aware of the clothes piling up on the recently vacated armchair, he began to take an interest. He liked Darrell's powerful chest and arms. The man's legs, covered with straggly dark hair, were solid looking but of greater interest was his cock; a very big cock, standing out stiffly and pulsating.

"Ready?" he asked.

Luke didn't reply. Mr. Simpson pulled him backwards so that he was lying flat on his back. He concentrated on the elaborately moulded ceiling. His mother had told him what the refurbishment had cost. He couldn't remember the figure but it was a hell of a lot.

Darrell lay on the bed beside him. "Open your legs a bit. That's right," he said. Then, to Luke's amazement, he started to lick him; lick him all over. He felt the man's tongue on his belly, lapping into his navel...moving down.

His heart began to beat faster. That felt nice. A warm, wet feeling enveloped his cock and, for a moment, brought a memory of the old man. That had been different. Darrell was young - quite good-looking too. Was he going to swallow it as the old man had done? Should he warn him when the time came? Fortunately it was some way off yet. It was a nice feeling. He hoped Darrell would...

"Keep going!" He hadn't meant to say it. It just slipped out. He needn't have said it. Darrell's tongue seemed to be working in several places at once. He felt it against his balls. Extraordinarily, his feet came into sight. Had he raised his legs or had Darrell?. Not that it mattered. Nothing mattered. Or did it? "A nice fuckable little ass," the old man had said and that tongue was getting nearer and nearer. It was a nice feeling though. Nothing wrong with a tongue but if Darrell had the same idea as that horrible old man he could think again.

Heavy breathing and little moaning noises seemed to fill the room. For a moment Luke thought they were coming from Darrell. He held his breath. They stopped. He exhaled and, as he did so, experienced a most peculiar feeling. It was as if a great wave of warmth had sucked him under. Something made him squirm. He didn't know what it was but one of the pillows fell onto the floor.

The feeling stopped. He closed his eyes. Something else dropped onto the floor. Then there was a cold feeling. Oh no! He wasn't going to have that!

"No! Oh!"

There was nothing he could do about it. It didn't actually hurt. Not really. It was more uncomfortable than painful. Not painful at all. The sort of feeling you could get used to.... He opened his eyes again. There was a strange geometrical pattern on the ceiling surrounded by a wreath. With a bit of imagination it could be a 'D.' Darrell, surrounded by a wreath. That was a nice thought. The wreath was a continuous, tight oval. Darrell couldn't get out of it.

Something happened. He didn't know what it was. His whole body went tense. His fingers ached as they dug into the bedclothes. A strange sensation ran along his spine to his head. He yelled. Darrell said something but he didn't hear what it was. Darrell was a nice person. Not at all like the dirty old man. Darrell wasn't a dirty old man at all. Darrell was nice. He was gentle. He deserved to have a wreath. He wondered what sort of leaves they were. Enclosing Darrell, wrapping round Darrell, protecting him.

The pain was agonizing – at first. He shouted. He tried to wriggle free but that made it worse. Again, Darrell said something in a soothing voice. It hurt again. He lay still. It wasn't so bad then.... in fact it felt quite nice. A sort of warm, full feeling. A bit like Christmas.... A wreath on the door. Quite unlike the wreath which enclosed Darrell's initial, holding Darrell in.

"Darrell!.... in!" Was that really his voice?

"Darrell! Darrell! Darrell!" He couldn't stop himself. The pattern on the ceiling became a blur and seemed to fade out altogether.

"Darrell! Darrell! Oh! Darrell!"

The man's face seemed to loom out of the mist, framed by a pair of legs. His mouth was wide open and he seemed to be grinning. Luke reached up and grasped the man's shoulders. Darrell was his!

It felt good to be holding on to Darrell. It felt good to have Darrell inside him, pushing that full feeling further and further into him.

"Darrell! Darrell!" he groaned. It was going to happen. There was nothing he could do to stop it. This wasn't the bedroom at home where you could leave off for a few seconds to grope in the dark for a tissue before going on. There was no leaving off here. No tissues either. But why leave off? Who cared?

"I... Oh! Oh! Aaah!" Again that strange feeling in his spine. He shuddered and a warm damp feeling spread over his belly. He was suddenly conscious of strange squishy noises and of Darrell's laboured breathing. He could smell the man's breath. Something happened inside him. A strange feeling as though someone was pushing a wet sponge up there. Instinctively he contracted himself round it to squeeze it dry. Darrell sank down on him and kissed him.

"Jeez! You're good!" said Darrell. Luke felt the wet sponge sliding out of him and a strange, empty, cold feeling took its place.

He had never felt so tired. Every muscle in his body ached. Worse still was the feeling that he had done it. How could he face Bert and laugh at the man's jokes about 'queers' and 'nancy - boys' when he had done it himself? Well.... he hadn't actually done it. It had been done to him. That made him feel better. And why had he allowed it to be done to him? Well, he couldn't very well get out of it and he had earned money...... quite a lot of money. Why else would a person allow that to be done to him?

He felt Darrell's arms go round him. He knew he ought to struggle but he was tired... very, very tired.

It happened again twice. The first time was three o'clock in the morning.

"What's the time?" he murmured sleepily as Darrell's wandering hand woke him.

"Three o'clock. Feel like another one?"

Luke let him. It didn't hurt that time. In fact, he thought afterwards as Darrell wiped the spunk off him, it had been quite nice.

At seven o'clock in the morning, his raised legs framed the sunlit window and he could see the moulding on the ceiling much more clearly. It was nothing like a 'D' he decided, and he tried to study it with detachment as the man pumped away at his ass. There was no doubt that it was a nice feeling. The incident in the ruin had been a nice feeling but this... this was something else.

Darrell finished, panting over his face again. A drop of sweat from the man's brow landed on Luke.

"Jeez! Am I one lucky guy!" he said. He rolled off and lay close to Luke. "And Richard is a genius," he added. "How did he actually persuade you to come."

"It was nothing to do with him," Luke said.

"How so?"

Luke told him the whole story.

"You came here to look at cars?" Darrell asked

incredulously.

"Yes. I'm interested in cars. I thought there would be some good ones."

"Can you drive?"

"Well, yes. I took the test last year but I can't afford one of my own."

Darrell put a hairy arm round his waist. "You can now," he said.

"How do you mean?"

"On Monday morning, we're going out to buy you a car."

"Do you mean that? You're not just saying it?"

"I never say anything I don't mean. How much do they pay you in that crummy firm?"

Luke told him.

"And you've gotten yourself a job too. If you want it, that is."

"What sort of job?"

"Chauffeur and handyman to Darrell J. Simpson. How does that sound to you?"

"It sounds brilliant. Er... what does the 'handyman' bit entail?

Darrell chuckled and hugged him tight. "Just being handy and doing odd jobs in the daytime," he said, "and possibly a bit of screwing at night. What do you say?"

"Yes please," said Luke happily, and for the first time in his life, he kissed a man. "Er, you'd have to provide the tools," he said.

"Is one enough?"

Luke reached down to feel it. "Oh, more than enough!" he said.

MISSING YOU

John Patrick

You are right on time. Walk in and look around, smile when you see me, come to the table, slid into the booth.

"Hi," you say, your eyes avoiding mine.

You touch your fingers to the menu, and the waitress comes right over. You order coffee and pie, pecan pie. We always used to come here for the pie. You love pecan pie.

But still, you have to ask the slutty, peroxided blonde waitress if it is good. My teeth are clenched so tight they hurt, watching you smile at that cheap bitch, play with her, flirt. She takes your menu, turns, and leaves, and you look at me, waiting for me to speak. I am biting on the inside of my mouth, trying to get control, not wanting to cry.

"You're disgusting," I mutter, finally.

"What?"

"You and pussy."

You glare at me. "*What?*"

Something snaps inside me. "You never change."

"*What?*"

"You know what I'm talkin' about! I'm talkin' about you and *pussy*."

You gulp. "Why did you invite me here?"

"To see you. I miss you."

"Look, Jeff, I've got obligations now."

"Of course. And how is the new Mrs. Andersen?"

"She's fine."

"You're happy then?"

"Sure."

Yeah, sure. But I knew that if you accepted my invitation to meet me over pie and coffee, you couldn't be all *that* happy.

The pie and coffees arrive. You flirt with the waitress again. She's smitten with you, like everyone.

I sip my coffee while you enjoy the pie. You eat the whole piece without stopping. When you are done, you push the plate away and wipe your fingers with your paper napkin.

"Man, that's the best damn pecan pie in the world!"

"Glad you enjoyed it."
"You know what else I'd enjoy?"
Suddenly you are all sweetness and light. Must have been the pie.
"But I don't have a pussy."
Your eyes search mine, concerned, as if I have lost my mind, as if *I* was the one. I sit here shock-still.
"C'mon, let's go back to your place."
"You're crazy," I say. The waitress won't leave us alone for a second; she re-fills our coffees. I put my paper napkin in my water glass and wipe my face, trying to get control of myself.
"Well, thank you, sweetheart," you say to the waitress. "That was just fine." She smiles back, pleased you're happy. Then she walks away. She never glances my way. Not once!
"I love Rita and the baby," you say, quietly. You put your coffee cup down. Something about the set of your shoulders scares me. I don't know what it is, but I can feel something happening that I can't stop. Tears are blurring everything. I want to touch your hand, but I don't. I pick up my car keys. They are making a racket, my hand is shaking so. I stand up. Your big dark eyes stay right on mine. My knees are trembling.
"Well, let's go then," I say.

In my car, you say, "I never said I was perfect. Never." A little smile crosses the corners of your mouth. You put your hand over my fingers that are clutching at the wheel, pat my fingers with your hand, and then push down on them tight. I try to pull my hand out from under you, but you won't let me. Like when I was a kid playing that game where you slide your hand out from under the other person's, only you would grab mine, hold on to it until you'd hurt me, until you'd make me yell.
"I'm gonna fuck the hell out of you today. You fuckin' deserve it." Your fingers are white on mine, you are pushing down so hard. My lip catches on my tooth; I am trying not to cry out. I want you so badly, sweat stands up on my face.
"What do you mean, Stefan?" I say.
You are breathing hard. "Keeping me waiting six months for it."
"But you're a married man now."

"So?"

I don't answer you. I have no answer. If it doesn't make any difference to you, why should it to me? You take your fingers away and begin massaging my thigh.

I start the car. "You said you'd given up things like that."

You sigh. "The way I look at it, what she don't know won't hurt her."

I want to go into my rant about "but what about me?" but I can't, not now. I want you too much to let anything change what is about to happen.

You have had me right where you want me. You were my first. Most people lose touch, forget, move on. But not us. You wouldn't let me. There were always girls but I could handle it, because you always came back. But then there came that night you didn't.

"You've played hard to get right from the start," you go on, reminiscing again. It's always turned you on to remember it, so I let you go on.

. . .

Jeff had a certain appeal that fascinated me for several months before I first let him suck me off. He had just moved into the neighborhood and I said to my football squad teammates that if Jeff were a girl, I'd be in love. They all laughed.

Jeff did act kinda nellie, but that was his charm for me. He was everything I thought a gay kid was. He was pretty, short, soft, sang in the school chorus, kinda swished when he walked. And he wore tight, tailored clothes, pants which accentuated his ass. I had never noticed another guy's ass before, and I couldn't explain why it turned me on, seeing Jeff's ass, but it did.

One night we were all over at Rosie's house. Everybody was invited, including Jeff, since Jeff was Rosie's new best friend. I was sitting with my football teammate Bud at a table next to the pool table watching the object of my secret crazy desire play pool. He was incredible! I asked Rosie where the kid learned to play like that. She said his father bought him a pool table when he was very little and he'd discovered something he could do without leaving the house. And something he could play by himself. He and Rosie often had matches that lasted all night. In between Jeff's pool shots Bud was calling him names. Bud was a genius at creating scenes and this was to be his biggest triumph. He was making lewd remarks about how Jeff used his "stick" and on and on.

Watching the tip of his cue while he chalked it with detachment, Jeff answered, "What'd you say, Bud?"

"I said, I've been wondering if you've had any other experience getting in holes," Bud prodded.

"I'll bet more than you, Bud," Jeff kidded back.

I laughed, much too loudly, trying to ease the tension that seemed to be developing between them. Finally, my gang left the party, but not before I took Jeff aside and made a date for the next night, to go over to his house and shoot some pool. Of course, pool was the last thing I wanted to shoot.

We went into the basement where he had his pool table. We shot a game and he let me beat him. He said he couldn't concentrate. I said I understood, and trapped him between the wall and the table, forcing his hand down onto my bulge.

He opened my belt buckle, then one by one undid the buttons of my jeans. My breathing became deep and labored – I knew what would happen next. My cock was only slightly exposed in the process, but finally my jeans were opened enough to let Jeff get closer to his goal.

The first touch was electric and resounded throughout the room as I moaned, even as my mind cried out against this perversion. I had learned early on the value of a hot moment, and this was supremely simple and erotic. There had been no preparation or elaborate talk – this was pure surrender. Jeff was absorbed by the hugeness of my erection and my writhing body. I was doing battle with myself. A battle I knew I would lose, but I couldn't live with myself if I didn't fight. As Jeff pulled my cock completely from my jeans and began fondling my balls, my body became stronger in its demand for the pleasure and release the kid could give it. Jeff kissed the head, licked the shaft, then began. Passion mounted as he began moving back and forth – in and out.

When he pulled it all the way out, my cock glistened in the light. I watched the throbbing hardness with new interest. I had never seen my cock adored this much. No girl had ever sucked it, really sucked it, at least not like this. I bit my lip trying to contain my moans. My hand crept around to Jeff's skull and dug in for the physical support I was going to need. Suddenly I exploded with a screaming, godless orgasm. I all but doubled over with the force of it.

"Ohhh, Jeff. Oh, damn you," came my hoarse curse.

Jeff ignored me and kept on, holding me tight as I caught my breath and recovered from the assault.

I knew Jeff had a good memory and he would play this scene out in his mind again and again, jerking off to the thought of it day after day.

Me, I had to have more of the real thing. The next day, we were at it again. Jeff just slurped my entire cock into his mouth and then settled down to work on it for a good long time.

I tried to hold on to my erection as long as possible, and Jeff helped by varying his speed and strength, and the motions of his head. He finally let it come, shooting so hard I couldn't even keep my head up. His sucking, swallowing mouth gently surrounded my glans, licking, finally letting the cock fall slowly back against my thigh. "I could really get used to this," I told him.

And I did get used to it. I'm not sure how many times Jeff blew me. I remember I was reluctant every time. I had my upbringing in America to overcome. My relatives back in Europe have a different attitude, and they had tried things with me whenever I would visit. In their view, "sex is just sex." As much as I liked that idea, doing anything at home made me nervous. Jeff helped me overcome it by saying it was our secret; no one would ever know.

The place for our sex was always the same: in the basement at his folks' place, where Jeff had his pool table. I knew we were going to do it beforehand, of course, but I never acted as if I was eager for it, although I was.

It amused me how Jeff wore this mask of innocence so that his parents would not become suspicious. I didn't feel comfortable when Jeff's father was in town and watching TV in the living room above us. I sensed he was curious why a jock was hanging out with his fruity son.

"We'll have to hurry now," Jeff said one night, and he took

me downstairs, which was dark except for the light over the pool table. We didn't even shot a game. He went right to his knees in front of me, shoving my pants around my ankles. I was quickly aroused and then Jeff stood and revealed himself to me for the first time. He had a nice cock, average in size, but it was his ass that he wanted to show me. Although it was his ass that had attracted me initially, I had forgotten about it, so entranced was I by his skill as a cocksucker.

He stepped over to a table and got some grease. He turned towards me while he applied some lube to his fingers and then began fucking his asshole with them. "I want you to try this," he said.

"Have you ever – ?" I asked, stroking my erection.

"Yeah, a couple of times. But they weren't as big as yours."

I had never thought my cock was anything special until Jeff started playing around. I liked the way he made me feel. He held my pulsing cock and bent his knees just a bit, parting the lips of his asshole. I rubbed my cock up and down his asscrack for a while, almost staggering, until he leaned over, bracing himself on the pool table.

I'd fucked maybe a dozen girls, usually in my car in one of several secluded places around town, but this was like the time I fucked Chrissie in the woods. Jeff turned to look at me over his shoulder, and snarled, "Stick it in!" He reached between his legs, grabbed my penis by its length, hung on to it as he felt it slide into him without stopping. I held his buttocks and I moved into him. He welcomed me by squeezing my cock inside of him. We gasped together. I folded my arms around his waist, drawing his arched back into my stomach. My teeth found the back of his neck. He flexed all at once and then began to change the tempo, coming back to meet my thrusts with such determined force that I had to step back to brace myself. He pounded back into me and began to moan. Then I convulsed, my belly slipping on his now sweaty back, gasping. He'd taken more than I ever knew I had.

I pulled out and leaned back against the table. In my thick sensual stupor, I couldn't resist him sucking my cock again, stroking my thighs. I could feel my cock, still slick from before, begin to throb heavily once more. He turned and bent forward slightly, rubbing his ass against my groin, and I could feel, with each movement, my cock growing harder. I put my arms around his waist, and pushed my crotch deeply against his ass. My hands worked their way upward, starting at his thighs, moving across his pubes, over his smooth stomach, to his taut nipples. I rubbed his nipples until he let out a deep moan, and his knees buckled.

I lifted him up and turned him around to face me. I smiled at him, then pulled him to my chest and kissed him. I don't know what possessed me to do that, but I was treating him as if he was a girl and I loved kissing my girlfriends. He kissed me back, but it was a brief kiss, broken as I gently eased him down to the cold concrete floor.

Crouching on top of him, sweaty and feverish, I stroked my cock. He took my balls in his hand and began to nibble on the tip of my cock. I moaned as he eased it deep into his mouth, and shouted when he suddenly shoved the last few inches in and gave me a tremendous upward suck. My body shook as he licked the exposed base of my dick with his tongue. I straddled his face with my legs while he continued sucking hard on my cock and fondling my balls. He twitched as my fingers massaged his asshole and then entered it, slowly, surely forcing their way inside. He threw his pelvis onto my fingers, grinding himself against them, and let out a little cry. I pushed him away and positioned him on all fours, spreading his legs from behind.

Holding my cock in my hands, I rubbed the head in the asscrack. Jeff was shaking with pleasure as I inserted the first several inches of my dick with a slow, deft push. Inch after inch poured into him, not stopping until my bush was against his ass. I began to fuck him, retreating and entering in long motions, my balls slapping against Jeff's butt as I pumped, the fingers biting into his skin where I held his thighs.

I thrust harder, forcing my cock deep into his asshole, pulling almost all of the way out before sinking in again. Then I rolled him over and knelt between his thighs and pulled his legs up over my shoulders.

As I shoved into him, Jeff cried out in pain. The thick shaft tore at his insides, and he started to cry. He looked up at me and his blue eyes remained clear and bright, even as I plowed into the tender ass beneath me. I touched his face, let him take my hand, suck my fingers. He spread his legs wider to give me better access, and, a few moments later, I came deep inside him. I kissed him again, taking him in my arms and rolling on the cold floor with him, my cock still in him. I started fucking him again but I could tell I was hurting him, so I pulled out and lay quietly beside him.

"I remember when I was a little kid, I saw a bunch of the older kids in a circle in the playground. I went over to see what they were doing." Jeff got up on one elbow to listen. "There was this big beetle. The kids were poking it with a stick. The bug just kind of curled up to protect itself."

Jeff snorted, "God knows I been poked with enough sticks."

I smiled, then kissed him on the forehead, as if he is one of my girlfriends.

"God," he went on, "by the time you're really old enough to have sex, we're already fucked, you know what I mean?"

I shrugged. No, I didn't know what he meant.

He smiled about this little secret, the one we have kept. Then he began licking me, slowly, teasingly, moving in small circles with his lips and tongue, his kisses pelting me, gentle as the rain that had started to fall outside.

. . .

I had gone to Catholic schools until my father was transferred and we moved into your neighborhood. If truth be known, my father had asked for the transfer, and he understood it would be best that I attend public school. We had left a scandal behind, or what would have become a scandal if they had not sent Father John away to a place where he could be "rehabilitated." I laughed at that, sensing he loved it too much to ever want to give it up. And there were others, too. I had been passed from priest to priest and even a few lay brothers. I was godless, they said, and everyone had to try to save me. For me, it is a simple journey from religious to sexual ecstasy.

After the move, we stopped going to church altogether and I was struggling with my emerging gay identity in those days, desperate for an older brother or a friend in whom I could confess my secrets as I had done to my priests. I began to fantasize that you were just like me, that because you loved fucking me that you were gay. Shows you what I know.

You fucked me for over a year before you met Rita. In all that time, no one found out about us. There were a couple of close calls, but for the most part it was a blissful time.

Now we are back in the basement, the little place where we have made love so often, and you say you want to play a game of pool. I go to the bathroom. When I come back you're standing next to the table, jacking off. I knew pool was the last thing on your mind.

"You're beautiful," I say reflexively before I really look at you. You grin, keep jacking off.

Now I stare at you. You are quite a beauty, though not in the way I have learned about beauty from the gay magazines. You are dark, your nose in crooked, your eyes heavy-lidded. And your penis is uncut. Maybe that's why I find it so exotic, so sublime. Certainly it was the biggest cock I have ever sucked. You have grown a lot of pubic hair, which is lustrous and coarse, and suddenly I bury my face in it and you give a surprised, pleased cry. I suck you for a good ten minutes before I hear you say, "Now, let me see you. See if you've grown any."

I stand and you motion me away a few steps. "There," you say, as though I have found center stage. "Go ahead," he says. "Pull 'em down."

I am a little embarrassed, but I quickly get out of my clothing. I stand before you, a little chilly, looking down at myself, then over at your incredible cock, which looks bigger than ever.

"You're beautiful, too," you say, and I can tell that you mean it. "For a boy." You have to add that. I understand that.

What I can't understand is why, when I'm on my knees and about to slip your cock in my mouth, you push me away.

You look at me as if I am a stranger, as if you hate me. I feel your anger like a physical blow. I shake, watching as you jerk your shorts on, tearing them in your haste. You look at me once more, your expression gentling as you see my hurt and confusion. "It's not you, Jeff...it's my fault. I shouldn't have tried this."

I start to cry, and you stand still. "Oh, god, don't do that."

I can't speak. I feel so stupid, kneeling here, my cock losing its hardness, tears streaming down my face.

"Oh, fuck!" you scream. You take my hand, none too gently, and with hardly any effort lift me up and lay me across the pool table.

As your body covers mine, I feel the thrill of our two cocks pressed together. Your lips find mine. You suck deeply at my mouth while your hands reach up to gently stroke my hair. Tugging on my hair, you pull my head back to expose my neck. Those big, soft lips devour the tender flesh of my neck and ears as they travel all over my body – slowly moving down to kiss and suck my chest, my nipples, my armpits. Your hands and lips seem to be everywhere as they burn a trail across my yearning flesh, the weight of your body keeping me pinned helpless beneath you. One hand works its way down beneath my balls and into the sweaty hollow between my asscheeks. Your fingers probe my hole.

Without warning you shove two fingers deep in my asshole. At the shock of the penetration, my body arches up – lifting us both off the pool table.

In an instant you tear your mouth from mine as your head dives between my legs. I am stunned as your tongue replaces your fingers as you roughly push yourself deep into my aching hole. You are using me as you would Rita's pussy, and I don't mind a bit.

You stand, strip off your shorts. Now wearing nothing but the smell of your sweat, your cock is hard again, ready for me, as if it has nothing to do with your brain. My hips shift so slightly and my heart beats so fast. How I have waited for this! You are perfect, physically at least.

You love my low moans, my sighs, my silent mouthing of your name with my head thrown back, loving it as you make yourself comfortable between my thighs. And I won't disappoint you today. No sense arguing anymore. No sense at all. You are the most beautiful man ever created. In fact, now, after six months apart, you are even more beautiful than I remember, if that is possible. There's not an ounce of fat on your six-foot frame. Lifting all those cartons every day at your father's wine shop must agree with you. I'll admit that you put on a few pounds while you were away, flunking out at college, only learning how to fuck better, as you used to say, not that you needed to know anything about that. Yes, all that fat is gone now; in fact, you've added some definition in six months.

Six months! Why did you make me wait so long? This is the driest spell we've ever had. Of course, I wasn't faithful. Not completely. I don't want to tell you how many times I've said your name as others have moved against me, slid it into me, drove their cocks into my ass. But they don't count. Not really. The last one was taller than you, a bear of a man really. I knew he was following me, but I didn't speed up. I let him catch up with me at the corner. He smiled and led the way. I followed him to an open garage. When he got out of his pick-up, I saw he was wearing tight blue jeans and black boots. He had a tremendous bulge at the crotch. I wanted him so bad.

I smelled old oil, gasoline, dust and the sweat under his arms. He was rough with me. I knew he would be. I could tell by the way he drove his pick-up. It's what I wanted. What I needed after you got married and said you couldn't see me anymore. He shoved me all the way to the back and slammed me, face down, onto the hood of an old Ford station wagon. He pulled my pants down, down to my ankles. I wasn't wearing any underwear; my ass was bare. He spread my legs with the toe of his boot. He unbuttoned his jeans and laid his cock inside the crack of my ass. Pre-cum dripped down from his cock hole onto my pants.

He spread my cheeks and tried to push his dick into me, but it was too tight and too dry. His dick wouldn't go in, not even the tip. He spit in the crack, then on his cock. He tried a finger. Then two. Finally he jammed his cock into me, hard. His cock was not as big as yours, of course, but it was big, and I felt as if I was being ripped apart. I whimpered. He slapped his hand over my mouth and pulled me up to his chest. Sweat dripped off his forehead onto my face. "Quiet, asshole. We have to be quiet."

He started to groan like he was about to come. I felt him pull out. Warm cum shot onto my ass and dripped onto my trousers. But he was not through. He started again.

God, it was incredible; the second fuck was even more savage than the first. When he began that now-familiar groaning, I reached down and jacked off. This time he came inside me, pulled out and left me in the garage. I pulled myself together as best I could. I stood, trembling from the shock of it. I pulled my pants up and buttoned them. I stumbled out to the street, to my car.

A couple of days later, I drove by the house and the garage door was closed. I did see him, though, mowing the lawn. His wife and two kids were playing in the yard. I slowed down, but I didn't stop.

Oh, but you're making up for it now, you gorgeous stud, shoving that nine-incher into my face, making me lift up to lick it, fondle the balls while I begin to suck. You position a pillow from the old couch behind my head. I know what is coming: You're going to fuck my face first. Today you'll probably even come, then want me to keep sucking till you're hard again, and I won't mind. Not a bit.

Oh, yeah, hold my head as you slide it in. God, I've missed it. It tastes so good. I chew on the foreskin. Now I'm sorry I've cheated on you. I remember when I admitted the long affair with the man who owned the florist shop where I worked after I graduated from high school, but you forgave me the moment I opened my mouth. You said all the practice blowing the boss had made me even better.

Yeah, that's it, get good and hard. Rita doesn't do this, I know. And even if she did, it wouldn't be the same.

Oh, don't come, not so soon! Oh, shit!

There, I swallowed it all. Make you happy?

I love it when you move down there and stick those fingers in. You don't have to prepare it, but you like to anyway. Yes, three fingers. Yes, yes.

You're hard again – it's just fantastic, that cock of yours. You guide it in, right to the edge of its head. It is only just inside my sloppy ass. Then out again. Then a little further in. I don't move. Now it's coming again.

We lie down on our side, with the prick still in. We turn round so I lie below, with my legs together, and your legs on each side of me, almost sitting up. I lift myself up a little. I press my ass up towards the prick. I screw it firm with thighs and muscles. The whole time soft, and hard. We can keep on. I want to feel you. I get a hand in and hold two fingers to the underside of the prick, just at the root, where the balls knock at each movement. I take hold of the hot, sticky tube, under the skin, where now, and now, the semen passes and plunges into my ass, far inside me. I have to scream. I too come. We can breathe again. I try to get up, but I can't. My legs shake under me. You get up, staggering.

Still, you want more. I lift up my legs. Right up to my neck. My asshole is open, right in front of the eye of an enormous prick. A drop of cum emerges from the crack in the prick-head and falls straight down into the asshole, which is wet itself. The asslips close around the falling drop and your cock throbs as it moves toward the target. Then you push it down into me in one movement, right to the bottom. It does not move but is so big that my ass is almost splitting. I am almost out of my mind.

After you fuck me for a few minutes, we roll on our sides, my ass against your groin. I lift my leg, as I love to do. You take hold of your prick and rub it along the crack. This will have to be the last one. Your wife will be holding dinner.

I tug at your prick. It stands up at once, and I sit up on it. I feel as if it's the last time in my life I'm going to be fucking. It's the last chance, I think, and slam down hard on the prick. You grab my buttocks with your calloused hands and massage them like balls. I shall come soon. I can feel it. You scratch my back with your nails. That's just what it needed. Now I come. You kiss, suck on my neck as I come. Gobs of cum.

You lift me off and up on my knees and enter me again.

You are merciless as you shove it in, completely savage now, desperate for it.

I grab your balls from below. And hold on to them so hard you have to yell.

You tear at my ass. It hurts.

You scratch my back and my sides. You hold on to my hips, lift up my ass, and shove it in all the way. When you come, you howl.

You ask if you can take a shower.

I tell you my mom is upstairs, somewhere. You understand and do the best you can in the lavatory I helped my father build in the basement.

You stand hard by the door and thank me for the pie and coffee. I laugh. You laugh.

I start to tell you how beautiful you are, and much I love

you, but I stop myself.

It is late. I lie in the jumble of my filthy sheets. I am alone again, but filled with you. I no longer miss you. You are gone, but you are coming back. Everything will be all right.

From now on I will say that to myself every morning when I wake up, missing you.

STRIP BOY

Dan Veen

It's closing time and here I am naked in the elevator of this office building.
Totally, completely, stark, buck naked.
They will ask me what I'm doing here, naked in an elevator like some orgiastic bellboy.
Thanks to Tom, my humiliation doesn't soften my hard-on. In fact this is my most intense hard-on since I met Tom at the New York Public Library. It aches. God, how it aches at the thought of being discovered here. Some business-suited executive, working late, leers at my helpless hard-on. He gets ideas. Or a security guard making his rounds. Maybe he'll take me back to the office. *Looky what I found here, boys! Wonder what he wants?* A little pink naked surprise for the night crew to screw.
They will ask me what I'm doing here, how I got this way, naked in a public elevator with my hard cock dripping pre-cum on my bare feet.
They will ask me and I will have to tell them about Tom.
I'll have to tell how I met Tom at the New York Public Library. How, in the middle of my student paper on nuclear fission, we both reach for the same encyclopedia.
"Nudist culture," Tom winks. "Sort of a hobby."
I should run. I should run, but I'm already making sort of a hobby of Tom, already undressing Tom with my eyes. Tom has that look of clothed nudity. The fact that Tom is wearing no belt makes him seem half-undressed.
Tom starts talking about nude beaches. Skinnydipping. *Der Nacktkultur.* Nude sunbathing. Nude volleyball. Nudist colonies. Naked fraternity initiations. Tom shows me a Polaroid of a naked Asian pledgeboy being made to sit in a tub of icecubes.
My face...warms.
Tom says how it's a scientific fact that when you blush, only your unclothed body parts redden.
Tom is in his mid-thirties with sun-gilded hair and a bronze

body you just know shows no tan seam. I easily picture Tom surfing naked, basking over my blushing body. Tom's peach-fuzz arm chairs, sugared with yellow sand, radiate with solar energies. In Tom I see nude beaches aswim with robust waves of blonds. Randy fauns frisk in ripe forests, pagan rites of spring pulse in Tom's pants. But –

"I've never had the nerve," I mumble.

"It doesn't take nerve." Tom punctures my politeness. "It takes balls." And when I smile bashfully, Tom says: "It takes...desire."

Desire.

That word. Desire. As if Tom photocopied my lewd thoughts. Desire paralyzes me there at the Reference Desk.

"Maybe you'd make a good strip boy." I hear Tom say.

Strip boy?

It is the first, but not the last, time I will hear the phrase.

Strip boy.

It sounds like some exotic Mediterranean island. But it is in no almanac. I know what it means, this 'strip boy', and yet I don't. It can't possibly mean what I think it might possibly mean, can it? The words, half-commanding, part-descriptive, hang upon Tom's lips. My body reads Tom's lips. My nipples stand attentive beneath my shirt. My balls get restless. My cock prods me.

"What's a...strip boy?"

Tom smirks, as if I'm hopelessly naive. "Well if you have to ask," and seems to turn away.

"No. I'd – " For a chance at Tom's cock, I'd be anything, anything Tom wants. Cocksucker.

Buttpunk.

Bootlick.

Asswipe.

Strip Boy.

"I'd like to know. No kidding. What's a strip boy?"

"Nah. It's not for you. You seem like the shy type."

He's getting away. Tom's door is shutting! I have to stick my foot in.

"*Please*."

The magic word. My imploring, needy tone pricks Tom's attention.

"Please tell me," I beg-whisper for Tom's raw forbidden knowledge.

Tom looks me over, looks through me, inside me. Reads me like a cheap paperback.

"Maybe I'll *show* you," Tom threatens.

With a mischievous glint in his eye and a lump in his pants, Tom leads me to the third level of Periodical Storage -- a hushed labyrinth of magazines lighted like some seedy basement bar.

"So you want to be my strip boy?"

"Well, sure." I make my pact with blond Satan. Anything, my soul, for this man now.

"So strip." Tom crosses his arms, looks down at me. "Strip...*boy*."

"Here? Now?" I check over my shoulder.

Tom rolls his eyes. *Amateurs.* Starts to leave.

"Wait." I start.

I unbutton.

My shirt comes off before I know it. Anything to recapture Tom's attention.

Unbuckling.

Unfastening.

Disrobing.

Stripping.

My mind unbuckles too.

A memory unzips of the time I was accidentally locked in my junior high school after-hours. I stood alone under the fluorescent lights of that long empty hallway where hundreds of students gathered in the normal course of the day. Now here I was in this empty school building. The urge to strip naked overwhelmed me. I shucked free my clothes. I felt...brand new. I felt free. I felt raunchy. Naked, I ran from one end of the echoing hall to the other, confident no one monitored my jubilant body.

Naked, I streaked past the windows.

Naked, I sat upon the water fountain where a thousand students bowed their heads and sucked during the day.

Naked, I let the cool water lick at my balls.

Naked, I sprinted up the stairs, slid down the banisters, my thrill-hardened cock flapping rebelliously.

What my teachers and classmates would say if they knew! Right by Billy Mullinix's locker I squatted, naked, and I jerked off, inhaling the scents of Billy's sweaty jockstraps. My cum splashed all over Billy's locker door. After that afternoon of my naked romp through the school, I got hard whenever I looked at Billy Mullinix, or whenever I saw my dried cumstains on Billy's locker. When I saw Billy drinking from the water fountain, I thought of Billy's tongue lapping at my balls and asshole.

So I had a talent for being a Strip Boy, even in junior high, and I didn't realize it!

Forget nuclear fission – I've found my calling.

My hard-on is now free of my undershorts. My clothes lay scattered upon the library floor.

Anybody can come along here at any minute and catch me standing here, buck naked, cowering under the gaze of this commanding, superior blond giant. My hard-on is raging red, blushing with the galvanized electric embarrassment of my forced humiliation.

I have never been this naked before. Here in public, where any taxpayer can see me, stripped by Tom's command, I am naked to my very core.

"Not bad for a virgin strip boy." Tom pets my cock. Tom can hide my cock with one large palm of his, his caress a momentary figleaf for my prick.

"Please," I whimper. "Can I please get dressed now?"

People are walking all around us in the stacks. Aisles of eyes.

"Fuck no, Strip Boy. Not yet you can't."

Tom is holding me and my throbbing cock in the palm of his hand. He is rubbing the flanged netherside of my cock gently with his lifelines.

"I'd like you to fetch me a magazine, Strip Boy."

"Please, Tom – " I'm like a fidgeting schoolboy dreading discipline.

"Fetch me a copy of "Outdoorsman Monthly." It's just down that aisle. The June issue."

"Like...this?"

"Of course. That's the only way natural for a good Strip Boy." Tom molds the front of his pants with his hand. His thick crease of cockmeat shows. "And you do want to be my

Strip Boy, don't you?"

"Yes." I swallow, "I want to be your Strip Boy."

Stealthily – a wild animal loose from the zoo – I pad down the aisles.

Someone approaches, one row away, pauses, passes. Secret-bright, I hold my breath, my hand covers my red-hard pee-pee. I sidestep into the stacks, then scurry to fetch the magazine back to Tom.

"Very good." Tom accepts my offering with a superior sneer. "Maybe you will make a good Strip Boy. With a little more practice. Now you can jerk off while I read."

He spits on my prick.

My prick can't wait. On my knees before Tom, admiring Tom's crotch, I writhe and scour my cock – a sizzling firecracker ready to blow. I try to perform for Tom, humping the cold floor, bruising my flopping balls. When I shoot, my cream spatters. Jism saturates my wadded up clothes. My draining cum leaves me a wriggling quivering shell, hunching the air and drooling spastically. Tom watches my cumshot like I'm a horny monkey spurting my jizm-load.

The fireworks clear. Tom is already striding down the stacks, leaving me to wallow in the aftermath of my depravity. But I must have more, more of Tom, more of Tom's kind of degradation and debasement, so I hurry to dress. I follow Tom out to Fifth Avenue in my cum-slimed clothes.

Tom barely acknowledges me, as if he knows I will tag eagerly upon his heels, craving more intense mistreatment.

Get in the car, Tom tells me.

"Now take your clothes off." He says matter-of-factly, as if he were telling me to fasten my seatbelt.

"Dammit, Tom, why can't we have a normal tawdry fling like everyone else?"

But Tom's silence shuts me up.

Tom's eyes are on the street, speeding down the Queensborough Bridge out of the city.

I fumble out of my clothes – these things that separate me and Tom. Hot vinyl seats sizzles my buttcheeks.

"Your shorts, Strip Boy." Tom demands, concentrating on the expressway.

"What about my shorts?"

Tom holds his hands out, ready to confiscate them.
I struggle free of my shorts. Cars are verging all around us -- drive-by spectators to my unwilling striptease. Kids peer out of rear windows. Truckers leer down from their eighteen-wheelers.
I surrender my shorts to Tom.
Tom throws my shorts out the car window.
"Hey!"
No use. They are gone, shed with any remaining dignity I might've had.
"You know I could put you out right here, Strip Boy." Tom is yelling over the rushing wind, jettisoning the rest of my clothes out the window. "It's a long walk back to NYU, college boy. Mmm, maybe if you shake that fine pink ass of yours somebody might be tempted to give you a lift."
Tom grins. I am trapped. Tom fingers my goosebumpy balls between my legs.
A busload of Japanese tourists rolls by us, Nikons clicking. I want to disappear in my seat. But my hard-on has become more obvious than ever. There's no hiding its red and waxy stiffness. Tom clutches my dick like a stickshift, bending it back and forth as he accelerates down the expressway.
"Rubbers are in the glove compartment." Tom finally says. I shiver at what's coming while he drives his finger up into my asshole.
A fifty-five mile-an-hour fuck is what's coming. He skewers me with his finger and tells me to fish his cock out of his fly with my tongue.
"Get it wet, Strip Boy. Suck it good. Lick that rubber on it." He smacks my ass, gropes it and splits my buns apart, shows my hole to the drivers in the next lane, shows how his big finger slides in my asshole to the knuckle.
He pulls me up for a breather. His cock vibrates and glistens with my spittle.
"Time to fill in your pothole!" He spanks me. "Now squeeze in here, Strip Boy. That's it. Get your ass up on this cock. Spread those legs and open your ass wide for my cock. Slide down on it."
Tom eases me down onto his lap, fitting his cock into my ass socket like a hot-wired spark plug. He loves fucking me on the

road. Pressed against the hot steering wheel, I feel his cock revving up into my naked ass while he tools up into my chocolate highway.

"Just relax and let me drive," Tom pumps his thick dick into me and tweaks my tits. "Don't worry, I've done this *lots* of times before. Hell, one time I fucked one of my Strip Boys from here on down to Miami! You should've seen him squirm every time I shot off into his ass, I didn't take my dick out of him once!"

Tom has me pinned and cumming all over the front seat. By the time we reach Queens, I am getting turned on being Tom's public plaything. I love being his dickhole. My cum shoots all across the dashboard. Tom stops the car by the roadside. He makes me get out and lick the windshield off with my tongue.

"That's right! Let'em see that hot ass I just fucked! Better'n a carwash!" Tom says, re-stuffing my mouth with his cock.

Tom drops me off at my apartment. He leaves me to fend for myself. Tom doesn't care if I spend the night hiding naked in the bushes. I don't know how I get in my bathroom window without the neighbors calling the cops. Relieved as I am to be back in the safety of my apartment, it seems claustrophobic now. None of my clothes fit. I try to sleep naked. But I can't sleep. Not with this unbearable throbbing erection. I stand in the window, cock in hand, hoping some Peeping Tom, maybe *my* peeping Tom, is watching.

Why am I the willing slave of another man's fantasy? Am I really some guy's Strip Boy? Some sex toy made to strip whenever and wherever Tom pleases?

When Tom pulls up in his car the next day, I know my answer is yes.

Tom orders me never to buy new clothes. I can wear whatever I already own, but I am never to add to my wardrobe. Why would I need clothes, when Tom makes me take them off as soon as he sees me? And that is every day now. Hurrying to meet him in front of Grand Central Station, I look up at the golden naked Mercury, God of Tourists and Strip Boys everywhere. The minute I see Tom he orders me to throw away my last pair of Nikes. Newly barefoot, I wonder if this is how Mercury got started.

Occasionally Tom grants me some temporary shred of

dignity. Like when he strips me to my undershorts and has me go into the drugstore and tells me to ask for the Super-Lube Kondoms so my boyfriend can fuck my ass super-hard.

And Tom does, too.

As naked as he likes me, I never ask Tom why he doesn't take off his clothes. One by one my own clothes disappear. My closet is emptying. But Tom is always fully dressed. Tom's clothes symbolize supremacy over me, his Strip Boy, his buck naked, ass fuck Strip Boy. It is only his dick that Tom allows me to suck and get fucked by. If I am real good, Tom will show me his gorgeous balls and let me mouth them as a special reward. Whether he fucks me in the subway, or in Central Park, the dressingroom at Macy's, on a fire-escape, or on the top of a bar during happy hour, I am more than willing to serve Tom's golden branding-iron cock. Getting it pumped up me like the cockslut I am, I especially like it when people watch me taking Tom's cock. They seem as entranced with Tom's cock as I am.

When he finally fucks all my pants off, Tom says that's OK.

He says a Strip Boy like me doesn't need pants any more anyways.

From that day on, I have to go practically everywhere in my white undershorts and T-shirts. Of course, the T-shirts don't last for long either, what with Tom stripping me and fucking me every chance he gets. My last T-shirt disappears the night Tom has me take a late night bus to Rockerfeller Center. Waiting for the bus in front of Lord & Taylor's, I look at the fashion-conscious mannequins in the windows -- all clothes and no flesh. I catch my reflection, an earnest student turned into a man's two-bit just-enslaved fucktoy, a wholesome young man transformed into a whoreboy cumslut. Oh well, you have to shed some of your self for any relationship.

The only people on the bus are me and a few Chicano construction workers who start laughing at me and making little kissy-sucky noises.

They tease me and grab my ass. They snap the elastic on my shorts, stinging my butt and my poor, cum-heavy balls pounce in their pouch. They laugh about how I must be somebody's fuckboy. How I must really love dick for him to make me go around like this. *You like dick, fuckboy? You like a mouth full of big hot cockmeat?* They start to tear at my last skintight T-shirt. I beg them don't, telling them it's the only shirt I own. They say they won't if I suck them off. *See? Look at it, fuckboy. I got a big juicy one for you. C'mere, don't you want to suck your mouth around this meat? Look how big it gets. Lick the cheese off. Suck me off good and then you can suck my brother's.* So I get down on my knees in hopes of saving the shirt off my back. After they both dump their stud loads out of their hot dicks, they take my T-shirt anyway, as a souvenir, calling me a stupid cocksucker who'd do anything to suck a guy's *pinga.*

I have to tell Tom about all this while I sit on his cock. It turns Tom on more than ever to fuck my ass while the rivets of his jeans pound my buttmounds.

So tonight I am down to my last pair of shorts. Tom takes me to the roof of this office building. It is chilly now. It is autumn and the wind is blowing stronger.

I think he is going to fuck me here, but Tom orders me to remove my last pair of shorts and literally has me kiss them goodbye. He flings them off the building and they disappear on the wind like a white flag of surrender. I feel exposed in front of all of Manhattan now. You can't get any more naked than this.

"Maybe I can take you back to my place on Long Island." Tom speculates, almost tenderly. "It's a fenced-in place. A big yard with plenty of room for you to run around naked. Lots of trees to exercise in. And if you're careful, the neighbors won't see you. Of course, you'll be required to rake the leaves and mow the lawn. But you can do that at night in the moonlight, if that makes you feel more comfortable. Wouldn't want to sunburn anything, would we? Oh, I'll provide the materials for you to build a little treehouse if you like. You'll probably want to do that before winter comes. 'Course, rain or shine, I'll expect you to have your ass up on the picnic table in the patio to fuck in the mornings and evenings. Maybe we can have a few selected guests over for a barbecue and you can entertain them. Some fraternities like to initiate their pledgeboys there. Would you like that?"

I nod eagerly. My cock stands out like a lightning rod.

Tom says wait here fifteen minutes. Then I am to follow him

down in the elevator. Maybe he'll be waiting for me at the bottom, maybe he won't. I am to tell Tom exactly what happens to me on the way down. Who sees me, who gets turned-on, who I suck off, who fucks me.

And that is why I am naked on this elevator.

Totally, completely, stark, buck naked.

Gears whir. Motors throb.

The groin-thrill of a plunging elevator surges through my balls.

My hard-on hardens.

Pause.

Elevator doors open – like a theater curtain.

My new life as a Strip Boy is about to begin.

Going down?

THE GENIUS OF ALL BEAUTIFUL BOYS

Orland Outland

"Oh, *that* boy," Ted responded in a deep, languorous murmur. "I met him at Colossus. Tits of *death*. He took me home and fucked me *silly*. He's the one I told you about, remember, his boyfriend came home and fucked me, too. Those boys were *hot!*"

The boy in question passed center stage at Cafe Flore, appearing nonchalant to his admirers; in truth, he'd walked around from the Noe Street side and, with the singular genius of all beautiful boys, already noted who was there, who was interesting, who to avoid. Ted, already had, was in the last category.

"He didn't even look at me!" Ted's voice rose in pitch. The boy *had* looked at Ted, and *had* chosen to ignore him, just as Ted would have ignored him had it not for Ted's ardent desire to be double pronged again. The problem was, when he first told Skip the story, he'd made it sound as if that boy was hot to have him again. "Boys play so many games," Ted airily dismissed him.

His reputation was intact, though Skip was paying no attention, having turned his own magnetic glamour on a blond boy several tables away, so immersed in what he was reading that his lips were moving. The blond boy felt the waves of Skip's stare and turned slowly, to allow Skip to look away before contact, one of many ornate rules of the Hot Boy Mating Dance. The boy got up and eyed Skip through his imitation Armani sunglasses. Skip was well trained to recognize both the direction of the hidden gaze and the authenticity of the sunglasses before sauntering inside. Skip got up. "I'm going to go see what that boy's having for *dessert.*"

Ted absently watched Skip go in, registering the current state of his body, hair and wardrobe. The body, of course, was perfect and perfectly tan; his tattoo, revealed by a sleeveless flannel shirt, was hot (one tattoo was hot; more than one was dirty and sleazy and too expensive to have removed later). His hair was slightly updated regulation porn-star – he'd done a movie for Falcon recently, less for the money than the celebrity and date bait. Ted absently brushed something from his own sleeveless flannel shirt, and noted his own tattoo and well-muscled arm with reassurance.

It wouldn't do to look around while sitting by oneself in Flore; it made you look desperate, a mortal sin. Like all boys, Ted kept a little notebook and pen in his gym bag for such occasions. He opened it to a blank page and put the pen thoughtfully to his lips. He would write a few words, carefully consider his next, and write a little more. Then and only then, as if suddenly pulled out of his deep reverie and recalled to the world, could he look around. He looked down at the page, well pleased: "Dry cleaning! BMer to shop (should I get a Jeep like Brad's?) Wolverines in yet? Disposable contacts. *Nordstrom* bill! Call that boy with great X from Endup last Sun. AM."

Skip returned to the table, his triumph at securing a date with the blond boy already eclipsed by more momentous news. "Guess who's inside?"

"Who?"

"*Ryan!*"

Ted paled. "I can't believe it. I can't believe he has the nerve to come here and show his face! God, I *loved* that boy and he hurt me so *bad!*" he said, raising his voice just enough to communicate his anguish to those nearby – not totally conscious of the effect, but not unconscious either. Since to have loved and lost showed greatness of soul and Ted had been informed that some people found this attractive, any opportunity to display its gestures should be taken.

Ryan came out and passed their table. Ted had forgotten what a hot boy he really was. Still, the fact was, being desirable was about being unattainable. Ryan had had Ted, so, Ted was therefore no longer desirable. Ted wanted Ryan again, which made Ted even less desirable. Ryan came out onto the patio with sunglasses on. Ted could have said something to catch his attention, but that...just wasn't done.

Today Ryan favored the abstracted "I really didn't notice anybody on my way out" look, way of snubbing Ted that was not as humiliating to Ted's reputation as it might have been.

After he was gone, Ted sighed, looked around. Boys had been watching, had overheard enough of the earlier conversation to have watched Ryan's passing with interest. Now they were looking at Ted. He began to bask in the attention. He put on his sunglasses in the fading afternoon light, leaned back, and stretched in a calculatedly lazy manner.

"Boys!" he said to nobody in particular. "Always playing games!"

THE SMELL OF SEX

Bruce Lee

I was a bus passenger riding South. At twenty-three I'd started in a small town on the west coast; setting out in a Greyhound across the Nevada desert and the vast yellow dirt of Texas till the bus was swallowed by the delta lands of the deep south, choking with green and smothered by vines – abandoned fields fallow with persistent kudzu vines dragging power lines and even the poles down to the ground. I was a little drowsy – daydreaming – thinking about Gracia Lorca's *One Hundred Years of Solitude*, which had got me through the long road of Texas where time stood still. Before I left I'd thought going by bus was romantic, but so far it had been depressing. We'd already rolled through Little Rock. The no-shirt, no-shoes, no-service sign looked suspiciously like it used to have "Whites Only" in the fresh area of paint at the bottom of the sign. We'd crossed the oily brown Mississippi, stopped long enough at the bus station in Memphis to load our cafeteria trays with golden brown fried things and tip our hats to the Elvis shrine at the end of the line. And also in Memphis just outside across the busy hot street the block-long adult cinema winked blue and white, chasing lights into the windows of the cool air-conditioned bus station.

Now we were in the pitch-black moonless darkness somewhere between Memphis and Birmingham, damp southern summer kept safely outside by our stale recycled breath and cigarettes. There were only a few reading lights throwing out cones of yellow light when the driver geared down in the middle of nowhere and crunched off onto the gravel shoulder.

Most of us had been on the bus since Texas, and we had started to think possessively of the added room in the aisle seats. I could feel the atmosphere thicken as the bus started to slow down. Passengers began to push packages onto the seats beside them, or spread their legs into the space below the aisle seats and pretend to be asleep.

When the doors opened, immediately the smell of the night rolled in. Hot gravel, baked in the day, released its dry barren smell into the bus, and the exhaust of the bus, the butyl rubber of the floormats, the smokey polyester upholstery, the bitter green smell of the milkweed on the bank of the highway, and somewhere far off, deep water. We heard the big doors underneath the seats open and close, the driver murmuring, the swaying from side to side as first the driver and then our unwelcome guest entered our cocoon.

At first I wanted to repel this rude interloper as much as everyone else – and then I smelled him.

There is no way really to describe the pheremonic power of the cloud of hormones that preceded him by at least ten feet. As soon as he stepped on board, his smell cloaked us, conquered us, his smell raced ahead of him, extending its fingers to our cheeks, enlarging him to superhuman stature, and as I later realized, distorting his true shape. The instant I smelled him, I wanted him next to me. I softened and released my arms. My shoulders relaxed, and my heart began pounding in my throat. My tongue thickened in my mouth, and I swallowed repeatedly. How can I describe a smell that drew out every detail of this man; painted in detail the tight line of his hip, that delicate furrowed bow that runs from waist to leg. A smell that measured just exactly how strong his arm, how powerful his chest, how he could hold both my crossed wrists with one hand, hold them down with so little effort, while he fucked me. How to describe a smell that screamed and whimpered like a thousand dogs in a light speed of rut, the pounding slamming screaming, and the throaty exhausted breathing afterward.

How can I describe how all of this came in an instant, and took me and mesmerized me and made me want this complicated intoxicating arabesque of scent next to me, how I wanted to drink the source of it, and how he slowly made his way down the aisle, trying to figure out where to sit, where to put this smell of sex and a thousand unwashed days, and I was screaming inside my head, here, here, you want to sit here?

And he paused for a moment next to my seat. I looked up.

He was tall, about 19, his shoulders looked just the way I knew they would; broad the way that a roofer or construction worker's shoulders are broad, from having to carry heavy things a great distance. His shirt seemed stretched over his chest, as if he'd dressed when he was a little boy, and forgotten ever to change clothes again.

"Anybody sitting here?" he asked.

"No," I choked out.

If I'd been clever, I would have said something like "you are!" or been friendly enough to strike up a conversation right away, but I was a deer in the path of an oncoming car, and I couldn't do anything but stare into the headlights and hope he would sit down next to me. His smell was so strong, I already felt like part of him had entered me through my nose.

It never occurred to me at the time that anyone would think he smelled like an unwashed bum, but they probably did. I could not imagine that he did not hold the whole bus in his power.

His smell had surrounded me like an envelope so secure, I felt like we were the only two people on the bus. I felt protected and warm, like he was already touching me, so when his head rolled over onto my shoulder in sleep, it seemed like something that had happened before. We had been on this bus a hundred times and each time, his head rolling onto my shoulder as he slept. I wanted to reach up and touch his cheek, but I didn't dare wake him. Putting his head there seemed a thing to please me, to put me at ease, but later, I would learn that he had just been careless. Men do careless and selfish things, not because they think only of themselves, but because it never occurs to them to think of others. His head rolled onto my shoulder because he was asleep and he didn't know or care where his head was.

But I didn't know about carelessness at this time, on this bus. When his head rolled onto me it seemed endearing that he would trust me so much, that he would feel at ease enough with me to allow his head to roll onto my shoulder. I immediately tried to make my shoulder more accommodating. I regretted its bony angularity, and tried to move very little for fear of waking him.

The bus stopped at 2 a.m. in Birmingham. He asked me to borrow a dollar, because his money was in his bag which was underneath the bus and he couldn't get to it.

The Birmingham bus station was all chest high blue counter with brightly wrapped, strangely named snacks winking and mooning behind vending machine glass, and those coffee machines where grinding gears gurgle out ersatz hot chocolate and instant coffee into tiny paper cups. The kitchen where you could get greasy fries and cheeseburgers was closed. I gave him a five, he said he'd pay me back when we got to Atlanta. I didn't care about the money. I wanted him to owe me more, but I didn't have any more. He scarfed down a white bread sandwich like he hadn't eaten in a week, and kept the change. I got a Thousand Dollar bar. It was hard to let him out of my sight, but he disappeared for a few minutes, and I felt alone. I realized that the smell of him was addictive, that I needed it, that the air smelled dry and metallic without it. Some people got off in Birmingham, and I was afraid he would use the opportunity to get a seat alone, but he didn't. He came right back and sat down next to me.

Somehow it felt very private, the two of us, sleeping on the bus, the sound of engine droning us on to dream.

And I did dream. About him. About his tan back and shocking white legs slogging through the swampy delta, wood shack by the creek, climbing trees, trying to be a good boy but getting beat no matter what, seeing his daddy with a belt looped in half, just standing there holding it. I seen his girls, white soft thighs and a softer place, tight home, whistle stop for his flesh. Explosion in pink, seashell to ride, a tide a river, ocean of hot nights when you can't sleep and what're you doin' in there, Roy, What's all that noise? And me, waiting for him behind the shed, enacting some frightening promise, the air crackling with sex, his hard smooth cock standing up, hips thrusting automatically like a dog's and me saying, "What do you want me to do?"

When I woke it was orange green dawn. The dirty yellow midsummer sun was filtered through the leaves of so many trees, it made me sad.

His head was still on my shoulder. I wondered if he had dreamed the same thing I did, if any of the stuff in the dream was true, and what he was running away from.

Since I woke before he did I watched the tobacco fields and little shacks rise and fall from view, with those women in the south who are always just walking along the road with no place in particular to go. The road is the highway, and it goes clean out of the state, and they are just walking down it with no place to go.

He woke and apologized for sleeping on my shoulder.

"It's okay," and I caught myself before I said "I kind of like it."

He seemed nervous. He fidgeted with his hands for a while and began to tell me about his family. He was from a little town in rural Georgia that I had never heard of. After a few years in Georgia I thought I'd heard the names of all those little towns. He was coming back home after a trip out west. I was never sure that he wasn't a bum or an escaped convict because even though he talked about himself, he never talked about his work, what he did, about anything but his family. Maybe it was just safer territory for him.

He called his grandmother "my granny" and he said she lived a long time. She'd married his granddaddy and spent her whole life with him. Lived in a little house they had built. I now try to imagine it big, but I can't, it was a little two-room house. I don't remember if he told me that or if I just knew, but he said when granddaddy died he never saw my granny cry. She moved out of the house though just as soon as he died. She moved just across the field up on a little hill and put the trailer so she could see the house. Then she watched the kudzu vines grow up over it, grow up through the floorboards, in through the windows and walls, and she watched the house rot from the dirt, the rains, the worms, and the muggy days and nights. She watched that house until it was just a big black mound covered in vines. Then she just died. No particular reason for it. She was old.

I could tell that he loved his granny (he was her favorite grandson), that he knew how odd her behavior might seem to be. It seemed abnormally important to him and I almost thought it was a code for something else because after this, I knew he was a bad man, at least to the law. He told me some other stories, too, but none was as vivid or moving as this. I wondered if Granny secretly hated Granddaddy, or whether she just wanted to prove that there was no cell or deed of his left before she died herself. Did she watch his ghost till it faded away or was it nothing but convenience to live in a smaller place with a smaller sphere? He didn't know, but he did know his granny and there was something going on.

He stayed with me all the way to Atlanta. We told each other stories, laughed. Since he didn't seem to have any place to go, I considered asking him to share a hotel room, so we could "both get cleaned up", and truthfully I can't remember whether I actually mentioned this to him or not. I knew my father and my brothers were going to be waiting on me when the bus arrived, but somehow I thought we could get away with it. I don't know what I thought I'd tell my dad.

When the bus pulled into the station, he got up right away. On the way into Atlanta the bus had filled with people, so I didn't see him off the bus. I knew it would take a while to get our bags out, and he owed me five bucks, right? When I walked off, there was my family, standing there like they had been there for a hundred years. I greeted them absentmindedly and looked for my friend. I walked around the bus two, three times.

He was gone.

I felt abandoned, betrayed. Hadn't we had had something special? Hadn't I given him five dollars? He could have at least stuck around to let me tell him he didn't have to pay back the money. He could have said goodbye!

On the drive home from the bus station I thought about him. Did I even know his real name?

It was late afternoon, and clobbering up to rain. The dark sky closed over me and I felt wedged and claustrophobic between my brothers in the car.

The hot air and the green suffocated me, so I insisted on rolling the windows all the way down till the muggy wind whipped our hair.

What had happened to me on the bus?

Who was granny? Her own family didn't know why she moved on the hill and watched the house go like that.

I knew my friend on the bus had told me something special and important about his own life, the whole truth about himself.

I felt he had left me a coded message consisting of smell, the story, every gesture he made, but I've never been able to decode that message.

The trees on the side of the highway loomed forward and back in the darkening sky like they were on a turntable and we were sitting still; the same trees coming back over and over but nobody else but me could see. I felt a drop of cool rain from the high clouds hit my arm.

— *This story originally appeared in the Lavender Reader.*

HIS FAVORITE PHOTO

Kevin Bantan

When I got the phone call from Rodney, I realized that I hadn't heard from him for several weeks. Nor he from me, honestly. He invited me to supper the following Saturday, and I accepted enthusiastically. Rodney and I have been friends for nearly ten years. We had been lovers briefly, but we found that our intellectual attraction for each other was much stronger than the physical one. So we nurtured our friendship through frequent phone calls, dinner dates and shopping forays, which made it highly unusual for us to be out of touch for that length of time. I couldn't wait to see my friend.

After a heartfelt hug and kiss, we settled in with drinks to catch up on each other's lives. I didn't have much to relate outside of my job. I was still getting over my husband Clete's death fourteen months earlier. It wasn't AIDS, but it wasn't pretty, either. He had been shot in the head on our apartment balcony by a racist punk out to have a good time at someone of color's expense. For five weeks he was in a coma, and I slowly resigned myself to losing him. Then he suddenly rallied and regained consciousness, and my joy knew no bounds. Just as suddenly a few days later he died of a stroke. My life collapsed with his last breath.

Since then, my social calendar had consisted of occasional dinner invitations from friends, who felt sorry for me, but who also felt uncomfortable hearing about my sorrow. It was weird how friends I thought I knew avoided acknowledging my loss. Those of us who mourn hunger for the recognition of our misfortune. We need to be validated. Rodney was not that way. He had been there for me, had cried with me, had held my hand on many a late night of unbearable grief. I knew that he would be comfortable with whatever mood I showed up in, and it turned out to be a cheery one.

He told several anecdotes related to his work at the studio. He's what's known politely as a boudoir photographer. He takes pictures of people in various states of undress, and frequently in the nude. Most of his clientele were men, but occasionally a woman would hire him to take some sexy photos for her girlfriend or lover. He regaled me with descriptions of his more interesting clients, and for the first time in long while, I was interested in hearing every graphic detail. At one point, he got up and went into his study, bringing back what looked like a photo album. I was curious about what it contained, not only because I enjoyed seeing the results of Rodney's work, but I was suddenly horny and hoped that a few hunks would grace some of the pages. Failing that, the strange outfits some of the customers wore would be worth a few laughs. The first model was an absolutely gorgeous, tanned blond. "Still partial to white boys, I see."

"You should talk. I don't recall ever seeing you with a white guy."

"It happened once."

"Obviously a weak moment."

"That wasn't all that was weak." We laughed. It was true, though. We were both irresistibly drawn to members of each other's race. I looked back to the album. The client was lying naked on a purple velvet Victorian sofa, one of Rodney's great props. The young man's genitals were obscured by his bent knee. It only added to the boy's erotic appeal.

On the next page, he appeared again, wearing a gold lame' thong. His body was turned slightly to show his preciously-round buttocks. I wondered if this guy's ass was the reason for Rodney's long silence, then thought better of it. He wouldn't compromise his professionalism by having sex with a client. Although this one had to have stretched his ethics to the limit, I suspected. The facing page showed the young man in a white G-string attached to white suspenders. The color looked great against his tanned, sleekly-muscled torso. On the fourth and fifth pages, I saw a trend. It was the same model. Sitting on a chair in a pair of knee-high engineer's boots, one sole planted firmly on the seat, obscuring his goods. A leather collar encircled his neck. He was looking to his left. What a great profile. On the facing page, he stood before a mirror in a pair of black tights and white ballet slippers, his hands crossed over his chest. The photo teased the viewer with the vague outline of his sheathed equipment. I looked up. "Seems you're partial to this one."

"Wouldn't you be?"

"Yeah, I have to admit I'd make an exception in his case. If only all of your clients were that beautiful."

"I wish. Keep going."

I turned the page. The bombshell was in chaps, top harness, cycle cap, his back to the camera. The chaps framed those cheeks of his perfectly. The companion photo featured hot pink swim briefs.

It went on and on. Sailor's uniform. Shiny black bike shorts. Long white mesh T-shirt. Red thong slingshot. Filmy pink negligee with matching stockings and garter belt. Baseball uniform. Jockstrap and shoulder pads holding a football. This kid looked great in everything. Plaid flannel shirt, logging boots and heavy socks sitting on a log, the open shirt inconveniently falling to obscure his equipment, which by now I desperately wanted to see.

"My god, Rodney. How many weeks did it take to do this shoot? It looks as if you could retire on this one client."

Rodney smiled. "Keep going." There was certainly more to go. Hockey shirt and matching long socks. The shirt, of course, hung low enough to frustrate this voyeur. Silver leather hot pants and matching newsboy cap. A rear shot in black stay-up stockings and black pumps. He's bending over as if he's smoothing his left leg. That one was really sexy, and I could see his rear window. Crotch-high waders with strategically-placed fishing net. West Point cadet. To me, that is the sexiest uniform on earth. Black satin Everlast boxing shorts with white side stripes, white gloves and high white boxing shoes. The last photo finally rewarded me with what I sought. I gasped when I saw it. It was a frontal shot. He was wearing the white suspenders, his arms folded over his chest, smirking at the camera. With good reason, too. Even at rest, his sex hung pendulously between his legs. The suspenders running on either side and underneath his genitals made them irresistibly the focal point of the picture. I knew that Rodney was good at what he did. I was ready to bestow greatness on him at that moment. "Geez, Rodney. Who is this kid?"

Just then the door opened and someone called from the foyer, "I'm home, dear". Before he could answer, the incredible blonde appeared in the living room doorway. "Alex, this is Brian." I stared at Alex, my mouth rudely agape. Alex said hello and shook my hand, while I managed only to stare at the life-sized translation from the photo album. The brown eyes were as piercing in real life. The pug upturned nose, the square chin, the prominent cheekbones had materialized in the flesh. The one thing missing was the smirk. It was replaced by a genuinely open smile, which hinted that he was a very happy man. I finally recovered sufficiently to laugh at my reaction to seeing him in the flesh. Alex was speaking to Rodney. "I don't know how or why you guys never became a couple, but I'm eternally grateful you didn't."

My friend chuckled. "If you must know, darling, we love each other for our minds."

"If his is anything like yours, it must be a hell of a relationship."

"It is, trust me."

Further discourse was interrupted by the doorbell. "That must be Jeff," Alex said and went to answer the door.

"You sly fox."

"You don't know how sly, Brian." The blond adonis returned with an equally devastating brown-haired one. They couldn't be called twins, exactly. Jeff's nose flared slightly more than Alex's, and his hair was in dreadlocks. Otherwise, they seemed to be cast from the same mold.

We were introduced, and I appreciated his firm handshake. Jeff plopped down next to me, even though there was abundant seating available.

We made small talk, while our hosts made a drink for Jeff and a refill for me. I felt a distinctive heat emanating from Jeff's body, the scent of which was intoxicating.

As we were chattering away, I was becoming enveloped in a lust I had once felt only for the lost love of my life. Still, I knew what I was feeling. I breathed more deeply than was necessary in order to inhale as much of Jeff as possible. Woodsy. I listened carefully to everything he said to me, searching for hidden messages, but there were none that I could discern. Suddenly the room began to darken. No doubt a thunderstorm was approaching. A weak cold front had struggled through yesterday and had stalled. Now it was pushing back north as a warm front. Its unstable air, fueled by an abundance of gulf moisture, threatened severe weather. Good luck to us.

Alex came into the room carrying a weather radio. "Repeating, a severe thunderstorm warning is in effect until 7:00 for Franklin County." The storm was fierce, drumming the windows with huge drops, which became sheets of water, rattling the panes with sudden bursts of high wind, and as if to dot the exclamation point of its fury, knocking out the power. We sat silently until Alex lit the candles in the candelabrum on Rodney's piano. Dinner would be delayed indefinitely, because the apartment was all-electric.

The candles created more than a pleasant ambience. Their presence was almost sinister in the darkened room, hinting at something vaguely threatening, as when the hairs on the back of one's neck suddenly stand up for no distinguishable reason. Scary but thrilling at the same time. Their flickering, smoldering dance, along with the unmistakable scent of sex pouring off the god sitting next to me, was fast raising the temperature in my crotch, having been so long below freezing. I could count the number of times I'd masturbated in the last fourteen months on one finger, so I was surprised and pleased by my reaction to Jeff.

We continued our conversation as the tempest outside abated and began to move away, its power reduced to distant rumblings. Just then the Weather Alert went off again. "The National Weather Service has issued a severe thunderstorm warning, effective until 8:15, for persons in Franklin County."

"What is going on here?"

"What is going on is we won't get power back for hours, at best. Let me get some more munchies and call the Colonel. Maybe they still have electricity," Alex said.

Fortunately, the grid where the Colonel was located had not been sabotaged by lightning. We would eat. When it was time to pick up the dinner, both of our hosts decided to go to retrieve it. It seemed odd that Rodney would abandon his guests like that.

It was out of character, given the attentive host that he was. Then it dawned on me. I had been set up. They had planned this all along. Well, they hadn't planned the storms, but they turned out to be a convenient cover for them to order out. They must have been thanking Mother Nature all the way to the car, when they weren't giggling about their cleverness. So Jeff was my blind date. Thank goodness I wasn't or I'd have missed ogling his rare beauty with my peripheral vision all evening.

"So, what do you do for a living, Brian?"

"I manage an electronics store. You?"

"Graduate school. And I work part time in the Department of Geography. That's my field of study."

"Interesting. I love geography, except I can never remember where Alsace-Lorraine is."

"I'd love to show you sometime."

"I'd love for you to do that." Our heads were moving slowly in each other's direction.

"Anytime." Contact. We wrapped our arms around each other and attacked each other's mouth. This was passion, which had been a stranger for far too long. I felt as if I were going positively incandescent on Jeff's sensuously abundant lips. We started undressing each other, heedless of the fact that we were in someone else's living room and that the someone elses could return at any minute.

Once my shirt was open, he was on my nipples like a lamprey. He had them rigid and me moaning in seconds. The feeling of his mouth on them rivaled the sensation lingering on my lips. From suckling, he went to teasing the newly hypersensitive nubs with his tongue. He sure was awfully talented for someone so young. He seemed absolutely delighted when my moans escaped from my throat more frequently and intensely. Satisfied that he had subdued my chest, Jeff's next assault was on my navel. I'd never had anyone take a serious interest in that part of me before, and now I couldn't understand why not. There sure seemed to be surfeit of nerves in the small concavity, and it was obvious that he knew that they were there. My squirming and whimpering told him that he'd hit paydirt. Well, close to it, because my erection was pointing at his chin as determinedly as a gun.

He didn't miss the cue, effortlessly moving his head to suck the knob of my shaft, as if he were extracting juice from an orange. I responded by making sounds that I'd never heard come from my mouth before. Spurred on, he coated my entire length with the wonderful saliva I had tasted minutes earlier.

I managed to unzip his baggy jeans and began to search for his cock. I found it right away, hard but lost in the folds of material. The process of concentrating on freeing it from its denim prison held my gathering orgasm at bay. After waiting more than a year for an encounter like this, I didn't want it to end so soon. Once revealed, Jeff's cock was beautiful. It's an overused term for this body part, but it was true. Uniformly dark brown, circumcised and ridged with numerous veins snaking just under the satiny skin, I wanted to return the favor of his mouth with mine. He had other ideas. His mouth slipped off my hard, wet sex.

"Please fuck me," he whispered urgently.

"Oh, yeah! You're on." I spit on my fingers and used them to massage Jeff's opening. He helped me with some of his own saliva, seeming as desperate to have me in him as I was to be there. I spit onto my cock in an act of pointless excess, spread it around and mounted him. He lay back, his head on the arm of the couch, his thighs resting on his torso. He accepted me easily, relaxing his muscle to let me slide all of the way in.

"When I had it in my mouth, I knew I had to feel you again this way. And I must say that I'm already glad I did. Take me hard, Tiger."

"You got it. Hang on." I fucked him at a frenzied pace, eager to possess his beauty. He held my buttocks, wanting to make sure he got all of me, and he did. Although I didn't stop my doomsday bucking, I began to lick his feet, which were planted on my pecs, teasing my nipples as I leaned into him. He had attractive wide ones with short, bent toes. I'm rarely turned on by feet, but Jeff's were too pretty to resist. I had sucked only three of them when I had to give up my ministrations, because I was on the steep downslope toward orgasm. Jeff literally touched his magnificent erection and shot his load onto his chest. I followed seconds later with a wrenching, seeing-stars climax. I collapsed on top of my sexmate. We were drenched from our exertions in the rapidly-warming apartment. We giggled like little kids. He licked my nose, I licked his. He licked me again. This was going to escalate into lovemaking again, except that our eyes both got big at the same time, remembering where we were and who could walk in and catch us *in flagrante delicto*.

We jumped off the sofa and dressed hurriedly. Then we used the remainder of our private time kissing soulfully. We sat down when we heard the door and pretended to look casual.

"It's not that hot in here yet for you two to be dripping with perspiration," Rodney said accusingly.

"I think it's hot. Seems very hot in here to me," I said.

"Yes, it's definitely very hot in here."

"Scorching."

"Like a furnace almost."

"Uh, huh. And I know where that furnace is located," Rodney said. We giggled. Why bother to deny it?

"That's better. Besides, do you think that Alex and I can't smell the heavy aroma of sex hanging in the air? Although I will admit that you two sure worked fast." We giggled again. We would become annoying shortly if we didn't control ourselves. "Eat up, guys. We got both white and dark meat." At least this time they giggled along with us.

Jeff and I did eat, but we spent more time mooning at each other than anything else. After the meal, we sat holding hands. When the evening was aging and more lightning flickered in the distance, we left together, deciding we were not at all ready to relinquish each other's company. In what I thought was a very nice gesture, Rodney gave me the album of Alex. While it wasn't necessary, considering that I had a potentially budding relationship with an equally hot man, I did appreciate Alex's beauty very much.

When we got to my place, I poured brandy into ridiculously large snifters and we sat on the sofa together, swishing the dark liquid around in their glass confinements. Jeff laughed. "What?"

"This snifter is so big. Like something else I know."

"I accept your adulation, modest though I am."

"And generous, too."

"It's the Christian thing to do."

"So is loving your neighbor," he said putting his glass down and recommencing licking my face.

"Well, we should all be charitable."

"Will you charitable to me again?" he asked as his mouth moved to cover mine. My 'you bet' was muffled by his lips.

It happened on the sofa again. Now I suspected that I knew why some of them were called loveseats. I was certainly inside the bottom of a lovely one. This time our union was prolonged, as we took it slow and relaxed. At least we did until after I had made love to each of his toes and licked the soles of his feet, which drove him crazy beneath me. At that point, I had no choice but to fuck him silly, the way he seemed to like it. Tiger, indeed. He begged and begged, and I pounded and pounded. He rewarded me for my good work by coming without even touching himself this time. I let out a banshee shriek as I started to pump my come into him, so wonderful had his body made my cock feel. Quietly, we lay holding each other, his calves resting on my ass cheeks. I raised my head, kissed him softly, and said "Bed?" Jeff grinned and nodded. As we got up he said, "Let me show you my favorite photo," pointing at the album. I picked it up and carried it to the bedroom. "You've seen the photos then," I said.

"Sure have."

"He's certainly dynamite-looking."

"I couldn't agree with you more," he said with a devilish smile. I wondered if that was a hint that he and Alex had at some point been intimate. I didn't allow that thought to linger in my head.

When we were comfortably snuggled together, a position I knew I could get used to easily, I opened the album, wondering which photo he liked best. My jaw dropped. I looked up at Jeff, who laughed, gleefully. "Surprise!" I turned the pages, and there he was in the same outfits that Alex had worn. They had switched albums when I wasn't looking. Man, what a beauty Jeffrey Anderson was! And, better yet, he was sitting next to me.

"So which one of these photos is your favorite?"

"This one," he said, kissing me.

A TIMELESS BEAUTY

Rick Jackson

I don't usually mind looking at naked men lying out in the sun — especially when they're tanned and buffed and glistening with drops of sweat. I certainly didn't mind how Jake was stretched out on his balcony — or that the condo didn't have a privacy divider to separate his balcony from mine. Before I saw what he had to offer, I had been sitting on the couch, looking out at white sails coasting along the blue horizon and musing on the glories of nature.

Once I saw the beads of sweat gather to form hot, salty trickles across his hard, muscular flesh, though, my musings upon nature grew plenty more personal. His broad, hairless chest and flat belly, his powerful arms and legs, and his handsome face all conspired to seduce my gaze away from the sea and to lock it firmly on the wonders of nature spread wide between his sweaty, yawning thighs.

Jake arrived a few days before. As I sat there, drinking a cool Foster's and watching the sun suck sweat from his naked flesh, I knew I was going to have trouble meditating on the glories of the sapphire horizon or the timeless beauty of a few fleecy clouds scudding past above the distant sails with him spread out on display.

Jake's shades shielded his eyes from mine; but the more I stared at his powerful young body, the more I felt his gaze — and his yearning. As if to prove what he had in mind, the big, thick dick which had been lying draped across his swollen balls began to twitch and, slowly, to inflate. For a brief moment, it stood tall as a mainsail spar, saluting the beauty of the seascape and then bent low over Jake's belly. As it bounced against the brown ridge of fur leading from his belly button down to his bushy brown pubes, that big dick developed a regular pulse that teased at the edges of my equanimity and incited me to a whole world of wild, wanton naughtiness.

I've never understood why big dicks turn me on. Maybe it's because my nine-inch nail has made me so happy over the years. I was born a top, so full-flaring glutes and tight, puckering holes obviously make my chimes clang. Unlike most of the men I pleasure, I don't get off on having my guts churned to tapioca or my asshole split wide by some over-sized rampaging freak of nature. On those rare occasions when I let a special man slip his dick up my tight little ass, the last thing I want is for him to have a dick as big and thick and painful as my own. For use in the sack, needledicks are fine with me. The only way I had ever even considered letting a dick near my asshole was if it was no bigger than Jesse Helms'.

There was no way Jake was ever going to fuck me. His thick, throbbing tool would send a fully-grown yak into cardiac arrest. Still, there was something so fascinating about watching his bone throb and bounce about above his belly that I couldn't move my eyes. He was like a freeway accident or the O.J. trial — a guy knows that he shouldn't gawk, but somehow can't help himself. My tongue twitched in anticipation of the taste of his sweat and the tangy musk of his crotch and hairy pits. My teeth tingled in anticipation of his swollen tits. Mostly, though, my mouth watered to get that big dick slammed down my throat where it belonged.

I'd never so much as said "Howdy" to the guy in the elevator, but the swell of his shank and the invisible yet hypnotic stare from behind those shades begged for us to seriously "meat" at last. The way our balcony was situated, only the gulls soaring out to sea could overlook us — and the way Jake was situated no mortal man could overlook his virile charms. If my new neighbor wanted to lie on his back with his legs spread wide to show off his stuff, I could play that game, too. I was wearing only an old pair of jeans and slipped them from my body without a second thought. Jake didn't move when I snagged some rubbers and stepped naked out onto our balcony. He didn't need to. He already had a damned fine view of everything a young neighbor could crave.

I padded over to him, planted my feet on his towel next to his ears, and bent over to pull the shades from his cute little nose. He squinted a bit in the harsh sunlight, but seemed to understand my need to see his eyes while I did him. He certainly used them to take stock of my advantages, running from my broad shoulders, down across my furry chest and belly to linger longingly at my throbbing loins before slipping down to my thighs. While his gorgeous green eyes were ruthlessly raping my body, his hands started a slow, seductive slide up my legs until they got just past my knees.

They might have kept on rising if I hadn't hunkered down over his face to drag my heavy nuts across his mouth. His lips were my favorite model: a thin Tom-Brockaw job on top with a full lower lip that pouted and parted to suck on my balls the way a young man deserves. After a quick preliminary chew on my nuts, Jake set to lapping at my hairy ballbag and sweaty crotch with all the frenzied, unrepentant relish of a lapsed Cistercian in a gladiator gang-bang. I let him have his way with me as I hung onto the metal balcony railing and let the sun lick at my naked body while Jake licked and sucked and chewed at what I had dragging low.

Somehow the view down the beach didn't hold my interest the way it usually does. I twisted myself around so I could lean down and play with his dick. I had seen it was thick and angry, but not until I took him in hand to give his monkey the spanking of its life did I realize that it was broader even than my own. I grabbed him underhanded and gave him a few gentle strokes to start him off and then picked up my pace until his hips were humping upwards into my fist. Jake's monster dick was a puzzle.

I had never had my hand around anything so hard and thick, yet every curve and inch of blue vein and sliding ripple of shank-skin seemed molded to hand as though by Destiny itself. Every stroke and twist of my paw along that massive tool was as exotic as it was erotic, yet it was somehow familiar, too — at once an adventure in the wickedest of excesses and the fulfillment of my soul's most secret and salacious imaginings.

That dick came alive in my hand and drew me towards it like a whole choir of Sirens. An instant before I was about to slip his naked knob into my mouth, I was jolted back to my senses — not by any awareness of the dangers involved, but by the sweet clouds of scent that wafted up from his sweat-soaked crotch. That musky man-smell lured me between his legs to lap and chew at his balls, even as he was tearing into mine. I had to drop his dick for the duration, but we both knew I would take it up again soon.

Jake and I rocked timelessly back and forth in the blazing

sunlight, heads shielded by the others' loins and hearts racing with the frenzy of approaching rut. In those rare flashes of feeling when something other than the firm texture of his nuts between my teeth or the tang of his musk on my tongue tore through the billowing veils of lust, I sensed his hands clawing at my ass-crack and his dick digging hard into my chest.

I must have instinctively returned the compliment, for I found Jake's tight, hot ass clenching away at two fingers of my right hand. Jake may have tried to dig deeper up my own hole, but that exit-only ass knew its nature well. As his fingers glided on an endless flood of sweat across my tender, shuddering shithole, I clenched down tight, determined to hold my virtue dear even as I did his deep.

His ass obviously wanted everything I had. Not only did his tight, hungry hole lunge up my fingers as his pelvis pounded his balls up into my mouth, but I heard the first of many nut-muffled moans of desperation echo upward from my crotch. Jake's body humped upwards, driving his big, thick dick up into my furry chest so hard I was sure he was about to spew spume. Normally, I wouldn't have minded his creaming my chest. I would have made him lick it up, of course, but I wouldn't have minded. With a mouthful of balls and my nose buried up his ass, though, I was almost sure to miss the show; and I couldn't have that.

I did the only thing I could under the circumstances: I ripped all that was left of my gonads out of his mouth and unhanded his shithole so I could rubber up and give him the hard dicking he needed so much. My hand was plenty busy sliding the slick latex down my shank, but my eyes saw nothing but his disheveled beauty and power and raw masculine sexuality. I must have stopped a moment to take it all in, because suddenly those dick-suckable lips of his parted and whispered their first words to me: "Please — hurry."

I lifted his legs enough to get at his ass and then shagged my shank home hard. Even through the rubber, I would swear I felt every fold of his buttpucker gape wide to caress my swollen dick as it dug in and got down to business. I didn't stop to take notes, but slammed on until all nine thick inches I had to give were duly shared with my next-neighbor in his time of need. By the time my cum-slit was scratching away at Jake's liver and the broad base of my bone had taught his ass the meaning of fear, I knew for sure that my new neighbor was one incredible fuck.

I usually watch my men's faces as I slam home because I get off almost as much on the power I wield over their bodies as the friction of their buttholes along my tool. Nothing gets me going as much as a man's eyes clenching shut in pain and opening wide in ecstasy — except maybe the sublime seizures that rock a man to wrack or, maybe, the raw, rippled despair as his body learns the full fury of my brutal need. By the time my boy-bitch is sucking air again and afraid that he might live after all, my meat is all but crisped and ready to juice.

In Jake's case, I managed to hold off for awhile, changing my tempo and position enough to keep my mind off how fucking fine he looked writhing around on the end of my dick. For a time, I sank my lips to his neck and chewed up a hickey that would brand him as mine for weeks. I sucked at his ear and played with his swollen tits. Mostly, though, I just slammed every inch I had up his ass and made him love it.

Just seconds before I ruptured the nut of a lifetime up his needy, neighborhood ass, I dropped one of his legs and held onto the other, fucking him sideways and jacking at his Godzilla-sized joint with my free hand. This new, lethal angle laid his prostate open to the most abject of cruelties, but I was long past being a good neighbor. Life is hard — but my dick and need were even harder. Selfish as I was, I kept busy at work, humping his hole like a pile-driver and lashing at his lizard with every five-fingered frolic I knew.

His tight ass suddenly seized up even tighter as his mouth gaped wide in a lupine howl of surrender and triumph and infinite incredulity. His monster meat jetted jism up past his face and out over the balcony, but not all of his whip-tailed seed fell to earth. Some splashed into his face and onto his broad, hairless chest. In the end, I suppose some even just drizzled down into his pubes or found a home on my hand, but I was gone by then — my soul soaring like Icarus' towards the glaring sun which seemed suddenly to shatter into searing shards of white-hot spunk that erupted from my balls and gushed up into Jake's tight, hot, hungry ass.

By the time my wings cooled and I found myself circling for a landing, my knees were rubbed raw and Jake's head had been fucked off the balcony. Fortunately, the railing was widely-spaced so we didn't have to call the fire department to free him. His ears gave him some trouble coming out, but between the slick sweat and the slicker jism he seemed to have sprayed so much of, we managed on our own.

We still are — and plan to keep at it indefinitely. Most of the time we save our out-door fucking for sunset or sometimes during a full moon when we can howl the way nature intended. Sharing a common balcony — along with everything else — means that we spend a lot of time together in his bed or mine, in a shower or on a kitchen floor.

In all the time we've been together, I still haven't let that monster dick up my ass and probably never will. Now that may seem selfish to you, but I think it's good. It keeps Jake hoping. And I've always thought that every young man needs some dream to keep him going.

MAGIC

Rick Jackson

I thought Buck was a odd sort of librarian the first time I saw him. Librarians are supposed to be look like Wally Cox, but Buck was about as wimpy as a marine battalion in a whisky warehouse. He was 22 years old, six-two and big-boned. The guy had the muscles of a weight-lifter and the face of a god doing a guest cover for *GQ*. Thick, curly blond hair eased down over one heavy brow, and delicious green eyes sparkled wit and intelligence below. He had a perfect nose and Hollywood-quality teeth, a cleft in his chin, and dimples the size of Wyoming on either side of his boyish grin. I discovered later that he started working in the University library as a freshman because he needed the bucks and stuck around because he liked to be able to read on the midnight shift – when he wasn't fucking around. Even before I came along, though, I don't think he got much reading done.

I stopped by the desk one night around 3 A.M. to ask if he could check the computer to see when an Oscar Wilde biography I needed was due back in. He looked up from a book, looked me up and down, and then barked in his quarterback voice, "Wilde was a faggot. What do you want a book about him for?"

I thought about getting pissed off and decided there wasn't much point. Besides, if Buck was as dumb as he was trying to pretend, I might be able to shame him into not being such a dick. I looked square into his delicious, cat-green eyes, suppressed a sigh, and snarled, "So am I. Are you taking a survey or running a library?"

Buck looked me up once more and then down again and loosened up as a huge grin slid across his face. He slammed his book shut, tossed it onto the counter, and asked if I felt like a good, solid fuck. As a matter of fact, looking at Buck had made me feel exactly like a good, solid fuck. He asked the geek behind the reference counter to cover for him at the main desk, and we were downstairs in periodicals storage before you could say *Hunks*. I expected us to drop trou and knock off a quickie, but Buck was in no hurry. Looking back, I suspect the bastard just wanted me to admire his body. I did. If he'd been a heart-stopper dressed, he was a walking wet-dream naked. His strong neck and shoulders; hard, hairless pecs and bulging arms; and rippling, washboard belly seemed to tower in front of a guy and reduce him to quivering, lust-struck jelly.

A few seconds later, I saw his ass and was in love forever. His macho-muscled mounds of man-meat didn't hang down slack like empty flour sacks along the back of his thighs the way most asses do these days, even on men who are otherwise well-built. No, Buck's hunks of muscle jutted proudly out at you and cast a spell as certain and absolute as any witches' brew, except Big Buck's perfect butt was more like a Medusa – one glance at that studly dick-twitcher and you went rigid. Great as his ass was, that shank of meat hanging between his legs was better! It was even longer and thicker than my own proud nine inches, but that wasn't a huge surprise. He was three inches taller than me, and much bigger-boned. What I didn't expect was the way his balls swung down low between his thighs to prove he hadn't creamed dick in days.

He stood naked and grinning, feet spread apart, while I did my inspection. I could tell from the way his eyebrows arched up that he realized I wasn't chopped chicken livers myself. I reached out to slide my hand up his thigh, but before I could get to his balls, he had me in his arms, caressing my quivering flesh, running his strong hands across the muscles of my back, and searing his kisses across my shoulders. I ran a hand through his thick blond curls and pulled his face to mine. My tongue pried open his lips and slithered inside his body while my flesh did everything but arc electricity. Buck's tongue wrapped around mine and made me plenty welcome. His hands continued to slide along my spine, up my flanks, down across my ass, and everywhere else I had a lusty itch that needs to be scratched by a strong, manly hand. Our bellies wriggled together in heat, introducing his dick to mine and letting them wrestle head to head.

I could tell Buck was especially interested in the thick carpet of red fur I have running from my chest down across the muscle I'll let anyone see to my private stock. On the other hand, maybe because my chest is so furry, I've always been turned on big-time by sweaty muscle-men with glistening, bare bodies. As our lips continued with their frenzied suck-fest, Buck rubbed his hard, savagely passion-tipped pecs through the forest of fur, grinding my own coarse hair into my flesh while he moaned and wriggled like a Tijuana whore on overtime. I felt his huge hands reach down to cup my ass, lifting me slightly to press my cock harder than ever against his lean, bare belly. His hips or mine instinctively began the rhythmic rocking that man has known since the dawn of time. Our blood-gorged butt-busters grated together as they slid relentlessly upwards to prod into our taut, gyrating bellies. Buck's hands shifted slightly on my ass, forcing me ever-harder into his belly-humping flesh and prying my mounds of muscle apart so his thumbs could twiddle along the hot, hairy crack between. I lifted my arms to his shoulders and wrapped them around his neck, lightening his load and adding my fuel to the fire engulfing us both. As I clenched my legs tight around his ass, I felt his thumbs begin to prod at my butthole. In any other lifetime, I'd have long since spread myself for him but these are not the times for careless love.

He seemed to read my mind – or maybe his own lust. His dick gave my belly a few last lashes of savage, thrusting need as his mouth tore at mine. Then he dropped my hungry, twitching ass onto a stack of recent issues of *The New York Times* while he deserted me for a shelf filled with magazines. Half insane with the need to shoot everything I had before his sweat dried on my body, before his lust cooled on my skin, I reached down to take myself in hand. I looked over at his naked body, his butt twitching as he reached behind the piles, searching for something. His jock body was so perfect, it was actually more of a turn-on ten feet away – because only at a distance could you see the whole thing and glory of the way muscle flowed into muscle or let your soul rejoice in the easy way he turned and moved and flexed with the natural grace of an unselfconscious animal. His classic jock body, a moving, breathing statue in muscle instead of marble, was so enthralling that I forgot my dick and watched him, struck insensible with lust and admiration. He finally turned around and lit the room with his grin and the twinkle of those green eyes as he pulled a rumpled paper bag from between the back-issue stacks of

American Heritage and *American Shepherd*. He was beside me again in a moment, digging into the bag like a schoolboy on Christmas morning. Frustrated, he ripped the bag open and sent rubbers, cock rings, cherry-flavored dick-oil, and all his other big-boy's toys rolling across the floor. Finally, triumphantly, he held up a huge flesh-colored dildo about the same size as his own impossibly hard cock. He grinned and asked if I liked it. He claimed it WAS a model of his cock he'd actually had a buddy mold for him. I started to dream of being that buddy, but before dreams could catch up with me, I was upside down on the *Times* with Buck's finger slithering lube up my fuckhole.

Almost before I knew what was happening, he'd rubbered his latex dick and shoved it so far up my tender shithole that I tasted latex for a week. His prosthetic pecker was no sooner up my butt than he'd flipped me back over, dropping my butt down onto the *Times* and making the brutal, glorious rape of my virtue complete as my own weight fucked me up the ass with his spare butt-buster. He wasn't going to let me just sit there and let his cock fester up my ass, though. He grabbed my head and pulled my face to his crotch, grinding my face-hole into his huge, hairy ballbag. I lapped the smell of man-crotch from his nuts and sucked at them until the bastard was dancing up and down on my face. He'd already slid a rubber over his massive male member and had even coated the fucker with his cherry-flavored lube – as if I needed anything artificial to turn me on.

I slipped my mouth around his huge, swollen manhood and felt my ass try to contract in a reflex of joy around his other fuck-tool, straining my fuckhole to the max. From the way his hands held my head as I slid across his mushroom-shaped dickhead, I knew the lube was the only thing cherry about his cock. This was meat that knew how to cook. His hands eased my head back and forth, shimmying my face up his vulcanized tongue-depressor. In return, I wrapped my hands around his ass, pulling his melon-shaped mounds apart as he had done mine, working my fuckfingers deep into his shithole as he ground his way down my throat. His cock was so huge and the taste of cherry so cloyingly overpowering that I almost forgot his dick up my ass – almost. Every movement of my head or his joint seemed to ripple down to my ass as I wriggled on yesterday's news, driving his second manhood up into my guts, straining the whole length of my love-tunnel to the breaking point, ramming and twisting its way into the muscle at the end of my fuckhole. My ass was so desperate to have him inside me that even Buck's second-best was good enough to make my body contract around him, squeezing and stroking, and rejoicing in his presence.

If his dick up my ass was a strain, his dick down my throat was too much of a good thing. I was able to get the whole of his head into my mouth, but when I tried to get all of his dick down my throat, we weren't so lucky. I got the first inch or two into my gullet, but after that, he was just too face-fucking big for me. He slammed his hips into my willing mouth, driving his dick hard against the back of my throat, grinding away with all the savagery of our race, but he wasn't able to make much head-way. Finally, he saw reason and worked my face off his brutal, beautiful marvel of a dick. For a second, I was afraid he was pissed that I couldn't take him down the throat, but most guys can't take me, either. We meaty men have a lot of disappointments in life. Life is hard.

If Buck couldn't ream one hole, he was doubly determined to ream the other. Fortunately, my ass had already been broken open and more than willing to meet his needs. He slid me over, jerked one dick out of my ass, and slid the other up. The real thing was better – bigger and hotter and more knowledgeable in giving a young stud what he craves. As I lay back on the *Times* and looked up into Buck's mask of animal ecstasy, I was so turned on by the thought of his perfect, studly body reaming me out that my ass forgot to be sore. As I hung off the end of his dick, Buck surprised me again. He took the dick he'd just pulled out of my butt, stripped the rubber from its long thick shaft, slid a fresh one on and, leaned over my body to expose his asshole. In a single, swift, sure, sadistic motion, he rammed the massive monster member up his own twitching butt! His cat-green eyes rolled back in his head and he started fucking me like an animal – harder and deeper and with a glorious fierceness unlike anything I'd ever experienced. His *GQ* mouth gaped open, partly to suck in great lungfuls of air to fan the flames of his fuck-frenzy, partly to let his moans and snarls of brutish mammalian rapture slide out. His hard pecs and broad shoulders contracted into knots of muscle but hung almost motionless above me; his hands pinched and twisted at my tits and grabbed great fistfuls of my chest hair. His hips, though, slid along his meaty monorail, heading straight for the pleasure of my tormented butthole. One sweaty thunderclap after another shook the room as his pelvis crashed into my butt, sliding me up along the *Times* until every slam of his dick was echoed with the thump of my head into the wall behind me. Every movement, every smell, every sight of the next several minutes has seared itself into my consciousness forever, but sorting through that stunning symphony of sensations is beyond the power of mortal man. My memory can only conjure especially savory images to convey the abandon and fierceness of our savage rut – for that is what our fuck had become. We were transported far beyond the mere basement of a temple of modern learning – far back through space and time to the jungle ruthlessness of our primitive, barbaric lusts. No longer creatures of the mind, we were guided only by the feral fierceness of Buck's untamed cock and my burning, all-consuming need to have it slammed up my desperate, hungry fuckhole. I felt his sweat dripping down onto my dick-racked body and smelt his heat as I writhed beneath him. I heard his breathing change as his cadence grew even more frenzied and irregular. His ballbag stopped slamming up against my ass and, as he shifted his weight more over me, I felt his thick, brutal butt-buster begin to pound into my prostate. Shivers of incomprehensible bliss radiated from his dickhead as it bolted and reamed and rammed its way up into my guts – and into my soul.

My legs wrapped tight and then tighter around his ass, pulling my willing fuckhole up his thick dick to stretch myself on the altar of his lust-driven immolation. Buck was barely conscious now, lost in the fog of frenzy that comes to men when they cum to men. His dick directed our destiny now, driving his hips against my ass, melding his flesh with mine. His upper body hung suspended by the same enchantment that enraptured my ass and wove the veil that hid from my brain the news that Buck was a major pain in the ass. That magic veil was not only the shroud of my pain, but also the scrim of my lust, letting only his beauty and power and the radiance of his hard masculinity shine through to light every dark corner of my being.

His massive manmeat was certainly firing up every dark corner of my butt. Every inch of my shit-chute slid tight against his rampaging dick, holding him steady on course. As his flying fuck-stick fed the friction fires up my ass, ground away at my prostate, and drilled through the end of my love tunnel, I pulled his handsome face down against mine. My heels prodded and sundered the hard-clenching muscles of his butt, working themselves down to his own overstuffed fuckhole to give his huge dildo-dick a kick in the ass, and I felt his teeth dig into my neck like a vampire.

Somehow, he still managed to bellow out the death-cry of a wounded mastodon as his body slipped into the fierce, final seizures I'd been expecting. I held him tight while his meaty dick did its nasty, sweet, wonderful work. His breathing stopped for a time and then started again in great gulps. The heat up my butt, unable to enjoy his creamy balm, grew from a glow to a fire that was completely out of control – but my craving for his dick was so frantic that I clenched down all the harder. We pounded and lashed together through the storm of our mutual need until his huge, cum-choked balls were drained flat as an empty promise.

When, at last, the storm had passed and the spasms abated, he released my shoulder from his relentless dental grip and collapsed atop me, all sliding, sweaty muscle and groping hands and lambent lips sliding across mine. Our bodies heaved together as we tried to recover our wind and keep the magic of his presence up my ass. Buck held me tight in his massive arms, but eventually had to pull his peg out of my hole and we were no longer one.

The hunky slut reached down with a grin, peeled the rubber from his cock, and slurped down every creamy drop of the load he'd just pumped up my butt. Watching him lick his chops in self-satisfaction, I knew I wouldn't be happy until I'd blasted everything I had down his gorgeous man-hole – just so I could suck my rubber dry, too. Now that his monster fucking dick was out of my ass, I felt my cock throbbing against my furry belly again, and knew there was no time like the present to get moving. He stood towering above me, legs apart, those green eyes of his twinkling his satisfaction. I reached up between his hard thighs, past his shriveled ballbag, and grabbed the rubber dick still clamped hard inside him. I yanked it out of his guts and started to smile myself: "Get another rubber, whore. You're about to learn what a fuck really is."

A terrible shudder rippled through his body as I took him seriously, but as I fucked the living shit out of his tight, jock ass over the next thirty minutes or so, he proved he could take it even better than he dished it out. Hanging over his perfect body, ramming my manhood up into his manhole and making him squirm and twist and moan with our pleasure, was probably the best thing that ever happened to me. When I'd finished and reached down to gobble my victory toast of frothy, fresh man-cream, it was even sweeter than I'd expected. Still, my own rich jism isn't as sweet as what we did next with the vibrator or how Buck used that rolled-up copy of *Life*. We kept on for hours, until the geek from the reference desk came down to complain about dawn happening. Buck just patted me on the butt and asked me to come back the next night for a rematch.

That was six weeks ago. My grades have slipped considerably since then, but considering the time I'm spending in the library, I'm not a bit surprised.

MIKEY LIKED IT

William Cozad

In high school I tried out for the football team in my senior year. I was crushed when I didn't make the it. Truth was, I just wasn't big enough. Seeing my disappointment, the coach offered me the position of team manager. He tried to convince me I'd still be a part of the team, could go to all the out-of-town games, and earn a letter to wear on my school jacket. But that wasn't why I took the job. The real reason was Mike, the quarterback, the star of the team. Handing out towels might've seemed pretty dull for a straight kid, but for a gay one like me the idea of hanging around in the locker room and showers with a whole team of hot football studs was just what the doctor ordered.

But Mike was my special favorite – a truly gorgeous hunk. Medium height, solid muscle, with sandy blond hair and blue-gray eyes. And he made my dick hard like only a teenager's dick can get. All the cheerleaders threw themselves at him.

The football season started poorly for our Winters Huskies. We'd lost a bunch of top players who'd graduated the year before, and lost the first two games. Coach Cole wasn't one to give up easily, though – especially when his butt was on the line. He worked the team hard in practice, kept them late memorizing new plays, and generally tried to build a fire under them. Well, it worked. Mike started running with the ball instead of just throwing it, and the team picked up some yardage, and their first win. By the end of the season, the Huskies were on a roll, and it was really coming together for them. They made the playoff for the conference championship against the undefeated Silver Creek Indians, and school spirit was running high. There was a lot of pressure on the team and the coach. The practice sessions for the championship game were intense. As team manager I felt like a shadowy figure, working behind the scenes, taking care of equipment and being a general gofer. But the players were nice to me, and at least I finally belonged somewhere on campus. As you might have guessed, I spent a lot of time fantasizing about my hero, Mike the quarterback. I was a chronic masturbator to start with, but nothing turned me on – not even the bodies of all the other hot players – like Mike did.

I hung around the showers until I was shrivelled, just to feast my eyes on that naked god. Even so, his cock was a monster slab of uncut meat, with pendulous balls. His body was smooth, with big pecs and washboard abs, but his pits, crotch and asscrack were hairy. I was spanking my little champ twice every night just to get to sleep, and most mornings I woke up with a raging boner that refused to go down until I drained my nuts. I couldn't get Mike off my mind. The painful reality was I'd never be able to do anything about it. There was no way I'd ever be able to touch Mike besides high fives, slaps on the back and sometimes the rump. How I yearned for the old days when guys goosed each other in junior high and asked you if you could shoot yet. There'd even been talk about circle jerks, but I was never invited and wasn't sure if they'd ever really happened. And then fate hunted me down. Suddenly I got my chance the day of the final practice before the championship game.

Mike had a charley horse. Nothing serious – he was so gung-ho he'd have played that last game with a broken leg. Coach usually took care of problem muscles himself or told the player to use rubbing alcohol. I'm sure the coach was totally straight – he never gave any hint that he was interested in anything except the players' condition. But the coach had a faculty meeting to attend and ordered me to massage Mike's leg muscle with alcohol. I told Mike to stick around, then killed time storing equipment, giving the other players time to shower and leave. Mike waited for me in his jockstrap, and his body was like the chiseled marble of a Greek statue. He was absolutely a young god. I pretended to be strictly business, although my cock was stirring in my pants. I'd seen the coach check players' muscles before. "Lie back on the bench, put your feet up. That's it."

A bag of supplies was sitting handy nearby.

I squeezed Mike's sinewy right leg until he winced, then splashed on the minty scented alcohol and rubbed it in.

"Just lie back, relax." He gave me a funny, but trusting look.

Rubbing Mike's leg gave me the same sensation as rubbing my dick. I was breathing heavy, although I tried to control it so it wouldn't be noticeable. "Close your eyes. Think about something peaceful, like a mountain stream where you're cooling off on a hot summer day. That's it. I'll take care of this charley horse."

I know this sounds crazy, but I couldn't take any chances. I'd never get another opportunity in my life like this. I had to do it. "You're moving around too much. Gotta stay still while I massage this leg." I was so distracted by the forest of sandy blond pubes that fanned out from his jockstrap – and the heaving pouch with his big jewels – that I could barely concentrate. "It'll work better if I secure you."

"What the fuck you talkin' about?"

Before Mike could object or get away, I managed to manacle his hands to the bench with a strip of Ace elastic bandage. In another quick movement I had his legs tied to the bench with another elastic strip. "What the fuck!"

"Trust me. This will keep you still while I concentrate on massaging your leg." I admired my handiwork. I'd had a recurring dream about tying up Mike and having my way with him.

"You're crazy! I've never heard of anything like this before."

"I plan to be a doctor someday. I've read about anatomy. I know a lot about the human body, about bones and muscles."

"I think you're full of shit.. Let me loose."

"Sorry, I can't do that. Coach's orders, you know, to take care of you."

"Untie me or I'll scream."

"Hey, that's not very macho. Besides I can gag you."

"The school janitor will be coming by to clean up. What if he sees me like this?"

"He's drunk, and in the boiler room sleeping it off. I've never seen him around before dark."

"Fuck, you've thought of everything. I think you've slipped a gear."

"I'll make you better, fit as a fiddle. You'll see." Splashing more alcohol on his leg, I massaged it in earnest.

With Mike tied to the bench like a killed deer on a car fender, you might say I pushed the envelope of my massage. I rubbed up his thigh right to where the leg joins the hip. It was doing the trick, too, because his cock was straining the pouch.

"Keep rubbing my crotch and I'll get a boner."

"You already got one, big boy."

"Hey man, you're queer, ain't you? I should have known, the way you hang around the showers, the way you gawk at me bare-ass naked."

"Oh, man, Mike. You're in excellent physical condition. I wish I had your body."

"Well, you'll never get it. You're not a girl."

"Is this some kind of discrimination?"

"You're nuts."

"But not stupid. Look who's tied up."

"I could get loose, you know."

"I could tie you up tighter."

Looking into Mike's eyes, I could see they were burning like a blue flame. He was excited.

"Hmmm," I moaned. "Yup, Mikey likes it!"

Making no pretense now, I rubbed his inner thighs and cupped his straining elastic pouch.

"Oooh fuck!"

"Feel good?"

"Oh man, that's where I live."

"Where I wanna live."

"What?"

"Never mind." I rubbed the jockstrap pouch until his cock was tenting it, stretching the fabric. I couldn't stand it any longer. Kneeling by the bench, I sniffed his jockstrap. It smelled like sweat, piss and dried cum – a delicious scent. Better than any of those designer colognes.

Sticking out my tongue, I started licking his jockstrap. "Oh wow, I don't fucking believe this."

While I lapped at his jockstrap, soaking it with spit, my own cock leaked like a sieve in my pants. Gazing at the football star strapped to the board, his eyes glazed with lust and beads of sweat forming on his forehead, I was drunk with power. He was all mine, to use however I wanted. If he got loose he might kill me in cold blood or tell the cops, accuse me of unlawful detainment. Jesus, maybe even rape. But I hadn't done anything yet, except lick his jockstrap. Now I was nibbling on it, chewing on it, feeling his love muscle underneath strain to the max. Maybe they'd put me in the funny farm, in the rubber room for safe sex. I was lost in lust.

In a frenzy, I bit into the jockstrap and tugged it down with my teeth.

I expected to see Mike's dick hard, with the head out of the foreskin, but nothing prepared me for the sudden spurts of hot cum. His cock was like a busted firehose – I couldn't believe it. He'd shot all over my face, and his steamy cum was dripping down my cheeks. I was licking it, tasting its sweet flavor.

"I fucking shot my load soon as my cock hit the air. Unreal. never even touched my pecker. You're such a fuckin' bastard."

"Oh, Mike. You weren't supposed to cum yet. That spoils everything. It's not the way it happened in my dreams."

"You dream of me? Of dicks?"

"Just your dick. There, I've said it."

"Then you are queer?"

"Look, if you take one drink it doesn't make you an alcoholic. If you suck one dick – and I didn't even do that."

"Shit! Untie me. Let's get outta here."

"You're not mad?"

"Hell, no. I just got my rocks off."

"Well, I didn't."

"You can go home and do it."

"I don't want to."

"Well, my leg feels better."

I reached over and touched Mike's silky smooth cockskin. I tugged on the foreskin and another drop of cum dribbled out of the pisshole. I cupped his balls. His cock pulsed and stayed stiff. "Looks like you still got cum in your balls."

"Go ahead, jack it some more." Mike was grinning. He wasn't supposed to.

In my dreams he got mad and threatened to tell everyone I was queer. He even told me to stay away from him, never speak to him again. I thought about pinching myself. Maybe this wasn't really happening. I blinked my eyes but Mike didn't disappear. Mesmerized by his cock, I knew I had to taste it. I stuck out my tongue and licked his dick, then held the pulsing shaft and swabbed its rosy crown, tasting the tangy cheese residue. I nibbled at the foreskin. "Oh Jesus, that feels so good.

You're a cocksucker. I know you are, man. No matter what you say I know you're a fuckin' fairy."

"So?"

"So, asshole, I've never had my dick sucked before. You're gonna blow me, ain't you?"

"That what you want?"

"Oh, *fuck* yeah."

"Naw. I want you to suffer a little, like you made me suffer, wanting you, longing for you, just living for a look, a smile, a hint of recognition. But you hardly knew I was alive, what with all them pussies."

"Do me, man."

I stood up. "No, I should just leave you here all tied up. The janitor's probably so drunk he wouldn't even notice."

"Suck me off first."

I couldn't believe it. Mike, the star football player, was begging me to suck his dick. But then I thought he was conning me. Maybe when I untied him he'd strangle me.

Kneeling beside the bench again, I fastened my lips around his bullet-shaped cockhead.

"Eat it. Eat my big dick."

I impaled my mouth on it, but I gagged. His dick was too big – he'd choke me to death for sure. This wasn't supposed to happen either.

My mind quickly switched gears. I'd do what I really wanted – whether Mike liked it or not. I wanted to be one of those cheerleaders I'd been sure he was plugging.

Yeah, I wanted him the way he had the girls. His teenaged prick was towering in the air. It was an eight-inch column of steel-hard dickmeat. I shucked my clothes.

"Whatcha doing?"

"Gonna give you a piece of ass. Cherry boy-pussy. You want it?"

"Shit, any port in the storm, man."

His pecker was not only raging, it was drooling pre-cum. Oh, I'd fingered my pucker a little, but I'd never stuck anything up my butthole before, but I never wanted anything as much as this. I straddled Mike's belly on the bench. Reaching back, I lubed the cock and impaled my ass on it.

"Jesus," he moaned.

"Fucking hurts. Your dick's so big."

"Sit on it. Do it for me."

Luckily, his pre-cum wet my pucker enough to take his dick up my shit chute without tearing it apart. His prick was like a hot poker up my hole, but I sat down on his meat until I felt his bristly pubes scratch my asscheeks. He thrust upwards. Just looking into Mike's cloudy blue-gray eyes, his tongue lolling, his breaths coming short and fast, knowing it was his prick in my butthole, was making me crazy.

My own prick was hard – not quite as long as Mike's but a bit thicker around. I fisted it while I humped his dick. Suddenly my cock just gushed all over the football player's belly. My hole clenched around his dick, which blasted cum deep into me.

When I lifted up, Mikey plopped out. He looked sexy with his jockstrap pulled down on his thighs and that big prick back in its hood, lying over those spent bullnuts. I cleaned the gunk off his prick with my tongue and even lapped up my own cum that I'd squirted into a puddle on his belly.

"You okay?" I asked.

"Never better," he managed. He was spent, breathing hard.

Cautiously, I untied him. He grabbed me and my heart lurched in my chest. I thought I was dead meat – but he just hugged me.

Both of us got dressed. He said he'd fucked the charley horse out of his leg, surely as beating off got rid of headaches.

Mike was totally awesome in the game against the Silver Creek Indians. He threw passes that connected, and even ran into the end zone. The Winters Huskies won the South Central Championship, and I won the chance to give Mike another massage. I never pressed him, but it seemed like I was able to give him "a good rubdown" at least once a week even though football season was over.

THE SECRET OF THE RUE ST. GERMAIN

Charles Willard Scoggins

Alfred Mock spent his second summer of a few weeks in Paris as a man of sixty. When he was seventeen, before he went for duty in the Merchant Marines during World War I, he spent several weeks in Paris with a lifelong friend from London where both of them were born and grew up. William was Alfred's friend's name. They were both seventeen and loved each other as friends with passion that never died – though William was killed in France and Alfred never saw him again.

After the War, in 1920, Alfred came to America where he married, settled in Morristown, New Jersey, and at sixty had an estate there, a son graduated from Yale Law School, a daughter married to a New York doctor, a wife, and the executive vice presidency in charge of advertising at a national finance company located also in Morristown. Through all the years the memory of William stayed pure and unchanged with Alfred.

"He was the sweetest boy on earth," Alfred said of him. "I've never loved anyone nor has anyone ever meant more to me than William. He had blond hair, blue eyes, and a simple clean face. I can still see him that summer in Paris sitting at the sidewalk cafes with me on the Rue St. Germain on the Left Bank – as simple-hearted and beautiful as he was; and as friends – I mean real friends – we were so important to each other. I shall never forget how it crushed me when I heard he'd died. I couldn't believe it. I didn't believe it though I knew it was true. You'll never know how tortured I was to know I'd never see William again."

To the Parisians – the Left Bank Parisians – the sidewalk cafes of the Rue St. Germain were a commonplace; but to Alfred when he returned to Paris for the first time in over forty years and came to the Rue and sat at the tables of the open cafes, they had an air of mystery, intrigue, and adventure.

In the years since he and William had sat at these tables, Alfred's blissful, pure, and noble friendship with William would in memory be churned over and over through the years with the lust that came to Alfred to mangle his adult manhood and maturity with the search in its more pleasant bodily form what he so purely had found in his youth and kept intact in his memory of William. Over and over in the years he found again and again in other young men the sanctity and loving memory of his friend William – in the many vast cities of the States he travelled in his work, in Greenwich Village, in the bars and other cruising places he frequented he found memories of William.

On the Rue Alfred, he picked a table at one of the cafes and sat watching everything around him, drinking all of it in, intrigued by the half overheard voices in French of the people at the tables on either side of him or close behind him. After awhile – a half hour or so – since one can sit undisturbed by the waiters for hours just sipping a demitasse of black coffee – he got up and walked down St. Germain, past other crowded cafes where if it struck him he would stop at one, sit and sip a cup of coffee and move on again. He was alone in Paris and staying at a hotel on the Left Bank not far from the Rue itself. His wife, Katherine, was in Scotland and would join him in a couple of days.

In the late afternoon sunshine of that first lazy summer day in June, 1968, Alfred sat relaxed and quietly happy at his sidewalk cafes – watching the people; watching the shadows of evening gather around the towers and buttresses of the Catholic Church, St. Germain des Pres, from which the street took its name.

Alfred Mock was a handsome man, stout and trimly built with a head of silvery white hair receding and wavy straight back without a part from the front, thicker and darker in the back; distinguished, gentlemanly, and prosperous-looking in his pinstriped gray suit and vest with the golden watch chain swinging in a loop down from his chest over his flat stomach. His eyes were sky blue, clear, sensitive, compassionate, and alert. They were a man's mature eyes. His hands were useful-looking, strong, and sure. His walk and even the way he sat in a chair was positive. He was – and his whole life was – a positive and aggressive thing.

Alfred had noticed as he strolled from one cafe to the next a French boy in the shadows of a doorway.

Further along, another boy was leaning against a tree.

Then he passed a French boy who looked him in the eyes and murmured as he went by, "Good evening, monsieur." Then there were two boys standing at the street curb with their backs to the traffic which was moderate in the late afterwork hours.

Alfred saw another fellow standing beyond the two boys at the curb and as he approached him he decided to stop and talk to him if he too said, "Good evening." As he came closer to the boy – he was tall, rather thin, about nineteen or twenty, with a pale complexion and classic features – Alfred looked right at him and said with his eyes what he knew the boy would understand.

The boy's eyes answered back. With just a little smile, he greeted Alfred. In his amateur French, Alfred said, "Hello. Good evening," and waited.

There was a pause and then the boy said, "*Voulez vous couche avec moi?*"

The words startled Alfred. He left the boy when he said it would cost him ten dollars! A little dazed by the brazen experience of this young man, Alfred went back to what he'd selected as his favorite sidewalk cafe near the St. Germain Cathedral; and on the way he passed several more young men most of whom looked at him with knowing eyes and many of whom said, "Bon soir, monsieur!" How many did he pass – twenty or thirty, all willing to go to bed with any chance passerby so long as he had the money!

The Rue St. Germain suddenly changed in front of Alfred's eyes. It was no longer just another busy street in Paris crowded with sidewalk cafes; it was a street of boys who were all for sale! The surge of excitement that went through Alfred made his hands shake so much he could hardly trust himself to lift his demitasse to sip his coffee. All around him at the cafe tables they sat – in pairs, in groups; some singles; all of them hunting the hunters! Alfred knew he'd been marked by them as a hunter, and an American hunter at that.

The boy Alfred had stopped and spoken to strolled past, this time with a friend. They came over to his table and the boy explained to Alfred that his friend spoke English and perhaps they'd be able to understand each other better if his friend acted as interpreter, since, he said politely in French, "Your English is better that your French."

Alfred suddenly made up his mind that he'd now discovered the "secret" of the Rue St. Germain (as it had changed in the forty years he and William had been there), and he was going to savor the hunt to the fullest. He was going to stroll up and down and look and stare, classify, select, and reject until finally he'd find the one that he could say to himself, "Yes, that's the one I want," and go with him. He'd have to be one who wasn't like the others, throwing themselves at anybody who gave them a second glance and ten dollars. The money part of it aggravated Alfred. He wanted something pure, and money shouldn't be a part of it.

Alfred got rid of the two French fellows and set out, keyed up to a high emotional pitch at being so completely surrounded on all sides by boys and fellows and men who were all so unashamed and natural, open and frank about it all. He crossed over to the other side of the street from where his favorite cafe was to get away from those he'd already passed and looked at and been looked at in return – several times as he'd hopscotched from cafe to cafe. As he set his foot on the curb on the opposite side, directly in front of him, his back to Alfred, looking in a store window, was a tasseled-haired young boy about seventeen. Alfred stopped. From the back he could see the boy had a shapely attractive body, and Alfred's heart beat faster as his imagination painted the details of the boy's face and features in his mind he couldn't yet see. Alfred strolled over and stood beside the boy, glancing over at him.

Alfred stood there a minute and then at last, unable to bear it any longer, he turned his head full in the boy's direction. Just as he did, the boy looked at him and then swung around and walked off down the street. But in that one instant he'd held Alfred's eyes, fleetingly, just one swift second, "And spoken to me?" Alfred asked himself. "Had he? Had his eyes, that quick glance said anything to me or had I read into them what my own wishes hoped?" In that one instant Alfred had drunk in the beauty of the boy's face and thought he heard him speak; and now he knew he had to follow him--anywhere he went--to find out if indeed he'd spoken to him. Alfred walked a few paces behind the boy, keeping him well in sight lest he lose him in the crowds. He tried to think of ways to open up a conversation: should he speed up, catch up with him and offer him an American cigarette? Should he just walk alongside him and see if he would speak first? The torment of the uncertainty of what to do; the fear that he might lose him; the burning desire that had been aroused in him by that one look into the boy's eyes – all combined to produce in Alfred an excitement, a rush of blood, a dryness in the mouth that had the boy stopped and spoken then, he would've only been able to stammer, his words would've been slurred and thick, and he would've been reduced to incoherency!

The young French boy hadn't turned around to look, yet Alfred felt he knew he was following him. After a short distance of a block or so, the boy turned into a side street leading off the Rue, walked a short way, then crossed the narrow roadway to the opposite curb. Alfred followed him. The boy still hadn't turned around to see if Alfred had followed. The side street was quiet. Most of the shops were closed, some with lighted windows advertising their wares. There were a few pedestrians; and Alfred knew the boy could hear his footsteps in the quietness of the street as he walked a respectable distance behind the boy. The grace and the ease of the young man's walk, the suppleness of his body, the reflected glints from his dark hair as he passed a lighted window – all these caused Alfred's heart to pound even that much more! Then came the meeting – the trick of which was as old as cities were: the boy stopped at a lighted bookstore window waiting, Alfred knew, for him to catch up and stop beside him. Alfred walked past the boy, afraid to stop. Maybe he wasn't a pickup. He feared the embarrassment if he did stop and tried to approach the boy and was rejected by him. Yet, as he passed him, his back to Alfred, Alfred had the distinct feeling that the boy knew he was there and was listening to his footsteps – listening so he could gauge his own movements and whereabouts on the street.

Crossing in front of the entrance to an alley just a few paces further on, Alfred stopped and boldly turned around and looked back. As he did so, the young man walked slowly away from the book store and turned into the alley. For Alfred, it was now or never. From where he stood he could look down the alley – more of a narrow street than an alley, with a sidewalk on one side and hardly wide enough for a car to go down – and he saw that the boy was walking ever so slowly looking back himself now.

    The alley led down a hundred feet or so, then turned sharply to the left. At the bend was a dim sign over a doorway advertising the entrance to a small bistro. High up on the side of one of the buildings a single streetlight barely illuminated the small side street so that the whole little area had an air of murkiness and shadows, and, well, to Alfred, solitude was the word.

    The boy stood right in the span of light from the streetlamp – handsome, inviting, his features softly lit from above, his hair catching the full rays of the light so it shone and stood out, emphasized against the background of the dark buildings, giving the effect to Alfred of an actor standing in the spotlight of a dimly lit stage. The boy stood alone. No one else could be seen on this little side alley in the heart of Paris except Alfred's little French boy.

    Alfred walked down the alley toward the boy and as he came close, Alfred said, "Bon soir, monsieur."

    The boy smiled and said, "Bon soir. How are you this evening?" Alfred could never begin to tell how the boy's smile sent the blood rushing to his head – the pitch of excitement, the emotions that welled up inside him, all compounded by the sound of the boy's voice. He'd spoken to Alfred in just those few words, drawing Alfred to him and embracing him – just in the tone, the sound to Alfred of his sweet voice. What made Alfred say the next thing he never knew. Maybe it was the surge of emotions coursing through him. Maybe it was the boy's smile, his beautiful lips, his trusting eyes that made love to Alfred. Maybe everything about him had let Alfred know instinctively that he'd say yes: "Voulez vous couche avec moi?"

    Never before had he said anything like that to anyone; yet it didn't seem strange after he'd said it. It sounded like one person declaring his love to another. It seemed to Alfred the most natural thing in the world to have said.

    "Oui, monsieur," the boy said; and the lights deepened and softened in his eyes and his lips trembled ever so lightly as he smiled. It was all Alfred could do to restrain himself from kissing the boy right there. They were alone and no one would've seen; and in that moment of acceptance, that mutuality of emotion, the pleasure and joy and sheer delight of such a kiss would've been unmatched! The boy accepted Alfred's invitation to go to his hotel room with him and they set off walking slowly, talking to each other softly. The boy's name was Francis. In English the name is pronounced "Fran-cis"; but in French, the name has a much softer sound, more musical in tone in the way it's pronounced. To Alfred one might almost say that the name had a caressing tone to it. The first part of the name is pronounced in French with the long "a" – FRAN, through the nose slightly. Then the last part is pronounced "CEASE." The harsh sharp English name "FRANcis" becomes the beautiful name "FRAN-CEASE." What notes of music lay in the French pronunciation of the name, waiting only for the instrument of an orchestra to bring it to life and sound and soaring song of love and joy to Alfred! That's how excited he was.

Alfred locked the door of his hotel room behind him and turned to Francis. The young man had preceded him and stood in the middle of the room, his arms outstretched to Alfred, a look of earnestness in his eyes; a half smiling, half serious set to his lips; his body leaning forward ever so slightly so that in the soft glow of the light from the bedside table his whole being spoke of deep yearning.

"Maybe he didn't have a father," Alfred thought, "and that's why he looks at me so longingly."

Alfred liked father-son relationships; they could be so warm and human between an older man like himself and a boy like Francis. Then Francis said very softly, very quietly, "Love me. Please love me like a son, Father Monsieur."

Alfred knew he'd been right. They both needed something they were both looking for; and for Alfred, he felt they'd both found their own individual needs. How many steps from where he stood at the door to being in the boy's arms? He flew! In an instant they were together, each clasping the other to him in an embrace that would've hurt were it not for the joy that sang through their bodies. The boy's lips found Alfred's and Alfred felt him swooning with emotion as he himself was, the boy's body trembling against Alfred's own trembling body.

Alfred took the boy's face between his hands gently as they

drank deeply of each others kisses; then very slowly, still holding him, Alfred moved the boy's head back so he could look into his eyes. Could one ever read someone else's soul by looking into their eyes? Not unless they let you and showed their soul to you through their eyes. As Francis did. Alfred looked into the innermost depths of his eyes and knew he and the boy were one; and Alfred let the boy see deeply into his own soul, into the secret places of his past as a human being so the boy would know too that they were interlocked lovers together sharing souls as well as bodies. "I want to get undressed for you so I can hold you closer to me," Francis said. "I want you to rock me in your arms like a little child." They took off their clothes together without seeming to Alfred to let go of each other without for an instant being out of each others arms, kissing each other; and then the next moment they were pressed naked against each other; and Alfred could feel the boy's body on fire because his face was flush and his lips were burning hot!

They embraced with passion now – a gentle but furious passion charged high with emotion. The boy's hands grasped Alfred's buttocks pulling Alfred against him as Alfred held the boy tightly around his bare shoulders crushing his chest to him while they kissed each other passionately. Somehow, tightly entwined though they were, oblivious as they were to everything around them, conscious as they were of only their own passionate feelings for each other and that they were alone, they somehow moved toward the bed and fell upon it together so they wouldn't break their embrace nor lose a moment of the searing joy that was within them. Alfred could feel the boy's every muscle tensed against him with longing and joy – just how Alfred himself felt melded into the boy's presence. They explored each other's bodies with their hands, adding through a delicate sense of touch more fuel to their already searing desire for each other: The roundness of the boy's shoulders; the firmness of his biceps; the smoothness of his thighs – the sensitive secret part of his thighs close up to his body where they met. The boy's hands stroking Alfred's buttocks, letting his fingers play between and down till it drove Alfred mad! And changing his position, Alfred caught the boy's head and though the boy needed no urging, Alfred pressed his face against his stomach so he could feel his kisses there and lower and lower.

This moment was Alfred's and Francis's – no others. It was private and personal, just between the two of them. It was something not to be shared with others – not to be told to others. Alfred had the feeling that the very telling of it to someone else would take away from Francis and him what they'd so secretly shared – that he would bring down on his head a sense of deep guilt at having violated the cherished secrets of the passions they felt and shared that were theirs alone. He feared too that this sense of guilt, if engendered, would insidiously creep into the memories he held so dear of this night they spent together and spoil them beyond recognition. If he told it to anyone, never again would he be able to look back on these few hours and feel the quickened heartbeat, the flush of intense emotion that suffused him when he saw in the mind's eye of his heart the beautiful body of his lover Francis and heard his sweet voice and felt his lips on his own. But then, what could Alfred tell? In truth, he didn't remember events and happenings – that Francis did this and he did that. Alfred could only remember a beautiful song in his heart. He remembered the beauty of the boy's body and the way their bodies seemed to be one. He remembered the beauty of his eyes and how he looked deeply into them and how they spoke to each other this way – of emotions that words could never say. He remembered the yielding softness of the boy's lips; the giving of himself to Alfred with his lips so that each of them together were no longer in that room. How could Alfred say it? How could he describe the emotions, feelings, passions, and joys in each other that carried them outside themselves?

Alfred remembered the blaze of fire that went through his body at the climatic moment; though when exactly the boy's lips had first started to caress Alfred's; and when Alfred's lips had found Francis's, Alfred couldn't remember – the blaze of fire that leapt out of all bounds with the bursts of knowing that he, Alfred, was sharing his moment of joyous climax with him, Francis, and at the same time. Then the blissful peace as they lay quietly still in each other's arms. The long slow descent from that heaven they'd both visited together. Alfred's reluctance to break the spell: he so wanted this hour to last forever; but he wanted to say it out loud. The words formed on his lips; then he held them back. Again; then hushed them.

Then, unable to bear it any longer, Alfred said ever so softly, "I love you, Francis."

Kissing Alfred first, the boy answered, "I love you."

Alfred buried his face in the curve of the boy's neck and felt the slow hot tears that come only at moments of great and boundless joy – a joy he could no longer hold within himself and that could only find expression in soft tears.

The next morning Alfred went again to the Rue St. Germain and found again the store where he'd first seen Francis. He walked down St. Germain to the side street Francis had turned into, down that street until he came to the alley, the little narrow street where Francis had stopped under the street light that had shown upon his hair and he'd looked back at Alfred waiting for him. Francis. It was broad daylight now and there were many people about crowding the little alley. There was the noise of traffic, the sound of hurrying footsteps, of voices. Alfred pushed his way through, unseeing, yet still seeing Francis standing there, the lamplight a halo in his hair, his face turned toward Alfred, a smile on his lips. Someone pushed past Alfred as he walked through the crowd to the spot where Francis had stood. Alfred murmured, "Pardon, monsieur," and kept on. He reached the place where Francis had stood when he first spoke to Alfred; and for a moment Alfred paused. He didn't say the words too loud for fear the passing Frenchmen would hear him. He was saying the words to Francis: "*Bon soir, Francis. Voulez vous couche avec moi?*"

Then Alfred hurried on. He came back to the sidewalk cafes of the Rue, found his favorite cafe and in the late morning sunshine had a demitasse of coffee sitting alone. The cafe was nearly empty. He didn't remember William right at first, the memory of Francis was so overpowering; and then he did remember William. "Poor dear William," he thought. "He would've been an old man like me now if he'd lived. Would he have understood if I'd told him of Francis? He probably wouldn't have, so good and so pure was his heart."

Alfred got up and walked back to his hotel room where he waited for his wife who would arrive from Scotland that afternoon.

There was only one thing he didn't like about the previous night with Francis. Francis had lingered in his room after he'd gotten up and dressed; and to save the boy embarrassment, Alfred had offered him the ten dollars first.

He didn't mind; he was glad to give him the money. He'd received so much in return. A memory of love, the experience of which he would carry with him to the day he died.

− *This story was based on a 1968 letter to the author from Alfred.*

FEASTING WITH PANTHERS

Thomas C. Humphrey

As I jockeyed the heavy tour bus around fallen limbs and debris on the ice-coated streets, already I was second-guessing my impulsive offer to take Billy Hawthorne in for the night. He had completely disconcerted me since I first glimpsed him that afternoon when I picked up the Panthers football team for their final road game of the season. He was so much like my old high school teammate, Richie Hawthorne, that the hair on the nape of my neck stood up and a sudden enervating hollowness washed through the pit of my stomach when he first climbed on the bus. Every time I looked at Billy the rest of the trip, my groin tightened, and I had an eerie feeling that I was in the presence of a ghost, a ghost I had tried unsuccessfully for years to put to rest.

But when we were introduced in the gym after we got back to town, he had avoided eye contact with me and muttered and mumbled and shuffled around like he was about to piss his pants. Alone with me on the empty bus, he responded to my attempts at conversation with monosyllabic replies in a voice so low I could hardly hear him from the seat directly behind me. I've had better conversations with people talking in their sleep. Whatever nostalgia for the past and growing sexual urgency he had aroused earlier quickly began to fade.

His whole demeanor really began to piss me, because I was no more than five years older than him, not some withered old fogy who was out of touch with young people. He'd almost certainly seen me play for the Panthers when I was in high school, and I was good enough that he'd have remembered who I was. It wasn't as if I'd drifted down from outer space; I was home folks, for Christ's sake.

Like it or not, though, I was stuck with him, at least for the night, because he had nowhere else to go. A sudden early December storm of driving rain mixed with sleet had plummeted the central Georgia temperature into the low teens, snapped trees and power lines, and completely closed some narrow roads to outlying communities. Especially team members who lived out at Harper's Mill were stranded at least for the night, if not for most of the weekend. When those of us huddled in the Pelham County High gym had been asked to take some of them in, I had jumped at the opportunity to spend the night with Billy. Now I was stuck with him.

After I parked the bus, Billy and I trudged precariously across the icy asphalt to my tiny apartment, which occupied part of a storage shed on the back of my dad's building supply company lot. Since I came out of the Army, I had turned the place into a pretty cozy lair, but so far I had been unable to entice anyone to share it with me, even for a night. Billy was to be my first guest.

We stood just inside the door to brush particles of ice off our hair. I hurriedly kicked up the thermostat and lit the gas logs in the fake fireplace to thaw the place out. Then I went for towels and tossed one to Billy. "I'm gonna have a beer," I said, rubbing my hair vigorously. "You want a soda?"

"Got an extra beer?" he surprised me.

"You're not old enough to drink," I lectured.

"Come on, man!" he bristled. "Don't treat me like some little kid."

Impressed by this unexpected show of balls, I went to the fridge for two Buds. After all, I figured, if he was anything like Richie and the other Hawthornes I had known, he had been drinking stronger stuff than beer since he was ten or twelve. I'd grown up out toward Harper's Mill and had been best friends with Richie, who I knew had to be a cousin or some relative of Billy. All the Hawthornes in the county are closely related. Most of them run stills in the pine woods and sell what shine they don't drink themselves all over the county.

By the time I got back with the beers, Billy had draped his athletic jacket over a chair and was taking off his wet sneakers. As he sat on the couch guzzling the Bud too fast and screwing up his face in distaste like a kid trying to come across as a pro, I nursed my beer and tried not to stare at him too openly.

The Hawhornes had Indian blood in them, and the genes were especially prominent in Billy. His coarse straight hair, now standing askew from the toweling, was as black as a raven's breast, with the same shiny, blue-purple tinge. His high cheek bones were wide and prominent, his nose slightly hooked, his jaw square and firm, his lips thin and even. Set against his unblemished, weathered-copper skin, his deep-set doe eyes were so brown they seemed almost black.

While I continued to strain at conversation and kept crashing against grunts and monosyllables, I was struck by how slightly built he was. He was not skinny, and his chest showed definition through his tight shirt, but I would have bet that one of my hands would more than three-quarters span it side to side. His arms were well-toned, but not overly muscular, and his long, thin neck was more typical of a freshman than a senior athlete. Altogether, he appeared almost fragile, and, recognizing this, I was impressed by his tenacity on the football field.

Within minutes, his beer can resounded emptily on the end table and he looked at me expectantly. "Help yourself," I offered. "And bring me one," I added as he moved toward the kitchen.

Halfway through his second and, I had decided, last beer, he actually had begun to talk in complete sentences, and not just in response to my questions. By the time he set the empty down, he had lost his scared animal look and had relaxed enough to be enjoying himself.

On a return trip from taking a piss, he stopped to pick up a framed picture of the Panther team I'd quarterbacked my senior year, the only Pelham High team to win a state championship. "I saw every game that year," he said. "It was fantastic. We don't play worth shit compared to you guys."

"Yeah, things did come together for us that year," I agreed.

"You and Richie were good friends, weren't you?"

"Good friends," I nodded. "How were you related?"

"First cousins. It totally wrecked me when he died."

"It got to me, too," I said. For the thousandth time, my mind flashed back to Richie running like the wind after catching one of my passes. As the image formed, I was acutely conscious again of just how much Billy reminded me of him.

"Yeah, I remember how you were at the funeral," he said quietly.

Then it all swept back over me. Richie and I had not been just friends. He had seduced me and introduced me to sex when we were twelve and playing Little League together. Before that first time with him, I hadn't known enough even to masturbate. Over the next six years, under his expert guidance, I learned it all. While keeping up a super-macho jock image, which included making it with a few girls, Richie and I balled each other every chance we got. Although he had a cavalier attitude toward our relationship, by the time we finished high school, he had become the first and, so far, only love of my life.

When he was killed a few weeks after graduation in a drunken auto accident, I went crazy. I showed up for the funeral almost falling-down drunk and created a scene after the service when I wouldn't let the mortician close his casket and had to be dragged out of the church by our teammates. After that, I tried to drown myself in alcohol. Although I had an academic scholarship to college, shortly after his death, I ran away to the Army, and I had been drifting ever since, succumbing to too much liquor and too many memories.

When I forced myself back to the present, I noticed that Billy was deep in thought, too. I was about to offer him a penny for them when we were plunged into darkness by a power outage. "Damn," I said. "There goes the central heat. Good thing the fireplace is gas." I lit a kerosene lamp filled with scented oil and set it on the coffee table. In the lambent glow across the ceiling, we both again retreated into reverie. The only sounds were the wind whistling and howling around the storage sheds and the sporadic "crack, crack" of pine saplings snapping under their burden of ice in the woods out back.

After waiting quite a while for the power to come back on, I gave up. "I think we'd better move a mattress out here by the heater," I said. "We'll freeze our balls off without heat in the bedroom tonight."

Billy helped me shift furniture to make room and lug out the mattress and covers. We stripped to our briefs, but neither of us was ready for sleep. Billy stretched out on his stomach and propped on elbows to stare at the hissing blue flames of the fireplace, and I sat on the edge of the mattress pinching at my temples, battling a headache that neither the beer nor three aspirins had eased.

"What's the matter?" Billy asked.

"Tension headache," I muttered.

"Would a massage help?" he asked, sitting up to squeeze my deltoid.

I stretched full length on the mattress, and Billy straddled my back and rubbed, kneaded, pinched, and pounded on my neck and shoulders like a professional masseur. I was surprised at the strength in his long, thin fingers, and I luxuriated in his touch.

"You are stiff," he said, shifting down until he practically sat on my ass. The tingle in my groin signaled that my back muscles were not my only stiffness. As he rocked back and forth, rubbing and kneading, the increasing heat and pressure from the front of his briefs soon clued me in that he was becoming aroused by our contact, too.

"Just how close were you and Richie?" he asked out of left field, completely discomfiting me. I detected a new huskiness in his voice and read exciting possibilities into his question.

"Close," I said. "Very close."

After a slight hesitation, he cleared his throat. "Richie told me some things about you and him," he said, his voice quivering with fear or excitement, or both.

"Oh? What things?" I queried.

"You know. Things," he said.

"Just how close were you and Richie," I asked.

"Close," he said. "Very close."

He went back to rubbing my back, but the force of his hands had softened into a caress. He worked his way around my sides and underneath to my nipples. He bent to kiss me lightly between the shoulder blades. "Do we have to play games with this?" he asked with a note of desperation.

I rolled out from under him and sat up beside him, our faces inches apart. In the spectral light, for a moment it was Richie and not Billy beside me. I shivered involuntarily, as if someone had walked over my grave. An agonized groan welled up from deep inside and escaped from my lips. Billy reached to caress my cheek and brought me back to the present.

"Are you sure about this?" I asked.

"I'm sure," he said, pushing me back onto the mattress. He leaned in to kiss me, his lips barely touching mine.

I pulled him atop me, and, as our kiss intensified, he emitted a soft animal whimper, and his entire body quivered faintly under my touch. At first, his own hands moved over my body with feline stealth and caution, fingers barely grazing my skin with maddening delicacy. When I grasped his buttocks and ground our pelvises together, he clawed at me hungrily and his whimper changed to a low growl. We became a tangle of arms and legs and hands and lips, tossing and turning and wrestling and exploring.

I managed to get first his and then my briefs off and held him down on his back as I mapped his lithe body with my hands. It was silk beneath my fingers, smooth and unflawed. Except for a small, coarse thatch in his crotch, he was completely hairless, even under his armpits. His baby-soft face had never known the touch of a razor. When I tongued one of his small nipples, the nub stood up a quarter of an inch, rock solid. As I explored, he lay trembling and mewling little animal sounds. When I reached his cock, so rigidly flattened against his abdomen that I had to force my fingers beneath it, he tensed his whole body and arched his back. As I took him in my mouth, he moaned, "It's been so long!" and clutched roughly at my hair with both hands, guiding me farther down on him.

I had hardly begun to savor his long, thin cock before he was shoving me away. "Not yet!" he said urgently. He twisted out from under me and wrestled me to my back. In the dim light, his black mane obscured his forehead, and his doe eyes had narrowed into dark, feline slits. When he touched my cock for the first time, he whispered, "Oh, god! Richie said it was big, but – oh, god!" Then he lowered his mouth on it.

I was practically delirious with excitement. I wanted to force myself completely into his warm, eager mouth and dissolve my entire being into the acute pleasure point of my throbbing cock. But I also did not want the pleasure to end, not too quickly. I forced myself to pry his mouth off me and to become the aggressor again. He did not submit easily, and for a long time we grappled and fought, each staving off climax after climax by striving to give the other the ultimate pleasure before our own became too acute. We wrestled and struggled like feral beasts vying over downed prey, each refusing to succumb to the defeat of orgasm before the other was vanquished.

After half an hour of this near-ecstatic duel, Billy whispered, "I want you to fuck me," and added plaintively, "but use a rubber."

As I fumbled in the darkness of my icy bedroom for condoms and lubricant, I recalled that Oscar Wilde once said that the uninhibited sex act was like feasting with panthers. For the second time in my life, my own Pelham Panther was waiting, and I hurried back to the feast.

"Go slow," he begged as I positioned his legs over my shoulders and pressed against him. When I eased in, he sucked in his breath and shrank away from the intrusion, then relaxed and shoved forward to meet me. I patiently worked my full length into him, freed his legs, and lowered my chest against his body. He wrapped his legs about me tightly, and his hands traced urgent patterns on my back as I established slow, shallow, rhythmic thrusts. As they deepened and sped up, he clawed at my back desperately, nails digging in, and chewed hungrily at my shoulders and neck. All the while he was making low growling animal sounds deep in his throat.

All too soon, he cried out, "Oh, god, I'm coming!" and bit down on my shoulder, hard, drawing blood. His ass pulsed and tightened around my cock, and his own cock twitched and thrashed against my abdomen and spilled out copiously between our bodies. A moment later, I buried myself as deeply as possible and shot burst after burst into the confining rubber. I collapsed against him and we lay unmoving, breathing heavily and both purring like big cats who have been stroked into contentment.

"I hope you're not disappointed," he said as he lay with his head on my chest and I ruffled his hair lethargically while we rested for what we both knew would be an equally grueling second course.

"It was beautiful," I assured him. "How could I possibly be disappointed?"

"It's just that - it's been so long. I've never done anything, except with Richie. I don't have anything to compare it to," he said.

"You had a good teacher, the same one I had, and you sure haven't forgotten any of the lessons," I said. "But you couldn't have been more than fourteen when Richie died. You mean you've gone that long? Why?"

"I don't know. You don't get many chances in Harper's Mill," he said. "I was so broken up about Richie, I didn't even want anybody else for a long time, and then when I did, I knew what other guys thought about it and I couldn't let them find out. And I was afraid of AIDS and things. Then I knew you were back in town and I sort of hoped something like tonight would happen."

"Thank god for ice storms," I said.

"Yeah," he agreed. "When I found out I was coming home with you, I was so nervous I couldn't even talk to you. You must have thought I was a retard. I don't even like beer, but I knew I had to do something to get my nerve up."

"Thank god for beer," I said.

"And for power failures," he laughed.

"So Richie told you all about me, huh?" I asked.

"Yeah. I guess he figured if I knew you did things with him, he could persuade me to do them, too."

"He was good at talking people into things."

"Yeah. He managed to screw me for the first time ever the day of your championship game. He'd been pressuring me to let him do it, but I was afraid it would hurt too much. That day he convinced me by saying it would relax him and make him play better."

I laughed out loud, remembering. "And he screwed me that night after we won. He said it would calm him down and help him sleep. Of course, that was about the thousandth time for me, but he talked me into it the first time, too. He talked me into everything the first time."

"I guess we have a lot in common, then," Billy said.

"Yeah," I agreed, "but that's all in the past. What's important is now. Come here." I pulled him close for a kiss to begin the second course of our feast.

. . .

Because of the weather, Billy couldn't make it home until Monday, and our feasting lasted the entire iced-in weekend, with little time out for sleep. Not long afterward, I took him with me on a ten-day charter to Florida during his winter vacation. We did all of Disney/Epcot, plus a lot of feasting in bed. By the time we got back home, we knew we were committed to each other.

After that trip, I managed to quit drinking, and Billy and I both have been accepted at the same college for the fall term. We plan to live together and build a future.

We talk about Richie once in awhile and laugh over shared memories, but except briefly that first night, his ghost has not intruded. I have buried the past and no longer dream of ghosts. Billy is too alive and too vibrant for ghosts to compete.

THE LAWNMOWER BOY

Jesse Monteagudo

I had just moved into my new house in a nice, lower-middle class, ethnically-mixed neighborhood in southwestern Plantation, a far cry from the mansions along Broward Boulevard or the condos west of University Drive. Most of my neighbors are single families, which is fine with me as long as they mind their own business. Kids played under the watchful eyes of their parents as I moved my belongings into my new home.

When I had finally settled in, I turned on my computer, and began to work. That's when the doorbell rang. I love the freedom of working around the house in the nude, so I had to go to the bedroom and get a pair of shorts. A loud knocking replaced the ringing of the bell.

Swearing under my breath, I put on a pair of shorts and hurried to the door, expecting to see a Jehovah's Witness or Mormon missionary trying to save my soul. Instead I found a beauty in a tank top and tight shorts, and a battered power lawnmower sat in my driveway. He was a swarthy boy in his late teens, I guessed, with dark curly hair, dark eyes and lips that begged to be kissed. His tank top pressed against his smooth, muscular chest and his shorts caressed his hard thighs and firm round buns. A bulge in his shorts hinted at a tasty set of cock and balls that I tried to ignore. "Yes?" I said, impatience to my tone.

"Good morning, mister," said the boy, with a soft Brazilian accent. "My name is Luiz. I live down the street and I mow some of the lawns in the neighborhood."

"So?"

"Your lawn could use some cutting," he said, pointing at the front yard.

"Thank you, but I really don't need any help. In fact, I just want to be left alone. I'm sure the grass can take care of itself."

Luiz smiled. Looking behind him, I saw a group of neighbors gathered across the street, no doubt staring at the strange man who would henceforth be known as the man who refused to have his lawn cut. Did they set Luiz up, I wondered? In any case, only his looks kept me from slamming the door in his face. My eyes kept drifting to the bulge in his shorts.

"You probably don't know it, sir," the boy persisted, "but the neighborhood association is very particular as to what your lawn should look like. In fact, they called the cops when my uncle Sergio kept a goat in his back yard. He said..."

"Well, thank you very much but I really don't care what your uncle Sergio said, or what he did about his goat. I am very busy. If I ever need your services I'll give you a call." I eased door shut, catching one last glimpse of Luiz's bulge.

"That should be the end of him," I thought, as I removed my shorts and sat down again in front of my computer. Still, Luiz remained on my mind during the next two weeks as I began to work on a novel that I hoped would repeat the success of my Lambda Award-winning novel *Apricots in June*. I also sent a series of letters to my agent and reviewed a couple of books for a gay publication out of Tampa Bay. Meanwhile summer showers came every day and the grass continued to grow.

The length of my grass seemed to bother everybody except me. Mrs. Gomez, my next door neighbor, who also happened to be the president of the neighborhood association, rang my bell one afternoon.

"You know, Mr. Prescott, we like our neighborhood to be clean and trim," said Mrs. Gomez, as she pointed her chin at my unruly lawn. "We don't care what you do inside the house but your yard is a mess. It reminds me of the time Mr. Ribeiro kept a goat in his back yard..."

There goes that goat again, I thought. But I had to agree. Not only was my lawn a mess, but my nerves were frazzled at the thought of a gang of neighborhood busybodies coming by to disturb my work. There was only one thing I could do. "I just haven't had a chance to go buy a mower. I lived in an apartment before."

"I see."

"Now where can I find that lawnmower boy?"

"He's mowing my lawn right now, as a matter of fact." She looked in the direction of her house and added, "He's a good boy."

I stepped out into the grass to see Luiz, wearing the same

tanktop and the same tight shorts, steering the power mower through my neighbor's grass. He smiled triumphantly when he saw me. He cut the motor and raced over.

He told me he would mow my lawn "first thing Saturday."

"No, no," I said, not willing to go down to defeat too easily, "make it ten."

Saturday morning came around soon enough, and I was drinking my first cup of coffee when the door bell rang. I put on my pair of cutoff shorts and opened the door to find Luiz, wearing his now-familiar tight shorts but now shirtless. A dark pair of perky nipples rested against his beautiful, brown, muscular torso, hairless except for a patch of hair that popped out of each underarm. "I'm ready to start, Mr. Prescott. Is there anything I need to know?"

This was truly bizarre, I thought. I felt like telling him all he needed to know was how to use a power mower, but I decided to play along. There was more going on here than met the eye.

"Not really, Luiz, and please call me Jason, I'm only a few years older than you." Actually I was 28 years old, almost a decade older than the boy, but I look pretty good for my age. I'm also in great shape, thanks to the gym and nutritional supplements. "Just let me know when you're done."

"That'll be fine with me," said Luiz, as he placed a Walkman around his ears. I smiled as Luiz revved his lawnmower and began to move around my front yard, singing along with the radio. "There he goes," I smiled, as boy and machine alike made their way around the yard. "He'll be done in no time," I thought, as I closed the door, removed my shorts and began to work. . .

"All finished!," cried Luiz, now outside my back door. Putting on my shorts, I approached the back door, groaning at the fact that Luiz mowed my front *and* back yards during the time that it took me to write a single paragraph. Luiz was sweaty, glistening in the bright sun. His body gave off a pungent smell, the powerful odor of young Brazilian boyflesh.

"How much do I owe you?"

"Fifty dollars."

"Fifty dollars?! That's a hundred dollars an hour!"

"No, no. I keep your lawn trim all month for that. Year 'round I work."

"Year 'round?"

"It's a service."

This was getting better by the moment. "Do you take a check?"

He nodded.

"Okay, then come in and I'll write it."

"While you do that, could I wash up, Mr. Prescott?"

"Jason. Call me Jason, remember?"

"Yes, of course."

"Let me show you to the bathroom." As I led my young guest further into the house, I struck up a conversation. "Where are you from originally?"

"Sao Paulo. But my family came over when I was six. I went to school here all my life. I'm now nineteen," he added, "and plan to go to college in the fall. Someday I'll become a U.S. citizen." Luiz stopped in front of a bookcase packed with author's copies of *Apricots in June*. "Did you write this?"

"I sure did. It made me enough money to buy this house and it won me a Lambda Literary Award. That's an award that's given to gay writers." There was no response. "I'll give you an autographed copy of the book if you want."

"That would be great. I don't get to read as much as I'd like. I go to class and I play on the soccer team and I mow lawns on the weekends. So I don't have much of a social life. Do you?"

"Not really. I had a lover once, but he died. And I moved out of South Beach to get *away* from a social life." Again there was no response. "Here is the bathroom," I said, pointing towards a door that stood next to the bookcase.

"Thanks," said Luiz, as he closed the door behind him, leaving me with my thoughts. "I shouldn't have been so open," I thought to myself. "Perhaps it turned him off." Luiz's voice rose above the water's noise as he sang in the shower. "He is smart for his age. And cute. Just like my lover was." I was lost in my thoughts when the bathroom door opened. I turned around to find Luiz standing there, naked: "I ran out of soap."

I stared. Soap was the last thing on this boy's mind! Where once was a lawnmower boy now stood dark, sexy young dude, prick in hand, inviting me to share in the pleasures of his body. Luiz's cock was hard and thick and covered with a rich brown foreskin, while his balls were like round brown eggs that hung low beneath his powerful man-organ. His was an offer I could not refuse.

As I approached the object of my desire, I took Luiz's hard cock with one hand and his plump balls with the other. We kissed passionately, our tongues intertwined as we shared in our common lust. Luiz's experienced hands went down my body as we kissed, playing with my hard nipples with one hand while pulling down my shorts with the other. I sighed with pleasure as Luiz worked my restless cock, pulling back the loose foreskin to stroke the sensitive cockhead within. Like two young savages, we continued to kiss, while our hands kept busy exploring each other's hard tits, low-hanging balls, and thick, uncut cocks. Luiz and I almost reached the point of no return when I begged him to stop.

"Let's go to bed," I said, as I led Luiz out of the bathroom. "We can do better lying down." Luiz awakened my hunger for young cock, an addiction that I indulged in when I lived in South Beach but which I suppressed when I moved to Plantation. Cocksucking is a total sensory experience that combines the taste of cock, precum, and cum in your mouth; the pungent odor of young manhood; and the force of a young prick as it pushes hard inside your mouth, past your tongue, and down your throat. Luiz's cock was young, thick and uncut; the kind that drives an experienced cocksucker wild.

Once in bed, everything came into place. I took Luiz's powerful *pinga* inside my mouth, licking the hard organ with my eager tongue as it found its way down my hungry throat. Luiz moaned with pleasure as I worked my way around his man-pole. After sucking his cock for awhile I moved my experienced mouth to his plump balls, taking both man-eggs inside me.

"Don't stop," groaned Luiz. "You suck cock like *no one!*" I groaned as well, for I was in cocksucking heaven. Though I've had my share of young Cuban and Puerto Rican dick while I lived in South Beach, they could not compare with this young Brazilian's thick prick and tasty balls. The world around me disappeared as I fed on my young lover's manhood.

"Man, you're a great cocksucker," cried Luiz. "[...] pretty good, too." To my surprise, Luiz reached o[ver and] began to suck on my own hard pole. Luiz's strong [hands] spread my muscular thighs apart as he swallowed m[y cock,] surrounding it with the warmth of his mouth and throat. The pleasure I received from Luiz's expert cocksucking only spurred me to take his dick deeper into my mouth. We were two young animals, satisfying our insatiable lusts by feeding on each others' hard, uncut man-muscles.

While Luiz continued to suck my cock, his hands began to explore my nether regions. Taking some lubricant from the night stand, Luiz's hands found their way beneath my balls to play with my tight round ass. I gasped as my lawnmower boy thrust one finger and then another into my tender rectum. Finding his way to my prostate, Luiz began to massage it with such great skill and force that he almost brought me to the brink of orgasm.

"You're driving me out of my mind, Luiz," I exclaimed, as he continued to fingerfuck my tender *culo*. "I need more than your fingers up my ass, man. I need your hard *pinga* inside me. Now!" Luiz looked up as I continued to beg for mercy. "Please fuck me, Luiz, please! I know you can do it! There's a condom on the nightstand."

Luiz sighed. Though he insisted he had never fucked a man before, he was turned on by what he called my "hot ass." He said even his uncle Sergio, with whom he played many times before, didn't have an ass an inviting as that of the young writer who lay next to him, desperately begging to be fucked. Taking a condom from the nightstand, Luiz slipped it over his hard cock and tossed my muscular legs over my shoulders, leaving my tender bunghole open and vulnerable to a full-frontal attack from his young, Brazilian man-missile.

Luiz's cock was all that I expected, and more. Though I've taken it up the ass many times before, I was not ready for Luiz's forceful fucking. I yelled with pain and pleasure as this young Brazilian love-god shoved his powerful peter inside my eager man-hole. Thrust followed thrust as my young lover plowed inside me with one expert fuck after another. I began to stroke my own cock, trying to keep pace with my lawnmower boy's pulsating thrusts.

"Fuck me, Luiz, fuck me! My asshole is yours, now and forever!" Luiz grabbed my nipples hard as he continued to fuck me, adding to the ecstatic pleasure that coursed through my body. Luiz's cock up my ass, his hands on my tits, and my own hand on my cock soon brought me to the point of no return. As Luiz's dick continued to pound on my prostate, my sperm began to gather in the base of my balls and find its way up my restless cock. I couldn't hold it any longer.

"I am cummin', Luiz!" I yelled, as buckets of sperm spewed out of my tense cock onto my stomach. Almost immediately, Luiz pulled his own cock out of my ass, breaking the condom as he shot spurt after spurt of man-juice in every direction. "Shiiit!," he cried, as he fell over me, as thoroughly spent as I was.

"You do quite a job," I said, as we shared a kiss. "Outdoors and indoors!"

We smiled.

"And you're not bad either. But now we *both* need a shower."

Though Luiz left for college that fall, he got his younger brother Pedro to cut my lawn on a regular basis. Pedro does not share in his brother's proclivities, as he made sure to let me know the first time that I hired him, but he mows a good lawn.

However, when Luiz comes home on a holiday, he makes sure to drop by my place for some serious sucking and fucking. I even got to fuck *his* ass a couple of times.

In the meantime, I completed my second novel, which matched the notoriety and profits of *Apricots in June*. Critics were especially intrigued by the title, which I adopted as a tribute to my young Brazilian lover: *Lawnmower Boy*.

ABSOLUTE BEAUTY

John Palgrave

"It's like some old legend," he said. "I don't know if I can explain it."

"Try," I asked. We were sitting at the base of one of the great pines which surrounded the small clearing. I had done this very well, I thought, and it rose out of sight until its branches blended with the canopy of dark green far above us. I had made it very quiet, too. At the moment that suited the situation and our mood admirably. He broke dried pine needles in his fingers, two or three at a time, and the bits fell to the ground between his legs. He leaned against the trunk and seemed to gaze at nothing particular, apparently barely aware of my reply. He had heard me, all right, it was just one of his silences, and there wasn't anything to be done about it except wait.

Al spoke when he felt like it, and that wasn't often. He had his own personality, after all, which was the way it had to be, and allowances have to made for that. My question hadn't surprised him. It was one I had asked many times, referring to this or that, and he had always shrugged it off or ignored it before. Now, for the first time, he seemed ready to speak about it so all I could do was be patient. "Why are we doing this?" I had grumbled, meaning this in particular – a flight begun in the middle of the night for no apparent reason. It wasn't the first. Many times before he had come home to wherever it was we were staying at the time and said nothing more than "let's go," and we had gone. That's why we didn't have anything with us that couldn't be carried in the backpacks. They were badly worn by now. I leaned back against the trunk and waited. He was listening again. I didn't know for what.

He isn't much to look at, I admit. At the beginning I'd worked hard on appearance. That isn't easy and the result isn't what I had wanted at first. Of course we don't always realize what we truly want and our subconscious starts to play its own game.

Before long I began to see the interest contained in the very irregularity of his boney features, and now I live with it without any problems. Though he's not ugly he is very plain. There's something wrong with his nose, though I can't figure out exactly what. On second thought, the nose itself is okay, really, it just seems stuck on the wrong face. Well, it's too late to worry about that now, and I've gotten to like it that way. He has a large mouth, sexy though, with full, precisely defined lips. I look at him when he is asleep and think it could be expressive if he chose, but he doesn't choose.

Perhaps he can't. Mouths are really difficult because they are so mobile. I've learned to interpret his moods in other ways. The lips are very smooth. It's the kind of mouth you want to be kissed by if you're the kisser type, which I am. There aren't many really sensual ones around, and when I do spot one then it isn't always interested in kissing me. Al is, and when he kisses me I come unstuck and start dribbling. His brows are very heavy and dark, unusually so for a man that doesn't have much hair on him anywhere else. They give him a threatening look. At least it seems that way at first, until you notice that his eyes have almost no expression about them. Like mouths, that's one hurdle I haven't been able to surmount yet. I will, someday. He has a funny way of turning his head to look at you, as though his neck is stiff or he doesn't have much peripheral vision, and then when he sees you he doesn't seem to be looking at very much. It gives me the creeps. Doesn't help my self-esteem any, either, if it comes to that. At least he doesn't pretend anything, like everybody else. There are only two parts in this movie and he plays it straight. That's probably good but it's not easy to live with. It's not a movie, either, but that's another story.

"Is there any coffee left?" he asked. I knew there was because it's up to me to keep track of things like that, so I dug out the Thermos and poured a cup. We passed it back and forth.

"Do you want to set up here?" I asked. The grove of old pines was quite pleasant, I was tired, and it was as good a place as any to stop. We'd been at it since before dawn and it would be dark in another hour. Day-long hikes almost killed me at first but I was used to them now. Not that I liked them any better, but I could handle it. For a while, when they first started, I had to stop every few miles. Carrying a fifty-pound pack wasn't something I did every day. He tried to be patient, and was, really, but irritation leaked through the cracks. Sometimes he'd let me stop, but then sometimes he wouldn't and would pull my arm over his shoulder and half carry me instead. That was a real hoot. He could pick me right up and throw me over his shoulder if he wanted to – God knows he's strong enough – but I couldn't imagine why he wanted to drag me along in the first place. Well, that's not entirely true. I knew, all right. It's just that I didn't have much of an opinion about myself then, though I've learned better since. Except for brains, perhaps, I'm not really anything to brag about – my mother loved me and that was about it – but Al wanted me. After that first night my whole life turned around one hundred eighty degrees. Before he came into my life I had been like everybody else, not getting what I wanted and either pretending I was, which is dumb, or pretending it didn't matter, which is dumber. Of course it matters. Like everybody I knew, I settled for what I could get. You too, I bet. What I got never turned out to be very much – mostly what the world seemed full of, guys just like myself, plain and dull. You must know what it's like, sitting across the breakfast table from someone just as blah as yourself. Not stupid necessarily, just blah. That's if you're lucky. If you're not then worse, and that's truly depressing. Two blahs don't add up to much. You can't stay very long with anyone as uninspiring as that or you'd blah yourself to death, so I hadn't. In my estimation, most guys are like wallpaper. They may have a snappy pattern but it's all they can do to just hang there, so if you expect anything more from them you're wasting your time. And that's in the real world, too, where you'd expect infinite variety so that custom would not stale, to paraphrase a little Shakespeare. It's different with Al, though. With him I'm beginning to feel a little like a prince and a lot less like a frog. That's prince. Al doesn't think much of boys trying to be girls so I don't, even though he keeps my knees pushed up around my ears a lot. Whichever way it is I like it. That's not true. I love it. No other two guys could fit together as perfectly as we do. Perfectly.

"Sure, why not. We made good time today," he said, and immediately busied himself getting out the tent. He could talk if he wanted to, or he could sit for hours, not saying a word. But when he wanted something done then he did it, quickly and efficiently in that way of his. It had taken me quite a while to learn to do the same. He's a patient man – he has to be with somebody like me – and trains me carefully. That's not entirely true, because we interact in a way I never expected at first. It's in the program of course, but not to the extent I find now. It can grow as well, and change, which I find fascinating. I should have paid more attention to that but he kept me in such a whirl that I didn't. I'm on my way, whichever way that is, and soon I'll be almost as good as he is. Almost. Well, perhaps not almost, but at least I can keep up with him now, and for me that's quite an accomplishment. Do I seem to be crapping on myself a lot? I'm not, actually, just being realistic. I'm trying real hard not to be wallpaper. Maybe I'll win this time. Maybe. I've been a lot more careful in setting this up than I ever had before. They don't come any more ordinary than me, except for my sole advantage. Since that advantage doesn't show, nobody would look at me twice, and until Al came into my life they hadn't. As he told me in his sweet, romantic way, the only reason he'd picked me up was because he wanted it and I happened to be standing next to him and looked available. He tells the exact truth without any bull. That's the way I wanted it but takes a lot of getting used to, let me tell you. I got back at him by telling him the same thing, more or less. He wasn't my type at all, being very tall and really plain, but I was frustrated and desperate, so when he said how about it then I said sure why not. The delicacy of his approach overwhelmed me. He was better than nothing, especially if that's what he wanted. He did, and does. That's one thing I made certain of from the start.

I took him home, and I'd hardly got the door closed before he pulled me against him. I played my part, throwing my arms around his neck for a kiss. Not many guys know how to glue mouths together for really serious kissing, but of course he does. We kissed like two suction-cups, which is the only way to do it. However carefully the plans are made, one never really knows exactly how they'll turn out. When he got his clothes off I saw that I'd actually done it right this time. Santa Claus had finally answered all my letters, and then some. He said essentially the same thing about me because he'd never met anybody who could take it all before. When I first saw it I didn't believe I could. I've been around the track quite a bit, but when he started then I thought I'd made a mistake and was in trouble. For a second I was sure I was being split. I wasn't. He thought he was going to hit bottom right away, the same way he always had with everybody else. He didn't, because I took it all. That's the whole point of it, and it worked. I knew I could take a lot but I'd never had the chance to try one as big as his. He's a freak. He's thirty-five, ten years older than me, and started his top-man career when he was twelve. By fourteen it had grown so much that boys his own age couldn't take him, so he moved to older guys. Even most of them yelled. By fifteen it had reached its present dimensions. Everybody wanted it of course, but few were stretched enough. Even those that were couldn't take all of it. He said he always thought he'd been cursed, because there's nothing worse than being hot to do it and having to settle for halfway in. He'd gone through a lot of guys, trying to find one who could take him. His story may not be unique but I don't think it's a bad one.

As for me, I was initiated into the usual stuff when I was thirteen, just a couple of kids playing around. That was fun but it didn't do much to open me up. At sixteen I met somebody more dangerous but a lot more interesting. I was still so tight that it took him half the night to get to the point where he could shake hands with my lower intestine. It made me yell a lot but it was a true revelation and I discovered it to be exactly what I needed. Nobody else had to tie me down after that. It was the only way I could get the thickness and length I wanted – until I met Al. At twenty-five I had become so accommodating that he could slide right in, exactly the way he was supposed to. In a manner of speaking I was his first real piece, and he was the only guy I'd ever found who could truly satisfy me. After that, for obvious reasons, we stuck together – figuratively and literally. We spend a lot of our time in the sack as he tries to make up with me what he'd been missing out on for so many years. I can't begin to tell you what it feels like. That part of the program works like a charm.

I cleared a large spot down to bare dirt, free of pine needles so we could have a fire without starting a bigger blaze than we wanted, then began fixing some supper while he unpacked the sleeping bag. Every few minutes he stopped to look out into the trees, his ears perked, listening. I couldn't hear anything but the wind moving in the branches far above. I wasn't sure he did either but didn't say so. He did that a lot, wherever we were, sometimes stopping in the middle of a sentence to turn his head like radar, alert to pick up whatever it was. I didn't know what he was listening for and he wouldn't talk about it so eventually I stopped asking. I finally concluded that in spite of the care I took in setting up the program he was just a little strange, that's all. It was either put up with it or leave, and I certainly wasn't going to do that. Not then, not now. Not ever. It's taken me a while to get used to freeze-dried food, too, but I have. It's all we can carry for long distances. It isn't our sole diet because when we camp near a lake we fish, and sometimes get rabbits with the squirrel-gun. I said I'd cook them if he skinned them. He buys fresh stuff whenever we pass near enough to a town to do that. Since all this started I don't go into towns. This setup as it is took me two years. If I'd put in towns too then it would have taken me ten. Whether I put them in or not, he heads off for a quick shop then I have to sit and wait until he comes back. I don't like being away from him, but it's more than that. It seems that he's listening for somebody following us, though I can't be sure. If somebody is, then I don't want him to be away from me when our camp is found, if that ever happens. Who or what might be looking I haven't a clue. That part must be in his imagination anyway because it isn't in the program.

Being always on the move like this, neither of us has a job. I gave mine up when I met him. In spite of that he always seems to have money when we need it. I left all that pretty vague and had set up only that he had done something and was on the run. I'm not running from anything, but I didn't have anything to tie me down, either, so I followed wherever he wanted to go. There didn't seem to be any particular direction – we just went. It isn't exactly a comfortable life, especially in the rain, but I got used to it, the same way you can learn to walk with a crutch if you have to. I'm a city-boy and didn't know one tree from another so I had a lot to learn. In spite of bad weather, flies, and mosquitos, there's a lot to be said for wilderness or the deep forest. Some guys I used to know played at camping-out on vacations and weekends, but this is more than that. We're out for weeks at a time and we aren't playing. I can't imagine doing this with anybody but Al. Roughing it with one person is okay only if it's somebody like him. Most guys would drive you crazy because they can't do anything in life but talk, so once they run out of things to say then they're dead. Sometimes living like this is bad, but then again sometimes it's spellbinding, like swimming together in some remote still lake with nothing around but trees and maybe an elk staring warily at us from across the water – that was a nice touch – or lying warm together in the sleeping-bag, watching the embers die out; or counting stars in the night. That's not as easy as it sounds because unless you're careful you end up counting the same ones over and over. I got up to more than three hundred once, but then lost track when Al stuck his tongue in my ear. He knows that drives me crazy. He also knows exactly what he's got for me and how much I want it. It's not one-sided, either, because by now I know what I've got for him, too. Well, let's face it, we have each other thoroughly hooked because nobody else could give either of us what the other's got. It's that simple. Why else would I stay with it all this time when he acted so peculiar?

Al is the seriously horny type. I never had all my buttons pushed before, but he pushes every one plus some I didn't even know I had. As I'm sure you've discovered for yourself, big ones are rare, and freaky huge ones about as common as true virtue. From all reports, the percentage of big ones that can stand up stiff is minuscule, though before Al I'd never had a chance to do that kind of research myself. With my encouragement it gets as hard as a steel pipe, which makes him one in a billion. Chances of winning three or four lotteries in a row are better than finding somebody like that. Looks or fancy conversational footwork don't tell you what a guy has in his pants, which is why people write fantasies about such things I guess, or write programs like his. I never had anybody with much more than half Al's size before, and neither had any of the guys I know. That's why we used to sit around in bars talking about it all the time. If we actually had anything like that then we'd be home with our arms around it. That's about all most guys could do, too, because it's too big around to suck and not many can take a baseball bat up their butt. Only little me. Before Al came into my life I took on anybody, always hoping. Because I was skinny and plain I didn't get much, and none of that was anything to write home about. Just wallpaper. Anyway, Al is a complete change from my usual, which is the way I wanted it. I'd experimented for years on other programs but none of them had been as satisfactory as this because they were too primitive. I learned a lot working on them, though, and Al is the result. It took two years of very hard work, but now I have the perfect man. For me, at least. The night I took him home I got the surprise I told you about, then we had a first-class, number-one time, better than either of us had ever experienced before. I was ready for lots more but I was surprised when he pulled his clothes on and left without a word. That was the first change in the script. There were others later, but that first one upset me more than I care to admit.

I felt like an abandoned child. I'd never had anything like that, never, and you better believe my butt felt like it had been blow-torched. Wonderful feeling. I was very unhappy when the door closed behind him, but, free-will is free-will, and since that's the way I'd set it up then I had to live with the way it turned out. I knew I'd never get anything like him again because each attempt is unique, with its own virtues and problems, but I was grateful because in that one night I had been completely satisfied for the first time in my life. Then, glory be, two hours later he was back, carrying all his stuff. He dropped it in the middle of the floor and said he was moving in, just like that. He didn't even ask me if he could, he just said he'd never had anybody like me before, and that was that. He took me back to bed and we stayed there until he finally pulled out after his third orgasm, somewhere around four o'clock in the afternoon. It nearly killed me, but oh man, that's the way I want to die! That was a year ago, and I've followed him ever since. I'd never been able to get enough before, so I take it as often as he wants, and he wants it all the time. What a glorious life! It's working! I'm a genius!

He didn't say much as he ate. Sometimes he talks easily enough, then again sometimes he's silent and away, off on some journey inside his head. Sometimes he's silent and right here, like tonight, listening. I've given up wondering what for. Twice before, instead of just listening, he must have heard something. The first time, in the deep woods, he scared the hell out of me. As usual I hadn't heard anything, so I almost jumped out of my shoes when he threw dirt on the fire to douse it and told me to be very quiet. He picked up the squirrel-gun then vanished into the dark two seconds later, back in the direction we had come from. He was so quiet I didn't even hear him move away, but I know he did because I could feel the emptiness. That was the second change in the script, and a big one. I sat alone and shook for almost four hours and nearly went crazy. When he came back he didn't say a word but just crawled into the sleeping bag. He was too tired to do anything, which was really unusual, and went right to sleep. I lay awake half the night but he was out of it. He knew I was wondering what the hell was going on because in the morning I asked him right out, but he went silent again and ignored me. Al doesn't like questions.

That was two weeks after we met. He didn't bother to listen for several days after that. It happened again a month later – almost exactly the same except it was only two hours this time. I guess I don't have to tell you how upset I was and how weird it seemed to have matters go off at unexpected tangents that way. Every few weeks after that I'd be left alone while he vanished into the dark to check out something. Those were short ones and he was back within an hour. He'd never talk about it. Today he's been listening again and it bothers me.

He isn't always silent and we do talk, but it's usually in bed or else after supper. If it's after supper, then lighting his pipe is the signal, though I don't think he means it to be that. He lit his pipe now.

"Just like some old legend," he repeated, then puffed quietly for several minutes. He'd come out with it if I waited and didn't try to push him. Al will not be pushed. That's the way I wanted him and that's what I got.

"What do you know about beauty?" he asked. Philosophy? That was a switch.

"Just what I see in the mirror when I shave," I joked.

He wasn't amused. "Real beauty," he said.

"Not much," I admitted.

"People say 'love' a lot, only because they don't know what it is," he said. "Everybody says 'beautiful,' too, but they don't know what that is, either."

"You do?" I asked.

He puffed a few minutes. "Yes, unfortunately."

"Unfortunately?" I had no idea where this was going. He looked at me.

"What would you do," he asked, "if one day you met a guy so beautiful it made you wet your pants?"

"Huh?" I admit I was startled. I wouldn't have thought that to be a usual response to a pretty face. Like anybody, I'd seen handsome men before, and drooled over them like a lesser mortal in front of the gods, but I'd never felt inclined to urinate because of it.

"Let's start all over again," he said patiently. "You know something about art. People disagree so much about it because most of it is crap. Even at best the majority of it is no more than cute, or interesting, or matches the decor. But you know that there are a few things everyone agrees on, and those are the standards by which serious people judge everything else, right?"

I nodded.

"There are people like that," he continued."Very few, but some." He puffed again, then spoke as if he was a long way away. "A guy so beautiful that he could walk into a convention hall and all conversation would stop. Everybody would just stand around feeling ugly."

"Really?" I asked. "I thought that was only in the movies."

"They try to show us but nobody really believes it," he remarked. "The director tells Joe Pie-face to come in the door then he tells everyone else to turn and look at his beautiful curly hair and shut up. That's easy. I mean the real thing."

"You know somebody like that," I said, drawing the obvious conclusion.

He nodded. "As I said, unfortunately." It took several minutes this time. "If you were beautiful then what do you think you'd be like?" he asked suddenly.

"Lucky," I replied, feeling sorry for myself.

"You think so?" he remarked with a wry expression. "Try again."

"What are you getting at?" I asked, feeling uncomfortable. I had the uneasy suspicion that the script was writing itself now and I didn't like it. "Most people don't see anything truly beautiful one year to the next. Others see a good sunset once in a while, or something in a good museum if they're the kind to go to museums. Their usual reaction is silence. Sometimes, if they're really young or stupid, they feel so ashamed of themselves they giggle. Sometimes they even hate."

He looked at me again. "What do you think you'd feel like if everybody looked at you as though you were beyond their experience, beyond even their imagination."

"You mean the same way guys must look at you when they first see your dick?"

He was surprised at that, but then he smiled. "Not exactly, but I guess you get the point."

"I don't know," I said. "How do you feel?"

"It's not the same and you know it. A lot of guys stare at big tits, too, but so what. Nobody pisses their pants over big tits."

I didn't have anything to say to that.

"His name is Laurence."

Laurence, I thought? Who the hell is that? There's no Laurence in the script. There's nobody but Al and me. What's going on? I was confused but I played along so I could find out. "He's very beautiful, I take it."

"There's no very to beautiful. The word is absolute. Yes, he is."

"I'd still feel lucky," I sighed.

"You think so?" he asked, raising one of those heavy brows.

"Is there something wrong with him, then?"

"If you abhor a vacuum, then yes, there is."

"Vacuum?" I must have looked surprised.

"I asked what you thought you would be like if you were truly beautiful," he said. "I'll tell you. You would command everything and everybody merely because of your looks. How much personality do you think would develop under a condition like that? How much patience, understanding, consideration, courtesy, or moral sense? How much anything?" The questions were unexpected from somebody like Al, but complications like this made it interesting.

"I guess you're trying to tell me not much."

"None. What possible use would they be when you already had what everybody else thinks is the most important thing in life? You wouldn't even have to be polite. People would forgive you anything just to have you look at them, and if you smiled then they'd do whatever you asked. They'd give everything they had to do whatever it was you wanted them to. You wouldn't even have to be any good. They'd kill if they had to, just to be able to do it to you again and tell people they had. "

That was the longest speech I'd heard him make, but he wasn't through yet. "You think you wouldn't be like that, but you would. Anybody would. You're a lot luckier just as you are." He puffed his pipe for several minutes. "Ever since he was a little kid he's always gotten whatever he wanted. Usually people gave everything without being asked, and if they didn't, all he had to do was cut them off and they'd act as if the sun went out. He looks like what we think an angel must look like, if there were angels, but he's a pretty box with nothing inside." I had no idea where that story came from but it sounded interesting. As before, I went along with it.

"Lucifer was the brightest of them all," I reminded him, just beginning to get the idea.

"So he was," he said, giving me one of his few smiles. "I guess you fell for him, then," I said.

"I'm only human, in spite of what you think," he remarked, which really unsettled me. How much could he know? Then he continued, "I've looked in the mirror too, so how do you think I felt when I found out that the most beautiful guy in the world wanted me. I'd have given him anything he asked for, even though kissing him is like kissing the wall, and he's rotten in bed. Nobody cared and I didn't either, even though I could hardly get it in him. You're a lot better, in every department."

That's the kind of comment that cheers me up. "Except looks."

"True. You may be as plain as a pig's ass but you kiss like an angel and you're the only real fuck I ever had. So which would you rather be?"

"Joe Pie-face," I said. I guess I was shaking because he'd never said anything like that to me before. I sure as hell didn't mind that kind of improvising, but it was unexpected. "He's following us, isn't he," I asked. Apparently this Laurence was going to get into it whether I wanted him to or not, though I didn't know how.

"Usually he sends guys looking, but he's after me himself this time. I don't know where I got the strength, but I left. Nobody had ever done that to him before and he didn't know what to make of it. When I told him he threw a real tantrum then began taking away my tricks. That was easy. All he had to do was look at them. If he couldn't be bothered doing that then he'd hire some goons to scare them off. I couldn't hang onto anybody more than five minutes." His pipe was finished so he knocked it against the tree to empty it and carefully ground the ashes out with his shoe. "Most of the time it didn't bother me because I'd already had them, and once I find out a guy can't take it then I don't want him anymore. It made him real mad that I didn't care. Then you came along. I told him if he or any of his goons came anywhere near you I'd kill him. That was a bad mistake, because now he knows how he can get back at me."

"Huh?" was all I could say. He was glowering. "That's why you took your gun that time." He nodded. "Would you really?"

He looked down at his feet and started picking at pine-needles again. "Probably not," he answered. "Would you smash a Michelangelo or burn a Rembrandt? He'll lose his looks eventually. That will kill him, then maybe on the other side of the world there'll be another one."

"So what did happen?" I asked. I was just beginning seriously to suspect that this thing might be getting away from me. I wasn't scared yet, though I should have been.

"That first time it was a couple of stupid goons, making a lot of noise. I bushwhacked them and kicked the hell out of them. The second one was a real tracker, and that wasn't so easy, but I'm as good as he was and covered our trail well enough to lose him. I was lucky, though. He'll come himself next time."

"Are you in any real danger?" I asked.

"Me?" he asked in surprise. "No. He wouldn't do anything to me. It's you he's after."

"Huh?" I asked, and I confess I jumped when I heard that. Bringing in a Laurence was one thing, but having him interact with me was something else.

"If he can get me out of the way for five minutes he'll show himself to you, and if he does then you won't be able to help yourself."

"The Medusa," I said.

"Exactly. The Greeks made a mistake, though, the same one everybody else did. They portrayed evil as ugly. It isn't. It's beautiful. That's what makes it horrifying. You can turn away from ugliness but not from beauty. He likes getting guys so worked up they'll do anything. He'll tell you to eat him out. Maybe you think you wouldn't do that, but you would, and thank him for it. Others have. I was the only one he'd ever met who wouldn't do whatever he wanted. That fascinated him."

There was a long silence after that. He was thinking whatever he was thinking, and my mind was buzzing, whipping around like a mad snake, trying to figure out when all this had started to diverge from the program and why I had been so stupid as not to see it.

"How'd you meet somebody like that?" I asked. It had to be kept moving or I wouldn't discover anything at all.

"I was hustling the beach down in Belize when I was younger. Lots of money there, and with meat the size of mine I made plenty. That's what we're living on. You've never seen me in a bathing-suit."

I hadn't, but I knew very well what he would look like, all muscles, with the crotch of his suit bulging like a basketball, or maybe hanging out like a piece of fire-hose. I shivered.

"He picked me up for a joke, but he didn't think it was so funny when I rolled him over and stuck it in him, or tried to. He has the most beautiful butt in the world and I had to have him. He screeched like a banshee and I couldn't get more than half of it in, but I laid him anyway. I thought an angel would make an angelic piece. I was wrong. It was disappointing. It's for the best, though. If he was half as good as you then I'd be with him now." He sighed. Well, that was a nice thing to say. Al isn't given to compliments. "He'll get tired of chasing me eventually, especially out in the rough like this. Usually he gets bored as quickly as a child."

"Except for you," I said, even more confused but still going along. It seemed that this added character had as many complications as Al himself did. Where did they come from? Al kept talking.

"Apparently. Lucifer or not, I guess he's just like anybody else, wanting most what he can't have." He sighed deeply and scratched himself. "He said I could kill him if I really wanted to, but he knows I won't."

"Is he out there now?" I asked. He'd been listening all day. I should have suspected something when he started that.

"I don't know. Maybe, back there somewhere. Not close, though."

"He's crazy."

"Not really. He's never developed enough of a mind to lose. He got stuck somewhere around five years old, I think, when people first began seriously to adore him. He told me that when he first went to school none of the kids could keep their hands off him, boys and girls both. He let them if they gave him their toys and licked his pee-pee, which they did. By the time he got to tenth grade the girls had given up, but the boys kept fighting over him. The winner got to follow him into the bushes after school. That's when he found out they'd lick more than his pee-pee if he told them to. He dazzled everyone and got "A's" in everything."

"Jesus," I sighed. "What a life!"

"Not really," Al said.

"No, I guess not," I admitted. Out loud, anyway. His point made sense but I was racing around inside my head, looking hard but not finding any answers. Up until that moment there hadn't been a possibility of losing him, first because nobody else could take it, and second because that's the most fundamental part of the program. Now I was really worried. He must have been reading my mind.

"Don't worry about it," he said. Of course I promised I wouldn't. I will anyway, though. But why, you ask? Remember what I told you about me, and consider how I felt the night I took him home and he kissed me. I thought I knew which was the icing and which the cake. I was right, but to a different degree than I had planned.

When he took his shirt off and I saw all those muscles I felt weak as a kitten, and when he dropped his pants my heart nearly stopped. That was his surprise. I took it all, and that was mine. The minute his belly hit my butt we knew we're made for each other. If this Laurence number tries to screw this up I'll ruin his pretty face so bad no one will ever look at him again. I swear it.

Al saw me frowning and got up to come over to me. "Come on, baby," he said, then picked me up like a child and took me to bed, driving all other thoughts out of my mind, as usual.

Afterward we watched the last small glow of the fire for a while, until it died out, waiting until he'd be ready again. I always get it twice, and the sensations overwhelm me. He started moving and I began moaning, then suddenly he tensed and froze. "Listen!" he whispered.

I tried but could hear nothing but the pounding of my own blood for a moment. Then, from very far away I did. It was very faint but unmistakable. Music. A flute, or something. In the otherwise silent forest it was uncanny. "Hear it?" he asked. I nodded, feeling a sudden chill. Then it was gone. We didn't have our second one after all because he went soft. I felt so weird I began to shake, and even though he held me close most of the night I had wild confused dreams that kept waking me up. Now I really was frightened.

I came awake at dawn. Usually Al woke first but he was still sleeping soundly. I got up because I had to. I went a distance from our campsite to squat with a sigh of relief. I always hate to let it go but it was either that or blow up. I had just turned to reach for some leaves to wipe myself when I saw him. There was no mistaking who it was and it couldn't have been anyone else. Time just stopped. It could only have taken a couple of seconds but it seemed like many minutes. He was standing beside a tree, looking at me. He was about five-seven or five-eight, and naked. He looked about sixteen but I couldn't be sure. He must be older than that, though. He wasn't tanned but his skin glowed, a kind of beige-pink that made him look as if he had been dipped in gold-dust. Al had been right. I had no definition of absolute beauty in my mind because I had no idea what such a thing could be like. I did now, though I couldn't imagine where the data came from. I just stared, paralyzed. It was more than his face, it was everything; physical perfection, from the curve of perfect lips to the equally perfect body. He seemed very young but he didn't really look like an adolescent. Golden curls wrapped his head, echoed in a small bush in his crotch. Not blond, golden. The match of proportions was unbelievable: nothing out of the ordinary, yet everything fitting exactly and precisely as it should be if designed by someone with an eye for celestial symmetry. He wasn't hung any better than I was, and by now you know I ignore them unless they're big, but even there the net effect was equally beautiful. I couldn't have moved if my life depended on it. Compared to him I was a bag of blotchy skin filled with dog-shit. I didn't like that at all. "I wondered what you would look like," he said, and the spell broke just a little. It was human. For several seconds there I wasn't sure. His voice wasn't as extraordinary as the rest of him but it was pleasant. He came toward me. Somehow I managed to stand up. I knew I should call to Al to wake him but I couldn't. I wanted this vision all to myself. He stopped in front of me to examine me curiously, like a child.

"You're not much to look at," he said.

"No," I agreed.

"What is it, then?" he asked himself. I didn't say anything. He examined me for what seemed like several minutes. I felt smaller and more inconsequential every second. "Come on," he added, then turned to walk away. I followed. What else could I do? By now I was desperate for answers and would try anything. He led me a couple of miles through the trees, and I watched that perfect body move, each step. I'm not an ass-freak, but if I was I would have freaked out. Gloriously beautiful buns, simply glorious! I was so jealous I could have died.

We came to his own camp, just a sleeping-bag and a small back-pack beside it. What looked like a recorder was leaning against the pack, the flute we had heard the night before. His expression was as close to being blank as it could get without appearing actually lifeless. That's always the hardest part so I knew it was data after all. I kissed him and discovered that he wasn't like a mud-pie at all, regardless of what Al had said. We felt and groped and squeezed and pulled. It went on like that for some time. That was just the preliminary. Data or not, he was reacting so perfectly to me, and I to him, that I almost lost my mind.

His fingers were everywhere. I could hear myself sighing and moaning. He began exploring my butt, then continued his exploration in a manner I hadn't exactly anticipated.

"You're easy for him, that's what it is," he said. "I should have guessed."

He gave me some more. "Good Lord!" he whispered, "now I understand." I had half his forearm! I knew I could take a lot but that didn't seem possible! We eased down onto the sleeping bag to do it right, then he hit bottom. At least I found out I had a bottom. I had never felt anything as overpowering and exquisite as this! He paused every few minutes so I wouldn't come too soon, but finally I couldn't help myself and did, very hard, then he stopped, leaving it in me. It was then that I learned my true capacity, for I could feel the crook of his elbow pressed tight against me. Nobody could take that much! Nobody! But I had. I didn't dare move and I didn't want to.

I don't know low long we lay like that, but eventually he pulled out. I sure felt empty. "Now it's your turn," he said. "He told you what I want."

"Yes," I replied. I ran my tongue in where he wanted and lapped his insides for quite a while.

Now it was his turn to moan and sigh. He was a long way from being virgin. It happened just as Al had said, and when it did he blew up. We collapsed to lay side by side, panting hard.

"You're really good!" he exclaimed.

"So are you," I told him.

"Don't stop," he told me.

"No," I said.

I began with his ears and licked very slowly down his body. His drying sweat was honeysweet. I cleaned him down to his toes then he rolled over onto his stomach with a satisfied sigh and I did his back. I ended up at the same place, of course. He certainly loved my tongue. When he was ready again I took him. He tasted like sugar-syrup. I moved up to lie on top of him and he put his arms around me.

"Well!" he said with a big sigh. "You're perfect. I've never been eaten out that beautifully."

"Now what?" I asked, feeling a sudden but very sharp stab of both guilt and panic. I hadn't given Al a single thought since Laurence first touched me. I still didn't know how Laurence fit, but by now I had no doubt that he was a full player.

"You know what," he whispered. "We're going to do a lot more of that. I like it. You do too, isn't that right?"

"If that's what you want," I said, feeling helpless.

"It's what I want," he said. "It's what you want too."

"Yes," I said. Al was right about that, too. I'd have agreed to anything. Anything at all.

"You won't miss him," he said, as if reading my thoughts. "Even his dick isn't as long as my arm." He whispered in my ear, "I'll give it to you until you go out of your fuckin' mind. Then I'll push until you're against my armpit! That's the way you want to die, isn't it?"

I shuddered.

"Isn't it?" he insisted.

"Yes," I whispered. By now I knew that something had gone radically wrong with the whole program. Either that or I was out of my mind. Whichever it was, he was right.

I woke up with a start, drenched in sweat and completely disoriented. It took me several seconds to realize that the arm around me was Al's. It was still mostly dark, but a faint light was noticeable between the trees. I had never had so vivid a dream before in my life, so vivid that I could still taste and smell him. Hallucination? It had to be, which would explain everything, even though I felt exhausted and used. I got up carefully so as not to wake him, and slipped outside to relieve myself. There was no sign of anyone, but in among the first bird-calls I was almost sure I could hear a flute playing, somewhere a couple of miles away. I crawled back into the sack in a hurry and pulled Al's arm around me again. It took me several minutes to stop shivering, then I slipped into the dark pit of dreamless sleep.

I sat straight up, cracking my head against the tentpole. I looked outside in a panic but felt a flood of relief when I saw Al squatting naked by the fire. He had the coffee pot on. I was relieved but at the same time confused. He never got up like that, when I was asleep. He always wanted to do it first. No matter what we had done the night before he was always ready again in the morning. And getting coffee was my job. He glanced over and saw I was awake, then poured two tin cups. I got out of the sack and went to squat close to him. He didn't say anything, just handed me my cup. "I can smell him on you," he said.

I nearly fell over. "Huh?"

"He has a distinct odor. I can smell him."

"But it was a dream!" I gasped. He turned to look at me, then I recited it all to him. It was still very vivid. I didn't leave anything out.

"It was no dream," he said.

"It must have been," I replied. "I woke up right here, just before dawn, not after, and you had your arm around me."

"He can play tricks," he said. "You were tricked, that's all. He can't help himself. He gives guys whatever it is they want until they die of it. He's done it before." He looked at me. "Describe him."

I described what I had seen in my dream.

"Exactly right," he said. "How else would you know?" I was both dumbfounded and in a panic. I felt entirely weird because my head had been messed with, and frightened at whatever reaction that might arouse in Al. Who was messing with my head? He put his arm around me and I felt better. "Let's get out of here," I whispered.

"There's no point in that," he said. "He'll be here in a minute."

"What'll we do?"

"Nothing. Wait."

"Then what?"

Before he could answer I heard the flute. Al stood up and I did too. Laurence appeared briefly between the trees some distance away, coming toward us. He was naked, with a golden nimbus around him. He was carrying the flute, not playing it, but I could hear it nevertheless. The tune was plaintive but had no melody I could follow. He and it were both achingly beautiful. I was very afraid. I held onto Al's arm. He wasn't shaking the way I was but his skin was clammy.

"What is he?" I asked.

"Death," he answered.

Everything loosened and I pissed myself. I couldn't help it. Laurence came closer until he stood across the clearing from us, resplendent. He wasn't looking at me but at Al, and Al looked back. He seldom had any definable expression but he did now, though I couldn't tell whether it was love or hate. I was startled to see his cock sticking straight out, pulsing like a live thing as it rose slowly. I thought I knew him intimately, but I'd never seen it as large as this, swollen almost purple, with a head on it the size of my fist. The music stopped and the three of us just stood like that for what seemed an age. Laurence hardened as well, and a moment later so did I. "I like your boy," Laurence said softly. "He's very good. Just as we planned." He smiled. I wondered what he meant by that.

"I know," Al said.

"Come here, boy," Laurence said. He stretched out on his belly and spread his legs apart. "Come here and give me that beautiful long tongue."

I started to move toward him but Al held me back. "Please, let me go," I said, and tried to pull away. He wouldn't let go and I began to get angry.

"Stop it!" Al barked, and threw me backward so hard I stumbled and fell.

The rest of it was so quick I barely saw what was happening. He leaped across the clearing, jumped on Laurence, then rammed his enormously swollen cock between those perfect cheeks. Laurence began yelling as Al held him down and forced it in him. Laurence isn't a freak like me, and as the huge thing went up inside him it must be ripping everything in its path.

As Al shoved it all in, the yells became one long scream, then he began fucking him very hard. His cock was covered with blood. There was a wild blur as Laurence did everything he could to get out from under him but he was impaled. It would take him a minute to understand it, but to all intents and purposes he was already dead. I began screaming too. How could he destroy such a thing! I beat on Al, trying to pull him off. I thought I was succeeding when he pulled out, but then I realized he had come and was ready to do so anyway. Laurence stopped screaming and blood streamed from his ass. Al's dick and crotch were covered with it and he was panting like a crazy man, staring at what he had done. I have never hated anyone so much. I ran to get the squirrel-gun to kill him but he wrested it away from me, broke it, and threw the pieces into the woods.

"It's over," he said.

I fell apart. I dropped down beside Laurence, crying harder than I ever had for anything or anybody before, and watched him die. I thought he might say something but he didn't. He breathed raggedly for a while, like tearing small pieces of paper, then the light went out. Al just stood there. His cock began to droop, slowly. Blood dripped off the end of it.

I woke in a cold sweat, shaking like a leaf. It was still mostly dark, with a faint rim of light low between the trees in the east. I moved out from under Al's arm and went away from the tent to squat. There was just enough light so I could see across the glade. It was empty and peaceful and I sagged with relief. Another dream. But which one did I dream, the first or the second? Or both? Was I in a dream now? Which, for God's sake! What was happening to me? I couldn't stop shaking. I felt cold and was covered with goose-pimples but I didn't want to go back to the tent to get my clothes. I reached in just far enough to get the matches. Al was sleeping peacefully. It seemed that I was the only one in fragments. Somehow I got a fire going with my shaking fingers, and put the coffee-pot on.

Then I heard the flute. I froze again, unable to move, but this time, instead of being surprised and curious, I was terrified.

There was a glow among the trees, then Laurence appeared, smiling at me. For some reason I stopped shaking. He lay down on his stomach and I went to him at once. Neither of us said anything. I started by kissing his neck and licked down his back, then he spread his legs. He tasted of honey. It went on and on. I had orgasms, one after another, but they didn't seem to empty me. Through it all Laurence didn't say a word. He just writhed in my arms, and under me, and over me. I did things I'd never done with anyone, and eagerly, too. It seemed to last hours, and every minute a straining, gasping wonder.

Suddenly he jerked violently and fell over. I never even heard the shot. I looked up and saw Al standing with the squirrel-gun. Laurence had a small neat hole in one side of his skull, and a large red one on the other side. I threw up then I passed out.

I woke feeling very peculiar, bouncing like a limp doll. The ground below me rolled and boot-heels popped into my vision then out of it as they moved in a steady pace. I was being carried, thrown over Al's shoulder like a sack of dead meat. Our packs dragged along behind on the ground. Trees and pine-needles swirled as my head bobbed. I couldn't focus very well, but it was obvious that we weren't where we had been. He must have sensed I had come-to, for he stopped and lowered me carefully to the ground then propped me up against a tree.

We were by the shore of a lake. He looked exactly the same as always but I felt like an illustration in a comic-book, two-dimensional and garish. He got out the Thermos, filled the cap, and made me drink the hot coffee. It tasted wonderful.

"What happened?" I asked.

"You tell me," he said. "I woke up and found you keeled over next to the fire."

"Is he dead?" He just looked at me. "Well?" I asked.

"No," he said. "Did you think he was?"

I told him the third dream, or hallucination, or whatever. "Have I gone out of my mind?" I asked. I wasn't frightened any more, just limp. I didn't care. It seemed to be late afternoon.

"Not really," he said. He sat down beside me carefully. He refilled the Thermos cap and this time had some himself.

"More tricks?" I asked.

"Yes," he said, then he turned his head the way he does and looked at me, "but they weren't really dreams. You must remember that.

I was upset because that didn't explain anything. The events weren't dreams yet I had been dreaming them? It didn't make sense. He took another sip of coffee and continued. "Things that happen that intensely inside your head can be just as lethal as reality." There was a pause. Why would he tell me that? For a moment I felt like a ventriloquist that had been spoken back to. "I have a few tricks of my own," he said. "I could have used them except that I wanted you to learn something."

I just felt numb. "Is he gone now?" I asked.

He nodded.

"Where?" I asked, feeling a touch of panic. Would I ever have that beautiful boy-man-whatever again? I could still taste him in the back of my mouth. I understood that I was still in shock, but I wanted to eat him and never stop. Or did I? I'd never been that interested in doing that before. Wasn't that what Laurence wanted to make guys do? Had I wanted to do it or had I been made to? My head reeled. "Will he come back?" I asked.

"Possibly. I don't really know," Al said. "I hope he'll go off and play his games somewhere else. There's a long list and you're just an episode. I've known him for many years."

Laurence didn't look much over sixteen so how could he have known him many years? I felt some cold prickles on the back of my neck. "What is he?" I whispered. "You said that he was Death."

"In a manner of speaking," Al said.

Then it occurred to me to ask the obvious. "What are you, then?"

"Don't you know?" He asked, looking puzzled.

I shook my head.

"Well, you'll find out soon enough."

"Please!" I moaned. The program had evaporated.

"Later," he said very kindly, then he kissed me in that perfect way which sent shudders up and down my spine. He pulled me down with him gently and our mouths stayed stuck together as we undressed each other, then he pulled me tight against him. I could feel his hard-on press against my belly.

"Feel better?" he asked.

"Much," I sighed. I reached down and felt him. It seemed much bigger. How could that be? I bent down to take it even though I had never had been able to suck it properly.

This time I could barely get the head in my mouth. As I tried he felt my ass, then rolled me over. I thought I was used to it by now, but since it was so much bigger I wasn't. So beautiful. Like Laurence's arm, it went in deep. Much more than it ever had before. Wonderful. I was stuffed so full I was sure I was ready to burst. He hit bottom and his belly pressed tight. He left it like that for a minute. My butt buzzed sharply from being stretched so much wider than usual and I could feel it pulsing deep inside me. Very deep. I was all tunnel and he was all dick. Only yesterday we were made for each other.

Today I wasn't so sure. If he kept getting bigger then what would happen?

"Okay?" he whispered.

"Lovely," I sighed. "Oh, yes."

"Yes. Very," he said, then he fucked me.

It was twilight by the time he finally pulled out. He had

come three times and I had lost count of my orgasms. They had seemed continuous. My butt really hurt this time but somehow it was immensely satisfying.

He stood and stretched with a contented sigh. His soft dick hung almost to his knees, thicker and longer than I remembered. He bent down and picked me up then carried me to the lake and waded in. The water was slightly cool but felt wonderful.

When he was in up to his waist he stood me on my feet and washed me. Except for the splashing it was very quiet.

Suddenly he stopped. "Look!" he whispered. On the opposite shore across the water I could see an elk standing, looking at us warily. It was then that I finally understood.

Now in a complete panic I realized I had gone much too far. I reached up to pull the headset off. There wasn't one! I flailed my arms around to rip off the wires leading to my dick, nipples, and asshole, but I felt nothing and nothing changed. I would have fallen over if he hadn't held me up.

I screamed a while then began to cry.

After supper we sat naked before the fire. We've had lots of fires, here and there, but for the first time it gave off some heat I could feel. Al lit his pipe. Neither of us had said anything since we came out of the lake. He had seen me crying and knew that I knew.

"How long have we got?" I asked.

"A little while yet," he said quietly.

I laid back with my head in his lap and looked up at him. He puffed on his pipe. It was utterly silent.

"I love you," I told him.

"I know," he said. I turned my face and pressed against his belly to inhale his odor. It wasn't honey but I liked it.

When I turned again I saw Laurence sitting close beside him. He was beautiful; his golden curls glitter in the firelight.

They both looked at me and I looked back. "I love you both," I told them. "Yes," Al said.

"Which dream is this," I asked.

"The last one."

"I'm trapped, aren't I."

"Trapped?" he said in surprise. "No. It's where you were made to be."

"With beauty and the beast," I said.

He smiled. "That's one way of looking at it, I suppose." He looked at me, and for once there was some expression in his eyes. "Or perhaps Eden."

"Which side of the looking-glass am I on?" I asked.

"Does it matter? You give us what we want. Instead of fighting over you we decided to share. Is that okay? You have free-will, you know."

"I can have you both?"

He nodded.

"It will kill me."

"It already has."

"Then it's over?"

"No. It's just begun."

"Good."

"That's the way it's programmed," he told me.

I just stared at him. It took me a long time before I could say anything without stuttering. "But this is my program!" I said.

"Oh no," he replied, and smiled.

"Then what – " I started, but couldn't finish. Now Laurence spoke up.

"We designed you a foot deep for him and with that tongue like a snake for me. It took us three years, but you're perfect. So perfect that Al ran off with you because he had to have you all to himself. I was mad as hell, but now that I've had you too I can't blame him." He bent down and gave me a kiss. "You are precisely and exactly right." The shock I felt at finally understanding the truth was very severe – so bad in fact that I curled into a ball, rejecting everything. Al caressed me reassuringly and Laurence kept whispering in my ear.

"It's all right," he said. "It always will be, too, because that's the program. You could never get enough before but you will now."

The knot that tied my mind began to loosen slowly. My tongue came out to search for Laurence. I gave him all of it this time as Al got on me. The three of us melted together. It went on for hours.

At dawn I made fresh coffee and fixed us something to eat. For the remainder of the day they did things to me that no one could possibly withstand unless it was exactly as I had been told, but by that time I was so crazed with sensation that it didn't matter. They were inexhaustible and didn't stop until I collapsed.

After a rest I made supper, though where I found the strength to do that I didn't know. We sat for a while afterward, tired but so contented that none of us said very much.

When Al finished his pipe he picked me up. I put my arms around his neck, then he carried me to the lake, where we cleaned up.

We were all so worn that we went to bed early that night. There were a million stars and for some reason I began to count, then everything went black. "That's enough!" I heard. "What are you trying to do, kill yourself?" The set was pulled off my head.

"You must be crazy!" Jimmy said in exasperation.

I sat stupefied as he disconnected the wires one after the other. I ached all over.

"Jesus, you stink," he growled. I sniffed and he was right. I'd come so much I smelled like a dead fish. I watched with horror as he pushed the delete button, then I began to cry over what was lost.

"Oh shut up, for Christ's sake," he said, then pulled me down to the floor and I was being slapped across the face.

"Hey, what's the matter?" Al asked, trying to rouse me. He looked concerned.

"What....?" I gasped. I had just felt Jimmy pull off the headset and wires, so how...

"Fight it!" he said sharply. I tried. Jimmy was biting the back of my neck and screwing me so hard it was difficult to fight. Al slapped me again.

"Come on!" he shouted. His voice echoed.

I tried harder. Laurence kissed me. That was better.

Jimmy screeched and started to come.

I was being stretched thin. Very thin. I was looking up at a ceiling. A bee stung my arm.

"Jesus, I've never seen a guy ripped open this bad. Did they catch the one who did it?" I heard. I didn't recognize the voice. I could feel the stimulant try to rouse me. My guts were a volcano on fire.

Al and Laurence stared at me from a distance.

Jimmy was wiping off his dick.

"No," another voice said, then more softly, "I don't think he's going to make it."

I was floating on a sea of mud, then, very slowly. I sank. Wallpaper.

As usual the music is so loud you can't talk, and the place is packed with really dull numbers trying their best to look brutal or disinterested. I was bored and half-drunk but if I had a better place to go I'd be there. In the crush I was pushed back against some tall ugly guy standing at the wall. Before I could move away again a hand started feeling my butt. Oh well, why not, I thought to myself, and pulled back against it. The hand squeezed. "Want it?" he asked.

I nodded.

"Got a place?"

I nodded again, feeling much better.

"Then let's go."

"Sounds good to me," I said. I followed him into the dark and wondered if this time Santa Claus was going to answer any of my letters.

By now I was getting interested but had the uneasy feeling that somewhere I'd heard this song before. What did he mean by "it already has?"

- This story originally appeared in the Antinous Review.

PRACTICE MAKES PERFECT

John Patrick

"He *is* beautiful," my drinking buddy Larry exclaimed.

"Beauty is in the eye of the beholder," I countered.

"Confess, you're fuckin' bewitched," Larry pressed. "Confess!"

"Okay, I'm bewitched, bothered and bewildered," I crooned.

The corner of Larry's mouth twitched upward when I went on with, "Besides, since when is beauty the basis for love? I'm looking for love." I mournfully shoved some of the fish-shaped pretzels in my mouth.

It was a typical Friday – celebrating the body beautiful at the Boybar. Strippers were the main attraction, and the best of the bunch, Arnie, a well-formed 19-year-old, was gyrating in front of us. But my attention was riveted on a stranger, a muscular blond youth who was standing off to the side. He was not beautiful in the conventional sense, but he was what I would call farm-boy beautiful, rough at the edges. Just the way I like 'em.

"Oh, speaking of beauty," Larry went on, "I spoke with Buddy on the phone the other day. For some reason he was recalling his days spent stripping and he said when he first met his lover he noticed the way he walked. That's rather sexy, I think. He also added that this lover had a sweet smile so he figured he was a nice man."

"Arnie has a sweet... smile," I said, turning my attention to the matter at hand. Arnie's crotch was right in my face; I couldn't see his smile but I knew he was smiling at me and it was a sweet smile. I stuffed a dollar in the jockstrap and Arnie ruffed my hair as he moved on to Larry.

Larry didn't keep him waiting, but copped a feel as he stuffed the dollar in.

Arnie scampered off the bar and made his way to the tables. He was lost to us, but my attention had returned to the stranger in the corner.

Larry could sense I was preoccupied and left. Larry was the last hope. I knew no one else at the bar. It was off-season and almost everyone I knew had gone elsewhere for the summer. I felt abandoned, somewhat ashamed by the fact that I had to work for a living.

But I hadn't been abandoned entirely. As I was ordering another round, the stranger sat down at the far end of the bar and was staring at me. When he saw me return his stare, he ran his forefinger from his lips down to the middle of his stomach, unbuttoning his flimsy shirt with his left hand as he went along. I shivered.

Then he slipped his arms out of the shirt. His shoulders were broad and deeply tanned. He was muscular from all that toiling in the fields.

Carrying his shirt in his hand, he slowly made his way toward me. I remembered about what Larry said, about Buddy's lover and his walk. This kid had the sexiest walk I'd ever seen.

In moments we were inseparable. He had a Coke, I finished my drink. He said his name was Bill, and he was "between jobs." It seemed a deal of some kind was struck, but just what was involved I wasn't sure. Finally, I bluntly asked, "How much will this cost me?"

"How much you got?" he laughed.

"Ten inches," I joked.

His eyebrows arched. "In that case, you get a discount."

I bit his neck while dragging my fingernails all along his side. Goosebumps covered both of us, making us laugh in the middle of a kiss. I pushed Bill's long blond hair out of the way, kissing his forehead, cheeks, nose, and lips. I parted his teeth with a dart of the tongue. Bill moaned and held onto me with such force I groaned. He was even hornier than I was.

Pressing the small of his back, I welded us together, the sweat sliding from our torsos onto the bed. I felt his fingers on the back of my neck threading up through my hair and I put my forehead between his well-definbed pecs. He arched his back and brought his legs up around my waist. I could feel the muscles running along the inside of the thighs. He lifted me up off his body with strong tanned legs and rolled me over on my side.

"What do you want?"

"I want to make you come," he whispered in my ear.

"Don't worry. We'll get there soon enough," I whispered, slowly traveling up his thigh to take his erection in my hand. He strained against the long fingers, pointing his toes, carrying the sensation through his entire body. It was an heroic orgasm. I jacked off, my puddle joining his on his belly. We hung suspended in mutual pleasure but not knowing one another well enough to admit it. I began kissing his neck, then filling his mouth with my tongue.

All I could think was how I had hadn't turned anybody on this much in ages. "It's so good. I mean if we can do this first time out – " I said.

"Practice makes perfect," he said.

I pulled my hands down from his neck to his lush bottom and moved my body against the smooth skin. I could feel the muscles tightening and relaxing across both of our flat stomachs. The heat, the motion, the shiny hair washing against my face got me hard again.

He felt my erection. "You really are incredible," he gasped.

"No, I've just been practicing longer than you. Sex gets easier and better as you get older."

"And I thought you old farts just got boring."

I slid it into him eagerly. "Does that feel boring?"

"Oh, god, easy, easy."

I loved to torment him; he loved being tormented. Through an older man he would now learn the pleasures of restraint, of holding off for a bit, savoring it. But slowly I would turn him into an ocean of hot tides. The power of my own sexuality over this rough beauty made me heady. I pulled my fingernails along the boy's sides, then slid my arms under his shoulders and cradled the back of his head. With mounting force, I slammed into him.

When he groaned, "Now, man, now," I was close to the edge myself. Now I felt that I was riding out a tidal wave, what with both of us coming. I started to cry, it was such a perfect moment. Coming together like that made me cry. As often as I'd sought that, it happened so very rarely. My mind pushed words away and the tears rolled along my nose into my mouth. I engulfed the lad with affection, kissed him, licked him. Stroking his hair, I felt protective. I knew he could take care of himself but for that vulnerable moment I shielded him from any further torments. At that moment I was glad I had always chosen to live alone. In fact, I was quite unused to having a boy to hold in my bed. I had, for the most part, taken my pleasures as I travelled about the state, as manager of operations for Thirfty Drug state-wide. Having someone in my home usually made me nervous, but Bill was so laidback he fit right in, in more ways than one.

In the morning, Bill was in no hurry to leave. And as though the first flurry of emotion and sex of the night before had relieved me of that utter urgency, I was able to relax and I lay down amid the disarray of the bedsheets and played with his body with a great deal of gentleness. There was an animal sensuality about Bill as he slowly stretched out against me on the bed. I gasped at the studliness of his body, exploring the sturdiness of his arms and shoulders, the swell of his chest, as I had not had the freedom to do before.

I was glad it was Saturday. We had the weekend ahead. Whatever it would cost me, I decided, it would be worth it.

I kissed him more tenderly than I had the night before, parting his lips for the sweeping invasion of my tongue. He met it and offered me his very essence, winding his own around it and arching toward me, seeming to need far more than my kiss. I felt his greater need, to have another male, hard and strong, against him. We were well attuned to one another. I sat up, panting, and steadied myself as I drank of the passion-glow in his cheeks. His eyes held the undisguised, sweet joy of anticipation that expressed far more than the rapid rise and fall of his chest. He waited and watched as I prepared his anus for another assault. I had never remembered wanting a boy like this, had never remembered anyone needing to be touched so badly. The years had given me a maturity that added to every ounce of my appreciation of a youth such as this. So beautiful was he that my hands trembled under the strain of control. I could not deny the thrust of my own aching need.

I barely managed a scratching whisper as my hands traced the journey my eyes had just completed.

"Bill..."

He seemed to forget everything, whatever nightmare had driven him to the Boybar, as I moved toward him. "Oh, mister," he moaned, and when my erection entered him, he arched himself against me in dire need.

With slow deliberation I dropped my hands to his buns. The male perfection of him getting fucked was nearly more than I could bear. His own cock was vibrantly hard, and he was soon warning me of imminent explosion. I jacked it, but with regret because there was so much to touch – he was so damn studly!

And when he touched me, stroking the lines of my body, caressing the sensitive points that I couldn't deny, I knew at last the full measure of the power that he now held over me. "Oh, yes," I murmured as he came deep inside me. I had never enjoyed being passive before. Bill had converted me, but I had a feeling it was only because of him, I was drunk with passion. He stretched upward toward me. His arms circled my neck to bring our bodies flush against one another. His orgasm incited my ardor and our bodies meshed instinctively. When I had reached the limit of control, I cried aloud, "Oh, Bill," a fevered cry of victorious possession as I came.

For me, there had never been anything quite so rich as the sharing of sex with Bill. He had learned, somehow, somewhere, to be as good a top as a bottom. Although young, he was brilliant in his pace setting, positively masterful in his reading of my body. In turn, I responded to his knowing fingers with a height of arousal that lifted us both far beyond anything either of us had known in the past.

I noticed the marks on Bill's back and buttocks. I didn't mention them, but Bill noticed me noticing them. Slowly I was able to elicit the whole story from him. He was reluctant to tell it, and I didn't press him. I knew, however, that he sought to share the terror with someone and eventually I won him over.

Bill grew up on a farm in Minnesota. Farming, he learned, is too much hard work for too little return. His family was very poor. Bill said, "My dad wanted me to drop out of school and help him on the farm. I fought him; I didn't want to leave school, it was the only fun I had. My minister took an interest in me, so I felt like there was somebody who cared, and all I could think of was going to him. I left a note for my parents and ran away.

"At my minister's, I began crying and told him about my life at home. He held me as I sobbed. It was the first time I could remember anyone showing me physical affection.

"When the minister took me home, my dad accused him of kidnapping me. The minister hightailed it, leaving me there. Dad took me to the side of the barn where he tied my hands above my head. Then he pulled my pants down, beat me with his belt until I was bleeding. When I screamed, he stuck his bandanna in my mouth. He left me tied up outside all night. Near dawn, he came out, threw me a pair of overalls and told me to get used to them because that was all I would be wearing from now on. Mom kept quiet, fearing for her own life."

Bill went on, telling me a bit about the various men who "ministered" to him after he ran away from home.

Later, snuggling exhausted in my protective embrace, Bill marvelled at the rarity of our joint explosions and wondered why life couldn't always be so glorious. His eyes were closed, their dark lashes lying luxuriously above his cheekbones. There was a light sheen of perspiration on his forehead and nose, a similar dampness on his chest. "Ummmm?" His big dark brown eyes opened. He was warm still in the aftermath of our heated sex. Suddenly I didn't know what to say. What I *wanted* to say was "I love you," yet I couldn't permit myself that luxury. It would only complicate things. It would only make things worse. There was still Monday morning with which to contend . . . and the utter futility of our love. It was best that it was left unpledged. Lowering my lips, I feather-touched them to the flat dot of his nipple. His helpless gasp was emotionally satisfying.

"Practice just makes perfect, I guess," I said, finally.

He smiled, lifting a hand to caress my face. "You're the nicest thing that's happened to me in a very, very long time."

"Me, too." I hesitated, but went on oblivious to the consequences. "You must stay."

He was, after all, "between jobs." He told me he was thinking of getting a job at the Boybar, maybe a barback, even a dancer. No, I said. I decided to give him a job. Being a farm boy, he enjoyed the garden. In fact, he was my "gardener" for four months, before he left to seek his fortune in Miami. It was, after all, high season by that time. But during our weeks together, the drug company was going through a huge merger and I didn't even have time to fall in love with him.

...Take off your coat, my boy,
Out of your trousers!
...Hurry up, you wild lout
And don't laugh, you rascal!
Your looks, your curls
Would drive gods to a frenzy!
Off with your clothes! Handsome lad,
All fire and motion!
From your eyebrows to your knee
The least movement is graceful!
Every line a mystery
Every dimple a question mark.
Put your arm across my shoulder,
So I can carry you to bed!
Your member is shining,
Glowing like a pale rose
Under your white shirt,
Pure as a dove.
You drop from the sofa,
Nestle like an Adonis
Upon the soft purple carpet,
Your sweet charms
Like green ivy wind round me;
Drunk and hot as from Falerian wine
With erring hands,
I silently strip off your shirt,
From your hips, tender as lilies.
Now you are uncovered, lovely miracle -
Bashful, you're warding off my desire;
Exultant I embrace.
Blissful and profoundly anxious,
Alluring, you tremble with lust...

– Adolf Brand, "Inseln des Eros"

My Past

is a short string of beautiful
boys or young men I admired,
dragged to bed, left in ruins
on corners with taxi fare home.
Another of friends who were horny,
who I could have slept
with but didn't because they
were ugly, insane, or too much
like me to be sexy. We were
partners for sweeps of wild
parties, took dope till they felt
like museums which we
could pick over for bodies
to idealize with caresses.

The sun rose slowly. I was
still huffing and toiling
with them, like a sculptor
attempting to get things just
right - finally collapsing
in bed with some smeared,
smelly torso before me, and
a powerful wish to be left
alone. Take you, for example,
who I found throwing up in
the bathroom of some actor's
mansion and crowned my new
boyfriend. Your ass made me
nervous till I explored it...

- Dennis Cooper, "The Dream Police"

Illustration on the preceding page from the video "Possession," courtesy Falcon Studios.

*The family that lays together,
stays together!*

THE
BLESSING

An Erotic Novella By
LEO CARDINI

*STARbooks Press
Sarasota, Florida*

"Yes, a big penis does get you more work."
– London porn star and erotic dancer
F Roy, admitting to The Face magazine
that a ten-inch cock is an asset

I.

Dressed in nothing but a worn-out jockstrap, the broad-shouldered, narrow-waisted hunk on his hands and knees makes his way around the crude semi-circle of bare-chested men beating their meat. In this dimly-lit backroom at the Mineshaft, my eyes gradually adjust to the lack of light as I watch him suck off one guy after another.

Just as it's my turn, he looks up at me. I see his face for the first time.

"Uncle Vinnie!"

"Mike?"

I freeze, my right hand glued to my rockhard, upcurving hard-on throbbing for attention barely inches from his face.

My uncle rises to his feet, overwhelming me with this unexpected display of his muscular, six-foot-two physique. There's just too much of him to take in all at once. Somehow, I manage to focus on the tantalizing spread of black hair that fans out across his chest, and then, lowering my eyes, the provocative sag of his jockstrap as it struggles to contain the ample contents within.

I open my mouth to say something, but nothing comes out. I reach for my tee-shirt that I've stuffed into my back pocket, but abandon the effort as ridiculous, given the situation.

"So," says my Uncle, flashing me one of his devilish smiles, "read any good books lately?"

I laugh nervously, feeling greatly relieved, and try to shove my dick back into my 501's.

"No. You?"

"Nah. Too busy landscaping...and sucking cock. C'mon, let's get something to drink."

And with that, he readjusts his jockstrap, slaps me on the ass and leads the way out of the backroom and into the bar as I struggle with the buttons in my fly, battling against a hard-on that refuses to go down.

"You don't have to stuff that thing away on my account. No indeed. I'm glad to see you've inherited the DeAngelo legacy.

Big dicks are legendary in our family, you know. Your father, in fact..."

I've seen my father's dick and I know how extraordinarily endowed he is.

But whatever he was going to say about my dad gets diverted as we settle on the two vacant stools at the bar in the midst of men drinking beer, smoking grass, and playing around with each other. This brawny, bare-chested bartender with a huge dick hanging out of his Levi's comes over to take our order.

"I'll have a Bud. You Mike?"

"The same."

As the bartender gets our beers, my uncle says, "I know you're too young to drink..."

This was in the June of nineteen seventy-seven, barely days after I graduated from high school.

"...but what the fuck, I've been waiting for the right moment to discuss our mutual attraction to men."

"You knew I was gay?"

The bartender returns with our beers and Uncle Vinnie pays him with bills stashed away in his left sock. Then he picks up his can of beer, taps it against mine by way of a toast and we each take a swig.

"Yeah," he says, setting his can down on the bar. "I've known for some time now. I figure any kid who goes nosing around in his uncle's bureau and steals one of his jockstraps..."

"How'd you know that?"

"Well, it's a long story. Some other time, 'cause right now what I'd like to do..."

He bends over and pulls a joint out of his other sock, which he holds up for my inspection.

"...is get you good and stoned."

He lights up and inhales, the masculine contours of his prominent pecs rising into mouth-watering display, and then passes the joint to me.

Well, we silently toke away - I can hardly believe I'm getting stoned with my own uncle in a sleazy sexclub! - and just as I begin to feel the effects of the grass this tall, lean guy wearing nothing but construction boots, white socks and a metal cock ring that serves to emphasize the enormous dimensions of his soft, heavy-hanging dick, comes up to us.

"Hiya, Vinnie."

Uncle Vinnie's just taken another toke, so he simply nods hello and holds out the joint for him.

"No thanks. I'm already ripped to the tits. Besides, you know what I really want, don't you?"

And with that he falls to his knees behind my uncle. Uncle Vinnie passes me the joint and slides his ass sideways almost all the way off the barstool until he has to support himself with his outstretched right leg so his friend can - oh my God! - pull my uncle's asscheeks as far apart as they'll go and stick his tongue up his butthole! And while he works his tongue in and out, Uncle Vinnie just keeps the joint moving back and forth between the two of us while he pushes out his butt to accommodate his friend.

Some tongues have all the luck, I think, and I begin to imagine what it must be like for that fortunate, slithery muscle to snake its way deep inside my very favorite uncle, working its way up that dark, narrow, silky smooth passageway...

Oh, I think I'm getting very, very stoned! So much so that after my uncle's extinguished the roach, he takes me by surprise when he asks, "Look familiar?"

I realize that though my thoughts have turned inwards on the mysteries of his butthole, my eyes are glued to that poor, put-upon jockstrap of his, burdened with the bulk of so much meat nestled inside.

"Huh?"

"It's your jockstrap I'm wearing."

I can only stare speechlessly at him.

"Yeah. I figured if you could steal one of mine, I could steal one of yours. Yes sir," he continues, rubbing it with one hand, "it's my favorite. Why the stories I could tell you about our adventures together..."

But just then, urgent moans from below distract our attention.

Uncle Vinnie lifts his butt off the barstool, pulls his asscheeks wide apart and pushes himself onto his friend's face just as the guy shoots an enormous load of cum all over the floor in a series of milky white pools. And all the time he's spilling his seed, my uncle just stares at me right in the eyes with that seductively wicked smile of his.

"Gee thanks, Vinnie," his friend says once he's recovered from his orgasm, seating himself on the barstoop on the other side of my uncle, clutching his softening dick and staring out into the forest of all those men's legs.

"Thank you!" Uncle Vinnie says down to him, settling himself once more on his barstool.

"But it's not like you, Mike, to find your way out of the wilds of New Jersey into a place like this. So where's Derek?"

And right on cue, Derek, my best friend for as long as I can remember, comes sauntering out of the back room in his dirty, white sneakers and his low-rise cotton briefs that serve to emphasize the hugeness of his dick. Among our classmates it's reputed to be second in size only to mine. It forces the waistband so far down in front that not only can you see the incredible tautness of his lower abdomen, traversed by a narrow, descending line of silky blond hair, but also the upper portion of his pubic bush. Tall and tight-muscled with a swimmer's body, and blessed with blond hair, steel-blue eyes and remarkably large hands, he attracts the notice of a number of men.

By the time he reaches the pool table in the center of the barroom - three guys are busy on top of it in a three-way suckoff - he spots us. I see the surprised reaction on his face as it registers who I'm sitting with. Then a mischievous smile spreads over it as he comes over to join us.

"Mr. DeAngelo!"

"I think under the circumstances you can call me Vinnie."

"Sure thing...Vinnie. Well, this is quite a surprise."

He stares down at my uncle's crotch as one hand reaches into his own.

"Quite a..."

With his free hand, he tugs on his left nipple.

"...surprise indeed."

"I was just telling Mike I figured he didn't come here all by himself. No, the instigator would have to be someone with a talent for trouble."

I'd never heard Derek described as having a talent for trouble, but it impresses me that there's no more apt description of him. Not that he's a bad kid. He's just...adventuresome.

Always the first kid on the block to try anything. Drinking, drugs, sex, you name it.

"A talent for trouble.," Derek says beaming, "Thanks. I like that."

"Two bad you weren't here a few minutes earlier. We just smoked the last joint I had on me."

"Oh, that's okay. The bartender downstairs? In the Den?"

"You must mean Davey. Black leather boots and posing strap?"

"Yeah, and a six-foot snake he calls Baby draped around his arms and shoulders."

"That's Davey all right."

"Anyhow, he and I shared a joint. Real good stuff. And once he got me good and stoned, he let me get behind the bar to pet his snake and suck his cock. It was really far out."

This is what I mean. These sort of things happen to Derek all the time.

"The only thing about sucking dick, though," he continues, hungrily staring at my uncle's crotch again, "is that it just leaves me wanting more. Mike's the same way. There've been nights we've sixty-nined each other maybe half-a-dozen times. We'd swallow each other's cum and fifteen minutes later we'd be hard and working on each other's dicks all over again. Maybe we were just re-cycling the same cum, passing it back and forth between us. You know - down your throat and out your dick."

Derek loves it when he has an audience, and Uncle Vinnie's giving him his undivided attention.

"So," Derek goes on. "We've always wondered how big you were. You know, down there."

"You have, huh?"

"Yeah." And then turning to me, "I guess you wasted no time in finding out, huh?"

"As a matter of fact, no."

"You're kidding!"

He grabs the front of Uncle Vinnie's waistband and asks, "May I?"

"Be my guest."

He slowly pulls the waistband away from my uncle and the two of us lean forward to peek inside.

There, between my uncle's muscular legs, beneath a lush forest of bristly black hair that encroaches onto the base of his dick, rests a substantial mass of soft manmeat that takes our breath away. His fat dick, brown-shafted and veiny, with a huge, mushroom-shaped cockhead, lazily flops forward into the safety net of my stolen jockstrap.

"Jesus! I know they grow them big in your family. But...my god!"

He boldly digs a hand into my uncle's crotch, skillfully slipping his fingers under those two enormous balls, as if to gauge the weight of my uncle's remarkable equipment.

Uncle Vinnie's dick responds by slowly stretching upwards like a dormant monster roused from a deep sleep.

"Here," my uncle says as he maneuvers the back of the waistband down below his ass. Derek cooperatively takes over, pulling it down to his ankles.

Hitching his feet on the lower rung of the barstool, he spreads his legs wide apart. We're so awed by the rugged beauty of my uncle's upstanding, over-sized hard-on as it reaches what must be a good ten-plus inches we're absolutely speechless. Wide-eyed and open-mouthed we just stand there gaping.

"I don't know what you guys are waiting for," Uncle Vinnie coaxes, grabbing his dickshaft - he can barely get his fingers around it - and giving it a few long, slow showoff strokes. "I can see you're both cockhungry as hell."

He reaches out and slides his left hand behind my neck. Our eyes meet. The moment grows intense with compelling intimacy as he nearly whispers to me, "Your cousin Ronnie would never hesitate for so long. Whenever we're alone, he just pulls down my pants and dives right in."

"Ronnie sucks you off?"

"Every chance he gets. I see you've got a lot to learn about your family. A lot. Oh!"

While Uncle Vinnie's been encouraging me to suck on his dick, the same time piquing my curiosity about our large family - it's so extensive, there are branches I've hardly met, like the Vermont DeAngelos, who, to hear my uncle talk about them, seem to number in the hundreds - Derek's lowered himself onto his haunches. He now commences to lick my uncle's loose-hanging balls with that well-trained tongue of his.

Okay, so maybe I haven't been around as much as some, but one thing I know for sure is no one knows how to lick balls like Derek. He's turned it into a fucking art form. Believe me.

As he skillfully manipulates the left ball into his mouth, Uncle Vinnie goes "Oh!" again, staring at me with raised eyebrows.

Then Derek coaxes in the right nut, eliciting a "Whoa!" from my Uncle Vinnie as he slowly pushes my face down into his crotch.

In my stoned state, time slows down and my head reverberates with the thought "I'm going to suck on my Uncle Vinnie's dick!" as he guides my mouth onto his impatiently-twitching dick. When I wrap my lips around his cockhead, capturing it in mid-twitch, I issue a stifled moan and close my eyes to fully savor the remarkable diameter of my uncle's warm, fleshy cum-shooter.

"Oh, Mike. That feels so fucking good!"

He massages the back of my neck as I slide my lips down his fat dick, relishing its incredible thickness and the rough texture of all those swollen veins that run rampant all over it.

His cockhead presses against my throat. I feel a stab of anxiety as I question my ability to deepthroat such a huge dick. But I want it so much, and I so desperately want to please my uncle and impress him with my cocksucking skills that I determinedly will my gagging muscles to relax. His cockhead slips into my throat and even I'm amazed when I find my nose buried in the bristle of his sweatsmelly pubic hairs.

"You two guys make quite a team," my uncle practically moans at us.

And as I begin to slowly suck up and down his dick, he continues with, "Oh yeah, one hot fucking team! The two of you are going to be awfully popular here. Awfully popular!"

Spurred on by my uncle's approval, I work my way up and down his dick, greedily sampling every detail of its rugged terrain, one moment flicking my tongue across his piss slit, coaxing his cock to jerk inside my mouth, the next feeling the tickle of his pubic hairs brushing against my nose as my lips stretch like they never have before to encircle the immense base of his dick.

Finally, Uncle Vinnie pulls me off him. Spit shiny, his upstanding monster of a cock throbs between his legs.

Derek looks up at us. You should see him there, his mouth stuffed with my uncle's ballsac.

Uncle Vinnie makes a half-successful attempt at forcing his uncooperatively rigid dick down towards Derek, who eases my uncle's balls out of his mouth and takes over sucking him off, his noisy, slurpy suckstrokes announcing his understandable enthusiasm.

Then my uncle reaches for my nipples and tugs me towards him. I follow his lead until my lips press against his. His tongue works its way inside my mouth, boldly taking possession of me.

He abandons my nipples. The back of his right hand lightly brushes down my chest as the other grabs my Levi's, deftly unbuttoning me and reaching in.

I feel his hand on my cock. Fondling it, he slips his tongue out of my mouth, looks at me with open-eyed wonderment and says, "Jesus!"

His gaze descends into my crotch and he expertly eases out my cock and balls. My liberated dick springs upwards in arrogant, show-off display.

"Would you just look at that!" he says, lowering my Levi's to mid-thigh.

And two guys passing by stop to gape approvingly before moving on.

"Oh, yes, you are indeed a DeAngelo! Every fucking inch of you."

As he slides his palm down along the underside of my dick, reaching for my balls and fondling them, Derek jumps up with "Well I might not be a fucking DeAngelo, but...

And with that he pulls down his briefs. His long, pale dickshaft jerks upwards, buoyant and restless, his shiny, bluish cockhead towering above the dense overgrowth of his blond pubic bush.

"See? Second at Lyndon High only to Mike. We had this contest in the locker room one day. Was that ever something!"

"I can just imagine," my uncle says as he savors the sight of my best friend's dick and grabs his balls.

He's now got us both by our nutsacs. We stand there in front of him, our throbbing dicks desperately begging for his attention.

"So now that you got us by the balls, what are you going to do?" Derek asks eagerly.

"This."

He plunges into my crotch and goes down on me. With a dozen or so deepthroat suckstrokes he's already got me close to coming. Fortunately, he dismounts me and with equal enthusiasm immediately goes down on Derek, who moans with pleasure.

Raising his head again, he yanks the two of us close together by our ballsacs until our dicks press against each other. He pauses to examine this union of the two of us, and then goes down on both of us. Of course he can't get all of us into his mouth, but what he lacks in deepthroating he makes up for in tonguing.

"Wow!" Derek says. "Can I try that? With the two of you?"

"What do you say, Mike?" Uncle Vinnie asks me as he sits up again.

But he doesn't wait for an answer. No, he just rises off his barstool, pushing it behind him with one foot as he presses his dick against mine. This never-so-personal contact with my uncle electrifies me, sending waves of pleasure down my dickshaft and deep below my balls.

I look down. Trapped between our two taut abdomens, our warm throbbing dicks intimately hug each other like two passionate, incestuous lovers locked in blissful embrace, my own cock betraying its admiration of my uncle's with an abundant ooze of pre-cum.

"Notice the family resemblance, Derek?" Uncle Vinnie asks him, leaning slightly backwards to bring our dicks out into fuller display.

Actually, I was noticing it myself - the remarkable circumference of the roots of our cocks, the trespass of pubic hairs growing up along their bases, the rugged, veiny texture of our brownish dickshafts as they rise stiff and upcurving, and the graceful flare of the undersides of our neatly-cut, over-sized cockheads. Ah, yes! Makes me proud to be a DeAngelo.

"Mmm," is all Derek says before he wedges his head between our abdomens, sticking out his tongue and snaking it in-between our piss slits, slithering it all over the sensitive territory just below.

Then, without warning, he plunges down on us. But he tries for too much at once and an involuntary "mmph!" issues from his cock-filled mouth, causing my uncle to cast me a roguish wink.

Derek quickly adapts to the dimensions of our dicks, though, sucking up and down as he strokes our butts, slowly sliding his hands between our asscheeks.

"That sure feels good, doesn't it Mike?"

"Yeah."

"Though I expect he's sucked you off maybe hundreds of times?"

"Yeah, maybe. But this is different."

"Because of me?"

I nod.

"I'm glad. If you only knew how often I've fantasized about us making it with each other."

I feel a sudden flood of affection for my uncle. I reach up, take his head in my hands and kiss him, slipping my tongue between his lips to greedily explore inside.

When I finally pull away from him again he goes "Jesus! You've sure turned into one hot young man. Derek too," he adds, looking down at my best friend's bobbing head. "You guys ever fuck?"

"All the time."

"You know what it is to be Lucky Pierre?"

"Uh...No. "

"What about you, Derek?"

Derek nods no as best he can with the two of us in his mouth.

"Then I guess I'll just have to show you guys."

"I'm game."

Derek dismounts us with, "Me, too."

"You like getting fucked by my nephew?"

Derek nods eagerly.

"Is he good at it?"

"You kidding? The best!"

"Well, I'll have to find out for myself..."

The very thought of screwing my Uncle Vinnie!

"...someday. Now about this Lucky Pierre thing. First, Derek, I need Mike to stick his cock up your ass!"

"Right here?" Derek asks, looking around the room. I follow his gaze and realize that while the three of us have been involved in our own little world, there are countless other male-sex scenarios being played out all around us.

"Sure. Does that bother you?"

"In front of all these guys? No. Actually it's a real turn-on. Though half of them look too busy to notice."

"Good. So take off your shorts and sneakers. Socks, too, if you want. You too, Mike."

"Yes sir!" Derek says eagerly, and the two of us strip in no time, kicking our stuff under Uncle Vinnie's barstool.

"So now what?" Derek asks, impatiently stroking his dick.

Uncle Vinnie calls over the bar, "Say Butch, some Crisco?"

Bartender Butch scoops a huge gob of the stuff out of a gallon container next to the cash register into a small, white paper cup and sets it down in front of us.

My uncle positions Derek facing the bar. He compliantly leans over on his elbows with his legs spread apart, provocatively wriggling his beautiful butt until Uncle Vinnie pulls his firm, downy-haired asscheeks wide apart, exposing that pink, puckered hole of his that I know so well.

"Oh," Derek goes, closing his eyes and letting his head fall limp

"You ever rim him, Mike?"

"Uh...no." I reply, hoping he can't tell I don't know what the fuck "rimming" is.

He gets down on his haunches behind Derek and buries his face in my best friend's asscrack. Pausing to look up at me, he then snakes his tongue up Derek's butthole.

"Oh! Oh! OOOHHH!!" Derek moans as he squirms around and pushes out his ass to make things easy on my uncle.

Uncle Vinnie finally pulls away his face and turns to me with a satisfied smile on his face as he gets up again and says, "Now that's what's called rimming. Wanna take a turn at it?"

He holds Derek's asscheeks apart for me and I kneel beside him. Derek repeatedly clenches his butthole, enticing me to enter. My tongue slips in easily and the surge of sensual excitement of exploring my best friend in this entirely new way washes over me like too much of a good thing.

Derek's moans increase in intensity and soon I'm hopelessly addicted to the compelling cause and effect of tongue-into-hole and moan-out-of-mouth.

"That's it," Uncle Vinnie coaxes. "Nice hot butthole. Just think how good it's going to feel when you stick your dick up there."

"Oh!" Derek moans all the louder in anticipation.

"Now get out of there and hold him open," Uncle Vinnie orders, transferring Derek's asscheeks to me he greases up Derek's hole with a prolonged, over-generous application of Crisco. Then he slathers a gob of it all over my dick, bringing me once again close to the edge of orgasm.

"Okay. Now slide it in."

Which I do, slowly, familiarly, as Derek shuts his eyes and shakes his head from side to side, recording every inch of my entrance until my hips are pressed against his asscheeks.

"Now just keep it there, deep inside him," he orders as he gets down on his haunches behind me and works his own tongue up my ass.

Aw, shit! I can't believe the sensation of my Uncle's jackhammer tongue as it repeatedly drills its way up my hole. I feel like I'm going to lose my balance and I close my eyes as I grip Derek firmly by the waist to steady myself. And Derek, the little fucker, rotates his hips in the little room he has between me and the bar, massaging my cockshaft with his clenched spinchter.

My uncle's tongue retreats from my hole and I feel the skillful application of Crisco up my butt.

Next thing I know, he's got his hands on my hips and his dick pressing against my hole.

I think to myself "My Uncle Vinnie's going to fuck me!" and I savor the moment.

He slides the first few inches of his dick inside me.

For a moment I panic. It's so big. So thick! So seemingly endless!

I tense up.

"Just relax," he whispers reassuringly into my ear. "The last thing I would ever do is hurt you."

"It's just that I've never had anything that big up my ass

before."

But I trust in my uncle, and relax, rewarded by the blissful entry of inch after magnificent inch of his dick slowly sliding up inside my ass, transporting me to a new realm of ecstasy I'd never known before.

He moves his hands over to Derek's hips, sandwiching me tightly between the two of them.

"And now, my dear nephew, you know what it is to be Lucky Pierre - the man in the middle of a threesome fuck."

I'm learning so much from my Uncle Vinnie. First rimming. Now this. If this keeps up, I think soon I'll be the one showing Derek a thing or two.

But all I respond is "Oh!" and crane my head around to kiss my Uncle Vinnie. With his tongue in my mouth and his dick up my ass, our familial relationship reaches new dimensions.

"Okay, guys," he says when our lips part, "Just take it nice and easy. Niiiice and eeeeasy."

The three of us feel our way about, gradually finding the rhythm we need to fall into sync.

And as we're doing this, the guy who was rimming Uncle Vinnie before comes over to us.

"Hey, Kurt," Uncle Vinnie says to him, "Wanna join us?"

With an eager nod he manages to maneuver his ass onto the barstoop between Derek's spread-apart legs, licking Derek's balls while his strokes his own dick.

Derek responds with a pleased "Aw shit!" which encourages the guy to deepthroat Derek, and I feel a shift in his hipthrusts as he seeks to accommodate this new partner to our pleasure-making.

In seconds we're going at it with all the regularity of a perpetual motion machine. I get lost in time, overcome by the potent undertow of sensuality that overtakes us, our shared orgasm extracting moans and groans and gasps, more collective than individual in origin. Sweat begins to coat our skins, dampen our armpits, and bead up on our foreheads, as if all this effort required lubrication.

And then I feel the sweet surge of cum building up in my balls, coaxed out of my nuts by the slippery sensations up and down my dickshaft as I repeatedly ram my cock all the way up my best friend's butthole.

"Oh!" I exhale.

"Oh!!!" Derek echoes, tossing his head back and forth like a wild horse, acknowledging my oncoming orgasm and seconding it with the announcement of his own.

Out of the corners of my eyes I can see Kurt's accelerated jackoff strokes as he continues sucking on Derek's dick.

And from behind, I feel Uncle's Vinnie's grasp on my hips tighten as he drives his mighty cock in and out my hole with a measure and force I wouldn't've believed myself capable of withstanding even just a few minutes ago.

Soon all you can hear is "Oh!!"

"OOH!"

"Ah!"

"Mmmph."

"OH! MY! GOD!"

It's unclear who exactly's saying what, but it doesn't really matter. All that matters is this overwhelming, out-of-control stampede towards our shared orgasm.

Then it happens. I hold onto Derek for dear life, screaming out something that blends with everything else and a tidal wave of cum blasts out of my balls, speeding through my dickshaft and up my best friend's butthole.

And just as the first spurt of my cum's upstaged by a second, I feel the powerful eruption of my uncle's jism up my ass as he issues out a loud, "Ah, fuck!" ramming his cock all the way up my ass and holding it there a second before depositing further loads of cum inside me.

And as he drains his dick, Derek's flings his head high into the air, let's out a loud wail, while the loudest "mmph!" of all records the steamy-hot spurts of his jism down Kurt's throat.

The loud cries of our shared climax mingle and diffuse as our orgasms run their course, leaving us sweaty, exhausted and intimately entangled.

By the time we've recovered somewhat, we gradually disengage, our heavy-hanging, semi-flaccid dicks shiny with Crisco and sticky with cum.

It's then I realize we've attracted quite a crowd of jackoff onlookers, most with softening cocks in their own hands, some with beads of cum lodged in their piss slits, others with ropey strands of the stuff dripping towards the floor. And the ones who still have hard-ons; well, Kurt makes his way over to them on his knees, clearly intent on sucking them off.

"So," Derek says to my uncle, groping for his dick, "Aren't you glad I brought your nephew out to the Mineshaft? Maybe we can do it again next week, huh?"

"Oh, I don't think so."

I don't expect this reaction. And it's clear neither does Derek.

"No. Now that everything's out in the open between us, Mike," he says, patting me on the ass, "I think it's time for a long weekend visit to the Vermont DeAngelos."

"Oh" says Derek, betraying his disappointment over this exclusion.

"Oh, you're invited to join us. It wouldn't be the same without you. I mean, you're practically family. And there are uncles and cousins who'll be very pleased to meet the two of you."

"And each and every one of them..."

He gives his dick a significant shake while grabbing for my own.

"Shit," says Derek, cupping our balls, "I can hardly wait to sample all that DeAngelo dick!"

And to prove the point, he gets down on his knees between us, uncertain which one of our dicks to suck on first, while my uncle distracts me with another tongue-probing kiss.

II.

"So, Mike," my hunky cousin Vito says to me, slouching forward in his beach chair at the foot of the pier extending out over the lake, "Uncle Vinnie says you've got one of the biggest dicks in the family."

I lift myself up onto one elbow, shield my eyes and squint up at him from the beach towel I'd set out to take advantage of the warm July sun, rewarded with a mouth-watering view of the outrageous bulge in his snug-fitting Speedos. Considering I've just met cousin Vito for the first time last night, the familiarity of his remark takes me by surprise.

"He told you that?"

"Wouldn't he just," my best friend Derek comments as he turns over onto his stomach on the towel next to mine.

"Yeah. I know your father's got the biggest, because it's legendary in the family. Then there's Uncle Vinnie, as I'm sure you know. And then, he says, there's you."

The sudden vroom of a car starting up prompts Vito to rise from his chair, turning towards the cottage, barely yards away, up a stairway-flanked incline so steep the back porch has a perfectly unobstructed view of the lake. Lonnigan's Lake, that is, in the middle of Vermont. Nearest paved road two miles away; nearest telephone even further. At least that's the way it was back in nineteen seventy-seven. It's the Vermont DeAngelos' summer cottage.

Me and Uncle Vinnie; we're part of the New Jersey DeAngelos, which is a large enough family in itself. The night he discovered me and Derek were gay for sure (we ran into him at the Mineshaft, which we'd snuck into with fade I.D.s) he insisted on bringing us up to visit the Vermont DeAngelos.

I never really knew any of our Vermont relatives because years ago my father had this falling out with his...well, that's boring family history, I guess. So I'll just tell you it was pretty overwhelming arriving here late yesterday afternoon and meeting all these relatives who'd gathered for a family dinner.

"Good. That's the last of them," Vito says as the car

disappears into the pine forest.

Some of them slept over, you see.

And then, like it was the most natural thing in the world, he peels off his Speedos. Since he's facing away from me, I get this absolutely breathtaking view of his beautiful butt; so firm and well-rounded you could die. And oh, what an irresistible sneak-preview I get of his succulent, baseball-sized ballsac as he lifts one foot and then the other to rid himself of his briefs. And - good God! - he has no tanline!

Turning around, he puts his hands on his hips and plants his legs wide apart, clearly showing off for our benefit that thick piece of cut, brown-shafted meat that hangs so heavily between his legs.

"Notice the family resemblance?" he asks, aiming his gaze down at his dick and then back at us.

"Uh...you mean, your high cheekbones?" Derek teases.

"No I don't mean my high cheekbones."

"Your Roman nose?"

Vito nods no.

"That head of thick, wavy black hair that'll probably thin out in your mid-twenties?"

Vito rolls his eyes and nods no again.

"Oh, then you must mean...uh...that!" he says pointing at Vito's dick.

"Yeah, this," he says, grabbing his fat, rubbery shaft and aiming at us like it was a hose, making me ache with the desire to wrap my lips around it.

"Jesus," Derek says, "what do you DeAngelos do? Soak 'em in Miracle Gro, or something?"

Vito laughs and then says, "Anyhow, when the straights aren't around, we usually hang out bareass. So come on, you two."

Truth to tell, being among unfamiliar family on unfamiliar turf, I'm a little hesitant. But Derek, who never hesitates to plunge into the unknown, jumps up and immediately shucks the briefs he's wearing, showing off that long graceful cock of his, so pale and smooth in comparison to the dark, veiny dicks that all us DeAngelos are blessed with. He runs his fingers through his blond pubic bush and then gives his cock a tantalizing shake for Vito's sake. His over-sized, blue-tinted cockhead whiplashes out of control, and I see a gleam of interest in my cousin's eyes.

So under the influence of peer pressure and downright horniness I peel off my own Speedos.

"My God!" cousin Vito says, staring bug-eyed at my dick. "You really are number three in line!"

"Shit," Derek says, tugging on his dick. "To think I got nearly nine fucking inches, and you DeAngelos make me feel like a goddamn dwarf."

But we're not really paying much attention to him, since Vito boldly takes me into his embrace, wrapping his powerful arms around me and snaking his tongue between my lips. I close my eyes and the next thing I know his hands are on my butt and his teeth gently tug on my left nipple.

Now, Derek's not one to hang around on the sidelines, so I'm not surprised when I feel the familiar flick of his tongue across the nub of my right nipple. I am surprised, though when Vito joins him on my right pec.

And I'm further surprised when seconds later Vito drops to his knees and takes my half-hard dick in his mouth, followed immediately by Derek who expertly sucks my nuts into his own.

I look down, amazed at the turn this family reunion has taken as I watch my cousin and my best friend feast on my cock and balls, noticing with aroused interest their huge, hand-held hard-ons.

Having sucked on my ballsac to his heart's content, Derek leaves Vito in sole possession of my crotch, moving behind him to pull his asscheeks wide apart and plunge his tongue deep inside.

"Ommmph" cousin Vito says through a mouthful of my stiff dick, and commences to work on me with long, expert suckstrokes that get the cum churning in my balls in no time. I estimate it'll be mere seconds before I shoot my load, which I don't want to do so soon, since there's so much more I want to get to know about my cousin other than how well he can suck cock. For one thing, there's that remarkable curvature of his ass. For another, his luscious nipples. And for another, that huge DeAngelo dick of his that sticks up rigidly in front of him now that he's abandoned stroking it in favor of fondling my balls.

But he sucks cock so well, I can't help but give in to it, and I close my eyes to concentrate on my approaching orgasm.

"You guys don't waste any time, do you?"

Opening my eyes again I see Uncle Vinnie, shorts and tee shirt in hand, standing there watching us, a six-foot two vision of manly beauty, what with those broad shoulders and perfectly-sculpted pecs, that trim waist and, of course, that huge DeAngelo dick.

Vito dismounts me to say, "Would you?"

"Yeah," Derek echoes, momentarily pulling his face out of Vito's asscrack, "Would you?"

"Not on your life!"

And with that, he drops to his knees in front of me, shoves Vito aside, and takes over sucking on my cock.

"Hey, Uncle Vinnie! That's not fair!"

But fair or not, Uncle Vinnie ignores him and Vito contents himself by falling onto his back beside me while managing to pull a cooperative Derek on top of him.

Well, what follows is what you'd expect, I guess, given four bareass, over-sexed guys on a sun-drenched pier in the middle of nowhere with the afternoon stretching ahead of them. And once we've finally come (I shoot my load up Vito's ass while he stands there letting Derek suck him off, and then Uncle Vinnie fucks Derek, quickly repositioning himself after cumming to take Derek's jism down his throat) we sprawl across the pier on beach towels, soaking up the warm rays, lost in the lazy perfection of the moment.

I'd dozed off for I guess a few minutes when I'm awakened by an unfamiliar voice.

"Would you look at the size of that dick? Oh, yes. Definitely a DeAngelo."

I open my eyes, shade them from the sun and look up. The butt-naked man standing above me looks so much like my Uncle Vinnie I do a double-take.

"Hey Nick!" says Uncle Vinnie, rising to his feet to shake his hand. "How the hell ya been?"

"Oh, hanging in there," he says, absentmindedly tugging on his big fat dick with his free hand.

Now I become aware there are three other fellows looking in

their early twenties hesitantly standing at the foot of the pier.

"Well c'mon guys," Nick urges. "Nothing to be modest about here."

And as they begin to strip, he turns his attention to me with, "You must be Mike," as he bends over to shake my hand.

"Yeah."

"Well, I'm your Uncle Nick. I heard you'd be here this weekend. Here, let me help you up."

The handshake becomes a powerful lift to my feet.

"Oh, and these guys are Eric, Steve and Marty, fuck buddies of mine. Met 'em over the winter at the Escapade - that's this gay bar in Burlington. Once they got a sample of the DeAngelo legacy..."

He gives his fat dick a shake that makes my mouth water for the umpteenth time this afternoon.

"...and I told them about our family, they've been dying to pay a visit to one of our reunions. Anyhow, this is my cousin Vinnie and my nephews Vito and Mike. And this is...?"

"Derek. My best friend."

Well, Derek and Vito rise to their feet and we all shake hands and exchange hellos. If I've got it right - I've been meeting so many people lately it's getting a little difficult - Eric's the tall, freckled redhead with a flaming pubic bush and a flushed, heavy-hanging dick looks like it's in for a severe sunburn, Steve's the short, brown-haired, body-builder type with an outrageously thick, uncut piece of meat, and Marty's the good-looking sandy blond with an All-American physique and a pale cock that curves slightly to the left, like it's trying to peek around his thigh.

"Oh," Nick recalls, "and we invited some other friends over tonight. That's okay, isn't it?"

"Auntie Gina will pretend to have a fit," Uncle Vinnie says, smiling at the thought of it, "but you know her; she's never so happy as when she's fussing over company."

Somehow I think this Auntie Gina is in for a surprise.

Well, of course, everyone's checking out everyone else, and everyone's pretending they're not, except that Eric and Marty are sporting telltale hard-ons growing by the second.

"You guys do what you like," Nick says to his friends. "I've never met my nephew Mike before and I'd like to get a chance to know him."

"Yeah. I'll bet," Derek says suggestively.

"C'mon," Vito prompts, about to dive off the pier. "Last one to the float gets gang-banged!"

And with that he dives in, swimming towards the wooden deck mounted on air-filled oil drums some twenty yards off. Everyone else follows, whooping up a bloody racket as they make their way to the raft.

All except Eric, that is.

"You can't swim?" Uncle Nick says to him in surprise.

"Oh, I can swim, all right. I just want to be last to the float!"

And with that he finally dives in, neatly cutting through the water with expert swimstrokes.

Me and Uncle Nick settle down sitting side by side at the end of the pier with our legs dangling in the water. I'm embarrassed that I'm getting a hard-on again and I try to cover it up with my hands.

But Uncle Nick gently removes them with, "Now that's nothing to be embarrassed about, Mike."

He wraps his hand around it and squeezes, prompting a moan I didn't expect to come out.

"See I'm getting one myself. Go ahead. Touch it."

Which I do. Responsively, it jerks upwards, growing enormously rigid in record time.

"Actually," he says, as we casually stroke each other's hard-ons, "you're my second cousin, since me and Vinnie are cousins. His parents, my Zia Sophy and Zio Dante..."

Well, he starts talking family. Far from being bored, he's got me spellbound. Our family's so extensive, and Nick's such a natural storyteller that I'm not that surprised when he tells me he's a writer.

Somehow we end up lying on the pier facing each other, each of us propped up on an elbow with his free hand in the other's crotch. I'm beginning to find it more and more difficult to concentrate on what he's saying as I fondle his balls and scan the contours of his broad, hairy chest.

"I could do this all afternoon," he says abandoning his narrative in favor of a more intense investigation of my throbbing, over-responsive dick. "Couldn't you?"

"Uh, yeah," I manage to reply through the haze of lust that

clouds my mind as I skate the tips of my fingers across his pre-cummy piss slit and then transfer the slick ooze to my lips.

"You know," he says, "it's grown awfully quiet over there on the raft."

"Yeah."

We look over. Derek's on his knees blowing Eric while he strokes himself a mile a minute. We see Vinnie pull out of Eric's ass with a softening cock, only to be replaced by a stiff-dicked Steve. Nearby, Vito and Marty are busy sixty-nining each other. So maybe Eric's not getting the full-fledged gang-bang he hoped for, but he looks quite contented with the way things are.

"Wanna join them?" Uncle Nick asks.

"Actually, I'd rather stay here with you."

And to prove the point, I lean over and kiss him. As I close my eyes, he slips his tongue between my lips. Like we're of one mind, I sink onto my back and he slowly rolls over on top of me.

And just as I'm about to ease into the pleasure of allowing my uncle to take possession of me, we're interrupted by two new guests tramping down the cottage steps. They're both tall and lean, with rolled-up bandannas tied around their shoulder-length hair. They're so engaged in an impassioned debate that once they reach the lake, they begin to strip without even acknowledging our presence.

"Shively's manifesto in the Fag Rag is one hundred percent right-on," says one, blessed with an unmistakable DeAngelo dick. "Cocksucking is an act of revolution."

"Jesus," says the other, so thin it looks like his fat sausage of a dick sucked up every extra ounce of flesh his body could spare, "your politics are so fucked up I don't know why I stay lovers with you."

"This is why," he throws back giving his beefy cock a shake, "you fucking reactionary."

"Me a reactionary! Me? The one who..."

"Hey, guys," Nick yells, "can't the two of you stop long enough to meet your cousin from New Jersey?"

The inevitable introductions and comments on my DeAngelo dick follow and I meet cousin Sergio, his boyfriend Ray.

As they untie the sailboat alongside the pier and jump in, Sergio beckons to me with, "C'mon. Wanna join us?"

"Yeah, we won't even talk politics. Promise."

"That'll be the day," mutters Uncle Nick.

"No thanks," I say, thinking of the feel of my uncle's body pressing down on mine. "Maybe some other time."

"Course he doesn't want to join us," says Ray, "and listen to all your simplistic revolutionary bullshit."

"Bullshit! How dare you..."

But a thoughtful breeze blows their conversation in the opposite direction as they sail away, and Uncle Nick once more takes me into his embrace with, "But where were we?"

Seconds later he's once again on top of me. His tongue makes its way into my mouth, I close my eyes, and I give myself up to him.

"Ahem!" someone discreetly interrupts what seems like barely seconds later.

"Don't let us disturb you!" someone else adds, and the two of us look up.

Am I seeing things? Twins? They've discarded their clothes already except for pale blue short sleeve shirts unbuttoned all the way down the front, fluttering in the light breeze. Each is a little over six feet tall with uncommonly fair skin, a lean, graceful body a model would envy, steel blue eyes and a mop of curly blond hair.

"Nat! Dan! Good to see the two of you," Uncle Nick says, dismounting me. "Here, meet your cousin Mike."

As I get up to shake hands with them, I think they sure don't look like DeAngelo's, although their dick's are just as big, only paler and smoother, like Derek's.

Uncle Nick reads my mind and explains, "Their mother, your Zia Adella, married your Zio Klaus, who's from Switzerland. They take after him."

"Oh, and we invited some friends over tonight," says Nat or Dan.

"We're sure Auntie Gina won't mind," says Dan or Nat, though his attention's focused on Derek who's just swum over from the raft and is now lifting himself up onto the pier.

Now both twins turn attention towards Derek and I see it in their eyes that it's lust at first sight between the three of them.

So I introduce Derek to the twins. They haven't even finished shaking hands with him when Nat or Dan asks, "Have you seen the back bedroom up at the cottage?

"Yeah," the other continues eagerly. "It's got a king size bed. Sleeps three comfortably."

"So what are we waiting for?" Derek asks.

And as the twins lead the way up towards the cottage, Derek turns to sing softly in my ear, "Double your pleasure..." before following them up the steps.

Well, Uncle Nick and I once again resume our lovemaking, and fall gratefully uninterrupted into a prolonged feast of sixty-nining until we simultaneously shoot our loads down each other's throats. Then we rest side by side, blissfully lulled into a post-orgasm lethargy under the warm sun until I doze off again, cozy in the knowledge I'm surrounded by this remarkable family of mine.

That is until, "Well, don't you two make a pair!"

I look up. The man standing foremost among this quartet of new visitors, the first to totally strip, lights up a joint, which he inhales and then steps forward to offer to Uncle Nick. The thing is, besides the DeAngelo black hair, high cheekbones and huge, veiny dick, he's a dead ringer for Rocky Angel. Sure, everyone agrees his movies are nothing but sex and violence, but, what with that ruggedly handsome face and that body even straight guys cream over, who the hell cares?

"This," says Uncle Nick over a lungful of smoke, "is your uncle Sylvester."

"Well, I'm glad to meet you. Mike, isn't it?" he asks, flashing me a smile to die as he bends over to shake my hand.

"But of course," Nick informs me, "Everyone calls him Rocky."

"As in Rocky Angel?" I dare to say.

"Well considering I am Rocky Angel..."

He sees the look of amazement on my face and his smile widens with easily-forgivable egotism.

"Here, let me help you up and introduce you to these ne'er-do-wells I brought along with me."

And with that my Uncle Rocky - can you just imagine! - takes my hand and effortlessly pulls me to my feet with a flex of his bulging biceps and a pendulous swing of his heavy-hanging dick that momentarily mesmerizes me.

His friends have finally managed to pull off all their clothes and they stand there waiting for introductions.

"This is Kurt," Rocky says, indicating this stud who looks an awful lot like him. "He's a stunt man. My double. And this is his 'boy' Danny," he continues indicating a dark-skinned, short but well-built kid looking my age with a fat, uncut dick with foreskin to spare, and a completely shaved chest and crotch. "And this is Tommy. Tommy's spending the summer with us..."

"Us," Uncle Nick explains is Rocky and his lover Ian, who's a professor at the University of Vermont."

"Yeah, he's over at the quarry - that's this swimming hole in the middle of the woods that used to be a granite quarry - with one of the bartenders from the Escapade. That's this gay bar in Burlington. They'll be joining us later. Anyhow, Tommy's my second cousin, which makes him your..."

He stops, trying to figure out the relationship, and then continues with, "oh what the fuck, what matters is we're all DeAngelos. So Mike..."

"Yoo hoo!" interrupts a singsong contralto from the cottage. "Is anyone ho-ooome!"

The pond echoes with a riot of enthusiastic greetings like none I've heard this afternoon and the occasional "Auntie Gina!" makes it clear this relative I've heard so much about has finally arrived.

The back porch door swings open and, with all the flair of a celebrated actress who knows she's a star, Auntie Gina makes her appearance. But - good God! - Auntie Gina's this soft-faced, gray-haired, roly-poly man in his fifties dressed in white Bermuda shorts and a pink LaCoste shirt! He bounces down the steps buoyant as a beach ball with hands aflutter to greet the appreciative audience of DeAngelos and their friends.

Talking nonstop to anyone and everyone, he gradually makes his way to me with "And you must be my dear, dear nephew Mikey. I'm your Auntie Gina. I mean," he continues, pulling in his chins and baritoning his voice, "I'm your Uncle Gino. But of course," he continues, his voice returning to contralto, "everyone calls me Auntie Gina. Anyhow, I'm so glad..."

He takes me by the shoulders and kisses me on the right cheek.

"...I finally get to meet you."

He kisses me on the left.

And then standing back to look me up and down, his gaze comes to rest in my crotch.

"Ooooh! You are a DeAngelo. Every luscious inch of you. If only I was twenty years younger! But I'm not, and I live the life of a nun. Well, we must have a nice long chat. Sometime. But first things first, my dear. Now, let's see how many for dinner?"

He does a limp-wristed head count.

"Oh dear! So many mouths to feed! Thank God there's food, food and more food in the trunk of my car. But it's not going to walk itself into the kitchen, you know!"

"Why don't you ask the twins?" Nick suggests. "They're in the bedroom."

"Don't I know it! Who's their scrumptious friend?"

"Derek. My best friend."

"Oh? Well, aren't you the lucky one! So anyone have any idea how many others are coming over tonight?"

Vito's just swum over from the raft and offers, "A hundred maybe?"

"Well!" Gina says, acting all put out. "Someone's going to have to make a liquor run. And munchies, too."

"I will," Vito volunteers, toweling himself dry. "C'mon Danny boy," he says, giving him a playful slap on the ass, "we can ride naked until we get to Owl's Head."

"Just don't you guys go running around bare-assed up at Lookout Point," Gina nags with waving forefinger. "You know what happened last time!"

Well, those who know laugh and those of us who don't are left to ponder the possibilities as they grab their clothes and ascend to the cottage with Auntie Gina huffing and puffing behind them with, "And no sucking on the driver's dick when he's behind the wheel! And don't..."

But I miss the rest, since Nick and Tommy have plunged into the water, heading for the raft, leaving me alone with my Uncle Rocky and his stuntman lookalike, Kurt.

I feel kind of awkward in the presence of my celebrity uncle. Awkward and turned-on. And when I feel my dick growing hard I try to will it back to softness. But it doesn't escape Rocky's attention. He steps towards me with an eager smile animating his stunning face and closes his hand around it. Then he leans forward and kisses me right on the lips. A lightening bolt of desire speeds through my chest and I feel my dick stiffen in his hand.

"Kurt and I were planning to spend some time together in one of the bedrooms," he purrs into my ear.

Kurt approaches, sliding a hand across my butt as he seconds my uncle with, "We'd sure like to have you join us."

No response is really necessary, and with a bouncing hard-on that won't go away I follow them up the steps and into the cottage, passing Auntie Gina in the kitchen chopping up vegetables and fussing out loud to himself...uh, herself...uh, whatever!...a mile a minute. We successfully avoid drawing attention to ourselves and quietly pass into the rear of the cottage.

"Let's see what the twins are up to," Uncle Rocky says with a mischievous gleam in his eye.

Quietly opening their bedroom door, we see the three of them busily engaged in a three-way suckoff. We don't escape their notice for long and the twins momentarily disengage to greet Rocky and Kurt. Derek, slow to give up Nat or Dan's fat nine-incher, gapes at my Uncle Rocky in astonishment. But before he has a chance to say anything, Rocky shuts the door and leads us into the next bedroom.

We step inside. Kurt closes the door behind us and Rocky takes me in his arms, overwhelming me with the press of his tall, muscular body against mine, the several inches he has on me in height forcing me to lean backwards, secure in his powerful embrace as he plunges his tongue deep into my mouth.

And then Kurt approaches me from behind, sandwiching me between the two of them.

The next half-hour or so passes like a dream. Who hasn't ever jacked off fantasizing about making it with a movie star? And who hasn't ever jacked off imagining what it would be like making it with some hot relative? And here I am doing both at once!

Is this really Rocky Angel - my very own uncle - down on his knees sucking my dick? And is that really his stuntman Kurt who now kneels next to him to lick my balls, so I look down beyond all this activity in my crotch to see double fists stroking double hard-ons with oversized cockheads oozing pre-cum?

Oh, but now Rocky's turned me around to stick his tongue up my butthole, his strong hands pulling my asscheeks wide apart while I bend over to suck on his stuntman's monster of a lookalike dick, now that he's risen from his knees.

And now, me and my uncle look deep into each other's eyes as we work as a team on a reclining Kurt's cock and balls, who all the while moans nonstop in encouraging response while he tugs on his nipples. That is, until Uncle Rocky leaves me to solo in Kurt's crotch as he kneels with spreadapart legs over Kurt's face, sinking his cock into Kurt's mouth and taking over his nipples.

Then I go nuts for my uncle, and with a lot of shifting that sets the poor bed a-creaking, I manage to push my he-man, matinee idol of an uncle down onto the bed. As he raises himself up on his elbows, I take his veiny, rockhard erection in my mouth, deepthroating it with surprising ease while Kurt, on his knees beside us leans into my ear, encouraging me with hotbreath whispers.

How many guys in how many darkened theaters across America have wished for as little as a single kiss from this stud, and here I am with my mouth full of his huge DeAngelo dick. Whoops, not any more! Now he's on his knees again sucking me off while his stuntman double first lubricates my butthole and then slowly sticks his dick up my ass.

And that's when the three of us come. I shoot my load down Uncle Rocky's throat at just about the same time Kurt shoots his own abundant supply of hot, steamy cum up my ass. And while Kurt lets his monster of a dick soften inside me, Rocky rises to his feet so I can now suck him off, in seconds the explosion of his salty, scalding cum making its welcomed way down my throat.

And then, while the three of us recuperate, Uncle Rocky whispers to me, "Next time, I want that load of yours up my ass."

Exhausted from the events of this remarkable afternoon, I blissfully doze off, entangled in the confusion of arms and legs between these two Hollywood heartthrobs.

That is, until "Yoo hoo! Dinner time! Come out, come out

wherever you are!"

The three of us disengage. Uncle Rocky goes to the bureau, opening a drawer full of men's underwear.

"Most of these are mine, I think" he says, tossing me a pair of briefs and Kurt a jockstrap, sliding on a pair of silk boxer shorts himself. Then tee-shirts from the drawer below.

"We always kind of dress for dinner," he informs me.

Making our way out into the main room of the cottage there are my uncles and cousins and second cousins and friends...and a few new faces...all dressed with the same informality.

The food's laid out buffet style on the dining table with Auntie Gina standing beside it, beaming with motherly pride while Vito and Danny pour out glasses of red wine and pass them around.

When they're done, Auntie Gina raises her glass.

"To the DeAngelos, and all their fabulous friends. Let us all be thankful for how fortunate we are to have each other. Those of us here who were out before the Stonewall Riots - and my dears I was - know what a blessing it is to have family to see you through the hard times as well as the good. And, of course we should all be thankful that our men are hung like... well, DeAngelos!"

Well, this gets a few laughs.

Auntie Gina raises her glass higher with "To us!" and then downs the wine in a most unladylike manner. And as everyone follows suit, she steps behind the buffet, all bustling with energy again.

"Now eat up!" she commands. "We've got a big night ahead of us!"

And with this I fall into the boisterous crush of family and friends helping themselves to dinner.

Uncle Vinnie winks at me from across the room. Uncle Nick, standing next to him, smiles at me and then says something to him. Uncle Vinnie looks at me again and then nods with raised eyebrows in agreement to whatever it is Uncle Nick said.

Uncle Rocky gives me an affectionate slap on the ass and leans into my ear with, "Kurt and I were thinking after dinner, before the guests arrive, maybe you'd like to join us and..."

Before I can respond to what he proposes, there's Derek

tugging on my arm, saying into my other ear, "The twins are so fucking hot, you won't believe it! They were thinking that while everyone else is having dessert, the four of us make off with that can of whipped cream in the fridge and..."

He's barely finished telling me what they had in mind when he redirects his attention towards Rocky with, "Say, did anyone ever tell you look a lot like..," pushing me aside, up against Ray who says, "Bet you've never been out on the lake under the moonlight. If you, me and Sergio slip away, we could take the sailboat and..."

So many relatives! So many propositions! So little time!

But Fairy Godmother Gina pulls me away from Ray with, "Now, I hope you're not planning to go back down to New Jersey tomorrow night. You should really stay the week. Oh, we'll get you home safe and sound. And we've lots of room since there'll hardly be anyone here. Just..." She silently mouths names as she counts up to eight on her fingers. "...well, just a few of the men in our family. And if you meet anyone at the party tonight you'd like to have stay over..."

Somehow I think I'm just beginning to appreciate what a blessing it is to be a DeAngelo!

III.

The well-built kid leaning next to me against the pool table with his jockstrap down around his ankles turns his head to whisper into my ear, "Doesn't that guy over there at the bar look just like Rocky Angel?"

I don't tell this stunning muscleboy with short black hair, dark eyes gleaming with excitement, and a dick almost as big as mine, that the hunk leaning against the bar on one elbow is Rocky Angel. Yeah, really, right here in the Mineshaft, barely five yards away from us, dressed in a black leather vest and tight, faded-blue 501's that show off his powerful, he-man physique millions of filmgoers cream over. And I sure don't tell him that the reason I know this is because he's my uncle.

"And the one standing next to him..."

...who's my uncle Vinnie, Rocky's cousin, also dressed in a leather vest and snug 501's...

"...could be his brother."

"Umm," is all I say, more interested in the gym-sculpted contours of his nearly hairless chest than in his understandable attraction to my uncles.

"Could you just imagine," he says after a meditative pause, "like, actually sucking on Rocky Angel's dick?"

I don't have to imagine. But I don't tell him that, either.

When he slowly exhales with a moan, I'm not sure it's because he's picturing himself all bare-chested and sweaty in some Rocky Angel adventure flick, where the distinctions between sex and violence blur, or because my best friend Derek, who's been down on his knees in front of the kid for the last ten or fifteen minutes sucking on his dick and licking his balls, reaches up without missing a suckstroke and tugs on the gold rings that pierce the kid's nipples.

He leans into my ear again with, "God, what I wouldn't give to blow him."

Derek rises from the floor, raising his white, low-rise briefs back up into his crotch to struggle with the burden of his stiff eight-incher.

"So why don't you just go over and do it?" he asks like it was no big deal.

The kid hesitates. Then, as if resolved to take action, he pulls up his well-worn jockstrap, making a poor job of covering up his thick, upcurving erection. But then he hesitates again.

"C'mon," Derek says impatiently, grabbing his hand and leading him over to the bar.

I, of course, follow, forcing my half-hard-on back up into the left leghole of my short denim cutoffs.

"Hi," Derek says to Rocky like he's never met him before in his life. "This is...uh..."

"Joey," the kid says.

"Joey. He wants to ask you something."

Rocky looks Joey up and down, and then lets his gaze linger in Joey's crotch, where his poor put-upon jockstrap struggles to contain the rebellious contents within.

"Uh-huh?" Rocky asks with a provocative glimmer of interest.

"Could I...uh..."

His eyes descend to Rocky's huge horsedick and egg-sized nuts as they rest in tight, denim-enclosed confinement against his left inner thigh.

"Yeah?" Rocky prompts.

"...uh..."

"He wants to suck you off," Derek matter-of-factly completes for him.

A smile makes its way across Rocky's face.

"Well, it's not like me to turn down a blowjob when a hot dude like you offers to give me one. But," he continues, slowly undoing his 501's, top button and all, and reaching in, "are you sure you can handle something like this?"

He whips out his huge, over-sized dick with one hand, and then reaches in with the other to pull out his enormous balls.

"Jesus!" Joey says half to himself, mesmerized by the sight of Rocky's thick, brown-shafted cock and his two grade-A, extra-large low-hangers.

As Joey worshipfully lowers himself down onto his knees, his eyes never leaving my uncle's dick, I seat myself on the bar stoop, lost in the shadows, where I can see in close-up profile, barely inches apart, Joey's boyishly handsome face and my uncle's ruggedly masculine dick.

Joey kneads his jockstrapped crotch with both hands as he examines my uncle's cock from several different angles. Watching him, I try to imagine what it must be like to see it for the first time.

Ah, the DeAngelo dick! You see, big dicks are legendary in my family, and though Rocky's professional name might be Angel, he's a DeAngelo through and through, like me and Uncle Vinnie and the other DeAngelos hanging out tonight at the Mineshaft. His real name's Sylvester, but like he always says, whoever heard of a he-man with a name like Sylvester? So Sylvester became Rocky and DeAngelo was shortened to Angel.

So there I am trying to see my Uncle Rocky's dick through Joey's eyes, sharing in his admiration of that rubbery shaft of thick, veiny meat, neatly cut with an over-sized mushroom of a cockhead. It hangs down between his legs against the backdrop of his Levi's that have slipped half-way down his hips, the bottom of his fly hitched up behind his nuts.

And his piss slit! I swear it has a life of its own. Right now, basking in Joey's rapt attention, it proudly manufactures a precious drop of pre-cum, knowing perfectly well the seductive force of this tiny drop of manjuice gleaming in the faint light.

Now, I might be only eighteen - yeah, class of '77 - but I've been around enough to know from the spellbound expression on Joey's face as he stares at my uncle's monster of a dick, that he's a dedicated cocksucker, so hopelessly addicted to the sensation of hot, hard manmeat making its way into his mouth and down his throat, I'll bet you he's all but lost his gagging reflexes. Though a DeAngelo dick, it occurs to me, will probably prove the exception.

How do I know this? Because I share Joey's obsession with cock, as does Derek, who now kneels opposite me to witness Joey's understandable fascination with my uncle's dick. "Once you've sucked one cock," Derek's always fond of saying, "you've only sucked one cock. And there's so many more out there, thank God." And Derek manages to find them, blessed as he is with a mischievous smile, a hard, lean body, a talent for trouble, and a complete lack of self-consciousness when he's horny, which is most of the time.

The bead of pre-cum on my uncle's dick hangs suspended below his piss slit from a slender strand of liquid that thins and lengthens, elongating several inches, ready at any moment to drop down onto the sawdusty floor. But it doesn't because Joey comes to the rescue, leaning forward and flicking it into his mouth with the tip of his tongue like a fucking expert. Then, sticking out his tongue again, he teases the moist, tender lips of my uncle's piss slit. Rocky's half-hard dick responds with a lazy, buoyant uptwitch and Joey quickly captures Rocky's cockhead with his lips and resumes tongue-teasing the hell out of it. My uncle's cockshaft lengthens, the large blue veins that run riot along his shaft swelling until they look fit to burst.

Once he's got my uncle's dick well on the way to complete erection, he slides his lips down Rocky's rugged cockshaft until he's got about five inches of it in his mouth. He begins to slowly suck up and down Rocky's still-stiffening shaft with the tight-lipped suckstrokes of an accomplished cocksucker. At the same time, he frees his dick from his overstretched jockpouch, deftly slipping it off and dropping it onto the floor, all the time never letting up on my uncle's dick.

Clutching his liberated, upcurving cock - almost as big, veiny and mushroom-headed as a DeAngelo's - his every suckstroke takes more and more of my uncle in his mouth until he's deepthroating the entire thing with surprising ability. And I'm wrong in my prediction; never once does he gag.

Soon he's working on all ten inches of my uncle's stiff, rugged manmeat. One moment he's got all of it in his mouth and his nose presses against my uncle's black, bristly pubic bush, and the next he's practically dismounted it, exposing it spit-shiny in the dim light, all those bulging veins thrown into shadowy relief.

"Yeah. That's it kid," my uncle says in that deep, gravelly baritone of his that means he's really getting turned on. "Suck on it. That's what you come here for, isn't it?"

Joey nods as well as he can considering his mouth's stuffed with a hearty portion of DeAngelo dick.

"Thought so. Probably sucked off lots of guys tonight, I'll betcha."

Joey manages to nod again.

"But you just can't get enough, huh?"

"No sir," Joey says, dismounting my uncle's dick long enough to look up at him with a face flushed with cockhunger. "Especially," he continues, gripping my uncle's dick mid-shaft and holding it up to admire its underside, "when it's..."

But however he was going to describe it, he lets out with a groan instead because just then my uncle takes a swig of his beer, holding the can so bottomhigh he's forced to lean back, thrusting out his dick, which slides spit-slippery through Joey's grip until my uncle's cockhead rests between Joey's lips.

And then Rocky surprises Joey by pushing him all the way down on his dick with his free hand. Joey responds with a not-so-unwelcome-sounding "mmph!" and enthusiastically throws himself into a double-time cocksuck.

At the sight of my uncle's enormous dick in and out Joey's mouth, I lean forward, irresistibly drawn towards his crotch. At the same time, I see Derek also leaning into my uncle. We've been here before ("No one'd ever believe me if I told them how often I get to lick Rocky Angel's nuts, never mind suck his dick," he loves to complain to me.) and, as a team used to working together on our knees, we furiously lick his hairy balls until I manage the one closest to me into my mouth. Derek goes for the other, but I beat him to it, aware for a split second, like I always am on such occasions, of the miracle it is that two such impossibly large nuts can fit inside your mouth when you really want them to.

With my mouth full of Rocky's ballsac, I see Derek's face close-up as his works his tongue as far behind my uncle's nuts as he can get it. Then, looking up, I see my uncle Vinnie step over to stand next to Rocky, unbuttoning his 501's and yanking out his own remarkable dick, huge even in its present state of half-hardness, proving that Rocky and Vinnie could still pass for brothers if you could see nothing but their cocks.

Vinnie pulls Derek out from between Rocky legs, forcefully redirecting him onto his own dick. Derek deepthroats the entire thing with no sign of difficulty and, noisily sucking on it, repositions himself facing Vinnie, at the same time sliding his cutoffs down to his ankles.

I release Rocky's balls to see the sight of these two uncles of mine standing there towering above us, their stiff dicks serviced with greedy enthusiasm.

Joey reaches out towards my crotch with his right hand, searching the air until he finds my dick. I wonder if he notices the remarkable similarities between the cock he's so busy deepthroating, the cock in his hand he struggles to stroke with some semblance of an even-paced rhythm, and the cock that Derek's so eagerly sucking on as he kneels next to him.

My uncles' unbuttoned jeans have managed to slide halfway down their firm, appetizing butts. In a display of cousinly affection, they further lower each other's Levi's in back, running their hands across into each other's asscheeks.

"Yes sir," Rocky says while he fingers his cousin's hole, "nothing like a good blowjob, hey Vinnie?"

"You can say that again."

There's a few moments' silence while they look down at the bobbing heads in front of them, appreciating all the attention lavished on their dicks, and then Vinnie asks Rocky, "So how's he doing?"

"Gives head like a real pro. Surprising for someone who looks so young."

He pulls Joey off his dick, tilting his head up until they meet eye to eye.

"Just how old are you, anyhow?"

"Uh, nineteen? Almost?" he replies, tugging on his nipple rings as he silently begs with pleading eyes for my uncle's dick again.

"Not even nineteen and you suck dick that good?"

"I've had a lot of practice. Believe me. But I've never had one like..."

He stops. His eyes are on my uncle's dick again and he lunges for it. But Rocky pushes him off. He wraps his fingers around his cock and holds it up in front of Joey's face, smiling down at him, knowing perfectly well what he's doing to the poor, cockhungry kid. Joey sticks out his tongue to make contact with Rocky's dickhead, but Rocky lifts it away from him and asks, "How many dicks would you guess you've sucked?"

"Uh, like hundreds?"

"Hundreds, and you're not even nineteen?" Vinnie questions.

"Well, I started at an early age. And then when I began coming here..."

His voice trails off as he continues to stare longingly at my uncle's dick.

"Yeah?" Rocky prompts.

"Please let me have it again?" he implores. "I'll do anything you want. Anything!"

"Anything? Anything's a mighty big word. But I suppose if you want it so badly..."

He directs his cock once more into Joey's willing mouth. Joey gobbles it right up and furiously sucks on it as if to make up for lost time.

Well, as I sit and watch, lazily stroking my pre-cummy nine-and-a-half-incher, Joey and Derek work on my two uncles while tugging on their own dicks. They close their eyes, their foreheads cover over with sweat and they suck away to their heart's content. Up above, Rocky and Vinnie have their arms around each other, running their free hands across each other's chest, sharing a cousinly moment enjoying, hardly for the first time, the pleasure of two cocksuckers down on their knees giving them head at the main bar in the Mineshaft.

This goes on for several minutes until Vinnie goes "Oh! Ohh! Ohhhh!" the cum clearly building up in this balls, ready to erupt. He clamps his hands down on either side of Derek's head, holding it stationary as he violently works his dick in and out of Derek's mouth, taking control of his own orgasm.

"I'm getting close!" Rocky announces, upstaging his cousin as he tenses his legs and butt in a wonderful display of hard muscle rallying to support his need to shoot his load.

"Mmmph!" Joey manages to reply while Rocky rams his cock deep down his throat.

Which Derek seconds, with a mouth just as full of dick.

And then with one loud, prolonged "Ohhh!" Rocky roughly pushes Joey off his dick. He grabs his cock and with just a few handstrokes his scalding hot cum shoots out. Lots of it. He directs the first abundant spurt of it right into Joey's wide-open mouth, and then aims the rest all over his face and chest.

Barely have the last few jets of his jism found their way onto Joey when Vinnie roughly pushes Derek off his dick and aims his own rapid-fire explosions of cum into Joey's mouth, though as much lands on his face as in his mouth.

I'm ready to shoot myself, so I stand up, steady myself with an arm around Rocky and let my cum join my uncles', the feeling of orgasm so strong my upper body jerks out of control until I'm spent.

Derek, the enterprising cocksucker that he is, makes up for the loss of Vinnie's cum by crouching down low, pushing Joey's hand away from his dick, and deepthroating the entire thing, working on it with a fury of passion.

Just as I've deposited the last drops of my cum onto Joey's chest, his eyes open wide and his breathing grows urgently ragged. Then with sharp gasps and heaving chest he shoots his own load into Derek's mouth. And as he does this I see his eyes dart crazily back and forth between the three DeAngelo dicks aimed at him with discharged loads.

When Derek's swallowed all Joey's cum - he makes an incredible racket doing it - he sits up on his knees, a stream of jism dribbling out of the left side of his mouth. Below, a drool of cum from his piss slit that makes us realize while he was swallowing Joey's load, he was also depositing his own onto the floor, which explains why he was so noisy about it.

As we slowly recover, Joey studies our three softening DeAngelo dicks. Does he question the coincidence they look so similar, I wonder.

When we stuff out dicks back into our jeans and cutoffs, Rocky graces Joey with that famous smile of his that rises slightly higher up one cheek than the other in an expression of shared, intimate wickedness. Then he gives Joey his even more-famous wink, and tousles his hair.

"Thanks a lot, kid. I appreciate it"

"Don't mention it, sir," Joey replies gratefully, burying his face in Rocky's crotch and inhaling deeply, looking like he might just stay there.

"C'mon," I say, pulling him away and helping him up, "Let's go into the backroom."

I'd meant to include Derek, since I was just sorta in the mood to hang out a little, but he'd already moved down to the end of the bar, already busy sucking more cock.

Joey picks his jockstrap up off the floor, shakes it free of sawdust, slips it on again, and we walk through the corridor that leads into the second-floor backroom which is, like most of the Mineshaft, all dim red lights and walls painted black.

Groups of men cluster about in the various areas, some talking, some watching, but most engaged in sex. In the middle of the room, a steep, narrow flight of wooden steps leads down to the first floor. At the far end, a makeshift wall of plywood and two-by-fours separates the final third of the room from the rest of it, allowing a yard or so on either side for access. The wall's riddled with glory holes at various heights. Two guys are down on their knees sucking dicks coming through, a third bends over with his sweat pants down around his ankles and his butt flush against one of the lower holes, and one enormous horsedick downcurves in semi-erection out one of the highest holes, waiting - but not for long - for anonymous cockworship.

I lead Joey to the small bar that looks out onto the open space between the wooden steps and the glory-hole wall. Here, *another* Kurt, blond-haired, blue-eyed, tends bar. Tonight he's dressed in cycle boots and a black leather posing strap. His fair skin positively glows with good health and he stands there looking like the statue of a Greek god come to life. Rick, his young dogboy of a boyfriend - black hair, large, dark eyes and a lean, tight-muscled body like a swimmer's - kneels butt-on-heels in a corner behind the bar, naked except for a black leather dog collar attached to a leash secured to the bar.

Kurt sees me and graces me with a smiling nod of recognition. I melt inside like I do every time he acknowledges my presence and order two beers.

He serves us and then unleashes Rick, who crawls on his hands and knees out from behind the bar to sniff at our crotches as we lean against the front counter, looking out at all the activity going on around us.

"You know, I think that really was Rocky Angel," Joey says, petting Rick like you would a real dog. "No one but Rocky winks like that. And to think I sucked him off," he says drifting into the recollection of what just occurred.

Well, while Rick sniffs and licks our crotches, I pull out a joint, light up and pass it between us, including Kurt whenever he's not busy. And while we get stoned, I can't resist bragging that Sly - that's what we call him, especially when he's hanging out in incognito places like this - and Vinnie are my uncles, and Derek my best friend.

When he gets over the surprise of all of this, he says, "I'll tell you one thing. Your uncle sure looks like Rocky Angel. Jesus this is good grass! I'm so high I could..."

But his words dry up as he surveys the room with stoned interest while Rick coaxes his cockhead out of the side of his jockpouch to lick it

Finally he says, "You know, I thought I was hallucinating or something after you guys shot your loads, the way you stood there with your dicks hanging out, like the same dick reflected in one of those three-way mirrors you see in clothing stores. And I guess you realize you and your uncles are like really hung."

"Oh, well, when you're a DeAngelo..."

"DeAngelo?"

"Yeah, that's our family name."

"It is?"

"Uh-huh."

I go on to explain there's tons of us in New Jersey and Vermont and Massachusetts. Not that I know all of them. I mean, I've grown up with the New Jersey DeAngelos, and this summer I've gotten to meet I guess most of the Vermont DeAngelos, but as for the ones in Massachusetts, I haven't met a single one of them yet, though if they're like the rest of my family, visiting Boston for the first time's gonna be some experience.

"Anyhow," I continue, "big dicks run in my family."

"Well, I'd sure like to be at one of your family reunions sometime."

"Well, you are, sort of."

"Huh?"

So I explain how a bunch of us - the gay ones, anyhow - are spending the week in the Big Apple, and that those of us who aren't at the Mineshaft yet tonight will be sooner or later, except for Auntie Gina - I mean Uncle Gino - who'd never make it past the doorman, even if she - I mean he - wanted to.

"So who else's here now, besides your uncles?"

As if on cue, Nat and Dan, my twin cousins from Vermont, make their way from behind the glory hole wall, stripped down to the white, low-rise jockey shorts they'd borrowed from Derek (don't ask why; that's a story in itself) that emphasize their long, lean bodies while straining against their double-your-pleasure claim to the DeAngelo legacy contained within.

After introductions Joey observes, "You guys don't look like DeAngelos."

"Because we're so fair-skinned?"

"With blond hair and blue eyes?"

"Yeah."

"That's because we're half Swiss."

"Yeah. But there's one thing about us that's every inch a DeAngelo."

They exchange looks and then lower their briefs mid-thigh, clearly delighted to show off their beautiful twin dicks that flop down fat and heavy in front of their large, low-hanging nuts.

"I see what you mean," Joey says, reaching out to balance their soft shafts, one in each hand, as if weighing them like so much sausage at a meat market, "though they're paler...and not as veiny...and..."

He forgets what he's saying as he watches them elongate, their twin, blue-tinged cockheads crawling over the edge of each palm as if curious about what lurked on the floor below, and then rising up as if now to check out Joey.

"You guys ever get into threesomes?" Joey asks looking up at them hopefully.

Nat and Dan exchange looks again. Then Nat gets down on his knees in front of Joey, gently shooing Rick out of his way. He lowers Joey's jockstrap down to his ankles and slips it off as Joey cooperatively lifts one foot and then the other. No sooner is he done than Rick tugs it out of his grip with his teeth.

When they see Joey's dick, half-hard with expectation, Nat looks up at his brother with, "God! Would you look at the size of that!"

Now it's their turn to examine Joey, and their busy hands all over his cock and balls encourage a rapidly-rising, pre-cummy hard-on.

"You sure you're not a DeAngelo?" Nat asks with a mischievous smile. Then, without waiting for a response, he goes down on him all the way to the base of his shaft. When he finally dismounts him, Joey's cock springs up stiff as a rock, throbbing for more attention.

"Jesus!" Dan exclaims. And then, turning around, he lowers

his briefs while bending over. Pulling his asscheeks apart, he cranes his neck around to look at Joey.

"Go ahead," he says. "Stick it in. It's okay, I'm already greased up."

But Rick's tired of chewing on Joey's jockstrap and his nose makes its way into Dan's asscrack before Joey has a chance. Joey pushes him away, grabs Dan by the hips and presses his cockhead against Dan's hole.

"Ohhh!" Dan groans as Joey slowly slides his dick inside him. "That feels so fucking good. Sooo fucking gooood!"

Without forfeiting an inch of Joey's dick, Dan manages to reposition himself until he's bent over the bar leaning on his elbows with his legs spread apart.

As the two of them work into a relaxed, slow-paced fuck, I get down on my haunches, pull Nat's briefs down to his ankles and suck him into an erection. In my stoned state I feel like I could go on sucking him all night long, but once he's hard, he pushes me off his dick and helps me to my feet.

"Grease my dick up, huh?" he asks, reaching for the can of Crisco on the bar.

I reach in, scoop out a gob of the stuff, and slather it all over his responsively-twitching cock.

When I'm done, he pulls Joey's asscheeks apart and says to me, "Better grease him up, too."

When Joey feels me fingering his hole, he halts his fucking, pulling half-way out of Dan with an outthrust of his butt to make it all the easier for me to stick one, two and finally three Crisco-coated fingers up inside him. Joey closes his eyes, his mouth falls open, and he moans in response to my probing.

When I finally slip my fingers out, Nat wastes no time pressing his stiff dick against Joey's hole. With his hands on Joey's hips, he slowly slides it in as far it it'll go, then begins working it in and out Joey's hole. Joey, in turn, does the same to Dan, and the three of them gradually find the rhythm they need for this threesome double-fuck.

"Oh, Baby!" Joey intones, sandwiched between my cousins. And while they go at it, a resourceful Rick manages his way in-between Dan's legs. Sitting on the floor with his back against the bar, he swallows Dan's dick, at the same time jacking himself off with Joey's jockstrap wrapped around his cock.

As my cousins and Joey moan and groan in ecstasy, they begin to attract a small crowd of a half-dozen or so men drawn to the irresistible spectacle of a well-built stud bookended by a pair of tall, tight-muscled twins. Even Kurt watches, idle since everyone's too interested to buy a drink, standing behind the bar with his armor-like legs spread apart and his powerful arms crossed over his chest, looking on with obvious interest.

Someone reaches out to tug on one of Joey's nipple rings. Someone else gets down on his knees to watch this double-fuck up close. A third guy gets down on his haunches behind Nat, unsuccessfully attempting to stick his tongue up Nat's hole since he's in non-stop motion thrusting his dick up Joey's ass, and so contenting himself with licking Nat's butt and then making his way down Nat's legs with the outstretched flat of his lick.

Eventually everyone has his dick out, stroking it. Even Kurt slips off his posing strap, revealing his smooth-shaven crotch, his big nuts snugly encased in a furrowed, hairless ballsac, and his thick, impossibly rigid eight-incher, beerbottle fat at the base, and curving upwards with so little taper it dwarfs his cockhead.

Me? I just lean against the bar facing them and watch, thinking in a corner of my mind what an unexpectedly extraordinary summer I've had getting to know my relatives. Soon someone behind me reaches around to pull down my cutoffs, and the next thing I know, one guy's sucking me off while a second one rims me. Then a third man joins them, helping me out of my cutoffs and then feasting on my nuts.

Someone passes around poppers. Then there's two bottles circulating. The group of us pass into a popper high and I drown in the sweet sensations of all the wetmouth, hypertongue attention lavished on my dick, my ballsac and my butthole. I see Nat plunging his dick in and out of Joey's ass, aware that not only is he fucking this hunk with a dick nearly as big as his, but that in some headtrippy way, he's also fucking his brother (not that they've ever needed a middleman for that!) in that his every cockthrust promotes a similar dick-plunge up his brother's ass.

Nat and Dan are the first to announce their oncoming orgasms as if not only identical in appearance, but also in the time it takes them to reach climax. Their breathy moans mingle and entwine. Some of the men surrounding them join in while others encourage them with the likes of "That's it babe," and "Yeah, man," and "Shoot it up his fucking ass!"

Suddenly, Joey howls "Oh! Oh! Ohhh!" ramming his cock up Dan's ass with powerful thrusts, depositing his load. Nat squeezes his eyes closed and shakes his head back and forth to work off the excess of his own orgasm, Dan loudly announces his discharge of cum down Rick's throat, and Rick works on his own dick with jackhammer cockstrokes until he shoots his seed into Joey's jockpouch.

As my own load blasts it way out of my nuts, warm and tongue-teased within this guy's mouth, it races through my shaft and explodes down the throat of this other guy in my crotch. And while the feeling of orgasm overcomes me, I watch the men surrounding us shoot their own loads. Some cum lands on the floor, and some on my cousins and Joey, directed towards them as if in a rite of pagan worship. And when Kurt shoots his own load, he surprises us with the power of his cumshots as they speedily arc over the bar, landing on Dan's face.

Sweaty and exhausted, Joey and my cousins slowly disentangle and recover. Nat slides his dick out of Joey and it flops down between his legs, semi-hard and heavy-hanging. Joey then does the same, and when Dan, in turn, eases his dick out of Rick's mouth, the little dogboy contents himself playing with Joey's cum-soaked jockpouch, rubbing it all over his face.

Dan dips his fingers into Kurt's cum on his face and then sticks them in his mouth. Kurt grips his dick and holds it up for Dan to admire. A final drool of jism, makes its slow way down the underside of his cock which Dan leans across the bar to lick off. When he's done, Kurt hands him the roll of paper towels behind the bar, and Joey and the twins clean each other off, spending much longer than necessary, though who can blame them?

By now, the crowd that surrounded them's dispersed. Nat and Dan pull up their briefs while I slide my cutoffs back into place and button up.

Joey goes to retrieve his jockstrap, but Rick refuses to give up. The harder Joey tries to tug it out of his mouth, the more firmly he clamps his teeth down on it, growling in protest.

"Let him have it," says Kurt. "Here."

And with that, he hands Joey his posing strap.

"Thanks," says Joey with privileged surprise in his voice. He rubs the inner pouch against one cheek, sniffs at the narrow back string, and then slips it on. As thick-dicked as Kurt might be, the pouch can barely contain his cock and balls.

When we step away a few minutes later, we leave Nat and Dan leaning against the bar talking with Kurt. Their briefs have already been lowered to their ankles again, this time by two blowboys down on their knees sucking on their dicks, looking like they rather appreciate the fact no one, the twins included, seems to be paying them much attention.

Now, Kurt's not just a bodybuilder and a bartender, but he's also an artist. Yeah, he's that Kurt, creator of that popular series of illustrations titled Mineshaft Knights, each drawing set in a different clubroom and packed with well-built men with over-sized dicks involved in just about every sexual act you could imagine. So before Joey and I make our way downstairs, we hear him entice Nat and Dan into agreeing to model sometime for him. A posing session with Kurt is a distinction some guys can only dream about. And rumors abound about these off-hour, daytime events, where Kurt and his subjects meet in the empty Mineshaft, the entire place at their disposal, a fitting backdrop for the hot-and-heavy, down-and-dirty activity he's so fond of portraying.

We make our way downstairs into The Den, where the real heavy-duty leathermen hang out. It's darker than any of the other rooms, the music Davey the bartender plays sounds like Philip Glass on acid and the several pieces of pleasure-pain equipment in the room look both forbidding and irresistible.

As we weave our way through the crowd, we pass one he-man in leather pants with a gag in his mouth tied to a post, his prominently protruding nipples receiving a thorough workout from his broad-chested buddy in tight jeans with his dick hanging out, and an even tighter T-shirt that stops short just above his navel. Another stud, a Titan of a man, faces away from us, spread-eagled and shackled to a scaffold, naked except for a leather ballstretcher and metal cockring, his firm asscheeks rosy from the whipping administered to him by a brother Titan in tall boots, a black jockstrap and a leather mask.

And after we pass by several groups of men deep in conversation, cockworship and buttfucking, we reach the sling in a corner of the room. There's my cousin Sergio lying naked in it. His big dick rests soft, heavy and inviting on his firm abdomen, obscuring, even in its flaccid state, the sight of his navel. His lover Ray stands at the foot of the sling facing Sergio's spreadapart legs wearing black, square-toed cowboy boots, a studded leather cockring and similarly-styled armbands, his huge dick hanging down between his legs, fat and flaccid, in dramatic contrast to his lean body.

Ray has one well-greased fist up Sergio's ass. Sergio rests open-mouthed and heavy-lidded in silent bliss. He slowly shakes his head from side to side as Ray carefully works his fist back and forth and in and out while holding a bottle of poppers in his free hand, periodically bringing it up to their noses for a hit.

It strikes me as odd to see Sergio and Ray, the impassioned gay activists that they are, engaged in something so purely non-political, but then I recall their enthusiastic interest in the recent six-part manifesto Cocksucking As An Act Of Revolution that appeared in Boston's Fag Rag, and its sequel Fistfucking as an Act of Revolution, though it took Sergio some time to bring Ray around to his point of view.

Ray sees me and silently offers me his bottle of poppers. I take a hit, pass them on to Joey, and when I feel their effect, my interest in Sergio's cock upstages my fascination with fistfucking and I lean over him, relishing the suppleness of his deliciously deadweight dick as I take it in my mouth. Sergio moans and I don't know if its because of my attention to his dick or Ray's to his hole. Whatever the case, when the popper high passes, I let his cock slide out from between my lips, plopping down moist and semi-hard on his abdomen.

"That's my cousin Sergio and his boyfriend Ray," I explain in a whisper to Joey, getting down on my haunches to whisper it into his ear, since while I was feasting on Sergio's dick, he'd dropped to his knees to manage Ray's dick into his mouth.

"Oh," he say, dismounting my cousin's dick and rising. "I should've guessed it was something like that."

We make our way close to the bar where Derek's down on

his knees sucking off Davey. You see, Derek's got it bad for Davey, and every time we go to the Mineshaft, though he's in and out of every room, in the thick of one sexscene after another, he spends most of his time down in the Den hanging around Davey, tending to his every need, be it licking his dick, his armpits or his butthole, or fetching a bucket of ice from the ice machine. Can't say I blame him, though, considering Davey's this tall, sinewy bartender, square-jawed with short black hair and dark, piercing eyes that always seem to be looking into some remote dimension of madness only he has access to. Tonight he's shirtless with a leather harness across his chest and leather chaps that exposes his big, brownish dick and melon-mound asscheeks.

When Joey sees the size of Davey's cock, he whispers to me jokingly, "Maybe he's a DeAngelo, too."

"Maybe he is," I say provocatively, covering up that I don't really know. You see, once he said he was and explained the connection, but the music was loud and we were sharing a joint of really potent grass and I was too stoned to know whether or not he's serious, since you can't always tell with Davey.

"Jesus! Just how many DeAngelos are there here tonight?"

As I begin to enumerate them, he interrupts with, "Did it ever occur to you, there might be DeAngelos here you don't even know about. Like some of those Massachusetts DeAngelo's?"

"Hmm," is all I say, pondering the interesting possibility that I could've have had sex tonight with a relative without even realizing it.

A leatherman steps up to the bar and orders a beer, forcing Davey to slide his dick out of Derek's mouth to step over to the beer bin, his mighty cock swinging between his legs, fat and heavy and gleaming with Derek's spit.

After he serves the leatherman he announces in his resonant bass voice, "Last call. The Den closes in fifteen minutes."

No one seems to need another drink and so he moves back over to Derek, who takes Davey's dick back in his mouth. While Derek works on him, Davey notices me and motions me over to him.

"You can stay. Once everyone leaves, we're gonna have a private party here. DeAngelos only. And their friends, of course," he adds with a nod towards Derek.

"Wow! Think of it, a den of DeAngelos!" Joey enthuses, overhearing as he joins us.

"Hey, cuz," Davey says, shaking hands with him revolutionary style.

"Hey yourself, cuz," he says back.

"Huh?" from me.

"Davey's my cousin," Joey explains with a wide grin. "We grew up together in the North End of Boston. We've got tons of family there, you know."

Just then, my Uncle Nick and cousin Vito, who I'd yet to see this evening, make their way towards us through the thinning crowd.

We make our hellos and then I say, "Oh, and this is Joey."

"Joey DeAngelo," he says, shaking hands with them. "Of the Massachusetts DeAngelos."

Kevin Kramer, photographed by the famed Douglas Cloutier

The good, the bad, and the beautiful...

FANTASY LOVERS

The Secret Lives of Porn Stars, Starring KEVIN KRAMER

An Expose
Edited by
JOHN PATRICK

STARbooks Press
Sarasota, Florida

Contents

Part One
GORGEOUSNESS-TO-GO

Part Two
STARRING
KEVIN KRAMER

One
Small and Tight
Two
The Big and the Beautiful
Three
A Day in the Life...
Four
A Cock's Pleasure
Five
Twenty Questions
Kevin: In His Own Words
Self Portrait
A Life in Pictures
Six
Sex, Sex, and Still More Sex...

Part Three
BODIES FOR SALE
Straight Stud's Confessions

"Fantasy may be the most empowering tool in our lives. It's how we reshape the world into playgrounds where we can work out our sexual natures. As gay people, we find ourselves constantly at play on these private fields of fantasy. We create worlds at once accessible and forbidden, all the time holding tight to the precious danger of longing for our own kind."

– Joe Bauer, writing in The Advocate

"Assume the mask appropriate. If you're hustling, then act like a hustler should. Don't let a trick know how much you hate him. Don't let him know that he, not you, is the piece of shit. And don't, under any circumstances, flaunt your beautiful body."
"Don't say that, about beautiful and all. I don't like that. I'm not a broad and I ain't a faggot."
"But you are beautiful and tricks resent hustlers who use their beauty to humiliate."
"I don't know what the fuck you're talking about."
"I think you do."

- Paul T. Rogers, "Saul's Book"

Part One
GORGEOUSNESS-TO-GO

"If you have to ask how much it costs, you can't afford it."
– Famous old saying

In the early '70s, even though I was married to a lovely young girl, I still had an seemingly unquenchable need for guy-to-guy sex. Luckily, I travelled a good deal with another married man who also fancied guys, and I discovered the places where boys meet other boys.

However, after a couple of years of cruising in bars, I discovered that, what with my limited time and hectic schedule, it was far simpler, and much more efficient, to hire some companionship.

Even for movie stars, hiring those who play-for-pay is a viable alternative. Consider Hugh Grant. In covering his infamous tryst with a prostie in his BMW, Susan Ager of the *Detroit Free Press* said, "A prostitute who spends 20 minutes with Hugh Grant will not think this is the beginning of something. She will not expect a phone call the next day. She will not tell all her friends, or if she does they will shrug and say, 'So? I did (fill in the blank) the other night."

"Even for a movie star like Mr. Grant," Roxanne Roberts in the *International Herald Tribune* suggested, "a Sunset Boulevard hooker is, well, less labor intensive than other women. No emotions. No pouting. No dinner or small talk. No introductions to his agent. No promises to read her screenplay."

In short, no complications.

Like Grant, I wanted to "see" and perhaps even "touch" the merchandise before purchase. While I did indulge in a bit of curbside service when the spirit moved me, I preferred the hustler bars to the streets.

Later I was to discover the possibilities of hiring porn stars who worked as escorts and advertised their services. The advantages were great: I already knew what they looked like so it was easy to just pick up the phone, and, without fail, the porn star was always clean and on-time. But I was lucky, I started at the top: I began with Casey Donovan. Casey was a fantasy come true.

And I am not alone. Thanks to the various gay classifieds, the ability to engage a porn star continues to be big business. In fact, during certain periods, you can get some real bargains. For instance, around tax deadline time, business is slow and you will find even the most celebrated of porn stars openly advertising in the classified sections of the *Advocate*, *Frontiers*, or the *Bay Area Reporter*. Last spring, videomaker Bob Jones announced a "Sale" on his various kink videos and, in his cover letter, commented, "The models – these guys are really the barometer of the gay economy. The phone is ringing constantly here at our offices – every model on the west coast and models as far away as New York City are calling begging for work. Strip clubs are cutting back, older gay gentlemen are not hiring 'models' for as many private shows, tips are down at the gay strip shows, massage and escort ads are not bringing in what they normally do. (Even Donny Russo has placed an ad in the escort section of a nationally distributed gay journal!) Times are tough!"

Bargain rates or not, even though I occasionally would meet a porn star (such as the incredibly hung Nick Jarrett) in a bar in Manhattan, this "hobby" has naturally involved considerable expense. But it has, upon reflection, been well worth it, because, to paraphrase Will Rogers, I never met a porn star I didn't like.

At least for a couple of hours.

One

Occasionally I would get lucky and find a likely renter on the road. It was easy to spot those willing to play.

One of the better descriptions of this phenomenon of gay life is found in *Pryor Rendering,* wherein Gary Reed has his narrator say, "Hustling is a lot like hitchin'."

He goes on, "A lot of standin' around in the middle of nowhere with your thumb out tryin' to look casual and harmless instead of like some kind of perv. After a while, you learn to read people from a far distance. You know who's cruisin' by how fast they're goin', how straight they're drivin', even what they're drivin'. You can just tell whether they're goin' to slow down for a closer look or speed on by like you're not even there. Sometimes a ride'll stop a ways off, make you walk a little 'cause they haven't quite decided to pick you up yet. They've still got the doors locked, and you can see by the brake lights that their minds are goin' back and forth, off and on as you come closer. You know a woman'll never stop; with men you can never be sure. They might peel out just as your hand reaches the door.

"I was always on the lookout for police, and sometimes that meant leavin' the streets. I was too young to get into the bars.

"I knew without even tryin' to know that the toilets could be a hustling' place and not just the bus station.... Almost any of 'em, anywhere.

"If I couldn't pick up cash, I'd settle for a ride across town or a joint or beer, maybe a drive-in hamburger or just a single night in a real house. It was like barterin' what I had for what I could get.

"Well, what it finally got me was busted for solicitation. You know that fancy word? I know it from my official record. It means a fuckin' lyin' cop.

"But, since I was a minor and a runaway and my folks refused custody, I was sent here to the Home until they change their minds or until I'm eighteen or until I die of boredom."

Another venue for quick sex I found convenient and sure-fire was the Gaiety Theater in New York. In her book *Working Sex,*

Marianne Macey says, "The Gaiety Theater is located above the Times Square Howard Johnson's, on Broadway. One flight above street level, it's got a stage with a runway where men with the bodies of professional body builders, dancers, and models dance for men. The rules are strict, no touching on the ass, cock, or balls. Other clubs have different rules. A more conservative area like Maine has a no-touch policy for the dancers, and bouncers strictly enforce it. Dancers work weekly shifts at the Gaiety. Many of the dancers supplement with hustling on the side. They're paid hourly, but unlike women strippers, the male dancers aren't tipped as they dance. It makes a serious financial difference."

"I'm fed up with the whole ordeal," a male dancer named Kirk told Macey. "All hassles. It's not as easy as everyone who's not in the business thinks it is. I did movies and magazines and that gets me better jobs in gay clubs. In straight clubs I have no credits. Maybe if I did a calendar. But women don't come out to see certain men the way men go to see feature centerfolds or female porn stars. Women go out to see groups of men dancers."

Kirk danced at the Gaiety in New York and hustled. "I don't like hustling for a living, but I'm safe about it," Kirk said. "I wear condoms, they wear condoms. They know I'm straight. Most of them even know I have a girlfriend."

For Kirk, the experience raised questions about his sexuality, about sexuality in general. "I'd rather be with my girlfriend. It's a job and I treat it like a job, but it got weird for me in the beginning when I found I could enjoy what was going on. I think everyone has bisexual tendencies, but not everyone acts on them.

"Many of the guys who work at the Gaiety are straight. When a woman comes in they'll bust their balls trying to impress her. And because they're trying so hard to impress her, when they're backstage all they can think about is, 'There are girls in the audience!' and then they can't get hard. Nerves. I had the same problem, it's psychological, performance anxiety." People seem afraid of their sexuality, Kirk said: "I think people know how much they are capable of, and that scares them, as if they think they won't be able to control it if they ever let go. People hide from themselves, not just society."

Macey talked about Kirk's time with Chippendales in New York, where men dance for women. It's an extravagant show, with choreographed routines, music, loudspeakers, costumes. And, Kirk said, they are built around fantasy themes, male prototypes like military uniforms or marshal arts. The audiences consist mostly of bachelorette parties, girls getting married next week with their friends, or divorcees getting remarried next week with their friends. They scream as guys in neon G-strings work the floor for money.

Macey told of visiting the Gaiety: "At the top of the stairs is a glass-enclosed ticket booth. Inside, Denise, the red-haired proprietress, sells tickets. There's a small theater with a stage that extends out to the audience on a short runway platform. The audience is all men, ranging in age from young boys to seniors. As quietly as I tried to enter, I was always stared at. The curtain over the stage was silver lame. It's dark except for small aisle lights and a spotlight. Over the loudspeaker, the DJ announced each performer. 'Please welcome . . . Devon!' The music started, unbearably plaintive. A woman sings in a low voice, 'Are you happy now? I could never make you so. You are a hard man, no harder in this world....' Erections get a big hand at the Gaiety. The audience clapped when Devon, a big blond, walked out with his. The man's beauty and sexuality is rated by applause. Unlike the frenetic theatrics of Chippendales, this was more like a horse show where the whole idea is to study the specimen in the spotlight. He was nude except for white socks, which accentuated the nudity. He had a perfect long body, slightly tanned, his ass the color of pale cream. He posed, knees bent and arm muscles flexed. He knelt down within touching distance of two men next to the stage. The music had a primitive drumbeat over electronic scales. A woman's voice rose over it in a wailing cry. Devon lifted his arm up to the sky, stretched his torso and took a deep breath, rippling from his chest up the line of his throat. He had an ethereal, angelic expression. The music throbbed, rushing like blood. He stopped in the middle of the stage under the light and pretended to pull a rope down from the sky. Muscles rippled his arms, shoulders, and chest. He sank to the floor in a hamstring stretch that left his cock pointing at the audience.

He sat up, closed his hand between his legs, and ran it down the shaft. His hand traveled up his abdomen and chest with slow twisting, moves. He looked down and his hair, the color of wheat, fell over his eyes. He turned his back and offered his rear to view, spreading his legs and sliding back and forth on his white socks. He stood straight, pirouetted, lifted his arms up and rotated his hips in an undulating series of thrusts. The audience clapped as he exited.

"The pace of this was so different than Chippendales. This was for slow, luxurious looking. I found myself settling in like a cat in front of a warm fire. The next dancer, a big, solid, Italian-looking guy, came out wearing a black sweatshirt and loose drawstring pants. His music was cheerily philosophical: 'Some people can hold it together....' He caressed the front of his shirt, his hand moving up and down his chest. He had a classic Roman head, thick short dark hair. He looked like someone you'd see behind the wheel of a large truck, but his movements were languid and flowing as he removed his clothing, particularly sexy because his rhythms belied his appearance. His body language was receptive, tentative even. He put his hands on his stomach, slid his pants up and down, and rolled his buttocks. His next song was a soft, guitar solo ballad. 'The night . . . the night is yours alone . . .' The guitar strummed slowly. 'Are you sure . . . you've had enough of desire?' He was totally nude except for black sneakers. He was large, very toned. He brought his hand slowly down his body to the shaft of his penis, and held himself as if for a moment's study. He lowered himself on the stage as if joining another body. He traced his fingertips as if touching a face. When he regained his feet, this big lovely man exhibited his body, showing himself off the way we expect of a woman. Looking at these men, I realized why men love looking at strippers. The pleasure of looking over nude bodies is to enter a state of altered consciousness, a sort of erotic visual drunkenness in which you can take your time. I felt as if I'd had sex with all of them. My painter friend Elliot and I once talked about why when we came back from art museums we were completely exhausted, and he said, 'Because it's active to really look at art.' So was this. Looking at every part of them was as active as touching every part of them. The body language was different from the presentation at Chippendales, which was so assertive. In their relation to the viewer, the Chippendale's dancers never seemed to lose the dominant position even when they had their clothes off. Chippendales was in your face, not in your eyes. This was more about being seen, which was calmer, more open. What Kirk said about being surprised by how many different sexual things men could do is true. But you don't get to see them all in society's limited presentations of men, which focus on images of hardness and masculinity rather than vulnerable sensuality. I found this incredibly sexy and intimate.

"When Kirk came out, his body was so perfect it was hard to accept, as if one of the statues from the museum had hopped off a stand and strode over. He stood in the lights and turned, slowly offering every muscle, every part, as if the beauty of a man was something to be celebrated, too."

"If women do pay men," Jay, a pimp, told Macey, "I think it's probably part of something on-going. The pool boy. Someone at a club. More like a relationship or at least familiar territory."

Jay went on to talk about his male escorts: "You wouldn't believe what I have to go through, even personal hygiene with these boys," he said. He talked about the young men who came to New York and were living in cars before they worked for him. We spoke of broken families and economics and class backgrounds. "You and I were raised to have a dream, and the American idea is to obtain the dream," he said. "I ask them what they're going to do and it's 'huh?' Many blow the money. They don't have anything in a few years. Car, Rolex, clothes, whatever they made, gone." Jay insisted that there was a right way and a wrong way to run an escort service. Drugs were the wrong way, but some places tried to hold on to boys that way. "You should see the handsome guys who have a good body but not a great body who I have to turn away all the time. My clients know exactly what they want: beef, big cock, beauty."

Macey asked Jon, an escort, if he enjoyed the sessions and he said he did. "He said when he was young, he was beautiful. On nights when he didn't pick anyone up, he would face the mirror, look at his own perfection, be his own sex object and masturbate. Hiring young men for body worship provided a mirror, a sort of Narcissus looking in his pool, an autoeroticism transformation."

Jon started as an exotic dancer in Atlanta, working the male dance review Chippendales. From the start, women approached him in many different ways. "They're not like a man," he said. "Men are . . . well, men are just pigs. Women are very slinky about everything...." His soft Georgian voice made this information more entertaining. "They say, 'May I take you to dinner' and this and that. 'I'll pay you this and that.' When you go out, if you show a lot of interest in her and be nice . . . you know ... they .... initiate things..."

Asked if the dates would end up in bed the first night or if the ladies would want some courtship, he reckoned it was eighty percent that had sex the first night. It was up to him if he wanted to repeat the encounter from that point, because most of the women did. He had a few clients, just a few, where things had worked out nicely. "I have one married lady in Atlanta that I've been seeing for five years now. I have a lady in L.A. who I've been seein' six months. She's married, too.

"Sometimes people get so much money, that they think they're so happy, when actually they're really so sad. Sometimes I feel bad cause I'm manipulatin' them in some way, in a fashion. Some become good friends of mine. It's different. You get an attraction to them, but most of the women I see *are* married.

"One woman said, 'I wish you were a blowup doll I could take home to my bedroom to show my husband what to do!'

"A lot of people are looking for somebody just to care, more than sex," he said. Currently, he had three regular clients, plus the occasional client who sent for him from places like Paris. When I asked if his work paid well, he laughed softly. "Ah have a place in L.A. and a home in Atlanta and cars paid for in both," he answered. He was a model who had done commercials. He was in his late twenties. He started exotic dancing when he was in college. He was dubious about the idea of male escorts working like female escorts, with hourly rates and clients calling for people to be sent over. ...Here in L.A. you get invited to all these parties if you're attractive and all. It's the only way you meet people here. People might tell you otherwise nine ways till Sunday, but they're lyin' to you. The most important thing is, you have to go to parties. I've been to so many, and I hate to be there. It's like you're a toy being paraded around. You get shown to these wealthy people, and there are going to be one or two who find you attractive. So they'll ask one person and ask another person, and someone's going to know your number. It's not as if you could come off the street and do this. Someone with ten million dollars is not going to be with someone who has no class. It has to do with how you present yourself. You better have a thousand-dollar suit on."

There were many married, divorced, or even single women with a lot of money. There were discreet circles through which these things happened. The fantasy involved was essential to the client, he explained. They wanted to feel they were buying things that other people couldn't afford.

"The lady I see in Atlanta, the first time I was with her she gave me $2,000 for the night," he explained. "After that, they don't pay you for every time, they help you with things you need." For him, those things had included $5,000 worth of fancy fixtures for his car, or the occasion when the lady had said, "Give me the mortgage book for your house, I'll take care of that."

"My car here, a brand-new BMW, is paid for," he said. "Just things like that. They ask what you need, and it's only a phone call away. Women are different than how men are with the escort business." Another problem was that some of his clients expected him to be Superman in bed. "They want it ten times a night. I may be potent, but I'm just human. I can only do so much. That's kind of hilarious, considering my age, twenty-nine. My clients are in their forties."

Asked if in addition to the affection and attention he'd mentioned, did the women also act aggressively? He said yes, that he'd even get emergency calls that needed to be satisfied.

TWO

"It all started for me when a man gave me three hundred dollars for sex," one of the girls says in *You'll Never Make Love In This Town Again*. "It felt good at the time. It was quick, easy money. I was actually paid for something I had readily done before for free. I felt like I had something of value. I was completely unaware of the effects prostitution would ultimately have on me, but after my first few tricks I knew I was getting sucked into a bad situation. Even then, I felt filthy."

Filthy or not, it wasn't long before the girl was introduced to drugs and full-on prostitution with Heidi Fleiss. "I rode the roller coaster high, until I took a ten-story fall, with Heidi's arrest – which I helped to bring about. Suddenly my income dropped to nothmg. Times were very difficult, yet to this day I know I did the right thing.

"Hollywood is an exciting place. But to have a fighting chance to survive, you need to keep your wits about you and play the game from a position of control over your own mind, body, soul, spirit, and destiny. If you don't, you can end up like so many young women I know, addicted to drugs and looking to prostitution to support your habit.

"When people have promised me the sun and the moon, I've had to learn the hard way that it's unlikely I will get them. Now I try to figure out what they're looking for – they may end up wanting Jupiter and Venus in return.

"Another painful lesson I learned was that people who acted like I was the greatest thing since the universe began often didn't bother to say hello once they finished using me. I've been lucky to have the friendship of some terrific people, and for that I am grateful. Others, who don't take my calls anymore, are probably taking calls from the new batch of hopeful starlets. And friends like that I can certainly do without.

"I look at life as a learning experience. But in my short life, I've learned too many lessons from too many people. Some of them, I'd rather forget...

"I used to feel guilty about the fact that I brought three girls into prostitution who more than likely would never have been there if it weren't for me. One of them, Kiki, wanted to be a stripper.

"'Kiki, why be a stripper for $75 a night?' I said. 'You lose all self-esteem, dancing nude up there on a stage for everyone to see. If you become a prostitute you do what you do behind closed doors, and the chances of keeping your profession anonymous are greater. Not to mention the money is good. With what you make in one hour you could pay your rent, and more.'

"Looking back on it now, I realize that it's a shame Kiki listened to me. She and I had good times together but she got in way over her head. She isn't the person she was when she began. For that matter, neither am I. If I could feel guilty or sadness or pain over having turned her out, I'd at least feel more human. But I can't really feel anything anymore. Not even remorse."

Esquire said that another of Heidi's girls, Liza Greer, was "a Stradivarius in a city of fiddles. The power of desire has significant investment potential. But she was too young to realize that it's the spiritual capital that gets spent first. Liza Greer attempted suicide many times."

"I'd always get into character before a trick," she told *Esquire*. "I'd become Domino, the gorgeous prostitute from 'Sharky's Machine.' In character, I could seduce – no, molest – any man into the little boy I needed him to be so that I could gain control. By becoming a controlling sex machine, I perfected how to give men orgasms.... I trained myself to escape emotion by staying in character.... I could time a rnan's orgasm to the minute – I was that sure of myself. You withhold all pleasure in yourself so that you can rnaintain the hatred that gets you through.... I always cried after a trick the minute I walked out the door. It was because Domino left so quickly and I suddenly experienced the emotion of being left alone with Liza."

"...There are two kinds of hookers: those who took control, like me, or those, like my friend Monday, who throw themselves into the work 'cause they're so desperate to be used. Girls like that are just dyin' to be dominated.... Then they start to pick tricks who beat them – and worse.... I guess you'd call them masochists. Which kind of hooker would you rather be?"

"If you ask me," says the indomitable Heidi Fleiss, "it's scary out there.... What we have now are low-rent madams and rinky-dink pimps pushing $300 hookers at hotel bars and clubs. The A-list of sex has retreated big time. I'm staying at home. I'm selling T-shirts. The tabloids have won! Face it, the nights are not electric."

Even for gay customers, the nights are dim and getting

dimmer. Chuck Edwards, editor of *Obsessions* magazine, says, "When CBS News announced they had details at 11:00 p.m., I perked up because I wanted to know who the male Heidi Fleiss was who was arrested. Apparently, an undercover vice cop answered an ad in *Frontiers* for one of Brad's Boys. Brad's Boys are current popular porn stars you can talk to or hire as an 'escort.' Well the undercover cop hired a boy from Brad and he showed up and got busted. Then the ball started to roll, this one got arrested, that one got arrested, and before you knew what was happening, every male prostitute in Hollywood and surrounding cities was scared to death. The ring leader was an agent who handled many of the boys for movies who were also, as the police describe, male prostitutes. This man, or ring leader, I will identify as David, had a computer filled with names, addresses, and activities of many male celebrities who have used these male prostitutes. Who are they? that is the question on everyone's lips at the moment.

"It seems that for years we have seen ads in local magazines for male escorts and we were to assume that they hung onto to the arm of the customer for dinner and dancing and then a quick kiss goodnight and payment for services rendered. No way. These guys were male prostitutes who started at 300 dollars for a quickie and could spend the entire weekend for as much as $5,000. No doubt it was safe sex, but it was sex and the police know each and every one of David's clients. Hard to believe that we are approaching the 21st Century and we still have the problem of a victimless crime that could be shoved under the table because there will always be a need for prostitutes. Lovers can't meet every sexual need of a partner. Wives can't meet all of the sexual needs of a husband. In fact, I doubt if anyone can prove The Sacred Married Couple that are true to each other really exists. I can't find a couple who can prove they have never lusted for someone other than their partner and most have ventured into the bar, the park, the alley, or the sex club looking for a quick someone other than the one they are committed to. If you know one, write to me and tell me about it.

"Prostitution will always be a concern unless it is legalized. Drugs have the same problems and some day probably will be legalized as well. When you think of the billions of dollars each year that gets spent on drugs and hookers, no taxes are paid on the income because who is going to report it: Do you know a hooker who files an honest tax return...or even files at all?

The male Heidi Fleiss is out of jail at the moment and it is not him people are worried about, it is his list of names. When the police hit his apartment they took all the files from his computer and it was where they found names that read like a Who's Who of Hollywood...

"So one piece of advice to get around the problem is to use a different name, pay cash and meet them at someone else's house, or pick them up in a limo."

You can say that again! Last fall, David Widmer in *4-Front* broke the news that "everybody's talking about the latest legal problems for agent and one-time producer David Forest. According to my source, Forest, who plea-bargained a pandering charge about a year ago, has been formally charged similarly again. Two telephones calls to a friend of this column are revealing that Chad Connors, who worked for Forest's escort service, says he was caught in an LAPD vice sting while on a call arranged by Forest. Connors is cooperating with the police and plans to testify against Forest. Not surprisingly, he admits his motivation is to get the law off his own back. Forest has long been a controversial figure attached to the gay porn biz. He blames Connors for his current legal problems and tells my friend that he hopes Connors ultimately chooses not to testify against him. I'm sure this will be an interesting drama as it plays out." Indeed.

THREE

*"I might not be able to possess him,
or anyone so beautiful,
but I can borrow him for a while..."*
— *Journalist Frank DeCaro*

Generally, male escorts don't have an easier time of it, of course. What we present here are several views of this part of the porn business with which I have first-hand experience: The Star-Fuck.

My first star-fuck was the realization of one of my greatest fantasies up to that time: Casey. After that fulfillment, I moved on to Roger. As many of my readers know well by now, I have had the pleasure of the company of many porn performers since, but my time with Roger remained a vivid memory that kept me warm on many a long winter's night. I would take the photo book of him created in his heyday with the old *Blueboy* and get off on the pictures that had been culled from magazine layouts. When I was with Roger in New Orleans, he autographed the book to me, "To Slim. Thanks for everything."

He was thanking me for giving him the opportunity to see New Orleans (where I had gone on business) and spending a weekend being wined and dined.

As I recounted in my book *Legends*, I finally struck a deal with the star's agent to have Roger make a stopover in New Orleans on his way to Hollywood to make a film. During that long weekend in the spring of 1978, I was to observe the phenomenon of the big basket as I had never experienced it before. No one on the street recognized Roger, but the splendidly skin tight clothes he always wore clung enticingly to his bulging biceps and crotch, attracting the stares of men and women alike even in no-holds-barred New Orleans.

He let me know right off that he didn't get fucked (he saved that for the screen and special occasions) but everything else was okay. I was so in awe of that mighty organ that all I really wanted to do was worship and adore it. It was the first time I had encountered one that large and I quickly discovered one of the problems a man so well endowed might have: it seems the meat rarely hardens to the extent it does with "normal" equipment. This is not much of a problem for these men when they are fucking women because cunts are designed to accept most anything. But for men with tight assholes, as we well know, it can be an excruciating experience.

After a few attempts to take Roger anally, I opted just to suck on it. Roger didn't have to but he eagerly got into a 69 position and proved a superb fellatist.

His posing for *Blueboy* pictorials led to a special issue devoted exclusively to the emerging star. And then, inevitably, came films. We first encountered him in a loop from Bullet called "Good Neighbors" (now available as part of Bullet's Pac 7). His first co-star was Bruno. In the loop, Roger needs some help with his geraniums on his patio but gets far more than that from the hugely developed he-man hero of the day. They go down on each other and then Bruno fucks Roger with his usual quick, powerful jabbing. Having also been with Bruno during a trip to New York, this loop is always a turn-on.

Oh, yes, I admit I am an unabashed size queen and when a boy comes along who is well-endowed, my gaydar goes on overdrive. I was able to meet Rick Donovan, Tom Steele, Kris Lord, even Ryan Idol. Nowadays I would give anything for a half-hour with Kevin Dean.

My fantasies are not limited to big-dicked wonders, however. I also admire a terrific bottom. Although I met Joey Stefano on several occasions, I was never able to arrange to take him to bed. I could have because we had a mutual pal in Gino Colbert, but it just never happened. I was a bit turned-off because every time I met him he was a different person. Drugs had him in a terrible grip. But he was a star, so we forgave him everything – excepting killing himself, of course.

"Style, self-display, and commodification converge on Warhol's central film interest: stars. Like hustlers, prostitutes, and fashion models, stars are the epitome of the commodification of the body and of personal style, since their whole behavior and looks can be framed as marketable items," says Juan A. Suarez in his book *Bike Boys, Drag Queens and Superstars*. In Edgar Morin's words: "The star is a total item of merchandise; there's not an inch of her body, not a shred of her soul, not a memory of her life that cannot be thrown into the market." In *The Philosophy,* one finds a comparable quote: "Movie stars get millions of dollars for nothing, so when someone asks them to do something for nothing, they go crazy – they think that if they are going to talk to somebody at the grocery store they should get fifty dollars an hour."

"Not only stars' bodies and personalities, but even their touch has market potential," says Suarez. "Since the consolidation of the star system in the mid-1990s, manufacturers cashed in on the stars' Midas-like touch by marketing their styles, the sex. His being a hustler seems to frame everything he does – or could do as a potential commodity. As one of Joe Dallesandro's tricks (awkwardly) puts it in an Andy Warhol flick: 'Money is all it's about with you, isn't it Joe?' Even in the one scene where Joe gives it away – when he is orally serviced by Geri Miller while drag queens Candy Darling and Jackie Curtis flick through old fan magazines – the conversation is still haunted by the specters of appearance and value: Jackie and Candy discuss star glamour while Geri confers about enlarging her breasts, which might increase her cachet as topless dancer and part-time 'girl of the night.'"

The many delights of "gorgeousness-to-go" is explained by Frank DeCaro. "I am not a john," he proclaimed in *Time Out.* "I am a journalist.

"At least that is what I tell myself as I dial his number. A couple of sevens. A three.

"'Hello?' It's him. His deep voice – a Canadian accent cobwebbed with sleepiness from a too-late night of doing what he does – tells me he is glad I called and, yes, he's free on Saturday morning. It's a date.

"Actually he's coming on Saturday morning and it isn't really a date. "But for my money, I will get 45 minutes of body worship (his), one orgasm (mine) and the chance to live out the masturbatory fantasy of every man – gay or straight – who ever kept a porn magazine hidden under his Posturepedic: a wet dream come to life in his bedroom. It will be what Robin Byrd calls a 'private show,' and early enough that I can be humming 'Love Hangover' in time for a 2 o'clock Broadway curtain. His name is Doug. At the strip club where we met one afternoon after his performance, he was using a *nom de porn.*

But when he introduced himself and said he was from Vancouver, I knew where I'd seen him before. A year and a half ago in a skin magazine, this delicious wad of north-of-the-border manliness was splashed across seven pages – including a glorious double-page spread of him with a maple leaf flag unfurled behind his scruffy-chinned, hard-nippled, perfectly fluffed splendor. 'You have no idea of the good times you and I have had together,' I say. He laughs. A good sign. In person, especially when he's smiling, Doug is even more dazzling than he is in print. Smoother, harder, and – thank God – with a better haircut than he had in that magazine. He is the Chelsea ideal, a tan, brown-haired specimen of physical perfection: broad shoulders, huge pecs, washboard abs, amazingly strong legs, an ass that's all it's cracked up to be. Of all the muscle boys living in New York and all the go-go dancers who, like Doug, just pass through, he is the best, at least for me. Although he looks like Hercules, he wears glasses, even while he dances, and I find this single trait irresistible. Doug is nearsighted, and that smidgen of human frailty, that myopic vulnerability, shows me a way into the soul behind his chiseled beauty. He is the one I want. I might not be able to possess him, or anyone so beautiful, but I can borrow him for a while, and I'm going to. He is to be my virgin foray into the business of sex-for-hire, an aesthetic diversion into the world of gorgeousness-to-go. Doug, I will learn, is worth every penny.

"What is $200 anyway?, I ask myself. Not much in New York City. Fast Cash, twice. Big deal. One sleeve of the Yohji jacket I've craved all spring and would wear only once a year. Dinner for two at the Gotham. Been there, ate that. With Doug, I am buying a fantasy and a memory. And, by the inch, it doesn't seem like such a bad deal when I get down to it. But paying for sex changes your life forever. From that morning on, I would be someone who, for 45 minutes at least, was a john – and a stage-door one, at that.

"'Is this what your life has come to?' my brain asked. 'So fucking what,' my dick replied. 'He's gorgeous.' When the doorbell sounds, it is 11:10 a.m. Doug is late, but not too. 'Hi, it's me,' he says over the intercom. He's coming up. The elevator rings as it passes each floor, and with each little ding, my heart races a bit faster. If I don't have a stroke before this guy reaches my floor, everything will be fine. The elevator door opens and he rounds the corner. He is wearing a navy blue-and-white striped polo shirt, blue jeans, hiking boots and, yes, his gold-rimmed Armani spectacles. 'Got any orange juice?' he asks, barely inside my apartment. I pour him a tall one. At that point, I would have made him eggs Benedict. But juice and small talk is all he wants.

"'You have to sign my centerfold,' I tell him, producing the magazine and a fine-point sharpie. He sits on my bed with its leopard-print cases and black-and-ivory gingham duvet – 'Nice sheets" he says – thinks a minute, and then writes an inscription beside his photographic nakedness.

"Then it begins. Chatting, he takes off his shoes, then his white athletic socks and then his shirt (which, it turns out, is from Structure). He stands at the foot of my bed, going on about what his day will hold – three shows, plus private clients--and undoes the top button of his jeans. Then, silently, he unbuttons the buttons of his fly, one at a time. Slowly. Sexily. Well-rehearsed.

"Underneath, he is wearing a black rayon thong bikini. It is my first – and only – disappointment with Doug. It reminds me that this all-American (Canadian) boy really is a prostitute. Not the boxer-wearing preppy next door I romanticized him to be. In a minute, Doug is posing in his G-string, catching a glimpse of himself in the gilt-framed mirror above the dresser and rubbing his fingertips across the body he loves most, his own. Then he teases me by shifting his skivvies to reveal the main attraction. Doug begins to touch himself. The results are instantly noticeable. For him and, especially, for me. What had seemed impressive on stage is exquisitely superhuman up close. Doug is, as Olive Oyl once said of Bluto, large. In fact, he has the kind of genitalia you could use to choose up sides on a baseball team – about two and a half handfuls.

"'How big are you?' I ask him.

"'I don't know,' he says.

"'Don't give me that. Every man knows *exactly* how big he is.'

"'Between nine-and-a half and ten inches,' Doug admits.

"'Well, you do get what you pay for,' I say. What you don't get – strictly speaking – is fucked. The rules of the game: Anal is out – pitching or catching – and he will not go down on you. I can go down on him, if I want to. Any bodily fluids I produce are mine to keep. He will not be having an orgasm, unless I come up with another $150. Truth be told, I want to see him come, *very* much. But not at that price. 'Oh, please, even Beluga isn't $150 a tablespoon!' I want to say, but I hold my tongue, which, by now, is busy anyway. Doug is lying on his back, a pillow behind his head, and I have become the human Dirt Devil. I look up to see an ear-to-ear smile on his face. But his eyes are closed. Who is he fantasizing about? I wonder. He has a girlfriend at home, he said. Perhaps it's her. Or maybe it's that handsome dancer he was talking to the day we met. That guy, named Dean, had a ten-inch dick and a girlfriend back home, too, but it was clear he and Doug liked each other. Labels – gay, straight, bisexual – mean nothing to either of them, they said. They are who they are and do what they do. Their parents know that they dance for a living, but not that they perform private shows. Their girlfriends know everything and really don't mind. That's that.

"'You're both handsome. You're both well hung. You guys really have it all, don't you?' I had asked that afternoon at the strip club.

"'If we had it all, we wouldn't be here,' Dean said. Would Doug be in my bedroom if *he* had it all?

"Of course not. But he is a man who has found his calling. He spotted a niche in the market and fills it the best way he knows how. Most guys he visits, he said, don't expect him to do very much other than show up, look beautiful, and let them touch him until they have what is usually a self-induced orgasm. And yet, despite Doug's laissez faire role in all of this, few would disagree that he is worth the money. For a man in his profession he's sweet instead of sleazy; strong, and seemingly unencumbered by guilt when it comes to sex. And, he is more beautiful a man than most men or women will ever see between their sheets – *unless* they pay for that person to be there. That's just the way things are. The hard reality of sexual attraction is that you *can* always get what you want, but it'll cost you. I learned that the good and hard way that morning.

"After a half hour, I finish myself off looking in Doug's eyes, then let my eyes wander down his naked, hairless body. Once

I've toweled off, he takes me in his arms and holds me close. This is what most men really want, he says. A little bit of affection, a feeling of safety, however fleeting. The orgasm is just icing.

"'May all your writing experiences come up with a fairy-tale ending,' Doug had written on my magazine centerfold. In his arms, he makes his clients' happily ever-after dreams seem tangible for one brief moment. Then, he gets up and gets dressed and goes on with his day like anyone else.

"'My friends are taking me shopping,' he says.

"'Yeah, with my money,' I kid.

"Making his way to my door, he says, 'I'll be back in New York in a couple of months. Can I call you?'

"We embrace, kissing each other on the cheek, me on tip toes to reach. 'Sure,' I say, quite confident of the fact that he won't ever call again. He's a man, after all, and not calling is what we do best.

"But, if by chance he does ring me up, what will I do? I don't know. I'll either say no, or – more likely – try to rationalize spending another $200 on 45 more minutes of bliss. I watch Doug walk down the hall and then turn out of sight into the elevator, and I wonder if I will ever see him again. But I can't worry about that just now. I've got to get showered and dressed. I've got another matinee to catch."

FOUR

Writer Mark Walder visited Thailand for *Gay Times* and in Patong Beach he found all the boys make their living by providing sex and companionship to gay tourists. "Unfortunately for the bar boys," Walder says, "they outnumber the punters by about six to one.

"...I meet a number of the other gay tourists. They seem to be quite a wealthy lot, mainly over 40 and nearly all European. The bar boys arrive for lunch wearing the skimpiest lycra imaginable. They chatter away in Thai and you assume they are exchanging the most salacious gossip from the way they shriek and laugh. Later on in the afternoon, they exercise their oh-so-desirable bodies with an enthusiastic game of volleyball. This is a humorous and engaging spectacle involving equal amounts of mincing and muscularity. The beauty and grace of the boys in this part of southern Thailand is only matched by the splendor and magnificence of the scenery.

"...Each bar employs about six boys to attract customers and act as hosts. The boys actually are men, usually in their late teens or early twenties. They are friendly, attractive and very adept at giving their punters a good time, albeit at a price. The bar owner will encourage the customer to buy the boys drinks throughout the evening and then take the boy off for sex. The off-fee is normally 200 baht (£6 approx.) and in addition the boy will expect to receive a tip of at least 500 baht. If you are into paying for sex and good-looking company, these bars offer an excellent service. However, if for reasons of pride or principle you are not willing to shell out for sex, and get fed up with being viewed as a walking wallet, you may find that the initial warm welcome rapidly turns tepid. Unfortunately, there are no gay places to go where you can hope to meet local guys on a non-commercial basis.

"If (like me) all you desire is a quiet drink and a little conversation, you will pay through the nose for it here, and once. So you get the reputation for not wanting to pay for sex your popularity will wither faster than a scrotum rubbed in snow.

"Looking at it from the sex worker's point of view, wages in

Thailand are very low. A waiter or hotel worker will earn 2,500 baht per month, on average (about £85). A 'bar boy' might hope to earn an equivalent amount in a single week, or even in one night if he gets lucky. The most successful boys can earn a lot more. Many of these have acquired foreign boyfriends who send them a generous allowance. The more unscrupulous boys are said to have several of these doting benefactors who are duped into believing that their boy loves them faithfully and exclusively."

Walder eventually does meet some boys willing to go with him to his room. "I learn to point out that the invitation to go back to my hotel room is not a financial proposition. Once this is clearly established and accepted I feel the friendship can continue on a more equal footing. Although when you get to know the boys and perceive how comparatively poor they really are you will feel very mean if you don't offer to support them in some way. The other ploy I adopt to beat the bar boy monopoly on sex is to try to meet other gay tourists. Patong attracts a lot of guys from Singapore, Malaysia and Japan who find the subtle climate of sexual tolerance in Thailand very attractive compared to the iron-fisted bigotry in their own countries. My liaisons do not go unnoticed by the beady-eyed bar boys, but it seems to earn a grudging respect from them. After a while, one or two stop giving me the frosty treatment and start to be friendly once again. They even offer me sex for free! Which I take as a sign that they now view me as a person rather than a customer, and in turn I stop seeing them as rent boys and perceive them more as individuals with problems, aspirations and needs the same as me."

FIVE

"Being a bottom is a very core part of my entire being."
– David Christopher in Drummer magazine

Luckily, unlike Mr. Walder, I have no hang-ups about paying for sex. In fact, most of the time I prefer it. Also, I consider myself versatile sexually, allowing me tremendous latitude when it comes to partners. Such is not the case with everyone. Consider what David Christopher admitted in *Drummer*: "I'm a bottom." David's observations help us understand superbottoms such as Joey Stefano and Kevin Kramer. "But there are many definitions of what a 'bottom' (or even a 'Top' for that matter) really is," David said. "I can tell you what definition applies to me, but that's not to say mine is the right one. There isn't a right one. If you know me at all, you know I do not presume to be the one to tell you what I think. What I do know, and what this piece is all about, is some of the different meanings of the word 'bottom.' I am using my viewpoint to explain; agree with or don't, but look at my purpose, not my perspective. Onward.

"Being a bottom is a very core part of my entire being. My first introduction to the world (used in this context) was also my first realization of it. I was in high school, and the person explaining the usage to me was assuming I understood that 'it' referred to fucking when he told me, 'The Top' does it and the bottom takes it.' This made perfect sense to me. I wanted someone to do certain things to me and for me to be expected to take it. At the time I didn't care too much about it. I like it, but there were too many other things I had wanted to give. This brings us to the first group's definition of a bottom: the one who gets fucked. Anyone whose top priority in a sexual encounter is fucking is in a completely different world. Sexually speaking. Fucking doesn't have any direct connection to the purpose of sex by my estimation. It is an optional road to stop in a very long journey. It's like taking a trip to the Grand Canyon for the mule ride.

"Now the 'I don't like labels' definition: a bottom is someone locked into a way of thinking and acting and allows himself no flexibility in his approach to a scene. Please! I am a bottom. It is unquestionable. I have played Top for other's enjoyment, but now that is as much a waste of his time as it is mine. Why should anyone lose out to make someone else happy when there is always someone out there who would be happy to indulge in the particular scene, leaving both parties satisfied? (This does not include people in relationships fulfilling *occasional* fantasies for the pleasure of their significant other.) I have never in my entire life had a fantasy in which I was the Top. NEVER. I have never in my entire life played the Top in a scene and been fulfilled. NEVER. So please, don't presume to tell me I am wrong to categorize myself. I didn't do it. God did. I have fallen for the old 'versatile' line once too often. I've never been with someone versatile enough to really be the Top, in one way or another, then play the bottom at some point in the scene. This makes me so uncomfortable, I can't tell you. I am not versatile, I don't pretend to be versatile, so don't try to make me play Top when I've been up-front about my head all along. Versatile should go with versatile, Tops with bottoms and bottoms with Tops. Don't mistake 'versatile' with mutual.

"In my relationship there is a time for mutual play and I won't deny either of us that. To many versatile people, what they really want is to switch back and forth within a scene. That's fine, I am honest about my desires and appreciate, though rarely get, the same in return. That's what I don't get. Why should anyone misrepresent themselves to go to bed with someone they are not suited to? I just don't understand."

Yes, while most of my own star fucks and other paid encounters have been with well-hung studs, I occasionally have a hankering for a splendid bottom. I have fantasized about Chad Knight, Danny Sommers, and, long ago, Kevin Williams and Jon King. Once I saw Kevin Kramer getting fucked, I began to fantasize about him. I rented every video he appeared in. Often the fuck of Kramer was the only thing certain videos had going for them.

Colbert, best known for directing "one-day wonders," often using the same bedroom over and over ("If they remember the furniture, I know I'm in trouble," Gino jokes) was instrumental in my actually meeting Kevin.

I was originally to meet the performer on the weekend of the

Gay Video Guide awards in Hollywood, but illness caused me to cancel. By January, I was well enough to start thinking about Kevin again. I called him and, to my great amusement, he was coming East to appear at a rich man's birthday party. I jumped at it. So on his way to New York and the birthday party, Kevin visited me in Florida.

What follows is Kevin's story, and that of other fantasy fulfillers. It says a lot about those boys, but I think it says even more about those who fuck the stars.

*"I am the diva.
You better roll out the red carpet
Because here I come.*

*I'm a diva
From head to toe,
And it's getting better every day.*

*...You have to work to get this good.
Stand on line to kiss my ... hand.*

*You better watch out because
Here I come!"*

*– Selected lyrics to one of
Kevin Kramer's favorite songs, by Club 69*

Part Two
STARRING
KEVIN KRAMER

One
SMALL & TIGHT

"Kevin Kramer is a very small, tight, adorable lad with a penchant for fucking," Dave Kinnick said once. Perhaps *too much* of a penchant for some, if that's possible. That hairy hellraiser Hunter Scott (and now retired porn star) says, "In my first video (for Chi Chi LaRue), I fucked Kevin Kramer, which was OK. Don't get me wrong – I love Kevin Kramer. He's a nice guy and a buddy of mine but not someone I'd wanna stick my dick into. I was really nervous, and it took me eight hours to do one scene. But I have to say, that Kramer was so patient with me. He was understanding and instructional with the camera angles. It was a great experience, and I really liked it."

But it was worth it, at least for us fans. In "The Look of A Man," Brandon West jerks himself off to thoughts of Hunter getting a major-league blowjob from Kevin. "Kramer grabs onto Hunter's barouche chest as Hunter commands him to chew on his huge, spit-covered dick, all the while throwing his hips forward while leaning back against a table," says Joe McKenna. "The view is tremendous as he thrusts his cock deeper into Kramer's mouth. Kramer's long, thin cock, meanwhile, gets a good work over by Kramer himself, who quickly drives himself wild with Hunter's piece of meat. Hunter then forces Kramer to rim him, getting increasingly verbal along the way: 'Come on, make it hurt! Make it sting!' he yells as Kramer slaps his ass. When Hunter finally fucks the kid, it's not too shabby either, especially the high-angle shots of Hunter's flat, hairy belly covered with sweat as he rams his meat into Kramer's sweet ass."

Sweet ass indeed! Eight hours fucking Kevin Kramer after getting one of those "major league blowjobs" – now, that's *my* idea of heaven! And Justin Young, star of Bob Jones fetish videos, agrees with me. Says he, "I don't want to swallow everyone's cum. It's probably a risky thing to do if you don't know the person extremely well. But then, if I had the chance to work with Kevin Kramer tomorrow and had to swallow his cum, I'd do it!"

We were likewise captivated by Kevin's smile, his cum, and his slutty reputation. Upon meeting Kevin, Kinnick remarked,

"Kevin is a little tramp. There's just no other way to put this." But who would want to?

After seeing Kevin in one of his first, and best, performances we've been in lust ever since. The event is the scene with Devyn Foster and Kevin in "Center Spread." Preston Richie in *Manshots* says, "They are on a huge bed, surrounded by foliage and latticework screens, devouring each other. Both deeply tanned, they fuck and suck with total abandon. In rapid-fire succession, Kramer sucks Foster's uncut pole, they sixty-nine, Kramer eats Foster's butt, and Foster throws a hard, missionary fuck into Kramer's eager hole. In response, Kramer pushes hard to meet every stroke, as they both unload."

At his house in Studio City, Kevin greeted Kinnick wearing "short, short, short denim shorts" that were strategically frayed at the bottom and had at least one other button in between that had missed its mark. "A bandanna was tied coquettishly around his neck and on the lapel of his long-sleeved shirt, open to the navel, was a button reading 'Fuck me. I did!'"

"I love living in the Valley," Kramer told Kinnick. "You really have to travel a ways to get yourself in trouble."

"Why," Kinnick wondered, "do I get the feeling he manages?"

Manages indeed, especially on a film set.

His "wonderfully sweet ass" got a workout with another "sweet ass" in All Worlds' "Tales From the Backlot," in which Rob Cryston plays the producer of GTelevision, who needs to put together a porn flick on a day when everything goes wrong. Kevin has a sizzling hot scene with the legendary bottom Chad Knight. "This scene alone makes the video worth seeing," *In Touch* raved. "These two sex-studs work up to a explosive conclusion...." It takes awhile though. At first, Chad doesn't seem to respond to Kevin's oral talents, but when he's finally in him, Knight jabs heatedly and, once Kevin is on his back, Chad fucking him enthusiastically, Kevin is able to come and the two great bottoms kiss in a nice fade-out.

"I'm in it just to have some fun," Kramer said after the filming. "I'm not going to worry about what happens or where it'll go but, hopefully it'll go somewhere, and I'll get something out of it. I really like this kind of entertainment - it's fun and I really enjoy the sex. It also makes me feel good knowing there are people out there who enjoy watching me perform. I'm a bit of an exhibitionist. At some point, though, I plan to finish my schooling, studying business administration and liberal arts."

Kevin's open-minded when it comes to his partners: "I'm attracted to men. But lately I've been attracted to younger boys. Ones of legal age, of course, but younger ones." No matter what the age, he likes nice, healthy guys with big dicks who love to fuck. "And," he adds, "who do it like they really mean it. It spooks me sometimes, because the harder it is, the better it is. Real hard – like pounding into the ground – I always like that best.

"I like to be aggressive, and like a partner that is also. I guess that labels me a bottom, at least until further notice."

He found a guy who really fucks like he means it in Marco Rossi, in "Masquerade." "...(And) it seems there's a trend toward porn romance," Joe McKenna in *Inches* says. "It's nice, actually; some affection really adds to the heat. And Kevin Kramer is especially good at it. He confesses his love for Marco in a later scene, and amazingly enough the kid can act! It's the prelude to a really hot scene, as Marco lets himself get worshipped by a guy who adores him."

Kevin says, "I think my best performance is my scene with Marco Rossi. That was the first time that I ever had the full-blown urge to fuck anyone on a movie set. I spread his ass open, and I had never seen a pink boy pussy like that in my entire life. He just looked like he had never ever been fucked before, and that made it even worse. But he was slated to fuck me. I was into it totally 110%. I liked the way the bedroom was set up, and I liked Marco very much. (Licking his butt was) feast time! I like being in this industry because I find that you discover a lot of things that you like that you never really did before. Things like eating ass."

This scene was indeed one of the best duos of the year. It was nice to see both boys sporting big erections and having Kevin lying across Marco's backside, rubbing his cock along the crack, and Marco reacting passionately – hinting of the incredible fuck that will someday come. Then Kevin puts the condom over Marco's cock and the fuck begins. Marco takes Kevin doggie to start and then missionary. After Kevin comes,

Marco slips off the latex and follows suit. The finale has Marco lying across Kevin and taking Kevin's head in his hands and kissing him as if he really meant it. Wow.

And then there's Nathan Rocco, who was paired with Kevin in "Hellknight." "The incredibly talented Kramer," Kinnick reported, "was put to work in a major role on David Babbitt's latest porn shoot, matched with Nathan Rocco, another of those boys we've seen a lot of (but not often enough in good productions). It seems this new work will confirm something we've long suspected, which is that young Nathan's nine-inch-plus tool is good for something other than garnishing his butt hole. He's always been a confirmed bottom, but apparently no more." Kramer got on the receiving end and said it was some of the best sex he's had since he started in the business. "Nathan has a quiet sort of sexuality. But once he gets going, there's no stopping him," Kramer says. "We couldn't keep our hands off each other. And that dick!"

In fact, Kevin told Kinnick he enjoyed all of his co-stars – and it showed.. About Kramer's appearance in "Smoke Screen," Michael Lynch in *The Guide* said, "the video feels like a quickie. Which is not to say that it has nothing to offer but rather that it has a superficial, not-quite complete quality to it that gives it an urgency but not an air of professionalism. The plot is rather convoluted – a gay man reads his lover's journal and problems ensue – but it is so labyrinthine that we have a hard time following (or caring about) it. On the other hand the sex is well-photographed and Skip Johnston and Kevin Kramer as the leads are handsome, well-hung and efficient in their sexual activity."

The busy Kevin appeared in one of Derek Powers' better offerings, appropriately titled, "The Rumpsters." The film has a total of six sequences of sex, silly and otherwise, starting off with Sean Hunter, who's "just in from out-of-town" at the Hollywood Bus Station and is picked up by Kramer who invites him to stay over, just buddies, you understand. Uh-huh. "The seduction scene isn't very realistic in that Hunter's completely asleep while Kramer does a 7.0 earthquake on his nude body, yowling all the while," Wesley Harris notes. "It's sexy, but inadvertently funny."

You get the idea that Kevin is game for anything. Listen to

what Joe McKenna in *Inches* says: "'XXX Oil Wars' begins with some behind-the-scenes shots of its stars, Kevin Kramer and Ren Adams, posing for publicity photos. Kramer is a hard little blond with a flat gut and a firm round ass; Adams is dark and thicker, with some hair on his belly. They both pose in various states of undress for the photographer, striking flexing postures that are typical but hot nonetheless ... making the video camera seem like a kind of secret voyeur ... and we're just lucky to have caught the show on the sly.

"Soon we begin to see spectators showing up for the fight-- real guys who are eager to get their rocks off on these two wrestling studs. Adams starts off by spreading oil all over Kramer's torso, his hands sliding across Kramer's smooth stomach, chest, and legs. He then squirts some down Kramer's underwear, first in the front, then behind, making his balls, cock, and ass crack shine through the flimsy wet material. I don't know about you, but I find it incredibly hot to watch a fighter service his opponent before taking him on. And Kramer likes to be serviced; he flexes every muscle in his already taut body as Adams' palms roam all over him. They each get to admire the body they're about to pummel worship the muscles that might overpower and defeat them. I found myself cumming before the fight even started.

"...Finally, the fight begins, and it is absolutely fantastic. Adams quickly gets Kramer spreadeagled on the mat, pinning him and sliding his glistening body all over the squirming little stud. Kramer starts to rally, but Adams is all over him again. You can see both of their cocks clearly through their wet, oily straps, and every cut in their glistening muscles shines in the light. And the camera keeps panning over to the audience, where one of the guys is actually blowing another while others are busy pounding their meat and showing each other their hard cocks....When Adams pulls Kramer's slick strap tightly through his crack and slaps his hard round ass with his palm, I just about passed out."

When not being paid to get fucked by some of the hottest studs in the business, Kevin says he loves to talk on the phone with friends and family. "Family is very important to me, because I believe very strongly in trust and love. I also love to travel, you know, escape and be by myself. I love amusement parks and parties." Kevin also enjoys donating his time to worthy causes, such as the safesex brochure directed at gay youth produced by AIDS Project Los Angeles (APLA) and Thor Productions.

And speaking of gay youth, Kevin's first sex experience was with a woman. "I was 16, and I was modeling in San Francisco. I was also in high school, of course, but I was living in the city on my own because the agency I was working for told my parents that I had to live there. So I was on my own, and my mom was helping with the rent and everything. She didn't like this whole idea, but she allowed me to be independent. But there was this 24-year-old girl I was working with that my mom liked very much. So she would ask the girl to peek in on me every once in a while. One day I was at home doing my homework. This girl came in, and we had a couple of glasses of wine, and she said, 'Let me show you something.' She just sucked down on my dick and said, 'Do you wanna do it?' She didn't know it was my first time."

Oh, and about that little button on his shirt: Dave asked Kramer where he got it. Kevin replied, "In Atlanta. Me and Chip Daniels found this shop there that had huge racks of nothing but sexually oriented buttons. And this was the one for me."

"Yes, but are you really able to fuck yourself?"

"Yes, I can!"

"With your very own penis?"

"Uh-huh."

"How much of your dick can you get up your butt?"

"I really haven't thought about it. When I do it I'm not really thinking about how much is going in as long as – "

"You're not a size queen when it comes to your own dick!"

"Right! But there's enough to get a little back-and-forth motion going."

"Can you come that way?"

"I've never, but I'm sure if I did it long enough, I could."

"I'm jealous. I've tried that, but it's never worked for me. I guess I'm not built right."

"I have a downward curve in my dick."

"Oh, so you have a head start?"

"Right."

"...I don't think I've seen you do that yet on-screen."

"There's a lot on the screen that I haven't done that I want to do."

"Do you have a shopping list that you keep under your mattress?"

"No, but it's always something in the back of my mind."

Foremost on his mind, it would seem, is pleasuring an increasing number of fans, who end up becoming longtime benefactors.

Because of his personal appearance schedule and his heavy advertising, it's easier to meet Kevin than it is some other porn stars. Kevin met Kinnick just after he had returned from a vacation in Europe. "I was in New York performing at the Show Palace and went on Robin Byrd's show," Kevin said. "A gentleman saw me on that show and came to the club and asked me to do a private show for him afterward. And we got along very well. After the sex and before the cigarette, he said, 'Do you want to go to Greece with me?' I said, 'What?' I'm, like, 'Uh-oh, this is a kinky one.' I really had to look at him to see if I could take his company for 18 days. But I figured I could. I flew back here to L.A., and within 48 hours I was back in New York and we were off. I went to the island of Mykonos, then the city of Athens, and then to Barcelona. In Barcelona the big disco clubs have dark rooms and mazes in them. 'Screw having a couple of drinks, getting to know one another, and going back to the apartment and fucking! I wanna fuck here! And I mean we're gonna fuck right now!' That's basically how it was.

"So, I had separated myself from the gentlemen I was staying with, and, uh, ended up in this dark room with two of the most gorgeous men I had ever seen. I just walked in, and they followed me. They were both about six-footers. One had a real pretty face. The other had really pretty eyebrows. I know that sounds really weird. But I have an eyebrow fetish.

"We were going to fuck, but I wanted to see what it was going to look like when it was going in. So, uh, we went into a bathroom, into one of the stalls. In fact, I fell and scraped my shoulder. Every time I look at it, I just kind of laugh about it. At night in Europe the men don't come out until after 12:30 or 1 a.m. So from 1 till 7 in the morning, it's a huge, huge party. There is dick everywhere in Mykonos. There's a beach called

Super Paradise, and I swam out to these rocks in, like, a cove? It was neat. It was like being on another planet. When you got around this one huge rock, there were nude men lying everywhere. I mean, all over the place. I swam up on a rock and just kind of hung out and looked around. Pinched myself just to make sure that I was actually there, on the spot, you know? I saw this guy that I thought was really hot. We didn't say a word to one another at all. He swam up to my rock and we ended up having lots of oral sex.

"Another guy was just standing there and watching from a rock only a few feet away. It might sound boring actually, but I think it was exciting to me because it was a completely different place. It was something you see in a movie.

"(My gentleman friend is) a lot of fun to be around: He really is. We kind of bonded and formed a friendship. We're actually really good friends now."

Kevin seems to be on good terms with everybody. You have to be, you know, to earn the Leo Ford Humanitarian Award.

The Advocate's gossip maven reported, "Those of you who continue to obsess over winners of the Leo Ford Humanitarian Award will be overjoyed to know that the current titleholder, Kevin Kramer, can be seen up close and personal dancing at Axis on Sundays. (Officially, that is. He's probably in there all the rest of the time dancing just for the hell of it, but don't quote us. Or make any plans.) Young K.K. hosted, not so very long ago, an evening at Axis honoring our trendelicious sister mag, *Freshmen*, and somehow our young and enterprising bottom deluxe latched on to a whole cartload of the May issue, which features – why, which features none other than Kevin Kramer himself! In big, white-white boxer shorts. And nerdy glasses on the cover. Correction: On the *shocking-pink* cover. And what's inside is guaranteed to send any red-blooded male with a discernible pulse right over the edge."

And speaking of going over the edge, to maintain his reputation as a Great Humanitarian, Kevin is often asked to make personal appearances. *The Advocate's* gossip maven was attending a pride day fest in West Hollywood and made note of the "official state visit by Kevin Kramer, who signed several copies of his notorious May diaperfest issue of *Freshmen*. The mobs snatched those up like hotcakes, believe you me.

"Of course it's also possible that Kevin didn't really stand in the next booth and wiggle in and out of scarcely legal ensembles while wrapped in a tablecloth (or a sarong), either, in full view of all the juiced-up passersby. (But) we choose to believe that he *did*. That's our story, and we're sticking with it. Although we wonder why Kevin would make such a feeble attempt at modesty in the middle of the largest assembled mass of homosexuals in the known universe."

Then the maven heard that Jeff Stryker had come out of his semi-retirement "or whatever you call it" long enough to "pork" – who else? – Kevin Kramer. "Which news," the maven gushed, "put those naked buns we'd seen the day before in a whole new light."

Yes indeed, Jeff was Kevin's fantasy lover for some years. But porn stars seldom get to live their fantasies out onscreen, unless they are aggressive about it.

"My fantasy always was to be in a Joe Gage movie," Roy Garrett of the Golden Age of Porn once said. "Working with him was terrific. He's so easy with the actors. When I think about how it all started, my introduction to him, it was all chance. I'd been in some films but my career as a porn star was not all that hot. Someone had asked me to partake in a promotion of *Hotter Than Hell*, a French film opening at the 55th Street Playhouse in New York. As none of the stars were available they needed someone to stand around in a T-shirt. And that's when I caught the attention of someone who knew Joe Gage."

Another of Roy's fantasies was to star in a film opposite the late performer and writer Richard Locke. That happened when he co-starred with the actor in *Heatstroke*. "But you know," he said, "reality and fantasy are different. I imagined Richard to be twelve feet tall. He is tall...but you know what fantasy does."

Yes we do, and it helps to be a whore. Sallie Tisdale, in her book *Talk Dirty to Me*, says: "The sexual fantasy, not of going to a whore, but of being one, is quite common. There is a whore in each of us, the whore who conquers our desire by selling it, conquers our fear of abandonment by controlling the risks of all her relations. The urge to romanticize the prostitute and her life is just like the urge to imagine her as infinitely sordid or as an inevitable victim – more about us than the whore. The whore scares us, the happy whore most of all, because she doesn't need conventional rules to survive and thrive. She makes up her own."

Kevin once told me that he can only deal with one fantasy at a time, so after he realized his fantasy fucking by Stryker, he moved on. The fantasy this time was big black dick. When I heard this, I realized how many fantasies the blond bottom and I had in common. The fantasy of the big black stud was one we shared with several celebrities, including Halston and Cole Porter. While celebrities live in the spotlight, love in the shadows, Porter took few precautions to avoid scandal. He and his close buddy Monty ("The Man Who Came to Dinner") Woolley used to cruise the streets of New York (or whatever city they were in together) for the kind of potentially dangerous sexual encounters they favored. Cole liked the tall, burly unwashed truck driver or longshoreman type, the kind of man who would as likely knock his teeth out with his fist as with his genitals. Cole naturally paid for this kind of sex, which was also a kick for him, because his attitude toward sex was tied up with his attitude toward money. He was deeply titillated by the idea of paying for sex.

Cole knew that the kind of men he favored could never fit in with the international high society in which he was a leading figure. He was not about to give up either sex or society. He also was not the kind of person who could be pigeonholed or categorized. Although he loved picking up or sending out for the kind of man that would have a teamster's union card, Cole also liked to surround himself with the more usual types of homosexual coteries that fit the stereotype: bright clothes, flamboyance, fun, and laughs.

His attitude toward his "tricks" was that they were purchases, not unlike his clothes, his champagne, and his houses, and he treated them as such. In *Genius and Lust*, Joseph Morella tells this tale about Porter and his pals: "In Harlem black people and white people were more segregated than in Paris except in one arena: sex. New York in the Roaring Twenties had brothels for men who wanted women and for men like Cole Porter. One of these houses in Harlem specialized in young black males. Both Cole and Monty Woolley shopped there. So did Jack Wilson.

"The pimp Clint Moore 'dealt' in mahogany merchandise. His house in Harlem was fully and richly furnished in this wood and with the mahogany male beauties who serviced the rich homosexuals who frequented the place. It was an exclusive and expensive club comparable to the fabled houses of female prostitution in old New Orleans. Nude black men mingled with the elegantly dressed famous and wealthy males who came to spend the evening. The only attire allowed the prostitutes were white terry cloth robes. Boys in training acted as servants, and guests could watch sexual training sessions through peepholes as older prostitutes taught newer ones the ropes.

"Cole was one of the regular and favored customers drinking and dining with Moore, along with Woolley and Lorenz Hart. Cole became friends with Clint Moore. In later years Moore would sometimes send one of the prostitutes to deliver a fake package to Cole's penthouse at the Waldorf. (This was in the 1930's when his legs had been crippled and he had lost the ability to go out in public without help.) The location of Moore's house was a closely guarded secret. Cole would go there and spend the night steeped in fantasies. Never mind that many of the boys available were fifteen years old, or that the actual 'employees' of the place led lives of virtual slavery and degradation. In those days the social consciousness was different; the idea that rich people could buy anything they wanted was a time-honored tradition."

Kevin Kramer achieved his latest fantasy by "acting" with Troy Maxwell in "Private Parts." It was unusual for Mustang (a Falcon cheapo label) to display a huge black erection on the frontpiece of a brochure, but when it's Maxwell's dong, well, they couldn't resist.

And size-queen Kramer couldn't resist the opportunity to have his first interracial scene when he saw it was Maxwell who would be doing him. Kevin disdains appearing with straight boys, and he didn't know Maxwell was straight until he showed up to do the video. He went along, true pro that he is, and in the resulting scene, Kramer sucked Maxwell and then took him in both doggie and missionary positions. For those of us who fantasize about being taken by a black dude, it is a fucking for the ages.

Now Kevin will move on to yet another fantasy, not yet fully formulated in his mind.

Two
THE BIG & THE BEAUTIFUL

Kevin lost out to Ken Ryker as Newcomer of the Year at the Gay Video Awards last December, but he wasn't too upset. After all, he says he taught Ken everything he knows!

Now, seeing a Ken Ryker video you may not think Ken knows much at all about gay sex. He just stands there and lets others adore him, and his tool never seems to get hard. But, believe Kevin, Ryker knows a lot more now than he did just a year ago.

Ken was a photographic model for Rip Colt and many other name photographers, yet he said he hankered to get into the video biz. His Sugar Daddy at the time didn't want him to and every time Ken thought he'd made a deal, SD would outbid the video company! Finally Ken did make a deal, with Studio 2000, whose big shots decided that Ken definitely needed to learn the fine points. And who better to teach him than Kramer? After all, Kevin makes far more being a sex therapist than he could ever make doing videos. The studio put KK up in a nice hotel and had Ken visit him. After two sessions, KK thought Ken was as ready as he would ever be and on the third session gave Ken a pep talk about really wanting to do video or get out.

Of course, either Ken decided he didn't really want to do videos or his SD came up with more cash because the Studio 2000 deal was suddenly off. Eventually, Ken ended up at Falcon, and, as they say, the rest is history.

Still, Ken has an incredibly tough time on camera. Kevin says that the "third eye" makes the hunk nervous and he can't "perform" the way he does when he's in a locked hotel room. Kevin certainly knows what he's talking about, having been a photographer's model since the age of seven.

Having met many of the great porn "sex workers" over the years, I know Kevin has what it takes to become the Leo Ford of the '90s. Leo, as you'll recall, was one of most successful performer-turned-escorts in the adult entertainment world. He parlayed his popularity into a health food business that survived until his death.

The beauty of video is that we get to see a worker working.

Seeing Kevin working sent me over the edge into fantasyland. As a long-time rump aficionado, I think Kevin is sheer perfection. But more than his physical beauty, he knows what to do with his assets and therein lies all the difference.

Kevin is, however, a maverick. He has what one director we know wants to be spared from: ATTITUDE. Joey Stefano had more attitude than any video performer we've ever met, except perhaps Ryan Idol, but Joey was just so crazy that everybody forgave him. Kramer, on the other hand, is so professional, so much the perfectionist, that he is fast becoming the Barbra Streisand of porn. (He'd love my calling him that so I'm leaving it in.) Directors just want their performers to be dumb and, indeed, most of them fill the bill admirably.

Granted Kevin is no rocket scientist but he doesn't need to be. He's got smarts that most rocket scientists would envy, in and out of bed. And you don't have to go to Hollywood and hire him to see that, either. Just look at him on your TV screen. If you love to watch someone loving their work, then there can be no greater joy than a Kevin Kramer sex scene, unless, of course, it would appearing with him. Take it from Jeff Stryker, gay porn's legendary top, who paged Kevin to co-star in "JS Big Time." Jeff did his usual masterful job of fucking as he pleasures himself and Kevin. What made it so exciting was that Kevin had been looking forward to it for so long. He watched all of Jeff's videos so that when it came to sucking and fucking, he would be the best Jeff had ever had. Jeff never publicly said what a good time he had but it's obvious from the smile on his face he got into Kevin – in every which way!

Kevin also posed for a sex products company, doing funny things with a pump. ("I told them they'd have to make a bigger one if I was going to demonstrate it," he says.)

Plus Kevin appeared with his pal Madame Dish (Stephen J. McCarthy) in "STRIP! Bare-ly Legal," on stage in WeHo, playing, of course, a stripper.

Dish calls his show "an environmental comedy where the audience becomes part of the action." Dale Reynolds in *Frontiers* said: "Ostensibly, the audience is attending the 18th anniversary party of David and Todd. David's Uncle Mortie has made a special arrangement to host the party at the infamous Cat Club, run by Ms. Kitty (played by McCarthy). The lovers aren't aware, nor are their guests, that the club is infamous for the Tom Cats: beautiful male strippers from all over the world; men who just love to strip naked for customers... All of the above frivolity will benefit a charity with which McCarthy is associated: Aunt Bee's Free Laundry and Housekeeping Service for People with AIDS. A portion of the proceeds will go to the business, and, in keeping with the theme of the evening, the audience may buy 'Kitty Kash' with which they may tip the dancers as they prance in their skimpies among the 'customers.'"

Reynolds reported that McCarthy, from Cleveland, is not shy about talking up his show and his own checkered background as a male prostitute, and, during grad school, a serious drug abuser. McCarthy says, "I did what I needed to do at the time and because of it I am a positive influence on younger gays: I've done drugs, and the prostitution, and survived. It lead me, or more accurately, Madame Dish, into becoming a spokesperson for AIDS groups."

After the play opened, Madame Dish wrote in her column in *Nightlife*, "Dearest friends, I do need to start our date this week by thanking all of you who came out to support my opening weekend of 'STRIP! Bare-ly Legal,' at The Globe Playhouse in West Hollywood. And what a grand opening night – it was Friday the 13th! - with the likes of Stella Stevens (ever so radiant), Sally Kirkland (ever so effervescent), Betty Garrett (ever so charming), Mr. Blackwell (ever so Mr. Blackwell), Eleanor Mondale, Tanya Hart from E-Entertainment, Skip E. Lowe, The Sisters of Perpetual Indulgence, papparazzis, critics galore, dear friends and fans (too many to mention and dare I forget to mention one, oh, my!)

"A sold out house – with a cancellation line stretching to the corner – and repeated with the same enthusiasm on Saturday night. Dear, dear friends, 'STRIP!' is selling out...

"'STRIP!' is indeed late night adult entertainment featuring some of the finest looking men in Southern California! Each night, we convert The Globe Playhouse into the infamous Cat Club to recreate the 18th anniversary of 'David and Todd,' played brilliantly by Jamie St. Anthony and Nick Salamone. You, dear fans, play party guests amidst David's wonderfully funny family – the charming Bob Prest as Uncle Mortie (a regular club patron), Bethany Carpenter (David's zany mother, Zeida), Penny Peyrot (David's ex-wife, Felicia), the adorable Eddie Shapiro (David's and Felicia's son), and the ruggedly handsome Thomas Potter sporting colorful and spectacular tatoos [Felicia's fiancee, Matt).

"Oh, but there is so much more with the entertainment (it is a party) yet to begin hosted by yours truly as the seductively dangerous Ms. Kitty and her gorgeous Tomcats played by internationally renown adult video stars, stud puppy Kevin Kramer as Golden Boy and the exquisite muscle god Bo Stallion (fans, he is built like a brick shithouse!) as my bodyguard, Zeus, together with the truly beautiful Joe Elvis Alway as Beau, the warm and sexy Kris Andersson as Jimmy Bob, Fabricio Gamboa as Precious (audiences, his character name says it all!), and my own hot Latin lover Euri as Ms. Kitty's hot Latin lover (art imitating life!), Julio!

"And indeed, my Tomcats display the BEAUTY AND MAGNIFICENSE (sic) OF THE MALE BODY in their solo erotic dances, choreographed so perfectly by my dear Euri with original music by my friend and master composer, Alex Varden. My Tomcats show no inhibitions, DISPLAYING THEIR NUDE PHYSIQUES IN EXQUISITE FORM."

You'll note the capitalization was also in bold face in the review, lest the reader not get the idea.

Indeed, John Price, publisher of a competitive L.A. publication, *4-Front*, said, "This was a hard show to review. As the proceeds benefit Aunt Bea's Laundry Service for PWAs, I don't want to be overly critical. However, this is a review after all. 'Strip!' is a fun evening where cute guys dance and take off their clothes - ALL their clothes. If that's what you want, that's what you'll get. If you want to see a play - with a story; with a beginning, a middle or an end; or even some clever dialogue or interesting music - steer clear. In spite of having said that, I still think Strip! will run forever in West Hollywood. Why? Nudity! As you may know, it is against the law for a go-go dancer in a club to strip down any further than his G-string. This show gets around that law by not serving alcohol. So, what in a bar would be 'illegal' at worst, sleazy at best; in the Globe Playhouse, is 'art.' This is an old fashioned lap dancing show, where the strippers work the room for tips and end up nude. Perhaps the future of small theater in Los Angeles. On the positive side, actors/strippers are adorable. Their personalities are bright and charming. They're gorgeous and there are enough of them so that anyone who comes will find just their type. My favorite was Joe Elvis Alway as the romantic Beau. I'm sure you'll have a favorite, too. Kevin Kramer is stunning as Golden Boy and there is plenty of 'eye candy' around to keep you titillated.

"As for the rest of the play, since Stephen J. McCarthy is credited as writer, director, creator, producer and star, I supposed he, and he alone, must bear the burden of criticism. I'm assuming that you know who McCarthy is. He is best known as Madame Dish ... a friend that I like and respect. However, this show needs a hostess with a million campy, hilarious, bawdy, suggestive, innuendo packed one-liners. Where is the camp? Where is the ad-lib? You can't find a drag queen hosting a strip show anywhere who doesn't have the naughty, funny, laugh lines flying. Where are the laughs? This Miss Kitty has the comic timing of Dr. Kevorkian.

"As for direction, the pace of the evening was far from up-beat. The show plods along with lengthy strip numbers to sluggish music. The cast does an excellent job of trying to keep the energy up, but it's hard. As for the writing, there are plot points introduced that don't make sense and never appear again. It's as if they tried to write a story, but didn't even bother to finish. Quite frankly, as theater, 'Strip!' is sloppy. I also found the billing offensive. McCarthy is the only actor whose name appears on the poster (five times) and above the title. I consider this insulting when the play also features other fine actors such as Nick Salamone, who plays the character Todd thoroughly from beginning to end; even though he had no real material to work with, and was forced to strip naked, for no apparent reason. Eddie Shapiro, as young Lawrence also does a great job with limited material. However, none of this changes the fact that it was fun. AND, if you like nudity... I overheard someone say, 'I can't remember the last time I had a ten dick night. I thought I was at the Hollywood Spa!' I'm happy for Miki Jackson and Aunt Bea's because I'm sure they'll get a lot of needed money. The nakedness alone will keep WeHo audiences lining up until L.A. shakes off the continent and sinks into the sea. And, if Jesse Helms is right, that should be very soon!"

In *Frontiers*, Dave Depino said, "CABARET meets CHIPPENDALES' in Steven J. McCarthy's bawdy, new, 'Bare-ly Legal environmental/comedy, STRIP.' This show doesn't lay any claim to being great 'theatre'. It is an old fashioned strip-show . . . a male strip-show . . . a fun, male strip-show with banter, a slight script and audience participation.

"When first invited, I suspected this would just be a 'campy', gay romp with a bunch of guys taking off their clothes. Surprise! These guys, Kitty's 'Tom Cats,' can really dance a la Chippendales and Ms. Kitty McCarthy (a.k a. 'Madame Dish') turns out to be a sultry, talented chanteuse. More of Ms. Kitty singing some 30's Europeanesque cabaret numbers would be a welcomed addition to the proceedings."

About the Tom Cats, the reviewer said: "Julio (Euri) a hot latin, Golden Boy (Kevin Kramer) sporting a 50's hair style, Jimmy Bo (a charismatic Kris Andersson), Beau (Joe Elvis Alway) the soap stud, Zeus (musclman Bo Stallion) and Precious (perky Fabricio Gambala) a Tom-Cat-in-training. The boys dance into the audience inviting members to put 'Kitty Cash'/money into their skimpy 'G' strings (which come off at the end of each number). And a good time is had by all."

And no better time than on Halloween, when patrons were requested to come to the theater dressed as their favorite "Cat," with prizes for best costume, and New Year's Eve with Kevin as "Baby New Year," complete with powdered butt and diaper. About the New Year's performance, McCarthy, as Madame Dish in *Nightlife*, wrote: "'Happy New Year' announced dear Kevin Kramer, appearing as The Baby New Year, sporting a diaper (it is amazing how adorable men can wear just anything and still look absolutely gorgeous) at the special New Year's Eve performance... I stood on the balcony with a glistening smile on my face, as my dear holiday revelers dined on chicken marabella, wild rice and pecans, crisp vegetables with mint sauce and homemade breads. Others embraced each other, toasting with fine champagne and delicious homemade sweets. 1997 had begun and I was in the company of some of the finest individuals a person could wish for as the old year exits and a new beginning chimes. Oh, indeed STRIP! has developed a very regular following lead by the likes of my dearest patrons, Martin Townsend and Kevin Rettig. So many others also returned for their 7th, 8th, 9th, and 10th time to share this special night together and with my brilliantly talented cast..."

Local critics were kind to the play generally, but Palm Springs' *Bottom Line* reviewer Dr. Hal Bargelt was anything *but* kind: "What evidently started out as this drag queen's dream has emerged as an audience nightmare. The only thing mildly professional or interesting about this 'theater experience' is the advertising and hype. Much of the time, one is actually embarrassed for the actors.

"The audience was asked this particular night to be there by 10:30 for the preshow. Everyone stood in the crowded lobby until 11:00. The theater was opened, and the strippers, wearing briefs, ushered the patrons to their seats. The strippers then served the audience a taste of a weak orange drink. At 11:15 the drag queen, Ms. Kitty, appeared in a nothing gown and the show began. Ms. Kitty started the show singing, in her less-than-average voice, 'Sweet Fornication,' which she had written. One by one, she proceeded to introduce 'her boys,' the strippers. Most were fair looking, poorly costumed, and couldn't dance. After gyrating around the floor for what seemed like an eternity, each finally shed his costume and appeared naked. Later, non-descript members of the cast, who were planted in the audience, were coaxed on stage where they, too, stripped, showing their tired arrangements. All of this action was built around a thin thread of a plot. Two men, who had been together for 18 years, were having an anniversary party and the audience were their guests. Ms. Kitty was on stage most of the time as mistress of ceremonies, constantly injecting her anal-banal humor. It wasn't interesting or clever.

"This evening of a 'hilariously seductive theater experience' as the ads called it, was not worth two hours of anyone's time or money. If one wanted to see naked men, he could do far better in a bathhouse. The major fault with this production is that it was written, produced and performed by many of the same people and their friends. Next time they would be well advised to get outside, professional help in all aspects of the production." It isn't surprising that when Kevin read this review, he thought the Dr., whoever he is, was the one in need of professional help!

While men cannot legally strip completely in clubs in L.A., they can do it in the context of a staged performance. McCarthy says, "As I value the artistic beauty of a man, I believe they should be displayed as exquisite works of art."

"Work of art" Kevin's video work continued sporadically while he appeared in "STRIP," danced at gay bars throughout the country, and entertained his clients.

Occasionally Kevin will make an appearance at one of those infamous parties held by the studios to promote their latest release. One such party heralded the "Hot Firemen" video from Cinetaur. Gossip maven Jack Francis in *Advocate Classifieds* attended and duly reported on Kevin's appearance: "Yes, I'm crazy about Chip Daniels, and his director of marketing, Shane Nelson, is a doll. And I had already seen some shots from 'Firemen' in which Johnny Hanson was putting his big fire hose up J.T. Sloan's butt, so there was that to look forward to. Plus just going to these things always gives me something to write about, for which I'm eternally grateful. I showed up at Axis – the place, it seems, for porn-related functions in West Hollywood – a good half hour later than the invitation dictated, figuring, as I told My Date, on the vagaries of porn-star time. Obviously I still can't tell time accurately by the porn-star clock, because we walked into an absolutely deserted club. ...Upstairs there was a big spread of food and Chad Donovan, who was slinging cocktails behind the bar. I titillated My Date with stories of Chad's enormous appendage until Vince Harrlngton (a.k a. Lana Luster) showed up and I was able to switch to a discussion of a different monster cock. ...I finally introduced myself to Kevln Kramer, who was charming and perky in a sparkly vest that should have come equipped with Polaroid lenses for the light-sensitive."

Kevin appeared because the party was the project of Shane Nelson, who is Kevin's best buddy.

A few weeks later, Chip Daniels was again in a party mood once again, and naturally *Advocate Classifieds* was invited. This provided yet another column for Kevin to be not only mentioned but also pictured, yet again from the infamous *Freshmen* "Underwear Fetish" layout. Columnist Jack Francis said, "Kevin Kramer was atop a high platform doing his best

Judy Carne (or was it Goldie Hawn?) imitation – that is, if *Laugh-In* had ever featured go-go dancers who'd escaped from the Mineshaft. Sporting a black biker's cap and various leather straps and buckly things, all of which led up to an inky studded leather codpiece, Kevin was decked out to give a rude awakening to all those not-quite NAMBLA members who so got off on his diapered appearance in Freshmen several moons ago...

"Frankly, as compelling a layout as that was, this version of Kevin, I thought as he leaned down to give me a very sweaty, out-of-breath (but nonetheless juicy) kiss, was much more up my slatternly alley. Not that you can't be an out-and-out whore in Depends."

And speaking of slatternly, among Kevin's on-screen sexual highlights was his appearance in V.C.A.'s video "Crystal Crawford's Coverboys," which follows the action on stage and off, at a contest to select a gay pin-up boy. *Urge's* reviewer commented, "Meanwhile, in the men's room, the contest has Kevin Kramer and Anthony Dillon all excited. They blow each other, then dark-haired Anthony screws blond Kevin, who takes a whorish delight in getting boned." Very well said.

Another ardent fan is "Unkle Lloyd" at *Videoview*. Mark Adams, in *Videoview*, said, "For those of you who prefer your men to be boys, check out the new YMAC release 'Secret Rituals,' featuring Kevin Kramer, Unkle Lloyd's personal delight, who also appeared in the frightening 'Hustler White,' a recent theatrical release that played at the Coolidge Corner Theatre, where blue-haired matrons were walking out in droves..."

In another column a week later, Adams brings Kevin up once again: "Not to be outdone, Mustang's new release, 'Private Parts' stars Troy Maxwell and Kevin Kramer, who will soon be running off with Unkle Lloyd, if he has anything to say about it. This one contains the controversial chain scene. Need I say more?"

Proving once again that you can't please everybody, in their review of "Coverboys," *Manshots* found the action pedestrian at best: "Antony Dillon comes on to Kevin Kramer in the men's room. They exchange blowjobs, and then Dillon predictably tops Kramer. After they both shoot, it's on to the grand finale."

In "Playing to Win," with a script penned by Mickey Skee,

studly Steven Sax portrays a self-centered egotist who *"wants those whom he can't have"* and will go to any length to get what he wants. His boyfriend, Tony Piagi, isn't enough for him, and he jumps at the chance to have sex when his pal Pagan Prince invites him to join him at a seminar designed to improve one's sex life. *Fig Leaf's* reviewer comments, "The workshop is attended by insatiable cock hounds J.T. Sloan, Hunter Scott, Kevin Kramer, Joshua Sterling, Aaron Austin, Steven, and Pagan, and is conducted in the nude to allay any inhibitions. The candid talk evolves around sex and is filled with funny double entendres. This top-quality scene gives the viewer the chance to appreciate each man's penis in its natural flaccid state – and a mighty fine bevy of cocks and balls it is! Steven and Joshua bolt before the communal sex begins, deciding to go to Steven's apartment for a night cap – sex. They are swiftly followed by J.T., Hunter, and Aaron, who leave Pagan and Kevin squatting naked, holding hands, and murmuring a tantric chant.

"From hand holding to cock-sucking in the time required to take a deep breath, Kevin engulfs Pagan's huge prick in his cock-hungry mouth giving him a stellar blowjob in several positions, including from behind which enables Kevin to sniff Pagan's *very* hairy asshole at the same time. After Pagan comes, he loosens Kevin's sphincter with several fingers then fucks the smooth-bodied blond with profound fervor producing simultaneous cum-shots."

For us, this ass-stuffing with eager fingers was the best part of this uneven video. Prince manages to get *four* fat fingers up Kevin, but the finger-fucking doesn't last nearly as long as it should have. Still, it's always a joy to see Kevin getting fucked by a big dick.

In person, Kevin resembles the child actor (and now esteemed director) Ron Howard. As such, he could well be cast with newcomer Wil Clark in a "brother love" video. But for Wil, like Kevin, looking like a kid is only part of the act. Says Clark, "Even though I actually look like Opie (from 'The Andy Griffith Show'), I can wear leather and be that really tough motorcycle guy. It's a role I can play in an SM situation that I will never get to be in real life because I just don't look like that. Playing different roles can be fun. In sex, or in drama, or in life, it's a nice psychological release." Performing in porno flicks is an opportunity to explore different sides of his personality, he told *The Guide*. "It's not that I'm bringing out anything that's not already there," he explains. "I'm just emphasizing one aspect of me. Like, the part of me that would like to be a huge, jock-type football player. Or the other part of me that is the wholesome, boy-next-door."

Meanwhile, Kevin's work as a "sex therapist" continues, and Kevin is about the only porn star I can think of who makes news by NOT being at an event! Jack Francis in *Advocate Classifieds* reported on what he termed "the biggest porn bash of the year," otherwise known as Chi Chi LaRue's birthday blowout. Said Jack, "Some might say the Black Party or the White Party or the Puce Party (well, whatever) was a bigger blast, but I'm talking about events that don't require you to purchase a ticket. ...Top prize for distance traveled, however, must go to genius couturier Thierry Mugler, who makes his home in Paris. And I don't mean Texas. Swathed in real brown python from fashionably buzzed head to impeccably shod toe - Thierry could give any porn daddy a run for his money. (I guess I should also mention at this time that Kevin Kramer was nowhere to be found. Apparently, Golden Boy, as he's known in 'Strip! Bare-ly Legal,' about which local cabaret show don't ask, was out of town. On business. Or so his pal, Centaur Films' Shane Nelson, told me. Which could mean, well, *anything.)*"

This item followed Jack's "breaking news" that it had been rumored for some time that among Kevin's most devoted clients was "Parisian couture's greatest showman Thierry Mugler," Jack said. Francis reminded us that Mugler was the first man to send Jeff Stryker down a fashion runway-clothed, in London." Francis called Mugler "very porn adjacent these days, what with his ongoing dalliance with Kevin Kramer, which should also tell you that there's truth to the rumor that Thierry is hung *comme un cheval!"*

Yes, like most great bottoms, Kevin does prefer a massively-hung stud. And how they love him! One of the many who sing Kramer's praises is Chad Donovan, with whom he shared the best scene in "Nights in Eden." In his interview with *Manshots,* Donovan admitted Kramer was his favorite sex partner. So good was the sex, the two carried on a short but torrid affair after the filming.

Chad went on to bottom himself. "You know, I was asked by my agent what I would and wouldn't do, and I said, 'Above all, I will not get fisted.' I did not say, 'I will not get fucked.' And he said, 'I don't care what you say. You're not getting fucked, period!' (Laughs) He said, 'There's no sense with a boy like you who has a dick like that gettin' fucked.'"

And no one would agree with that more than Kevin!

Three
A DAY IN THE LIFE...

Kevin Kramer's day begins around two in the afternoon, normal hours for people of the night. *Details* editor Stephen Saban, who never retires before 4 a.m., quotes another night person, Billy, who says, "In L.A., it's all about sidewalk sales. Everything goes on sale after two, when they pour out of the bars onto the sidewalk."

Kevin certainly doesn't need to put it on sale on the sidewalk. His phone starts ringing in earnest around five or six, after he has had his coffee, watched his soap, and returned from the gym and the tanning salon.

He averages a dozen pages on his digital pager a day.

And then the parade of johns begins.

We want sex and romance both, but not necessarily together. Most of us still think somewhere in our secret hearts that sex is nasty, and we hesitate to link it irrevocably with intimacy, love, and cherishing. But because of our training and because we long for love and intimacy, we hesitate to accept free sexual relations *without* intimacy and love. So prostitutes, who have cheerfully made the separation in their own minds, evoke a lot of hostility, much of it illogical and inconsistent. How dare they codify so bluntly that sex can be a product? And how dare they attract us to that idea so much?

I have always lusted after the whore-with-a-heart-of-gold, longing for love. One prostitute said, "It was clear to me when I did finally start doing sex work, after thinking about it for many years, that all the fears and ideas I had about it weren't true. Sometimes it does feel like I'm doing something spiritual and healing and sacred, and I do like knowing the history, that there was a tradition of temple prostitutes. At another time I could have been totally respected for this."

I totally respect the boys I buy. Some, of course, more than most. Kevin was one of those I respected even before I met him.

A streetboy named Snoopy told a reporter for *Frontiers* magazine: "Hustling was easy for me. I was good at it. Scary!" When picking up dates, said Snoopy, "You wait for them to speak. Look for a gay flag or anything gay in the car.

I was very good at it; never been busted. Cops rent cars (to throw off hustlers). I turned down a couple of people; once you know it isn't a cop, you say, 'What you into?'

"When they say, then you say, 'I do this for this.'

"The thing that gets me is there's a lot of money out there. You can make a lot, and then go out and get more; you're insensitive to it – just block it out – it's addictive for the money." Although he is off the streets now, Snoopy said the decision to hustle is a personal choice. "I don't think there's anything wrong with it if that's what you want to do, (but it's) not what I want to do. You can make $300-400 a night." Snoopy said four years ago he hustled for about a year and got caught up in using crack until he, "just realized it was a big nothing."

It would seem the cops are kinder to those who advertise than those who are so visible on the streets. The populace, you see, doesn't read *Frontiers'* classified section. And the cops are probably busy doing other things (or should be) and perhaps realize that hookers will always be with us. "Throughout history, wherever there were money and power, there were hookers," critic Stanley Kauffmann says in his review of the film biography of infamous Hollywood Madam Heidi Fleiss. Kauffmann observes that Hollywood whoring is "ramified out of elements that characterize Movieland. The homes of the principal people look like Lana Turner settings. Chat and atmosphere continually make us feel that the studios are just outside the frames of many scenes. The porno players and hookers who are interviewed are ultra-consciously in Movieland.

"It's all as if we were looking at the film industry through a sewer grating." Kauffman notes that the film makes us aware of the collusion between the prostitution business and the Los Angeles police, who use the madams and the girls as informants. "Whenever I read about a police bust of a pimping ring anywhere, I suspect that some higher-up wasn't paid off or that some unusual urgency prevailed. How could it be otherwise? If the police aren't blind and dumb, they know what's going on. Usually, between the police and pimps, it's footsie time; occasionally, it's revenge time. So it is in the Fleiss story, though somewhat complexly."

"Prostitution is an omnipresent social reality. As the cliche goes, it's the world's oldest profession. Male prostitution, homosexual prostitution by men for men, is probably just as old and proportionately as widespread as its female, heterosexual counterpart.

"While true, these statements carry an unspoken untruth about them. America's hypocritical values insist that prostitution is a sleazy affair with nameless johns using desperate, ill-educated, or evil bodies for a moment's sexual release. Paradoxically, there is also another perception of the prostitute as a highly exotic sexual superstar."

Of course, our view of Hollywood hustlers has been framed from years of porn films depicting the lives of supposedly "typical" ones. For instance, in his review of "Beverly Hills Hustlers" in *Advocate Men*, Floyd Johnson notes The Five Sacred Laws of Hustling, but first he sets the scene: "It's a long way from Miami, Fla., to Santa Monica Boulevard – at least for Erik Knight, who's fresh off the turnip truck and pulling a meager $25 a night until the kindly Holly Woodlawn (Warhol pal, playing a back-alley psychic) intervenes. By reading Knight's crotch like so many tea leaves, Woodlawn prophesies three possible futures for him: 1) hustling his way to financial security; 2) hosting a daytime talk show on NBC; 3) ending up as lifeless flotsam in the L.A. River.

"'How am I going to avoid Futures 2 and 3?' asks Knight, understandably concerned. Why, by learning the Five Sacred Laws of Hustling, of course!

"I. Let Them Know Who's Boss: Streetwalker Tony Cummings learns this when he turns the wrong trick: Kurt Young, an undercover cop. Halfway through his blow job, Young slaps the cuffs on Cummings, who then regains control of the situation by offering his ass for his freedom. Young gladly accepts and pokes Cummings but good. Afterward, they share a cigarette and become the best of buddies.

"II. Take the Money and Run: Knight is picked up by a sleazy sex-club owner who puts him in a live show with Wes Parker and Vic Hall. (This scene was shot at an actual Hollywood sex club with a live audience of 30 lucky patrons. Where was I that day, damn it?) When it comes compensation time, though, the owner won't pay up, so Knight and Parker help themselves to a wad of bills and exit, stage left. They then return to Parker's place for a more private encounter.

"III. Know When to Play Your Ace: And what an ace Kevin Dean has 14 inches' worth. Chris Yeager is the fortunate recipient of Dean's ace in his hole, and Dean – whose French-Canadian grasp of English has improved to where he's actually given lines now – pounds him in a variety of positions. Guys who are fucked by Dean have such a genuine tone to their moaning and groaning; we should all be so lucky!

"IV. Watch What You're Getting Into: Baby-faced Troy Dillion learns this the hard way, finding his ass quite literally in a sling. He's turned every which way, especially loose, in an orgy with leathermen Jake Taylor, Chad Donovan, Brett Winters, and Blou Clover. The scene includes some ass play with Dillion taking a series of large anal balls and some brief spanking.

"V. There's Always a Richer Daddy Up the Hill: And Knight finds him, dumping sugar daddy Vince Skylar for a benefactor with more benefits. Skylar makes do, though, finding a quick replacement in Dillion, whose butt just can't seem to get enough stuffing. Having taken Woodlawn's wisdom to heart, Knight becomes a self-made success and moves into a posh Beverly Hills hotel. There he hires his own callboy, former *Teen* cover model Austin Ashley, and they perform for the JO pleasure of voyeuristic bellhop Clay Maverick. "Yes, hustling's been good to young Knight, a millionaire at only 19. Only in America. 'Hustling's the life for me,' he opines. 'It embraces all the true American values: freedom, competition, opportunity – all the joys of a free-market economy. I consider it my way to serve my country.'

"All young men should be so patriotic."

"The male hustler is seldom called upon only to provide orgasm," John Preston says in *Hustling, A Gentleman's Guide to the Fine Art of Homosexual Prostitution*, (a Richard Kasak Book). Preston agrees that while it may be true when the client seeks only a quick blow job from a street hustler, but even then a contact may be established that is more than one-dimensional.

"The modern male hustler meets his clients through ads or

discreet introductions. He doesn't stand on street corners in dangerous neighborhoods. He entertains in his own apartment or visits clients in their hotel rooms or homes. He has more in common with image of the Japanese geisha than with the *National Enquirer's* sensational headlines about white slavery. Expert sensuality is a part of the gay prostitute's reality, but so too are his social skills."

Preston quotes his pal, author and artist Gavin Geoffrey Dillard, a one-time whore: "Now, with mortgage, taxes, garden, and cats to feed, I find myself more behooved than ever to participate in the trials of money-gathering, selling my time, my passions and my sensibilities in more wearisome and much more emotion-consuming manners than ever I did as a paid tart.

"Let's face it, in this exhausted ruin of an industrial society we are all conscripted to prostitute ourselves though seldom do we garner the satisfaction of a good buck, nor even the strokes that accompany the affirmations that one is attractive, sensual, and desired by another.

"As a professional writer, I can find few justifications for the drudgery of word processing, for spreading my creative cheeks for inane corporate policies, for writing a song or an article that in my heart of hearts I know is not worthy of being written – who is the better for it?

"But in a romantic tete-a-tete, even of the basest and most mercenary sort, souls are obliged to touch souls, human energies mingle, and passions, however restrained, do surface. Besides, a hundred bucks for an hour of trolloping beats the heck out of the same wage for a grisly nine-to-five within the toxic air, Muzak and lighting of our modern high-rise whorehouse. And the rest of the day is left available for poetry, prayer and meditation."

Preston says he learned many things from hustling, one of them being that labor in any form can be exploitative and degrading, but the self-employed person can at least have some control over his dignity. "I was a bank teller when I was in my twenties," Preston recalled, "and I held a number of other similar service jobs. Believe me, all of them were much more demeaning than being a hustler.

"The basic problem with being a male prostitute is your own

and other people's perceptions of the occupation, not the reality of it. It can be difficult to overcome the internalized interpretation that only people with low self-esteem would sell themselves to a stranger. Forget it. Laugh all the way to the bank and, if your self-image is in bad shape, remember that someone else thought you were hot enough that he was willing to pay for the privilege of sucking your cock. That fact has a lot more reality to it than any New Age bullshit."

Four
A COCK'S PLEASURE

"A cock's pleasure is like a fist, concentrated; anal pleasure is diffused, an open palm, and the pleasure of an anal orgasm is founded on relaxation. It's hard to understand how a man can write well if he doesn't like to be fucked."
— Robert Gluck, 1982

In his essay "Cocksucking as an Act of Revolution," Charles Shively analyzed sex acts in the context of the Gay Liberation Movement, seeking to construct an ideological foundation for gay rights. The premise of Shively's two-year series was that sex is fundamental to being gay, and gay men should celebrate, rather than be embarrassed by, the sexual acts they enjoy. But Shively chastised Gay America, arguing that most men are uncomfortable talking about those acts that, in the eyes of most people, define them. "In a faggot bar," he observed, "a cocksucker is considered less honorable than a cocksuckee." Shively further supported his argument by pointing out that gay men had not even created a word to describe the man who is the passive participant in anal intercourse, or, as Shively put it, "a male who takes it up the ass."

Shively applauded group sex. Specifically, he said orgies helped build a sense of community among gay men. One essay began: "Each faggot has a mouth, anus, and penis which can all be used at once." Because all of these parts of the male anatomy can be used for homosexual activity, Shively suggested that gay men were intended not to make love only to one man at a time but to many. He further theorized that, just as sex with a partner is better than masturbation, sex among three men is better than sex between two. He ended the essay more concretely with a personal endorsement of group sex: "I know of no sensation so pleasant as having someone fuck me while I'm sixty-nineing with another person."

In "The Searcher," Takahashi Mutsuo says, "Between the inserter and the receiver, at first glance it appears that the person who inserts his penis is the active one, the 'top' and the aggressor, but that's probably not the case. The one choosing his indispensable partner to engage in this behavior is the one with the pliant rectum who is always looking for a thick dick; it is probably not the owner of the thick dick who is looking for a pliant rectum. The aggressor, then, from the time he chooses his partner, is always the passive one (the 'bottom') while the top is just a servant to pleasure – as if the top is nothing more than a servant to the bottom's *out-of-this-world* feelings. This sort of awakened aggressor *could* be a woman or a sensible man, but common sense has it that in male-female relationships, the woman is the passive one. This, however, is nothing more than habitual passivity and is certainly far from conscious passivity.

"One of the important reasons that the aggressor is particularly aware is that this sexual act is always accompanied by the danger of death. Since the rectum is an organ for expulsion and is not an organ for insertion, it has no defenses against invasive elements. It's extremely easy to injure the rectum and, if one does injure it even a little, it's easy for various kinds of germs to enter those wounds and damage various vital centers. In order to prevent that, one usually cleanses the rectal wall beforehand, but the result of the cleansing is that one also erodes the rectal membrane making it easier to injure."

"If you ask a bunch of bottoms," Dossie Easton says in *The Topping and Bottoming Books*, "you will hear heartfelt and often bitter complaints about the scarcity of tops in the S/M community. The good news (if you're a top) is that this is often true – particularly in heterosexual communities or those in smaller cities and rural environments. The bad news is that it's changing: both of us have noticed that more and more of the new young players coming into the scene are top-identified.

"However, for the time being, there are more bottoms than tops – often many more." Easton remembers learning to top because in the women's community in which she came of age as a player, there essentially were no tops, so bottoms politely took turns topping one another so that everybody got to get played with.

"What that means to you, particularly if you're a heterosexual female, a lesbian or a gay man, is that you as a top are in something of a buyer's market. That certainly doesn't mean, however, that all you have to do is lean back and casually choose from a parade of eager bottoms who are all dying to throw themselves at your feet. Quality tops get quality bottoms - it's up to you, not only to be a quality top, but to make sure your potential bottoms know it.

"This goal is not accomplished by boasting about your true master... or by acting pushy and bossy outside scene space in order to demonstrate your natural gin for domination, or by hauling around a bunch of toys that you had to take out a second mortgage to buy. The best tops we know are quite modest, soft-spoken, and always scrupulously polite - until they've finished their negotiations and the scene begins... then, watch out!

"...One of the most important qualifications you need in order to become a bottom is - a top. For many folks, unfortunately, this is easier said than done. There are typically more bottoms than tops in any given S/M scene, and good tops - skilled, empathetic, ethical and uninhibited - are a rare and precious commodity."

"...Most bottoms will support you enthusiastically while you're acting like a top, especially if you're acting like the kind of top they like. But a good bottom will also be supportive when you're not acting like a top - when you're feeling tired, vulnerable, confused, depressed or simply *untoppy*."

With Kevin Kramer in the offing, I felt very *toppy*. In fact, that was the point. Suffering with liver disease, I was able to keep a full erection for only a few moments. I could, eventually, orgasm, but I had not been able to enjoy what is to me the greatest thrill man can have: topping a compliant bottom. Having had two lovers in my salad days who wanted that – and only that – when I didn't have it I missed it greatly.

Seeing Kevin on screen I knew that if I ever had the chance, he would be the one to grant an old man's dying wish. Little did I know.

Later, in bed, there was only skin. Kevin, his bronze chest glistening, put his hand on my cock. It swelled. I was surprising myself as to how out of control Kevin became. No.

Kevin was in control. He was doing what he wanted, which was what I wanted.

He licked the tip. My cock stood up, burning a little. It was like the dead coming to life. I had forgotten what it was like, the sensations of someone wanting my cock.

Kevin was luscious in his nakedness, with that firm flesh that, at a certain age, comes with little effort. It was once like that for me. But it didn't seem to matter to Kevin that I had become flabby as he nudged his way along my body.

He was so young, and yet it was as if there is some ancient understanding between us. Now as he took me in his arms and we embraced, our bodies fit so well together, like molded parts of the same figure. I could not draw away. I didn't even want to. My mind warned me that acting impulsively can so easily end in disappointment, but I found myself rolling him over onto his back. "I want you," I said, as I felt my penis bore into him. "I want you so bad!"

I anchored him firmly against the coverlet, and began to sear him everywhere – licking him under the armpits and behind the ears and on his forehead. I pelted him with kisses and tiny bites, then rejoiced in the satin smoothness of his penis, hard, throbbing, ready.

And it was real – every minute of it. Kevin was really good. Excellent, in fact. Better than most anyone – girl or guy – that I could remember having suck me, including the masseur in Tampa who loved uncut cocks and gave me a superb blowjob at no extra charge. Kevin just slurped my entire cock into his mouth and then settled down to work on it for a good long time. This was heaven, I thought, throwing my head back. I didn't care if he stayed all week.

And then, finally, I was between his legs. The anus was prepared and it soon embraced my cock. And then his mouth was on mine and he pleaded, in muffled cries, that I stick it all the way in.

But the pulsing had already started, and I was seeing spots before my eyes, like after the camera flashes, which Kevin said happened to him a lot.

Now this boy-like man opened up to me, and the scent, the taste, was right. The brain said, don't give in to impulse, but I couldn't help it. No, I was growing larger between his legs, crushing out any air remaining between us.

Kevin came without touching himself. Such kamikaze arousal with a client was rare, he said, but this is no ordinary situation. I was only too happy to oblige him by fucking him even harder. And soon he seemed to be on another plane of existence, completely free of the pall of guilt and withdrawal I imagined he usually carried when he was paid for sex.

When I could bear it no longer, I withdrew from him, slid down his body, knelt with him, stifled his protest with a kiss, tasted myself on his tongue. He pulled away, breathless. "I am not used to this, to being loved so much by somebody. Let me, now. Let me make love to you. I know how to do that."

My answer was a sigh, a lingering kiss. His hand crept round my back and pulled me closer. He lifted me up slightly so that he could slide between my thighs, his erection pulsing against my sweaty crack. He slid back and forth, across but not in, and I gripped my thighs tight around him. My head fell back; he kissed my throat, traced with his tongue the stubble on my jawline.

"Please," I whispered against his mouth, and he entered me, paused there to listen to my quickened breathing, to his own, then he slid it in all the way.

Yes, a bottom can be a superb top, if given half a chance. As his pace intensified, I could feel him inside me, swelling. I began undulating with all my might, working him all the way in. I closed my eyes, waiting, until he started in earnest, giving me a fucking I will never forget.

He brought me to the brink several times, then let me come as he had. Exhausted, I lay beside him remembering how often I had fantasized about a night like this. And now the fantasy was this night.

Twenty Questions for Kevin Kramer

What do you consider your greatest achievement?
My independence.

What is your most marked characteristic?
My eyes.

Which talent would you most like to have?
To be able to sing.

What do you regard as the lowest depth of misery?
Living without credit cards.

What is your greatest fear?
Running out of hot lube.

What is your current state of mind?
Confident.

When and where were you happiest?
Now, everywhere.

What is your idea of perfect happiness?
Being able to continue to make myself and everyone around me smile, laugh, be happy, and live life to the fullest.

What is the trait you most deplore in other people?
Lying.

What is your greatest extravagance?
Long bubble baths.

What is your favorite journey?
Visiting San Diego; Black's Beach by day, Club San Diego by night.

What do you consider the most overrated virtue?
Humility.

On what occasion do you lie?
Never, although I do exaggerate occasionally.

What do you dislike most about your personal appearance?
My ankles and wrists.

Which words or phrases do you most overuse?
"Like;" "Period. The End;" "Ya know what I mean?"

What is your greatest regret?
Not knowing who Jerry Douglas was when he called me.

What is your most treasured possession?
My award as the "Leo Ford Humanitarian of the Year."

What or who is the greatest love of your life?
My "family."

What is the quality you like most in a man?
Perfect hygiene. (And no fingernails – that hurts!)

Which living person do you most admire?
Madonna.

Which living person do you most despise?
I don't despise people, I ignore them.

If you were to die and come back as a person or thing, what would it be?
"Kevin Kramer."

Five
KEVIN: IN HIS OWN WORDS

"Here's to L.A., city of whores."
– Hustler in the porn video "Beverly Hills Hustlers"

To understand me, it helps for people to know I've been experiencing these camera flashes before my eyes since birth. It's why I'm so ditzy.

It also helps to know that I was born in that Gay Mecca San Francisco.

And that I spent four years as an altar boy at St. Paul's. No, I was not seduced by a priest, although that might have been fun. I just loved the pageantry of mass, as if I was part of a show.

And that my dad was killed in a car accident when I was 12. Some think the loss of Dad at such a tender age contributed to my desire for men, but that had taken shape long before my dad's passing. What the death of my father taught me was that you could be taken away from this life at any moment, so you might as well enjoy it while you have it.

It's also important to know that I had a sense I was different when I was four. At fourteen I thought about gay sex occasionally, but I suppressed it. I liked girls and I dated them, but I knew the gay thing was always going to be there. All my friends were girls. When I did get together with other guys it was to drink beer and look at girlie magazines.

I didn't have my first gay experience until I was 19. I was attending Columbia Junior College in Sonora. I was a business major, and I worked part-time at Wendy's. One day a man came through the drive-thru. He managed a small supermarket behind the high school. He let guys hang out in the back of the supermarket. Everybody liked him. He was 29. We dated for six months. He asked me to marry him, but I wasn't ready for that. We stayed lovers for three years, but I finally outgrew him. My mom loved him. She thought he was good for me.

I always considered myself lucky that he was the first one to fuck me. At least I didn't have to get fucked by some stranger in a bath house for the first time. I learned what relationships were about, what ingredients go into that cake. I still haven't found anybody strong enough to handle me.

The last six months of our relationship, I strayed. I discovered that sex can get you everywhere. Especially in Hollywood. After I broke up with my lover, I decided I needed a change.

I was working as a booker at a modeling agency in Modesto so I took it upon myself to respond to an ad in the *Advocate Classifieds*. My cousin took some pictures of me and I sent them to Hollywood. Three days later I was making "Olympic Proportions." The director, J. D. Kidd, said I could stay at his place for 10 days. He said he would call people, get me more work. I don't even remember who I was paired with. All I remember about it was that I couldn't help but come. Ooops. But they didn't seem to mind. Then I saw an ad in *Edge*, and I called Tommy Tanner. I took the bus to the Valley. I liked the place. I also did the video "Fresh Men," for Vision Video, with Ted Matthews. (Matthews is a stud who advertises regularly as "gorgeous bdy-bldr top...hung huge, friendly...available for travel or overnight.") Being with Ted was a lot of fun, but I still didn't have a lot of control. The boxcover photos ended up in *Blueboy*. That was really exciting.

I returned to San Francisco, only to get a call that I was wanted for "Smoke Screen," being filmed in Hollywood for Mustang. It was very uncomfortable doing it all in this tiny bathroom. I was still having a problem controlling my orgasm. Then I went back to San Francisco to discover the modeling agency had closed. I began dancing. I became a transient, partying till dawn and go-go dancing, just bouncing around for about three months. By then my mom had moved to Nevada. I called her and told her I wanted to go back to Hollywood. She left a one-way ticket to Los Angeles at the counter at the airport. She said, "Be careful. Call me when you get a place. I love you, son." And I knew she really did.

This is when it becomes the classic Hollywood story. I had ten outfits, $25 in cash, and a pair of go-go boots. J. D. Kidd said I could stay with him. He lived in Hollywood and it took me four hours and seven buses to get to his house! Of course, it should have taken only 45 minutes and two buses, but what did I know? After three days in Hollywood, I moved to the

Valley and I have been there ever since.

I guess it all boils down to what door you happen to walk through. Tommy Tanner was still on the scene and took me to Studio One. I met Chi Chi LaRue but he was occupied. Besides, I had no idea who he was! Eventually I did work for him, on "Coach's Boys." I was with Tanner Reeves and we shot it at the Midtown Spa, during the day. I had to get up at 4 am! It was a really professional shoot. I took a dildo for the first time. It was a huge dildo and I had to sit on it. I didn't particularly care for it and don't to this day. It just ripped me open and I had my first embarrassing moment on a set. But they calmed me down and I was able to jack off for them.

I moved in with Tommy but that didn't work out. Trouble is I had appeared in three cheap videos and couldn't find work. Somebody suggested I call Chip Daniels. We talked on the phone for six months. We had phone sex once a week and he kinda took me under his wing. I fell in love with him actually. He was the one who booked me into the Campus in San Francisco.

But first I got a part in "Biggest Piece I've Ever Had." Jason Reddy was my partner and we hit it off. He invited me to go back to Palm Springs with him for the White Party. I was in a discovery mode, and at the Desert Palms we were standing next to a scaffolding that was empty because the dancer who was supposed to be performing hadn't showed up. So we thought, what the hell. So we just started dancing on the scaffolding. I was playing around with Jason and begged him to whip out his dick. Damned if he didn't, and I started sucking it. The management climbed up and told us to stop. We wouldn't – the crowd loved it and we were being tipped very generously. People still talk about that! It was quite amateur, but it was gutsy. And, when you consider how fabulous Jason's cock is, it was absolutely fabulous!

It was there that I met my friend Shane Nelson, who was manager at the Desert Palms. This is where it gets real soapy – and its been sudsy ever since.

Back in Hollywood, I discovered *Blueboy* was on the newsstands and for the first time I was being recognized on the street. We went to Circus of Books to buy a copy but they were closed. We banged on the door and the manager opened it and sold us a copy. What a thrill!

Anyhow, I took off for my engagement at the Campus. I had no music and nothing to wear. I worried about getting a hard-on, coming on stage. A regular dancer there, Rick, taught me what to do. The Campus billed me as a "Kevin Kramer, Go Go God. Come and meet the youngest, sexiest gay erotic star of the decade." I came out in a black leather jacket and motorcycle boots, acting as if I was a little boy playing in Daddy's closet.

It was there in San Francisco that I started doing private shows. Having paid sex, I was there, but I wasn't there. I was not sophisticated enough to do it properly. But I was going to the school of Chip Daniels and so it had to be taken in little steps. He told me I had to have a pager ("because everyone has one"). The Campus gives their visiting stars a "corporate apartment" and pays the airfare. They are great. They bring a star back for three reasons: the numbers at the door, the work performance, and attitude. Basically, Chip had said their only rule was "come to work." They wanted guys who were there to put on a show, not just trying to turn tricks. "You have to be nice to the fans," Chip told me. The Campus was certainly nice to me, giving me a great review in their magazine for my work in "Fresh Men": "See the video and you will find out why the title of this article fits so well. He definitely has what I call a candy apple ass. That's only part of the package. Blond hair and blue eyes are a couple of his other attributes. Did I mention that he's also single! What does he like about his new career? 'The Men!' Sex is fun but Safe Sex is even better,' says Kevin."

When I returned to Los Angeles, Shane had moved back to the city from Palm Springs and we grew very close. He has become my parent, my friend, the brother I never had. He really does care. He said he was going to put me through "the School of Shane" and I was to be his "last model." We've never had sex. I don't mind that; I find it less complicated. But Shane would not be my agent. I had no one representing me. Finally, in late 1993, Chip booked me into the Show Palace in New York. I appeared in "Masquerade" and left for New York. I was supposed to be on the boxcover of the video with Marco Rossi, but I couldn't be in two places at once (they used a chimp instead!).

The flight to New York was eventful. One of the flight attendants was *very* friendly! My longtime pal Dave Kinnick reported it in *Advocate Classifieds*: "The flight attendant in question stood 6 feet 2 inches tall and had sandy-blond hair. Kevin's initiation into the famed mile-high club took place late in the flight after the passengers had been fed and were drifting off to sleep. The steward served young Kevin a steady stream of vodka tonics before bluntly asking, 'Do you wanna fool around?' and making a beeline for an aft lavatory. The two went at it for 'close to an hour,' exploring many oral sex possibilities in the lofty realm of aluminum toilet bowls and signs warning of the many dire consequences resulting from the improper disposal of sanitary napkins." I would have loved to have ass-fucked; his dick was a beauty, nine-inches long and very thick, but there was just no way to maneuver into a fuck position. Now I always try to fly Continental!

I had never been to New York before and I was stunned. There were so many people wanting me.

What guys found out was that, "oh, god, this guy really wants to do this." They'd been screwed over so many times, I felt sorry for them. I told them, "I can be rented, but I can't be bought."

One guy I met wanted me to go to Europe with him. He said, "You don't know how unaffected you are."

When I got back to California, business was slow. It was the hardest winter I ever lived through. I'd spend Friday and Saturday nights at Numbers trying to get tricks. It was a big-time head game. Finally I said, "This is not healthy."

I continued dancing, many times for charity. In Dave Kinnick's column he commented about one of my performances: "He spent a good part of the afternoon standing up on a bar, making the usual charming spectacle of himself while doing his quite commendable boogie-for-charity act. He also proved to be one of the best-dressed men in attendance, decked out in leather from his windswept bow to his outward-jutting stern, which constantly wallowed and occasionally breached amid his rolling ocean of admirers, many of them new to the "Kramer experience."

Finally I got more work in video. All Worlds was very nice and took care of me. For them I did "Tales of the Backlot" and

"Hard Bargains." At Catalina I did "Too Damn Big." "Tales of the Backlot" was memorable because of Chad Knight. *In Touch* magazine said this scene alone "made the video worth seeing." Chad was some of the best sex I ever had. We did the scene all in one take, without stopping. He was very passionate. I guess it takes a great bottom to be a great top. Someday maybe somebody will let me prove what I can do!

One of my best reviews came for my work in "The Rival" for Jim Steel. I was on the boxcover for this one, and Hank Ferguson, writing in *Adult Video News*, said I stole the show! "While Kramer's looks may not stand out in gay porn's ever-expanding sea of pretty faces, this young sandy-haired pup knows how to throw down some sizzling sex. After a blistering alley encounter, Kramer's second scene has him going at it on a bed with a hot blond. Nearby video monitors show close-ups of the fuck 'n' suck activity as it takes place."

Before I went back to the Campus, I signed with Brad's Buddies. When I returned to Los Angeles, I did two clients because a friend of mine didn't want to do them. It was quick and painless, but I didn't consider doing it as a business at that time. I was having too much fun.

One of the defining moments of my life was meeting Madame Dish (Stephen McCarthy) at the 1993 Erotic Video Awards. We clicked and I eventually became her second permanent Naughty Boy. We do one or two functions per month and tape a local access program twice a month. The show plays in eight states and doesn't offend straight people. It's designed to educate young gays and increase HIV awareness. The story of Madame Dish and her Naughty Boys became a part of gay Hollywood folklore. Madame Dish lives high in the Hollywood Hills. She has been married seven times, and is looking for husband number eight. She is terribly wealthy, what with all that alimony, and lives with her two sons, Tony and Kevin. Tony's father was a performer who never quite made it on Broadway, explaining why he frequently breaks out in song. My father was abducted by aliens, never to be seen again, and I am the white trash of the family. I can do no wrong in Madame's eyes, and if I do, it is always Tony's fault. Early one morning, Tony found Ned in the bushes at Griffith Park and brought him home. Lo and behold, it turned out that Ned indeed was our long lost brother! You see, ages ago, Madame, when she was touring the bars as Candy Dish, had an affair, and gave up the product of that affair to adoption! God knows how many other brothers are out there. Madame isn't talking.

What Madame does all day is interview people for the TV show, people who have done wonderful things for the gay community. All we Naughty Boys do is interview pool boys. We go through pool boys like crazy!

I posed for a layout in *Freshmen* featuring underwear and they put me on the cover. I suddenly became even more visible. One fan from Michigan wrote the magazine, "Just when I thought you couldn't get any better! Kevin Kramer is hot, hot, hot! Am I weird, or is there anybody else who thinks the sexiest picture is the one where Kevin still has clothes on? And his smile!"

I also started to advertise on my own and the peak was over the Memorial Day weekend I did seven tricks a day for four days. It wore me out! I hate it when someone says that bottoms have it easier. That's not so. You have to be very clean and that means not eating solid food. With the release of "Hustler White" and Madame Dish's "STRIP" stage show, I seem to be getting a better class of client. Recently, a man in San Jose flew me up, entertained me royally, let me drive his new Mercedes roadster, gave me a great massage, and made love to me. It was almost as if I should have been paying him. Then he gave me a generous tip!

I guess my clients appreciate me. With me, it's everything or nothing. I *make* my johns come. They say they've never met another one like me. You see, I've always followed my mom's advice: "Don't rush it."

Self Portrait: Kevin Kramer

Height: *Five nine*

Weight: *160#*

Date and place of birth: *San Francisco, on September 14.*

Sun sign: *Virgo*

Flower: *Roses. Longstem. Any color.*

Birthstone: *Sapphire.*

Occupation: *Entertainer.*

Best day I've ever had was: *The Gay Video Awards in 1994, when I was given the humanitarian award.*

Worst job I ever had was: *None so far.*

My pet peeve is: *Indecisiveness.*

I'm proudest of: *My accomplishments.*

My favorite kind of music:
Music that you FEEL, not just hear.

My favorite movie stars:
Jean Harlow, Patrick Swayze, Bette Midler.

My favorite movie:
"Strictly Ballroom" and "Mr. Holland's Opus."

My ideal vacation:
Far away in a hot climate with my friends.

The best advice I would give a teenager:
Live everyday as if it were your last (and use a condom).

My most embarrassing moment:
When I got a condom stuck in my butt on a movie set. I passed it a month later!

My favorite food:
Chocolate.

My favorite drink:
Cocksucker shots.

I drive a:
Depends on what day it is!

I'm superstitious about:
Letting people know about a project I'm working on before I've completed it.

My friends like me because:
I am REAL.

If I could invite anyone to dinner it would be:
My mom.

My hero is:
My pal Shane Nelson. My rock.

My worst habit is:
Going shopping.

The worst mistake I ever made was:
Accepting that first credit card approval!

A LIFE IN PICTURES...

"You must've been a beautiful baby..."

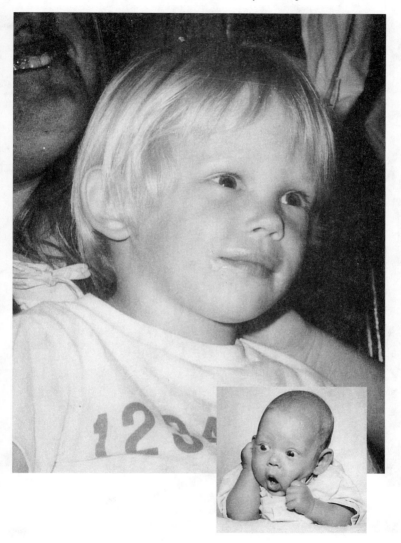

Kevin, surprised at three months, and at almost four.

Kevin at 15

Kevin at 16

Kevin at 17

Bondage Go-Go, San Francisco (pre-porn)

Kevin and his best pal, Shane, backstage at Axis in WeHo and Kevin with Madame Dish and Naughty Boy Tony

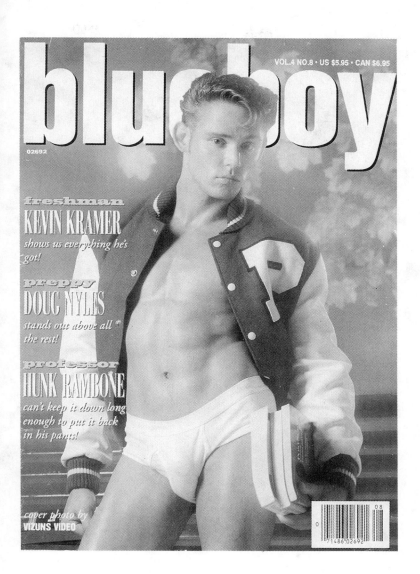

Kevin's First Cover, for Blueboy

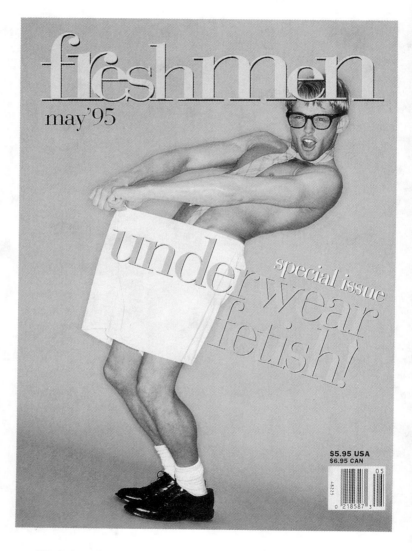

Kevin's infamous underwear fetish cover for Freshmen

Nightlife magazine used one of the shots from the underwear fetish layout for its cover

Kevin with Jeff Stryker in "JS Big Time" and (inset) as he appeared in "Private Parts"

Kevin was on the prowl in "JS Big Time"

Kevin gets cozy with Pagan Prince in "Playing to Win"

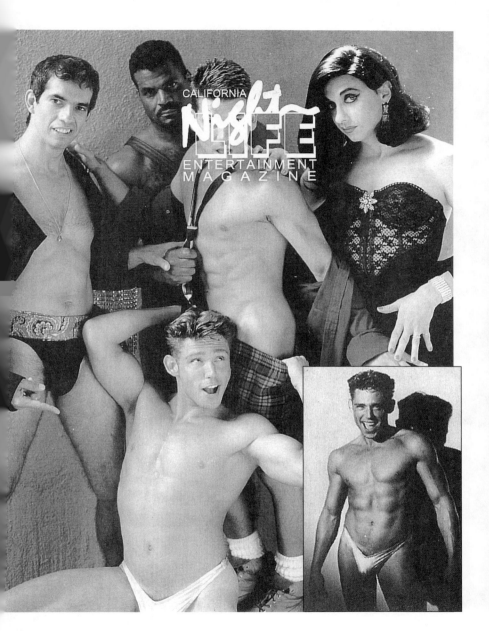

Kevin appeared in "STRIP" on stage in West Hollywood

Frontiers coverboy, photo by Martin Ryter

Six
SEX, SEX, AND STILL MORE SEX...

Of all of the performers I have met over the years, Kevin was one of the few I wanted to see again. So when he called in late November inviting me to come to California to see him in "STRIP!" I jumped at the chance.

In an indulgent mood, having refrained from sex for a week, I was ready for anything. Kevin, however, was tired. I had arrived just after the Gay Video Awards ceremonies and he had gone to the annual bash with Stephen J. McCarthy (as Madame Dish) who interviewed the arrivals for his cable TV program and later use in a video about the show. Kevin was nominated for the Leo Ford Humanitarian award again, but lost out to Troy Steele. He did get some client action from the show, however, and had been very busy before I arrived.

The big buzz around town was about the "gay Heidi Fleiss" David Forest calling in his participation in the show from County Jail! Forest was out of prison on bond while appealing the mandatory three-year sentence he was facing. When the court heard testimony that Forest was still operating in a manner that violated his bond, he was immediately handcuffed and ordered to begin serving his sentence. The new charges involved Forest's escort Chad Connors, who agreed to cooperate with authorities. Connors was in court when Forest was taken away. Forest's appeal of the sentence (not the conviction) is still pending. In a recent interview in *Genre* magazine Forest was asked to describe what services an escort from his Brad's Buddies and Superstars would provide. He replied, "This may be a *dinner* engagement, *or, shall we say a fan-appreciation meeting like an afternoon tea or whatever.*" David Widmer of *Nightlife* says that Forest will "now have three years (if his appeal is unsuccessful) to join his fellow prisoners for an afternoon tea – or whatever."

Also generating lots of talk was the fact that Jeff Browning had become gay porn's version of Traci Lords. Browning's agent, Johnny Johnston, had no comment about the problem. Widmer says, "I could never figure out why anyone used this dog-faced boy in the first place. This, I suspect, comes from the fierce competition that forces producers to keep costs low. When you get a chance to hire a guy for a ham sandwich and a hot shower, you may not be looking too closely at his documentation."

Since Kevin is also represented by Forest, he had to visit the house to pick up a check for a recent dance gig. While there, I was pleased to see Scott Baldwin and Tom Katt looking so well. I was surprised to see Johnny Hanson hanging around the house, dressed only in a bathrobe. He said he had left the cast of "Making Porn" in Manhattan to fly in for the awards and to promote his new dance record, "Mr. Fantasy." Our spy in New York said the show, which starred Rex Chandler, had become tired until Blue Blake joined the cast. "Johnny is still giving his same monotone performance (but what great equipment!)," our spy said. "But Blue is great!"

Blue's pal, and mine, Gino Colbert was in Manhattan to see him the week I was in L.A. so we missed each other. However, Gino was there in spirit since his videos are unspooling in a "film festival" at the Tomkat Theater, where he had premiered his legendary fuckfest "Night Walk."

While in L.A., Hanson was basking in the glow of a huge publicity push from *All-Man* magazine. Readers were invited to subscribe and be entered in a sweepstakes for a date with Johnny. Then, in the Christmas issue, they presented Johnny as "the perfect gift," in a stunning layout by Anneli Adolfsson.

Meanwhile, my own "perfect gift" – Kevin – was in perfect form at the Globe in West Hollywood acting as the host as playgoers arrived. I was delighted to see the show, especially when I was introduced by executive producer/creator McCarthy (in full drag as Miss Kitty) as a "world-famous author!"

Kevin was, of course, perfect as "Golden Boy," and I was also taken with Hawk McAllistar, who is quickly making a name for himself in porn. The slim, handsome boy from Idaho is in the aforementioned "Idol in the Sky" and *Gay Video Guide's* best video of the year, "Flesh and Blood."

What a thrill it was to leave the show with the star, and go home to bed with him! By this time, Kevin had rested and was ready for me. We started kissing and I had to confess to Kevin that while he was out shopping earlier in the day, I had come watching Jason Reddy's cock sliding in and out of his ass. But that didn't deter determined Kevin, and before long I was imitating Reddy to the best of my ability. Kevin lives in what can only be described as a "love nest," with mirrors all around the elevated, queen-sized bed.

He showered and came to bed nude. With gentle hands I turned Kevin so that we were facing each other. Softly, I touched his cheek. Speechless, we held each other, warm bodies pressing tighter as seconds became minutes. Then, with the advantage of height, I began kissing his hair, slowly moving my lips down until they covered his waiting mouth. We kissed softly at first, then, as desire mounted, kissing wasn't enough. After Kevin demonstrated his incredible oral ability once again, I was shuddering with excitement as his hands explored my body, began urging more.

Eagerly, he rolled over and offered his ass to my warm tongue. Step by tiny step, I licked and sucked the smooth young skin. His flesh was on fire.

After a time, Kevin wanted a much more intimate touch. His ass was squirming as I greased and fingered the hole.

We were both breathing hard in anticipation and my cock begin to ease slowly through moisture. Unable to hold still, Kevin jerked his hips upward in invitation. The heat flowed through me toward him, drawing out intense, almost unbearable pleasure. I was able to watch myself in the mirrors as if in a video, taking him doggie as Jason had. But thoughts of those other studs who had been here before me did not enter my mind. I concentrated on my own pleasure.

Then we turned again so that he lay on his back, caressing me as I was speeding toward climax.

"Don't come yet," he whispered.

But I was unable to slow the tide thumping through me, and I drowned my cries of pleasure against his naked shoulder.

Moments later, while I still lay in spasms, he growled loudly and began convulsing himself.

He jerked himself, squeezing my cock. What ensued was the most intense orgasm I have ever witnessed. It rolled up the boy's body in waves, a sight to behold.

We lay pooled in drying sweat and sperm until our breathing returned to normal, then I took him in my arms. "You are a wonderful lover," I said, realizing that I could never get enough of this kind of loving.

"Mmm," he said, kissing my chin.

We kissed and, as our lips parted, Kevin said, "I want to ask a favor – "

"Oh, god, here it comes," I joked.

"Can we cuddle?" he asked.

And, of course, we did. All night long.

My fantasy lover was flesh.

Porn Industry Watcher Mickey Skee's Put-Their-Name-on-the-Box-and-It-Sells List

Rex Chandler
Gino Colbert
Rob Cryston
Karen Dior
Chris Green
Ryan Idol
Kevin Kramer
Mike Lamas
Ted Matthews
Johnny Rey
Ken Ryker
Jeff Stryker
Dallas Taylor

- Courtesy Mickey Skee of URGE and AVN magazines, circa 1995.

Kevin Talks About His Videos
With Commentary by John Patrick

Note: This is as complete a list of Kevin's video appearances we could come up with. Some are obscure and not available at some rental outlets.

Big Shooters - "I really don't remember a thing about it."

Biggest Piece I Ever Had - "One of the best times I ever had. Jason Reddy really was the biggest piece I'd ever had at that point. We saw each other a lot after that and are friends still." (This is my personal favorite of all the Kevin Kramer fuckings on screen. Jason's really into it, in more ways than one!)

Bridegroom's Cherry - "I got to top Michael Brawn in this, but not for long. This was not a good experience."

Centerspread - (Devyn Foster and Kevin make love under Jim Steel's direction for Vivid.) "Devyn was very nice," Kevin says now.

The Coach's Boys - "Tanner Reeves was a good top."

Coverboys - (Antony Dillon topped Kevin, but it wasn't memorable.)

Double Dare - (A cheapie from Image Video, with Kevin in a rare three-way with the always dependable Karl Thomas and Troy Robinson fucking him.)

Fresh Men - "This was my first boxcover and they turned it into my first magazine cover. Ted Matthews topped me."

Hard Bargains - "This was a costume-us-to-death video for All-Worlds. I was the devil."

Hellknight - (A poor Kevin Aames' video memorable for Kevin's "exploding like a volcano" while getting plugged by Nathan

Rocco, to quote *Next* magaine.)

JS Big Time - (Kevin achieved one his personal fantasies with this pairing with the legendary Jeff Stryker.) "A wonderful memory," Kevin says now.

Hot Reunion - "I don't remember this at all."

Imagination - "I met Tony Belmonte on this Sam Abdul shoot."

Look of a Man - (Hairy stud Hunter Scott has his way with Kevin for Mustang.)

Malerotic II - "A wonderful shoot. I love this video."

Masquerade - "One of my best performances, I think, with Marco Rossi. This was the first time I ever had the full-blown urge to fuck someone on a movie set. But I couldn't, because Marco was supposed to fuck me! And fuck me he did! At least on this set I learned that I really loved eating ass, if it was Marco's ass!"

Mind Blower - "Sean Hunter was my partner, for Derek Powers."

Moving Target - "My first time with York Powers. Hmmmm."

Nights in Eden - "I really feel in lust with Chad Donovan and saw him a lot after this."

Ninety Dirty Minutes - "I'll never forget this one. It was the last of several hundred videos shot at one of my friend's houses. The crew lit a fire in the fireplace and we were having sex. Suddenly the place was filled with smoke. It was then that they realized the fireplace was fake! Ryan Block was my co-star and we just finished the scene!"

Oh! So Tender - "I took this because I was flat broke at the time, but everyone likes this scene (with Mike Dixon)."

Olympic Proportions - "This is the first video I ever did. It's so bad that I buried my copy in my front yard back in Modesto so nobody would ever see it!"

Playing to Win - (Pagan Prince manages to get four fingers up Kevin, but the finger-fucking doesn't last as long as it should have).

Powerdriver - "Jamie Hendrix directed this and I rather enjoyed it."

Private Parts - "I could hardly wait to get it over with."

Proud 2 - "Alex Kincaid was fun. He didn't say much. I like it when they don't say very much."

Reflections 2 - "Jeff Dillon said he was straight but, my oh my!"

Rival - "I had two scenes in this. Eric Marks was very good, but J.T. Sloan was too much like me to make our scene together effective."

Rumpsters - "Another by the late Derek Powers, again with Sean Hunter. Chris Stone played Sean's lover so we had a three-way. Not bad." (This one may be hard to find now that Jeff Browning's videos have been pulled from shelves.)

Secret Rituals - "YMAC held this for two years. I have no idea why." (Refer to full review.)

Sexposure II - "The Australian guy who fucked me was fun and I was on the boxcover."

Sex Stories - (It is in this Image Video cheapie that Kevin utters the immortal line, "Don't worry, I'll do alll the work," and boy does he ever. Poor Kevin, try as he might, cannot get Wade Cole, who was introduced with this video and enever seen again, hard. This is why Kevin says bottoms really have the *hardest* time in video! Cole holds his cock at its base while he stuffs the head into Kevin. The grimaces on Kevin's face are real as Wade attempts to do the nasty and hopelessly fails. Any other studio would have said, "Come back tomorrow, Kevin, and we'll have a real stud for you," but no, they released this anyway.)

Stiff - "My *second* one with York Powers. Hmmmmm."

Tales From the Backlot - "They just let Chad go at it. We never stopped till we both came. One of the best fucks I've ever had." (You have to envy Kevin this one, watching one of my all-time favorites Chad Knight prove he's versatile as all get out. One of my own fantasies is that Chad will someday do escort work.)

Too Damn Big - "My first Catalina video. Cutter West was the top and he was a lot of fun. I look really good in this."

Weekend with Howie - "They kinda buried this. It's like, the worst."

XXX Oil Wars - "They call these wrestling videos 'recreation.'"

Kevin can also be seen in Bruce LaBruce's "Hustler White," wherein he is gang-banged by a group of actors and actual hustlers dragged off the street by LaBruce. "The sex was simulated," he says, wistfully.

Kevin, The Sex-Pig
A Special Review

What follows is an excerpt from a recent Fig Leaf review of Kevin's "The Secret Rituals of the Westside Boys," released by YMAC. Although hyperbolic in the extreme (as most Fig Leaf reviews are), this is perhaps the most complete review of a Kramer performance ever published and succinctly sums up the essence of this unique sex performer.

With a rare combination of humor and fiery gaysex, *The Secret Rituals of the Westside Boys is* a charismatic, light-hearted sociological treatment of the affluent, blond and golden-skinned dissembling subculture of pampered and stunning young men who reside in the fabulous environs west of Los Angeles – a "nabe" where the streets seem lined with gold and "golden boys." You see these bright, handsome seniors hanging out, on the beaches, cruising in their Corvettes and Mercedes, shooting baskets made of platinum... and they attract at a glance. J. Press, Gap and Rodeo Drive attired, they are a catch for every panties-soaked deb. The natives refer to this southern region of the semi-arid California plains braggingly as the Westside golden oasis, we are informed by an earnest old sociology professor who entertains and enlightens us with a clever voice-over narration during our sojourn in this lotus land. Brunet, rabbit-toothed, smooth, doll-faced Boots McKay; small, smooth, hunky, blond, distinctively sultry, carnally cute, Kevin Kramer; alabaster, blond, hairless, sexy jock Billy Roberts (aka Taz Action); tall and smooth, handsome and proud, very-light-brown-haired and startlingly trim, Jonny Ford; and tall blond bombshell, self-admiring and sexy, smooth Jason Nikas, are the denizens of this diamond mecca whom we get to meet and "study."

"A strange and curious sub-species," our anthropologist narrator describes these appealing California males, tongue-in-cheek, "the Westside boy has almost universally been admired as an ideal sexual trophy. While it has long been suspected that these desirable studs engage extensively in sexual contact amongst their own kind, their activities have never before been documented.

"Extreme social pressures within the status-conscious and upwardly-mobile Westside families impact profoundly on the behavior of our sexual subjects".

So we are treated to a blazing playing-out of the ritual of these seniors wherein one student tries to convince the other of his *heterosexual* intentions for the coming weekend. It's 3:30 p.m. on a Spring Friday and unpretentious Jonny and preening pal Jason are headed home from school in Jonny's modest car--a two-year-old BMW (Jonny's humble by Westside standards a veritable egalitarian). Classmate Jason regales Jonny about the date he's got with a perfect "36-24-36" – a girl from out of town, *of course*. But Jonny's humbler spirit is not immune from the deceptive ritual: his weekend sexual conundrum concerns which of three young ladies he should service. Bidding adios and a reminder to meet on time Monday morning, the fellows he'd off for their hot conquests. Following Jason home, we discover that his romantic object ain't shaped "36-24-36" – it's long, lanky heartthrob Boots McKay, who lounges on the sofa feasting his eyes on Jason's stimulating, sensual and steamy strip-dance, every bump, grind, and nuance directed straight at him. Boots' attraction is tangible, and as Jason disrobes, Boots has got to free his immense cock and balls, his hand irresistibly drawn to his manhood. The more he sees of Jason's flesh the harder his blunderbuss strains. Jason's erotic dance exposes the glories of his pale and perfectly sculpted cock and lean white ass, and Boots sheds his clothes, the fire inside undeniable.

Just as they are to pounce – we're swished a mile away to the tony backyard pool at Jonny's home where, strange to say, the object to choose for his weekend debauch seems already solved – and the choice sports a dick. It' s hunky, hunky-dory Kevin Kramer. A special bonus of this sexcapade filmed in December, 1994, is the affording his legions of fans an early, and most indicative, performance by the now justly celebrated sexpig, Kevin Kramer.

When Jonny takes his clothes off he reveals an astoundingly attractive slenderness, wiry and smooth, and a cock to die for. The ritual of the suntan lotion commences, Kevin smoothing sunscreen over tall Jonny's back as Jonny reaches behind him to kneed Kevin's crotch. As he extends his arm, his huge cock extends, growing to an enormity as it juts out from that trim physique. He unstrings Kevin's briefs and removes them freeing his shorter, humpier lover's ample endowment and monumentally popular, prominent, taut ass. And Jonny lotions those cheeks, lingering on the pale, smooth, memorable muscles. Jonny's dick reaches for heaven. Facing each other now, Jonny's pole pokes Kevin in the gut and keeps them distant – and it's killing Kevin to be so far apart. He kneels to worship the fabulous phallus; kiss it, lick it, suck it, trying desperately to swallow deeply a cock so big it makes Kevin's head look tiny. Fearful of exploding, Jonny raises his worshipper, and in a sweet embrace, leads him inside.

(The scene shifts momentarily before we return to) Jonny's bedroom where pretty Kevin has his tongue shoved high inside his host's hot heiny. Then Kevin's tantalizing tongue lavishes Jonny's monster, his anus again, back to cock, back and forth, cock to ass, feasting on his tall, darkish, slender, wiry, smooth, exotically handsome pal with an abandon so wanton that it stirs the blood. Finally, as Kevin's eyes roll around in his head, Jonny inserts his giant fuck pole between those notorious cheeks and Kev is happily torn asunder. But he can't get enough of this or that, and he again eats cock, shoves his tongue up Jonny's ass, stuffing his insatiable, pretty mouth with cock and ass juice, then wanting to get fucked again begging that the beautiful penis stuff first his ass and now his throat, over and over, an alternation of dizzying delight. At last deciding for them, Jonny plunders the pretty provocateur's butthole passionately as he fondles Kevin's tool and kissing, the overtaxed dams of these lusters let loose their floods all over Kevin's hunky bod.

IFEDS MODELS

SO. CALIFORNIA

The Nation's Finest

BRAD'S BUDDIES AND SUPERSTARS

STARRING
(COAST TO COAST)

TOM KATT
KEN RYKER
ADAM HART
CHRIS GREEN
LEX BALDWIN
MIKE HENSEN
MARCO ROSSI
DEVYN FOSTER
CHASE HUNTER
CHRISTIAN FOX
KEVIN KRAMER
SEAN DIAMOND

Huge 6' 240# BB
4% bodyfat Very tan very friendly! Ric (310) 473-4822

San Diego
Exceptional blond Great body & face (619) 685-0788

Hot Porn Star
BOTTOM STUD PUPPY
KEVIN (818) 819-0129

It pays to advertise: Kevin's own ad runs in The Advocate alongside an ad featuring many superstars, and Kevin's frequent "stud boy" ad in Frontiers generates lots of calls.

Part Three
BODIES FOR SALE

While the story of Kevin Kramer is, generally, a joyous, playful one, the story of a boy who became a star in straight porn provides a revealing contrast. The one-time porn stud Bill Landis, a pal of one-time gay porn idol George Payne, tells his story (originally published in the pages of The Village Voice). A few names have been changed to protect privacy.

By high school I'd been skipped two years. It traumatized me! Any of the normal peer initiations – hanging out, dating, learning to drive – were ruined by the age difference. The girls I met in my classes were too old to go out with me. In college I briefly went out with a well-meaning but neurotic girl my own age. I wantd to get kinky, but couldn't even undress in front of her. By then I knew that my proclivity was known as s/m and I felt guilty. I didn't know whether it was a weird sex drive or mental illness. What I enjoyed about visiting my girlfriend as when I'd be the only man in the house, the enter of attention for her, her younger sister, and her youngish divorcee mother, a real Erica Jlong type. I wanted them to gang up and get as tough as they wanted on me.

After splitting with my girlfriend, I became obsessed with hardcore pornographic movies. I wanted to get the act right. I saw hundreds of sex acts; there was something educational about people fucking 50 feet high, as if they were under a magnifying glass. I also read s/m books like *Story of O*, so I no longer felt like a total nut. After I saw enough films, I finally jumped over the sex hurdle by going to a prostitute. It was an apartment situation, a phone number from a new ad. I didn't want to be with a nervous teen. I never liked the thought of a girl collecting my cherry, so I collected it myself.

During the day I was ostensibly attending NYU. Then for a year my parents attempted to groom me into a Wall Street superstar by making me go to night school while working nine to five. I'd see Kelly on the train going to her Catholic high school and it would break my heart. She was still enjoying her teen years and I was forced to be a junior adult with a briefcase. I got angry. I stopped going to school; I just read the books and passed the tests. It was New York in the late 1970s. I had just turned 18. There were all sorts of freaky scenes to explore. Clubs for every persuasion. I participated in gang bangs, pissed on strangers lying in troughs, fisted masochists in front of enthralled voyeurs. I punched, kicked, and shoved. There was never a shortage of willing victims, although more of them were male than female. Manhattan was a floating Roman orgy, but it was a cold and anonymous party. In two or three months I got bored. I dabbled in hustling faceless male tricks. I tried to give myself confidence; I seemed to need a lot of it. My one consistent admirer was one of my mother's friends, a schoolteacher who would slip me $50 bills when I'd tell her salacious stories about New York's wild side. She never demanded any sex. I never offered. But I did get the "Midnight Cowboy" delusion of getting kept by an older woman. I graduated college with a business degree I never wanted, and took a few desk jobs just to move to Manhattan, but I just couldn't deal with the prison of an office. The hourglass of my life was always in my face. Apart from that vague childhood ambition of becoming a movie star, an international sex symbol like Ursula Andress, I didn't know what to do with my life, but I wanted to feel free again. I drifted out of the nine-to-five world into acid, quaaludes, and bar hustling. Eventually I got a job working as a cashier in a big old dirty movie house on 42nd Street.

Suddenly I found an escape from straight society that also seemed to solve my financial problems: I'd become a porn star. I was a consenting adult who never considered the consequences. I didn't think I'd live long enough to see any. I thought it meant easy money, basking in my own glory, and having tons of sex partners approach me with cash in their hands. I had no patience for talking girls into things, which made me feel like a cad. I didn't want to hurt anyone's feelings. I studied the m.o. of stars like George Payne, Jim Cassidy, and Wade Nichols, steel-eyed men who had gotten their starts marketing carefully tailored sexual personas to the gay audience. These actors were icons. They got billing above the women in straight movies and had their faces in newspaper ads for the gay ones. People threw themselves at them. I couldn't imagine a better position in life.

A hustler friend told me that the notorious "chicken classic" auteur Toby Ross was scouting for talent at the Ninth Circle bar. Toby's operating company, Hornbill Films, specialized in quintessential huge-dicked, boy-next-door types, slightly retarded and vaguely underaged. Toby's movies, which when they were converted to videotape and sold for $100, included *Reflections of Youth*, *Boys of the Slums*, and *Do Me Evil*, a speed-inspired masterwork about two hustler brothers. Disturbingly, it featured a five-year-old boy as a clothed extra peeking through a keyhole at two clean-cut teenaged boys making out and giving each other head. That summed up the shock, prurience, and casting philosophy of Toby Ross. I found Toby in the basement of the Ninth Circle. We bonded over acid and quaaludes, followed by strong candy-store grass.

Toby was a great talker, full of weird stories, and we went back to my apartment and rapped for hours about mutual acquaintances and sex-industry gossip. A balding man with a vaguely Austrian accent who spoke seven languages and had a talent for invisibility, he had spent time in Eastern Europe and Israel, where, he told me, she was a child prostitute and had witnessed much illegal behavior. I knew that Toby's endorsement would immediately bring me two flights up on the golden porn pyramid, above Deuce grunt workers like live-sex-show performers and male dancers.

Toby took some test shots of me against drawing table in sun-shadowy natural light. I loved the way I came out. I was 23, but I looked 13 and my dick seemed bigger than I had ever seen it before, straining against Fruit of the Loom boxers. Toby had a fetish for boxers, Fruit of the Looms in particular. He also shot a masturbation loop of me, and used my test stills on a flyer promoting his videos. At this point I chose my professional name, Spector in honor of Phil, Bobby for a vaguely doo-wop feel.

Working at the theater I encountered the actor I had admired so much as a teenager. George Payne was a drifter of indeterminate age from somewhere out west who had been looking out for himself since age 14. His cinematic career began with fucking in hotel room loops, and he progressed to playact everything from midnight cowboys, a regular guy having a midlife crisis, a bearded Spartacus, and clean-shaven sadist psychos. He was a man of a thousand faces, always offering a new angle, a new look, another refracted image. He had the hands of a man of advanced years, and those hands were known for pushing sex partners to the limit.

I was sitting in the box office listening to tinny oldies on WCBS-FM when George popped up brandishing a $100 bill and demanding change. One of George's movies was playing inside; not five minutes before I had witnessed him spitting on his own penis, verbally abusing a girl, and performing rough anal sex on her. I was surprised to see George was my height, five-seven, and had slimmed down from the tiny Atlas look of his early films. I had the eerie feeling I was looking at myself grown older. I locked eyes with him through the glass as I buzzed the bookkeeper for approval, and introduced myself, sliding George the Toby Ross flyer with my photo on it.

Shortly thereafter, we got better acquainted while I was managing another Deuce theater that George was using as a home base. He lived nowhere in particular and spent most of his time waiting for the pay phone to ring. He told me of repeated incestuous molestation as a child. His current act wasn't far from that angry kid trapped in a middle-aged body – spitting, cursing, pinching, punching, attacking. I couldn't bear the thought of my idol living so close to the edge, so I invited George to crash with me. This was the business school I had always wanted to attend.

Right after George moved in, I passed through the initiation rite of all sex workers: completing a sex act watched by multiple strangers. April, an Asian-black-Hispanic live sex-show performer with whom I had shared a mellow platonic friendship for about six months, showed up at the theater without her male partner. Besides live shows, April moonlighted as a booth girl and in-house prostitute. Her brother usually watched her two kids. For a woman on the chaotic Times Square grind, witnessing a steady parade of flashers each day, April had remained surprisingly whole – not at all hard-bitten or cold-blooded, which is the Darwinist road female sex workers are usually forced to take if they don't want to get killed. But the only empowerment she felt was that she had survived another day. One show partner had a cocaine jones and would sponge off her. Ultimately, the story goes, he gave April the twisted knife in the heart when he molested her children.

I volunteered to do the live show and April was relieved. I was nervous, but I had six friends in the audience, people who worked at the theater with me. George sat in the back row. About three dozen oldster regulars were paying customers. A white spotlight hit the stage and April did a quick gyrating strip, spreading her legs in a split beaver. April always did her shows to good music, and Mtume's "Juicy Fruit" was thumping out of the loudspeakers when I made my entrance. I was the legendary Cuban Superman, one of those guys who did shows for tourists in pre-Castro Havana, only I was American. I was where it was at. The public humiliation gave me a charge. I climbed on top of a dirty mattress, undressed, and kicked my clothes to the side, out of the audience's reach so no one could steal them. April and I performed virtually every sexual act within 15 minutes, and I came on cue. George gave me a standing ovation. By the end of the night, my show had become mythologized in its retelling by my coworkers. I was in the gang!

George then began trotting me around to various porn directors as "the new kid." I gave up casual hustling, but I did have a morbid curiosity about trading on my new persona for cash as an escort. This was a scene George knew too well. When I inquired, the inscrutable Mr. Payne looked me up and down and said matter-of-factly, "They'll eat you alive. Like piranhas." He also mentioned new social diseases like GRID and AIDS, surrounded by myth, confusion, and no cure.

George and I obtained leads in one of those porn spoofs on a popular Hollywood title. It was my rent money, two days out of my life. I immediately experienced a loss of control when we got bused up to Nyack, New York. I had no bread and no idea how to return to Manhattan. Everything went wrong. I hated the girl. I had to do a scene with her and the super-competitive Jerry Butler. Jerry had only spent two years in the business and was already so mad that everyone had to pay for his misery. He was a regular Brooklyn guy, but he was so high and upset that he lived on the verge of snapping into a violent rage. I thought he was going to strangle me with all of us naked on a bed. Another hassle was my cocaine and Percodan habit. I was still new to drugs and made the mistake of not taking any Percs during the sex, which left my mind in a shambles. For a long time I had searched for the ideal self-medication. My mother used to steal my painkillers, supposedly because I didn't know how to use them, and I'd get back at her by drinking her cough medicine and helping myself to her Valiums. Pot always clicked with me. Cocaine was everywhere around the Deuce and in the sex business; it made things glow, intensified them, but I could never prolong the euphoria. A security guy in the theater sold Percs...which give a sudden manic surge of euphoria and a sense of sexual excitement, producing an involuntary erection in some males. They also kill mental anguish. Percs can give you the courage of a lion, but your tolerance rises very quickly and the crash is devastating.

I felt my first big shoot had gone very badly. But George, pragmatist that he was, told me they only really cared about the come shot, and I had come. Women can fake it. Men must ejaculate or they have no business in the sex business. George took care of this requirement personally, with baby oil, not asking his co-star for anything. People teased him about it, but it always worked. Most male actors end up using masturbatory cum shots anyway. The fluff girl is a myth on straight sets – your erection is up to you.

This shoot solidified my bond with George. We would start each day with a manic jolt, sharing an entire Entenmann's chocolate marshmallow cream cake for breakfast and playing on the telephone like children, pranking enemies in the sex business. Then we'd make an exhaustive run hitting up directors for the work. We soon wound up in another badly titled Hollywood spoof. On this shoot I took the Percs, but by the time I was called for my scene 10 hours later, they'd worn off. Nevertheless, I got the job done.

Soon the stress from my sex-kitten career grew too much for my system. I was an anorexic, bulimic 105 pounds, with an agonizing manic drive. My Percodan tolerance was shot to hell; I needed eight pills – $40 worth – to feel something. So I joined the long line of porn performers who were IV-drug users. The Molotov cocktail of heroin and cocaine, never pharmaceutically consistent when purchased off the streets, made me feel calm, collected, distant, eliminating all my superficial guilt. But the gnawing feeling that I was wasting my life reemerged. Although I thought the speedballs were preserving my youth, they were actually embalming me, and no matter what the medication I'd see the hourglass again. But the rush – the warm feeling from the dope and the excitement of coke – was better than any orgasm I had experienced with another human, and I was aware enough to regret it.

The next gig that came our way was with a fat slob, a one-eyed cheesy swing enthusiast. We were taken by van to a dominatrix's lair on a Latino street just outside Newark. We were told that the woman we'd be working over was a willing submissive and were commanded to "lay some real force into her."

While to some personalities this might have been an outlet, George and I were disgusted. George compensated by making loud whip noises and ogre-like faces out of a bad B-movie. The dominant woman aiding our assault was pretty bruised – she calmed her frayed nerves with so many quaaludes that she'd knock into the sharp edges of furniture in her apartment.

Our best job that summer was for the original porno-chic auteur, Gerry Damiano, director of *Deep Throat* and *Devil & Miss Jones*. We knew we were working with a legend. Damiano was one of the last directors to make the job as comfortable as possible. It was 1983 and he was still trying to cultivate a 1970s bacchanal atmosphere. He played to our vanity and flattered us. If you were working well with the girl, he went for a John Cassavetes effect that struck the viewer as cinema verite.

Finally I landed my first major lead in a big-budget 35mm production by David Darby. You got very big after working as a lead for him. As a kid I had seen the Darby film he made starring porno-chic out-there masochist C. D. Laing, one of the few actresses who seemed to enjoy getting whipped for real. For a grand finale she got fistfucked by a ring-wearing "gypsy" lady while deep-throating a 13-inch dick!

...I went to Darby's office in the garment center, a mass of cubicles decorated with posters of his current hits and populated by tough, grim, nasty, gray-haired men. Darby had his own rather large office and looked like what he was: a big ex-trucker with a huge gut. His hair was dyed an unconvincing brown and he sported a sloppy emulation of a Bob Guccione noodle to mask his creeping baldness. I presented my credentials – the Toby Ross flyer, a few mentions of my prior roles, and my dick. He asked me to rub it and get it hard. To be blunt, this horrified me, but it wasn't out of the norm. That's the thing about the sex business. Acts that would otherwise be unthinkably dehumanizing become a way of life. So I sat on his couch and got a hard-on. It took little time but felt scary and suspicious.

"Feel comfortable," he said as he eyeballed me.

I had heard about actors in straight movies getting fucked in the ass by openly gay directors. That I would never have tolerated. But this was getting punked with eyes. Darby seemed like a deeply closeted and angry guy. Once I was hard, I stopped, knowing that's all he superficially wanted. I wasn't about to give him a free come shot. He told me he'd get back to me.

I felt that a sick trick had gotten one over on me. George dismissed Darby as a kook but noted that he did actually make a lot of films. And eventually he did call me. I went back to his office and he gave me a script in which I was to portray a dim-witted underage boy who was also a deaf-mute. Maybe I should have been insulted, but in fact I was relieved I didn't have to memorize any dialogue. I had never been to a set without George, but Darby nixed Mr. Payne. The male umbilical cord had finally been severed. Since I didn't trust Darby, I got a bit part for April. At least if I was found dead or mutilated maybe she'd whisper it in someone's ear, and perhaps George would repeat it to other performers, who'd then know to avoid Darby. They always train you not to go to the police in the sex business. If I did get killed, what could April do? Show up at the stationhouse and incriminate herself as a prostitute and accessory to a crime? This is why no one in the industry can give an honest interview. Nothing bad can be revealed, and the performer turns into a porch nigger. Interviews with sex workers are just ads to get more work.

We all showed up in the garment district early Saturday morning and got taken by van four hours into Suffolk County. The set was an ordinary suburban home. Since this was a four-day affair, we were stationed in a cheap truckers' motel nearby.

Trapped far from Manhattan yet again, I was subjected during this shoot to cheap ego-shattering tactics, kept awake at different hours, and fed joints to keep me off balance. Kentucky Fried Chicken or cheap Chinese takeout were brought to the set at the director's whim. Darby would thuggishly shout instructions, then tell me a story about being raped by an older woman as a little kid, assigning me the task of recreating this experience. There I was recreating this nutso's fantasy on the same turf where several porno-chic superstars had gotten busted in the 1970s. Darby bullied me constantly. He snatched one of my last joints, smoked it in front of me, pausing as the smoke swirled in front of his swollen slit dark eyes, repeating, "Bobby, you have to give good acting. But you also have to give good sex."

Every time I'd have to do a scene, he'd stare at my dick and say, "I wish I was an actor." Fucking an older woman in the pussy and the ass on a car hood under blaring lights for four hours in the middle of a hot summer night was no easy task. One of the comic-relief episodes had me beat up, but for real by the guy playing my father. He then threw me out of a second-story window. Also for real. I hated heights anyway, but this was too much. I wanted Darby dead. Still do.

When the nightmare ended I was back in Manhattan and high out of my mind for several days. I began to black out. My phone would ring, I'd talk, but later I'd remember none of the conversations. My showbiz illusions were permanently shattered after a year. The drug use took its course. The speedballs would provide a glimpse of clarity, helping me realize that the movies were merely photographed acts of prostitution, but at the same time put a tourniquet on my emotions. I also began timing my injections so that they'd produce an automatic come shot the following day if I was going to a shoot. My personal sex life became nonexistent.

When George Payne got hospitalized for ulcers, my life turned into a shambles. I was overrun by obnoxious, loser, drug-addicted and alcoholic roommates who would leech sex, drugs, and sympathy. I became resigned to never finding a permanent relationship. I didn't want to drag any regular girl into a weird scene where her boyfriend went out and fucked strangers for money.

Surprisingly, when George got better, he became adamant about "hooking up with an old lady," as he'd bellow to me whenever he was within earshot of Deirdre, an assistant to a well-known pornographer who frequently employed all of us. George particularly enjoyed telling of an aging muscleman who bamboozled a Miami Beach oldster into marriage and joyfully received his first facelift as a wedding gift. Deirdre would lock eyes with George and respond with bemused curiosity and surprise. George was direct in a greaser, doo-wop way. I found it a beautiful courtship, and it gave me some hope that I'd find someone. I knew it worked when I saw George sitting in the projection booth at the theater wearing an outtasight sheepskin coat Deirdre had bought him. He wore it like a shawl, like he was growing a second skin. The sadness in his face was heartbreaking. He just couldn't believe anyone would be that nice to him. As soon as they held hands, they inspired catty remarks and jealous sexual speculation.

The more I worked, the more the situations seemed like replays. The directors always wanted the same scenes: a double penetration with a woman getting fucked in the ass and the pussy by two guys; three guys getting a blowjob from one girl; a straight fuck; two girls and a guy. During the sex scenes people would shout orders like drill sergeants. It's a trained dog act – there's nothing "sex-positive" about it. The women are your coworkers, and you hope that you have some kind of rapport so you can get the job done as easily as possible.

Perhaps one out of 20 times you'll hit a groove where you'll actually get turned on, but mostly you have to invent crazy mental scenarios to achieve the come shot. The come shot rules your life. It's your existence. You're just fluid in the universe. Your seeds, never to reproduce, are a means to an end. A "sex magick" act has been performed, but the energy released is a negative current. After the sex scenes I'd run to the shower at top speed. If I had done an anal to a woman, I'd vomit immediately. There would be a pileup of women behind me shouting stuff like "Bobby, please hurry up. I've got three guys' come all over me. It's cold and it's drying. It's stuck in my hair! Hurry!" Very empowered.

I worked with girls who I learned after the fact were either barely legal or slightly underage. Usually, in a different context, this would make me hot. Very salacious, ordinary, and true – the sweet, fuckable 16-year-old is a prized trophy in this culture. But the reality on the sets was that these girls were children, plagued by homelessness, pimps, drug addiction. They were usually completely freaked out and hard to work with. The most despicable thing I saw was a mother pimping her "19"-year-old daughter and bringing her 15-year-old onto the sets to get her used to the atmosphere. On that shoot they all shared a motel room with the 15-year-old's boyfriend and a little kid. God knows what happened to the younger ones afterward, but I later saw the "19"-year-old in magazines catering to pregnancy fetishists.

By 1984, the David Darby movie I starred in had become a huge inner-city and video hit, and I was flooded with work, generally as a juvenile. Late that year, Wade Nichols, the porno-chic icon turned soap-opera star, committed suicide. No one knew for certain whether he was dying of AIDS, whether he'd lost the soap job when the producers found out about his X-rated past, or both. Wade, who'd started as an escort, was the guy everybody looked up to for clawing his way out of the sex-for-sale ghetto. His death sent a shock wave through the industry. All of a sudden people realized they could contract AIDS in the line of duty, but that didn't stop filmmakers from demanding even more anal sex.

By 1985, an increasing number of directors had turned to video because of the huge savings in film development. As theatrical venues close and home video boomed, features went directly to videotape anyway. And with home video came the amateurs, ugly people who had such X-rated star illusions they worked for well below the going rates. When Josey Duvall arrived on the scene, it was the beginning of the end. To know Josey was to loathe him. He was an old swinger who looked no less than 65, wore leather pants, and sniffed coke constantly. Josey claimed to be from Belgium and to have been a mercenary in Africa for the French Foreign Legion, but all he had to show for it was sleazy tattoo of an anchor. Although he appeared in straight movies, Josey seemed homosexually inclined as well. Basically, his big charge was a compulsive, exhibitionistic masochism and impaling actresses on a half-hard dick while screaming, "Ride me, baby!" After about four hours, the actress would sink into nervous exhaustion and Josey would be on the brink of heart attack from priapism. I was virtually guaranteed stunt cock work every time Josey was cast.

The constant presence of Ron Jeremy, a fat, obnoxious failed Catskills comedian, was a blight everyone lived with. I've seen girls screaming in pain as he did anals to them. They didn't yell to stop. They'd just scream. Later during the editing, moans and music were cut in. After 10, 15 years in the business, women get physically banged up – even with no anals – and suffer severe gynecological troubles. Hysterectomies are the norm, and a few of the better-off actresses pay for surgery to restore their vaginal elasticity. It was heartbreaking to see how these women were damaged, physically as well as psychologically.

By 1986 I was paranoid about AIDS and drifted into the gray s/m world, which required no sexual contact. S/M was an underground scene populated by high-frequency personalities, far from the safe-sex cure-all it's seen as today. I played in videos shot under the auspices of the legendary Eric Stanton, America's most famed and prolific heterosexual fetish artist, although Stanton wasn't personally present on the shoots. Nothing heavy happened in the Stanton tapes. They were a throwback to the Betty Page days, what would now be called vanilla. I had personally enjoyed Stanton's art as a horny thrill, but acting it out never turned me on.

...When it came down to cases, I was getting paid to be battered. I later discovered that Stanton had not only shot a videotape, but created stills and traced comic strips from the session. I received $75 – my lowest rate – for two hours of work. Although I've met guys who told me they would have paid for the experience, bondage work is among the most exploitative and worst-paying for men.

The last sets I made it through were very rough. Filmmakers no longer cared about quality. Directors gave their sons jobs, and professional producers had been replaced by indie fly-by-nights, causing many fights over payment. Horribly, Josey Duvall and Ron Jeremy had both become directors, and needless to say, both paid shit. George Payne had been taken off active sex duty by Deirdre and I was relying on baby oil for the come shot. I was so tracked up that my arms were filled with pinpoints on a road to nowhere; filmmakers often had me work in long sleeves.

As long as I could get the pop shot I didn't even have to feign interest in my partner. I was dying from neglect. Drug addiction, depersonalized sex, and the dark illegal realm I lived in had taken their toll.

My pictures were playing everywhere, from home video to the remaining Times Square grindhouses, and were shown in softcore versions on cable TV. Like all my colleagues I received not a penny in residuals. But I felt I was too recognizable to go straight. Now turning 27, I was refusing parts because I could no longer stand playing a 14-year-old boy to an old lady.

David Darby called me like the pig he was, asking me to accept a job taking a dildo from a methadone-addicted, crack-smoking actress who worked as an escort. I told him to do the job himself and slammed the phone down. I later discovered that this actress, who was a nice person despite her plethora of problems, had died of AIDS. Soon the Meese Commission was witch-hunting the porn industry. Performers were being interrogated. I did not need this trouble. The last job I pulled took place in Queens. I smelled trouble from minute one. No one knew the filmmakers – they seemed like college kids – and the shoot was being overseen by a director's son, so we were vague about who was in charge. I was acting very passive aggressive, chewing codeine tablets and drifting into seminods. I'd been told I'd be doing a straight fuck scene. When I got there, it turned into sex on a rooftop with a crackhead I despised. She was so spazzed she looked like she had Parkinson's disease. They said they wanted to get as much open-air sex footage as possible. All I could see was a *Post* headline: PORN ACTORS BUSTED DURING ROOFTOP ORGY. This wasn't California, where you could get away with outdoor stuff: it seemed like an invite to a bust. I talked one of the filmmakers out of $100 and ran to the subway, fleeing back to Manhattan as fast as the IRT would carry me. I did a rollercoaster of drugs – black-market methadone, IV speedballs, codeine, and Valium. This binge started as a celebratory fuck-you to a job I hated. In the end it almost killed me.

After I came out of a 24-hour stupor George Payne gave me

one more bit of advice: find a girl and quit the business. He was right once again. Eventually, I did find my wife in Florida, but she was a younger girl, not in the industry, who really turned me on. I love her. We've been married nine years. My sex life isn't a performance anymore.

Since I quit the sex business, it's proven very hard for the survivors to talk to each other. If you tracked us to our various hiding places and put us in a room together, you'd get nothing but arguments, tears, recriminations, and slammed doors. George Payne and I touch base from time to time, but it's difficult to reach out even to people that you felt closest with. I don't know if George remembers the night he saved my life during an OD, but I never forgot it.

People need sexual fantasies, and I don't think all pornography is bad for them. Unfortunately, it's bad for the people who make it. We're all deeply upset individuals who entered the business with our own emotional baggage, but the new scars never quite heal. If you try to talk to outsiders, what you went through is so different from anything they've ever encountered that you can't explain without shocking them or eliciting moral judgments. The empowerment theorists, all wishful academicians or ex-performers with a hustle, have an interest in suppressing any negative comment. I never felt empowered for a second. What I did was nothing more than hooking, with the familiar business expense of self-tranquilization through hard drugs. The only sense of power I felt was a vicarious power over other men unable to live up to my image. A hollow victory.

My advice to any individual wanting to enter the sex industry in any capacity is that old maxim: Is the fucking you get worth the fucking you get?

"Y'know, Forty-Second Street's really changed.

"I remember that you could walk down this block and there were all these beautiful kids hanging out. Occasionally I go up to those bars in the Upper Forties...

"They have some great music and the dancing kids are wild. Good looking kids moving in a great-looking way...

"But I have to keep telling myself to remember I'm a man with responsibilities... an outstanding job and a wonderful family that I really love, I can't afford to get arrested. I'd lose it all.

"But I can't help it. All those beautiful kids."

-David Wojnarowicz
"Seven Miles a Second"

Contributors
(Other Than the Editor, John Patrick)

"The Twins"
Grant Adams

This is the first story by this author to be published by STARbooks.

Lead Poem
Antler

The poet lives in Milwaukee when not traveling to perform his poems or wildernessing. His epic poem *Factory* was published by City Lights. His collection of poems *Last Words* was published by Ballantine. Winner of the Whitman Award from the Walt Whitman Society of Camden, New Jersey, and the Witter Bynner prize from the Academy and Institute of Arts & Letters in New York, his poetry has appeared in many periodicals (including *Utne Reader*, *Whole Earth Review* and *American Poetry Review*) and anthologies (including *Gay Roots*, *Erotic by Nature*, and *Gay and Lesbian Poetry of Our Time*).

"His Favorite Photo"
Kevin Bantan

The author lives in "the Gay Capitol of the Midwest," Columbus, Ohio, providing him with many opportunities for new literary masterpieces. He is currently working on "Showboys," a novella for a future STARbooks volume.

"Portrait of a Freshman"
David Patrick Beavers

The author's books are published by Millivres, London. He resides in Los Angeles.

"The Red-Haired Professor"
Greg Bowden

The author, who lives in California, has contributed many stories to gay magazines.

"Hard All Over"
Frank Brooks

The author is a regular contributor to gay magazines. In addition to writing, his interests include figure drawing from the live model and mountain hiking.

"The Blessing" and "The Boys in the Fens"
Leo Cardini

Author of the best-selling *Mineshaft Nights*, Leo's short stories and theatre-related articles have appeared in numerous magazines. An enthusiastic nudist, he reports that, "A hundred and fifty thousand people have seen me naked, but I only had sex with half of them."

"Mikey Liked It"
William Cozad

The author is a regular contributor to gay magazines and his startling memoirs were published by STARbooks Press in the best-selling anthologies *Lover Boys* and *Boys of the Night*.

"First Lesson"
Kent Dawson

This is the second story of the author's to be published by STARbooks. The author lives in Australia.

"Son of Dakota"
Peter Eros

The author is a 45-year-old Seattle native. He has been a farm-workerm gardener, merchant seaman, hustler, and porn movie performer. He now lives in Vermont with his current lover and five dogs.

"Tools"
Peter Gilbert

"Semi-retired" after a long career with the British Armed Forces, the author now lives in Germany but is contemplating a return to England. A frequent contributor to various periodicals, he also writes for television. He enjoys walking, photography and reading.

"Doogie"
Jarred Goodall

When he is not accepting sabbatical appointments abroad, the author teaches English in a Midwestern university. Born in Wisconsin, he loves back-packing, mountain-climbing, chess and Victorian literature. His favorite color: blue-green; favorite pop-star: Leonard Bernstein; favorite car: WWII Jeep; favorite drink: water, preferably recycled; favorite actor: River Phoenix (alas); favorite hobby: "If you want to know that, read my stories."

"Notorious"
Thomas Holm

The author lives in London.

"Magic"
Rick Jackson, USMC

The oft-published author specializes in jarhead stories. When not travelling, he is based in Hawaii.

"The Smell of Sex"
Bruce Lee

This story originally appeared in *Lavender Review*.

"The Lawnmower Boy"
Jesse Monteagudo

The author is a regular columnist for *The Gazette* and other gay news journals and is noted for his non-fiction writing, including a passage in John Preston's *Hometowns*.

"Seduce Me, Please!"
Thom Nickels

The Cliffs of Aries, the author's first novel, was published in 1988 by Aegina Press. His second book, *Two Novellas: Walking Water & After All This*, was published in 1989 by Banned Books. A collection of his writing, *The Boy on the Bicyle*, was published by STARbooks Press. Thom also reviews literature for the *Lambda Book Report* and writes for the *Philadelphia Forum* and *The City Paper*.

"The Genius of All Beautiful Boys"
Orland Outland
This story originally appeared in HOMOture magazine.

"Absolute Beauty"
John Palgrave
This story originally appeared in *Antinous Review*.

"The Secret of the Rue St. Germain"
Charles Willard Scoggins
The author, who lives in Iowa, wrote poetry from 1956 to 1966 before turning his hand to prose. He is currently finishing a novel, *My Real and Last Earth*.

"The Company of Beautiful Boys"
P. K. Warren
The writer is currently "on retreat," courtesy of the State of New York. A graphic story about what goes on where he is now living will be in an upcoming STARbooks anthology.

"Couplings"
James Wilton
The author, who resides in Connecticut, has contributed stories to various gay magazines. The story in this collection was written especially for STARbooks Press.

"Strip Boy"
Dan Veen
The author's first stories were based on his experiences as a hustler in San Francisco and New Orleans. He has written erotic fiction for *Honcho, Mandate, Playguy, Torso, Inches, and First Hand* magazines. He writes regular film articles and erotic video reviews for *Honcho* under the name of V.C. Rand. He has a PhD. in English Literature and Germanic Languages.

ACKNOWLEDGEMENTS AND SOURCES

Kevin Kramer's photographs are from his private collection.

Other coverboys appear through the courtesy of the celebrated English photographer David Butt. Mr. Butt's photographs may be purchased through Suntown, Post Office Box 151, Danbury, Oxfordshire, OX16 8QN, United Kingdom. Ask for a full catalogue.

George Duroy's models appear through the courtesy of Bel-Ami Video. Write them at their U.S. offices: 484-B Washington Street #342, Monterey CA 93940-3030.

Mr. Duroy's models also appear in the videos from International Collection distributed by Falcon Studios, which can be contacted at 1-800-227-3717; catalogue is $15, refundable with purchase.

Other cover models courtesy Brown Bag Co. (Avalon Video), P.O. Box 91257, Los Angeles CA 90009. 1-800-222-9622. Shipment restricted in certain states.

SPECIAL OFFER

STARbooks Press now offers two very special international gay magazine packages: You can get the hottest American gay magazines, including *GAYME*, *All-Man*, *Torso*, *Advocate Men*, *Advocate Fresh Men*, *In Touch*, and *Playguy*, either singly for $6.95, or in a very special deluxe sampler package for only $25 for six big issues.

We also offer the sizzling British and European magazines, including *Euros*, *Euroboy*, *Prowl*, *Vulcan*, *HUNK*, and *Steam* for $9.95 each or only $49.95 for sampler of six fabulous issues. Please add $2.75 post per issue or sampler. Order from: STARbooks, P.O. Box 2737-B, Sarasota FL 34230-2737 USA.

He's waiting for you...
IN THE BOY ZONE

Another erotic classic, *In the BOY Zone*, edited by John Patrick and featuring many of your favorite authors and some interesting new writers, is now available at your local bookseller, or by mail from STARbooks Press: $14.95 U.S. Plus $2.75 postage and handling. Address: STARbooks Press, P. O. Box 2737, Sarasota FL 34230-2737.

ABOUT THE EDITOR

The editor with Kevin Kramer.

John Patrick is a prolific, prize-winning author of fiction and non-fiction. One of his short stories, "The Well," was honored by PEN American Center as one of the best of 1987. His novels and anthologies, as well as his non-fiction works, including *Legends* and *The Best of the Superstars* series, continue to gain him new fans every day. One of his stories appears in the Badboy collection *Southern Comfort*.

A divorced father of two, the author is a longtime member of the American Booksellers Association, the Florida Publishers' Association, American Civil Liberties Union, and the Adult Video Association. He resides in Florida.